Christie, Agatha
Perilous journeys of Hercule
Poirot

PERILOUS JOURNEYS OF HERCULE POIROT

IN THIS GENEROUS omnibus Hercule Poirot, the dynamic little Belgian detective, appears in diverse places—in the famous Blue Train which runs across France, in a little desert village north of Baghdad and aboard an excursion steamer on the Nile. In the Blue Train a girl has been murdered and the fabulous "Heart of Fire" ruby stolen. In Mesopotamia the wife of the leader of an archeological expedition dies under circumstances that rival a sealed room mystery. On the Nile, Poirot's dire forebodings are realized in a multiple tragedy. Everywhere the little grey cells work at full pressure. Always Agatha Christie is unrivaled in every department of the puzzler's art.

The three novels included are: THE MYSTERY OF THE BLUE TRAIN, MURDER IN MESOPOTAMIA and DEATH ON THE NILE.

Perilous Journeys of
HERCULE POIROT

including *The Mystery of the Blue Train,*
Death on the Nile and *Murder in Mesopotamia*

BY AGATHA CHRISTIE

DODD, MEAD & COMPANY · NEW YORK

The characters, places, incidents and situations in this book are imaginary and have no relation to any person, place or actual happening.

CONTENTS

The Mystery of the Blue Train

CHAPTER I

THE MAN WITH THE WHITE FACE

It was close on midnight when a man crossed the [illegible] Concorde. In spite of the handsome fur coat wh[illegible] form, there was something essentially weak a[illegible]

A little man with a face like a rat. A man [illegible] could never play a conspicuous part, or rise [illegible] sphere. And yet, in leaping to such a conclusion [illegible] have been wrong. For this man, negligible and [illegible] seemed, played a prominent part in the destiny [illegible] Empire where rats ruled, he was the king of the [illegible]

Even now, an Embassy awaited his return. [illegible] to do first—business of which the Embassy w[illegible] zant. His face gleamed white and sharp [illegible] the least hint of a curve in the thin nose. [illegible] journeyman tailor. It was business [illegible] loved that took him abroad to-night.

He came to the Seine, crossed it, and [illegible] atable quarters of Paris. Here he stopped before [illegible] house and made his way up to an apartment [illegible] had barely time to knock before the door [illegible] who had evidently been awaiting his arrival. [illegible] ing, but helped him off with his overcoat and [illegible] the tawdrily furnished sitting-room. The [illegible] with dirty pink festoons, and it softened, [illegible] girl's face with its mask of crude paint. [illegible] the broad, Mongolian cast of her countenance. [illegible] of Olga Demiroff's profession, nor of her nationality.

"All is well, little one?"

"All is well, Boris Ivanovitch."

He nodded murmuring: "I do not think [illegible]"

But there was anxiety in his tone. He went [illegible] the curtains aside slightly, and peering [illegible] away violently.

"There are two men—on the opposite [illegible]" He broke off and began gnawing at his nails [illegible] anxious.

CHAPTER I

THE MAN WITH THE WHITE HAIR

It was close on midnight when a man crossed the Place de la Concorde. In spite of the handsome fur coat which garbed his meagre form, there was something essentially weak and paltry about him.

A little man with a face like a rat. A man, one would say, who could never play a conspicuous part, or rise to prominence in any sphere. And yet, in leaping to such a conclusion, an onlooker would have been wrong. For this man, negligible and inconspicuous as he seemed, played a prominent part in the destiny of the world. In an Empire where rats ruled, he was the king of the rats.

Even now, an Embassy awaited his return. But he had business to do first—business of which the Embassy was not officially cognizant. His face gleamed white and sharp in the moonlight. There was the least hint of a curve in the thin nose. His father had been a journeyman tailor. It was business such as his father would have loved that took him abroad to-night.

He came to the Seine, crossed it, and entered one of the less reputable quarters of Paris. Here he stopped before a tall, dilapidated house and made his way up to an apartment on the fourth floor. He had barely time to knock before the door was opened by a woman who had evidently been awaiting his arrival. She gave him no greeting, but helped him off with his overcoat and then led the way into the tawdrily furnished sittingroom. The electric light was shaded with dirty pink festoons, and it softened, but could not disguise, the girl's face with its mask of crude paint. Could not disguise, either, the broad Mongolian cast of her countenance. There was no doubt of Olga Demiroff's profession, nor of her nationality.

"All is well, little one?"

"All is well, Boris Ivanovitch."

He nodded murmuring: "I do not think I have been followed."

But there was anxiety in his tone. He went to the window, drawing the curtains aside slightly, and peering carefully out. He started away violently.

"There are two men—on the opposite pavement. It looks to me——" He broke off and began gnawing at his nails—a habit he had when anxious.

The Russian girl was shaking her head with a slow, reassuring action.

"They were here before you came."

"All the same, it looks to me as though they were watching this house."

"Possibly," she admitted indifferently.

"But then——"

"What of it? Even if they *know*—it will not be *you* they will follow from here."

A thin, cruel smile came to his lips.

"No," he admitted, "that is true."

He mused for a minute or two and then observed.

"This damned American—he can look after himself as well as anybody."

"I suppose so."

He went again to the window.

"Tough customers," he muttered, with a chuckle. "Known to the police, I fear. Well, well, I wish Brother Apache good hunting."

Olga Demiroff shook her head.

"If the American is the kind of man they say he is, it will take more than a couple of cowardly Apaches to get the better of him." She paused. "I wonder——"

"Well?"

"Nothing. Only twice this evening a man has passed along this street—a man with white hair."

"What of it?"

"This. As he passed those two men, he dropped his glove. One of them picked it up and returned it to him. A threadbare device."

"You mean—that the white-haired man is—their employer?"

"Something of the kind."

The Russian looked alarmed and uneasy.

"You are sure—the parcel is safe? It has not been tampered with? There has been too much talk . . . much too much talk."

He gnawed his nails again.

"Judge for yourself."

She bent to the fireplace, deftly removing the coals. Underneath, from amongst the crumpled balls of newspaper, she selected from the very middle an oblong package wrapped round with grimy newspaper, and handed it to the man.

"Ingenious," he said, with a nod of approval.

"The apartment has been searched twice. The mattress on my bed was ripped open."

"It is as I said," he muttered. "There has been too much talk. This haggling over the price—it was a mistake."

He had unwrapped the newspaper. Inside was a small brown paper parcel. This in turn he unwrapped, verified the contents, and quickly wrapped it up once more. As he did so, an electric bell rang sharply.

"The American is punctual," said Olga, with a glance at the clock.

She left the room. In a minute she returned ushering in a stranger, a big, broad-shouldered man whose transatlantic origin was evident. His keen glance went from one to the other.

"M. Krassnine?" he inquired politely.

"I am he," said Boris. "I must apologize for—for the unconventionality of this meeting-place. But secrecy is urgent. I—I cannot afford to be connected with this business in any way."

"Is that so?" said the American politely.

"I have your word, have I not, that no details of this transaction will be made public? That is one of the conditions of—sale."

The American nodded.

"That has already been agreed upon," he said indifferently. "Now, perhaps, you will produce the goods."

"You have the money—in notes?"

"Yes," replied the other.

He did not, however, make any attempt to produce it. After a moment's hesitation, Krassnine gestured towards the small parcel on the table.

The American took it up and unrolled the wrapping paper. The contents he took over to a small electric lamp and submitted them to a very thorough examination. Satisfied, he drew from his pocket a thick leather wallet and extracted from it a wad of notes. These he handed to the Russian, who counted them carefully.

"All right?"

"I thank you, Monsieur. Everything is correct."

"Ah!" said the other. He slipped the brown paper parcel negligently into his pocket. He bowed to Olga. "Good evening, Mademoiselle. Good evening, M. Krassnine."

He went out, shutting the door behind him. The eyes of the two in the room met. The man passed his tongue over his dry lips.

"I wonder—will he ever get back to his hotel?" he muttered.

By common accord, they both turned to the window. They were just in time to see the American emerge into the street below. He turned to the left and marched along at a good pace without once turning his head. Two shadows stole from a doorway and followed noiselessly. Pursuers and pursued vanished into the night. Olga Demiroff spoke.

"He will get back safely," she said. "You need not fear—or hope—whichever it is."

"Why do you think he will be safe?" asked Krassnine curiously.

"A man who has made as much money as he has could not possibly be a fool," said Olga. "And talking of money——"

She looked significantly at Krassnine.

"Eh?"

"My share, Boris Ivanovitch."

With some reluctance, Krassnine handed over two of the notes. She nodded her thanks, with a complete lack of emotion, and tucked them away in her stocking.

"That is good," she remarked, with satisfaction.

He looked at her curiously.

"You have no regrets, Olga Vassilovna?"

"Regrets? For what?"

"For what has been in your keeping. There are women—most women, I believe, who go mad over such things."

She nodded reflectively.

"Yes, you speak truth there. Most women have that madness. I—have not. I wonder now——" She broke off.

"Well?" asked the other curiously.

"The American will be safe with them—yes, I am sure of that. But afterwards——"

"Eh? What are you thinking of?"

"He will give them, of course, to some woman," said Olga thoughtfully. "I wonder what will happen then. . . ."

She shook herself impatiently and went over to the window. Suddenly she uttered an exclamation and called to her companion.

"See, he is going down the street now—the man I mean."

They both gazed down together. A slim, elegant figure was progressing along at a leisurely pace. He wore an opera hat and a cloak. As he passed a street lamp, the light illumined a thatch of thick white hair.

CHAPTER II

M. LE MARQUIS

THE MAN WITH the white hair continued on his course, unhurried, and seemingly indifferent to his surroundings. He took a side turning to the right and another one to the left. Now and then he hummed a little air to himself.

Suddenly he stopped dead and listened intently. He had heard a certain sound. It might have been the bursting of a tyre or it might have been—a shot. A curious smile played round his lips for a minute. Then he resumed his leisurely walk.

On turning a corner he came upon a scene of some activity. A representative of the law was making notes in a pocket-book, and one or two late passers-by had collected on the spot. To one of these the man with the white hair made a polite request for information.

"Something has been happening, yes?"

"*Mais oui*, Monsieur. Two Apaches set upon an elderly American gentleman."

"They did him no injury?"

"No, indeed." The man laughed. "The American, he had a revolver in his pocket, and before they could attack him, he fired shots so closely round them that they took alarm and fled. The police, as usual, arrived too late."

"Ah!" said the inquirer.

He displayed no emotion of any kind.

Placidly and unconcernedly he resumed his nocturnal strolling. Presently he crossed the Seine and came into the richer areas of the city. It was some twenty minutes later that he came to a stop before a certain house in a quiet but aristocratic thoroughfare.

The shop, for shop it was, was a restrained and unpretentious one. D. Papopolous, dealer in antiques, was so known to fame that he needed no advertisement, and indeed most of his business was not done over a counter. M. Papopolous had a very handsome apartment of his own overlooking the Champs Élysées, and it might reasonably be supposed that he would have been found there and not at his place of business at such an hour, but the man with the white hair seemed confident of success as he pressed the obscurely placed bell, having first given a quick glance up and down the deserted street.

His confidence was not misplaced. The door opened and a man stood in the aperture. He wore gold rings in his ears and was of a swarthy cast of countenance.

"Good evening," said the stranger. "Your master is within?"

"The master is here, but he does not see chance visitors at this time of night," growled the other.

"I think he will see me. Tell him that his friend M. le Marquis is here."

The man opened the door a little wider and allowed the visitor to enter.

The man who gave his name as M. le Marquis had shielded his face with his hand as he spoke. When the man-servant returned with the information that M. Papopolous would be pleased to receive the visitor a further change had taken place in the stranger's appearance. The man-servant must have been very unobservant or very well trained for he betrayed no surprise at the small black satin mask which hid the other's features. Leading the way to a door at the end of the hall, he opened it and announced in a respectful murmur: "*M. le Marquis.*"

The figure which rose to receive this strange guest was an imposing one. There was something venerable and patriarchal about M. Papopolous. He had a high domed forehead and a beautiful white beard. His manner had in it something ecclesiastical and benign.

"My dear friend," said M. Papopolous.

He spoke in French and his tones were rich and unctuous.

"I must apologize," said the visitor, "for the lateness of the hour."

"Not at all. Not at all," said M. Papopolous—"an interesting time of night. You have had, perhaps, an interesting evening?"

"Not personally," said M. le Marquis.

"Not personally," repeated M. Papopolous, "no, no, of course not. And there is news, eh?"

He cast a sharp glance sideways at the other, a glance that was not ecclesiastical or benign in the least.

"There is no news. The attempt failed. I hardly expected anything else."

"Quite so," said M. Papopolous; "anything crude——"

He waved his hand to express his intense distaste for crudity in any form. There was indeed nothing crude about M. Papopolous nor about the goods he handled. He was well known in most European courts, and kings called him Demetrius in a friendly manner. He had the reputation for the most exquisite discretion. That, together with the nobility of his aspect, had carried him through several very questionable transactions.

"The direct attack——" said M. Papopolous. He shook his head. "It answers sometimes—but very seldom."

The other shrugged his shoulders.

"It saves time," he remarked, "and to fail costs nothing—or next to nothing. The other plan—will not fail."

"Ah," said M. Papopolous, looking at him keenly.

The other nodded slowly.

"I have great confidence in your—er—reputation," said the antique dealer.

M. le Marquis smiled gently.

"I think I may say," he murmured, "that your confidence will not be misplaced."

"You have unique opportunities," said the other, with a note of envy in his voice.

"I make them," said M. le Marquis.

He rose and took up the cloak which he had thrown carelessly on the back of a chair.

"I will keep you informed, M. Papopolous, through the usual channels, but there must be no hitch in your arrangements."

M. Papopolous was pained.

"There is *never* a hitch in my arrangements," he complained.

The other smiled, and without any further word of adieu he left the room, closing the door behind him.

M. Papopolous remained in thought for a moment stroking his venerable white beard, and then moved across to a second door which opened inwards. As he turned the handle, a young woman, who only too clearly had been leaning against it with her ear to the keyhole, stumbled headlong into the room. M. Papopolous displayed neither surprise nor concern. It was evidently all quite natural to him.

"Well, Zia?" he asked.

"I did not hear him go," explained Zia.

She was a handsome young woman, built on Junoesque lines, with dark flashing eyes and such a general air of resemblance to M.

Papopolous that it was easy to see they were father and daughter.

"It is annoying," she continued vexedly, "that one cannot see through a keyhole and hear through it at the same time."

"It has often annoyed me," said M. Papopolous, with great simplicity.

"So that is M. le Marquis," said Zia slowly. "Does he always wear a mask, father?"

"Always."

There was a pause.

"It is the rubies, I suppose?" asked Zia.

Her father nodded.

"What do you think, my little one?" he inquired, with a hint of amusement in his beady black eyes.

"Of M. le Marquis?"

"Yes."

"I think," said Zia slowly, "that it is a very rare thing to find a well-bred Englishman who speaks French as well as that."

"Ah!" said M. Papopolous, "so that is what you think."

As usual, he did not commit himself, but he regarded Zia with benign approval.

"I thought, too," said Zia, "that his head was an odd shape."

"Massive," said her father—"a trifle massive. But then that effect is always created by a wig."

They both looked at each other and smiled.

CHAPTER III

HEART OF FIRE

RUFUS VAN ALDIN passed through the revolving doors of the Savoy, and walked to the reception desk. The desk clerk smiled a respectful greeting.

"Pleased to see you back again, Mr. Van Aldin," he said.

The American millionaire nodded his head in a casual greeting.

"Everything all right?" he asked.

"Yes, sir. Major Knighton is upstairs in the suite now."

Van Aldin nodded again.

"Any mail?" he vouchsafed.

"They have all been sent up, Mr. Van Aldin. Oh! wait a minute."

He dived into a pigeon hole, and produced a letter.

"Just come this minute," he explained.

Rufus Van Aldin took the letter from him, and as he saw the handwriting, a woman's flowing hand, his face was suddenly transformed. The harsh contours of it softened, and the hard line of his mouth relaxed. He looked a different man. He walked across to the lift with the letter in his hand and the smile still on his lips.

In the drawing-room of his suite, a young man was sitting at a desk nimbly sorting correspondence with the ease born of long practice. He sprang up as Van Aldin entered.

"Hallo, Knighton!"

"Glad to see you back, sir. Had a good time?"

"So so!" said the millionaire unemotionally. "Paris is rather a one-horse city nowadays. Still—I got what I went over for."

He smiled to himself rather grimly.

"You usually do, I believe," said the secretary, laughing.

"That's so," agreed the other.

He spoke in a matter-of-fact manner, as one stating a well-known fact. Throwing off his heavy overcoat, he advanced to the desk.

"Anything urgent?"

"I don't think so, sir. Mostly the usual stuff. I have not quite finished sorting it out."

Van Aldin nodded briefly. He was a man who seldom expressed either blame or praise. His methods with those he employed were simple; he gave them a fair trial and dismissed promptly those who were inefficient. His selections of people were unconventional. Knighton, for instance, he had met casually at a Swiss resort two months previously. He had approved of the fellow, looked up his war record, and found in it the explanation of the limp with which he walked. Knighton had made no secret of the fact that he was looking for a job, and indeed diffidently asked the millionaire if he knew of any available post. Van Aldin remembered, with a grim smile of amusement, the young man's complete astonishment when he had been offered the post of secretary to the great man himself.

"But—but I have no experience of business," he had stammered.

"That doesn't matter a cuss," Van Aldin had replied. "I have got three secretaries already to attend to that kind of thing. But I am likely to be in England for the next six months, and I want an Englishman who—well, knows the ropes—and can attend to the social side of things for me."

So far, Van Aldin had found his judgment confirmed. Knighton had proved quick, intelligent, and resourceful, and he had a distinct charm of manner.

The secretary indicated three or four letters placed by themselves on the top of the desk.

"It might perhaps be as well, sir, if you glanced at these," he suggested. "The top one is about the Colton agreement——"

But Rufus Van Aldin held up a protesting hand.

"I am not going to look at a durned thing to-night," he declared. "They can all wait till the morning. Except this one," he added, looking down at the letter he held in his hand. And again that strange transforming smile stole over his face.

Richard Knighton smiled sympathetically.

"Mrs. Kettering?" he murmured. "She rang up yesterday and to-day. She seems very anxious to see you at once, sir."

"Does she, now!"

The smile faded from the millionaire's face. He ripped open the envelope which he held in his hand and took out the enclosed sheet. As he read it his face darkened, his mouth set grimly in the line which Wall Street knew so well, and his brows knit themselves ominously. Knighton turned tactfully away, and went on opening letters and sorting them. A muttered oath escaped the millionaire, and his clenched fist hit the table sharply.

"I'll not stand for this," he muttered to himself. "Poor little girl, it's a good thing she has her old father behind her."

He walked up and down the room for some minutes, his brows drawn together in a scowl. Knighton still bent assiduously over the desk. Suddenly Van Aldin came to an abrupt halt. He took up his overcoat from the chair where he had thrown it.

"Are you going out again, sir?"

"Yes; I'm going round to see my daughter."

"If Colton's people ring up——"

"Tell them to go to the devil," said Van Aldin.

"Very well," said the secretary unemotionally.

Van Aldin had his overcoat on by now. Cramming his hat upon his head, he went towards the door. He paused with his hand upon the handle.

"You are a good fellow, Knighton," he said. "You don't worry me when I am rattled."

Knighton smiled a little, but made no reply.

"Ruth is my only child," said Van Aldin, "and there is no one on this earth who knows quite what she means to me."

A faint smile irradiated his face. He slipped his hand into his pocket.

"Care to see something, Knighton?"

He came back towards the secretary.

From his pocket he drew out a parcel carelessly wrapped in brown paper. He tossed off the wrapping and disclosed a big, shabby, red velvet case. In the centre of it were some twisted initials surmounted by a crown. He snapped the case open, and the secretary drew in his breath sharply. Against the slightly dingy white of the interior, the stones glowed like blood.

"My God! sir," said Knighton. "Are they—are they real?"

Van Aldin laughed a quiet little cackle of amusement.

"I don't wonder at your asking that. Amongst these rubies are the three largest in the world. Catherine of Russia wore them, Knighton. That centre one there is known as Heart of Fire. It's perfect—not a flaw in it."

"But," the secretary murmured, "they must be worth a fortune."

"Four or five hundred thousand dollars," said Van Aldin nonchalantly, "and that is apart from the historical interest."

"And you carry them about—like that, loose in your pocket?"

Van Aldin laughed amusedly.

"I guess so. You see, they are my little present for Ruthie."

The secretary smiled discreetly.

"I can understand now Mrs. Kettering's anxiety over the telephone," he murmured.

But Van Aldin shook his head. The hard look returned to his face.

"You are wrong there," he said. "She doesn't know about these; they are my little surprise for her."

He shut the case, and began slowly to wrap it up again.

"It's a hard thing, Knighton," he said, "how little one can do for those one loves. I can buy a good portion of the earth for Ruth, if it would be any use to her, but it isn't. I can hang these things round her neck and give her a moment or two's pleasure, maybe, but——"

He shook his head.

"When a woman is not happy in her home——"

He left the sentence unfinished. The secretary nodded discreetly. He knew, none better, the reputation of the Hon. Derek Kettering. Van Aldin sighed. Slipping the parcel back in his coat pocket, he nodded to Knighton and left the room.

CHAPTER IV

IN CURZON STREET

THE HON. MRS. DEREK KETTERING lived in Curzon Street. The butler who opened the door recognized Rufus Van Aldin at once and permitted himself a discreet smile of greeting. He led the way upstairs to the big double drawing-room on the first floor.

A woman who was sitting by the window started up with a cry.

"Why, Dad, if that isn't too good for anything! I've been telephoning Major Knighton all day to try and get hold of you, but he couldn't say for sure when you were expected back."

Ruth Kettering was twenty-eight years of age. Without being beautiful, or in the real sense of the word even pretty, she was striking looking because of her colouring. Van Aldin had been called Carrots and Ginger in his time, and Ruth's hair was almost pure auburn. With it went dark eyes and very black lashes—the effect somewhat enhanced by art. She was tall and slender, and moved well. At a careless glance it was the face of a Raphael Madonna. Only if one looked closely did one perceive the same line of jaw and chin as in Van Aldin's face, bespeaking the same hardness and determination. It suited the man, but suited the woman less well. From her childhood upward Ruth Van Aldin had been accustomed to having her own way, and any one who had ever stood up against her soon realized that Rufus Van Aldin's daughter never gave in.

"Knighton told me you'd 'phoned him," said Van Aldin. "I only got back from Paris half an hour ago. What's all this about Derek?"

Ruth Kettering flushed angrily.

"It's unspeakable. It's beyond all limits," she cried. "He—he doesn't seem to listen to anything I say."

There was bewilderment as well as anger in her voice.

"He'll listen to me," said the millionaire grimly.

Ruth went on.

"I've hardly seen him for the last month. He goes about everywhere with that woman."

"With what woman?"

"Mirelle. She dances at the Parthenon, you know."

Van Aldin nodded.

"I was down at Leconbury last week. I—I spoke to Lord Leconbury. He was awfully sweet to me, sympathized entirely. He said he'd give Derek a good talking to."

"Ah!" said Van Aldin.

"What do you mean by 'Ah!', Dad?"

"Just what you think I mean, Ruthie. Poor old Leconbury is a wash-out. Of course he sympathized with you, of course he tried to soothe you down. Having got his son and heir married to the daughter of one of the richest men in the States, he naturally doesn't want to mess the thing up. But he's got one foot in the grave already, every one knows that, and anything he may say will cut darned little ice with Derek."

"Can't *you* do anything, Dad?" urged Ruth, after a minute or two.

"I might," said the millionaire. He waited a second reflectively, and then went on. "There are several things I might do, but there's only one that will be any real good. How much pluck have you got, Ruthie?"

She stared at him. He nodded back at her.

"I mean just what I say. Have you got the grit to admit to all the world that you've made a mistake. There's only one way out of this mess, Ruthie. Cut your losses and start afresh."

"You mean——"

"Divorce."

"Divorce!"

Van Aldin smiled drily.

"You say that word, Ruth, as though you'd never heard it before. And yet your friends are doing it all round you every day."

"Oh! I know that. But——"

She stopped, biting her lip. Her father nodded comprehendingly.

"I know, Ruth. You're like me, you can't bear to let go. But I've learnt, and you've got to learn, that there are times when it's the only way. I might find ways of whistling Derek back to you, but it would all come to the same in the end. *He's no good,* Ruth; he's rotten through and through. And mind you, I blame myself for ever letting you marry him. But you were kind of set on having him, and he seemed in earnest about turning over a new leaf—and well, I'd crossed you once, honey . . ."

He did not look at her as he said the last words. Had he done so, he might have seen the swift colour that came up in her face.

"You did," she said in a hard voice.

"I was too durned soft hearted to do it a second time. I can't tell you how I wish I had, though. You've led a poor kind of life for the last few years, Ruth."

"It has not been very—agreeable," agreed Mrs. Kettering.

"That's why I say to you that this thing has got to *stop!*" He brought his hand down with a bang on the table. "You may have a hankering after the fellow still. *Cut it out.* Face facts. Derek Kettering married you for your money. That's all there is to it. Get rid of him, Ruth."

Ruth Kettering looked down at the ground for some moments, then she said, without raising her head:

"Supposing he doesn't consent?"

Van Aldin looked at her in astonishment.

"He won't have a say in the matter."

She flushed and bit her lip.

"No—no—of course not. I only meant——"

She stopped. Her father eyed her keenly.

"What did you mean?"

"I meant——" She paused, choosing her words carefully. "He mayn't take it lying down."

The millionaire's chin shot out grimly.

"You mean he'll fight the case? Let him! But, as a matter of fact, you're wrong. He won't fight. Any solicitor he consults will tell him he hasn't a leg to stand upon."

"You don't think"—she hesitated—"I mean—out of sheer spite against me—he might try to make it awkward?"

Her father looked at her in some astonishment.

"Fight the case, you mean?"

He shook his head.

"Very unlikely. You see, he would have to have something to go upon."

Mrs. Kettering did not answer. Van Aldin looked at her sharply.

"Come, Ruth, out with it. There's something troubling you—what is it?"

"Nothing, nothing at all."

But her voice was unconvincing.

"You are dreading the publicity, eh? Is that it? You leave it to me. I'll put the whole thing through so smoothly that there will be no fuss at all."

"Very well, Dad, if you really think it's the best thing to be done."

"Got a fancy for the fellow still, Ruth? Is that it?"

"No."

The word came with no uncertain emphasis. Van Aldin seemed satisfied. He patted his daughter on the shoulder.

"It will be all right, little girl. Don't you worry any. Now let's forget all about this. I have brought you a present from Paris."

"For me? Something very nice?"

"I hope you'll think so," said Van Aldin, smiling.

He took the parcel from his coat pocket and handed it to her. She unwrapped it eagerly, and snapped open the case. A long-drawn "Oh!" came from her lips. Ruth Kettering loved jewels—always had done so.

"Dad, how—how wonderful!"

"Rather in a class by themselves, aren't they?" said the millionaire, with satisfaction. "You like them, eh?"

"Like them? Dad, they're unique. How did you get hold of them?"

Van Aldin smiled.

"Ah! that's my secret. They had to be bought privately, of course. They are rather well known. See that big stone in the middle? You have heard of it, maybe; that's the historic 'Heart of Fire.'"

"Heart of Fire!" repeated Mrs. Kettering.

She had taken the stones from the case and was holding them against her breast. The millionaire watched her. He was thinking of the series of women who had worn the jewels. The heartaches, the despairs, the jealousies. "Heart of Fire," like all famous stones, had left behind it a trail of tragedy and violence. Held in Ruth Kettering's assured hand, it seemed to lose its potency of evil. With her cool, equable poise, this woman of the western world seemed a negation to tragedy or heart-burnings. Ruth returned the stones to their case; then, jumping up, she flung her arms round her father's neck.

"Thank you, thank you, thank you, Dad! They are wonderful! You do give me the most marvellous presents always."

"That's all right," said Van Aldin, patting her shoulder. "You are all I have, you know, Ruthie."

"You will stay to dinner, won't you, father?"

"I don't think so. You were going out, weren't you?"

"Yes, but I can easily put that off. Nothing very exciting."

"No," said Van Aldin. "Keep your engagement. I have got a good deal to attend to. See you to-morrow, my dear. Perhaps if I 'phone you, we can meet at Galbraiths'?"

Messrs. Galbraith, Galbraith, Cuthbertson, & Galbraith were Van Aldin's London solicitors.

"Very well, Dad." She hesitated. "I suppose it—this—won't keep me from going to the Riviera?"

"When are you off?"

"On the fourteenth."

"Oh, that will be all right. These things take a long time to mature. By the way, Ruth, I shouldn't take those rubies abroad if I were you. Leave them at the bank."

Mrs. Kettering nodded.

"We don't want to have you robbed and murdered for the sake of 'Heart of Fire,'" said the millionaire jocosely.

"And yet you carried it about in your pocket loose," retorted his daughter, smiling.

"Yes——"

Something, some hesitation, caught her attention.

"What is it, Dad?"

"Nothing." He smiled. "Thinking of a little adventure of mine in Paris."

"An adventure?"

"Yes, the night I bought these things."

He made a gesture towards the jewel case.

"Oh, do tell me."

"Nothing to tell, Ruthie. Some Apache fellows got a bit fresh and I shot at them and they got off. That's all."

She looked at him with some pride.

"You're a tough proposition, Dad."

"You bet I am, Ruthie."

He kissed her affectionately and departed. On arriving back at the Savoy, he gave a curt order to Knighton.

"Get hold of a man called Goby; you'll find his address in my private book. He's to be here to-morrow morning at half-past nine."

"Yes, sir."

"I also want to see Mr. Kettering. Run him to earth for me if you can. Try his Club—at any rate, get hold of him somehow, and arrange for me to see him here to-morrow morning. Better make it latish, about twelve. His sort aren't early risers."

The secretary nodded in comprehension of these instructions. Van Aldin gave himself into the hands of his valet. His bath was prepared, and as he lay luxuriating in the hot water, his mind went back over the conversation with his daughter. On the whole he was well satisfied. His keen mind had long since accepted the fact that divorce was the only possible way out. Ruth had agreed to the proposed solution with more readiness than he had hoped for. Yet, in spite of her acquiescence, he was left with a vague sense of uneasiness. Something about her manner, he felt, had not been quite natural. He frowned to himself.

"Maybe I'm fanciful," he muttered, "and yet—I bet there's something she has not told me."

CHAPTER V

A USEFUL GENTLEMAN

Rufus Van Aldin had just finished the sparse breakfast of coffee and dry toast, which was all he ever allowed himself, when Knighton entered the room.

"Mr. Goby is below, sir, waiting to see you."

The millionaire glanced at the clock. It was just half-past nine.

"All right," he said curtly. "He can come up."

A minute or two later, Mr. Goby entered the room. He was a small, elderly man, shabbily dressed, with eyes that looked carefully all round the room, and never at the person he was addressing.

"Good morning, Goby," said the millionaire. "Take a chair."

"Thank you, Mr. Van Aldin."

Mr. Goby sat down with his hands on his knees, and gazed earnestly at the radiator.

"I have got a job for you."

"Yes, Mr. Van Aldin?"

"My daughter is married to the Hon. Derek Kettering, as you may perhaps know."

Mr. Goby transferred his gaze from the radiator to the left-hand drawer of the desk, and permitted a deprecating smile to pass over his face. Mr. Goby knew a great many things, but he always hated to admit the fact.

"By my advice, she is about to file a petition for divorce. That, of course, is a solicitor's business. But, for private reasons, I want the fullest and most complete information."

Mr. Goby looked at the cornice and murmured:

"About Mr. Kettering?"

"About Mr. Kettering."

"Very good, sir."

Mr. Goby rose to his feet.

"When will you have it ready for me?"

"Are you in a hurry, sir?"

"I'm always in a hurry," said the millionaire.

Mr. Goby smiled understandingly at the fender.

"Shall we say two o'clock this afternoon, sir?" he asked.

"Excellent," approved the other. "Good morning, Goby."

"Good morning, Mr. Van Aldin."

"That's a very useful man," said the millionaire as Goby went out and his secretary came in. "In his own line he's a specialist."

"What is his line?"

"Information. Give him twenty-four hours and he would lay the private life of the Archbishop of Canterbury bare for you."

"A useful sort of chap," said Knighton, with a smile.

"He has been useful to me once or twice," said Van Aldin. "Now then, Knighton, I'm ready for work."

The next few hours saw a vast quantity of business rapidly transacted. It was half-past twelve when the telephone bell rang, and Mr. Van Aldin was informed that Mr. Kettering had called. Knighton looked at Van Aldin, and interpreted his brief nod.

"Ask Mr. Kettering to come up, please."

The secretary gathered up his papers and departed. He and the visitor passed each other in the doorway, and Derek Kettering stood aside to let the other go out. Then he came in, shutting the door behind him.

"Good morning, sir. You are very anxious to see me, I hear."

The lazy voice with its slightly ironic inflection roused memories in Van Aldin. There was charm in it—there had always been charm in it. He looked piercingly at his son-in-law. Derek Kettering was thirty-four, lean of build, with a dark, narrow face, which had even now something indescribably boyish in it.

"Come in," said Van Aldin curtly. "Sit down."

Kettering flung himself lightly into an arm-chair. He looked at his father-in-law with a kind of tolerant amusement.

"Not seen you for a long time, sir," he remarked pleasantly. "About two years, I should say. Seen Ruth yet?"

"I saw her last night," said Van Aldin.

"Looking very fit, isn't she?" said the other lightly.

"I didn't know you had had much opportunity of judging," said Van Aldin drily.

Derek Kettering raised his eyebrows.

"Oh, we sometimes meet at the same night club, you know," he said airily.

"I am not going to beat about the bush," Van Aldin said curtly. "I have advised Ruth to file a petition for divorce."

Derek Kettering seemed unmoved.

"How drastic!" he murmured. "Do you mind if I smoke, sir?"

He lit a cigarette, and puffed out a cloud of smoke as he added nonchalantly:

"And what did Ruth say?"

"Ruth proposes to take my advice," said her father.

"Does she really?"

"Is that all you have got to say?" demanded Van Aldin sharply.

Kettering flicked his ash into the grate.

"I think, you know," he said, with a detached air, "that she's making a great mistake."

"From your point of view she doubtless is," said Van Aldin grimly.

"Oh, come now," said the other; "don't let's be personal. I really wasn't thinking of myself at the moment. I was thinking of Ruth. You know my poor old Governor really can't last much longer; all the doctors say so. Ruth had better give it a couple more years, then I shall be Lord Leconbury, and she can be châtelaine of Leconbury, which is what she married me for."

"I won't have any of your darned impudence," roared Van Aldin.

Derek Kettering smiled at him quite unmoved.

"I agree with you. It's an obsolete idea," he said. "There's nothing in a title nowadays. Still, Leconbury is a very fine old place, and, after all, we are one of the oldest families in England. It will be very annoying for Ruth if she divorces me to find me marrying again, and some other woman queening it at Leconbury instead of her."

"I am serious, young man," said Van Aldin.

"Oh, so am I," said Kettering. "I am in very low water financially; it will put me in a nasty hole if Ruth divorces me, and, after all, if she has stood it for ten years, why not stand it a little longer? I give you my word of honour that the old man can't possibly last out another eighteen months, and, as I said before, it's a pity Ruth shouldn't get what she married me for."

"You suggest that my daughter married you for your title and position?"

Derek Kettering laughed a laugh that was not all amusement.

"You don't think it was a question of a love match?" he asked.

"I know," said Van Aldin slowly, "that you spoke very differently in Paris ten years ago."

"Did I? Perhaps I did. Ruth was very beautiful, you know—rather like an angel or a saint, or something that had stepped down from a niche in a church. I had fine ideas, I remember, of turning over a new leaf, of settling down and living up to the highest traditions of English home-life with a beautiful wife who loved me."

He laughed again, rather more discordantly.

"But you don't believe that, I suppose?" he said.

"I have no doubt at all that you married Ruth for her money," said Van Aldin unemotionally.

"And that she married me for love?" asked the other ironically.

"Certainly," said Van Aldin.

Derek Kettering stared at him for a minute or two, then he nodded reflectively.

"I see you believe that," he said. "So did I at the time. I can assure you, my dear father-in-law, I was very soon undeceived."

"I don't know what you are getting at," said Van Aldin, "and I don't care. You have treated Ruth darned badly."

"Oh, I have," agreed Kettering lightly, "but she's tough, you know. She's your daughter. Underneath the pink-and-white softness of her she's as hard as granite. You have always been known as a hard man, so I have been told, but Ruth is harder than you are. You, at any rate, love one person better than yourself. Ruth never has and never will."

"That is enough," said Van Aldin. "I asked you here so that I could tell you fair and square what I meant to do. My girl has got to have some happiness, and remember this, I am behind her."

Derek Kettering got up and stood by the mantelpiece. He tossed away his cigarette. When he spoke, his voice was very quiet.

"What exactly do you mean by that, I wonder?" he said.

"I mean," said Van Aldin, "that you had better not try to defend the case."

"Oh," said Kettering. "Is that a threat?"

"You can take it any way you please," said Van Aldin.

Kettering drew a chair up to the table. He sat down fronting the millionaire.

"And supposing," he said softly, "that, just for argument's sake, I did defend the case?"

Van Aldin shrugged his shoulders.

"You have not got a leg to stand upon, you young fool. Ask your solicitors, they will soon tell you. Your conduct has been notorious, the talk of London."

"Ruth has been kicking up a row about Mirelle, I suppose. Very foolish of her. I don't interfere with her friends."

"What do you mean?" said Van Aldin sharply.

Derek Kettering laughed.

"I see you don't know everything, sir," he said. "You are, perhaps naturally, prejudiced."

He took up his hat and stick and moved towards the door.

"Giving advice is not much in my line." He delivered his final thrust. "But, in this case, I should advise most strongly perfect frankness between father and daughter."

He passed quickly out of the room and shut the door behind him just as the millionaire sprang up.

"Now, what the hell did he mean by that?" said Van Aldin as he sank back into his chair again.

All his uneasiness returned in full force. There was something here that he had not yet got to the bottom of. The telephone was by his elbow; he seized it, and asked for the number of his daughter's house.

"Hallo! Hallo! Is that Mayfair 81907? Mrs. Kettering in? Oh, she's out, is she? Yes, out to lunch. What time will she be in? You don't know? Oh, very good; no, there's no message."

He slammed the receiver down again angrily. At two o'clock he was pacing the floor of his room waiting expectantly for Goby. The latter was ushered in at ten minutes past two.

"Well?" barked the millionaire sharply.

But little Mr. Goby was not to be hurried. He sat down at the table, produced a very shabby pocket-book, and proceeded to read from it in a monotonous voice. The millionaire listened attentively, with an increasing satisfaction. Goby came to a full stop, and looked attentively at the wastepaper-basket.

"Um!" said Van Aldin. "That seems pretty definite. The case will go through like winking. The hotel evidence is all right, I suppose?"

"Cast iron," said Mr. Goby, and looked malevolently at a gilt armchair.

"And financially he's in very low water. He's trying to raise a loan now, you say? Has already raised practically all he can upon his expectations from his father. Once the news of the divorce gets about, he won't be able to raise another cent, and not only that, his obligations can be brought up and pressure can be put upon him from that quarter. We have got him, Goby; we have got him in a cleft stick."

He hit the table a bang with his fist. His face was grim and triumphant.

"The information," said Mr. Goby in a thin voice, "seems satisfactory."

"I have got to go round to Curzon Street now," said the millionaire. "I am much obliged to you, Goby. You are the goods all right."

A pale smile of gratification showed itself on the little man's face.

"Thank you, Mr. Van Aldin," he said; "I try to do my best."

Van Aldin did not go direct to Curzon Street. He went first to the City, where he had two interviews which added to his satisfaction. From there he took the tube to Down Street. As he was walking along Curzon Street, a figure came out of No. 160, and turned up the street towards him, so that they passed each other on the pavement. For a moment, the millionaire had fancied it might be Derek Kettering himself; the height and build were not unlike. But as they came face to face, he saw that the man was a stranger to him. At least—no, not a stranger; his face awoke some call of recognition in the millionaire's mind, and it was associated definitely with something unpleasant. He cudgelled his brains in vain, but the thing eluded him. He went on, shaking his head irritably. He hated to be baffled.

Ruth Kettering was clearly expecting him. She ran to him and kissed him when he entered.

"Well, Dad, how are things going?"

"Very well," said Van Aldin; "but I have got a word or two to say to you, Ruth."

Almost insensibly he felt the change in her; something shrewd and watchful replaced the impulsiveness of her greeting. She sat down in a big arm-chair.

"Well, Dad?" she asked. "What is it?"

"I saw your husband this morning," said Van Aldin.

"You saw Derek?"

"I did. He said a lot of things, most of which were darned cheek. Just as he was leaving, he said something that I didn't understand. He advised me to be sure that there was perfect frankness between father and daughter. What did he mean by that, Ruthie?"

Mrs. Kettering moved a little in her chair.

"I—I don't know, Dad. How should I?"

"Of course you know," said Van Aldin. "He said something else, about his having his friends and not interfering with yours. What did he mean by that?"

"I don't know," said Ruth Kettering again.

Van Aldin sat down. His mouth set itself in a grim line.

"See here, Ruth. I am not going into this with my eyes closed. I am not at all sure that that husband of yours doesn't mean to make trouble. Now, he can't do it, I am sure of that. I have got the means to silence him, to shut his mouth for good and all, but I have got to know if there's any need to use those means. What did he mean by your having your own friends?"

Mrs. Kettering shrugged her shoulders.

"I have got lots of friends," she said uncertainly. "I don't know what he meant, I am sure."

"You do," said Van Aldin.

He was speaking now as he might have spoken to a business adversary.

"I will put it plainer. Who is the man?"

"What man?"

"*The* man. That's what Derek was driving at. Some special man who is a friend of yours. You needn't worry, honey, I know there is nothing in it, but we have got to look at everything as it might appear to the Court. They can twist these things about a good deal, you know. I want to know who the man is, and just how friendly you have been with him."

Ruth didn't answer. Her hands were kneading themselves together in intense nervous absorption.

"Come, honey," said Van Aldin in a softer voice. "Don't be afraid of your old Dad. I was not too harsh, was I, even that time in Paris? —By gosh!"

He stopped, thunderstruck.

"That's who it was," he murmured to himself. "I thought I knew his face."

"What are you talking about, Dad? I don't understand."

The millionaire strode across to her and took her firmly by the wrist.

"See here, Ruth, have you been seeing that fellow again?"

"What fellow?"

"The one we had all that fuss about years ago. You know who I mean well enough."

"You mean"—she hesitated—"you mean the Comte de la Roche?"

"Comte de la Roche!" snorted Van Aldin. "I told you at the time that the man was no better than a swindler. You had entangled yourself with him then very deeply, but I got you out of his clutches."

"Yes, you did," said Ruth bitterly. "And I married Derek Kettering."

"You wanted to," said the millionaire sharply.

She shrugged her shoulders.

"And now," said Van Aldin slowly, "you have been seeing him again—after all I told you. He has been in the house to-day. I met him outside, and couldn't place him for the moment."

Ruth Kettering had recovered her composure.

"I want to tell you one thing, Dad; you are wrong about Armand—the Comte de la Roche, I mean. Oh, I know there were several regrettable incidents in his youth—he has told me about them; but—well, he has cared for me always. It broke his heart when you parted us in Paris, and now——"

She was interrupted by the snort of indignation her father gave.

"So you fell for that stuff, did you? You, a daughter of mine! My God!"

He threw up his hands.

"That women can be such darned fools!"

CHAPTER VI

MIRELLE

Derek Kettering emerged from Van Aldin's suite so precipitantly that he collided with a lady passing across the corridor. He apologized, and she accepted his apologies with a smiling reassurance and passed on, leaving with him a pleasant impression of a soothing personality and rather fine grey eyes.

For all his nonchalance, his interview with his father-in-law had shaken him more than he cared to show. He had a solitary lunch, and after it, frowning to himself a little, he went around to the sumptuous flat that housed the lady known as Mirelle. A trim Frenchwoman received him with smiles.

"But enter then, Monsieur. Madame reposes herself."

He was ushered into the long room with its Eastern setting which he knew so well. Mirelle was lying on the divan, supported by an incredible number of cushions, all in varying shades of amber, to harmonize with the yellow ochre of her complexion. The dancer was a beautifully made woman, and if her face, beneath its mask of yellow, was in truth somewhat haggard, it had a bizarre charm of its own, and her orange lips smiled invitingly at Derek Kettering.

He kissed her, and flung himself into a chair.

"What have you been doing with yourself? Just got up, I suppose?"

The orange mouth widened into a long smile.

"No," said the dancer. "I have been at work."

She flung out a long, pale hand towards the piano, which was littered with untidy music scores.

"Ambrose has been here. He has been playing me the new Opera."

Kettering nodded without paying much attention. He was profoundly uninterested in Claud Ambrose and the latter's operatic setting of Ibsen's *Peer Gynt*. So was Mirelle, for that matter, regarding it merely as a unique opportunity for her own presentation as Anitra.

"It is a marvellous dance," she murmured. "I shall put all the passion of the desert into it. I shall dance hung over with jewels—ah! and, by the way, *mon ami*, there is a pearl that I saw yesterday in Bond Street—a black pearl."

She paused, looking at him invitingly.

"My dear girl," said Kettering, "it's no use talking of black pearls to me. At the present minute, as far as I am concerned, the fat is in the fire."

She was quick to respond to his tone. She sat up, her big black eyes widening.

"What is that you say, Dereek? What has happened?"

"My esteemed father-in-law," said Kettering, "is preparing to go off the deep end."

"Eh?"

"In other words, he wants Ruth to divorce me."

"How stupid!" said Mirelle. "Why should she want to divorce you?"

Derek Kettering grinned.

"Mainly because of you, *chérie!*" he said.

Mirelle shrugged her shoulders.

"That is foolish," she observed in a matter-of-fact voice.

"Very foolish," agreed Derek.

"What are you going to do about it?" demanded Mirelle.

"My dear girl, what can I do? On the one side, the man with unlimited money; on the other side, the man with unlimited debts. There is no question as to who will come out on top."

"They are extraordinary, these Americans," commented Mirelle. "It is not as though your wife were fond of you."

"Well," said Derek, "what are we going to do about it?"

She looked at him inquiringly. He came over and took both her hands in his.

"Are you going to stick to me?"

"What do you mean? After——"

"Yes," said Kettering. "After, when the creditors come down like wolves on the fold. I am damned fond of you, Mirelle; are you going to let me down?"

She pulled her hands away from him.

"You know I adore you, Dereek."

He caught the note of evasion in her voice.

"So that's that, is it? The rats will leave the sinking ship."

"Ah, Dereek!"

"Out with it," he said violently. "You will fling me over; is that it?"

She shrugged her shoulders.

"I am fond of you, *mon ami*—indeed I am fond of you. You are very charming—*un beau garçon*, but *ce n'est pas pratique*."

"You are a rich man's luxury, eh? Is that it?"

"If you like to put it that way."

She leaned back on the cushions, her head flung back.

"All the same, I am fond of you, Dereek."

He went over to the window and stood there some time looking out, with his back to her. Presently the dancer raised herself on her elbow and stared at him curiously.

"What are you thinking of, *mon ami?*"

He grinned at her over his shoulder, a curious grin, that made her vaguely uneasy.

"As it happened, I was thinking of a woman, my dear."

"A woman, eh?"

Mirelle pounced on something that she could understand.

"You are thinking of some other woman, is that it?"

"Oh, you needn't worry; it is purely a fancy portrait. 'Portrait of a lady with grey eyes.'"

Mirelle said sharply, "When did you meet her?"

Derek Kettering laughed, and his laughter had a mocking, ironical sound.

"I ran into the lady in the corridor of the Savoy Hotel."

"Well! what did she say?"

"As far as I can remember, I said, 'I beg your pardon,' and she said, 'It doesn't matter,' or words to that effect."

"And then?" persisted the dancer.

Kettering shrugged his shoulders.

"And then—nothing. That was the end of the incident."

"I don't understand a word of what you are talking about," declared the dancer.

"Portrait of a lady with grey eyes," murmured Derek reflectively. "Just as well I am never likely to meet her again."

"Why?"

"She might bring me bad luck. Women do."

Mirelle slipped quickly from her couch, and came across to him, laying one long, snake-like arm round his neck.

"You are foolish, Dereek," she murmured. "You are very foolish. You are *beau garçon*, and I adore you, but I am not made to be poor—no, decidedly I am not made to be poor. Now listen to me; everything is very simple. You must make it up with your wife."

"I am afraid that's not going to be actually in the sphere of practical politics," said Derek drily.

"How do you say? I do not understand."

"Van Aldin, my dear, is not taking any. He is the kind of man who makes up his mind and sticks to it."

"I have heard of him," nodded the dancer. "He is very rich, is he not? Almost the richest man in America. A few days ago, in Paris, he bought the most wonderful ruby in the world—'Heart of Fire' it is called."

Kettering did not answer. The dancer went on musingly:

"It is a wonderful stone—a stone that should belong to a woman like me. I love jewels, Dereek; they say something to me. Ah! to wear a ruby like 'Heart of Fire.'"

She gave a little sigh, and then became practical once more.

"You don't understand these things, Dereek; you are only a man. Van Aldin will give these rubies to his daughter, I suppose. Is she his only child?"

"Yes."

"Then when he dies, she will inherit all his money. She will be a rich woman."

"She is a rich woman already," said Kettering drily. "He settled a couple of millions on her at her marriage."

"A couple of million! But that is immense. And if she died suddenly, eh? That would all come to you?"

"As things stand at present," said Kettering slowly, "it would. As far as I know she has not made a will."

"*Mon Dieu!*" said the dancer. "If she were to die, what a solution that would be."

There was a moment's pause, and then Derek Kettering laughed outright.

"I like your simple, practical mind, Mirelle, but I am afraid what you desire won't come to pass. My wife is an extremely healthy person."

"*Eh, bien!*" said Mirelle; "there are accidents."

He looked at her sharply but did not answer.

She went on.

"But you are right, *mon ami,* we must not dwell on possibilities. See now, my little Dereek, there must be no more talk of this divorce. Your wife must give up the idea."

"And if she won't?"

The dancer's eyes widened to slits.

"I think she will, my friend. She is one of those who would not like the publicity. There are one or two pretty stories that she would not like her friends to read in the newspapers."

"What do you mean?" asked Kettering sharply.

Mirelle laughed, her head thrown back.

"*Parbleu!* I mean the gentleman who calls himself the Comte de la Roche. I know all about him. I am Parisienne, you remember. He was her lover before she married you, was he not?"

Kettering took her sharply by the shoulders.

"That is a damned lie," he said, "and please remember that, after all, you are speaking of my wife."

Mirelle was a little sobered.

"You are extraordinary, you English," she complained. "All the same, I dare say that you may be right. The Americans are so cold, are they not? But you will permit me to say, *mon ami,* that she was *in love with him* before she married you, and her father stepped in and sent the Comte about his business. And the little Mademoiselle, she wept many tears! But she obeyed. Still, you must know as well as I do, Dereek, that it is a very different story now. She sees him nearly every day, and on the fourteenth she goes to Paris to meet him."

"How do you know all this?" demanded Kettering.

"Me? I have friends in Paris, my dear Dereek, who know the Comte intimately. It is all arranged. She is going to the Riviera, so she says, but in reality the Comte meets her in Paris and—who knows! Yes, yes, you can take my word for it, it is all arranged."

Derek Kettering stood motionless.

"You see," purred the dancer, "if you are clever, you have her in the hollow of your hand. You can make things very awkward for her."

"Oh, for God's sake be quiet," cried Kettering. "Shut your cursed mouth!"

Mirelle flung herself down again on the divan with a laugh. Kettering caught up his hat and coat and left the flat, banging the door violently. And still the dancer sat on the divan and laughed softly to herself. She was not displeased with her work.

CHAPTER VII

LETTERS

"Mrs. Samuel Harfield presents her compliments to Miss Katherine Grey and wishes to point out that under the circumstances Miss Grey may not be aware——"

Mrs. Harfield, having written so far fluently, came to a dead stop, held up by what has proved an insuperable difficulty to many other people—namely, the difficulty of expressing oneself fluently in the third person.

After a minute or two of hesitation, Mrs. Harfield tore up the sheet of notepaper and started afresh.

"Dear Miss Grey,—Whilst fully appreciating the adequate way you discharged your duties to my Cousin Emma (whose recent death has indeed been a severe blow to us all), I cannot but feel——"

Again Mrs. Harfield came to a stop. Once more the letter was consigned to the wastepaper-basket. It was not until four false starts had been made that Mrs. Harfield at last produced an epistle that satisfied her. It was duly sealed and stamped and addressed to Miss Katherine Grey, Little Crampton, St. Mary Mead, Kent, and it lay beside that lady's plate on the following morning at breakfast-time in company with a more important looking communication in a long blue envelope.

Katherine Grey opened Mrs. Harfield's letter first. The finished production ran as follows:

"Dear Miss Grey,—My husband and I wish to express our thanks to you for your services to my poor cousin, Emma. Her death has been a great blow to us, though we were, of course, aware that her mind has been failing for some time past. I understand that her latter testamentary dispositions have been of a most peculiar character, and they would not hold good, of course, in any court of law. I have no doubt that, with your usual good sense, you have already realized this fact. If these matters can be arranged privately it is always so much better, my husband says. We shall be pleased to recommend you most highly for a similar post and hope that you will also accept a small present. Believe me, dear Miss Grey, yours cordially, Mary Anne Harfield."

Katherine Grey read the letter through, smiled a little, and read it a second time. Her face as she laid the letter down after the second reading was distinctly amused. Then she took up the second letter. After one brief perusal she laid it down and stared very straight in front of her. This time she did not smile. Indeed, it would have been hard for any one watching her to guess what emotions lay behind that quiet, reflective gaze.

Katherine Grey was thirty-three. She came of good family, but her father had lost all his money, and Katherine had had to work for her living from an early age. She had been just twenty-three when she had come to old Mrs. Harfield as companion.

It was generally recognized that old Mrs. Harfield was "difficult." Companions came and went with startling rapidity. They arrived full of hope and they usually left in tears. But from the moment Katherine Grey set foot in Little Crampton, ten years ago, perfect peace had reigned. No one knows how these things come about. Snake-charmers, they say, are born, not made. Katherine Grey was born with the power of managing old ladies, dogs, and small boys, and she did it without any apparent sense of strain.

At twenty-three she had been a quiet girl with beautiful eyes. At thirty-three she was a quiet woman, with those same grey eyes, shining steadily out on the world with a kind of happy serenity that nothing could shake. Moreover, she had been born with, and still possessed, a sense of humour.

As she sat at the breakfast-table, staring in front of her, there was a ring at the bell, accompanied by a very energetic rat-a-tat-tat at the knocker. In another minute the little maid-servant opened the door and announced rather breathlessly:

"Dr. Harrison."

The big, middle-aged doctor came bustling in with the energy and breeziness that had been foreshadowed by his onslaught on the knocker.

"Good morning, Miss Grey."

"Good morning, Dr. Harrison."

"I dropped in early," began the doctor, "in case you should have heard from one of those Harfield cousins. Mrs. Samuel, she calls herself—a perfectly poisonous person."

Without a word, Katherine picked up Mrs. Harfield's letter from the table and gave it to him. With a good deal of amusement she watched his perusal of it, the drawing together of the bushy eyebrows, the snorts and grunts of violent disapproval. He dashed it down again on the table.

"Perfectly monstrous," he fumed. "Don't you let it worry you, my dear. They're talking through their hat. Mrs. Harfield's intellect was as good as yours or mine, and you won't get any one to say the contrary. They wouldn't have a leg to stand upon, and they know it. All that talk of taking it into court is pure bluff. Hence this attempt to get round you in a hole-and-corner way. And look here, my dear, don't let them get round you with soft soap either. Don't get fancying it's your duty to hand over the cash, or any tomfoolery of conscientious scruples."

"I'm afraid it hasn't occurred to me to have scruples," said Katherine. "All these people are distant relatives of Mrs. Harfield's husband, and they never came near her or took any notice of her in her lifetime."

"You're a sensible woman," said the doctor. "I know, none better, that you've had a hard life of it for the last ten years. You're fully entitled to enjoy the old lady's savings, such as they were."

Katherine smiled thoughtfully.

"Such as they were," she repeated. "You've no idea of the amount, doctor?"

"Well—enough to bring in five hundred a year or so, I suppose."

Katherine nodded.

"That's what I thought," she said. "Now read this."

She handed him the letter she had taken from the long blue envelope. The doctor read and uttered an exclamation of utter astonishment.

"Impossible," he muttered. "Impossible."

"She was one of the original shareholders in Mortaulds. Forty years ago she must have had an income of eight or ten thousand a year. She has never, I am sure, spent more than four hundred a year. She was always terribly careful about money. I always believed that she was obliged to be careful about every penny."

"And all the time the income has accumulated at compound interest. My dear, you're going to be a very rich woman."

Katherine Grey nodded.

"Yes," she said, "I am."

She spoke in a detached, impersonal tone, as though she were looking at the situation from outside.

"Well," said the doctor, preparing to depart, "you have all my congratulations." He flicked Mrs. Samuel Harfield's letter with his thumb. "Don't worry about that woman and her odious letter."

"It really isn't an odious letter," said Miss Grey tolerantly. "Under the circumstances, I think it's really quite a natural thing to do."

"I have the gravest suspicions of you sometimes," said the doctor.

"Why?"

"The things that you find perfectly natural."

Katherine Grey laughed.

Doctor Harrison retailed the great news to his wife at lunch-time. She was very excited about it.

"Fancy old Mrs. Harfield—with all that money. I'm glad she left it to Katherine Grey. That girl's a saint."

The doctor made a wry face.

"Saints I always imagine must have been difficult people. Katherine Grey is too human for a saint."

"She's a saint with a sense of humour," said the doctor's wife, twinkling. "And, though I don't suppose you've ever noticed the fact, she's extremely good looking."

"Katherine Grey?" The doctor was honestly surprised. "She's got very nice eyes, I know."

"Oh, you men!" cried his wife. "Blind as bats. Katherine's got all the makings of a beauty in her. All she wants is clothes!"

"Clothes? What's wrong with her clothes? She always looks very nice."

Mrs. Harrison gave an exasperated sigh, and the doctor rose preparatory to starting on his rounds.

"You might look in on her, Polly," he suggested.

"I'm going to," said Mrs. Harrison promptly.

She made her call about three o'clock.

"My dear, I'm so glad," she said warmly, as she squeezed Katherine's hand. "And every one in the village will be glad too."

"It's very nice of you to come and tell me," said Katherine. "I hoped you would come in because I wanted to ask about Johnnie."

"Oh! Johnnie. Well——"

Johnnie was Mrs. Harrison's youngest son. In another minute she was off, retailing a long history in which Johnnie's adenoids and tonsils bulked largely. Katherine listened sympathetically. Habits die hard. Listening had been her portion for ten years now. "My dear, I wonder if I ever told you about that naval ball at Portsmouth? When Lord Charles admired my gown?" And composedly, kindly, Katherine would reply: "I rather think you have, Mrs. Harfield, but I've forgotten about it. Won't you tell it me again?" And then the old lady would start off full swing, with numerous details. And half of Katherine's mind would be listening, saying the right things mechanically when the old lady paused. . . .

Now, with that same curious feeling of duality to which she was accustomed, she listened to Mrs. Harrison.

At the end of half an hour, the latter recalled herself suddenly.

"I've been talking about myself all this time," she exclaimed. "And I came here to talk about you and your plans."

"I don't know that I've got any yet."

"My dear—you're not going to stay on *here*."

Katherine smiled at the horror in the other's tone.

"No; I think I want to travel. I've never seen much of the world, you know."

"I should think not. It must have been an awful life for you cooped up here all these years."

"I don't know," said Katherine. "It gave me a lot of freedom."

She caught the other's gasp, and reddened a little.

"It must sound foolish—saying that. Of course, I hadn't much freedom in the downright physical sense——"

"I should think not," breathed Mrs. Harrison, remembering that Katherine had seldom had that useful thing known as a "day off."

"But, in a way, being tied physically gives you lots of scope mentally. You're always free to think. I've had a lovely feeling always of mental freedom."

Mrs. Harrison shook her head.

"I can't understand that."

"Oh! you would if you'd been in my place. But, all the same, I feel I want a change. I want—well, I want things to happen. Oh! not to me—I don't mean that. But to be in the midst of things, exciting things—even if I'm only the looker-on. You know, things don't happen in St. Mary Mead."

"They don't indeed," said Mrs. Harrison, with fervour.

"I shall go to London first," said Katherine. "I have to see the solicitors, anyway. After that, I shall go abroad, I think."

"Very nice."

"But, of course, first of all——"

"Yes?"

"I must get some clothes."

"Exactly what I said to Arthur this morning," cried the doctor's wife. "You know, Katherine, you could look positively beautiful if you tried."

Miss Grey laughed unaffectedly.

"Oh! I don't think you could ever make a beauty out of me," she said sincerely. "But I shall enjoy having some really good clothes. I'm afraid I'm talking about myself an awful lot."

Mrs. Harrison looked at her shrewdly.

"It must be quite a novel experience for you," she said drily.

Katherine went to say good-bye to old Miss Viner before leaving the village. Miss Viner was two years older than Mrs. Harfield, and her mind was mainly taken up with her own success in outliving her dead friend.

"You wouldn't have thought I'd have outlasted Jane Harfield, would you?" she demanded triumphantly of Katherine. "We were at school together, she and I. And here we are, she taken, and I left. Who would have thought it?"

"You've always eaten brown bread for supper, haven't you?" murmured Katherine mechanically.

"Fancy your remembering that, my dear. Yes; if Jane Harfield had had a slice of brown bread every evening and taken a little stimulant with her meals she might be here to-day."

The old lady paused, nodding her head triumphantly; then added in sudden remembrance:

"And so you've come into a lot of money, I hear? Well, well. Take care of it. And you're going up to London to have a good time? Don't think you'll get married, though, my dear, because you won't. You're not the kind to attract the men. And, besides, you're getting on. How old are you now?"

"Thirty-three," Katherine told her.

"Well," remarked Miss Viner doubtfully, "that's not so very bad. You've lost your first freshness, of course."

"I'm afraid so," said Katherine, much entertained.

"But you're a very nice girl," said Miss Viner kindly. "And I'm sure there's many a man might do worse than take you for a wife instead of one of these flibbertigibbets running about nowadays showing more of their legs than the Creator ever intended them to. Good-bye, my dear, and I hope you'll enjoy yourself, but things are seldom what they seem in this life."

Heartened by these prophecies, Katherine took her departure.

Half the village came to see her off at the station, including the little maid of all work, Alice, who brought a stiff wired nosegay and cried openly.

"There ain't a many like her," sobbed Alice when the train had finally departed. "I'm sure when Charlie went back on me with that girl from the Dairy, nobody could have been kinder than Miss Grey was, and though particular about the brasses and the dust, she was always one to notice when you'd give a thing an extra rub. Cut myself in little pieces for her, I would, any day. A real lady, that's what I call her."

Such was Katherine's departure from St. Mary Mead.

CHAPTER VIII

LADY TAMPLIN WRITES A LETTER

"WELL," said Lady Tamplin, "well."

She laid down the continental *Daily Mail* and stared out across the blue waters of the Mediterranean. A branch of golden mimosa, hanging just above her head, made an effective frame for a very charming picture. A golden-haired, blue-eyed lady in a very becoming *négligée*. That the golden hair owed something to art, as did the pink-and-white complexion, was undeniable, but the blue of the eyes was Nature's gift, and at forty-four Lady Tamplin could still rank as a beauty.

Charming as she looked, Lady Tamplin was, for once, not thinking of herself. That is to say, she was not thinking of her appearance. She was intent on graver matters.

Lady Tamplin was a well-known figure on the Riviera, and her parties at the Villa Marguerite were justly celebrated. She was a woman of considerable experience, and had had four husbands. The first had been merely an indiscretion, and so was seldom referred to by the lady. He had had the good sense to die with commendable promptitude, and his widow thereupon espoused a rich manufacturer of buttons. He too had departed for another sphere after three years of married life—it was said after a congenial evening with some boon companions. After him came Viscount Tamplin, who had placed Rosalie securely on those heights where she wished to tread. She had retained her title when she married for a fourth time. This fourth venture had been undertaken for pure pleasure. Mr. Charles Evans, an extremely good-looking young man of twenty-seven, with delightful manners, a keen love of sport, and an appreciation of this world's goods, had no money of his own whatsoever.

Lady Tamplin was very pleased and satisfied with life generally, but she had occasional faint preoccupations about money. The button manufacturer had left his widow a considerable fortune, but, as Lady Tamplin was wont to say, "what with one thing and another——" (one thing being the depreciation of stocks owing to the War, and the other the extravagances of the late Lord Tamplin). She was still comfortably off. But to be merely comfortably off is hardly satisfactory to one of Rosalie Tamplin's temperament.

So, on this particular January morning, she opened her blue eyes extremely wide as she read a certain item of news and uttered that noncommittal monosyllable "Well." The only other occupant of the balcony was her daughter, the Hon. Lenox Tamplin. A daughter such as Lenox was a sad thorn in Lady Tamplin's side, a girl with no kind of tact, who actually looked older than her age, and whose peculiar sardonic form of humour was, to say the least of it, uncomfortable.

"Darling," said Lady Tamplin, "just fancy."

"What is it?"

Lady Tamplin picked up the *Daily Mail*, handed it to her daughter, and indicated with an agitated forefinger the paragraph of interest.

Lenox read it without any of the signs of agitation shown by her mother. She handed back the paper.

"What about it?" she asked. "It is the sort of thing that is always happening. Cheese-paring old women are always dying in villages and leaving fortunes of millions to their humble companions."

"Yes, dear, I know," said her mother, "and I dare say the fortune is not anything like as large as they say it is; newspapers are so inaccurate. But even if you cut it down by half——"

"Well," said Lenox, "it has not been left to us."

"Not exactly, dear," said Lady Tamplin; "but this girl, this Katherine Grey, is actually a cousin of mine. One of the Worcestershire Greys, the Edgeworth lot. My very own cousin! Fancy!"

"Ah-ha," said Lenox.

"And I was wondering——" said her mother.

"What there was in it for us," finished Lenox, with that sideways smile that her mother always found difficult to understand.

"Oh, darling," said Lady Tamplin, on a faint note of reproach. It was very faint, because Rosalie Tamplin was used to her daughter's outspokenness and to what she called Lenox's uncomfortable way of putting things.

"I was wondering," said Lady Tamplin, again drawing her artistically pencilled brows together, "whether—oh, good morning, Chubby darling; are you going to play tennis? How nice!"

Chubby, thus addressed, smiled kindly at her, remarked perfunctorily, "How topping you look in that peach-coloured thing," and drifted past them and down the steps.

"The dear thing," said Lady Tamplin, looking affectionately after her husband. "Let me see, what was I saying? Ah!" She switched her mind back to business once more. "I was wondering——"

"Oh, for God's sake get on with it. That is the third time you have said that."

"Well, dear," said Lady Tamplin, "I was thinking that it would be very nice if I wrote to dear Katherine and suggested that she should pay us a little visit out here. Naturally, she is quite out of touch with Society. It would be nicer for her to be launched by one of her own people. An advantage for her and an advantage for us."

"How much do you think you would get her to cough up?" asked Lenox.

Her mother looked at her reproachfully and murmured.

"We should have to come to some financial arrangement, of course. What with one thing and another—the War—your poor father——"

"And Chubby now," said Lenox. "He is an expensive luxury if you like."

"She was a nice girl as I remember her," murmured Lady Tamplin, pursuing her own line of thought—"quiet, never wanted to shove herself forward, not a beauty, and never a man-hunter."

"She will leave Chubby alone, then?" said Lenox.

Lady Tamplin looked at her in protest. "Chubby would never——" she began.

"No," said Lenox, "I don't believe he would; he knows a jolly sight too well which way his bread is buttered."

"Darling," said Lady Tamplin, "you have such a coarse way of putting things."

"Sorry," said Lenox.

Lady Tamplin gathered up the *Daily Mail* and her *négligée,* a vanity-bag, and various odd letters.

"I shall write to dear Katherine at once," she said, "and remind her of the dear old days at Edgeworth."

She went into the house, a light of purpose shining in her eyes.

Unlike Mrs. Samuel Harfield, correspondence flowed easily from her pen. She covered four sheets without pause or effort, and on rereading it found no occasion to alter a word.

Katherine received it on the morning of her arrival in London. Whether she read between the lines of it or not is another matter. She put it in her handbag and started out to keep the appointment she had made with Mrs. Harfield's lawyers.

The firm was an old-established one in Lincoln's Inn Fields, and after a few minutes' delay Katherine was shown into the presence of the senior partner, a kindly, elderly man with shrewd blue eyes and a fatherly manner.

They discussed Mrs. Harfield's will and various legal matters for some minutes, then Katherine handed the lawyer Mrs. Samuel's letter.

"I had better show you this, I suppose," she said, "though it is really rather ridiculous."

He read it with a slight smile.

"Rather a crude attempt, Miss Grey. I need hardly tell you, I suppose, that these people have no claim of any kind upon the estate, and if they endeavour to contest the will no court will uphold them."

"I thought as much."

"Human nature is not always very wise. In Mrs. Samuel Harfield's place, I should have been more inclined to make an appeal to your generosity."

"That is one of the things I wanted to speak to you about. I should like a certain sum to go to these people."

"There is no obligation."

"I know that."

"And they will not take it in the spirit it is meant. They will probably regard it as an attempt to pay them off, though they will not refuse it on that account."

"I can see that, and it can't be helped."

"I should advise you, Miss Grey, to put that idea out of your head."

Katherine shook her head. "You are quite right, I know, but I should like it done all the same."

"They will grab at the money and abuse you all the more afterwards."

"Well," said Katherine, "let them if they like. We all have our own ways of enjoying ourselves. They were, after all, Mrs. Harfield's only relatives, and though they despised her as a poor relation and paid no attention to her when she was alive, it seems to me unfair that they should be cut off with nothing."

She carried her point, though the lawyer was still unwilling, and she presently went out into the streets of London with a comfortable assurance that she could spend money freely and make what plans she liked for the future. Her first action was to visit the establishment of a famous dressmaker.

A slim, elderly Frenchwoman, rather like a dreaming duchess, received her, and Katherine spoke with a certain *naïveté.*

"I want, if I may, to put myself in your hands. I have been very poor all my life and know nothing about clothes, but now I have come into some money and want to look really well dressed."

The Frenchwoman was charmed. She had an artist's temperament, which had been soured earlier in the morning by a visit from an Argentine meat queen, who had insisted on having those models least suited to her flamboyant type of beauty. She scrutinized Katherine with keen, clever eyes. "Yes—yes, it will be a pleasure. Mademoiselle has a very good figure; for her the simple lines will be best. She is also *très anglaise.* Some people it would offend them if I said that, but Mademoiselle, no. *Une belle Anglaise,* there is no style more delightful."

The demeanour of a dreaming duchess was suddenly put off. She screamed out directions to various mannequins. "Clothilde, Virginie, quickly, my little ones, the little *tailleur gris clair* and the *robe de soirée 'soupir d'automne.'* Marcelle, my child, the little mimosa suit of crêpe de chine."

It was a charming morning. Marcelle, Clothilde, Virginie, bored and scornful, passed slowly round, squirming and wriggling in the time-honoured fashion of mannequins. The Duchess stood by Katherine and made entries in a small notebook.

"An excellent choice, Mademoiselle. Mademoiselle has great *goût.* Yes, indeed. Mademoiselle cannot do better than those little suits if she is going to the Riviera, as I suppose, this winter."

"Let me see that evening dress once more," said Katherine—"the pinky mauve one."

Virginie appeared, circling slowly.

"That is the prettiest of all," said Katherine, as she surveyed the exquisite draperies of mauve and grey and blue. "What do you call it?"

"*Soupir d'automne;* yes, yes, that is truly the dress of Mademoiselle."

What was there in these words that came back to Katherine with a faint feeling of sadness after she had left the dressmaking establishment.

"*'Soupir d'automne; that is truly the dress of Mademoiselle.'*" Autumn, yes, it was autumn for her. She who had never known spring or summer, and would never know them now. Something she had lost never could be given to her again. These years of servitude in St. Mary Mead—and all the while life passing by.

"I am an idiot," said Katherine. "I am an idiot. What do I want? Why, I was more contented a month ago than I am now."

She drew out from her handbag the letter she had received that morning from Lady Tamplin. Katherine was no fool. She understood the *nuances* of that letter as well as anybody and the reason of Lady Tamplin's sudden show of affection towards a long-forgotten cousin was not lost upon her. It was for profit and not for pleasure that Lady Tamplin was so anxious for the company of her dear cousin. Well, why not? There would be profit on both sides.

"I will go," said Katherine.

She was walking down Piccadilly at the moment, and turned into Cook's to clinch the matter then and there. She had to wait for a few minutes. The man with whom the clerk was engaged was also going to the Riviera. Every one, she felt, was going. Well, for the first time in her life, she, too, would be doing what "everybody did."

The man in front of her turned abruptly, and she stepped into his place. She made her demand to the clerk, but at the same time half of her mind was busy with something else. That man's face—in some vague way it was familiar to her. Where had she seen him before? Suddenly she remembered. It was in the Savoy outside her room that morning. She had collided with him in the passage. Rather an odd coincidence that she should run into him twice in a day. She glanced over her shoulder, rendered uneasy by something, she knew not what. The man was standing in the doorway looking back at her. A cold shiver passed over Katherine; she had a haunting sense of tragedy, of doom impending. . . .

Then she shook the impression from her with her usual good sense and turned her whole attention to what the clerk was saying.

CHAPTER IX

AN OFFER REFUSED

It was rarely that Derek Kettering allowed his temper to get the better of him. An easy-going insouciance was his chief characteristic, and it had stood him in good stead in more than one tight corner. Even now, by the time he had left Mirelle's flat, he had cooled down. He had need of coolness. The corner he was in now was a tighter one than he had ever been in before, and unforeseen factors had arisen with which, for the moment, he did not know how to deal.

He strolled along deep in thought. His brow was furrowed, and there was none of the easy, jaunty manner which sat so well upon him. Various possibilities floated through his mind. It might have been said of Derek Kettering that he was less of a fool than he looked. He saw several roads that he might take—one in particular. If he shrank from it, it was for the moment only. Desperate ills need desperate remedies. He had gauged his father-in-law correctly. A war between Derek Kettering and Rufus Van Aldin could end only one way. Derek damned money and the power of money vehemently to himself. He walked up St. James's Street, across Piccadilly, and strolled along it in the direction of Piccadilly Circus. As he passed the offices of Messrs. Thomas Cook & Sons his footsteps slackened. He walked on, however, still turning the matter over in his mind. Finally, he gave a brief nod of his head, turned sharply—so sharply as to collide with a couple of pedestrians who were following in his footsteps, and went back the way he had come. This time he did not pass Cook's, but went in. The office was comparatively empty, and he got attended to at once.

"I want to go to Nice next week. Will you give me particulars?"

"What date, sir?"

"The 14th. What is the best train?"

"Well, of course, *the* best train is what they call 'The Blue Train.' You avoid the tiresome Customs business at Calais."

Derek nodded. He knew all this, none better.

"The 14th," murmured the clerk; "that is rather soon. The Blue Train is nearly always all booked up."

"See if there is a berth left," said Derek. "If there is not——" He left the sentence unfinished, with a curious smile on his face.

The clerk disappeared for a few minutes, and presently returned. "That is all right, sir; still three berths left. I will book you one of them. What name?"

"Pavett," said Derek. He gave the address of his rooms in Jermyn Street.

The clerk nodded, finished writing it down, wished Derek good morning politely, and turned his attention to the next client.

"I want to go to Nice—on the 14th. Isn't there a train called the Blue Train?"

Derek looked round sharply.

Coincidence—a strange coincidence. He remembered his own half-whimsical words to Mirelle, *"Portrait of a lady with grey eyes. I don't suppose I shall ever see her again."* But he *had* seen her again, and, what was more, she proposed to travel to the Riviera on the same day as he did.

Just for a moment a shiver passed over him; in some ways he was superstitious. He had said, half-laughingly, that this woman might bring him bad luck. Suppose—suppose that should prove to be true. From the doorway he looked back at her as she stood talking to the clerk. For once his memory had not played him false. A lady—a lady in every sense of the word. Not very young, not singularly beautiful. But with something—grey eyes that might perhaps see too much. He knew as he went out of the door that in some way he was afraid of this woman. He had a sense of fatality.

He went back to his rooms in Jermyn Street and summoned his man.

"Take this cheque, Pavett, cash it first thing in the morning, and go around to Cook's in Piccadilly. They will have some tickets there booked in your name, pay for them, and bring them back."

"Very good, sir."

Pavett withdrew.

Derek strolled over to a side-table and picked up a handful of letters. They were of a type only too familiar. Bills, small bills and large bills, one and all pressing for payment. The tone of the demands was still polite. Derek knew how soon that polite tone would change if—if certain news became public property.

He flung himself moodily into a large, leather-covered chair. A damned hole—that was what he was in. Yes, a damned hole! And ways of getting out of that damned hole were not too promising.

Pavett appeared with a discreet cough.

"A gentleman to see you—sir—Major Knighton."

"Knighton, eh?"

Derek sat up, frowned, became suddenly alert. He said in a softer tone, almost to himself: "Knighton—I wonder what is in the wind now?"

"Shall I—er—show him in, sir?"

His master nodded. When Knighton entered the room he found a charming and genial host awaiting him.

"Very good of you to look me up," said Derek.

Knighton was nervous.

The other's keen eyes noticed that at once. The errand on which the secretary had come was clearly distasteful to him. He replied almost mechanically to Derek's easy flow of conversation. He declined a drink, and, if anything, his manner became stiffer than before. Derek appeared at last to notice it.

"Well," he said cheerfully, "what does my esteemed father-in-law want with me? You have come on his business, I take it?"

Knighton did not smile in reply.

"I have, yes," he said carefully. "I—I wish Mr. Van Aldin had chosen some one else."

Derek raised his eyebrows in mock dismay.

"Is it as bad as all that? I am not very thin skinned, I can assure you, Knighton."

"No," said Knighton; "but this——"

He paused.

Derek eyed him keenly.

"Go on, out with it," he said kindly. "I can imagine my dear father-in-law's errands might not always be pleasant ones."

Knighton cleared his throat. He spoke formally in tones that he strove to render free of embarrassment.

"I am directed by Mr. Van Aldin to make you a definite offer."

"An offer?" For a moment Derek showed his surprise. Knighton's opening words were clearly not what he had expected. He offered a cigarette to Knighton, lit one himself, and sank back in his chair, murmuring in a slightly sardonic voice:

"An offer? That sounds rather interesting."

"Shall I go on?"

"Please. You must forgive my surprise, but it seems to me that my dear father-in-law has rather climbed down since our chat this morning. And climbing down is not what one associates with strong men,

Napoleons of finance, etc. It shows—I think it shows that he finds his position weaker than he thought it."

Knighton listened politely to the easy, mocking voice, but no sign of any kind showed itself on his rather stolid countenance. He waited until Derek had finished, and then he said quietly.

"I will state the proposition in the fewest possible words."

"Go on."

Knighton did not look at the other. His voice was curt and matter-of-fact.

"The matter is simply this. Mrs. Kettering, as you know, is about to file a petition for divorce. If the case goes undefended you will receive one hundred thousand on the day that the decree is made absolute."

Derek, in the act of lighting his cigarette, suddenly stopped dead.

"A hundred thousand!" he said sharply. "Dollars?"

"Pounds."

There was dead silence for at least two minutes. Kettering had his brows together thinking. A hundred thousand pounds. It meant Mirelle and a continuance of his pleasant, carefree life. It meant that Van Aldin knew something. Van Aldin did not pay for nothing. He got up and stood by the chimney-piece.

"And in the event of my refusing his handsome offer?" he asked, with a cold, ironical politeness.

Knighton made a deprecating gesture.

"I can assure you, Mr. Kettering," he said earnestly, "that it is with the utmost unwillingness that I came here with this message."

"That's all right," said Kettering. "Don't distress yourself; it's not your fault. Now then—I asked you a question, will you answer it?"

Knighton also rose. He spoke more reluctantly than before.

"In the event of your refusing this proposition," he said, "Mr. Van Aldin wished me to tell you in plain words that he proposes to break you. Just that."

Kettering raised his eyebrows, but he retained his light, amused manner.

"Well, well!" he said, "I suppose he can do it. I certainly should not be able to put up much of a fight against America's man of millions. A hundred thousand! If you are going to bribe a man there is nothing like doing it thoroughly. Supposing I were to tell you that for two hundred thousand I'd do what he wanted, what then?"

"I would take your message back to Mr. Van Aldin," said Knighton unemotionally. "Is that your answer?"

"No," said Derek; "funnily enough it is not. You can go back to my father-in-law and tell him to take himself and his bribes to hell. Is that clear?"

"Perfectly," said Knighton. He got up, hesitated, and then flushed. "I—you will allow me to say, Mr. Kettering, that I am glad you have answered as you have."

Derek did not reply. When the other had left the room he remained for a minute or two lost in thought. A curious smile came to his lips.

"And that is that," he said softly.

CHAPTER X

ON THE BLUE TRAIN

"DAD!"

Mrs. Kettering started violently. Her nerves were not completely under control this morning. Very perfectly dressed in a long mink coat and a little hat of Chinese lacquer red, she had been walking along the crowded platform of Victoria deep in thought, and her father's sudden appearance and hearty greeting had an unlooked-for effect upon her.

"Why, Ruth, how you jumped!"

"I didn't expect to see you, I suppose, Dad. You said good-bye to me last night and said you had a conference this morning."

"So I have," said Van Aldin, "but you are more to me than any number of darned conferences. I came to take a last look at you, since I am not going to see you for some time."

"That is very sweet of you, Dad. I wish you were coming too."

"What would you say if I did?"

The remark was merely a joking one. He was surprised to see the quick colour flame in Ruth's cheeks. For a moment he almost thought he saw dismay flash out of her eyes. She laughed uncertainly and nervously.

"Just for a moment I really thought you meant it," she said.

"Would you have been pleased?"

"Of course." She spoke with exaggerated emphasis.

"Well," said Van Aldin, "that's good."

"It isn't really for very long, Dad," continued Ruth; "you know, you are coming out next month."

"Ah!" said Van Aldin unemotionally, "sometimes I guess I will go to one of these big guys in Harley Street and have him tell me that I need sunshine and change of air right away."

"Don't be so lazy," cried Ruth; "next month is ever so much nicer than this month out there. You have got all sorts of things you can't possibly leave just now."

"Well, that's so, I suppose," said Van Aldin, with a sigh. "You had better be getting on board this train of yours, Ruth. Where is your seat?"

Ruth Kettering looked vaguely up at the train. At the door of one of the Pullman cars a thin, tall woman dressed in black was standing —Ruth Kettering's maid. She drew aside as her mistress came up to her.

"I have put your dressing-case under your seat, Madam, in case you should need it. Shall I take the rugs, or will you require one?"

"No, no, I shan't want one. Better go and find your own seat now, Mason."

"Yes, Madam."

The maid departed.

Van Aldin entered the Pullman car with Ruth. She found her seat, and Van Aldin deposited various papers and magazines on the table in front of her. The seat opposite to her was already taken, and the American gave a cursory glance at its occupant. He had a fleeting impression of attractive grey eyes and a neat travelling costume. He indulged in a little more desultory conversation with Ruth, the kind of talk peculiar to those seeing other people off by train.

Presently, as whistles blew, he glanced at his watch.

"I had best be clearing out of here. Good-bye, my dear. Don't worry, I will attend to things."

"Oh, father!"

He turned back sharply. There had been something in Ruth's voice, something so entirely foreign to her usual manner, that he was startled. It was almost a cry of despair. She had made an impulsive movement towards him, but in another minute she was mistress of herself once more.

"Till next month," she said cheerfully.

Two minutes later the train started.

Ruth sat very still, biting her under lip and trying hard to keep the unaccustomed tears from her eyes. She felt a sudden sense of horrible desolation. There was a wild longing upon her to jump out of the train and to go back before it was too late. She, so calm, so self-assured, for the first time in her life felt like a leaf swept by the wind. If her father knew—what would he say?

Madness! Yes, just that, madness! For the first time in her life she was swept away by emotion, swept away to the point of doing a thing which even she knew to be incredibly foolish and reckless. She was enough Van Aldin's daughter to realize her own folly, and level headed enough to condemn her own action. But she was his daughter in another sense also. She had that same iron determination that would have what it wanted, and once it had made up its mind would not be balked. From her cradle she had been self-willed; the very circumstances of her life had developed that self-will in her. It drove her now remorselessly. Well, the die was cast. She must go through with it now.

She looked up, and her eyes met those of the woman sitting opposite. She had a sudden fancy that in some way this other woman had read her mind. She saw in those grey eyes understanding and—yes—compassion.

It was only a fleeting impression. The faces of both women hardened to well-bred impassiveness. Mrs. Kettering took up a magazine, and Katherine Grey looked out of the window and watched a seemingly endless vista of depressing streets and suburban houses.

Ruth found an increasing difficulty in fixing her mind on the printed page in front of her. In spite of herself, a thousand apprehensions preyed on her mind. What a fool she had been! What a fool she was! Like all cool and self-sufficient people, when she did lose her self-control she lost it thoroughly. It was too late. . . . Was it too late? Oh, for some one to speak to, for some one to advise her. She had never before had such a wish; she would have scorned the idea of relying on any judgment other than her own, but now—what was the matter with her? Panic. Yes, that would describe it best—panic. She, Ruth Kettering, was completely and utterly panic stricken.

She stole a covert glance at the figure opposite. If only she knew some one like that, some nice, cool, calm, sympathetic creature. That was the sort of person one could talk to. But you can't, of course, confide in a stranger. And Ruth smiled to herself a little at the idea. She picked up the magazine again. Really she must control herself. After all, she had thought all this out. She had decided of her own free will. What happiness had she ever had in her life up to now? She said to herself restlessly: "Why shouldn't I be happy? No one will ever know."

It seemed no time before Dover was reached. Ruth was a good sailor. She disliked the cold, and was glad to reach the shelter of the private cabin she had telegraphed for. Although she would not have admitted the fact, Ruth was in some ways superstitious. She was of the order of people to whom coincidence appeals. After disembarking at Calais and settling herself down with her maid in her double compartment in the Blue Train, she went along to the luncheon car. It was with a little shock of surprise that she found herself set down to a small table with, opposite her, the same woman who had been her *vis-à-vis* in the Pullman. A faint smile came to the lips of both women.

"This is quite a coincidence," said Mrs. Kettering.

"I know," said Katherine; "it is odd the way things happen."

A flying attendant shot up to them with the wonderful velocity always displayed by the Compagnie Internationale des Wagons-Lits and deposited two cups of soup. By the time the omelette succeeded the soup they were chatting together in friendly fashion.

"It will be heavenly to get into the sunshine," sighed Ruth.

"I am sure it will be a wonderful feeling."

"You know the Riviera well?"

"No; this is my first visit."

"Fancy that."

"You go every year, I expect?"

"Practically. January and February in London are horrible."

"I have always lived in the country. They are not very inspiring months there either. Mostly mud."

"What made you suddenly decide to travel?"

"Money," said Katherine. "For ten years I have been a paid companion with just enough money of my own to buy myself strong country shoes; now I have been left what seems to me a fortune, though I dare say it would not seem so to you."

"Now I wonder why you say that—that it would not seem so to me."

Katherine laughed. "I don't really know. I suppose one forms impressions without thinking of it. I put you down in my own mind as one of the very rich of the earth. It was just an impression. I dare say I am wrong."

"No," said Ruth, "you are not wrong." She had suddenly become very grave. "I wish you would tell me what other impressions you formed about me?"

"I—"

Ruth swept on disregarding the other's embarrassment.

"Oh, please, don't be conventional. I want to know. As we left Victoria I looked across at you, and I had the sort of feeling that you —well, understood what was going on in my mind."

"I can assure you I am not a mind reader," said Katherine, smiling.

"No; but will you tell me, please, just what you thought." Ruth's eagerness was so intense and so sincere that she carried her point.

"I will tell you if you like, but you must not think me impertinent.

I thought that for some reason you were in great distress of mind, and I was sorry for you."

"You are right. You are quite right. I am in terrible trouble. I—I should like to tell you something about it, if I may."

"Oh, dear," Katherine thought to herself, "how extraordinarily alike the world seems to be everywhere! People were always telling me things in St. Mary Mead, and it is just the same thing here, and I don't really want to hear anybody's troubles!"

She replied politely:

"Do tell me."

They were just finishing their lunch. Ruth gulped down her coffee, rose from her seat, and quite oblivious of the fact that Katherine had not begun to sip her coffee, said: "Come to my compartment with me."

They were two single compartments with a communicating door between them. In the second of them a thin maid, whom Katherine had noticed at Victoria, was sitting very upright on the seat, clutching a big scarlet morocco case with the initials R. V. K. on it. Mrs. Kettering pulled the communicating door to and sank down on the seat. Katherine sat down beside her.

"I am in trouble and I don't know what to do. There is a man whom I am fond of—very fond of indeed. We cared for each other when we were young, and we were thrust apart most brutally and unjustly. Now we have come together again."

"Yes?"

"I—I am going to meet him now. Oh! I dare say you think it is all wrong, but you don't know the circumstances. My husband is impossible. He has treated me disgracefully."

"Yes," said Katherine again.

"What I feel so badly about is this. I have deceived my father—it was he who came to see me off at Victoria to-day. He wishes me to divorce my husband, and, of course, he has no idea—that I am going to meet this other man. He would think it extraordinarily foolish."

"Well, don't you think it is?"

"I—I suppose it is."

Ruth Kettering looked down at her hands; they were shaking violently.

"But I can't draw back now."

"Why not?"

"I—it is all arranged, and it would break his heart."

"Don't you believe it," said Katherine robustly; "hearts are pretty tough."

"He will think I have no courage, no strength of purpose."

"It seems to me an awfully silly thing that you are going to do," said Katherine. "I think you realize that yourself."

Ruth Kettering buried her face in her hands. "I don't know—I don't know. Ever since I left Victoria I have had a horrible feeling of something—something that is coming to me very soon—that I can't escape."

She clutched convulsively at Katherine's hand.

"You must think I am mad talking to you like this, but I tell you I know something horrible is going to happen."

"Don't think it," said Katherine; "try to pull yourself together. You could send your father a wire from Paris, if you like, and he would come to you at once."

The other brightened.

"Yes, I could do that. Dear old Dad. It is queer—but I never knew until to-day how terribly fond of him I am." She sat up and dried her eyes with a handkerchief. "I have been very foolish. Thank you so much for letting me talk to you. I don't know why I got into such a queer, hysterical state."

She got up. "I am quite all right now. I suppose, really, I just needed some one to talk to. I can't think now why I have been making such an absolute fool of myself."

Katherine got up too.

"I am so glad you feel better," she said, trying to make her voice sound as conventional as possible. She was only too well aware that the aftermath of confidences is embarrassment. She added tactfully:

"I must be going back to my own compartment."

She emerged into the corridor at the same time as the maid was also coming out from the next door. The latter looked towards Katherine, over her shoulder, and an expression of intense surprise showed itself on her face. Katherine turned also, but by that time whoever it was who had aroused the maid's interest had retreated into his or her compartment, and the corridor was empty. Katherine walked down it to regain her own place, which was in the next coach. As she passed the end compartment the door opened and a woman's face looked out for a moment and then pulled the door to sharply. It was a face not easily forgotten, as Katherine was to know when she saw it again. A beautiful face, oval and dark, very heavily made up in a bizarre fashion. Katherine had a feeling that she had seen it before somewhere.

She regained her own compartment without other adventure and sat for some time thinking of the confidence which had just been made to her. She wondered idly who the woman in the mink coat might be, wondered also how the end of her story would turn out.

"If I have stopped any one from making an idiot of themselves, I suppose I have done good work," she thought to herself. "But who knows? That is the kind of woman who is hard-headed and egotistical all her life, and it might be good for her to do the other sort of thing for a change. Oh, well—I don't suppose I shall ever see her again. She certainly won't want to see *me* again. That is the worst of letting people tell you things. They never do."

She hoped that she would not be given the same place at dinner. She reflected, not without humour, that it might be awkward for both of them. Leaning back with her head against a cushion she felt tired and vaguely depressed. They had reached Paris, and the slow journey round the *ceinture*, with its interminable stops and waits, was very wearisome. When they arrived at the Gare de Lyon she was glad to get out and walk up and down the platform. The keen cold air was refreshing after the steam-heated train. She observed with a smile that her friend of the mink coat was solving the possible awkwardness of the dinner problem in her own way. A dinner basket was being handed up and received through the window by the maid.

When the train started once more, and dinner was announced by a violent ringing of bells, Katherine went along to it much relieved in mind. Her *vis-à-vis* to-night was of an entirely different kind—a small man, distinctly foreign in appearance, with a rigidly waxed moustache and an egg-shaped head which he carried rather on one side. Katherine had taken in a book to dinner with her. She found the little man's eyes fixed upon it with a kind of twinkling amusement.

"I see, Madame, that you have a *Roman Policier*. You are fond of such things?"

"They amuse me," Katherine admitted.

The little man nodded with the air of complete understanding. "They have a good sale always, so I am told. Now why is that, eh,

Mademoiselle? I ask it of you as a student of human nature—why should that be?"

Katherine felt more and more amused.

"Perhaps they give one the illusion of living an exciting life," she suggested.

He nodded gravely.

"Yes; there is something in that."

"Of course, one knows that such things don't really happen," Katherine was continuing, but he interrupted her sharply.

"Sometimes, Mademoiselle! Sometimes! I who speak to you—they have happened to *me*."

She threw him a quick, interested glance.

"Some day, who knows, *you* might be in the thick of things," he went on. "It is all chance."

"I don't think it is likely," said Katherine. "Nothing of that kind ever happens to me."

He leaned forward.

"Would you like it to?"

The question startled her, and she drew in her breath sharply.

"It is my fancy, perhaps," said the little man, as he dexterously polished one of the forks, "but I think that you have a yearning in you for interesting happenings. *Eh bien,* Mademoiselle, all through my life I have observed one thing—'All one wants one gets!' Who knows?" His face screwed itself up comically. "You may get more than you bargain for."

"Is that a prophecy?" asked Katherine, smiling as she rose from the table.

The little man shook his head.

"I never prophesy," he declared pompously. "It is true that I have the habit of being always right—but I do not boast of it. Good-night, Mademoiselle, and may you sleep well."

Katherine went back along the train amused and entertained by her little neighbour. She passed the open door of her friend's compartment and saw the conductor making up the bed. The lady in the mink coat was standing looking out of the window. The second compartment, as Katherine saw through the communicating door, was empty, with rugs and bags heaped up on the seat. The maid was not there.

Katherine found her own bed prepared, and since she was tired, she went to bed and switched off her light about half-past nine.

She woke with a sudden start; how much time had passed she did not know. Glancing at her watch, she found that it had stopped. A feeling of intense uneasiness pervaded her and grew stronger moment by moment. At last she got up, threw her dressing-gown round her shoulders, and stepped out into the corridor. The whole train seemed wrapped in slumber. Katherine let down the window and sat by it for some minutes, drinking in the cool night air and trying vainly to calm her uneasy fears. She presently decided that she would go along to the end and ask the conductor for the right time so that she could set her watch. She found, however, that his little chair was vacant. She hesitated for a moment and then walked through into the next coach. She looked down the long, dim line of the corridor and saw, to her surprise, that a man was standing with his hand on the door of the compartment occupied by the lady in the mink coat. That is to say, she thought it was the compartment. Probably, however, she was mistaken. He stood there for a moment or two with his back to her, seeming uncertain and hesitating in his attitude. Then he slowly turned, and with an odd feeling of fatality, Katherine recognized him as the same man whom she had noticed twice before—once in the corridor of the Savoy Hotel and once in Cook's offices. Then he opened the door of the compartment and passed in, drawing it to behind him.

An idea flashed across Katherine's mind. Could this be the man of whom the other woman had spoken—the man she was journeying to meet.

Then Katherine told herself that she was romancing. In all probability she had mistaken the compartment.

She went back to her own carriage. Five minutes later the train slackened speed. There was the long plaintive hiss of the Westinghouse brake, and a few minutes later the train came to a stop at Lyons.

CHAPTER XI

MURDER

KATHERINE WAKENED the next morning to brilliant sunshine. She went along to breakfast early, but met none of her acquaintances of the day before. When she returned to her compartment it had just been restored to its daytime appearance by the conductor, a dark man with a drooping moustache and melancholy face.

"Madame is fortunate," he said; "the sun shines. It is always a great disappointment to passengers when they arrive on a grey morning."

"I should have been disappointed, certainly," said Katherine.

The man prepared to depart.

"We are rather late, Madame," he said. "I will let you know just before we get to Nice."

Katherine nodded. She sat by the window, entranced by the sunlit panorama. The palm trees, the deep blue of the sea, the bright yellow mimosa came with all the charm of novelty to the woman who for fourteen years had known only the drab winters of England.

When they arrived at Cannes, Katherine got out and walked up and down the platform. She was curious about the lady in the mink coat, and looked up at the windows of her compartment. The blinds were still drawn down—the only ones to be so on the whole train. Katherine wondered a little, and when she re-entered the train she passed along the corridor and noticed that these two compartments were still shuttered and closed. The lady of the mink coat was clearly no early riser.

Presently the conductor came to her and told her that in a few minutes the train would arrive at Nice. Katherine handed him a tip; the man thanked her, but still lingered. There was something odd about him. Katherine, who had at first wondered whether the tip had not been big enough, was now convinced that something far more serious was amiss. His face was of a sickly pallor, he was shaking all over, and looked as if he had been frightened out of his life. He was eyeing her in a curious manner. Presently he said abruptly: "Madame will excuse me, but is she expecting friends to meet her at Nice?"

"Probably," said Katherine. "Why?"

But the man merely shook his head and murmured something that

Katherine could not catch and moved away, not reappearing until the train came to rest at the station, when he started handing her belongings down from the window.

Katherine stood for a moment or two on the platform rather at a loss, but a fair young man with an ingenuous face came up to her and said rather hesitatingly:

"Miss Grey, is it not?"

Katherine said that it was, and the young man beamed upon her seraphically and murmured:

"I am Chubby, you know—Lady Tamplin's husband. I expect she mentioned me, but perhaps she forgot. Have you got your *billet de bagages?* I lost mine when I came out this year, and you would not believe the fuss they made about it. Regular French red tape!"

Katherine produced it, and was just about to move off beside him when a very gentle and insidious voice murmured in her ear:

"A little moment, Madame, if you please."

Katherine turned to behold an individual who made up for insignificance of stature by a large quantity of gold lace and uniform. The individual explained. "There were certain formalities. Madame would perhaps be so kind as to accompany him. The regulations of the police——" He threw up his arms. "Absurd, doubtless, but there it was."

Mr. Chubby Evans listened with a very imperfect comprehension, his French being of a limited order.

"So like the French," murmured Mr. Evans. He was one of those staunch patriotic Britons who, having made a portion of a foreign country their own, strongly resent the original inhabitants of it. "Always up to some silly dodge or other. They've never tackled people on the station before, though. This is something quite new. I suppose you'll have to go."

Katherine departed with her guide. Somewhat to her surprise, he led her towards a siding where a coach of the departed train had been shunted. He invited her to mount into this, and, preceding her down the corridor, held aside the door of one of the compartments. In it was a pompous-looking official personage, and with him a nondescript being who appeared to be a clerk. The pompous-looking personage rose politely, bowed to Katherine, and said:

"You will excuse me, Madame, but there are certain formalities to be complied with. Madame speaks French, I trust?"

"Sufficiently, I think, Monsieur," replied Katherine in that language.

"That is good. Pray be seated, Madame. I am M. Caux, the Commissary of Police." He blew out his chest importantly, and Katherine tried to look sufficiently impressed.

"You wish to see my passport?" she inquired. "Here it is."

The Commissary eyed her keenly and gave a little grunt.

"Thank you, Madame," he said, taking the passport from her. He cleared his throat. "But what I really desire is a little information."

"Information?"

The Commissary nodded his head slowly.

"About a lady who has been a fellow-passenger of yours. You lunched with her yesterday."

"I am afraid I can't tell you anything about her. We fell into conversation over our meal, but she is a complete stranger to me. I have never seen her before."

"And yet," said the Commissary sharply, "you returned to her compartment with her after lunch and sat talking for some time?"

"Yes," said Katherine; "that is true."

The Commissary seemed to expect her to say something more. He looked at her encouragingly.

"Yes, Madame?"

"Well, Monsieur?" said Katherine.

"You can, perhaps, give me some kind of idea of that conversation?"

"I could," said Katherine, "but at the moment I see no reason to do so."

In somewhat British fashion she felt annoyed. This foreign official seemed to her impertinent.

"No reason?" cried the Commissary. "Oh yes, Madame, I can assure you that there *is* a reason."

"Then perhaps you will give it to me."

The Commissary rubbed his chin thoughtfully for a minute or two without speaking.

"Madame," he said at last, "the reason is very simple. The lady in question was found dead in her compartment this morning."

"Dead!" gasped Katherine. "What was it—heart failure?"

"No," said the Commissary in a reflective, dreamy voice. "No—she was murdered."

"Murdered!" cried Katherine.

"So you see, Madame, why we are anxious for any information we can possibly get."

"But surely her maid——"

"The maid has disappeared."

"Oh!" Katherine paused to assemble her thoughts.

"Since the conductor had seen you talking with her in her compartment, he quite naturally reported the fact to the police, and that is why, Madame, we have detained you, in the hope of gaining some information."

"I am very sorry," said Katherine; "I don't even know her name."

"Her name is Kettering. That we know from her passport and from the labels on her luggage. If we——"

There was a knock on the compartment door. M. Caux frowned. He opened it about six inches.

"What is the matter?" he said peremptorily. "I cannot be disturbed."

The egg-shaped head of Katherine's dinner acquaintance showed itself in the aperture. On his face was a beaming smile.

"My name," he said, "is Hercule Poirot."

"Not," the Commissary stammered, "not *the* Hercule Poirot?"

"The same," said Mr. Poirot. "I remember meeting you once, M. Caux, at the *Sûreté* in Paris, though doubtless you have forgotten me?"

"Not at all, Monsieur, not at all," declared the Commissary heartily. "But enter, I pray of you. You know of this——"

"Yes, I know," said Hercule Poirot. "I came to see if I might be of any assistance?"

"We should be flattered," replied the Commissary promptly. "Let me present you, Mr. Poirot, to"—he consulted the passport he still held in his hand—"to Madame—er—Mademoiselle Grey."

Poirot smiled across at Katherine.

"It is strange, is it not," he murmured, "that my words should have come true so quickly?"

"Mademoiselle, alas! can tell us very little," said the Commissary.

"I have been explaining," said Katherine, "that this poor lady was a complete stranger to me."

Poirot nodded.

"But she talked to you, did she not?" he said gently. "You formed an impression—is it not so?"

"Yes," said Katherine thoughtfully. "I suppose I did."

"And that impression was——"

"Yes, Mademoiselle"—the Commissary jerked himself forward—"let us by all means have your impressions."

Katherine sat turning the whole thing over in her mind. She felt in a way as if she were betraying a confidence, but with that ugly word "Murder" ringing in her ears she dared not keep anything back. Too much might hang upon it. So, as nearly as she could, she repeated word for word the conversation she had had with the dead woman.

"That is interesting," said the Commissary, glancing at the other. "Eh, M. Poirot, that is interesting? Whether it has anything to do with the crime——" He left the sentence unfinished.

"I suppose it could not be suicide," said Katherine, rather doubtfully.

"No," said the Commissary, "it could not be suicide. She was strangled with a length of black cord."

"Oh!" Katherine shivered. M. Caux spread out his hands apologetically. "It is not nice—no. I think that our train robbers are more brutal than they are in your country."

"It is horrible."

"Yes, yes"—he was soothing and apologetic—"but you have great courage, Mademoiselle. At once, as soon as I saw you, I said to myself, 'Mademoiselle has great courage.' That is why I am going to ask you to do something more—something distressing, but I assure you very necessary."

Katherine looked at him apprehensively.

He spread out his hands apologetically.

"I am going to ask you, Mademoiselle, to be so good as to accompany me to the next compartment."

"Must I?" asked Katherine in a low voice.

"Some one must identify her," said the Commissary, "and since the maid has disappeared"—he coughed significantly—"you appear to be the person who has seen most of her since she joined the train."

"Very well," said Katherine quietly; "if it is necessary——"

She rose. Poirot gave her a little nod of approval.

"Mademoiselle is sensible," he said. "May I accompany you, M. Caux?"

"Enchanted, my dear M. Poirot."

They went out into the corridor, and M. Caux unlocked the door of the dead woman's compartment. The blinds on the far side had been drawn half-way up to admit light. The dead woman lay on the berth to their left, in so natural a posture that one could have thought her asleep. The bedclothes were drawn up over her, and her head was turned to the wall, so that only the red auburn curls showed. Very gently M. Caux laid a hand on her shoulder and turned the body back so that the face came into view. Katherine flinched a little and dug her nails into her palms. A heavy blow had disfigured the features almost beyond recognition. Poirot gave a sharp exclamation.

"When was that done, I wonder?" he demanded. "Before death or after?"

"The doctor says after," said M. Caux.

"Strange," said Poirot, drawing his brows together. He turned to Katherine. "Be brave, Mademoiselle; look at her well. Are you sure that this is the woman you talked to in the train yesterday?"

Katherine had good nerves. She steeled herself to look long and earnestly at the recumbent figure. Then she leaned forward and took up the dead woman's hand.

"I am quite sure," she replied at length. "The face is too disfigured to recognize, but the build and carriage and hair are exact, and besides I noticed *this*"—she pointed to a tiny mole on the dead woman's wrist—"while I was talking to her."

"*Bon,*" approved Poirot. "You are an excellent witness, Mademoiselle. There is, then, no question as to the identity, but it is strange, all the same." He frowned down on the dead woman in perplexity.

M. Caux shrugged his shoulders.

"The murderer was carried away by rage, doubtless," he suggested.

"If she had been struck down, it would have been comprehensible," mused Poirot, "but the man who strangled her slipped up behind and caught her unawares. A little choke—a little gurgle—that is all that would be heard, and then afterwards—that smashing blow on her face. Now why? Did he hope that if the face were unrecognizable she might not be identified? Or did he hate her so much that he could not resist striking that blow even after she was dead?"

Katherine shuddered, and he turned at once to her kindly.

"You must not let me distress you, Mademoiselle," he said. "To you this is all very new and terrible. To me, alas! it is an old story. One moment, I pray of you both."

They stood against the door watching him as he went quickly round the compartment. He noted the dead woman's clothes neatly folded on the end of the berth, the big fur coat that hung from a hook, and the little red lacquer hat tossed up on the rack. Then he passed through into the adjoining compartment, that in which Katherine had seen the maid sitting. Here the berth had not been made up. Three or four rugs were piled loosely on the seat; there was a hat-box and a couple of suitcases. He turned suddenly to Katherine.

"You were in here yesterday," he said. "Do you see anything changed, anything missing?"

Katherine looked carefully round both compartments.

"Yes," she said, "there is something missing—a scarlet morocco case. It had the initials 'R. V. K.' on it. It might have been a small dressing-case or a big jewel-case. When I saw it, the maid was holding it."

"Ah!" said Poirot.

"But, surely," said Katherine. "I—of course, I don't know anything about such things, but surely it is plain enough, if the maid and the jewel-case are missing?"

"You mean that it was the maid who was the thief? No, Mademoiselle; there is a very good reason against that."

"What?"

"The maid was left behind in Paris."

He turned to Poirot.

"I should like you to hear the conductor's story yourself," he murmured confidentially. "It is very suggestive."

"Mademoiselle would doubtless like to hear it also," said Poirot. "You do not object, Monsieur le Commissaire?"

"No," said the Commissary, who clearly did object very much. "No, certainly, M. Poirot, if you say so. You have finished here?"

"I think so. One little minute."

He had been turning over the rugs, and now he took one to the window and looked at it, picking something off it with his fingers.

"What is it?" demanded M. Caux sharply.

"Four auburn hairs." He bent over the dead woman. "Yes, they are from the head of Madame."

"And what of it? Do you attach importance to them?"

Poirot let the rug drop back on the seat.

"What is important? What is not? One cannot say at this stage. But we must note each little fact carefully."

They went back again into the first compartment, and in a minute or two the conductor of the carriage arrived to be questioned.

"Your name is Pierre Michel?" said the Commissary.

"Yes, Monsieur le Commissaire."

"I should like you to repeat to this gentleman"—he indicated Poirot—"the story that you told me as to what happened in Paris."

"Very good, Monsieur le Commissaire. It was after we had left the Gare de Lyon I came along to make the beds, thinking that Madame would be at dinner, but she had a dinner-basket in her compartment. She said to me that she had been obliged to leave her maid behind in Paris, so that I only need make up one berth. She took her dinner-basket into the adjoining compartment, and sat there while I made up the bed; then she told me that she did not wish to be wakened early in the morning, that she liked to sleep on. I told her I quite understood, and she wished me 'good-night.'"

"You yourself did not go into the adjoining compartment?"

"No, Monsieur."

"Then you did not happen to notice if a scarlet morocco case was amongst the luggage there?"

"No, Monsieur, I did not."

"Would it have been possible for a man to have been concealed in the adjoining compartment?"

The conductor reflected.

"The door was half open," he said. "If a man had stood behind that door I should not have been able to see him, but he would, of course, have been perfectly visible to Madame when she went in there."

"Quite so," said Poirot. "Is there anything more you have to tell us?"

"I think that is all, Monsieur. I can remember nothing else."

"And now this morning?" prompted Poirot.

"As Madame had ordered, I did not disturb her. It was not until just before Cannes that I ventured to knock at the door. Getting no reply, I opened it. The lady appeared to be in her bed asleep. I took her by the shoulder to rouse her, and then——"

"And then you saw what had happened," volunteered Poirot. "*Très bien.* I think I know all I want to know."

"I hope, Monsieur le Commissaire, it is not that I have been guilty of any negligence," said the man piteously. "Such an affair to happen on the Blue Train! It is horrible."

"Console yourself," said the Commissary. "Everything will be done to keep the affair as quiet as possible, if only in the interests of justice. I cannot think you have been guilty of any negligence."

"And Monsieur le Commissaire will report as much to the Company?"

"But certainly, but certainly," said M. Caux impatiently. "That will do now."

The conductor withdrew.

"According to the medical evidence," said the Commissary, "the lady was probably dead before the train reached Lyons. Who then was the murderer? From Mademoiselle's story, it seems clear that somewhere on her journey she was to meet this man of whom she spoke. Her action in getting rid of the maid seems significant. Did the man join the train at Paris, and did she conceal him in the adjoining compartment? If so, they may have quarrelled, and he may have killed her in a fit of rage. That is one possibility. The other, and the more likely to my mind, is that her assailant was a train robber travelling on the train; that he stole along the corridor unseen by the conductor, killed her, and went off with the red morocco case, which doubtless contained jewels of some value. In all probability he left the train at Lyons, and we have already telegraphed to the station there for full particulars of any one seen leaving the train."

"Or he might have come on to Nice," suggested Poirot.

"He might," agreed the Commissary, "but that would be a very bold course."

Poirot let a minute or two go by before speaking, and then he said:

"In the latter case you think the man was an ordinary train robber?"

The Commissary shrugged his shoulders.

"It depends. We must get hold of the maid. It is possible that she has the red morocco case with her. If so, then the man of whom she spoke to Mademoiselle may be concerned in the case, and the affair is a crime of passion. I myself think the solution of a train robber is the more probable. These bandits have become very bold of late."

Poirot looked suddenly across to Katherine.

"And you, Mademoiselle," he said, "you heard and saw nothing during the night?"

"Nothing," said Katherine.

Poirot turned to the Commissary.

"We need detain Mademoiselle no longer, I think," he suggested.

The latter nodded.

"She will leave us her address?" he said.

Katherine gave him the name of Lady Tamplin's villa. Poirot made her a little bow.

"You permit that I see you again, Mademoiselle?" he said. "Or have you so many friends that your time will be all taken up?"

"On the contrary," said Katherine, "I shall have plenty of leisure, and I shall be very pleased to see you again."

"Excellent," said Poirot, and gave her a little friendly nod. "This shall be a '*Roman Policier*' *à nous*. We will investigate this affair together."

CHAPTER XII

AT THE VILLA MARGUERITE

"THEN YOU WERE really in the thick of it all!" said Lady Tamplin enviously. "My dear, how thrilling!" She opened her china blue eyes very wide and gave a little sigh.

"A real murder," said Mr. Evans gloatingly.

"Of course Chubby had no idea of anything of the kind," went on Lady Tamplin; "he simply could *not* imagine why the police wanted you. My dear, what an opportunity! I think, you know—yes, I certainly think something might be made out of this."

A calculating look rather marred the ingenuousness of the blue eyes.

Katherine felt slightly uncomfortable. They were just finishing lunch, and she looked in turn at the three people sitting round the table. Lady Tamplin, full of practical schemes; Mr. Evans, beaming with naïve appreciation, and Lenox with a queer crooked smile on her dark face.

"Marvellous luck," murmured Chubby; "I wish I could have gone along with you—and seen—all the exhibits."

His tone was wistful and childlike.

Katherine said nothing. The police had laid no injunctions of secrecy upon her, and it was clearly impossible to suppress the bare facts or try to keep them from her hostess. But she did rather wish it had been possible to do so.

"Yes," said Lady Tamplin, coming suddenly out of her reverie, "I do think something might be done. A little account, you know, cleverly written up. An eyewitness, a feminine touch: '*How I chatted with the dead woman, little thinking*——' that sort of thing, you know."

"Rot!" said Lenox.

"You have no idea," said Lady Tamplin in a soft, wistful voice, "what newspapers will pay for a little titbit! Written, of course, by some one of really unimpeachable social position. You would not like to do it yourself, I dare say, Katherine dear, but just give me the bare bones of it, and *I* will manage the whole thing for you. Mr. de Haviland is a special friend of mine. We have a little understanding together. A most delightful man—not at all reporterish. How does the idea strike you, Katherine?"

"I would much prefer to do nothing of the kind," said Katherine bluntly.

Lady Tamplin was rather disconcerted at this uncompromising refusal. She sighed and turned to the elucidation of further details.

"A very striking-looking woman, you said? I wonder now who she could have been. You didn't hear her name?"

"It was mentioned," Katherine admitted, "but I can't remember it. You see, I was rather upset."

"I should think so," said Mr. Evans; "it must have been a beastly shock."

It is to be doubted whether, even if Katherine had remembered the name, she would have admitted the fact. Lady Tamplin's remorseless cross-examination was making her restive. Lenox, who was observant in her own way, noticed this, and offered to take Katherine upstairs to see her room. She left her there, remarking kindly before she went: "You mustn't mind Mother; she would make a few pennies' profit out of her dying grandmother if she could."

Lenox went down again to find her mother and her stepfather discussing the newcomer.

"Presentable," said Lady Tamplin, "quite presentable. Her clothes are all right. That grey thing is the same model that Gladys Cooper wore in *Palm Trees in Egypt*."

"Have you noticed her eyes—what?" interposed Mr. Evans.

"Never mind her eyes, Chubby," said Lady Tamplin tartly; "we are discussing the things that really matter."

"Oh, quite," said Mr. Evans, and retired into his shell.

"She doesn't seem to me very—malleable," said Lady Tamplin, rather hesitating to choose the right word.

"She has all the instincts of a lady, as they say in books," said Lenox, with a grin.

"Narrow-minded," murmured Lady Tamplin. "Inevitable under the circumstances, I suppose."

"I expect you will do your best to broaden her," said Lenox, with a grin, "but you will have your work cut out. Just now, you noticed, she stuck down her fore feet and laid back her ears and refused to budge."

"Anyway," said Lady Tamplin hopefully, "she doesn't look to me at all mean. Some people, when they come into money, seem to attach undue importance to it."

"Oh, you'll easily touch her for what you want," said Lenox; "and, after all, that is all that matters, isn't it? That is what she is here for."

"She is my own cousin," said Lady Tamplin, with dignity.

"Cousin, eh?" said Mr. Evans, waking up again. "I suppose I call her Katherine, don't I?"

"It is of no importance at all what you call her, Chubby," said Lady Tamplin.

"Good," said Mr. Evans; "then I will. Do you suppose she plays tennis?" he added hopefully.

"Of course not," said Lady Tamplin. "She has been a companion, I tell you. Companions don't play tennis—or golf. They might possibly play golf-croquet, but I have always understood that they wind wool and wash dogs most of the day."

"O God!" said Mr. Evans; "do they really?"

Lenox drifted upstairs again to Katherine's room. "Can I help you?" she asked rather perfunctorily.

On Katherine's disclaimer, Lenox sat on the edge of the bed and stared thoughtfully at her guest.

"Why did you come?" she said at last. "To us, I mean. We're not your sort."

"Oh, I am anxious to get into Society."

"Don't be an ass," said Lenox promptly, detecting the flicker of a smile. "You know what I mean well enough. You are not a bit what I thought you would be. I say, you *have* got some decent clothes." She sighed. "Clothes are no good to me. I was born awkward. It's a pity, because I love them."

"I love them too," said Katherine, "but it has not been much use my loving them up to now. Do you think this is nice?"

She and Lenox discussed several models with artistic fervour.

"I like you," said Lenox suddenly. "I came up to warn you not to be taken in by Mother, but I think now that there is no need to do that. You are frightfully sincere and upright and all those queer things, but you are not a fool. Oh hell! what is it now?"

Lady Tamplin's voice was calling plaintively from the hall:

"Lenox, Derek has just rung up. He wants to come to dinner tonight. Will it be all right? I mean, we haven't got anything awkward, like quails, have we?"

Lenox reassured her and came back into Katherine's room. Her face looked brighter and less sullen.

"I'm glad old Derek is coming," she said; "you'll like him."

"Who is Derek?"

"He is Lord Leconbury's son, married a rich American woman. Women are simply potty about him."

"Why?"

"Oh, the usual reason—very good-looking and a regular bad lot. Every one goes off their head about him."

"Do you?"

"Sometimes I do," said Lenox, "and sometimes I think I would like to marry a nice curate and live in the country and grow things in frames." She paused a minute, and then added, "An Irish curate would be best, and then I should hunt."

After a minute or two she reverted to her former theme. "There is something queer about Derek. All that family are a bit potty—mad gamblers, you know. In the old days they used to gamble away their wives and their estates, and did most reckless things just for the love of it. Derek would have made a perfect highwayman—debonair and gay, just the right manner." She moved to the door. "Well, come down when you feel like it."

Left alone, Katherine gave herself up to thought. Just at present she felt thoroughly ill at ease and jarred by her surroundings. The shock of the discovery in the train and the reception of the news by her new friends jarred upon her susceptibilities. She thought long and earnestly about the murdered woman. She had been sorry for Ruth, but she could not honestly say that she had liked her. She had divined only too well the ruthless egoism that was the keynote of her personality, and it repelled her.

She had been amused and a trifle hurt by the other's cool dismissal of her when she had served her turn. That she had come to some decision, Katherine was quite certain, but she wondered now what that decision had been. Whatever it was, death had stepped in and made all decisions meaningless. Strange that it should have been so, and that a brutal crime should have been the ending of that fateful journey. But suddenly Katherine remembered a small fact that she ought, perhaps, to have told the police—a fact that had for the moment escaped her memory. Was it of any real importance? She had certainly thought that she had seen a man going into that particular compartment, but she realized that she might easily have been mistaken. It might have been the compartment next door, and certainly the man in question could be no train robber. She recalled him very clearly as she had seen him on those two previous occasions—once at the Savoy and once at Cook's office. No, doubtless she had been mistaken. He had not gone into the dead woman's compartment, and it was perhaps as well that she had said nothing to the police. She might have done incalculable harm by doing so.

She went down to join the others on the terrace outside. Through the branches of mimosa, she looked out over the blue of the Mediterranean, and, whilst listening with half an ear to Lady Tamplin's chatter, she was glad that she had come. This was better than St. Mary Mead.

That evening she put on the mauvy pink dress that went by the name of *soupir d'automne,* and after smiling at her reflection in the mirror, went downstairs with, for the first time in her life, a faint feeling of shyness.

Most of Lady Tamplin's guests had arrived, and since noise was the essential of Lady Tamplin's parties, the din was already terrific. Chubby rushed up to Katherine, pressed a cocktail upon her, and took her under his wing.

"Oh, here you are, Derek," cried Lady Tamplin, as the door opened to admit the last comer. "Now at last we can have something to eat. I am starving."

Katherine looked across the room. She was startled. So this—was Derek, and she realized that she was not surprised. She had always known that she would some day meet the man whom she had seen three times by such a curious chain of coincidences. She thought, too, that he recognized her. He paused abruptly in what he was saying to Lady Tamplin, and went on again as though with an effort. They all went in to dinner, and Katherine found that he was placed beside her. He turned to her at once with a vivid smile.

"I knew I was going to meet you soon," he remarked, "but I never dreamt that it would be here. It had to be, you know. Once at the Savoy and once at Cook's—never twice without three times. Don't say you can't remember me or never noticed me. I insist upon your pretending that you noticed me, anyway."

"Oh, I did," said Katherine; "but this is not the third time. It is the fourth. I saw you on the Blue Train."

"On the Blue Train!" Something undefinable came over his manner; she could not have said just what it was. It was as though he had received a check, a setback. Then he said carelessly:

"What was the rumpus this morning? Somebody had died, hadn't they?"

"Yes," said Katherine slowly; "somebody had died."

"You shouldn't die on a train," remarked Derek flippantly. "I believe it causes all sorts of legal and international complications, and it gives the train an excuse for being even later than usual."

"Mr. Kettering?" A stout American lady, who was sitting opposite, leaned forward and spoke to him with the deliberate intonation of her race. "Mr. Kettering, I do believe you have forgotten me, and I thought you such a perfectly lovely man."

Derek leaned forward, answering her, and Katherine sat almost dazed.

Kettering! That was the name, of course! She remembered it now —but what a strange, ironical situation! Here was this man whom she had seen go into his wife's compartment last night, who had left her alive and well, and now he was sitting at dinner, quite unconscious of the fate that had befallen her. Of that there was no doubt. He did not know.

A servant was leaning over Derek, handing him a note and murmuring in his ear. With a word of excuse to Lady Tamplin, he broke it open, and an expression of utter astonishment came over his face as he read; then he looked at his hostess.

"This is most extraordinary. I say, Rosalie, I am afraid I will have to leave you. The Prefect of Police wants to see me at once. I can't think what about."

"Your sins have found you out," remarked Lenox.

"They must have," said Derek; "probably some idiotic nonsense, but I suppose I shall have to push off to the Prefecture. How dare the old boy rout me out from dinner? It ought to be something deadly serious to justify that," and he laughed as he pushed back his chair and rose to leave the room.

CHAPTER XIII

VAN ALDIN GETS A TELEGRAM

On the afternoon of the 15th February a thick yellow fog had settled down on London. Rufus Van Aldin was in his suite at the Savoy and was making the most of the atmospheric conditions by working double time. Knighton was overjoyed. He had found it difficult of late to get his employer to concentrate on the matters in hand. When he had ventured to urge certain courses, Van Aldin had put him off with a curt word. But now Van Aldin seemed to be throwing himself into work with redoubled energy, and the secretary made the most of his opportunities. Always tactful, he plied the spur so unobtrusively that Van Aldin never suspected it.

Yet in the middle of this absorption in business matters, one little fact lay at the back of Van Aldin's mind. A chance remark of Knighton's, uttered by the secretary in all unconsciousness, had given rise to it. It now festered unseen, gradually reaching further and further forward into Van Aldin's consciousness, until at last, in spite of himself, he had to yield to its insistence.

He listened to what Knighton was saying with his usual air of keen attention, but in reality not one word of it penetrated his mind. He nodded automatically, however, and the secretary turned to some other paper. As he was sorting them out, his employer spoke:

"Do you mind telling me that over again, Knighton?"

For a moment Knighton was at a loss.

"You mean about this, sir?" He held up a closely written Company report.

"No, no," said Van Aldin; "what you told me about seeing Ruth's maid in Paris last night. I can't make it out. You must have been mistaken."

"I can't have been mistaken, sir; I actually spoke to her."

"Well, tell me the whole thing again."

Knighton complied.

"I had fixed up the deal with Bartheimers," he explained, "and had gone back to the Ritz to pick up my traps preparatory to having dinner and catching the nine o'clock train from the Gare du Nord. At the reception desk I saw a woman whom I was quite sure was

Mrs. Kettering's maid. I went up to her and asked if Mrs. Kettering was staying there."

"Yes, yes," said Van Aldin. "Of course. Naturally. And she told you that Ruth had gone on to the Riviera and had sent her to the Ritz to await further orders there?"

"Exactly that, sir."

"It is very odd," said Van Aldin. "Very odd, indeed, unless the woman had been impertinent or something of that kind."

"In that case," objected Knighton, "surely Mrs. Kettering would have paid her down a sum of money, and told her to go back to England. She would hardly have sent her to the Ritz."

"No," muttered the millionaire; "that's true."

He was about to say something further, but checked himself. He was fond of Knighton and liked and trusted him, but he could hardly discuss his daughter's private affairs with his secretary. He had already felt hurt by Ruth's lack of frankness, and this chance information which had come to him did nothing to allay his misgivings.

Why had Ruth got rid of her maid in Paris? What possible object or motive could she have had in so doing?

He reflected for a moment or two on the curious combination of chance. How should it have occurred to Ruth, except as the wildest coincidence, that the first person that the maid should run across in Paris should be her father's secretary? Ah, but that was the way things happened. That was the way things got found out.

He winced at the last phrase; it had arisen with complete naturalness to his mind. Was there then "something to be found out"? He hated to put this question to himself; he had no doubt of the answer. The answer was—he was sure of it—Armand de la Roche.

It was bitter to Van Aldin that a daughter of his should be gulled by such a man, yet he was forced to admit that she was in good company—that other well-bred and intelligent women had succumbed just as easily to the Count's fascination. Men saw through him, women did not.

He sought now for a phrase that would allay any suspicion that his secretary might have felt.

"Ruth is always changing her mind about things at a moment's notice," he remarked, and then he added in a would-be careless tone: "The maid didn't give any—er—reason for this change of plan?"

Knighton was careful to make his voice as natural as possible as he replied:

"She said, sir, that Mrs. Kettering had met a friend unexpectedly."

"Is that so?"

The secretary's practised ears caught the note of strain underlying the seemingly casual tone.

"Oh, I see. Man or woman?"

"I think she said a man, sir."

Van Aldin nodded. His worst fears were being realized. He rose from his chair, and began pacing up and down the room, a habit of his when agitated. Unable to contain his feelings any longer, he burst forth:

"There is one thing no man can do, and that is to get a woman to listen to reason. Somehow or other, they don't seem to have any kind of *sense*. Talk of woman's instinct—why, it is well known all the world over that a woman is the surest mark for any rascally swindler. Not one in ten of them knows a scoundrel when she meets one; they can be preyed on by any good-looking fellow with a soft side to his tongue. If I had my way——"

He was interrupted. A page-boy entered with a telegram. Van Aldin tore it open, and his face went a sudden chalky white. He caught hold of the back of a chair to steady himself, and waved the page-boy from the room.

"What's the matter, sir?"

Knighton had risen in concern.

"Ruth!" said Van Aldin hoarsely.

"Mrs. Kettering?"

"Killed!"

"An accident to the train?"

Van Aldin shook his head.

"No. From this it seems she has been robbed as well. They don't use the word, Knighton, but my poor girl has been murdered."

"Oh, my God, sir!"

Van Aldin tapped the telegram with his forefinger.

"This is from the police at Nice. I must go out there by the first train."

Knighton was efficient as ever. He glanced at the clock.

"Five o'clock from Victoria, sir."

"That's right. You will come with me, Knighton. Tell my man, Archer, and pack your own things. See to everything here. I want to go round to Curzon Street."

The telephone rang sharply, and the secretary lifted the receiver.

"Yes; who is it?"

Then to Van Aldin.

"Mr. Goby, sir."

"Goby? I can't see him now. No—wait, we have plenty of time. Tell them to send him up."

Van Aldin was a strong man. Already he had recovered that iron calm of his. Few people would have noticed anything amiss in his greeting to Mr. Goby.

"I am pressed for time, Goby. Got anything important to tell me?"

Mr. Goby coughed.

"The movements of Mr. Kettering, sir. You wished them reported to you."

"Yes—well?"

"Mr. Kettering, sir, left London for the Riviera yesterday morning."

"What?"

Something in his voice must have startled Mr. Goby. That worthy gentleman departed from his usual practice of never looking at the person to whom he was talking, and stole a fleeting glance at the millionaire.

"What train did he go on?" demanded Van Aldin.

"The Blue Train, sir."

Mr. Goby coughed again and spoke to the clock on the mantelpiece.

"Mademoiselle Mirelle, the dancer from the Parthenon, went by the same train."

CHAPTER XIV

ADA MASON'S STORY

"I CANNOT REPEAT to you often enough, Monsieur, our horror, our consternation, and the deep sympathy we feel for you."

Thus M. Carrège, the Juge d'Instruction, addressed Van Aldin. M. Caux, the Commissary, made sympathetic noises in his throat. Van Aldin brushed away horror, consternation, and sympathy with an abrupt gesture. The scene was the Examining Magistrate's room at Nice. Besides M. Carrège, the Commissary, and Van Aldin, there was a further person in the room. It was that person who now spoke.

"M. Van Aldin," he said, "desires action—swift action."

"Ah!" cried the Commissary, "I have not yet presented you. M. Van Aldin, this is M. Hercule Poirot; you have doubtless heard of him. Although he has retired from his profession for some years now, his name is still a household word as one of the greatest living detectives."

"Pleased to meet you, M. Poirot," said Van Aldin, falling back mechanically on a formula that he had discarded some years ago. "You have retired from your profession?"

"That is so, Monsieur. Now I enjoy the world."

The little man made a grandiloquent gesture.

"M. Poirot happened to be travelling on the Blue Train," explained the Commissary, "and he has been so kind as to assist us out of his vast experience."

The millionaire looked at Poirot keenly. Then he said unexpectedly:

"I am a very rich man, M. Poirot. It is usually said that a rich man labours under the belief that he can buy everything and every one. That is not true. I am a big man in my way, and one big man can ask a favour from another big man."

Poirot nodded a quick appreciation.

"That is very well said, M. Van Aldin. I place myself entirely at your service."

"Thank you," said Van Aldin. "I can only say call upon me at any time, and you will not find me ungrateful. And now, gentlemen, to business."

"I propose," said M. Carrège, "to interrogate the maid, Ada Mason. You have her here, I understand?"

"Yes," said Van Aldin. "We picked her up in Paris in passing through. She was very upset to hear of her mistress's death, but she tells her story coherently enough."

"We will have her in, then," said M. Carrège.

He rang the bell on his desk, and in a few minutes Ada Mason entered the room.

She was very neatly dressed in black, and the tip of her nose was red. She had exchanged her grey travelling gloves for a pair of black suède ones. She cast a look round the Examining Magistrate's office in some trepidation, and seemed relieved at the presence of her mistress's father. The Examining Magistrate prided himself on his geniality of manner, and did his best to put her at her ease. He was helped in this by Poirot, who acted as interpreter, and whose friendly manner was reassuring to the Englishwoman.

"Your name is Ada Mason; is that right?"

"Ada Beatrice I was christened, sir," said Mason primly.

"Just so. And we can understand, Mason, that this has all been very distressing."

"Oh, indeed it has, sir. I have been with many ladies and always given satisfaction, I hope, and I never dreamt of anything of this kind happening in any situation where I was."

"No, no," said M. Carrège.

"Naturally I have read of such things, of course, in the Sunday papers. And then I always have understood that those foreign trains——" She suddenly checked her flow, remembering that the gentlemen who were speaking to her were of the same nationality as the trains.

"Now let us talk this affair over," said M. Carrège. "There was, I understand, no question of your staying in Paris when you started from London?"

"Oh no, sir. We were to go straight through to Nice."

"Have you ever been abroad with your mistress before?"

"No, sir. I had only been with her two months, you see."

"Did she seem quite as usual when starting on this journey?"

"She was worried like and a bit upset, and she was rather irritable and difficult to please."

M. Carrège nodded.

"Now then, Mason, what was the first you heard of your stopping in Paris?"

"It was at the place they call the Gare de Lyon, sir. My mistress was thinking of getting out and walking up and down the platform. She was just going out into the corridor when she gave a sudden exclamation, and came back into her compartment with a gentleman. She shut the door between her carriage and mine, so that I didn't see or hear anything, till she suddenly opened it again and told me that she had changed her plans. She gave me some money and told me to get out and go to the Ritz. They knew her well there, she said, and would give me a room. I was to wait there until I heard from her; she would wire me what she wanted me to do. I had just time to get my things together and jump out of the train before it started off. It was a rush."

"While Mrs. Kettering was telling you this, where was the gentleman?"

"He was standing in the other compartment, sir, looking out of the window."

"Can you describe him to us?"

"Well, you see, sir, I hardly saw him. He had his back to me most of the time. He was a tall gentleman and dark; that's all I can say. He was dressed very like any other gentleman in a dark blue overcoat and a grey hat."

"Was he one of the passengers on the train?"

"I don't think so, sir; I took it that he had come to the station to see Mrs. Kettering in passing through. Of course he might have been one of the passengers; I never thought of that."

Mason seemed a little flurried by the suggestion.

"Ah!" M. Carrège passed lightly to another subject. "Your mistress later requested the conductor not to rouse her early in the morning. Was that a likely thing for her to do, do you think?"

"Oh yes, sir. The mistress never ate any breakfast and she didn't sleep well at nights, so that she liked sleeping on in the morning."

Again M. Carrège passed to another subject.

"Amongst the luggage there was a scarlet morocco case, was there not?" he asked. "Your mistress's jewel-case?"

"Yes, sir."

"Did you take that case to the Ritz?"

"*Me* take the mistress's jewel-case to the Ritz! Oh no, indeed, sir." Mason's tones were horrified.

"You left it behind you in the carriage?"

"Yes, sir."

"Had your mistress many jewels with her, do you know?"

"A fair amount, sir; made me a bit uneasy sometimes, I can tell you, with those nasty tales you hear of being robbed in foreign countries. They were insured, I know, but all the same it seemed a frightful risk. Why, the rubies alone, the mistress told me, were worth several hundred thousand pounds."

"The rubies! What rubies?" barked Van Aldin suddenly.

Mason turned to him.

"I think it was you who gave them to her, sir, not very long ago."

"My God!" cried Van Aldin. "You don't say she had those rubies with her? I told her to leave them at the bank."

Mason gave once more the discreet cough which was apparently part of her stock-in-trade as a lady's maid. This time it expressed a good deal. It expressed far more clearly than words could have done, that Mason's mistress had been a lady who took her own way.

"Ruth must have been mad," muttered Van Aldin. "What on earth could have possessed her?"

M. Carrège in turn gave vent to a cough, again a cough of significance. It riveted Van Aldin's attention on him.

"For the moment," said M. Carrège, addressing Mason, "I think that is all. If you will go into the next room, Mademoiselle, they will read over to you the questions and answers, and you will sign accordingly."

Mason went out escorted by the clerk, and Van Aldin said immediately to the Magistrate:

"Well?"

M. Carrège opened a drawer in his desk, took out a letter, and handed it across to Van Aldin.

"This was found in Madame's handbag."

"Chère Amie" (the letter ran),—"I will obey you; I will be prudent, discreet—all those things that a lover most hates. Paris would perhaps have been unwise, but the Isles d'Or are far away from the world, and you may be assured that nothing will leak out. It is like you and your divine sympathy to be so interested in the work on famous jewels that I am writing. It will, indeed, be an extraordinary privilege to actually see and handle these historic rubies. I am devoting a special passage to 'Heart of Fire.' My wonderful one! Soon I will make up to you for all those sad years of separation and emptiness.—Your ever-adoring,

"Armand."

CHAPTER XV

THE COMTE DE LA ROCHE

Van Aldin read the letter through in silence. His face turned a dull angry crimson. The men watching him saw the veins start out on his forehead, and his big hands clench themselves unconsciously. He handed back the letter without a word. M. Carrège was looking with close attention at his desk, M. Caux's eyes were fixed upon the ceiling, and M. Hercule Poirot was tenderly brushing a speck of dust from his coat sleeve. With the greatest tact they none of them looked at Van Aldin.

It was M. Carrège, mindful of his status and his duties, who tackled the unpleasant subject.

"Perhaps, Monsieur," he murmured, "you are aware by whom—er—this letter was written?"

"Yes, I know," said Van Aldin heavily.

"Ah?" said the Magistrate inquiringly.

"A scoundrel who calls himself the Comte de la Roche."

There was a pause; then M. Poirot leaned forward, straightened a ruler on the judge's desk, and addressed the millionaire directly.

"M. Van Aldin, we are all sensible, deeply sensible, of the pain it must give you to speak of these matters, but believe me, Monsieur, it is not the time for concealments. If justice is to be done, we must know everything. If you will reflect a little minute you will realize the truth of that clearly for yourself."

Van Aldin was silent for a moment or two, then almost reluctantly he nodded his head in agreement.

"You are quite right, M. Poirot," he said. "Painful as it is, I have no right to keep anything back."

The Commissary gave a sigh of relief, and the Examining Magistrate leaned back in his chair and adjusted a pince-nez on his long thin nose.

"Perhaps you will tell us in your own words, M. Van Aldin," he said, "all that you know of this gentleman."

"It began eleven or twelve years ago—in Paris. My daughter was a young girl then, full of foolish, romantic notions, like all young girls are. Unknown to me, she made the acquaintance of this Comte de la Roche. You have heard of him, perhaps?"

The Commissary and Poirot nodded in assent.

"He calls himself the Comte de la Roche," continued Van Aldin, "but I doubt if he has any right to the title."

"You would not have found his name in the *Almanac de Gotha*," agreed the Commissary.

"I discovered as much," said Van Aldin. "The man was a good-looking, plausible scoundrel, with a fatal fascination for women. Ruth was infatuated with him, but I soon put a stop to the whole affair. The man was no better than a common swindler."

"You are quite right," said the Commissary. "The Comte de la Roche is well known to us. If it were possible, we should have laid him by the heels before now, but *ma foi!* it is not easy; the fellow is cunning, his affairs are always conducted with ladies of high social position. If he obtains money from them under false pretences or as the fruit of blackmail, *eh bien!* naturally they will not prosecute. To look foolish in the eyes of the world, oh no, that would never do, and he has an extraordinary power over women."

"That is so," said the millionaire heavily. "Well, as I told you, I broke the affair up pretty sharply. I told Ruth exactly what he was, and she had, perforce, to believe me. About a year afterwards, she met her present husband and married him. As far as I knew, that was the end of the matter; but only a week ago, I discovered, to my amazement, that my daughter had resumed her acquaintance with the Comte de la Roche. She had been meeting him frequently in London and Paris. I remonstrated with her on her imprudence, for I may tell you gentlemen, that, on my insistence, she was preparing to bring a suit for divorce against her husband."

"That is interesting," murmured Poirot softly, his eyes on the ceiling.

Van Aldin looked at him sharply, and then went on.

"I pointed out to her the folly of continuing to see the Comte under the circumstances. I thought she agreed with me."

The Examining Magistrate coughed delicately.

"But according to this letter——" he began, and then stopped.

Van Aldin's jaw set itself squarely.

"I know. It's no good mincing matters. However unpleasant, we have got to face facts. It seems clear that Ruth had arranged to go to Paris and meet de la Roche there. After my warnings to her, however, she must have written to the Count suggesting a change of rendezvous."

"The Isles d'Or," said the Commissary thoughtfully, "are situated just opposite Hyères, a remote and idyllic spot."

Van Aldin nodded.

"My God! How could Ruth be such a fool?" he exclaimed bitterly. "All this talk about writing a book on jewels! Why, he must have been after the rubies from the first."

"There are some very famous rubies," said Poirot, "originally part of the Crown jewels of Russia; they are unique in character, and their value is almost fabulous. There has been a rumour that they have lately passed into the possession of an American. Are we right in concluding, Monsieur, that you were the purchaser?"

"Yes," said Van Aldin. "They came into my possession in Paris about ten days ago."

"Pardon me, Monsieur, but you have been negotiating for their purchase for some time?"

"A little over two months. Why?"

"These things become known," said Poirot. "There is always a pretty formidable crowd on the track of jewels such as these."

A spasm distorted the other's face.

"I remember," he said brokenly, "a joke I made to Ruth when I gave them to her. I told her not to take them to the Riviera with her, as I could not afford to have her robbed and murdered for the sake of the jewels. My God! the things one says—never dreaming or knowing they will come true."

There was a sympathetic silence, and then Poirot spoke in a detached manner.

"Let us arrange our facts with order and precision. According to our present theory, this is how they run. The Comte de la Roche knows of your purchase of these jewels. By an easy stratagem he induces Madame Kettering to bring the stones with her. He, then, is the man Mason saw in the train at Paris."

The other three nodded in agreement.

"Madame is surprised to see him, but she deals with the situation promptly. Mason is got out of the way; a dinner basket is ordered. We know from the conductor that he made up the berth for the first compartment, but he did not go into the second compartment, and that a man could quite well have been concealed from him. So far the Comte could have been hidden to a marvel. No one knows of his presence on the train except Madame; he has been careful that the maid did not see his face. All that she could say is that he was tall and dark. It is all most conveniently vague. They are alone—and the train rushes through the night. There would be no outcry, no struggle, for the man is, so she thinks, her lover."

He turned gently to Van Aldin.

"Death, Monsieur, must have been almost instantaneous. We will pass over that quickly. The Comte takes the jewel-case which lies ready to his hand. Shortly afterwards the train draws into Lyons."

M. Carrège nodded his approval.

"Precisely. The conductor without descends. It would be easy for our man to leave the train unseen; it would be easy to catch a train back to Paris or anywhere he pleases. And the crime would be put down as an ordinary train robbery. But for the letter found in Madame's bag, the Comte would not have been mentioned."

"It was an oversight on his part not to search that bag," declared the Commissary.

"Without doubt he thought she had destroyed that letter. It was —pardon me, Monsieur—it was an indiscretion of the first water to keep it."

"And yet," murmured Poirot, "it was an indiscretion the Comte might have foreseen."

"You mean?"

"I mean we are all agreed on one point, and that is that the Comte de la Roche knows one subject *à fond:* Women. How was it that, knowing women as he does, he did not foresee that Madame would have kept that letter?"

"Yes—yes," said the Examining Magistrate doubtfully, "there is something in what you say. But at such times, you understand, a man is not master of himself. He does not reason calmly. *Mon Dieu!*" he added, with feeling, "if our criminals kept their heads and acted with intelligence, how should we capture them?"

Poirot smiled to himself.

"It seems to me a clear case," said the other, "but a difficult one to prove. The Comte is a slippery customer, and unless the maid can identify him——"

"Which is most unlikely," said Poirot.

"True, true." The Examining Magistrate rubbed his chin. "It is going to be difficult."

"If he did indeed commit the crime——" began Poirot. M. Caux interrupted.

"If—you say *if?*"

"Yes, Monsieur le Juge, I say *if.*"

The other looked at him sharply. "You are right," he said at last, "we go too fast. It is possible that the Comte may have an alibi. Then we should look foolish."

"*Ah, ça par exemple,*" replied Poirot, "that is of no importance whatever. Naturally, if he committed the crime he will have an alibi. A man with the Comte's experience does not neglect to take precautions. No, I said *if* for a very different reason."

"And what was that?"

Poirot wagged an emphatic forefinger. "The psychology."

"Eh?" said the Commissary.

"The psychology is at fault. The Comte is a scoundrel—yes. The Comte is a swindler—yes. The Comte preys upon women—yes. He proposes to steal Madame's jewels—again yes. Is he the kind of man to commit murder? I say *no!* A man of the type of the Comte is always a coward; he takes no risks. He plays the safe, the mean, what the English call the low-down game; but murder, a hundred times no!" He shook his head in a dissatisfied manner.

The Examining Magistrate, however, did not seem disposed to agree with him.

"The day always comes when such gentry lose their heads and go too far," he observed sagely. "Doubtless that is the case here. Without wishing to disagree with you, M. Poirot——"

"It was only an opinion," Poirot hastened to explain. "The case is, of course, in your hands, and you will do what seems fit to you."

"I am satisfied in my own mind that the Comte de la Roche is the man we need to get hold of," said M. Carrège. "You agree with me, Monsieur le Commissaire?"

"Perfectly."

"And you, M. Van Aldin?"

"Yes," said the millionaire. "Yes; the man is a thorough-paced villain, no doubt about it."

"It will be difficult to lay hands on him, I am afraid," said the Magistrate, "but we will do our best. Telegraphed instructions shall go out at once."

"Permit me to assist you," said Poirot. "There need be no difficulty."

"Eh?"

The others stared at him. The little man smiled beamingly back at them.

"It is my business to know things," he explained. "The Comte is a man of intelligence. He is at present at a villa he has leased, the Villa Marina at Antibes."

CHAPTER XVI

POIROT DISCUSSES THE CASE

Everybody looked respectfully at Poirot. Undoubtedly the little man had scored heavily. The Commissary laughed—on a rather hollow note.

"You teach us all our business," he cried. "M. Poirot knows more than the police."

Poirot gazed complacently at the ceiling, adopting a mock-modest air.

"What will you; it is my little hobby," he murmured, "to know things. Naturally I have the time to indulge it. I am not overburdened with affairs."

"Ah!" said the Commissary shaking his head portentously. "As for me——"

He made an exaggerated gesture to represent the cares that lay on his shoulders.

Poirot turned suddenly to Van Aldin.

"You agree, Monsieur, with this view? You feel certain that the Comte de la Roche is the murderer?"

"Why, it would seem so—yes, certainly."

Something guarded in the answer made the Examining Magistrate look at the American curiously. Van Aldin seemed aware of his scrutiny and made an effort as though to shake off some preoccupation.

"What about my son-in-law?" he asked. "You have acquainted him with the news? He is in Nice, I understand."

"Certainly, Monsieur." The Commissary hesitated, and then murmured very discreetly: "You are doubtless aware, M. Van Aldin, that M. Kettering was also one of the passengers on the Blue Train that night?"

The millionaire nodded.

"Heard it just before I left London," he vouchsafed laconically.

"He tells us," continued the Commissary, "that he had no idea his wife was travelling on the train."

"I bet he hadn't," said Van Aldin grimly. "It would have been rather a nasty shock to him if he'd come across her on it."

The three men looked at him questioningly.

"I'm not going to mince matters," said Van Aldin savagely. "No one knows what my poor girl has had to put up with. Derek Kettering wasn't alone. He had a lady with him."

"Ah?"

"Mirelle—the dancer."

M. Carrège and the Commissary looked at each other and nodded as though confirming some previous conversation. M. Carrège leaned back in his chair, joined his hands, and fixed his eyes on the ceiling.

"Ah!" he murmured again. "One wondered." He coughed. "One has heard rumours."

"The lady," said M. Caux, "is very notorious."

"And also," murmured Poirot softly, "very expensive."

Van Aldin had gone very red in the face. He leant forward and hit the table a bang with his fist.

"See here," he cried, "my son-in-law is a damned scoundrel!"

He glared at them, looking from one face to another.

"Oh, I know," he went on. "Good looks and a charming, easy manner. It took me in once upon a time. I suppose he pretended to be broken-hearted when you broke the news to him—that is, if he didn't know it already."

"Oh, it came as a complete surprise to him. He was overwhelmed."

"Darned young hypocrite," said Van Aldin. "Simulated great grief, I suppose?"

"N—no," said the Commissary cautiously. "I would not quite say that—eh, M. Carrège?"

The Magistrate brought the tips of his fingers together, and half closed his eyes.

"Shock, bewilderment, horror—these things, yes," he declared judicially. "Great sorrow—no—I should not say that."

Hercule Poirot spoke once more.

"Permit me to ask, M. Van Aldin, does M. Kettering benefit by the death of his wife?"

"He benefits to the tune of a couple of millions," said Van Aldin.

"Dollars?"

"Pounds. I settled that sum on Ruth absolutely on her marriage. She made no will and leaves no children, so the money will go to her husband."

"Whom she was on the point of divorcing," murmured Poirot. "Ah, yes—*précisément*."

The Commissary turned and looked sharply at him.

"Do you mean——" he began.

"I mean nothing," said Poirot. "I arrange the facts, that is all."

Van Aldin stared at him with awakening interest.

The little man rose to his feet.

"I do not think I can be of any further service to you, M. le Juge," he said politely, bowing to M. Carrège. "You will keep me informed of the course of events? It will be a kindness."

"But certainly—most certainly."

Van Aldin rose also.

"You don't want me any more at present?"

"No, Monsieur; we have all the information we need for the moment."

"Then I will walk a little way with M. Poirot. That is, if he does not object?"

"Enchanted, Monsieur," said the little man, with a bow.

Van Aldin lighted a large cigar, having first offered one to Poirot who declined it and lit one of his own tiny cigarettes. A man of great strength of character, Van Aldin already appeared to be his everyday, normal self once more. After strolling along for a minute or two in silence, the millionaire spoke:

"I take it, M. Poirot, that you no longer exercise your profession?"

"That is so, Monsieur. I enjoy the world."

"Yet you are assisting the police in this affair?"

"Monsieur, if a doctor walks along the street and an accident happens, does he say, 'I have retired from my profession, I will continue my walk,' when there is some one bleeding to death at his feet? If I had been already in Nice, and the police had sent to me and asked me to assist them, I should have refused. But this affair, the good God thrust it upon me."

"You were on the spot," said Van Aldin thoughtfully. "You examined the compartment, did you not?"

Poirot nodded.

"Doubtless you found things that were, shall we say, suggestive to you?"

"Perhaps," said Poirot.

"I hope you see what I am leading up to?" said Van Aldin. "It seems to me that the case against this Comte de la Roche is perfectly clear, but I am not a fool. I have been watching you for this last hour or so, and I realize that for some reason of your own you don't agree with that theory?"

Poirot shrugged his shoulders.

"I may be wrong."

"So we come to the favour I want to ask you. Will you act in this matter for me?"

"For you personally?"

"That was my meaning."

Poirot was silent for a moment or two. Then he said:

"You realize what you are asking?"

"I guess so," said Van Aldin.

"Very well," said Poirot. "I accept. But in that case, I must have frank answers to my questions."

"Why, certainly. That is understood."

Poirot's manner changed. He became suddenly brusque and business-like.

"This question of a divorce," he said. "It was you who advised your daughter to bring the suit?"

"Yes."

"When?"

"About ten days ago. I had had a letter from her complaining of her husband's behaviour, and I put it to her very strongly that divorce was the only remedy."

"In what way did she complain of his behaviour?"

"He was being seen about with a *very* notorious lady—the one we have been speaking of—Mirelle."

"The dancer. Ah-ha! And Madame Kettering objected? Was she very devoted to her husband?"

"I would not say that," said Van Aldin, hesitating a little.

"It was not her heart that suffered, it was her pride—is that what you would say?"

"Yes, I suppose you might put it like that."

"I gather that the marriage had not been a happy one from the beginning?"

"Derek Kettering is rotten to the core," said Van Aldin. "He is incapable of making any woman happy."

"He is, as you say in England, a bad lot. That is right, is it not?"

Van Aldin nodded.

"*Très bien!* You advise Madame to seek a divorce, she agrees; you consult your solicitors. When does M. Kettering get news of what is in the wind?"

"I sent for him myself, and explained the course of action I proposed to take."

"And what did he say?" murmured Poirot softly.

Van Aldin's face darkened at the remembrance.

"He was infernally impudent."

"Excuse the question, Monsieur, but did he refer to the Comte de la Roche?"

"Not by name," growled the other unwillingly, "but he showed himself cognizant of the affair."

"What, if I may ask, was M. Kettering's financial position at the time?"

"How do you suppose I should know that?" asked Van Aldin, after a very brief hesitation.

"It seemed likely to me that you would inform yourself on that point."

"Well—you are quite right, I did. I discovered that Kettering was on the rocks."

"And now he has inherited two million pounds! *La vie*—it is a strange thing, is it not?"

Van Aldin looked at him sharply.

"What do you mean?"

"I moralize," said Poirot. "I reflect, I speak the philosophy. But to return to where we were. Surely M. Kettering did not propose to allow himself to be divorced without making a fight for it?"

Van Aldin did not answer for a minute or two, then he said:

"I don't exactly know what his intentions were."

"Did you hold any further communications with him?"

Again a slight pause, then Van Aldin said:

"No."

Poirot stopped dead, took off his hat, and held out his hand.

"I must wish you good-day, Monsieur. I can do nothing for you."

"What are you getting at?" demanded Van Aldin angrily.

"If you do not tell me the truth, I can do nothing."

"I don't know what you mean."

"I think you do. You may rest assured, M. Van Aldin, that I know how to be discreet."

"Very well, then," said the millionaire. "I'll admit that I was not speaking the truth just now. I *did* have further communication with my son-in-law."

"Yes?"

"To be exact, I sent my secretary, Major Knighton, to see him, with instructions to offer him the sum of one hundred thousand pounds in cash if the divorce went through undefended."

"A pretty sum of money," said Poirot appreciatively; "and the answer of Monsieur your son-in-law?"

"He sent back word that I could go to hell," replied the millionaire succinctly.

"Ah!" said Poirot.

He betrayed no emotion of any kind. At the moment he was engaged in methodically recording facts.

"Monsieur Kettering has told the police that he neither saw nor spoke to his wife on the journey from England. Are you inclined to believe that statement, Monsieur?"

"Yes, I am," said Van Aldin. "He would take particular pains to keep out of her way, I should say."

"Why?"

"Because he had got that woman with him."

"Mirelle?"

"Yes."

"How did you come to know that fact?"

"A man of mine, whom I had put on to watch him, reported to me that they had both left by that train."

"I see," said Poirot. "In that case, as you said before, he would not be likely to attempt to hold any communication with Madame Kettering."

The little man fell silent for some time. Van Aldin did not interrupt his meditation.

CHAPTER XVII

AN ARISTOCRATIC GENTLEMAN

"YOU HAVE BEEN to the Riviera before, Georges?" said Poirot to his valet the following morning.

George was an intensely English, rather wooden-faced individual.

"Yes, sir. I was here two years ago when I was in the service of Lord Edward Frampton."

"And to-day," murmured his master, "you are here with Hercule Poirot. How one mounts in the world!"

The valet made no reply to this observation. After a suitable pause he asked:

"The brown lounge suit, sir? The wind is somewhat chilly to-day."

"There is a grease spot on the waistcoat," objected Poirot. "A *morceau* of *Fillet de sole à la Jeanette* alighted there when I was lunching at the Ritz last Tuesday."

"There is no spot there now, sir," said George reproachfully. "I have removed it."

"*Très bien!*" said Poirot. "I am pleased with you, Georges."

"Thank you, sir."

There was a pause, and then Poirot murmured dreamily:

"Supposing, my good Georges, that you had been born in the same social sphere as your late master, Lord Edward Frampton—that, penniless yourself, you had married an extremely wealthy wife, but that that wife proposed to divorce you, with excellent reasons, what would you do about it?"

"I should endeavour, sir," replied George, "to make her change her mind."

"By peaceful or by forcible methods?"

George looked shocked.

"You will excuse me, sir," he said, "but a gentleman of the aristocracy would not behave like a Whitechapel coster. He would not do anything low."

"Would he not, Georges? I wonder now. Well, perhaps you are right."

There was a knock on the door. George went to it and opened it a discreet inch or two. A low murmured colloquy went on, and then the valet returned to Poirot.

"A note, sir."

Poirot took it. It was from M. Caux, the Commissary of Police. "We are about to interrogate the Comte de la Roche. The Juge d'Instruction begs that you will be present."

"Quickly, my suit, Georges! I must hasten myself."

A quarter of an hour later, spick and span in his brown suit, Poirot entered the Examining Magistrate's room. M. Caux was already there, and both he and M. Carrège greeted Poirot with polite *empressement*.

"The affair is somewhat discouraging," murmured M. Caux. "It appears that the Comte arrived in Nice the day before the murder."

"If that is true, it will settle your affair nicely for you," responded Poirot.

M. Carrège cleared his throat.

"We must not accept this alibi without very cautious inquiry," he declared. He struck the bell upon the table with his hand.

In another minute a tall dark man, exquisitely dressed, with a somewhat haughty cast of countenance, entered the room. So very aristocratic-looking was the Count, that it would have seemed sheer heresy even to whisper that his father had been an obscure corn-chandler in Nantes—which, as a matter of fact, was the case. Looking at him, one would have been prepared to swear that innumerable ancestors of his must have perished by the guillotine in the French Revolution.

"I am here, gentlemen," said the Count haughtily. "May I ask why you wish to see me?"

"Pray be seated, Monsieur le Comte," said the Examining Magistrate politely. "It is the affair of the death of Madame Kettering that we are investigating."

"The death of Madame Kettering? I do not understand."

"You were—ahem!—acquainted with the lady, I believe, Monsieur le Comte?"

"Certainly I was acquainted with her. What has that to do with the matter?"

Sticking an eyeglass in his eye, he looked coldly round the room, his glance resting longest on Poirot, who was gazing at him with a kind of simple, innocent admiration which was most pleasing to the Count's vanity. M. Carrège leaned back in his chair and cleared his throat.

"You do not perhaps know, Monsieur le Comte"—he paused—"that Madame Kettering was murdered?"

"Murdered? *Mon Dieu*, how terrible!"

The surprise and the sorrow were excellently done—so well done, indeed, as to seem wholly natural.

"Madame Kettering was strangled between Paris and Lyons," continued M. Carrège, "and her jewels were stolen."

"It is iniquitous!" cried the Count warmly; "the police should do something about these train bandits. Nowadays no one is safe."

"In Madame's handbag," continued the Judge, "we found a letter to her from you. She had, it seemed, arranged to meet you?"

The Count shrugged his shoulders and spread out his hands.

"Of what use are concealments," he said frankly. "We are all men of the world. Privately and between ourselves, I admit the affair."

"You met her in Paris and travelled down with her, I believe?" said M. Carrège.

"That was the original arrangement, but by Madame's wish it was changed. I was to meet her at Hyères."

"You did not meet her on the train at the Gare de Lyon on the evening of the 14th?"

"On the contrary, I arrived in Nice on the morning of that day, so what you suggest is impossible."

"Quite so, quite so," said M. Carrège. "As a matter of form, you would perhaps give me an account of your movements during the evening and night of the 14th."

The Count reflected for a minute.

"I dined in Monte Carlo at the Café de Paris. Afterwards I went to the Le Sporting. I won a few thousand francs," he shrugged his shoulders. "I returned home at perhaps one o'clock."

"Pardon me, Monsieur, but how did you return home?"

"In my own two-seater car."

"No one was with you?"

"No one."

"You could produce witnesses in support of this statement?"

"Doubtless many of my friends saw me there that evening. I dined alone."

"Your servant admitted you on your return to your villa?"

"I let myself in with my own latch-key."

"Ah!" murmured the Magistrate.

Again he struck the bell on the table with his hand. The door opened, and a messenger appeared.

"Bring in the maid, Mason," said M. Carrège.

"Very good, Monsieur le Juge."

Ada Mason was brought in.

"Will you be so good, Mademoiselle, as to look at this gentleman. To the best of your ability was it he who entered your mistress's compartment in Paris?"

The woman looked long and searchingly at the Count, who was, Poirot fancied, rather uneasy under this scrutiny.

"I could not say, sir, I am sure," said Mason at last. "It might be and again it might not. Seeing as how I only saw his back, it's hard to say. I rather think it *was* the gentleman."

"But you are not sure?"

"No–o," said Mason unwillingly; "n–no, I am not sure."

"You have seen this gentleman before in Curzon Street?"

Mason shook her head.

"I should not be likely to see any visitors that come to Curzon Street," she explained, "unless they were staying in the house."

"Very well, that will do," said the Examining Magistrate sharply. Evidently he was disappointed.

"One moment," said Poirot. "There is a question I would like to put to Mademoiselle, if I may?"

"Certainly, M. Poirot—certainly, by all means."

Poirot addressed himself to the maid.

"What happened to the tickets?"

"The tickets, sir?"

"Yes; the tickets from London to Nice. Did you or your mistress have them?"

"The mistress had her own Pullman ticket, sir; the others were in my charge."

"What happened to them?"

"I gave them to the conductor on the French train, sir; he said it was usual. I hope I did right, sir?"

"Oh, quite right, quite right. A mere matter of detail."

Both M. Caux and the Examining Magistrate looked at him curiously. Mason stood uncertainly for a minute or two, and then the Magistrate gave her a brief nod of dismissal, and she went out. Poirot scribbled something on a scrap of paper and handed it across to M. Carrège. The latter read it and his brow cleared.

"Well, gentlemen," demanded the Count haughtily, "am I to be detained further?"

"Assuredly not, assuredly not," M. Carrège hastened to say, with a great deal of amiability. "Everything is now cleared up as regards your own position in this affair. Naturally, in view of Madame's letter, we were bound to question you."

The Count rose, picked up his handsome stick from the corner, and, with rather a curt bow, left the room.

"And that is that," said M. Carrège. "You were quite right, M. Poirot—much better to let him feel he is not suspected. Two of my men will shadow him night and day, and at the same time we will go into the question of the alibi. It seems to me rather—er—a fluid one."

"Possibly," agreed Poirot thoughtfully.

"I asked M. Kettering to come here this morning," continued the Magistrate, "though really I doubt if we have much to ask him, but there are one or two suspicious circumstances——" He paused, rubbing his nose.

"Such as?" asked Poirot.

"Well"—the Magistrate coughed—"this lady with whom he is said to be travelling—Mademoiselle Mirelle. She is staying at one hotel and he at another. That strikes me—er—as rather odd."

"It looks," said M. Caux, "as though they were being careful."

"Exactly," said M. Carrège triumphantly; "and what should they have to be careful about?"

"An excess of caution is suspicious, eh?" said Poirot.

"*Précisément.*"

"We might, I think," murmured Poirot, "ask M. Kettering one or two questions."

The Magistrate gave instructions. A moment or two later, Derek Kettering, debonair as ever, entered the room.

"Good morning, Monsieur," said the Judge politely.

"Good morning," said Derek Kettering curtly. "You sent for me. Has anything fresh turned up?"

"Pray sit down, Monsieur."

Derek took a seat and flung his hat and stick on the table.

"Well?" he asked impatiently.

"We have, so far, no fresh data," said M. Carrège cautiously.

"That's very interesting," said Derek drily. "Did you send for me here in order to tell me that?"

"We naturally thought, Monsieur, that you would like to be informed of the progress of the case," said the Magistrate severely.

"Even if the progress was non-existent."

"We also wished to ask you a few questions."

"Ask away."

"You are quite sure that you neither saw nor spoke with your wife on the train?"

"I've answered that already. I did not."

"You had, no doubt, your reasons."

Derek stared at him suspiciously.

"I–did–not–know–she–was–on–the–train," he explained, spacing his words elaborately, as though to some one dull of intellect.

"That is what you say, yes," murmured M. Carrège.

A frown suffused Derek's face.

"I should like to know what you're driving at. Do you know what I think, M. Carrège?"

"What do you think, Monsieur?"

"I think the French police are vastly overrated. Surely you must have some data as to these gangs of train robbers. It's outrageous that such a thing could happen on a *train de luxe* like that, and that the French police should be helpless to deal with the matter."

"We are dealing with it, Monsieur, never fear."

"Madame Kettering, I understand, did not leave a will," interposed Poirot suddenly. His fingertips were joined together, and he was looking intently at the ceiling.

"I don't think she ever made one," said Kettering. "Why?"

"It is a very pretty little fortune that you inherit there," said Poirot —"a very pretty little fortune."

Although his eyes were still on the ceiling, he managed to see the dark flush that rose to Derek Kettering's face.

"What do you mean, and who are you?"

Poirot gently uncrossed his knees, withdrew his gaze from the ceiling, and looked the young man full in the face.

"My name is Hercule Poirot," he said quietly, "and I am probably the greatest detective in the world. You are quite sure that you did not see or speak to your wife on that train?"

"What are you getting at? Do you–do you mean to insinuate that I–I killed her?"

He laughed suddenly.

"I mustn't lose my temper; it's too palpably absurd. Why, if I killed her I should have had no need to steal her jewels, would I?"

"That is true," murmured Poirot, with a rather crestfallen air. "I did not think of that."

"If ever there were a clear case of murder and robbery, this is it," said Derek Kettering. "Poor Ruth, it was those damned rubies did for her. It must have got about she had them with her. There has been murder done for those same stones before now, I believe."

Poirot sat up suddenly in his chair. A very faint green light glowed in his eyes. He looked extraordinarily like a sleek, well-fed cat.

"One more question, M. Kettering," he said. "Will you give me the date when you last saw your wife?"

"Let me see," Kettering reflected. "It must have been—yes over three weeks ago. I am afraid I can't give you the date exactly."

"No matter," said Poirot drily; "that is all I wanted to know."

"Well," said Derek Kettering impatiently, "anything further?"

He looked towards M. Carrège. The latter sought inspiration from Poirot, and received it in a very faint shake of the head.

"No, M. Kettering," he said politely; "no, I do not think we need trouble you any further. I wish you good morning."

"Good morning," said Kettering. He went out, banging the door behind him.

Poirot leaned forward and spoke sharply, as soon as the young man was out of the room.

"Tell me," he said peremptorily, "when did you speak of these rubies to M. Kettering?"

"I have not spoken of them," said M. Carrège. "It was only yesterday afternoon that we learnt about them from M. Van Aldin."

"Yes; but there was a mention of them in the Comte's letter."

M. Carrège looked pained.

"Naturally I did not speak of that letter to M. Kettering," he said in a shocked voice. "It would have been most indiscreet at the present juncture of affairs."

Poirot leaned forward and tapped the table.

"*Then how did he know about them?*" he demanded softly. "Madame could not have told him, for he has not seen her for three weeks. It seems unlikely that either M. Van Aldin or his secretary would have mentioned them; their interviews with him have been on entirely different lines, and there has not been any hint or reference to them in the newspapers."

He got up and took his hat and stick.

"And yet," he murmured to himself, "our gentleman knows all about them. I wonder now, yes, I wonder!"

CHAPTER XVIII

DEREK LUNCHES

DEREK KETTERING WENT straight to the Negresco, where he ordered a couple of cocktails and disposed of them rapidly; then he stared moodily out over the dazzling blue sea. He noted the passers-by mechanically—a damned dull crowd, badly dressed, and painfully uninteresting; one hardly ever saw anything worth while nowadays. Then he corrected this last impression rapidly, as a woman placed herself at a table a little distance away from him. She was wearing a marvellous confection of orange and black, with a little hat that shaded her face. He ordered a third cocktail; again he stared out to sea, and then suddenly he started. A well-known perfume assailed his nostrils, and he looked up to see the orange-and-black lady standing beside him. He saw her face now, and recognized her. It was Mirelle. She was smiling that insolent, seductive smile he knew so well.

"Dereek!" she murmured. "You are pleased to see me, no?"

She dropped into a seat the other side of the table.

"But welcome me, then, stupid one," she mocked.

"This is an unexpected pleasure," said Derek. "When did you leave London?"

She shrugged her shoulders.

"A day or two ago."

"And the Parthenon?"

"I have, how do you say it?—given them the chuck!"

"Really?"

"You are not very amiable, Dereek."

"Do you expect me to be?"

Mirelle lit a cigarette and puffed at it for a few minutes before saying:

"You think, perhaps, that it is not prudent so soon?"

Derek stared at her, then he shrugged his shoulders, and remarked formally:

"You are lunching here?"

"*Mais oui*. I am lunching with you."

"I am extremely sorry," said Derek. "I have a very important engagement."

"*Mon Dieu!* But you men are like children," exclaimed the dancer. "But yes, it is the spoilt child that you act to me, ever since that day in London when you flung yourself out of my flat, you sulk. Ah! *mais c'est inoui!*"

"My dear girl," said Derek, "I really don't know what you are talking about. We agreed in London that rats desert a sinking ship, that is all that there is to be said."

In spite of his careless words, his face looked haggard and strained. Mirelle leaned forward suddenly.

"You cannot deceive me," she murmured. "I know—I know what you have done for me."

He looked up at her sharply. Some undercurrent in her voice arrested his attention. She nodded her head at him.

"Ah! have no fear; I am discreet. You are magnificent! You have a superb courage, but, all the same, it was I who gave you the idea that day, when I said to you in London that accidents sometimes happened. And you are not in danger? The police do not suspect you?"

"What the devil——"

"Hush!"

She held up a slim olive hand with one big emerald on the little finger.

"You are right; I should not have spoken so in a public place. We will not speak of the matter again, but our troubles are ended; our life together will be wonderful—wonderful!"

Derek laughed suddenly—a harsh, disagreeable laugh.

"So the rats come back, do they? Two million makes a difference—of course it does. I ought to have known that." He laughed again. "You will help me to spend that two million, won't you, Mirelle? You know how, no woman better." He laughed again.

"Hush!" cried the dancer. "What is the matter with you, Dereek? See—people are turning to stare at you."

"Me? I will tell you what is the matter. I have finished with you, Mirelle. Do you hear? Finished!"

Mirelle did not take it as he expected her to do. She looked at him for a minute or two, and then she smiled softly.

"But what a child! You are angry—you are sore, and all because I am practical. Did I not always tell you that I adored you?"

She leaned forward.

"But I know you, Dereek. Look at me—see, it is Mirelle who speaks to you. You cannot live without her, you know it. I loved you before, I will love you a hundred times more now. I will make life wonderful for you—but wonderful. There is no one like Mirelle."

Her eyes burned into his. She saw him grow pale and draw in his breath, and she smiled to herself contentedly. She knew her own magic and power over men.

"That is settled," she said softly, and gave a little laugh. "And now, Dereek, will you give me lunch?"

"No."

He drew in his breath sharply and rose to his feet.

"I am sorry, but I told you—I have got an engagement."

"You are lunching with some one else? Bah! I don't believe it."

"I am lunching with that lady over there."

He crossed abruptly to where a lady in white had just come up the steps. He addressed her a little breathlessly.

"Miss Grey, will you—will you have lunch with me? You met me at Lady Tamplin's, if you remember."

Katherine looked at him for a minute or two with those thoughtful grey eyes that said so much.

"Thank you," she said, after a moment's pause; "I should like to very much."

CHAPTER XIX

AN UNEXPECTED VISITOR

The Comte de la Roche had just finished *déjeuner,* consisting of an *omelette fines herbes,* an *entrecôte Bearnaise,* and a *Savarin au Rhum.* Wiping his fine black moustache delicately with his table napkin, the Comte rose from the table. He passed through the salon of the villa, noting with appreciation the few *objets d'art* which were carelessly scattered about. The Louis XV snuff-box, the satin shoe worn by Marie Antoinette, and the other historic trifles were part of the Comte's *mise en scène.* They were, he would explain to his fair visitors, heirlooms in his family. Passing through on to the terrace, the Comte looked out on the Mediterranean with an unseeing eye. He was in no mood for appreciating the beauties of scenery. A fully matured scheme had been rudely brought to naught, and his plans had to be cast afresh. Stretching himself out in a basket chair, a cigarette held between his white fingers, the Comte pondered deeply.

Presently Hippolyte, his man-servant, brought out coffee and a choice of liqueurs. The Comte selected some very fine old brandy.

As the man-servant was preparing to depart, the Comte arrested him with a slight gesture. Hippolyte stood respectfully to attention. His countenance was hardly a prepossessing one, but the correctitude of his demeanour went far to obliterate the fact. He was now the picture of respectful attention.

"It is possible," said the Comte, "that in the course of the next few days various strangers may come to the house. They will endeavour to scrape acquaintance with you and with Marie. They will probably ask you various questions concerning me."

"Yes, Monsieur le Comte."

"Perhaps this has already happened?"

"No, Monsieur le Comte."

"There have been no strangers about the place? You are certain?"

"There has been no one, Monsieur le Comte."

"That is well," said the Comte drily; "nevertheless they will come—I am sure of it. They will ask questions."

Hippolyte looked at his master in intelligent anticipation.

The Comte spoke slowly, without looking at Hippolyte.

"As you know, I arrived here last Tuesday morning. If the police or any other inquirer should question you, do not forget that fact. I arrived on Tuesday, the 14th—not Wednesday, the 15th. You understand?"

"Perfectly, Monsieur le Comte."

"In an affair where a lady is concerned, it is always necessary to be discreet. I feel certain, Hippolyte, that you can be discreet."

"I can be discreet, Monsieur."

"And Marie?"

"Marie also. I will answer for her."

"That is well then," murmured the Comte.

When Hippolyte had withdrawn, the Comte sipped his black coffee with a reflective air. Occasionally he frowned, once he shook his head slightly, twice he nodded it. Into the midst of these cogitations came Hippolyte once more.

"A lady, Monsieur."

"A lady?"

The Comte was surprised. Not that a visit from a lady was an unusual thing at the Villa Marina, but at this particular moment the Comte could not think who the lady was likely to be.

"She is, I think, a lady not known to Monsieur," murmured the valet helpfully.

The Comte was more and more intrigued.

"Show her out here, Hippolyte," he commanded.

A moment later a marvellous vision in orange and black stepped out on the terrace, accompanied by a strong perfume of exotic blossoms.

"Monsieur le Comte de la Roche?"

"At your service, Mademoiselle," said the Comte, bowing.

"My name is Mirelle. You may have heard of me."

"Ah, indeed, Mademoiselle, but who has not been enchanted by the dancing of Mademoiselle Mirelle? Exquisite!"

The dancer acknowledged this compliment with a brief mechanical smile.

"My descent upon you is unceremonious," she began.

"But seat yourself, I beg of you, Mademoiselle," cried the Comte, bringing forward a chair.

Behind the gallantry of his manner he was observing her narrowly. There were very few things that the Comte did not know about women. True, his experience had not lain much in ladies of Mirelle's class, who were themselves predatory. He and the dancer were, in a sense, birds of a feather. His arts, the Comte knew, would be thrown away on Mirelle. She was a Parisienne, and a shrewd one. Nevertheless, there was one thing that the Comte could recognize infallibly when he saw it. He knew at once that he was in the presence of a very angry woman, and an angry woman, as the Comte was well aware, always says more than is prudent, and is occasionally a source of profit to a level-headed gentleman who keeps cool.

"It is most amiable of you, Mademoiselle, to honour my poor abode thus."

"We have mutual friends in Paris," said Mirelle. "I have heard of you from them, but I come to see you to-day for another reason. I have heard of you since I came to Nice—in a different way, you understand."

"Ah?" said the Comte softly.

"I will be brutal," continued the dancer; "nevertheless, believe that I have your welfare at heart. They are saying in Nice, Monsieur le Comte, that you are the murderer of the English lady, Madame Kettering."

"I!—the murderer of Madame Kettering? Bah! But how absurd!"

He spoke more languidly than indignantly, knowing that he would thus provoke her further.

"But yes," she insisted; "it is as I tell you."

"It amuses people to talk," murmured the Comte indifferently. "It would be beneath me to take such wild accusations seriously."

"You do not understand." Mirelle bent forward, her dark eyes flashing. "It is not the idle talk of those in the streets. It is the police."

"The police—ah?"

The Comte sat up, alert once more.

Mirelle nodded her head vigorously several times.

"Yes, yes. You comprehend me—I have friends everywhere. The Prefect himself——" She left the sentence unfinished, with an eloquent shrug of the shoulders.

"Who is not indiscreet where a beautiful woman is concerned?" murmured the Count politely.

"The police believe that you killed Madame Kettering. But they are wrong."

"Certainly they are wrong," agreed the Comte easily.

"You say that, but you do not know the truth. I do."

The Comte looked at her curiously.

"You know who killed Madame Kettering? Is that what you would say, Mademoiselle?"

Mirelle nodded vehemently.

"Yes."

"Who was it?" asked the Comte sharply.

"Her husband." She bent nearer to the Comte, speaking in a low voice that vibrated with anger and excitement. "It was her husband who killed her."

The Comte leant back in his chair. His face was a mask.

"Let me ask you, Mademoiselle—how do you know this?"

"How do I know it?" Mirelle sprang to her feet, with a laugh. "He boasted of it beforehand. He was ruined, bankrupt, dishonored. Only the death of his wife could save him. He told me so. He travelled on the same train—but she was not to know it. Why was that, I ask you? So that he might creep upon her in the night—Ah!"—she shut her eyes—"I can see it happening. . . ."

The Count coughed.

"Perhaps—perhaps," he murmured. "But surely, Mademoiselle, in that case he would not steal the jewels?"

"The jewels!" breathed Mirelle. "The jewels. Ah! Those rubies . . ."

Her eyes grew misty, a far-away light in them. The Comte looked at her curiously, wondering for the hundredth time at the magical influence of precious stones on the female sex. He recalled her to practical matters.

"What do you want me to do, Mademoiselle?"

Mirelle became alert and business-like once more.

"Surely it is simple. You will go to the police. You will say to them that M. Kettering committed this crime."

"And if they do not believe me? If they ask for proof?" He was eyeing her closely.

Mirelle laughed softly, and drew her orange-and-black wrap closer round her.

"Send them to me, Monsieur le Comte," she said softly; "I will give them the proof they want."

Upon that she was gone, an impetuous whirlwind, her errand accomplished.

The Comte looked after her, his eyebrows delicately raised.

"She is in a fury," he murmured. "What has happened now to upset her? But she shows her hand too plainly. Does she really believe that Mr. Kettering killed his wife? She would like me to believe it. She would even like the police to believe it."

He smiled to himself. He had no intention whatsoever of going to the police. He saw various other possibilities; to judge by his smile, an agreeable vista of them.

Presently, however, his brow clouded. According to Mirelle, he was suspected by the police. That might be true or it might not. An angry woman of the type of the dancer was not likely to bother about the strict veracity of her statements. On the other hand, she might easily have obtained—inside information. In that case—his mouth set grimly—in that case he must take certain precautions.

He went into the house and questioned Hippolyte closely once more as to whether any strangers had been to the house. The valet was positive in his assurances that this was not the case. The Comte went up to his bedroom and crossed over to an old bureau that stood against the wall. He let down the lid of this, and his delicate fingers sought for a spring at the back of one of the pigeonholes. A secret drawer flew out; in it was a small brown paper package. The Comte took this out and weighed it in his hand carefully for a minute or two. Raising his hand to his head, with a slight grimace he pulled out a single hair. This he placed on the lip of the drawer and shut it carefully. Still carrying the small parcel in his hand, he went downstairs and out of the house to the garage, where stood a scarlet two-seater car. Ten minutes later he had taken the road for Monte Carlo.

He spent a few hours at the Casino, then sauntered out into the town. Presently he re-entered the car and drove off in the direction of Mentone. Earlier in the afternoon he had noticed an inconspicuous grey car some little distance behind him. He noticed it again now. He smiled to himself. The road was climbing steadily upwards. The Comte's foot pressed hard on the accelerator. The little red car had been specially built to the Comte's design, and had a far more powerful engine than would have been suspected from its appearance. It shot ahead.

Presently he looked back and smiled; the grey car was following behind. Smothered in dust, the little red car leaped along the road. It was travelling now at a dangerous pace, but the Comte was a first-class driver. Now they were going down hill, twisting and curving unceasingly. Presently the car slackened speed, and finally came to a standstill before a Bureau de Poste. The Comte jumped out, lifted the lid of the tool chest, extracted the small brown paper parcel and hurried into the post office. Two minutes later he was driving once more in the direction of Mentone. When the grey car arrived there, the Comte was drinking English five o'clock tea on the terrace of one of the hotels.

Later, he drove back to Monte Carlo, dined there, and reached home once more at eleven o'clock. Hippolyte came out to meet him with a disturbed face.

"Ah! Monsieur le Comte has arrived. Monsieur le Comte did not telephone me, by any chance?"

The Comte shook his head.

"And yet at three o'clock I received a summons from Monsieur le Comte, to present myself to him at Nice, at the Negresco."

"Really," said the Comte; "and you went?"

"Certainly, Monsieur, but at the Negresco they knew nothing of Monsieur le Comte. He had not been there."

"Ah," said the Comte, "doubtless at that hour Marie was out doing her afternoon marketing?"

"That is so, Monsieur le Comte."

"Ah, well," said the Comte, "it is of no importance. A mistake."

He went upstairs, smiling to himself.

Once within his own room, he bolted his door and looked sharply round. Everything seemed as usual. He opened various drawers and cupboards. Then he nodded to himself. Things had been replaced almost exactly as he had left them, but not quite. It was evident that a very thorough search had been made.

He went over to the bureau and pressed the hidden spring. The drawer flew open, but the hair was no longer where he had placed it. He nodded his head several times.

"They are excellent, our French police," he murmured to himself —"excellent. Nothing escapes them."

CHAPTER XX

KATHERINE MAKES A FRIEND

On the following morning Katherine and Lenox were sitting on the terrace of the Villa Marguerite. Something in the nature of a friendship was springing up between them, despite the difference in age. But for Lenox, Katherine would have found life at the Villa Marguerite quite intolerable. The Kettering case was the topic of the moment. Lady Tamplin frankly exploited her guest's connection with the affair for all it was worth. The most persistent rebuffs that Katherine could administer quite failed to pierce Lady Tamplin's self-esteem. Lenox adopted a detached attitude, seemingly amused at her mother's manœuvres, and yet with a sympathetic understanding of Katherine's feelings. The situation was not helped by Chubby, whose naïve delight was unquenchable, and who introduced Katherine to all and sundry as:

"This is Miss Grey. You know that Blue Train business? She was in it up to the ears! Had a long talk with Ruth Kettering a few hours before the murder! Bit of luck for her, eh?"

A few remarks of this kind had provoked Katherine that morning to an unusually tart rejoinder, and when they were alone together Lenox observed in her slow drawl:

"Not used to exploitation, are you? You have a lot to learn, Katherine."

"I am sorry I lost my temper. I don't, as a rule."

"It is about time you learnt to blow off steam. Chubby is only an ass; there is no harm in him. Mother, of course, is trying, but you can lose your temper with her until Kingdom come, and it won't make any impression. She will open large, sad blue eyes at you and not care a bit."

Katherine made no reply to this filial observation, and Lenox presently went on:

"I am rather like Chubby. I delight in a good murder, and besides—well, knowing Derek makes a difference."

Katherine nodded.

"So you lunched with him yesterday," pursued Lenox reflectively. "Do you like him, Katherine?"

Katherine considered for a minute or two.

"I don't know," she said very slowly.

"He is very attractive."

"Yes, he is attractive."

"What don't you like about him?"

Katherine did not reply to the question, or at any rate not directly. "He spoke of his wife's death," she said. "He said he would not pretend that it had been anything but a bit of most marvellous luck for him."

"And that shocked you, I suppose," said Lenox. She paused, and then added in rather a queer tone of voice: "He likes you, Katherine."

"He gave me a very good lunch," said Katherine, smiling.

Lenox refused to be side-tracked.

"I saw it the night he came here," she said thoughtfully. "The way he looked at you; and you are not his usual type—just the opposite. Well, I suppose it is like religion—you get it at a certain age."

"Mademoiselle is wanted at the telephone," said Marie, appearing at the window of the salon. "M. Hercule Poirot desires to speak with her."

"More blood and thunder. Go on, Katherine; go and dally with your detective."

M. Hercule Poirot's voice came neat and precise in its intonation to Katherine's ear.

"That is Mademoiselle Grey who speaks? *Bon.* Mademoiselle, I have a word for you from M. Van Aldin, the father of Madame Kettering. He wishes very much to speak with you, either at the Villa Marguerite or at his hotel, whichever you prefer."

Katherine reflected for a moment, but she decided that for Van Aldin to come to the Villa Marguerite would be both painful and unnecessary. Lady Tamplin would have hailed his advent with far too much delight. She never lost a chance of cultivating millionaires. She told Poirot that she would much rather come to Nice.

"Excellent, Mademoiselle. I will call for you myself in an auto. Shall we say in about three-quarters of an hour?"

Punctually to the moment Poirot appeared. Katherine was waiting for him, and they drove off at once.

"Well, Mademoiselle, how goes it?"

She looked at his twinkling eyes, and was confirmed in her first impression that there was something very attractive about M. Hercule Poirot.

"This is our own Roman Policier, is it not?" said Poirot. "I made you the promise that we should study it together. And me, I always keep my promises."

"You are too kind," murmured Katherine.

"Ah, you mock yourself at me; but do you want to hear the developments of the case, or do you not?"

Katherine admitted that she did, and Poirot proceeded to sketch for her a thumbnail portrait of the Comte de la Roche.

"You think he killed her," said Katherine thoughtfully.

"That is the theory," said Poirot guardedly.

"Do you yourself believe that?"

"I did not say so. And you, Mademoiselle, what do you think?"

Katherine shook her head.

"How should I know? I don't know anything about those things, but I should say that——"

"Yes," said Poirot encouragingly.

"Well—from what you say the Count does not sound the kind of man who would actually kill anybody."

"Ah! Very good," cried Poirot, "you agree with me; that is just what I have said." He looked at her sharply. "But tell me, you have met Mr. Derek Kettering?"

"I met him at Lady Tamplin's, and I lunched with him yesterday."

"A *mauvais sujet*," said Poirot, shaking his head; "but *les femmes*—they like that, eh?"

He twinkled at Katherine and she laughed.

"He is the kind of man one would notice anywhere," continued Poirot. "Doubtless you observed him on the Blue Train?"

"Yes, I noticed him."

"In the restaurant car?"

"No. I didn't notice him at meals at all. I only saw him once—going into his wife's compartment."

Poirot nodded. "A strange business," he murmured. "I believe you said you were awake, Mademoiselle, and looked out of your window at Lyons? You saw no tall dark man such as the Comte de la Roche leave the train?"

Katherine shook her head. "I don't think I saw any one at all," she said. "There was a youngish lad in a cap and overcoat who got out, but I don't think he was leaving the train, only walking up and down the platform. There was a fat Frenchman with a beard, in pyjamas and an overcoat, who wanted a cup of coffee. Otherwise, I think there were only the train attendants."

Poirot nodded his head several times. "It is like this, you see," he confided, "the Comte de la Roche has an alibi. An alibi, it is a very pestilential thing, and always open to the gravest suspicion. But here we are!"

They went straight up to Van Aldin's suite, where they found Knighton. Poirot introduced him to Katherine. After a few commonplaces had been exchanged, Knighton said, "I will tell Mr. Van Aldin that Miss Grey is here."

He went through a second door into an adjoining room. There was a low murmur of voices, and then Van Aldin came into the room and advanced towards Katherine with outstretched hand, giving her at the same time a shrewd and penetrating glance.

"I am pleased to meet you, Miss Grey," he said simply. "I have been wanting very badly to hear what you can tell me about Ruth."

The quiet simplicity of the millionaire's manner appealed to Katherine strongly. She felt herself in the presence of a very genuine grief, the more real for its absence of outward sign.

He drew forward a chair.

"Sit here, will you, and just tell me all about it."

Poirot and Knighton retired discreetly into the other room, and Katherine and Van Aldin were left alone together. She found no difficulty in her task. Quite simply and naturally she related her conversation with Ruth Kettering, word for word as nearly as she could. He listened in silence, leaning back in his chair, with one hand shading his eyes. When she had finished he said quietly:

"Thank you, my dear."

They both sat silent for a minute or two. Katherine felt that words of sympathy would be out of place. When the millionaire spoke, it was in a different tone:

"I am very grateful to you, Miss Grey. I think you did something to ease my poor Ruth's mind in the last hours of her life. Now I want to ask you something. You know—M. Poirot will have told you—about the scoundrel that my poor girl had got herself mixed up with. He was the man of whom she spoke to you—the man she was going to meet. In your judgment do you think she might have changed her mind after her conversation with you? Do you think she meant to go back on her word?"

"I can't honestly tell you. She had certainly come to some decision, and seemed more cheerful in consequence of it."

"She gave you no idea where she intended to meet the skunk—whether in Paris or at Hyères?"

Katherine shook her head.

"She said nothing as to that."

"Ah!" said Van Aldin thoughtfully, "and that is the important point. Well, time will show."

He got up and opened the door of the adjoining room. Poirot and Knighton came back.

Katherine declined the millionaire's invitation to lunch, and Knighton went down with her and saw her into the car which had been kept waiting. He returned to find Poirot and Van Aldin deep in conversation.

"If we only knew," said the millionaire thoughtfully, "what decision Ruth came to. It might have been any of half a dozen. She might have meant to leave the train at Paris and cable to me. She may have meant to have gone on to the south of France and have an explanation with the Count there. We are in the dark—absolutely in the dark. But we have the maid's word for it that she was both startled and dismayed at the Count's appearance at the station in Paris. That was clearly not part of the preconceived plan. You agree with me, Knighton?"

The secretary started. "I beg your pardon, Mr. Van Aldin. I was not listening."

"Day-dreaming, eh?" said Van Aldin. "That's not like you. I believe that girl has bowled you over."

Knighton blushed.

"She is a remarkably nice girl," said Van Aldin thoughtfully, "very nice. Did you happen to notice her eyes?"

"Any man," said Knighton, "would be bound to notice her eyes."

CHAPTER XXI

AT THE TENNIS

SEVERAL DAYS HAD ELAPSED. Katherine had been for a walk by herself one morning, and came back to find Lenox grinning at her expectantly.

"Your young man has been ringing you up, Katherine!"

"Who do you call my young man?"

"A new one—Rufus Van Aldin's secretary. You seem to have made rather an impression there. You are becoming a serious breaker of hearts, Katherine. First Derek Kettering, and now this young Knighton. The funny thing is, that I remember him quite well. He was in Mother's War Hospital that she ran out here. I was only a kid of about eight at the time."

"Was he badly wounded?"

"Shot in the leg, if I remember rightly—rather a nasty business. I think the doctors messed it up a bit. They said he wouldn't limp or anything, but when he left here he was still completely dot and go one."

Lady Tamplin came out and joined them.

"Have you been telling Katherine about Major Knighton?" she asked. "Such a dear fellow! Just at first I didn't remember him—one had so many—but now it all comes back."

"He was a bit too unimportant to be remembered before," said Lenox. "Now that he is a secretary to an American millionaire, it is a very different matter."

"Darling!" said Lady Tamplin in her vague reproachful voice.

"What did Major Knighton ring up about?" inquired Katherine.

"He asked if you would like to go to the tennis this afternoon. If so, he would call for you in a car. Mother and I accepted for you with *empressement*. Whilst you dally with a millionaire's secretary, you might give me a chance with the millionaire, Katherine. He is about sixty, I suppose, so that he will be looking about for a nice sweet young thing like me."

"I should like to meet Mr. Van Aldin," said Lady Tamplin earnestly; "one has heard so much of him. Those fine rugged figures of the Western world"—she broke off—"so fascinating," she murmured.

"Major Knighton was very particular to say it was Mr. Van Aldin's invitation," said Lenox. "He said it so often that I began to smell a rat. You and Knighton would make a very nice pair, Katherine. Bless you, my children!"

Katherine laughed, and went upstairs to change her clothes.

Knighton arrived soon after lunch and endured manfully Lady Tamplin's transports of recognition.

When they were driving together towards Cannes he remarked to Katherine: "Lady Tamplin has changed wonderfully little."

"In manner or appearance?"

"Both. She must be, I suppose, well over forty, but she is a remarkably beautiful woman still."

"She is," agreed Katherine.

"I am very glad that you could come to-day," went on Knighton. "M. Poirot is going to be there also. What an extraordinary little man he is. Do you know him well, Miss Grey?"

Katherine shook her head. "I met him on the train on the way here. I was reading a detective novel, and I happened to say something about such things not happening in real life. Of course, I had no idea of who he was."

"He is a very remarkable person," said Knighton slowly, "and has done some very remarkable things. He has a kind of genius for going to the root of the matter, and right up to the end no one has any idea of what he is really thinking. I remember I was staying at a house in Yorkshire, and Lady Clanravon's jewels were stolen. It seemed at first to be a simple robbery, but it completely baffled the local police. I wanted them to call in Hercule Poirot, and said he was the only man who could help them, but they pinned their faith to Scotland Yard."

"And what happened?" said Katherine curiously.

"The jewels were never recovered," said Knighton drily.

"You really do believe in him?"

"I do indeed. The Comte de la Roche is a pretty wily customer. He has wriggled out of most things. But I think he has met his match in Hercule Poirot."

"The Comte de la Roche," said Katherine thoughtfully; "so you really think he did it?"

"Of course." Knighton looked at her in astonishment. "Don't you?"

"Oh yes," said Katherine hastily; "that is, I mean, if it was not just an ordinary train robbery."

"It might be, of course," agreed the other, "but it seems to me that the Comte de la Roche fits into this business particularly well."

"And yet he has an alibi."

"Oh, alibis!" Knighton laughed, his face broke into his attractive boyish smile.

"You confess that you read detective stories, Miss Grey. You must know that any one who has a perfect alibi is always open to grave suspicion."

"Do you think that real life is like that?" asked Katherine, smiling.

"Why not? Fiction is founded on fact."

"But is rather superior to it," suggested Katherine.

"Perhaps. Anyway, if I was a criminal I should not like to have Hercule Poirot on my track."

"No more should I," said Katherine, and laughed.

They were met on arrival by Poirot. As the day was warm he was attired in a white duck suit, with a white camellia in his buttonhole.

"*Bon jour*, Mademoiselle," said Poirot. "I look very English, do I not?"

"You look wonderful," said Katherine tactfully.

"You mock yourself at me," said Poirot genially, "but no matter. Papa Poirot, he always laughs the last."

"Where is Mr. Van Aldin?" asked Knighton.

"He will meet us at our seats. To tell you the truth, my friend, he is not too well pleased with me. Oh, those Americans—the repose, the calm, they know it not! Mr. Van Aldin, he would that I fly myself in the pursuit of criminals through all the byways of Nice."

"I should have thought myself that it would not have been a bad plan," observed Knighton.

"You are wrong," said Poirot; "in these matters one needs not energy but finesse. At the tennis one meets every one. That is so important. Ah, there is Mr. Kettering."

Derek came abruptly up to them. He looked reckless and angry, as though something had arisen to upset him. He and Knighton greeted each other with some frigidity. Poirot alone seemed unconscious of any sense of strain, and chatted pleasantly in a laudable attempt to put every one at their ease. He paid little compliments.

"It is amazing, M. Kettering, how well you speak the French," he observed—"so well that you could be taken for a Frenchman if you chose. That is a very rare accomplishment among Englishmen."

"I wish I did," said Katherine. "I am only too well aware that my French is of a painfully British order."

They reached their seats and sat down, and almost immediately Knighton perceived his employer signalling to him from the other end of the court, and went off to speak to him.

"Me, I approve of that young man," said Poirot, sending a beaming smile after the departing secretary; "and you, Mademoiselle?"

"I like him very much."

"And you, M. Kettering?"

Some quick rejoinder was springing to Derek's lips, but he checked it as though something in the little Belgian's twinkling eyes had made him suddenly alert. He spoke carefully, choosing his words.

"Knighton is a very good fellow," he said.

Just for a moment Katherine fancied that Poirot looked disappointed.

"He is a great admirer of yours, M. Poirot," she said, and she related some of the things that Knighton had said. It amused her to see the little man plume himself like a bird, thrusting out his chest, and assuming an air of mock modesty that would have deceived no one.

"That reminds me, Mademoiselle," he said suddenly, "I have a little matter of business I have to speak to you about. When you were sitting talking to that poor lady in the train, I think you must have dropped a cigarette case."

Katherine looked rather astonished. "I don't think so," she said. Poirot drew from his pocket a cigarette case of soft blue leather, with the initial "K" on it in gold.

"No, that is not mine," Katherine said.

"Ah, a thousand apologies. It was doubtless Madame's own. 'K' of course, stands for Kettering. We were doubtful, because she had another cigarette case in her bag, and it seemed odd that she should have two." He turned to Derek suddenly. "You do not know, I suppose, whether this was your wife's case or not?"

Derek seemed momentarily taken aback. He stammered a little in his reply: "I—I don't know. I suppose so."

"It is not yours by any chance?"

"Certainly not. If it were mine it would hardly have been in my wife's possession."

Poirot looked more ingenuous and childlike than ever.

"I thought perhaps you might have dropped it when you were in your wife's compartment," he explained guilelessly.

"I never was there. I have already told the police that a dozen times."

"A thousand pardons," said Poirot, with his most apologetic air. "It was Mademoiselle here who mentioned having seen you going in."

He stopped with an air of embarrassment.

Katherine looked at Derek. His face had gone rather white, but perhaps that was her fancy. His laugh, when it came, was natural enough.

"You made a mistake, Miss Grey," he said easily. "From what the police have told me, I gather that my own compartment was only a door or two away from that of my wife's—though I never suspected the fact at the time. You must have seen me going into my own compartment." He got up quickly as he saw Van Aldin and Knighton approaching.

"I'm going to leave you now," he announced. "I can't stand my father-in-law at any price."

Van Aldin greeted Katherine very courteously, but was clearly in a bad humour.

"You seem fond of watching tennis, M. Poirot," he growled.

"It is a pleasure to me, yes," cried Poirot placidly.

"It is as well you are in France," said Van Aldin. "We are made of sterner stuff in the States. Business comes before pleasure there."

Poirot did not take offense; indeed, he smiled gently and confidingly at the irate millionaire.

"Do not enrage yourself, I beg of you. Every one his own methods. Me, I have always found it a delightful and pleasing idea to combine business and pleasure together."

He glanced at the other two. They were deep in conversation, absorbed in each other. Poirot nodded his head in satisfaction, and then leant towards the millionaire, lowering his voice as he did so.

"It is not only for pleasure that I am here, M. Van Aldin. Observe just opposite us that tall old man—the one with the yellow face and the venerable beard."

"Well, what of him?"

"That," Poirot said, "is M. Papopolous."

"A Greek, eh?"

"As you say—a Greek. He is a dealer in antiques of world-wide reputation. He has a small shop in Paris, and he is suspected by the police of being something more."

"What?"

"A receiver of stolen goods, especially jewels. There is nothing as to the re-cutting and re-setting of gems that he does not know. He deals with the highest in Europe and with the lowest of the riff-raff of the underworld."

Van Aldin was looking at Poirot with suddenly awakened attention.

"Well?" he demanded, a new note in his voice.

"I ask myself," said Poirot, "I, Hercule Poirot"—he thumped himself dramatically on the chest—"ask myself *why is M. Papopolus suddenly come to Nice?*"

Van Aldin was impressed. For a moment he had doubted Poirot and suspected the little man of being past his job, a *poseur* only. Now, in a moment, he switched back to his original opinion. He looked straight at the little detective.

"I must apologize to you, M. Poirot."

Poirot waved the apology aside with an extravagant gesture.

"Bah!" he cried, "all that is of no importance. Now listen, M. Van Aldin; I have news for you."

The millionaire looked sharply at him, all his interest aroused.

Poirot nodded.

"It is as I say. You will be interested. As you know, M. Van Aldin, the Comte de la Roche has been under surveillance ever since his interview with the Juge d'Instruction. The day after that, during his absence, the Villa Marina was searched by the police."

"Well," said Van Aldin, "did they find anything? I bet they didn't."

Poirot made him a little bow.

"Your acumen is not at fault, M. Van Aldin. They found nothing of an incriminating nature. It was not to be expected that they would. The Comte de la Roche, as your expressive idiom has it, was not born on the preceding day. He is an astute gentleman with great experience."

"Well, go on," growled Van Aldin.

"It may be, of course, that the Comte had nothing of a compromising nature to conceal. But we must not neglect the possibility. If, then, he has something to conceal, where is it? Not in his house—the police searched thoroughly. Not on his person, for he knows that he is liable to arrest at any minute. There remains—his car. As I say he was under surveillance. He was followed on that day to Monte Carlo. From there he went by road to Mentone, driving himself. His car is a very powerful one, it outdistanced his pursuers, and for about a quarter of an hour they completely lost sight of him."

"And during that time you think he concealed something by the roadside?" asked Van Aldin, keenly interested.

"By the roadside, no. *Ça n'est pas pratique.* But listen now—me, I have made a little suggestion to M. Carrège. He is graciously pleased to approve of it. In each Bureau de Poste in the neighbourhood it has been seen to that there is some one who knows the Comte de la Roche by sight. Because, you see, Messieurs, the best way of hiding a thing is by sending it away by the post."

"Well?" demanded Van Aldin; his face was keenly alight with interest and expectation.

"Well—*voilà!*" With a dramatic flourish Poirot drew out from his pocket a loosely wrapped brown paper package from which the string had been removed.

"During that quarter of an hour's interval, our good gentleman mailed this."

"The address?" asked the other sharply.

Poirot nodded his head.

"Might have told us something, but unfortunately it does not. The package was addressed to one of these little newspaper shops in Paris where letters and parcels are kept until called for on payment of a small commission."

"Yes, but what is inside?" demanded Van Aldin impatiently.

Poirot unwrapped the brown paper and disclosed a square cardboard box. He looked round him.

"It is a good moment," he said quietly. "All eyes are on the tennis. Look, Monsieur!"

He lifted the lid of the box for the fraction of a second. An exclamation of utter astonishment came from the millionaire. His face turned as white as chalk.

"My God!" he breathed, "the rubies."

He sat for a minute as though dazed. Poirot restored the box to his pocket and beamed placidly. Then suddenly the millionaire seemed to come out of his trance; he leaned across to Poirot and wrung his hand so heartily that the little man winced with pain.

"This is great," said Van Aldin. "Great! You are the goods, M. Poirot. Once and for all, you are the goods."

"It is nothing," said Poirot modestly. "Order, method, being prepared for eventualities beforehand—that is all there is to it."

"And now, I suppose, the Comte de la Roche has been arrested?" continued Van Aldin eagerly.

"No," said Poirot.

A look of utter astonishment came over Van Aldin's face.

"But why? What more do you want?"

"The Comte's alibi is still unshaken."

"But that is nonsense."

"Yes," said Poirot; "I rather think it is nonsense, but unfortunately we have to prove it so."

"In the meantime he will slip through your fingers."

Poirot shook his head very energetically.

"No," he said, "he will not do that. The one thing the Comte cannot afford to sacrifice is his social position. At all costs he must stop and brazen it out."

Van Aldin was still dissatisfied.

"But I don't see——"

Poirot raised a hand. "Grant me a little moment, Monsieur. Me, I have a little idea. Many people have mocked themselves at the little ideas of Hercule Poirot—and they have been wrong."

"Well," said Van Aldin, "go ahead. What is this little idea?"

Poirot paused for a moment and then he said:

"I will call upon you at your hotel at eleven o'clock to-morrow morning. Until then, say nothing to any one."

CHAPTER XXII

M. PAPOPOLOUS BREAKFASTS

M. PAPOPOLOUS WAS at breakfast. Opposite him sat his daughter, Zia.

There was a knock at the sitting-room door, and a chasseur entered with a card which he brought to Mr. Papopolous. The latter scrutinized it, raised his eyebrows, and passed it over to his daughter.

"Ah! said M. Papopolous, scratching his left ear thoughtfully, "Hercule Poirot. I wonder now."

Father and daughter looked at each other.

"I saw him yesterday at the tennis," said M. Papopolous. "Zia, I hardly like this."

"He was very useful to you once," his daughter reminded him.

"That is true," acknowledged M. Papopolous; "also he has retired from active work, so I hear."

These interchanges between father and daughter had passed in their own language. Now M. Papopolous turned to the chasseur and said in French:

"*Faites monter ce monsieur.*"

A few minutes later Hercule Poirot, exquisitely attired, and swinging a cane with a jaunty air, entered the room.

"My dear M. Papopolous."

"My dear M. Poirot."

"And Mademoiselle Zia." Poirot swept her a low bow.

"You will excuse us going on with our breakfast," said M. Papopolous, pouring himself out another cup of coffee. "Your call is—ahem! —a little early."

"It is scandalous," said Poirot, "but see you, I am pressed."

"Ah!" murmured M. Papopolous, "you are on an affair then?"

"A very serious affair," said Poirot: "the death of Madame Kettering."

"Let me see," M. Papopolous looked innocently up at the ceiling, "that was the lady who died on the Blue Train, was it not? I saw a mention of it in the papers, but there was no suggestion of foul play."

"In the interests of justice," said Poirot, "it was thought best to suppress that fact."

There was a pause.

"And in what way can I assist you, M. Poirot?" asked the dealer politely.

"*Voilà*," said Poirot, "I shall come to the point." He took from his pocket the same box that he had displayed at Cannes, and, opening it, he took out the rubies and pushed them across the table to Papopolous.

Although Poirot was watching him narrowly, not a muscle of the old man's face moved. He took up the jewels and examined them with a kind of detached interest, then he looked across at the detective inquiringly:

"Superb, are they not?" asked Poirot.

"Quite excellent," said M. Papopolous.

"How much should you say they are worth?"

The Greek's face quivered a little.

"Is it really necessary to tell you, M. Poirot?" he asked.

"You are shrewd, M. Papopolous. No, it is not. They are not, for instance, worth five hundred thousand dollars."

Papopolous laughed, and Poirot joined with him.

"As an imitation," said Papopolous, handing them back to Poirot, "they are, as I said, quite excellent. Would it be indiscreet to ask, M. Poirot, where you came across them?"

"Not at all," said Poirot; "I have no objection to telling an old friend like yourself. They were in the possession of the Comte de la Roche."

M. Papopolous' eyebrows lifted themselves eloquently.

"In-deed," he murmured.

Poirot leant forward and assumed his most innocent and beguiling air.

"M. Papopolous," he said, "I am going to lay my cards upon the table. The original of these jewels was stolen from Madame Kettering on the Blue Train. Now I will say to you first this: *I am not concerned with the recovery of these jewels. That is the affair of the police.* I am working not for the police but for M. Van Aldin. I want to lay hands on the man who killed Madame Kettering. I am interested in the jewels only in so far as they may lead me to the man. You understand?"

The last two words were uttered with great significance. M. Papopolous, his face quite unmoved, said quietly:

"Go on."

"It seems to me probable, Monsieur, that the jewels will change hands in Nice—may already have done so."

"Ah!" said M. Papopolous.

He sipped his coffee reflectively, and looked a shade more noble and patriarchal than usual.

"I say to myself," continued Poirot, with animation, "what good fortune! My old friend, M. Papopolous, is in Nice. He will aid me."

"And how do you think I can aid you?" inquired M. Papopolous coldly.

"I said to myself, without doubt M. Papopolous is in Nice on business."

"Not at all," said M. Papopolous, "I am here for my health—by the doctor's orders."

He coughed hollowly.

"I am desolated to hear it," replied Poirot, with somewhat insincere sympathy. "But to continue. When a Russian Grand Duke, an Austrian Archduchess, or an Italian Prince wish to dispose of their family jewels—to whom do they go? To M. Papopolous, is it not? He who is famous all over the world for the discretion with which he arranges these things."

The other bowed.

"You flatter me."

"It is a great thing, discretion," mused Poirot, and was rewarded by the fleeting smile which passed across the Greek's face. "I, too, can be discreet."

The eyes of the two men met.

Then Poirot went on speaking very slowly, and obviously picking his words with care.

"I say to myself, this: if these jewels have changed hands in Nice, M. Papopolous would have heard of it. He has knowledge of all that passes in the jewel world."

"Ah!" said M. Papopolous, and helped himself to a *croissant*.

"The police, you understand," said M. Poirot, "do not enter into the matter. It is a personal affair."

"One hears rumours," admitted M. Papopolous cautiously.

"Such as?" prompted Poirot.

"Is there any reason why I should pass them on?"

"Yes," said Poirot, "I think there is. You may remember, M. Papopolous, that seventeen years ago there was a certain article in your hands, left there as security by a very—er—Prominent Person.

It was in your keeping and it unaccountably disappeared. You were, if I may use the English expression, in the soup."

His eyes came gently round to the girl. She had pushed her cup and plate aside, and with both elbows on the table and her chin resting on her hands was listening eagerly. Still keeping an eye on her he went on:

"I am in Paris at the time. You send for me. You place yourself in my hands. If I restore to you that—article, you say I shall earn your undying gratitude. *Eh bien!* I did restore it to you."

A long sigh came from M. Papopolous.

"It was the most unpleasant moment of my career," he murmured.

"Seventeen years is a long time," said Poirot thoughtfully, "but I believe that I am right in saying, Monsieur, that your race does not forget."

"A Greek?" murmured Papopolous, with an ironical smile.

"It was not as a Greek I meant," said Poirot.

There was a silence, and then the old man drew himself up proudly.

"You are right, M. Poirot," he said quietly. "I am a Jew. And, as you say, our race does not forget."

"You will aid me then?"

"As regards the jewels, Monsieur, I can do nothing."

The old man, as Poirot had done just now, picked his words carefully.

"I know nothing. I have heard nothing. But I can perhaps do you a good turn—that is, if you are interested in racing."

"Under certain circumstances I might be," said Poirot, eyeing him steadily.

"There is a horse running at Longchamps that would, I think, repay attention. I cannot say for certain, you understand; this news passed through so many hands."

He stopped, fixing Poirot with his eye, as though to make sure that the latter was comprehending him.

"Perfectly, perfectly," said Poirot, nodding.

"The name of the horse," said M. Papopolous, leaning back and joining the tips of his fingers together, "is the Marquis. I think, but I am not sure, that it is an English horse, eh, Zia?"

"I think so too," said the girl.

Poirot got up briskly.

"I thank you, Monsieur," he said. "It is a great thing to have what the English call a tip from the stable. Au revoir, Monsieur, and many thanks."

He turned to the girl.

"Au revoir, Mademoiselle Zia. It seems to me but yesterday that I saw you in Paris. One would say that two years had passed at most."

"There is a difference between sixteen and thirty-three," said Zia ruefully.

"Not in your case," declared Poirot gallantly. "You and your father will perhaps dine with me one night."

"We shall be delighted," replied Zia.

"Then we will arrange it," declared Poirot, "and now—*je me sauve.*"

Poirot walked along the street humming a little tune to himself. He twirled his stick with a jaunty air, once or twice he smiled to himself quietly. He turned into the first Bureau de Poste he came to and sent off a telegram. He took some time in wording it, but it was in code and he had to call upon his memory. It purported to deal with a missing scarf-pin, and was addressed to Inspector Japp, Scotland Yard.

Decoded, it was short and to the point. "*Wire me everything known about man whose soubriquet is the Marquis.*"

CHAPTER XXIII

A NEW THEORY

IT WAS EXACTLY eleven o'clock when Poirot presented himself at Van Aldin's hotel. He found the millionaire alone.

"You are punctual, M. Poirot," he said, with a smile, as he rose to greet the detective.

"I am always punctual," said Poirot. "The exactitude—always do I observe it. Without order and method——"

He broke off. "Ah, but it is possible that I have said these things to you before. Let us come at once to the object of my visit."

"Your little idea?"

"Yes, my little idea." Poirot smiled.

"First of all, Monsieur, I should like to interview once more the maid, Ada Mason. She is here?"

"Yes, she's here."

"Ah!"

Van Aldin looked at him curiously. He rang the bell, and a messenger was dispatched to find Mason.

Poirot greeted her with his usual politeness, which was never without effect on that particular class.

"Good afternoon, Mademoiselle," he said cheerfully. "Be seated, will you not, if Monsieur permits."

"Yes, yes, sit down, my girl," said Van Aldin.

"Thank you, sir," said Mason primly, and she sat down on the extreme edge of a chair. She looked bonier and more acid than ever.

"I have come to ask you yet more questions," said Poirot. "We must get to the bottom of this affair. Always I return to the question of the man in the train. You have been shown the Comte de la Roche. You say that it is possible he was the man, but you are not sure."

"As I told you, sir, I never saw the gentleman's face. That is what makes it so difficult."

Poirot beamed and nodded.

"Precisely, exactly. I comprehend well the difficulty. Now, Mademoiselle, you have been in the service of Madame Kettering two months, you say. During that time, how often did you see your master?"

Mason reflected a minute or two, and then said:

"Only twice, sir."

"And was that near to, or far away?"

"Well once, sir, he came to Curzon Street. I was upstairs, and I looked over the banisters and saw him in the hall below. I was a bit curious like, you understand, knowing the way things—er—were." Mason finished up with her discreet cough.

"And the other time?"

"I was in the Park, sir, with Annie—one of the housemaids, sir, and she pointed out the master to me walking with a foreign lady."

Again Poirot nodded.

"Now listen, Mason, this man whom you saw in the carriage talking to your mistress at the Gare de Lyon, how do you know it was not your master?"

"The master, sir? Oh, I don't think it could have been."

"But you are not sure," Poirot persisted.

"Well—I never thought of it, sir."

Mason was clearly upset at the idea.

"You have heard that your master was also on the train. What more natural than that it should be he who came along the corridor."

"But the gentleman who was talking to the mistress must have come from outside, sir. He was dressed for the street. In an overcoat and soft hat."

"Just so, Mademoiselle, but reflect a minute. The train has just arrived at the Gare de Lyon. Many of the passengers promenade themselves upon the quay. Your mistress was about to do so, and for that purpose had doubtless put on her fur coat, eh?"

"Yes, sir," agreed Mason.

"Your master, then, does the same. The train is heated, but outside in the station it is cold. He puts on his overcoat and his hat and he walks along beside the train, and looking up at the lighted windows he suddenly sees Madame Kettering. Until then he has had no idea that she was on the train. Naturally, he mounts the carriage and goes to her compartment. She gives an exclamation of surprise at seeing him and quickly shuts the door between the two compartments since it is possible that their conversation may be of a private nature."

He leaned back in his chair and watched the suggestion slowly take effect. No one knew better than Hercule Poirot that the class to which Mason belongs cannot be hurried. He must give her time to get rid of her own preconceived ideas. At the end of three minutes she spoke:

"Well, of course, sir, it might be so. I never thought of it that way. The master is tall and dark, and just about that build. It was seeing the hat and coat that made me say it was a gentleman from outside. Yes, it might have been the master. I would not like to say either way, I am sure."

"Thank you very much, Mademoiselle. I shall not require you any further. Ah, just one thing more." He took from his pocket the cigarette case he had already shown to Katherine. "Is that your mistress's case?" he said to Mason.

"No, sir, it is not the mistress's—at least——"

She looked suddenly startled. An idea was clearly working its way to the forefront of her mind.

"Yes," said Poirot encouragingly.

"I think, sir—I can't be sure, but I think—it is a case that the mistress bought to give to the master."

"Ah," said Poirot in a non-committal manner.

"But whether she ever did give it to him or not, I can't say, of course."

"Precisely," said Poirot, "precisely. That is all, I think, Mademoiselle. I wish you good afternoon."

Ada Mason retired discreetly, closing the door noiselessly behind her.

Poirot looked across at Van Aldin, a faint smile upon his face. The millionaire looked thunderstruck.

"You think—you think it was Derek?" he queried, "but—everything points the other way. Why, the Count has actually been caught red-handed with the jewels on him."

"No."

"But you told me——"

"What did I tell you?"

"That story about the jewels. You showed them to me."

"No."

Van Aldin stared at him.

"You mean to say you didn't show them to me."

"No."

"Yesterday—at the tennis?"

"No."

"Are you crazy, M. Poirot, or am I?"

"Neither of us is crazy," said the detective. "You ask me a question; I answer it. You say have I not shown you the jewels yesterday? I reply—no. What I showed you, M. Van Aldin, was a first-class imitation, hardly to be distinguished except by an expert from the real ones."

CHAPTER XXIV

POIROT GIVES ADVICE

It took the millionaire some few minutes to take the thing in. He stared at Poirot as though dumbfounded. The little Belgian nodded at him gently.

"Yes," he said, "it alters the position, does it not?"

"Imitation!"

He leaned forward.

"All along, M. Poirot, you have had this idea? All along this is what you have been driving at? You never believed that the Comte de la Roche was the murderer?"

"I have had doubts," said Poirot quietly. "I said as much to you. Robbery with violence and murder"—he shook his head energetically—"no, it is difficult to picture. It does not harmonize with the personality of the Comte de la Roche."

"But you believe that he meant to steal the rubies?"

"Certainly. There is no doubt as to that. See, I will recount to you the affair as I see it. The Comte knew of the rubies and he laid his plans accordingly. He made up a romantic story of a book he was writing, so as to induce your daughter to bring them with her. He provided himself with an exact duplicate. It is clear, is it not, that substitution is what he was after. Madame, your daughter, was not an expert on jewels. It would probably be a long time before she discovered what had occurred. When she did so—well—I do not think she would prosecute the Comte. Too much would come out. He would have in his possession various letters of hers. Oh yes, a very safe scheme from the Comte's point of view—one that he has probably carried out before."

"It seems clear enough, yes," said Van Aldin musingly.

"It accords with the personality of the Comte de la Roche," said Poirot.

"Yes, but now——" Van Aldin looked searchingly at the other. "What actually happened? Tell me that, M. Poirot."

Poirot shrugged his shoulders.

"It is quite simple," he said; "some one stepped in ahead of the Comte."

There was a long pause.

Van Aldin seemed to be turning things over in his mind. When he spoke it was without beating about the bush.

"How long have you suspected my son-in-law, M. Poirot?"

"From the very first. He had the motive and the opportunity. Every one took for granted that the man in Madame's compartment in Paris was the Comte de la Roche. I thought so, too. Then you happened to mention that you had once mistaken the Comte for your son-in-law. That told me that they were of the same height and build, and alike in colouring. It put some curious ideas in my head. The maid had only been with your daughter a short time. It was unlikely that she would know Mr. Kettering well by sight, since he had not been living in Curzon Street; also the man was careful to keep his face turned away."

"You believe he—murdered her," said Van Aldin hoarsely.

Poirot raised a hand quickly.

"No, no, I did not say that—but it is a possibility—a very strong possibility. He was in a tight corner, a very tight corner, threatened with ruin. This was the one way out."

"But why take the jewels?"

"To make the crime appear an ordinary one committed by train robbers. Otherwise suspicion might have fallen on him straight away."

"If that is so, what has he done with the rubies?"

"That remains to be seen. There are several possibilities. There is a man in Nice who may be able to help, the man I pointed out at the tennis."

He rose to his feet and Van Aldin rose also and laid his hand on the little man's shoulder. His voice when he spoke was harsh with emotion.

"Find Ruth's murderer for me," he said, "that is all I ask."

Poirot drew himself up.

"Leave it in the hands of Hercule Poirot," he said superbly; "have no fears. I will discover the truth."

He brushed a speck of fluff from his hat, smiled reassuringly at the millionaire, and left the room. Nevertheless, as he went down the stairs some of the confidence faded from his face.

"It is all very well," he murmured to himself, "but there are difficulties. Yes, there are great difficulties." As he was passing out of the hotel he came to a sudden halt. A car had drawn up in front of the door. In it was Katherine Grey, and Derek Kettering was standing beside it talking to her earnestly. A minute or two later the car drove off and Derek remained standing on the pavement looking after it. The expression on his face was an odd one. He gave a sudden impatient gesture of the shoulders, sighed deeply, and turned to find Hercule Poirot standing at his elbow. In spite of himself he started. The two men looked at each other. Poirot steadily and unwaveringly and Derek with a kind of light-hearted defiance. There was a sneer behind the easy mockery of his tone when he spoke, raising his eyebrows slightly as he did so.

"Rather a dear, isn't she?" he asked easily.

His manner was perfectly natural.

"Yes," said Poirot thoughtfully, "that describes Mademoiselle Katherine very well. It is very English, that phrase there, and Mademoiselle Katherine, she also is very English."

Derek remained perfectly still without answering.

"And yet she is *sympathique*, is it not so?"

"Yes," said Derek; "there are not many like her."

He spoke softly, almost as though to himself. Poirot nodded significantly. Then he leant towards the other and spoke in a different tone, a quiet, grave tone that was new to Derek Kettering.

"You will pardon an old man, Monsieur, if he says to you something that you may consider impertinent. There is one of your English proverbs that I would quote to you. It says that 'it is well to be off with the old love, before being on with the new.'"

Kettering turned on him angrily.

"What the devil do you mean?"

"You enrage yourself at me," said Poirot placidly. "I expected as much. As to what I mean—I mean, Monsieur, that there is a second car with a lady in it. If you turn your head you will see her."

Derek spun round. His face darkened with anger.

"Mirelle, damn her!" he muttered. "I will soon——"

Poirot arrested the movement he was about to make.

"Is it wise what you are about to do there?" he asked warningly. His eyes shone softly with a green light in them. But Derek was past noticing the warning signs. In his anger he was completely off his guard.

"I have broken with her utterly, and she knows it," cried Derek angrily.

"You have broken with her, yes, but has *she* broken with you?"

Derek gave a sudden harsh laugh.

"She won't break with two million pounds if she can help it," he murmured brutally; "trust Mirelle for that."

Poirot raised his eyebrows.

"You have the outlook cynical," he murmured.

"Have I?" There was no mirth in his sudden wide smile. "I have lived in the world long enough, M. Poirot, to know that all women are pretty much alike." His face softened suddenly. "All save one."

He met Poirot's gaze defiantly. A look of alertness crept into his eyes, then faded again. "That one," he said, and jerked his head in the direction of Cap Martin.

"Ah!" said Poirot.

This quiescence was well calculated to provoke the impetuous temperament of the other.

"I know what you are going to say," said Derek rapidly, "the kind of life I have led, the fact that I am not worthy of her. You will say that I have no right to think even of such a thing. You will say that it is not a case of giving a dog a bad name—I know that it is not decent to be speaking like this with my wife dead only a few days, and murdered at that."

He paused for breath, and Poirot took advantage of the pause to remark in his plaintive tone.

"But, indeed, I have not said anything at all."

"But you will."

"Eh?" said Poirot.

"You will say that I have no earthly chance of marrying Katherine."

"No," said Poirot, "I would not say that. Your reputation is bad, yes, but with women—never does that deter them. If you were a man of excellent character, of strict morality who had done nothing that he should not do, and—possibly everything that he should do—*eh bien!* then I should have grave doubts of your success. Moral worth, you understand, it is not romantic. It is appreciated, however, by widows."

Derek Kettering stared at him, then he swung round on his heel and went up to the waiting car.

Poirot looked after him with some interest. He saw the lovely vision lean out of the car and speak.

Derek Kettering did not stop. He lifted his hat and passed straight on.

"*Ça y est,*" said M. Hercule Poirot, "it is time, I think, that I return *chez moi.*"

He found the imperturbable George pressing trousers.

"A pleasant day, Georges, somewhat fatiguing, but not without interest," he said.

George received these remarks in his usual wooden fashion.

"Indeed, sir."

"The personality of a criminal, Georges, is an interesting matter. Many murderers are men of great personal charm."

"I always heard, sir, that Dr. Crippen was a pleasant-spoken gentleman. And yet he cut up his wife like so much mincemeat."

"Your instances are always apt, Georges."

The valet did not reply, and at that moment the telephone rang. Poirot took up the receiver.

"'Allo—'allo—yes, yes, it is Hercule Poirot who speaks."

"This is Knighton. Will you hold the line a minute, M. Poirot? Mr. Van Aldin would like to speak to you."

There was a moment's pause, then the millionaire's voice came through.

"Is that you, M. Poirot? I just wanted to tell you that Mason came to me now of her own accord. She has been thinking it over, and she says that she is almost certain that the man at Paris was Derek Kettering. There was something familiar about him at the time, she says, but at the minute she could not place it. She seems pretty certain now."

"Ah," said Poirot, "thank you, M. Van Aldin. That advances us."

He replaced the receiver, and stood for a minute or two with a very curious smile on his face. George had to speak to him twice before obtaining an answer.

"Eh?" said Poirot. "What is that that you say to me?"

"Are you lunching here, sir, or are you going out?"

"Neither," said Poirot, "I shall go to bed and take a *tisane*. The expected has happened, and when the expected happens, it always causes me emotion."

CHAPTER XXV

DEFIANCE

As Derek Kettering passed the car, Mirelle leant out.

"Dereek—I must speak to you for a moment——"

But, lifting his hat, Derek passed straight on without stopping. When he got back to his hotel, the concierge detached himself from his wooden pen and accosted him.

"A gentleman is waiting to see you, Monsieur."

"Who is it?" asked Derek.

"He did not give me his name, Monsieur, but he said his business with you was important, and that he would wait."

"Where is he?"

"In the little salon, Monsieur. He preferred it to the lounge he said, as being more private."

Derek nodded, and turned his steps in that direction.

The small salon was empty except for the visitor, who rose and bowed with easy foreign grace as Derek entered. As it chanced, Derek had only seen the Comte de la Roche once, but found no difficulty in recognizing that aristocratic nobleman, and he frowned angrily. Of all the consummate impertinence!

"The Comte de la Roche, is it not?" he said. "I am afraid you have wasted your time in coming here."

"I hope not," said the Comte agreeably. His white teeth glittered.

The Comte's charm of manner was usually wasted on his own sex. All men, without exception, disliked him heartily. Derek Kettering was already conscious of a distinct longing to kick the Count bodily out of the room. It was only the realization that scandal would be unfortunate just at present that restrained him. He marvelled anew that Ruth could have cared, as she certainly had, for this fellow. A bounder, and worse than a bounder. He looked with distaste at the Count's exquisitely manicured hands.

"I called," said the Comte, "on a little matter of business. It would be advisable, I think, for you to listen to me."

Again Derek felt strongly tempted to kick him out, but again he refrained. The hint of a threat was not lost upon him, but he interpreted it in his own way. There were various reasons why it would be better to hear what the Comte had to say.

He sat down and drummed impatiently with his fingers on the table.

"Well," he said sharply, "what is it?"

It was not the Comte's way to come out into the open at once.

"Allow me, Monsieur, to offer you my condolences on your recent bereavement."

"If I have any impertinence from you," said Derek quietly, "you go out by that window."

He nodded his head towards the window beside the Comte, and the latter moved uneasily.

"I will send my friends to you, Monsieur, if that is what you desire," he said haughtily.

Derek laughed.

"A duel, eh? My dear Count, I don't take you seriously enough for that. But I should take a good deal of pleasure in kicking you down the Promenade des Anglais."

The Comte was not at all anxious to take offence. He merely raised his eyebrows and murmured:

"The English are barbarians."

"Well," said Derek, "what is it you have to say to me?"

"I will be frank," said the Comte, "I will come immediately to the point. That will suit us both, will it not?"

Again he smiled in his agreeable fashion.

"Go on," said Derek curtly.

The Comte looked at the ceiling, joined the tips of his fingers together, and murmured softly:

"You have come into a lot of money, Monsieur."

"What the devil has that got to do with you?"

The Comte drew himself up.

"Monsieur, my name is tarnished! I am suspected—accused—of foul crime."

"The accusation does not come from me," said Derek coldly; "as an interested party I have not expressed any opinion."

"I am innocent," said the Comte, "I swear before heaven"—he raised his hand to heaven—"that I am innocent."

"M. Carrège is, I believe, the Juge d'Instruction in charge of the case," hinted Derek politely.

The Comte took no notice.

"Not only am I unjustly suspected of a crime that I did not commit, but I am also in serious need of money."

He coughed softly and suggestively.

Derek rose to his feet.

"I was waiting for that," he said softly; "you blackmailing brute! I will not give you a penny. My wife is dead, and no scandal that you can make can touch her now. She wrote you foolish letters, I dare say. If I were to buy them from you for a round sum at this minute, I am pretty certain that you would manage to keep one or two back; and I will tell you this, M. de la Roche, blackmailing is an ugly word both in England and in France. That is my answer to you. Good afternoon."

"One moment"—the Comte stretched out a hand as Derek was turning to leave the room. "You are mistaken, Monsieur. You are completely mistaken. I am, I hope, a 'gentleman.'" Derek laughed. "Any letters that a lady might write to me I should hold sacred." He flung back his head with a beautiful air of nobility. "The proposition that I was putting before you was of quite a different nature. I am, as I said, extremely short of money, and my conscience might impel me to go to the police with certain information."

Derek came slowly back into the room.

"What do you mean?"

The Comte's agreeable smile flashed forth once more.

"Surely it is not necessary to go into details," he purred. "Seek whom the crime benefits, they say, don't they? As I said just now, you have come into a lot of money lately."

Derek laughed.

"If that is all——" he said contemptuously.

But the Comte was shaking his head.

"But it is not all, my dear sir. I should not come to you unless I had much more precise and detailed information than that. It is not agreeable, Monsieur, to be arrested and tried for murder."

Derek came close up to him. His face expressed such furious anger that involuntarily the Comte drew back a pace or two.

"Are you threatening *me?*" the young man demanded angrily.

"You shall hear nothing more of the matter," the Comte assured him.

"Of all the colossal bluffs that I have ever struck——"

The Comte raised a white hand.

"You are wrong. It is not a bluff. To convince you I will tell you this. My information was obtained from a certain lady. It is she who holds the irrefutable proof that you committed the murder."

"She? Who?"

"Mademoiselle Mirelle."

Derek drew back as though struck.

"Mirelle," he muttered.

The Comte was quick to press what he took to be his advantage.

"A bagatelle of one hundred thousand francs," he said. "I ask no more."

"Eh?" said Derek absently.

"I was saying, Monsieur, that a bagatelle of one hundred thousand francs would satisfy my—conscience."

Derek seemed to recollect himself. He looked earnestly at the Comte.

"You would like my answer now?"

"If you please, Monsieur."

"Then here it is. You can go to the devil. See?"

Leaving the Comte too astonished to speak, Derek turned on his heel and swung out of the room.

Once out of the hotel he hailed a taxi and drove to Mirelle's hotel. On inquiring, he learned that the dancer had just come in. Derek gave the concierge his card.

"Take this up to Mademoiselle and ask if she will see me."

A very brief interval elapsed, and then Derek was bidden to follow a *chasseur*.

A wave of exotic perfume assailed Derek's nostrils as he stepped over the threshold of the dancer's apartments. The room was filled with carnations, orchids, and mimosa. Mirelle was standing by the window in a *peignoir* of foamy lace.

She came towards him, her hands outstretched.

"Dereek—you have come to me. I knew you would."

He put aside the clinging arms and looked down on her sternly.

"Why did you send the Comte de la Roche to me?"

She looked at him in astonishment, which he took to be genuine.

"I? Send the Comte de la Roche to you? But for what?"

"Apparently—for blackmail," said Derek grimly.

Again she stared. Then suddenly she smiled and nodded her head.

"Of course. It was to be expected. It is what he would do, *ce type là*. I might have known it. No, indeed, Dereek, I did not send him."

He looked at her piercingly, as though seeking to read her mind.

"I will tell you," said Mirelle. "I am ashamed, but I will tell you. The other day, you comprehend, I was mad with rage, quite mad—"

she made an eloquent gesture. "My temperament, it is not a patient one. I want to be revenged on you, and so I go to the Comte de la Roche, and I tell him to go to the police and say so and so, and so and so. But have no fear, Dereek. Not completely did I lose my head; the proof rests with me alone. The police can do nothing without my word, you understand? And now—now?"

She nestled up close to him, looking up at him with melting eyes.

He thrust her roughly away from him. She stood there, her breast heaving, her eyes narrowing to a catlike slit.

"Be careful, Dereek, be very careful. You have come back to me, have you not?"

"I shall never come back to you," said Derek steadily.

"Ah!"

More than ever the dancer looked like a cat. Her eyelids flickered.

"So there is another woman? The one with whom you lunched that day. Eh! am I right?"

"I intend to ask that lady to marry me. You might as well know."

"That prim Englishwoman! Do you think that I will support that for one moment? Ah, no." Her beautiful lithe body quivered. "Listen, Dereek, do you remember that conversation we had in London? You said the only thing that could save you was the death of your wife. You regretted that she was so healthy. Then the idea of an accident came to your brain. And more than an accident."

"I suppose," said Derek contemptuously, "that it was this conversation that you repeated to the Comte de la Roche."

Mirelle laughed.

"Am I a fool? Could the police do anything with a vague story like that? See—I will give you a last chance. You shall give up this Englishwoman. You shall return to me. And then, *chéri*, never, never will I breathe——"

"Breathe what?"

She laughed softly. "You thought no one saw you——"

"What do you mean?"

"As I say, you thought no one saw you—but *I* saw you, Dereek, *mon ami; I saw you coming out of the compartment of Madame your wife just before the train got into Lyons that night. And* I know more than that. I know that when you came out of her compartment she was dead."

He stared at her. Then, like a man in a dream he turned very slowly and went out of the room, swaying slightly as he walked.

CHAPTER XXVI

A WARNING

"AND SO IT IS," said Poirot, "that we are the good friends and have no secrets from each other."

Katherine turned her head to look at him. There was something in his voice, some undercurrent of seriousness, which she had not heard before.

They were sitting in the gardens of Monte Carlo. Katherine had come over with her friends, and they had run into Knighton and Poirot almost immediately on arrival. Lady Tamplin had seized upon Knighton and had overwhelmed him with reminiscences, most of which Katherine had a faint suspicion were invented. They had moved away together, Lady Tamplin with her hand on the young man's arm. Knighton had thrown a couple of glances back over his shoulder, and Poirot's eyes twinkled a little as he saw them.

"Of course we are friends," said Katherine.

"From the beginning we have been sympathetic to each other," mused Poirot.

"When you told me that a 'Roman Policier' occurs in real life."

"And I was right, was I not?" he challenged her, with an emphatic forefinger. "Here we are, plunged in the middle of one. That is natural for me—it is my *métier*—but for you it is different. Yes," he added in a reflective tone, "for you it is different."

She looked sharply at him. It was as though he were warning her, pointing out to her some menace that she had not seen.

"Why do you say that I am in the middle of it? It is true that I had that conversation with Mrs. Kettering just before she died, but now —now all that is over. I am not connected with the case any more."

"Ah, Mademoiselle, Mademoiselle, can we ever say, 'I have finished with this or that'?"

Katherine turned defiantly round to face him.

"What is it?" she asked. "You are trying to tell me something— to convey it to me rather. But I am not clever at taking hints. I would much rather that you said anything you have to say straight out."

Poirot looked at her sadly. "*Ah, mais c'est Anglais ça,*" he murmured, "everything in black and white, everything clear cut and well defined. But life, it is not like that, Mademoiselle. There are the things that are not yet, but which cast their shadow before."

He dabbed his brow with a very large silk pocket-handkerchief and murmured:

"Ah, but it is that I become poetical. Let us, as you say, speak only of facts. And, speaking of facts, tell me what you think of Major Knighton."

"I like him very much indeed," said Katherine warmly; "he is quite delightful."

Poirot sighed.

"What is the matter?" asked Katherine.

"You reply so heartily," said Poirot. "If you had said in an indifferent voice, 'Oh, quite nice,' *eh bien,* do you know I should have been better pleased."

Katherine did not answer. She felt slightly uncomfortable. Poirot went on dreamily:

"And yet, who knows? With *les femmes,* they have so many ways of concealing what they feel—and heartiness is perhaps as good a way as any other."

He sighed.

"I don't see——" began Katherine.

He interrupted her.

"You do not see why I am being so impertinent, Mademoiselle? I am an old man, and now and then—not very often—I come across some one whose welfare is dear to me. We are friends, Mademoiselle. You have said so yourself. And it is just this—I should like to see you happy."

Katherine stared very straight in front of her. She had a cretonne sunshade with her, and with its point she traced little designs in the gravel at her feet.

"I have asked you a question about Major Knighton, now I will ask you another. Do you like Mr. Derek Kettering?"

"I hardly know him," said Katherine.

"That is not an answer, that."

"I think it is."

He looked at her, struck by something in her tone. Then he nodded his head gravely and slowly.

"Perhaps you are right, Mademoiselle. See you, I who speak to you have seen much of the world, and I know that there are two things which are true. A good man may be ruined by his love for a bad woman—but the other way holds good also. A bad man may equally be ruined by his love for a good woman."

Katherine looked up sharply.

"When you say ruined——"

"I mean from his point of view. One must be wholehearted in crime as in everything else."

"You are trying to warn me," said Katherine in a low voice. "Against whom?"

"I cannot look into your heart, Mademoiselle; I do not think you would let me if I could. I will just say this. There are men who have a strange fascination for women."

"The Comte de la Roche," said Katherine, with a smile.

"There are others—more dangerous than the Comte de la Roche. They have qualities that appeal—recklessness, daring, audacity. You are fascinated, Mademoiselle; I see that, but I think that it is no more than that. I hope so. This man of whom I speak, the emotion he feels is genuine enough, but all the same——"

"Yes?"

He got up and stood looking down at her. Then he spoke in a low, distinct voice:

"You could, perhaps, love a thief, Mademoiselle, *but not a murderer.*"

He wheeled sharply away on that and left her sitting there.

He heard the little gasp she gave and paid no attention. He had said what he meant to say. He left her there to digest that last unmistakable phrase.

Derek Kettering, coming out of the Casino into the sunshine, saw her sitting alone on the bench and joined her.

"I have been gambling," he said, with a light laugh, "gambling unsuccessfully. I have lost everything—everything, that is, that I have with me."

Katherine looked at him with a troubled face. She was aware at once of something new in his manner, some hidden excitement that betrayed itself in a hundred different infinitesimal signs.

"I should think you were always a gambler. The spirit of gambling appeals to you."

"Every day and in every way a gambler? You are about right. Don't *you* find something stimulating in it? To risk all on one throw—there is nothing like it."

Calm and stolid as she believed herself to be, Katherine felt a faint answering thrill.

"I want to talk to you," went on Derek, "and who knows when I may have another opportunity? There is an idea going about that I murdered my wife—no, please don't interrupt. It is absurd, of course." He paused for a minute or two, then went on, speaking more deliberately. "In dealing with the police and Local Authorities here I have had to pretend to—well—a certain decency. I prefer not to pretend with you. I meant to marry money. I was on the lookout for money when I first met Ruth Van Aldin. She had the look of a slim Madonna about her, and I—well—I made all sorts of good resolutions—and was bitterly disillusioned. My wife was in love with another man when she married me. She never cared for me in the least. Oh, I am not complaining; the thing was a perfectly respectable bargain. She wanted Leconbury and I wanted money. The trouble arose simply through Ruth's American blood. Without caring a pin for me, she would have liked me to be continually dancing attendance. Time and again she as good as told me that she had bought me and that I belonged to her. The result was that I behaved abominably to her. My father-in-law will tell you that, and he is quite right. At the time of Ruth's death, I was faced with absolute disaster." He laughed suddenly. "One *is* faced with absolute disaster when one is up against a man like Rufus Van Aldin."

"And then?" asked Katherine in a low voice.

"And then," Derek shrugged his shoulders, "Ruth was murdered—very providentially."

He laughed, and the sound of his laugh hurt Katherine. She winced.

"Yes," said Derek, "that wasn't in very good taste. But it is quite true. Now I am going to tell you something more. From the very first moment I saw you I knew you were the only woman in the world for me. I was—afraid of you. I thought you might bring me bad luck."

"Bad luck?" said Katherine sharply.

He stared at her. "Why do you repeat it like that? What have you got in your mind?"

"I was thinking of things that people have said to me."

Derek grinned suddenly. "They will say a lot to you about me, my dear, and most of it will be true. Yes, and worse things too—things that I shall never tell you. I have been a gambler always—and I have taken some long odds. I shan't confess to you now or at any other time. The past is done with. There is one thing I do wish you to believe. I swear to you solemnly that I did not kill my wife."

He said the words earnestly enough, yet there was somehow a theatrical touch about them. He met her troubled gaze and went on:

"I know. I lied the other day. It *was* my wife's compartment I went into."

"Ah," said Katherine.

"It's difficult to explain just why I went in, but I'll try. I did it on an impulse. You see, I was more or less spying on my wife. I kept out of sight on the train. Mirelle had told me that my wife was meeting the Comte de la Roche in Paris. Well, as far as I had seen, that was not so. I felt ashamed, and I thought suddenly that it would be a good thing to have it out with her once and for all, so I pushed open the door and went in."

He paused.

"Yes," said Katherine gently.

"Ruth was lying on the bunk asleep—her face was turned away from me—I could only see the back of her head. I could have waked her up, of course. But suddenly I felt a reaction. What, after all, was there to say that we hadn't both of us said a hundred times before? She looked so peaceful lying there. I left the compartment as quietly as I could."

"Why lie about it to the police?" asked Katherine.

"Because I'm not a complete fool. I've realized from the beginning that, from the point of view of motive, I'm the ideal murderer. If I once admitted that I had been in her compartment just before she was murdered, I'd do for myself once and for all."

"I see."

Did she see? She could not have told herself. She was feeling the magnetic attraction of Derek's personality, but there was something in her that resisted, that held back . . .

"Katherine——"

"I——"

"You know that I care for you. Do—do you care for me?"

"I—I don't know."

Weakness there. Either she knew or she did not know. If—if only——

She cast a look round desperately as though seeking something that would help her. A soft colour rose in her cheeks as a tall fair man with a limp came hurrying along the path towards them—Major Knighton.

There was relief and an unexpected warmth in her voice as she greeted him.

Derek stood up scowling, his face black as a thundercloud.

"Lady Tamplin having a flutter?" he said easily. "I must join her and give her the benefit of my system."

He swung round on his heel and left them together. Katherine sat down again. Her heart was beating rapidly and unevenly, but as she sat there talking commonplaces to the quiet, rather shy man beside her, her self-command came back.

Then she realized with a shock that Knighton also was laying bare his heart, much as Derek had done, but in a very different manner.

He was shy and stammering. The words came haltingly with no eloquence to back them.

"From the first moment I saw you—I—I ought not to have spoken so soon—but Mr. Van Aldin may leave here any day, and I might not have another chance. I know you can't care for me so soon—that is impossible. I dare say it is presumption anyway on my part. I have private means, but not very much—no, please don't answer now. I know what your answer would be. But in case I went away suddenly I just wanted you to know—that I care."

She was shaken—touched. His manner was so gentle and appealing.

"There's one thing more. I just wanted to say that if—if you are ever in trouble, anything that I can do——"

He took her hand in his, held it tightly for a minute, then dropped it and walked rapidly away towards the Casino without looking back.

Katherine sat perfectly still, looking after him. Derek Kettering—Richard Knighton—two men so different—so very different. There was something kind about Knighton, kind and trustworthy. As to Derek——

Then suddenly Katherine had a very curious sensation. She felt that she was no longer sitting alone on the seat in the Casino gardens, but that some one was standing beside her, and that that some one was the dead woman, Ruth Kettering. She had a further impression that Ruth wanted—badly—to tell her something. The impression was so curious, so vivid, that it could not be driven away. She felt absolutely certain that the spirit of Ruth Kettering was trying to convey something of vital importance to her. The impression faded. Katherine got up, trembling a little. What was it that Ruth Kettering had wanted so badly to say?

CHAPTER XXVII

INTERVIEW WITH MIRELLE

When Knighton left Katherine he went in search of Hercule Poirot, whom he found in the Rooms, jauntily placing the minimum stake on the even numbers. As Knighton joined him, the number thirty-three turned up, and Poirot's stake was swept away.

"Bad luck!" said Knighton; "are you going to stake again?"

Poirot shook his head.

"Not at present."

"Do you feel the fascination of gambling?" asked Knighton curiously.

"Not at roulette."

Knighton shot a swift glance at him. His own face became troubled. He spoke haltingly, with a touch of deference.

"I wonder, are you busy, M. Poirot? There is something I would like to ask you about."

"I am at your disposal. Shall we go outside? It is pleasant in the sunshine."

They strolled out together, and Knighton drew a deep breath.

"I love the Riviera," he said. "I came here first twelve years ago, during the War, when I was sent to Lady Tamplin's Hospital. It was like Paradise, coming from Flanders to this."

"It must have been," said Poirot.

"How long ago the War seems now!" mused Knighton.

They walked on in silence for some little way.

"You have something on your mind?" said Poirot.

Knighton looked at him in some surprise.

"You are quite right," he confessed. "I don't know how you knew it, though."

"It showed itself only too plainly," said Poirot drily.

"I did not know that I was so transparent."

"It is my business to listen and to observe the physiognomy," the little man explained, with dignity.

"I will tell you, M. Poirot. You have heard of this dancer woman —Mirelle?"

"She who is the *chère amie* of M. Derek Kettering?"

"Yes, that is the one; and, knowing this, you will understand that

Mr. Van Aldin is naturally prejudiced against her. She wrote to him, asking for an interview. He told me to dictate a curt refusal, which of course I did. This morning she came to the hotel and sent up her card, saying that it was urgent and vital that she should see Mr. Van Aldin at once."

"You interest me," said Poirot.

"Mr. Van Aldin was furious. He told me what message to send down to her. I ventured to disagree with him. It seemed to me both likely and probable that this woman Mirelle might give us valuable information. We know that she was on the Blue Train, and she may have seen or heard something that it might be vital for us to know. Don't you agree with me, M. Poirot?"

"I do," said Poirot drily. "M. Van Aldin, if I may say so, behaved exceedingly foolishly."

"I am glad you take that view of the matter," said the secretary. "Now I am going to tell you something, M. Poirot. So strongly did I feel the unwisdom of Mr. Van Aldin's attitude that I went down privately and had an interview with the lady."

"*Eh bien?*"

"The difficulty was that she insisted on seeing Mr. Van Aldin himself. I softened his message as much as I possibly could. In fact—to be candid—I gave it in a very different form. I said that Mr. Van Aldin was too busy to see her at present, but that she might make any communication she wished to me. That, however, she could not bring herself to do, and she left without saying anything further. But I have a strong impression, M. Poirot, that that woman knows something."

"This is serious," said Poirot quietly. "You know where she is staying?"

"Yes." Knighton mentioned the name of the hotel.

"Good," said Poirot; "we will go there immediately."

The secretary looked doubtful.

"And Mr. Van Aldin?" he queried doubtfully.

"M. Van Aldin is an obstinate man," said Poirot drily. "I do not argue with obstinate men. I act in spite of them. We will go and see the lady immediately. I will tell her that you are empowered by M. Van Aldin to act for him, and you will guard yourself well from contradicting me."

Knighton still looked slightly doubtful, but Poirot took no notice of his hesitation.

At the hotel, they were told that Mademoiselle was in, and Poirot sent up both his and Knighton's cards, with "From Mr. Van Aldin" pencilled upon them.

Word came down that Mademoiselle Mirelle would receive them. When they were ushered into the dancer's apartments, Poirot immediately took the lead.

"Mademoiselle," he murmured, bowing very low, "we are here on behalf of M. Van Aldin."

"Ah! And why did he not come himself?"

"He is indisposed," said Poirot mendaciously; "the Riviera throat, it has him in its grip, but me, I am empowered to act for him, as is Major Knighton, his secretary. Unless, of course, Mademoiselle would prefer to wait a fortnight or so."

If there was one thing of which Poirot was tolerably certain, it was that to a temperament such as Mirelle's the mere word "wait" was anathema.

"*Eh bien,* I will speak, Messieurs," she cried. "I have been patient. I have held my hand. And for what? That I should be insulted! Yes, insulted! Ah! Does he think to treat Mirelle like that? To throw her off like an old glove. I tell you never has a man tired of me. Always it is I who tire of them."

She paced up and down the room, her slender body trembling with rage. A small table impeded her free passage and she flung it from her into a corner, where it splintered against the wall.

"That is what I will do to him," she cried, "and that!"

Picking up a glass bowl filled with lilies she flung it into the grate, where it smashed into a hundred pieces.

Knighton was looking at her with cold British disapproval. He felt embarrassed and ill at ease. Poirot, on the other hand, with twinkling eyes was thoroughly enjoying the scene.

"Ah, it is magnificent!" he cried. "It can be seen—Madame has a temperament."

"I am an artist," said Mirelle; "every artist has a temperament. I told Dereek to beware, and he would not listen." She whirled round on Poirot suddenly. "It is true, is it not, that he wants to marry that English miss?"

Poirot coughed.

"*On m'a dit,*" he murmured, "that he adores her passionately."

Mirelle came towards them.

"He murdered his wife," she screamed. "There—now you have it!

He told me beforehand that he meant to do it. He had got to an *impasse*—zut! he took the easiest way out."

"You say that M. Kettering murdered his wife."

"Yes, yes, yes. Have I not told you so?"

"The police," murmured Poirot, "will need proof of that—er—statement."

"I tell you I saw him come out of her compartment that night on the train."

"When?" asked Poirot sharply.

"Just before the train reached Lyons."

"You will swear to that, Mademoiselle?"

It was a different Poirot who spoke now, sharp and decisive.

"Yes."

There was a moment's silence. Mirelle was panting, and her eyes, half defiant, half frightened, went from the face of one man to the other.

"This is a serious matter, Mademoiselle," said the detective. "You realize how serious?"

"Certainly I do."

"That is well," said Poirot. "Then you understand, Mademoiselle, that no time must be lost. You will, perhaps, accompany us immediately to the office of the Examining Magistrate."

Mirelle was taken aback. She hesitated, but, as Poirot had foreseen, she had no loophole for escape.

"Very well," she muttered. "I will fetch a coat."

Left alone together, Poirot and Knighton exchanged glances.

"It is necessary to act while—how do you say it?—the iron is hot," murmured Poirot. "She is temperamental; in an hour's time, maybe, she will repent, and she will wish to draw back. We must prevent that at all costs."

Mirelle reappeared, wrapped in a sand-coloured velvet wrap trimmed with leopard skin. She looked not altogether unlike a leopardess, tawny and dangerous. Her eyes still flashed with anger and determination.

They found M. Caux and the Examining Magistrate together. A few brief introductory words from Poirot, and Mademoiselle Mirelle was courteously entreated to tell her tale. This she did in much the same words as she had done to Knighton and Poirot, though with far more soberness of manner.

"This is an extraordinary story, Mademoiselle," said M. Carrège slowly. He leant back in his chair, adjusted his pince-nez, and looked keenly and searchingly at the dancer through them.

"You wish us to believe M. Kettering actually boasted of the crime to you beforehand?"

"Yes, yes. She was too healthy, he said. If she were to die it must be an accident—he would arrange it all."

"You are aware, Mademoiselle," said M. Carrège sternly, "that you are making yourself out to be an accessory before the fact?"

"Me? But not the least in the world, Monsieur. Not for a moment did I take that statement seriously. Ah no, indeed! I know men, Monsieur; they say many wild things. It would be an odd state of affairs if one were to take all they said *au pied de la lettre*."

The Examining Magistrate raised his eyebrows.

"We are to take it, then, that you regarded M. Kettering's threats as mere idle words? May I ask, Mademoiselle, what made you throw up your engagements in London and come out to the Riviera?"

Mirelle looked at him with melting black eyes.

"I wished to be with the man I loved," she said simply. "Was it so unnatural?"

Poirot interpolated a question gently.

"Was it, then, at M. Kettering's wish that you accompanied him to Nice?"

Mirelle seemed to find a little difficulty in answering this. She hesitated perceptibly before she spoke. When she did, it was with a haughty indifference of manner.

"In such matters I please myself, Monsieur," she said.

That the answer was not an answer at all was noted by all three men. They said nothing.

"When were you first convinced that M. Kettering had murdered his wife?"

"As I tell you, Monsieur, I saw M. Kettering come out of his wife's compartment just before the train drew into Lyons. There was a look on his face—ah! at the moment I could not understand it—a look haunted and terrible. I shall never forget it."

Her voice rose shrilly, and she flung out her arms in an extravagant gesture.

"Quite so," said M. Carrège.

"Afterwards, when I found that Madame Kettering was dead when the train left Lyons, then—then I knew!"

"And still—you did not go to the police, Mademoiselle," said the Commissary mildly.

Mirelle glanced at him superbly; she was clearly enjoying herself in the rôle she was playing.

"Shall I betray my lover?" she asked. "Ah no; do not ask a woman to do that."

"Yet now——" hinted M. Caux.

"Now it is different. He has betrayed me! Shall I suffer that in silence . . . ?"

The Examining Magistrate checked her.

"Quite so, quite so," he murmured soothingly. "And now, Mademoiselle, perhaps you will read over the statement of what you have told us, see that it is correct, and sign it."

Mirelle wasted no time on the document.

"Yes, yes," she said, "it is correct." She rose to her feet. "You require me no longer, Messieurs?"

"At present, no, Mademoiselle."

"And Dereek will be arrested?"

"At once, Mademoiselle."

Mirelle laughed cruelly and drew her fur draperies closer about her.

"He should have thought of this before he insulted me," she cried.

"There is one little matter"—Poirot coughed apologetically—"just a matter of detail."

"Yes?"

"What makes you think Madame Kettering was dead when the train left Lyons?"

Mirelle stared.

"But she *was* dead."

"Was she?"

"Yes, of course. I——"

She came to an abrupt stop. Poirot was regarding her intently, and he saw the wary look that came into her eyes.

"I have been told so. Everybody says so."

"Oh," said Poirot, "I was not aware that the fact had been mentioned outside the Examining Magistrate's office."

Mirelle appeared somewhat discomposed.

"One hears those things," she said vaguely; "they get about. Somebody told me. I can't remember who it was."

She moved to the door. M. Caux sprang forward to open it for her, and as he did so, Poirot's voice rose gently once more.

"And the jewels? Pardon, Mademoiselle. Can you tell me anything about those?"

"The jewels? What jewels?"

"The rubies of Catherine the Great. Since you hear so much, you must have heard of them."

"I know nothing about any jewels," said Mirelle sharply.

She went out, closing the door behind her. M. Caux came back to his chair; the Examining Magistrate sighed.

"What a fury!" he said, "but *diablement chic,* I wonder if she is telling the truth? I think so."

"There is *some* truth in her story, certainly," said Poirot. "We have confirmation of it from Miss Grey. She was looking down the corridor a short time before the train reached Lyons and she saw M. Kettering go into his wife's compartment."

"The case against him seems quite clear," said the Commissary, sighing; "it is a thousand pities," he murmured.

"How do you mean?" asked Poirot.

"It has been the ambition of my life to lay the Comte de la Roche by the heels. This time, *ma foi,* I thought we had got him. This other —it is not nearly so satisfactory."

M. Carrège rubbed his nose.

"If anything goes wrong," he observed cautiously, "it will be most awkward. M. Kettering is of the aristocracy. It will get into the newspapers. If we have made a mistake——" He shrugged his shoulders forebodingly.

"The jewels now," said the Commissary, "what do you think he has done with them?"

"He took them for a plant, of course," said M. Carrège; "they must have been a great inconvenience to him and very awkward to dispose of."

Poirot smiled.

"I have an idea of my own about the jewels. Tell me, Messieurs, what do you know of a man called the Marquis?"

The Commissary leant forward excitedly.

"The Marquis," he said, "the Marquis? Do you think he is mixed up in this affair, M. Poirot?"

"I ask you what you know of him."

The Commissary made an expressive grimace.

"Not as much as we should like to," he observed ruefully. "He works behind the scenes, you understand. He has underlings who do his dirty work for him. But he is some one high up. That we are sure of. He does not come from the criminal classes."

"A Frenchman?"

"Y—es. At least we believe so. But we are not sure. He has worked in France, in England, in America. There was a series of robberies in Switzerland last autumn which were laid at his door. By all accounts he is a *grand seigneur,* speaking French and English with equal perfection and his origin is a mystery."

Poirot nodded and rose to take his departure.

"Can you tell us nothing more, M. Poirot," urged the Commissary.

"At present, no," said Poirot, "but I may have news awaiting me at my hotel."

M. Carrège looked uncomfortable. "If the Marquis is concerned in this——" he began, and then stopped.

"It upsets our ideas," complained M. Caux.

"It does not upset mine," said Poirot. "On the contrary, I think it agrees with them very well. Au revoir, Messieurs; if news of any importance comes to me I will communicate it to you immediately."

He walked back to his hotel with a grave face. In his absence a telegram had come to him. Taking a paper-cutter from his pocket, he slit it open. It was a long telegram, and he read it over twice before slowly putting it in his pocket. Upstairs, George was awaiting his master.

"I am fatigued, Georges, much fatigued. Will you order for me a small pot of chocolate?"

The chocolate was duly ordered and brought, and George set it at the little table at his master's elbow. As he was preparing to retire, Poirot spoke:

"I believe, Georges, that you have a good knowledge of the English aristocracy?" murmured Poirot.

George smiled apologetically.

"I think that I might say that I have, sir," he replied.

"I suppose that it is your opinion, Georges, that criminals are invariably drawn from the lower orders."

"Not always, sir. There was great trouble with one of the Duke of Devize's younger sons. He left Eton under a cloud, and after that he caused great anxiety on several occasions. The police would not accept the view that it was kleptomania. A very clever young gentleman, sir, but vicious through and through, if you take my meaning. His Grace shipped him to Australia, and I hear he was convicted out there under another name. Very odd, sir, but there it is. The young gentleman, I need hardly say, was not in want financially."

Poirot nodded his head slowly.

"Love of excitement," he murmured, "and a little kink in the brain somewhere. I wonder now——"

He drew out the telegram from his pocket and read it again.

"Then there was Lady Mary Fox's daughter," continued the valet in a mood of reminiscence. "Swindled tradespeople something shocking, she did. Very worrying to the best families, if I may say so, and there are many other queer cases I could mention."

"You have a wide experience, Georges," murmured Poirot. "I often wonder having lived so exclusively with titled families that you demean yourself by coming as a valet to me. I put it down to love of excitement on your part."

"Not exactly, sir," said George. "I happened to see in *Society Snippets* that you had been received at Buckingham Palace. That was just when I was looking for a new situation. His Majesty, so it said, had been most gracious and friendly and thought very highly of your abilities."

"Ah," said Poirot, "one always likes to know the reason for things."

He remained in thought for a few moments and then said:

"You rang up Mademoiselle Papopolous?"

"Yes, sir; she and her father will be pleased to dine with you tonight."

"Ah," said Poirot thoughtfully. He drank off his chocolate, set the cup and saucer neatly in the middle of the tray, and spoke gently, more to himself than to the valet.

"The squirrel, my good Georges, collects nuts. He stores them up in the autumn so that they may be of advantage to him later. To make a success of humanity, Georges, we must profit by the lessons of those below us in the animal kingdom. I have always done so. I have been the cat, watching at the mouse hole. I have been the good dog following up the scent, and not taking my nose from the trail. And also, my good Georges, I have been the squirrel. I have stored away the little fact here, the little fact there. I go now to my store and I take out one particular nut, a nut that I stored away —let me see, seventeen years ago. You follow me, Georges?"

"I should hardly have thought, sir," said George, "that nuts would have kept so long as that, though I know one can do wonders with preserving bottles."

Poirot looked at him and smiled.

CHAPTER XXVIII

POIROT PLAYS THE SQUIRREL

POIROT STARTED TO KEEP his dinner appointment with a margin of three-quarters of an hour to spare. He had an object in this. The car took him, not straight to Monte Carlo, but to Lady Tamplin's house at Cap Martin, where he asked for Miss Grey. The ladies were dressing and Poirot was shown into a small salon to wait, and here, after a lapse of three or four minutes, Lenox Tamplin came to him.

"Katherine is not quite ready yet," she said. "Can I give her a message, or would you rather wait until she comes down?"

Poirot looked at her thoughtfully. He was a minute or two in replying, as though something of great weight hung upon his decision. Apparently the answer to such a simple question mattered.

"No," he said at last, "no, I do not think it is necessary that I should wait to see Mademoiselle Katherine. I think, perhaps, that it is better that I should not. These things are sometimes difficult."

Lenox waited politely, her eyebrows slightly raised.

"I have a piece of news," continued Poirot. "You will, perhaps, tell your friend. M. Kettering was arrested to-night for the murder of his wife."

"You want me to tell Katherine that?" asked Lenox. She breathed rather hard, as though she had been running; her face, Poirot thought, looked white and strained—rather noticeably so.

"If you please, Mademoiselle."

"Why?" said Lenox. "Do you think Katherine will be upset? Do you think she cares?"

"I don't know, Mademoiselle," said Poirot. "See, I admit it frankly. As a rule I know everything, but in this case, I—well, I do not. You, perhaps, know better than I do."

"Yes," said Lenox, "I know—but I am not going to tell you all the same."

She paused for a minute or two, her dark brows drawn together in a frown.

"You believe he did it?" she said abruptly.

Poirot shrugged his shoulders.

"The police say so."

"Ah," said Lenox, "hedging, are you? So there is something to hedge about."

Again she was silent, frowning. Poirot said gently:

"You have known Derek Kettering a long time, have you not?"

"Off and on ever since I was a kid," said Lenox gruffly.

Poirot nodded his head several times without speaking.

With one of her brusque movements Lenox drew forward a chair and sat down on it, her elbows on the table and her face supported by her hands. Sitting thus, she looked directly across the table at Poirot.

"What have they got to go on?" she demanded. "Motive, I suppose. Probably came into money at her death."

"He came into two million."

"And if she had not died he would have been ruined?"

"Yes."

"But there must have been more than that," persisted Lenox. "He travelled by the same train, I know, but—that would not be enough to go on by itself."

"A cigarette case with the letter 'K' on it which did not belong to Mrs. Kettering was found in her carriage, and he was seen by two people entering and leaving the compartment just before the train got into Lyons."

"What two people?"

"Your friend Miss Grey was one of them. The other was Mademoiselle Mirelle, the dancer."

"And he, Derek, what has he got to say about it?" demanded Lenox sharply.

"He denies having entered his wife's compartment at all," said Poirot.

"Fool!" said Lenox crisply, frowning. "Just before Lyons, you say? Does nobody know when—when she died?"

"The doctors' evidence necessarily cannot be very definite," said Poirot; "they are inclined to think that death was unlikely to have occurred after leaving Lyons. And we know this much, that a few moments after leaving Lyons Mrs. Kettering was dead."

"How do you know that?"

Poirot was smiling rather oddly to himself.

"Some one else went into her compartment and found her dead."

"And they did not rouse the train?"

"No."

"Why was that?"

"Doubtless they had their reasons."

Lenox looked at him sharply.

"Do you know the reason?"

"I think so—yes."

Lenox sat still turning things over in her mind. Poirot watched her in silence. At last she looked up. A soft colour had come into her cheeks and her eyes were shining.

"You think some one on the train must have killed her, but that need not be so at all. What is to stop any one swinging themselves on to the train when it stopped at Lyons? They could go straight to her compartment, strangle her, and take the rubies and drop off the train again without any one being the wiser. She may have been actually killed while the train was in Lyons station. Then she would have been alive when Derek went in, and dead when the other person found her."

Poirot leant back in his chair. He drew a deep breath. He looked across at the girl and nodded his head three times, then he heaved a sigh.

"Mademoiselle," he said, "what you have said there is very just—very true. I was struggling in darkness, and you have shown me a light. There was a point that puzzled me and you have made it plain."

He got up.

"And Derek?" said Lenox.

"Who knows?" said Poirot, with a shrug of his shoulders. "But I will tell you this, Mademoiselle. I am not satisfied; no, I, Hercule Poirot, am not yet satisfied. It may be that this very night I shall learn something more. At least, I go to try."

"You are meeting some one?"

"Yes."

"Some one who knows something?"

"Some one who might know something. In these matters one must leave no stone unturned. Au revoir, Mademoiselle."

Lenox accompanied him to the door.

"Have I—helped?" she asked.

Poirot's face softened as he looked up at her standing on the doorstep above him.

"Yes, Mademoiselle, you have helped. If things are very dark, always remember that."

When the car had driven off he relapsed into a frowning absorption, but in his eyes was that faint green light which was always the precursor of the triumph to be.

He was a few minutes late at the rendezvous, and found that M. Papopolous and his daughter had arrived before him. His apologies were abject, and he outdid himself in politeness and small attentions. The Greek was looking particularly benign and noble this evening, a sorrowful patriarch of blameless life. Zia was looking handsome and good humoured. The dinner was a pleasant one. Poirot was his best and most sparkling self. He told anecdotes, he made jokes, he paid graceful compliments to Zia Papopolous, and he told many interesting incidents of his career. The menu was a carefully selected one, and the wine was excellent.

At the close of dinner M. Papopolous inquired politely:

"And the tip I gave you? You have had your little flutter on the horse?"

"I am in communication with—er—my bookmaker," replied Poirot.

The eyes of the two men met.

"A well-known horse, eh?"

"No," said Poirot; "it is what our friends, the English, call a dark horse."

"Ah!" said M. Papopolous thoughtfully.

"Now we must step across to the Casino and have our little flutter at the roulette table," cried Poirot gaily.

At the Casino the party separated, Poirot devoting himself solely to Zia, whilst Papopolous himself drifted away.

Poirot was not fortunate, but Zia had a run of good luck, and had soon won a few thousand francs.

"It would be as well," she observed drily to Poirot, "if I stopped now."

Poirot's eyes twinkled.

"Superb!" he exclaimed. "You are the daughter of your father, Mademoiselle Zia. To know when to stop. Ah! that is the art."

He looked round the rooms.

"I cannot see your father anywhere about," he remarked carelessly. "I will fetch your cloak for you, Mademoiselle, and we will go out in the gardens."

He did not, however, go straight to the cloak-room. His sharp eyes had seen but a little while before the departure of M. Papopolous. He was anxious to know what had become of the wily Greek. He ran him to earth unexpectedly in the big entrance hall. He was standing by one of the pillars, talking to a lady who had just arrived. The lady was Mirelle.

Poirot sidled unostentatiously round the room. He arrived at the other side of the pillar, and unnoticed by the two who were talking together in an animated fashion—or rather, that is to say, the dancer was talking, Papopolous contributing an occasional monosyllable and a good many expressive gestures.

"I tell you I must have time," the dancer was saying. "If you give me time I will get the money."

"To wait"—the Greek shrugged his shoulders—"it is awkward."

"Only a very little while," pleaded the other. "Ah! but you must! A week—ten days—that is all I ask. You can be sure of your affair. The money will be forthcoming."

Papopolous shifted a little and looked round him uneasily—to find Poirot almost at his elbow with a beaming innocent face.

"*Ah! vous voilà,* M. Papopolous. I have been looking for you. It is permitted that I take Mademoiselle Zia for a little turn in the gardens? Good evening, Mademoiselle." He bowed very low to Mirelle. "A thousand pardons that I did not see you immediately."

The dancer accepted his greetings rather impatiently. She was clearly annoyed at the interruption of her *tête-à-tête.* Poirot was quick to take the hint. Papopolous had already murmured: "Certainly—but certainly," and Poirot withdrew forthwith.

He fetched Zia's cloak, and together they strolled out into the gardens.

"This is where the suicides take place," said Zia.

Poirot shrugged his shoulders. "So it is said. Men are foolish, are they not, Mademoiselle? To eat, to drink, to breathe the good air, it is a very pleasant thing, Mademoiselle. One is foolish to leave all that simply because one has no money—or because the heart aches. *L'amour,* it causes many fatalities, does it not?"

Zia laughed.

"You should not laugh at love, Mademoiselle," said Poirot, shaking an energetic forefinger at her. "You who are young and beautiful."

"Hardly that," said Zia; "you forget that I am thirty-three, M. Poirot. I am frank with you, because it is no good being otherwise. As you told my father, it is exactly seventeen years since you aided us in Paris that time."

"When I look at you, it seems much less," said Poirot gallantly.

"You were then very much as you are now, Mademoiselle, a little thinner, a little paler, a little more serious. Sixteen years old and fresh from your pension. Not quite the *petite pensionnaire*, not quite a woman. You were very delicious, very charming, Mademoiselle Zia; others thought so too, without doubt."

"At sixteen," said Zia, "one is simple and a little fool."

"That may be," said Poirot, "yes, that well may be. At sixteen one is credulous, is one not? One believes what one is told."

If he saw the quick sideways glance that the girl shot at him, he pretended not to have done so. He continued dreamily: "It was a curious affair that, altogether. Your father, Mademoiselle, has never understood the true inwardness of it."

"No?"

"When he asked me for details, for explanations, I said to him thus: 'Without scandal, I have got back for you that which was lost. You must ask no questions.' Do you know, Mademoiselle, why I said these things?"

"I have no idea," said the girl coldly.

"It was because I had a soft spot in my heart for a little pensionnaire, so pale, so thin, so serious."

"I don't understand what you are talking about," cried Zia angrily.

"Do you not, Mademoiselle? Have you forgotten Antonio Pirezzio?"

He heard the quick intake of her breath—almost a gasp.

"He came to work as an assistant in the shop, but not thus could he have got hold of what he wanted. An assistant can lift his eyes to his master's daughter, can he not? If he is young and handsome with a glib tongue. And since they cannot make love all the time, they must occasionally talk of things that interest them both—such as that very interesting thing which was temporarily in M. Papopolous' possession. And since, as you say, Mademoiselle, the young are foolish and credulous, it was easy to believe him and to give him a sight of that particular thing, to show him where it was kept. And afterwards when it is gone—when the unbelievable catastrophe has happened. Alas! the poor little pensionnaire. What a terrible position she is in. She is frightened, the poor little one. To speak or not to speak? And then there comes along that excellent fellow, Hercule Poirot. Almost a miracle it must have been, the way things arranged themselves. The priceless heirlooms are restored and there are no awkward questions."

Zia turned on him fiercely.

"You have known all the time? Who told you? Was it—was it Antonio?"

Poirot shook his head.

"No one told me," he said quietly. "I guessed. It was a good guess, was it not, Mademoiselle? You see, unless you are good at guessing, it is not much use being a detective."

The girl walked along beside him for some minutes in silence. Then she said in a hard voice:

"Well, what are you going to do about it, are you going to tell my father?"

"No," said Poirot sharply. "Certainly not."

She looked at him curiously.

"You want something from me?"

"I want your help, Mademoiselle."

"What makes you think that I can help you?"

"I do not think so. I only hope so."

"And if I do not help you, then—you will tell my father?"

"But no, but no! Debarrass yourself of that idea, Mademoiselle. I am not a blackmailer. I do not hold your secret over your head and threaten you with it."

"If I refuse to help you——" began the girl slowly.

"Then you refuse, and that is that."

"Then why——" she stopped.

"Listen, and I will tell you why. Women, Mademoiselle, are generous. If they can render a service to one who has rendered a service to them, they will do it. I was generous once to you, Mademoiselle. When I might have spoken, I held my tongue."

There was another silence; then the girl said, "My father gave you a hint the other day."

"It was very kind of him."

"I do not think," said Zia slowly, "that there is anything that I can add to that."

If Poirot was disappointed he did not show it. Not a muscle of his face changed.

"*Eh bien!*" he said cheerfully, "then we must talk of other things."

And he proceeded to chat gaily. The girl was *distraite,* however, and her answers were mechanical and not always to the point. It was when they were approaching the Casino once more that she seemed to come to a decision.

"M. Poirot?"

"Yes, Mademoiselle?"

"I—I should like to help you if I could."

"You are very amiable, Mademoiselle—very amiable."

Again there was a pause. Poirot did not press her. He was quite content to wait and let her take her own time.

"Ah bah," said Zia, "after all, why should I not tell you? My father is cautious—always cautious in everything he says. But I know that with you it is not necessary. You have told us it is only the murderer you seek, and that you are not concerned over the jewels. I believe you. You were quite right when you guessed that we were in Nice because of the rubies. They have been handed over here according to plan. My father has them now. He gave you a hint the other day as to who our mysterious client was."

"The Marquis?" murmured Poirot softly.

"Yes, the Marquis."

"Have you ever seen the Marquis, Mademoiselle Zia?"

"Once," said the girl. "But not very well," she added. "It was through a keyhole."

"That always presents difficulties," said Poirot sympathetically, "but all the same you saw him. You would know him again?"

Zia shook her head.

"He wore a mask," she explained.

"Young or old?"

"He had white hair. It may have been a wig, it may not. It fitted very well. But I do not think he was old. His walk was young, and so was his voice."

"His voice?" said Poirot thoughtfully. "Ah, his voice! Would you know it again, Mademoiselle Zia?"

"I might," said the girl.

"You were interested in him, eh? It was that that took you to the keyhole."

Zia nodded.

"Yes, yes. I was curious. One had heard so much—he is not the ordinary thief—he is more like a figure of history or romance."

"Yes," said Poirot thoughtfully, "yes; perhaps so."

"But it is not this that I meant to tell you," said Zia. "It was just one other little fact that I thought might be—well—useful to you."

"Yes?" said Poirot encouragingly.

"The rubies, as I say, were handed over to my father here at Nice. I did not see the person who handed them over, but——"

"Yes?"

"I know one thing. *It was a woman.*"

CHAPTER XXIX

A LETTER FROM HOME

"DEAR KATHERINE,—Living among grand friends as you are doing now, I don't suppose you will care to hear any of our news; but as I always thought you were a sensible girl, perhaps you are a trifle less swollen-headed than I suppose. Everything goes on much the same here. There was great trouble about the new curate, who is scandalously high. In my view, he is neither more nor less than a Roman. Everybody has spoken to the Vicar about it, but you know what the Vicar is—all Christian charity and no proper spirit. I have had a lot of trouble with maids lately. That girl Annie was no good—skirts up to her knees and wouldn't wear sensible woollen stockings. Not one of them can bear being spoken to. I have had a lot of pain with my rheumatism one way and another, and Dr. Harris persuaded me to go and see a London specialist—a waste of three guineas and a railway fare, as I told him; but by waiting until Wednesday I managed to get a cheap return. The London doctor pulled a long face and talked all round about and never straight out, until I said to him, 'I'm a plain woman, Doctor, and I like things to be plainly stated. Is it cancer, or is it not?' And then, of course, he had to say it was. They say a year with care, and not too much pain, though I am sure I can bear pain as well as any other Christian woman. Life seems rather lonely at times, with most of my friends dead or gone before. I wish you were in St. Mary Mead, my dear, and that is a fact. If you hadn't come into this money and gone off into grand society, I would have offered you double the salary poor Jane gave you to come and look after me; but there—there's no good wanting what we can't get. However, if things should go ill with you—and that is always possible. I have heard no end of tales of bogus noblemen marrying girls and getting hold of their money and then leaving them at the church door. I dare say you are too sensible for anything of the kind to happen to you, but one never knows; and never having had much attention of any kind it might easily go to your head now. So just in case, my dear, remember there is always a home for you here; and though a plain-spoken woman I am a warm-hearted one too.—Your affectionate old friend,

"AMELIA VINER.

"P.S.—I saw a mention of you in the paper with your cousin, Viscountess Tamplin, and I cut it out and put it with my cuttings. I prayed for you on Sunday that you might be kept from pride and vainglory."

Katherine read this characteristic epistle through twice, then she laid it down and stared out of her bedroom window across the blue waters of the Mediterranean. She felt a curious lump in her throat. A sudden wave of longing for St. Mary Mead swept over her. So full of familiar, everyday, stupid little things—and yet—home. She felt very inclined to lay her head down on her arms and indulge in a real good cry.

Lenox, coming in at the moment, saved her.

"Hello, Katherine," said Lenox. "I say—what is the matter?"

"Nothing," said Katherine, grabbing up Miss Viner's letter and thrusting it into her handbag.

"You looked rather queer," said Lenox. "I say—I hope you don't mind—I rang up your detective friend, M. Poirot, and asked him to lunch with us in Nice. I said you wanted to see him, as I thought he might not come for me."

"Did you want to see him then?" asked Katherine.

"Yes," said Lenox. "I have rather lost my heart to him. I never met a man before whose eyes were really green like a cat's."

"All right," said Katherine. She spoke listlessly. The last few days had been trying. Derek Kettering's arrest had been the topic of the hour, and the Blue Train Mystery had been thrashed out from every conceivable standpoint.

"I have ordered the car," said Lenox, "and I have told Mother some lie or other—unfortunately I can't remember exactly what; but it won't matter, as she never remembers. If she knew where we were going, she would want to come too, to pump M. Poirot."

The two girls arrived at the Negresco to find Poirot waiting.

He was full of Gallic politeness, and showered so many compliments upon the two girls that they were soon helpless with laughter; yet for all that the meal was not a gay one. Katherine was dreamy and distracted, and Lenox made bursts of conversation, interspersed by silences. As they were sitting on the terrace sipping their coffee she suddenly attacked Poirot bluntly.

"How are things going? You know what I mean?"

Poirot shrugged his shoulders. "They take their course," he said.

"And you are just letting them take their course?"

He looked at Lenox a little sadly.

"You are young, Mademoiselle, but there are three things that cannot be hurried—*le bon Dieu*, Nature, and old people."

"Nonsense!" said Lenox. "You are not old."

"Ah, it is pretty what you say there."

"Here is Major Knighton," said Lenox.

Katherine looked round quickly and then turned back again.

"He is with Mr. Van Aldin," continued Lenox. "There is something I want to ask Major Knighton about. I won't be a minute."

Left alone together, Poirot bent forward and murmured to Katherine:

"You are *distraite,* Mademoiselle; your thoughts, they are far away, are they not?"

"Just as far as England, no farther."

Guided by a sudden impulse, she took the letter she had received that morning and handed it across to him to read.

"That is the first word that has come to me from my old life; somehow or other—it hurts."

He read it through and then handed it back to her. "So you are going back to St. Mary Mead?" he said slowly.

"No, I am not," said Katherine; "why should I?"

"Ah," said Poirot, "it is my mistake. You will excuse me one little minute."

He strolled across to where Lenox Tamplin was talking to Van Aldin and Knighton. The American looked old and haggard. He greeted Poirot with a curt nod but without any other sign of animation.

As he turned to reply to some observation made by Lenox, Poirot drew Knighton aside.

"M. Van Aldin looks ill," he said.

"Do you wonder?" asked Knighton. "The scandal of Derek Kettering's arrest has about put the lid on things, as far as he is concerned. He is even regretting that he asked you to find out the truth."

"He should go back to England," said Poirot.

"We are going the day after to-morrow."

"That is good news," said Poirot.

He hesitated, and looked across the terrace to where Katherine was sitting.

"I wish," he murmured, "that you could tell Miss Grey that."

"Tell her what?"

"That you—I mean that M. Van Aldin is returning to England."

Knighton looked a little puzzled, but he readily crossed the terrace and joined Katherine.

Poirot saw him go with a satisfied nod of the head, and then joined Lenox and the American. After a minute or two they joined the others. Conversation was general for a few minutes, then the millionaire and his secretary departed. Poirot also prepared to take his departure.

"A thousand thanks for your hospitality, Mesdemoiselles," he cried; "it has been a most charming luncheon. *Ma foi,* I needed it!" He swelled out his chest and thumped it. "I am now a lion—a giant. Ah, Mademoiselle Katherine, you have not seen me as I can be. You have seen the gentle, the calm Hercule Poirot; but there is another Hercule Poirot. I go now to bully, to threaten, to strike terror into the hearts of those who listen to me."

He looked at them in a self-satisfied way, and they both appeared to be duly impressed, though Lenox was biting her under lip, and the corners of Katherine's mouth had a suspicious twitch.

"And I shall do it," he said gravely. "Oh yes, I shall succeed."

He had gone but a few steps when Katherine's voice made him turn.

"M. Poirot, I—I want to tell you. I think you were right in what you said. I am going back to England almost immediately."

Poirot stared at her very hard, and under the directness of his scrutiny she blushed.

"I see," he said gravely.

"I don't believe you do," said Katherine.

"I know more than you think, Mademoiselle," he said quietly.

He left her, with an odd little smile upon his lips. Entering a waiting car, he drove to Antibes.

Hippolyte, the Comte de la Roche's wooden-faced man-servant, was busy at the Villa Marina polishing his master's beautiful cut table glass. The Comte de la Roche himself had gone to Monte Carlo for the day. Chancing to look out of the window, Hippolyte espied a visitor walking briskly up to the hall door, a visitor of so uncommon a type that Hippolyte, experienced as he was, had some difficulty in placing him. Calling to his wife, Marie, who was busy in the kitchen, he drew her attention to what he called *ce type là.*

"It is not the police again?" said Marie anxiously.

"Look for yourself," said Hippolyte.

Marie looked.

"Certainly not the police," she declared. "I am glad."

"They have not really worried us much," said Hippolyte. "In fact, but for Monsieur le Comte's warning, I should never have guessed that stranger at the wineshop to be what he was."

The hall bell pealed and Hippolyte, in a grave and decorous manner, went to open the door.

"M. le Comte, I regret to say, is not at home."

The little man with the large moustaches beamed placidly.

"I know that," he replied. "You are Hippolyte Flavelle, are you not?"

"Yes, Monsieur, that is my name."

"And you have a wife, Marie Flavelle?"

"Yes, Monsieur, but——"

"I desire to see you both," said the stranger, and he stepped nimbly past Hippolyte into the hall.

"Your wife is doubtless in the kitchen," he said. "I will go there."

Before Hippolyte could recover his breath, the other had selected the right door at the back of the hall and passed along the passage and into the kitchen, where Marie paused open-mouthed to stare at him.

"*Voilà*," said the stranger, and sank into a wooden arm-chair; "I am Hercule Poirot."

"Yes, Monsieur?"

"You do not know the name?"

"I have never heard it," said Hippolyte.

"Permit me to say that you have been badly educated. It is the name of one of the great ones of this world."

He sighed and folded his hands across his chest.

Hippolyte and Marie were staring at him uneasily. They were at a loss what to make of this unexpected and extremely strange visitor.

"Monsieur desires——" murmured Hippolyte mechanically.

"I desire to know why you have lied to the police."

"Monsieur!" cried Hippolyte; "I—lied to the police? Never have I done such a thing."

M. Poirot shook his head.

"You are wrong," he said; "you have done it on several occasions. Let me see." He took a small notebook from his pocket and consulted it. "Ah, yes; on seven occasions at least. I will recite them to you."

In a gentle unemotional voice he proceeded to outline the seven occasions.

Hippolyte was taken aback.

"But it is not of these past lapses that I wish to speak," continued Poirot, "only, my dear friend, do not get into the habit of thinking yourself too clever. I come now to the particular lie in which I am concerned—your statement that the Comte de la Roche arrived at this villa on the morning of 14th January."

"But that was no lie, Monsieur; that was the truth. Monsieur le Comte arrived here on the morning of Tuesday, the 14th. That is so, Marie, is it not?"

Marie assented eagerly.

"Ah, yes, that is quite right. I remember it perfectly."

"Ah," said Poirot, "and what did you give your good master for *déjeuner* that day?"

"I——" Marie paused, trying to collect herself.

"Odd," said Poirot, "how one remembers some things—and forgets others."

He leant forward and struck the table a blow with his fist; his eyes flashed with anger.

"Yes, yes, it is as I say. You tell your lies and you think nobody knows. But there are two people who know. Yes—two people. One is *le bon Dieu*——"

He raised a hand to heaven, and then settling himself back in his chair and shutting his eyelids, he murmured comfortably:

"And the other is Hercule Poirot."

"I assure you, Monsieur, you are completely mistaken. Monsieur le Comte left Paris on Monday night——"

"True," said Poirot—"by the Rapide. I do not know where he broke his journey. Perhaps you do not know that. What I do know is that he arrived here on Wednesday morning, and not on Tuesday morning."

"Monsieur is mistaken," said Marie stolidly.

Poirot rose to his feet.

"Then the law must take its course," he murmured. "A pity."

"What do you mean, Monsieur?" asked Marie, with a shade of uneasiness.

"You will be arrested and held as accomplices concerned in the murder of Mrs. Kettering, the English lady who was killed."

"Murder!"

The man's face had gone chalk white, his knees knocked together. Marie dropped the rolling-pin and began to weep.

"But it is impossible—impossible. I thought——"

"Since you stick to your story, there is nothing to be said. I think you are both foolish."

He was turning towards the door when an agitated voice arrested him.

"Monsieur, Monsieur, just a little moment. I—I had no idea that it was anything of this kind. I—I thought it was just a matter concerning a lady. There have been little awkwardnesses with the police over ladies before. But murder—that is very different."

"I have no patience with you," cried Poirot. He turned round on them and angrily shook his fist in Hippolyte's face. "Am I to stop here all day, arguing with a couple of imbeciles thus? It is the truth I want. If you will not give it to me, that is your lookout. *For the last time, when did Monsieur le Comte arrive at the Villa Marina—Tuesday morning or Wednesday morning?*"

"Wednesday," gasped the man, and behind him Marie nodded confirmation.

Poirot regarded them for a minute or two, then inclined his head gravely.

"You are wise, my children," he said quietly. "Very nearly you were in serious trouble."

He left the Villa Marina, smiling to himself.

"One guess confirmed," he murmured to himself. "Shall I take a chance on the other?"

It was six o'clock when the card of Monsieur Hercule Poirot was brought up to Mirelle. She stared at it for a moment or two, and then nodded. When Poirot entered, he found her walking up and down the room feverishly. She turned on him furiously.

"Well?" she cried. "Well? What is it now? Have you not tortured me enough, all of you? Have you not made me betray my poor Dereek? What more do you want?"

"Just one little question, Mademoiselle. After the train left Lyons, when you entered Mrs. Kettering's compartment——"

"What is that?"

Poirot looked at her with an air of mild reproach and began again.

"I say when you entered Mrs. Kettering's compartment——"

"I never did."

"And found her——"

"I never did."

"*Ah, sacré!*"

He turned on her in a rage and shouted at her, so that she cowered back before him.

"Will you lie to me? I tell you I know what happened as well as though I had been there. You went into her compartment and you found her dead. I tell you I know it. To lie to me is dangerous. Be careful, Mademoiselle Mirelle."

Her eyes wavered beneath his gaze and fell.

"I—I didn't——" she began uncertainly and stopped.

"There is only one thing about which I wonder," said Poirot—"I wonder, Mademoiselle, if you found what you were looking for or whether——"

"Whether what?"

"Or whether some one else had been before you."

"I will answer no more questions," screamed the dancer. She tore herself away from Poirot's restraining hand, and flinging herself down on the floor in a frenzy, she screamed and sobbed. A frightened maid came rushing in.

Hercule Poirot shrugged his shoulders, raised his eyebrows, and quietly left the room.

But he seemed satisfied.

CHAPTER XXX

MISS VINER GIVES JUDGMENT

KATHERINE LOOKED OUT of Miss Viner's bedroom window. It was raining, not violently, but with a quiet, well-bred persistence. The window looked out on a strip of front garden with a path down to the gate and neat little flower-beds on either side, where later roses and pinks and blue hyacinths would bloom.

Miss Viner was lying in a large Victorian bedstead. A tray with the remains of breakfast had been pushed to one side and she was busy opening her correspondence and making various caustic comments upon it.

Katherine had an open letter in her hand and was reading it through for the second time. It was dated from the Ritz Hotel, Paris.

"CHÈRE MADEMOISELLE KATHERINE" (it began),—"I trust that you are in good health and that the return to the English winter has not proved too depressing. Me, I prosecute my inquiries with the utmost diligence. Do not think that it is the holiday that I take here. Very shortly I shall be in England, and I hope then to have the pleasure of meeting you once more. It shall be so, shall it not? On arrival in London I shall write to you. You remember that we are the colleagues in this affair? But indeed I think you know that very well.

"Be assured, Mademoiselle, of my most respectful and devoted sentiments.

"HERCULE POIROT."

Katherine frowned slightly. It was as though something in the letter puzzled and intrigued her.

"A choir boys' picnic indeed," came from Miss Viner. "Tommy Saunders and Albert Dykes ought to be left behind, and I shan't subscribe to it unless they are. What those two boys think they are doing in church on Sundays I don't know. Tommy sang, 'O God, make speed to save us,' and never opened his lips again, and if Albert Dykes wasn't sucking a mint humbug, my nose is not what it is and always has been."

"I know, they are awful," agreed Katherine.

She opened her second letter, and a sudden flush came to her cheeks. Miss Viner's voice in the room seemed to recede into the far distance.

When she came back to a sense of her surroundings Miss Viner was bringing a long speech to a triumphant termination.

"And I said to her, 'Not at all. As it happens, Miss Grey is Lady Tamplin's own cousin.' What do you think of that?"

"Were you fighting my battles for me? That was very sweet of you."

"You can put it that way if you like. There is nothing to me in a title. Vicar's wife or no vicar's wife, that woman is a cat. Hinting you had bought your way into Society."

"Perhaps she was not so very far wrong."

"And look at you," continued Miss Viner. "Have you come back a stuck-up fine lady, as well you might have done? No, there you are, as sensible as ever you were, with a pair of good Balbriggan stockings on and sensible shoes. I spoke to Ellen about it only yesterday. 'Ellen,' I said, 'you look at Miss Grey. She has been hobnobbing with some of the greatest in the land, and does she go about as you do with skirts up to her knees and silk stockings that ladder when you look at them, and the most ridiculous shoes that ever I set eyes on?'"

Katherine smiled a little to herself; it had apparently been worth while to conform to Miss Viner's prejudices. The old lady went on with increasing gusto.

"It has been a great relief to me that you have not had your head turned. Only the other day I was looking for my cuttings. I have several about Lady Tamplin and her War Hospital and what not, but I cannot lay my hand upon them. I wish you would look, my dear; your eyesight is better than mine. They are all in a box in the bureau drawer."

Katherine glanced down at the letter in her hand and was about to speak, but checked herself, and going over to the bureau found the box of cuttings and began to look over them. Since her return to St Mary Mead her heart had gone out to Miss Viner in admiration of the old woman's stoicism and pluck. She felt that there was little she could do for her old friend, but she knew from experience how much those seemingly small trifles meant to old people.

"Here is one," she said presently. "'Viscountess Tamplin, who is running her villa at Nice as an Officers' Hospital, has just been the victim of a sensational robbery, her jewels having been stolen. Amongst them were some very famous emeralds, heirlooms of the Tamplin family.'"

"Probably paste," said Miss Viner; "a lot of these Society women's jewels are."

"Here is another," said Katherine. "A picture of her, 'A charming camera study of Viscountess Tamplin with her little daughter Lenox.'"

"Let me look," said Miss Viner. "You can't see much of the child's face, can you? But I dare say that is just as well. Things go by contraries in this world and beautiful mothers have hideous children. I dare say the photographer realized that to take the back of the child's head was the best thing he could do for her."

Katherine laughed.

"'One of the smartest hostesses on the Riviera this season is Viscountess Tamplin, who has a villa at Cap Martin. Her cousin, Miss Grey, who recently inherited a vast fortune in a most romantic manner, is staying with her there.'"

"That is the one I wanted," said Miss Viner. "I expect there has been a picture of you in one of the papers that I have missed; you know the kind of thing. Mrs. Somebody or other Jones-Williams, at the something or other Point-to-Point, usually carrying a shooting-stick and having one foot lifted up in the air. It must be a trial to some of them to see what they look like."

Katherine did not answer. She was smoothing out the cutting with her finger, and her face had a puzzled, worried look. Then she drew the second letter out of its envelope and mastered its contents once more. She turned to her friend.

"Miss Viner? I wonder—there is a friend of mine, some one I met on the Riviera, who wants very much to come down and see me here?"

"A man," said Miss Viner.

"Yes."

"Who is he?"

"He is secretary to Mr. Van Aldin, the American millionaire."

"What is his name?"

"Knighton. Major Knighton."

"Hm—secretary to a millionaire. And wants to come down here. Now, Katherine, I am going to say something to you for your own good. You are a nice girl and a sensible girl, and though you have your head screwed on the right way about most things, every woman makes a fool of herself once in her life. Ten to one what this man is after is your money."

With a gesture she arrested Katherine's reply. "I have been waiting for something of this kind. What is a secretary to a millionaire? Nine times out of ten it is a young man who likes living soft. A young man with nice manners and a taste for luxury and no brains and no enterprise, and if there is anything that is a softer job than being a secretary to a millionaire it is marrying a rich woman for her money. I am not saying that you might not be some man's fancy. But you are not young, and though you have a very good complexion you are not a beauty, and what I say to you is, don't make a fool of yourself; but if you are determined to do so, do see that your money is properly tied up on yourself. There, now I have finished. What have you got to say?"

"Nothing," said Katherine; "but would you mind if he did come down to see me?"

"I wash my hands of it," said Miss Viner. "I have done my duty, and whatever happens now is on your own head. Would you like him to lunch or to dinner? I dare say Ellen could manage dinner—that is, if she didn't lose her head."

"Lunch would be very nice," said Katherine. "It is awfully kind of you, Miss Viner. He asked me to ring him up, so I will do so and say that we shall be pleased if he will lunch with us. He will motor down from town."

"Ellen does a steak with grilled tomatoes pretty fairly," said Miss Viner. "She doesn't do it well, but she does it better than anything else. It is no good having a tart because she is heavy handed with pastry; but her little castle puddings are not bad, and I dare say you could find a nice piece of Stilton at Abbot's. I have always heard that gentlemen like a nice piece of Stilton, and there is a good deal of father's wine left, a bottle of sparkling Moselle, perhaps."

"Oh no, Miss Viner; that is really not necessary."

"Nonsense, my child. No gentleman is happy unless he drinks something with his meal. There is some good pre-war whisky if you think he would prefer that. Now do as I say and don't argue. The key of the wine-cellar is in the third drawer down in the dressing-table in the second pair of stockings on the left-hand side."

Katherine went obediently to the spot indicated.

"The second pair, now mind," said Miss Viner. "The first pair has my diamond earrings and my filigree brooch in it."

"Oh," said Katherine, rather taken aback, "wouldn't you like them put in your jewel-case?"

Miss Viner gave vent to a terrific and prolonged snort.

"No, indeed! I have much too much sense for that sort of thing, thank you. Dear, dear, I well remember how my poor father had a safe built in downstairs. Pleased as Punch he was with it, and he said to my mother, 'Now, Mary, you bring me your jewels in their case every night and I will lock them away for you.' My mother was a very tactful woman, and she knew that gentlemen like having their own way, and she brought him the jewel-case locked up just as he said.

"And one night burglars broke in, and of course—naturally—the first thing they went for was the safe! It would be, with my father talking up and down the village and bragging about it until you might have thought he kept all King Solomon's diamonds there. They made a clean sweep, got the tankards, the silver cups, and the presentation gold plate that my father had had presented to him, *and* the jewel-case."

She sighed reminiscently. "My father was in a great state over my mother's jewels. There was the Venetian set and some very fine cameos, and some pale pink corals, and two diamond rings with quite large stones in them. And then, of course, she had to tell him that, being a sensible woman, she had kept her jewellery rolled up in a pair of corsets, and there it was still as safe as anything."

"And the jewel-case had been quite empty?"

"Oh no, dear," said Miss Viner, "it would have been too light a weight then. My mother was a very intelligent woman; she saw to that. She kept her buttons in the jewel-case, and a very handy place it was. Boot buttons in the top tray, trouser buttons in the second tray, and assorted buttons below. Curiously enough, my father was quite annoyed with her. He said he didn't like deceit. But I mustn't go chattering on; you want to go and ring up your friend, and mind you choose a nice piece of steak, and tell Ellen she is not to have holes in her stockings when she waits at lunch."

"Is her name Ellen or Helen, Miss Viner? I thought——"

Miss Viner closed her eyes.

"I can sound my h's, dear, as well as any one, but Helen is *not* a suitable name for a servant. I don't know what the mothers in the lower classes are coming to nowadays."

The rain had cleared away when Knighton arrived at the cottage. The pale fitful sunshine shone down on it and burnished Katherine's head as she stood in the doorway to welcome him. He came up to her quickly, almost boyishly.

"I say, I hope you don't mind. I simply had to see you again soon. I hope the friend you are staying with does not mind."

"Come in and make friends with her," said Katherine. "She can be most alarming, but you will soon find that she has the softest heart in the world."

Miss Viner was enthroned majestically in the drawing-room, wearing a complete set of the cameos which had been so providentially preserved in the family. She greeted Knighton with dignity and an austere politeness which would have damped many men. Knighton, however, had a charm of manner which was not easily set aside, and after about ten minutes Miss Viner thawed perceptibly. Luncheon was a merry meal, and Ellen, or Helen, in a new pair of silk stockings devoid of ladders performed prodigies of waiting. Afterwards, Katherine and Knighton went for a walk and they came back to have tea *tête-à-tête,* since Miss Viner had gone to lie down.

When the car had finally driven off Katherine went slowly upstairs. A voice called her and she went in to Miss Viner's bedroom.

"Friend gone?"

"Yes. Thank you so much for letting me ask him down."

"No need to thank me. Do you think I am the sort of old curmudgeon who never will do anything for anybody?"

"I think you are a dear," said Katherine affectionately.

"Humph," said Miss Viner mollified.

As Katherine was leaving the room she called her back.

"Katherine?"

"Yes."

"I was wrong about that young man of yours. A man when he is making up to anybody can be cordial and gallant and full of little attentions and altogether charming. But when a man is really in love he can't help looking like a sheep. Now, whenever that young man looked at you he looked like a sheep. I take back all I said this morning. It is genuine."

CHAPTER XXXI

MR. AARONS LUNCHES

"AH!" said Mr. Joseph Aarons appreciatively.

He took a long draught from his tankard, set it down with a sigh, wiped the froth from his lips, and beamed across the table at his host, Monsieur Hercule Poirot.

"Give me," said Mr. Aarons, "a good Porterhouse steak and a tankard of something worth drinking, and any one can have your French fallals and whatnots, your ordoovres and your omelettes and your little bits of quail. Give me," he reiterated, "a Porterhouse steak."

Poirot, who had just complied with this request, smiled sympathetically.

"Not that there is much wrong with a steak and kidney pudding," continued Mr. Aarons. "Apple tart? Yes, I will take apple tart, thank you, Miss, and a jug of cream."

The meal proceeded. Finally, with a long sigh, Mr. Aarons laid down his spoon and fork preparatory to toying with some cheese before turning his mind to other matters.

"There was a little matter of business I think you said, Monsieur Poirot," he remarked. "Anything I can do to help you I am sure I shall be most happy."

"That is very kind of you," said Poirot. "I said to myself, 'If you want to know anything about the dramatic profession there is one person who knows all that is to be known and that is my old friend, Mr. Joseph Aarons.'"

"And you don't say far wrong," said Mr. Aarons complacently; "whether it is past, present, or future, Joe Aarons is the man to come to."

"*Précisément.* Now I want to ask you, Monsieur Aarons, what you know about a young woman called Kidd."

"Kidd? Kitty Kidd?"

"Kitty Kidd."

"Pretty smart, she was. Male impersonator, song and a dance—— That one?"

"That is the one."

"*Very* smart, she was. Made a good income. Never out of an engagement. Male impersonation mostly, but, as a matter of fact, you could not touch her as a character actress."

"So I have heard," said Poirot; "but she has not been appearing lately, has she?"

"No. Dropped right out of things. Went over to France and took up with some swell nobleman there. She quitted the stage then for good and all, I guess."

"How long ago was that?"

"Let me see. Three years ago. And she has been a loss—let me tell you that."

"She was clever?"

"Clever as a cartload of monkeys."

"You don't know the name of the man she became friends with in Paris?"

"He was a swell, I know that. A Count—or was it a Marquis? Now I come to think of it, I believe it was a Marquis."

"And you know nothing about her since?"

"Nothing. Never even run across her accidentally like. I bet she is tooling it round some of these foreign resorts. Being a Marquise to the life. You couldn't put one over on Kitty. She would give as good as she got any day."

"I see," said Poirot thoughtfully.

"I am sorry I can't tell you more, Monsieur Poirot," said the other. "I would like to be of use to you if I could. You did me a good turn once."

"Ah, but we are quits on that; you, too, did me a good turn."

"One good turn deserves another. Ha, ha!" said Mr. Aarons.

"Your profession must be a very interesting one," said Poirot.

"So-so," said Mr. Aarons non-committally. "Taking the rough with the smooth, it is all right. I don't do so badly at it, all things considered, but you have to keep your eyes skinned. Never know what the public will jump for next."

"Dancing has come very much to the fore in the last few years," murmured Poirot reflectively.

"*I* never saw anything in this Russian ballet, but people like it. Too highbrow for me."

"I met one dancer out on the Riviera—Mademoiselle Mirelle."

"Mirelle? She is hot stuff, by all accounts. There is always money going to back her—though, so far as that goes, the girl can dance; I have seen her, and I know what I am talking about. I never ha much to do with her myself, but I hear she is a terror to deal with. Tempers and tantrums all the time."

"Yes," said Poirot thoughtfully; "yes, so I should imagine."

"Temperament!" said Mr. Aarons, "temperament! That is what they call it themselves. My missus was a dancer before she married me, but I am thankful to say she never had any temperament. You don't want temperament in the home, Monsieur Poirot."

"I agree with you, my friend; it is out of place there."

"A woman should be calm and sympathetic, and a good cook," said Mr. Aarons.

"Mirelle has not been long before the public, has she?" asked Poirot.

"About two and a half years, that is all," said Mr. Aarons. "Some French Duke started her. I hear now that she has taken up with the ex-Prime Minister of Greece. These are the chaps who manage to put money away quietly."

"That is news to me," said Poirot.

"Oh, she's not one to let the grass grow under her feet. They say that young Kettering murdered his wife on her account. I don't know, I am sure. Anyway, he is in prison, and she had to look round for herself, and pretty smart she has been about it. They say she is wearing a ruby the size of a pigeon's egg—not that I have ever seen a pigeon's egg myself, but that is what they always call it in works of fiction."

"A ruby the size of a pigeon's egg!" said Poirot. His eyes were green and catlike. "How interesting!"

"I had it from a friend of mine," said Mr. Aarons. "But, for all I know, it may be coloured glass. They are all the same, these women—they never stop telling tall stories about their jewels. Mirelle goes about bragging that it has got a curse on it. 'Heart of Fire,' I think she calls it."

"But if I remember rightly," said Poirot, "the ruby that is named 'Heart of Fire' is the centre stone in a necklace."

"There you are! Didn't I tell you there is no end to the lies women will tell about their jewellery? This is a single stone, hung on a platinum chain round her neck; but, as I said before, ten to one it is a bit of coloured glass."

"No," said Poirot gently; "no—somehow I do not think it is coloured glass."

CHAPTER XXXII

KATHERINE AND POIROT COMPARE NOTES

"YOU HAVE CHANGED, Mademoiselle," said Poirot suddenly. He and Katherine were seated opposite each other at a small table at the Savoy.

"Yes, you have changed," he continued.

"In what way?"

"Mademoiselle, these *nuances* are difficult to express."

"I am older."

"Yes, you are older. And by that I do not mean that the wrinkles and the crows' feet are coming. When I first saw you, Mademoiselle, you were a looker-on at life. You had the quiet, amused look of one who sits back in the stalls and watches the play."

"And now?"

"Now, you no longer watch. It is an absurd thing, perhaps, that I say here, but you have the wary look of a fighter who is playing a difficult game."

"My old lady is difficult sometimes," said Katherine, with a smile; "but I can assure you that I don't engage in deadly contests with her. You must go down and see her some day, Monsieur Poirot. I think you are one of the people who would appreciate her pluck and her spirit."

There was a silence while the waiter deftly served them with chicken *en casserole*. When he had departed, Poirot said:

"You have heard me speak of my friend Hastings?—he who said that I was a human oyster. *Eh bien*, Mademoiselle, I have met my match in you. You, far more than I, play a lone hand."

"Nonsense," said Katherine lightly.

"Never does Hercule Poirot talk nonsense. It is as I say."

Again there was a silence. Poirot broke it by inquiring:

"Have you seen any of our Riviera friends since you have been back, Mademoiselle?"

"I have seen something of Major Knighton."

"A-ha! Is that so?"

Something in Poirot's twinkling eyes made Katherine lower hers.

"So Mr. Van Aldin remains in London?"

"Yes."

"I must try to see him to-morrow or the next day."

"You have news for him?"

"What makes you think that?"

"I—wondered, that is all."

Poirot looked across at her with twinkling eyes.

"And now, Mademoiselle, there is much that you wish to ask me, I can see that. And why not? Is not the affair of the Blue Train our own 'Roman Policier'?"

"Yes, there are things I should like to ask you."

"*Eh bien?*"

Katherine looked up with a sudden air of resolution.

"What were you doing in Paris, Monsieur Poirot?"

Poirot smiled slightly.

"I made a call at the Russian Embassy."

"Oh."

"I see that that tells you nothing. But I will not be a human oyster. No, I will lay my cards on the table, which is assuredly a thing that oysters do not do. You suspect, do you not, that I am not satisfied with the case against Derek Kettering?"

"That is what I have been wondering. I thought, in Nice, that you had finished with the case."

"You do not say all that you mean, Mademoiselle. But I admit everything. It was I—my researches—which placed Derek Kettering where he is now. But for me the Examining Magistrate would still be vainly trying to fasten the crime on the Comte de la Roche. *Eh bien,* Mademoiselle, what I have done I do not regret. I have only one duty—to discover the truth, and that way led straight to Mr. Kettering. But did it end there? The police say yes, but I, Hercule Poirot, am not satisfied."

He broke off suddenly. "Tell me, Mademoiselle, have you heard from Mademoiselle Lenox lately?"

"One very short, scrappy letter. She is, I think, annoyed with me for coming back to England."

Poirot nodded.

"I had an interview with her the night that Monsieur Kettering was arrested. It was an interesting interview in more ways than one."

Again he fell silent, and Katherine did not interrupt his train of thought.

"Mademoiselle," he said at last, "I am now on delicate ground, yet I will say this to you. There is, I think, some one who loves

Monsieur Kettering—correct me if I am wrong—and for her sake—well—for her sake I hope that I am right and the police are wrong. You know who that some one is?"

There was a pause, then Katherine said:

"Yes—I think I know."

Poirot leant across the table towards her.

"I am not satisfied, Mademoiselle; no, I am not satisfied. The facts, the main facts, led straight to Monsieur Kettering. But there is one thing that has been left out of account."

"And what is that?"

"The disfigured face of the victim. I have asked myself, Mademoiselle, a hundred times, 'Was Derek Kettering the kind of man who would deal that smashing blow after having committed the murder?' What end would it serve? What purpose would it accomplish? Was it a likely action for one of Monsieur Kettering's temperament? And, Mademoiselle, the answer to these questions is profoundly unsatisfactory. Again and again I go back to that one point—'why?' And the only things I have to help me to a solution of the problem are these."

He whipped out his pocket-book and extracted something from it which he held between his finger and thumb.

"Do you remember, Mademoiselle? You saw me take these hairs from the rug in the railway carriage."

Katherine leant forward, scrutinizing the hairs keenly.

Poirot nodded his head slowly several times.

"They suggest nothing to you, I see that, Mademoiselle. And yet —I think somehow that you see a good deal."

"I have had ideas," said Katherine slowly, "curious ideas. That is why I ask you what you were doing in Paris, Monsieur Poirot."

"When I wrote to you——"

"From the Ritz?"

A curious smile came over Poirot's face.

"Yes, as you say, from the Ritz. I am a luxurious person sometimes —when a millionaire pays."

"The Russian Embassy," said Katherine, frowning. "No, I don't see where that comes in."

"It does not come in directly, Mademoiselle. I went there to get certain information. I saw a particular personage and I threatened him—yes, Mademoiselle, I, Hercule Poirot, threatened him."

"With the police?"

"No," said Poirot drily, "with the Press—a much more deadly weapon."

He looked at Katherine and she smiled at him, just shaking her head.

"Are you not just turning back into an oyster again, Monsieur Poirot?"

"No, no! I do not wish to make mysteries. See, I will tell you everything. I suspect this man of being the active party in the sale of the jewels of Monsieur Van Aldin. I tax him with it, and in the end I get the whole story out of him. I learn where the jewels were handed over, and I learn, too, of the man who paced up and down outside in the street—a man with a venerable head of white hair, but who walked with the light, springy step of a young man—and I give that man a name in my own mind—the name of 'Monsieur le Marquis.'"

"And now you have come to London to see Mr. Van Aldin?"

"Not entirely for that reason. I had other work to do. Since I have been in London I have seen two more people—a theatrical agent and a Harley Street doctor. From each of them I have got certain information. Put these things together, Mademoiselle, and see if you can make of them the same as I do."

"I?"

"Yes, you. I will tell you one thing, Mademoiselle. There has been a doubt all along in my mind as to whether the robbery and the murder were done by the same person. For a long time I was not sure——"

"And now?"

"And now I *know.*"

There was a silence. Then Katherine lifted her head. Her eyes were shining.

"I am not clever like you, Monsieur Poirot. Half the things that you have been telling me don't seem to me to point anywhere at all. The ideas that came to me came from such an entirely different angle——"

"Ah, but that is always so," said Poirot quietly. "A mirror shows the truth, but every one stands in a different place for looking into the mirror."

"My ideas may be absurd—they may be entirely different from yours, but——"

"Yes?"

"Tell me, does this help you at all?"

He took a newspaper cutting from her outstretched hand. He read it and, looking up, he nodded gravely.

"As I told you, Mademoiselle, one stands at a different angle for looking into the mirror, but it is the same mirror and the same things are reflected there."

Katherine got up. "I must rush," she said. "I have only just time to catch my train. Monsieur Poirot——"

"Yes, Mademoiselle."

"It—it mustn't be much longer, you understand. I—I can't go on much longer."

There was a break in her voice.

He patted her hand reassuringly.

"Courage, Mademoiselle, you must not fail now; the end is very near."

CHAPTER XXXIII

A NEW THEORY

"MONSIEUR POIROT wants to see you, sir."

"Damn the fellow!" said Van Aldin.

Knighton remained sympathetically silent.

Van Aldin got up from his chair and paced up and down.

"I suppose you have seen the cursed newspapers this morning?"

"I have glanced at them, sir."

"Still at it hammer and tongs?"

"I am afraid so, sir."

The millionaire sat down again and pressed his hand to his forehead.

"If I had had an idea of this," he groaned. "I wish to God I had never got that little Belgian to ferret out the truth. Find Ruth's murderer—that was all I thought about."

"You wouldn't have liked your son-in-law to go scot free?"

Van Aldin sighed.

"I would have preferred to take the law into my own hands."

"I don't think that would have been a very wise proceeding, sir."

"All the same—are you sure the fellow wants to see me?"

"Yes, Mr. Van Aldin. He is very urgent about it."

"Then I suppose he will have to. He can come along this morning if he likes."

It was a very fresh and debonair Poirot who was ushered in. He did not seem to see any lack of cordiality in the millionaire's manner, and chatted pleasantly about various trifles. He was in London, he explained, to see his doctor. He mentioned the name of an eminent surgeon.

"No, no, *pas la guerre*—a memory of my days in the police force, a bullet of a rascally Apache."

He touched his left shoulder and winced realistically.

"I always consider you a lucky man, Monsieur Van Aldin; you are not like our popular idea of American millionaires, martyrs to the dyspepsia."

"I am pretty tough," said Van Aldin. "I lead a very simple life, you know; plain fare and not too much of it."

"You have seen something of Miss Grey, have you not?" inquired Poirot, innocently turning to the secretary.

"I—yes; once or twice," said Knighton.

He blushed slightly and Van Aldin exclaimed in surprise:

"Funny you never mentioned to me that you had seen her, Knighton?"

"I didn't think you would be interested, sir."

"I like that girl very much," said Van Aldin.

"It is a thousand pities that she should have buried herself once more in St. Mary Mead," said Poirot.

"It is very fine of her," said Knighton hotly. "There are very few people who would bury themselves down there to look after a cantankerous old woman who has no earthly claim on her."

"I am silent," said Poirot, his eyes twinkling a little; "but all the same I say it is a pity. And now, Messieurs, let us come to business."

Both the other men looked at him in some surprise.

"You must not be shocked or alarmed at what I am about to say. Supposing, Monsieur Van Aldin, that, after all, Monsieur Derek Kettering did not murder his wife?"

"What?"

Both men stared at him in blank surprise.

"Supposing, I say, that Monsieur Kettering did not murder his wife?"

"Are you mad, Monsieur Poirot?"

It was Van Aldin who spoke.

"No," said Poirot, "I am not mad. I am eccentric, perhaps—at least certain people say so; but as regards my profession, I am very much, as one says, 'all there.' I ask you, Monsieur Van Aldin, whether you would be glad or sorry if what I tell you should be the case?"

Van Aldin stared at him.

"Naturally I should be glad," he said at last. "Is this an exercise in suppositions, Monsieur Poirot, or are there any facts behind it?"

Poirot looked at the ceiling.

"There is an off-chance," he said quietly, "that it might be the Comte de la Roche after all. At least I have succeeded in upsetting his alibi."

"How did you manage that?"

Poirot shrugged his shoulders modestly.

"I have my own methods. The exercise of a little tact, a little cleverness—and the thing is done."

"But the rubies," said Van Aldin, "these rubies that the Count had in his possession were false."

"And clearly he would not have committed the crime except for the rubies. But you are overlooking one point, Monsieur Van Aldin. Where the rubies were concerned, some one might have been before him."

"But this is an entirely new theory," cried Knighton.

"Do you really believe all this rigmarole, Monsieur Poirot?" demanded the millionaire.

"The thing is not proved," said Poirot quietly. "It is as yet only a theory, but I tell you this, Monsieur Van Aldin, the facts are worth investigating. You must come out with me to the south of France and go into the case on the spot."

"You really think this is necessary—that I should go, I mean."

"I thought it would be what you yourself would wish," said Poirot.

There was a hint of reproach in his tone which was not lost upon the other.

"Yes, yes, of course," he said. "When do you wish to start, Monsieur Poirot?"

"You are very busy at present, sir," murmured Knighton.

But the millionaire had now made up his mind, and he waved the other's objections aside.

"I guess this business comes first," he said. "All right, Monsieur Poirot, to-morrow. What train?"

"We will go, I think, by the Blue Train," said Poirot, and he smiled.

CHAPTER XXXIV

THE BLUE TRAIN AGAIN

"THE MILLIONAIRE'S TRAIN," as it is sometimes called, swung round a curve of line at what seemed a dangerous speed. Van Aldin, Knighton, and Poirot sat together in silence. Knighton and Van Aldin had two compartments connecting with each other, as Ruth Kettering and her maid had had on the fateful journey. Poirot's own compartment was further along the coach.

The journey was a painful one for Van Aldin, recalling as it did the most agonizing memories. Poirot and Knighton conversed occasionally in low tones without disturbing him.

When, however, the train had completed its slow journey round the *ceinture* and reached the Gare de Lyon, Poirot became suddenly galvanized into activity. Van Aldin realized that part of his object in travelling by the train had been to attempt to reconstruct the crime. Poirot himself acted every part. He was in turn the maid, hurriedly shut into her own compartment, Mrs. Kettering, recognizing her husband with surprise and a trace of anxiety, and Derek Kettering discovering that his wife was travelling on the train. He tested various possibilities, such as the best way for a person to conceal himself in the second compartment.

Then suddenly an idea seemed to strike him. He clutched at Van Aldin's arm.

"*Mon Dieu*, but that is something I have not thought of! We must break our journey in Paris. Quick, quick, let us alight at once."

Seizing suitcases he hurried from the train. Van Aldin and Knighton, bewildered but obedient, followed him. Van Aldin having once formed his opinion of Poirot's ability was slow to part from it. At the barrier they were held up. Their tickets were in charge of the conductor of the train, a fact which all three of them had forgotten.

Poirot's explanations were rapid, fluent, and impassioned, but they produced no effect upon the stolid-faced official.

"Let us get quit of this," said Van Aldin abruptly. "I gather you are in a hurry, Monsieur Poirot. For God's sake pay the fares from Calais and let us get right on with whatever you have got in your mind."

But Poirot's flood of language had suddenly stopped dead, and he had the appearance of a man turned to stone. His arm still outflung in an impassioned gesture, remained there as though stricken with paralysis.

"I have been an imbecile," he said simply. "*Ma foi,* I lose my head nowadays. Let us return and continue our journey quietly. With reasonable luck the train will not have gone."

They were only just in time, the train moving off as Knighton, the last of the three, swung himself and his suitcase on board.

The conductor remonstrated with them feelingly, and assisted them to carry their luggage back to their compartments. Van Aldin said nothing, but he was clearly disgusted at Poirot's extraordinary conduct. Alone with Knighton for a moment or two, he remarked:

"This is a wildgoose chase. The man has lost his grip on things. He has got brains up to a point, but any man who loses his head and scuttles round like a frightened rabbit is no earthly darned good."

Poirot came to them in a moment or two, full of abject apologies and clearly so crestfallen that harsh words would have been superfluous. Van Aldin received his apologies gravely, but managed to restrain himself from making acid comments.

They had dinner on the train, and afterwards, somewhat to the surprise of the other two, Poirot suggested that they should all three sit up in Van Aldin's compartment.

The millionaire looked at him curiously.

"Is there anything that you are keeping back from us, Monsieur Poirot?"

"I?" Poirot opened his eyes in innocent surprise. "But what an idea."

Van Aldin did not answer, but he was not satisfied. The conductor was told that he need not make up the beds. Any surprise he might have felt was obliterated by the largeness of the tip which Van Aldin handed to him. The three men sat in silence. Poirot fidgeted and seemed restless. Presently he turned to the secretary.

"Major Knighton, is the door of your compartment bolted? The door into the corridor, I mean."

"Yes; I bolted it myself just now."

"Are you sure?" said Poirot.

"I will go and make sure, if you like," said Knighton smiling.

"No, no, do not derange yourself. I will see for myself."

He passed through the connecting door and returned in a second or two, nodding his head.

"Yes, yes, it is as you said. You must pardon an old man's fussy ways."

He closed the connecting door and resumed his place in the right-hand corner.

The hours passed. The three men dozed fitfully, waking with uncomfortable starts. Probably never before had three people booked berths on the most luxurious train available, then declined to avail themselves of the accommodation they had paid for. Every now and then Poirot glanced at his watch, and then nodded his head and composed himself to slumber once more. On one occasion he rose from his seat and opened the connecting door, peered sharply into the adjoining compartment, and then returned to his seat, shaking his head.

"What is the matter?" whispered Knighton. "You are expecting something to happen, aren't you?"

"I have the nerves," confessed Poirot. "I am like the cat upon the hot tiles. Every little noise it makes me jump."

Knighton yawned.

"Of all the darned uncomfortable journeys," he murmured. "I suppose you know what you are playing at, Monsieur Poirot."

He composed himself to sleep as best he could. Both he and Van Aldin had succumbed to slumber, when Poirot, glancing for the fourteenth time at his watch, leant across and tapped the millionaire on the shoulder.

"Eh? What is it?"

"In five or ten minutes, Monsieur, we shall arrive at Lyons."

"My God!" Van Aldin's face looked white and haggard in the dim light. "Then it must have been about this time that poor Ruth was killed."

He sat staring straight in front of him. His lips twitched a little, his mind reverting back to the terrible tragedy that had saddened his life.

There was the usual long screaming sigh of the brake, and the train slackened speed and drew into Lyons. Van Aldin let down the window and leant out.

"If it wasn't Derek—if your new theory is correct, it is here that the man left the train?" he asked over his shoulder.

Rather to his surprise Poirot shook his head.

"No," he said thoughtfully, "no *man* left the train, but I think—yes, I think, a *woman* may have done so."

Knighton gave a gasp.

"A woman?" demanded Van Aldin sharply.

"Yes, a woman," said Poirot, nodding his head. "You may not remember, Monsieur Van Aldin, but Miss Grey in her evidence mentioned that a youth in a cap and overcoat descended on to the platform ostensibly to stretch his legs. Me, I think that that youth was most probably a woman."

"But who was she?"

Van Aldin's face expressed incredulity, but Poirot replied seriously and categorically.

"Her name—or the name under which she was known, for many years—is Kitty Kidd, but you, Monsieur Van Aldin, knew her by another name—*that of Ada Mason*."

Knighton sprang to his feet.

"What?" he cried.

Poirot swung round to him.

"Ah!—before I forget it." He whipped something from a pocket and held it out.

"Permit me to offer you a cigarette—out of your own cigarette-case. It was careless of you to drop it when you boarded the train on the *ceinture* at Paris."

Knighton stood staring at him as though stupefied. Then he made a movement, but Poirot flung up his hand in a warning gesture.

"No, don't move," he said in a silky voice; "the door into the next compartment is open, and you are being covered from there this minute. I unbolted the door into the corridor when we left Paris, and our friends the police were told to take their places there. As I expect you know, the French police want you rather urgently, Major Knighton—or shall we say—Monsieur le Marquis?"

CHAPTER XXXV

EXPLANATIONS

"Explanations?"

Poirot smiled. He was sitting opposite the millionaire at a luncheon table in the latter's private suite at the Negresco. Facing him was a relieved but very puzzled man. Poirot leant back in his chair, lit one of his tiny cigarettes, and stared reflectively at the ceiling.

"Yes, I will give you explanations. It began with the one point that puzzled me. You know what that point was? *The disfigured face.* It is not an uncommon thing to find when investigating a crime and it rouses an immediate question, the question of identity. That naturally was the first thing that occurred to me. Was the dead woman really Mrs. Kettering? But that line led me nowhere, for Miss Grey's evidence was positive and very reliable, so I put that idea aside. The dead woman *was* Ruth Kettering."

"When did you first begin to suspect the maid?"

"Not for some time, but one peculiar little point drew my attention to her. The cigarette-case found in the railway carriage and which she told us was one which Mrs. Kettering had given to her husband. Now that was, on the face of it, most improbable, seeing the terms that they were on. It awakened a doubt in my mind as to the general veracity of Ada Mason's statements. There was the rather suspicious fact to be taken into consideration, that she had only been with her mistress for two months. Certainly it did not seem as if she could have had anything to do with the crime since she had been left behind in Paris and Mrs. Kettering had been seen alive by several people afterwards, but——"

Poirot leant forward. He raised an emphatic forefinger and wagged it with intense emphasis at Van Aldin.

"But I am a good detective. I suspect. There is nobody and nothing that I do not suspect. I believe nothing that I am told. I say to myself: how do we know that Ada Mason was left behind in Paris? And at first the answer to that question seemed completely satisfactory. There was the evidence of your secretary, Major Knighton, a complete outsider whose testimony might be supposed to be entirely impartial, and there was the dead woman's own words to the conductor on the train. But I put the latter point aside for the moment, because a very curious idea—an idea perhaps fantastic and impossible—was growing up in my mind. If by any outside chance it happened to be true, that particular piece of testimony was worthless.

"I concentrated on the chief stumbling-block to my theory, Major Knighton's statement that he saw Ada Mason at the Ritz after the Blue Train had left Paris. That seemed conclusive enough, but yet, on examining the facts carefully, I noted two things. First, that by a curious coincidence he, too, had been exactly two months in your service. Secondly, his initial letter was the same—'K.' Supposing—just supposing—that it was *his* cigarette case which had been found in the carriage. Then, if Ada Mason and he were working together, and she recognized it when we showed it to her, would she not act precisely as she had done? At first, taken aback, she quickly evolved a plausible theory that would agree with Mr. Kettering's guilt. *Bien entendu,* that was not the original idea. The Comte de la Roche was to be the scapegoat, though Ada Mason would not make her recognition of him too certain, in case he should be able to prove an alibi. Now, if you will cast your mind back to that time, you will remember a significant thing that happened. I suggested to Ada Mason that the man she had seen was not the Comte de la Roche, but Derek Kettering. She seemed uncertain at the time, but after I had got back to my hotel you rang me up and told me that she had come to you and said that, on thinking it over, she was now quite convinced that the man in question *was* Mr. Kettering. I had been expecting something of the kind. There could be but one explanation of this sudden certainty on her part. After my leaving your hotel, she had had time to consult with somebody, and had received instructions which she acted upon. Who had given her these instructions? Major Knighton. And there was another very small point, which might mean nothing or might mean a great deal. In casual conversation Knighton had talked of a jewel robbery in Yorkshire in a house where he was staying. Perhaps a mere coincidence—perhaps another small link in the chain."

"But there is one thing I do not understand, Monsieur Poirot. I guess I must be dense or I would have seen it before now. Who was the man in the train at Paris? Derek Kettering or the Comte de la Roche?"

"That is the simplicity of the whole thing. *There was no man.* Ah—*mille tonnerres!*—do you not see the cleverness of it all? Whose word have we for it that there ever was a man there? Only Ada

Mason's. And we believe in Ada Mason because of Knighton's evidence that she was left behind in Paris."

"But Ruth herself told the conductor that she had left her maid behind there," demurred Van Aldin.

"Ah! I am coming to that. We have Mrs. Kettering's own evidence there, but, on the other hand, we have not really got her evidence, because, Monsieur Van Aldin, a dead woman cannot give evidence. It is not *her* evidence, but the evidence of the conductor of the train—a very different affair altogether."

"So you think the man was lying?"

"No, no, not at all. He spoke what he thought to be the truth. But the woman who told him that she had left her maid in Paris was not Mrs. Kettering."

Van Aldin stared at him.

"Monsieur Van Aldin, Ruth Kettering was dead before the train arrived at the Gare de Lyon. It was Ada Mason, dressed in her mistress's very distinctive clothing, who purchased a dinner basket and who made that very necessary statement to the conductor."

"Impossible!"

"No, no, Monsieur Van Aldin; not impossible. *Les femmes,* they look so much alike nowadays that one identifies them more by their clothing than by their faces. Ada Mason was the same height as your daughter. Dressed in that very sumptuous fur coat and the little red lacquer hat jammed down over her eyes, with just a bunch of auburn curls showing over each ear, it was no wonder that the conductor was deceived. He had not previously spoken to Mrs. Kettering, you remember. True, he had seen the maid just for a moment when she handed him the tickets, but his impression had been merely that of a gaunt, black-clad female. If he had been an unusually intelligent man, he might have gone so far as to say that mistress and maid were not unlike, but it is extremely unlikely that he would even think that. And remember, Ada Mason, or Kitty Kidd, was an actress, able to change her appearance and tone of voice at a moment's notice. No, no; there was no danger of his recognizing the maid in the mistress's clothing, but there *was* the danger that when he came to discover the body he might realize it was not the woman he had talked to the night before. And now we see the reason for the disfigured face. The chief danger that Ada Mason ran was that Katherine Grey might visit her compartment after the train left Paris, and she provided against that difficulty by ordering a dinner basket and by locking herself in her compartment."

"But who killed Ruth—and when?"

"First, bear it in mind that the crime was planned and undertaken by the two of them—Knighton and Ada Mason, working together. Knighton was in Paris that day on your business. He boarded the train somewhere on its way round the *ceinture*. Mrs. Kettering would be surprised, but she would be quite unsuspicious. Perhaps he draws her attention to something out the window, and as she turns to look he slips the cord round her neck—and the whole thing is over in a second or two. The door of the compartment is locked, and he and Ada Mason set to work. They strip off the dead woman's outer clothes. Mason and Knighton roll the body up in a rug and put it on the seat in the adjoining compartment amongst the bags and suitcases. Knighton drops off the train, taking the jewel-case containing the rubies with him. Since the crime is not supposed to have been committed until nearly twelve hours later he is perfectly safe, and his evidence and the supposed Mrs. Kettering's words to the conductor will provide a perfect alibi for his accomplice.

"At the Gare de Lyon Ada Mason gets a dinner basket, and shutting herself into the toilet compartment she quickly changes into her mistress's clothes, adjusts two false bunches of auburn curls, and generally makes up to resemble her as closely as possible. When the conductor comes to make up the bed, she tells him the prepared story about having left her maid behind in Paris; and whilst he is making up the berth, she stands looking out of the window, so that her back is towards the corridor and people passing along there. That was a wise precaution, because, as we know, Miss Grey was one of those passing, and she among others, was willing to swear that Mrs. Kettering was still alive at that hour."

"Go on," said Van Aldin.

"Before getting to Lyons, Ada Mason arranged her mistress's body in the bunk, folded up the dead woman's clothes neatly on the end of it, and herself changed into a man's clothes and prepared to leave the train. When Derek Kettering entered his wife's compartment, and, as he thought, saw her asleep in her berth, the scene had been set, and Ada Mason was hidden in the next compartment waiting for the moment to leave the train unobserved. As soon as the conductor had swung himself down on to the platform at Lyons, she follows, slouching along as though just taking a breath of air. At a moment when she is unobserved, she hurriedly crosses to the other platform, and takes the first train back to Paris and the Ritz Hotel. Her name has been registered there as taking a room the night before by one of Knighton's female accomplices. She has nothing to do but wait there placidly for your arrival. The jewels are not, and never have been, in her possession. No suspicion attaches to him, and, as your secretary, he brings them to Nice without the least fear of discovery. Their delivery there to Monsieur Papopolous is already arranged for and they are entrusted to Mason at the last moment to hand over to the Greek. Altogether a very neatly planned coup, as one would expect from a master of the game such as the Marquis."

"And you honestly mean that Richard Knighton is a well-known criminal, who has been at this business for years?"

Poirot nodded.

"One of the chief assets of the gentleman called the Marquis was his plausible, ingratiating manner. You fell a victim to his charm, Monsieur Van Aldin, when you engaged him as a secretary on such a slight acquaintanceship."

"I could have sworn that he never angled for the post," cried the millionaire.

"It was very astutely done—so astutely done that it deceived a man whose knowledge of other men is as great as yours is."

"I looked up his antecedents too. The fellow's record was excellent."

"Yes, yes; that was part of the game. As Richard Knighton his life was quite free from reproach. He was well born, well connected, did honourable service in the War, and seemed altogether above suspicion; but when I came to glean information about the mysterious Marquis, I found many points of similarity. Knighton spoke French like a Frenchman, he had been in America, France, and England at much the same time as the Marquis was operating. The Marquis was last heard of as engineering various jewel robberies in Switzerland, and it was in Switzerland that you had come across Major Knighton; and it was at precisely that time that the first rumours were going round of your being in treaty for the famous rubies."

"But why murder?" murmured Van Aldin brokenly. "Surely a clever thief could have stolen the jewels without running his head into a noose."

Poirot shook his head. "This is not the first murder that lies to the Marquis's charge. He is a killer by instinct; he believes, too, in leaving no evidence behind him. Dead men and women tell no tales.

"The Marquis had an intense passion for famous and historical jewels. He laid his plans far beforehand by installing himself as your secretary and getting his accomplice to obtain the situation of maid with your daughter, for whom he guessed the jewels were destined. And, though this was his matured and carefully thought-out plan, he did not scruple to attempt a short cut by hiring a couple of Apaches to waylay you in Paris on the night you bought the jewels. That plan failed, which hardly surprised him, I think. This plan was, so he thought, completely safe. No possible suspicion could attach to Richard Knighton. But like all great men—and the Marquis was a great man—he had his weaknesses. He fell genuinely in love with Miss Grey, and suspecting her liking for Derek Kettering, he could not resist the temptation to saddle him with the crime when the opportunity presented itself. And now, Monsieur Van Aldin, I am going to tell you something very curious. Miss Grey is not a fanciful woman by any means, yet she firmly believes that she felt your daughter's presence beside her one day in the Casino Gardens at Monte Carlo, just after she had been having a long talk with Knighton. She was convinced, she says, that the dead woman was urgently trying to tell her something, and it suddenly came to her that what the dead woman was trying to say was that Knighton was her murderer! The idea seemed so fantastic at the time that Miss Grey spoke of it to no one. But she was so convinced of its truth that she acted on it—wild as it seemed. She did not discourage Knighton's advances, and she pretended to him that she was convinced of Derek Kettering's guilt."

"Extraordinary," said Van Aldin.

"Yes, it is very strange. One cannot explain these things. Oh, by the way, there is one little point that baffled me considerably. Your secretary has a decided limp—the result of a wound that he received in the War. Now the Marquis most decidedly did not limp. That was a stumbling-block. But Miss Lenox Tamplin happened to mention one day that Knighton's limp had been a surprise to the surgeons who had been in charge of the case in her mother's hospital. That suggested camouflage. When I was in London I went to the surgeon in question, and I got several technical details from him which confirmed me in that belief. I mentioned the name of that surgeon in Knighton's hearing the day before yesterday. The natural thing would have been for Knighton to mention that he had been attended by him during the War, but he said nothing—and that little point, if nothing else, gave me the last final assurance that my theory of the crime was correct. Miss Grey, too, provided me with a cutting, showing that there had been a robbery at Lady Tamplin's hospital during the time that Knighton had been there. She realized that I was on the same track as herself when I wrote to her from the Ritz in Paris.

"I had some trouble in my inquiries there, but I got what I wanted —evidence that Ada Mason arrived on the morning after the crime and not on the evening of the day before."

There was a long silence, then the millionaire stretched out a hand to Poirot across the table.

"I guess you know what this means to me, Monsieur Poirot," he said huskily. "I am sending you round a cheque in the morning, but no cheque in the world will express what I feel about what you have done for me. You are the goods, Monsieur Poirot. Every time, you are the goods."

Poirot rose to his feet; his chest swelled.

"I am only Hercule Poirot," he said modestly, "yet, as you say, in my own way I am a big man, even as you also are a big man. I am glad and happy to have been of service to you. Now I go to repair the damages caused by travel. Alas! my excellent Georges is not with me."

In the lounge of the hotel he encountered a friend—the venerable Monsieur Papopolous, his daughter Zia beside him.

"I thought you had left Nice, Monsieur Poirot," murmured the Greek as he took the detective's affectionately proffered hand.

"Business compelled me to return, my dear Monsieur Papopolous."

"Business?"

"Yes, business. And talking of business, I hope your health is better, my dear friend?"

"Much better. In fact, we are returning to Paris tomorrow."

"I am enchanted to hear such good news. You have not completely ruined the Greek ex-Minister, I hope."

"I?"

"I understand you sold him a very wonderful ruby which—strictly *entre nous*—is being worn by Mademoiselle Mirelle, the dancer?"

"Yes," murmured Monsieur Papopolous; "yes, that is so."

"A ruby not unlike the famous 'Heart of Fire'."

"It has points of resemblance, certainly," said the Greek casually.

"You have a wonderful hand with jewels, Monsieur Papopolous. I congratulate you. Mademoiselle Zia, I am desolate that you are returning to Paris so speedily. I had hoped to see some more of you now that my business is accomplished."

"Would one be indiscreet if one asked what that business was?" asked Monsieur Papopolous.

"Not at all, not at all. I have just succeeded in laying the Marquis by the heels."

A far-away look came over Monsieur Papopolous' noble countenance.

"The Marquis?" he murmured; "now why does that seem familiar to me? No—I cannot recall it."

"You would not, I am sure," said Poirot. "I refer to a very notable criminal and jewel robber. He has just been arrested for the murder of the English lady, Madame Kettering."

"Indeed? How interesting these things are!"

A polite exchange of farewells followed, and when Poirot was out of earshot, Monsieur Papopolous turned to his daughter.

"Zia," he said, with feeling, "that man is the devil!"

"I like him."

"I like him myself," admitted Monsieur Papopolous. "But he is the devil, all the same."

CHAPTER XXXVI

BY THE SEA

THE MIMOSA WAS nearly over. The scent of it in the air was faintly unpleasant. There were pink geraniums twining along the balustrade of Lady Tamplin's villa, and masses of carnations below sent up a sweet, heavy perfume. The Mediterranean was at its bluest. Poirot sat on the terrace with Lenox Tamplin. He had just finished telling her the same story he had told to Van Aldin two days before. Lenox had listened to him with absorbed attention, her brows knitted and her eyes sombre.

When he had finished she said simply:

"And Derek?"

"He was released yesterday."

"And he has gone—where?"

"He left Nice last night."

"For St. Mary Mead?"

"Yes, for St. Mary Mead."

There was a pause.

"I was wrong about Katherine," said Lenox. "I thought she did not care."

"She is very reserved. She trusts no one."

"She might have trusted me," said Lenox, with a shade of bitterness.

"Yes," said Poirot gravely, "she might have trusted you. But Mademoiselle Katherine has spent a great deal of her life listening, and those who have listened do not find it easy to talk; they keep their sorrows and joys to themselves and tell no one."

"I was a fool," said Lenox; "I thought she really cared for Knighton. I ought to have known better. I suppose I thought so because—well, I hoped so."

Poirot took her hand and gave it a little friendly squeeze. "Courage, Mademoiselle," he said gently.

Lenox looked very straight out across the sea, and her face, in its ugly rigidity, had for the moment a tragic beauty.

"Oh, well," she said at last, "it would not have done. I am too young for Derek; he is like a kid that has never grown up. He wants the Madonna touch."

There was a long silence, then Lenox turned to him quickly and impulsively. "But I *did* help, Monsieur Poirot—at any rate I did help."

"Yes, Mademoiselle. It was you who gave me the first inkling of the truth when you said that the person who committed the crime need not have been on the train at all. Before that, I could not see how the thing had been done."

Lenox drew a deep breath.

"I am glad," she said; "at any rate—that is something."

From far behind them there came a long-drawn-out scream of an engine's whistle.

"That is that damned Blue Train," said Lenox. "Trains are relentless things, aren't they, Monsieur Poirot? People are murdered and die, but they go on just the same. I am talking nonsense, but you know what I mean."

"Yes, yes, I know. Life is like a train, Mademoiselle. It goes on. And it is a good thing that that is so."

"Why?"

"Because the train gets to its journey's end at last, and there is a proverb about that in your language, Mademoiselle."

"'Journeys end in lovers meeting.'" Lenox laughed. "That is not going to be true for me."

"Yes—yes, it is true. You are young, younger than you yourself know. Trust the train, Mademoiselle, for it is *le bon Dieu* who drives it."

The whistle of the engine came again.

"Trust the train, Mademoiselle," murmured Poirot again. "And trust Hercule Poirot. He knows."

Death on the Nile

PART I
ENGLAND

CHAPTER I

"LINNET RIDGEWAY!"

"That's *her!*" said Mr. Burnaby, the landlord of the Three Crowns.

He nudged his companion.

The two men stared with round bucolic eyes and slightly open mouths.

A big scarlet Rolls Royce had just stopped in front of the local post office.

A girl jumped out, a girl without a hat and wearing a frock that looked (but only *looked*) simple. A girl with golden hair and straight autocratic features—a girl with a lovely shape—a girl such as was seldom seen in Malton-under-Wode.

With a quick imperative step she passed into the post office.

"That's her!" said Mr. Burnaby again. And he went on in a low awed voice: "Millions she's got. . . . Going to spend thousands on the place. Swimming pools there's going to be, and Italian gardens and a ballroom and half of the house pulled down and rebuilt. . . ."

"She'll bring money into the town," said his friend. He was a lean seedy-looking man. His tone was envious and grudging.

Mr. Burnaby agreed.

"Yes, it's a great thing for Malton-under-Wode. A great thing it is."

Mr. Burnaby was complacent about it.

"Wake us all up proper," he added.

"Bit of a difference from Sir George," said the other.

"Ah, it was the 'orses did for him," said Mr. Burnaby indulgently. "Never 'ad no luck."

"What did he get for the place?"

"A cool sixty thousand, so I've heard."

The lean man whistled.

Mr. Burnaby went on triumphantly: "And they say she'll have spent another sixty thousand before she's finished!"

"Wicked!" said the lean man. "Where'd she *get* all that money from?"

"America, so I've heard. Her mother was the only daughter of one of those millionaire blokes. Quite like the Pictures, isn't it?"

The girl came out of the post office and climbed into the car.

As she drove off the lean man followed her with his eyes. He muttered:

"It seems all wrong to me—her looking like that. Money *and* looks—it's too much! If a girl's as rich as that she's no right to be a good-looker as well. And she *is* a good-looker. . . . Got everything, that girl has. Doesn't seem fair. . . ."

II

Extract from the Social column of the *Daily Blague*.

Among those supping at Chez Ma Tante I noticed beautiful Linnet Ridgeway. She was with the Hon. Joanna Southwood, Lord Windlesham and Mr. Toby Bryce. Miss Ridgeway, as everyone knows, is the daughter of Melhuish Ridgeway who married Anna Hartz. She inherits from her grandfather, Leopold Hartz, an immense fortune. The lovely Linnet is the sensation of the moment and it is rumoured that an engagement may be announced shortly. Certainly Lord Windlesham seemed very épris! !

III

The Hon. Joanna Southwood said:

"Darling, I think it's going to be all perfectly *marvellous!*"

She was sitting in Linnet Ridgeway's bedroom at Wode Hall.

From the window the eye passed over the gardens to open country with blue shadows of woodlands.

"It's rather perfect, isn't it?" said Linnet.

She leaned her arms on the window sill. Her face was eager alive, dynamic. Beside her, Joanna Southwood seemed, somehow, a little dim—a tall thin young woman of twenty-seven, with a long clever face and freakishly plucked eyebrows.

"And you've done so much in the time! Did you have lots of architects and things?"

"Three."

"What are architects like? I don't think I've ever seen any."

"They were all right. I found them rather unpractical sometimes."

"Darling, you soon put *that* right! You are the *most* practical creature!"

Joanna picked up a string of pearls from the dressing-table.

"I suppose these are real, aren't they, Linnet?"

"Of course."

"I know it's 'of course' to you, my sweet, but it wouldn't be to most people. Heavily cultured or even Woolworth! Darling, they really are *incredible*, so exquisitely matched. They must be worth the *most* fabulous sums!"

"Rather vulgar, you think?"

"No, not at all—just pure beauty. What *are* they worth?"

"About fifty thousand."

"What a lovely lot of money! Aren't you afraid of having them stolen?"

"No, I always wear them—and anyway they're insured."

"Let me wear them till dinner time, will you, darling? It would give me such a thrill."

Linnet laughed.

"Of course if you like."

"You know, Linnet, I really do envy you. You've simply got *everything*. Here you are at twenty, your own mistress, with any amount of money, looks, superb health. You've even got *brains!* When are you twenty-one?"

"Next June. I shall have a grand coming-of-age party in London."

"And then are you going to marry Charles Windlesham? All the dreadful little gossip writers are getting so excited about it. And he really is frightfully devoted."

Linnet shrugged her shoulders.

"I don't know. I don't really want to marry anyone yet."

"Darling, how right you are! It's never quite the same afterward, is it?"

The telephone shrilled and Linnet went to it.

"Yes? Yes?"

The butler's voice answered her.

"Miss de Bellefort is on the line. Shall I put her through?"

"Bellefort? Oh, of course, yes, put her through."

A click and a voice, an eager, soft, slightly breathless voice: "Hullo, is that Miss Ridgeway? *Linnet!*"

"*Jackie darling!* I haven't heard anything of you for ages and *ages!*"

"I know. It's awful. Linnet, I want to see you terribly."

"Darling, can't you come down here? My new toy. I'd love to show to you."

"That's just what I want to do."

"Well, jump into a train or a car."

"Right, I will. A frightfully dilapidated two-seater. I bought it for fifteen pounds, and some days it goes beautifully. But it has moods. If I haven't arrived by tea time you'll know it's had a mood. So long, my sweet."

Linnet replaced the receiver. She crossed back to Joanna.

"That's my oldest friend, Jacqueline de Bellefort. We were together at a convent in Paris. She's had the most terribly bad luck. Her father was a French Count, her mother was American—a Southerner. The father went off with some woman, and her mother lost all her money in the Wall Street crash. Jackie was left absolutely broke. I don't know how she's managed to get along the last two years."

Joanna was polishing her deep-blood-coloured nails with her friend's nail pad. She leant back with her head on one side scrutinizing the effect.

"Darling," she drawled, "won't that be rather *tiresome?* If any misfortunes happen to my friends I always drop them *at once!* It sounds heartless, but it saves such a lot of trouble later! They always want to borrow money off you, or else they start a dressmaking business and you have to get the most terrible clothes from them. Or they paint lampshades, or do Batik scarves."

"So if I lost all my money, you'd drop me tomorrow?"

"Yes, darling, I would. You can't say I'm not honest about it! I only like successful people. And you'll find that's true of nearly everybody—only most people won't admit it. They just say that really they can't put up with Mary or Emily or Pamela any more! 'Her troubles have made her so *bitter* and peculiar, poor dear!' "

"How beastly you are, Joanna!"

"I'm only on the make, like everyone else."

"*I'm* not on the make!"

"For obvious reasons! You don't have to be sordid when good-looking, middle-aged American trustees pay you over a vast allowance every quarter."

"And you're wrong about Jacqueline," said Linnet. "She's not a sponge. I've wanted to help her, but she won't let me. She's as proud as the devil."

"What's she in such a hurry to see you for? I'll bet she wants something! You just wait and see."

"She sounded excited about something," admitted Linnet. "Jackie always did get frightfully worked up over things. She once stuck a penknife into someone!"

"Darling, how thrilling!"

"A boy who was teasing a dog. Jackie tried to get him to stop. He wouldn't. She pulled him and shook him but he was much stronger than she was, and at last she whipped out a penknife and plunged it right into him. There was the *most* awful row!"

"I should think so. It sounds most uncomfortable!"

Linnet's maid entered the room. With a murmured word of apology, she took down a dress from the wardrobe and went out of the room with it.

"What's the matter with Marie?" asked Joanna. "She's been crying."

"Poor thing. You know I told you she wanted to marry a man who has a job in Egypt. She didn't know much about him, so I thought I'd better make sure he was all right. It turned out that he had a wife already—and three children."

"What a lot of enemies you must make, Linnet."

"Enemies?" Linnet looked surprised.

Joanna nodded and helped herself to a cigarette.

"Enemies, my sweet. You're so devastatingly efficient. And you're so frightfully good at doing the right thing."

Linnet laughed.

"Why, I haven't got an enemy in the world!"

IV

Lord Windlesham sat under the cedar tree. His eyes rested on the graceful proportions of Wode Hall. There was nothing to mar its old-world beauty; the new buildings and additions were out of sight round the corner. It was a fair and peaceful sight bathed in the Autumn sunshine. Nevertheless, as he gazed, it was no longer Wode Hall that Charles Windlesham saw. Instead, he seemed to see a more imposing Elizabethan mansion, a long sweep of park, a more bleak background. . . . It was his own family seat, Charltonbury, and in the foreground stood a figure—a girl's figure, with bright golden hair and an eager confident face . . . Linnet as mistress of Charltonbury!

He felt very hopeful. That refusal of hers had not been at all a definite refusal. It had been little more than a plea for time. Well, he could afford to wait a little. . . .

How amazingly suitable the whole thing was. It was certainly advisable that he should marry money, but not such a matter of necessity that he could regard himself as forced to put his own feelings on one side. And he loved Linnet. He would have wanted to marry her even if she had been practically penniless, instead of one of the richest girls in England. Only, fortunately, she *was* one of the richest girls in England. . . .

His mind played with attractive plans for the future. The Mastership of the Roxdale perhaps, the restoration of the west wing, no need to let the Scotch shooting. . . .

Charles Windlesham dreamed in the sun.

V

It was four o'clock when the dilapidated little two-seater stopped with a sound of crunching gravel. A girl got out of it—a small slender creature with a mop of dark hair. She ran up the steps and tugged at the bell.

A few minutes later she was being ushered into the long stately drawing-room, and an ecclesiastical butler was saying with the proper mournful intonation, "Miss de Bellefort."

"Linnet!"

"Jackie!"

Windlesham stood a little aside, watching sympathetically as this fiery little creature flung herself open-armed upon Linnet.

"Lord Windlesham—Miss de Bellefort—my best friend."

A pretty child, he thought—not really pretty but decidedly attractive, with her dark curly hair and her enormous eyes. He murmured a few tactful nothings and then managed unobtrusively to leave the two friends together.

Jacqueline pounced—in a fashion that Linnet remembered as being characteristic of her.

"Windlesham? Windlesham? *That's* the man the papers always say you're going to marry! Are you, Linnet? *Are* you?"

Linnet murmured, "Perhaps."

"Darling—I'm so glad! He looks nice."

"Oh, don't make up your mind about it—I haven't made up my own mind yet."

"Of course not! Queens always proceed with due deliberation to the choosing of a consort!"

"Don't be ridiculous, Jackie."

"But you *are* a queen, Linnet! You always were. *Sa Majesté, la reine Linette. Linette la blonde!* And I—*I'm* the Queen's confidante! The trusted Maid of Honour."

"What nonsense you talk, Jackie darling! Where have you been all this time? You just disappear. And you never write."

"I hate writing letters. Where have I been? Oh, about three parts submerged, darling. In JOBS, you know. Grim jobs with grim women!"

"Darling, I wish you'd—"

"Take the Queen's bounty? Well, frankly, darling, that's what I'm here for. No, not to borrow money. It's not got to that yet! But I've come to ask a great big important favour!"

"Go on."

"If you're going to marry the Windlesham man, you'll understand, perhaps."

Linnet looked puzzled for a minute; then her face cleared.

"Jackie, do you mean—"

"Yes, darling, *I'm engaged!*"

"So that's it! I thought you were looking particularly alive somehow. You always do, of course, but even more than usual."

"That's just what I feel like."

"Tell me all about him."

"His name's Simon Doyle. He's big and square and incredibly simple and boyish and utterly adorable! He's poor—got no money. He's what you call 'county' all right—but very impoverished county—a younger son and all that. His people come from Devonshire. He loves country and country things. And for the last five years he's been in the city in a stuffy office. And now they're cutting down and he's out of a job. Linnet, I shall *die* if I can't marry him! I shall die! I shall die! I shall *die*. . . ."

"Don't be ridiculous, Jackie."

"I shall die, I tell you! I'm crazy about him. He's crazy about me. We can't live without each other."

"Darling, you *have* got it badly!"

"I know. It's awful, isn't it? This love business gets hold of you and you can't do anything about it."

She paused for a minute. Her dark eyes dilated, looked suddenly tragic. She gave a little shiver.

"It's—even frightening sometimes! Simon and I were made for each other. I shall never care for anyone else. And *you've* got to help us, Linnet. I heard you'd bought this place and it put an idea into my head. Listen, you'll have to have a land agent—perhaps two. I want you to give the job to Simon."

"Oh!" Linnet was startled.

Jacqueline rushed on: "He's got all that sort of thing at his fingertips. He knows all about estates—was brought up on one. And he's got his business training too. Oh, Linnet, you will give him a job, won't you, for love of me? If he doesn't make good, sack him. But he will. And we can live in a little house, and I shall see lots of you, and everything in the garden will be too, too divine."

She got up.

"Say you will, Linnet. Say you will. Beautiful Linnet! Tall golden Linnet! My own very special Linnet! Say you will!"

"Jackie—"

"You will?"

Linnet burst out laughing.

"Ridiculous Jackie! Bring along your young man and let me have a look at him and we'll talk it over."

Jackie darted at her, kissing her exuberantly:

"*Darling* Linnet—you're a real friend! I knew you were. You wouldn't let me down—ever. You're just the loveliest thing in the world. Good-bye."

"But, Jackie, you're *staying*."

"Me? No, I'm not. I'm going back to London, and tomorrow I'll come back and bring Simon and we'll settle it all up. You'll adore him. He really is a *pet*."

"But can't you wait and just have tea?"

"No, I can't wait, Linnet. I'm too excited. I must get back and tell Simon. I know I'm mad, darling, but I can't help it. Marriage will cure me, I expect. It always seems to have a very sobering effect on people."

She turned at the door, stood a moment, then rushed back for a last quick birdlike embrace.

"Dear Linnet—there's no one like you."

VI

M. Gaston Blondin, the proprietor of that modish little restaurant Chez Ma Tante, was not a man who delighted to honour many of his *clientèle*. The rich, the beautiful, the notorious and the well-born might wait in vain to be signalled out and paid special attention.

Only in the rarest cases did M. Blondin, with gracious condescension, greet a guest, accompany him to a privileged table, and exchange with him suitable and apposite remarks.

On this particular night, M. Blondin had exercised his royal prerogative three times—once for a Duchess, once for a famous racing peer, and once for a little man of comical appearance with immense black moustaches, who, a casual onlooker would have thought, could bestow no favour on Chez Ma Tante by his presence there.

M. Blondin, however, was positively fulsome in his attentions. Though clients had been told for the last half hour that a table was not to be had, one now mysteriously appeared, placed in a most favourable position. M. Blondin conducted the client to it with every appearance of *empressement*.

"But naturally, for *you* there is *always* a table, Monsieur Poirot! How I wish that you would honour us oftener."

Hercule Poirot smiled, remembering that past incident wherein a dead body, a waiter, M. Blondin, and a very lovely lady had played a part.

"You are too amiable, Monsieur Blondin," he said.

"And you are alone, Monsieur Poirot?"

"Yes, I am alone."

"Oh, well, Jules here will compose for you a little meal that will be a poem—positively a poem! Women, however charming, have this disadvantage: they distract the mind from food! You will enjoy your dinner, Monsieur Poirot; I promise you that. Now, as to wine—"

A technical conversation ensued. Jules, the *maître d'hôtel*, assisting.

Before departing, M. Blondin lingered a moment, lowering his voice confidentially.

"You have grave affairs on hand?"

Poirot shook his head.

"I am, alas, a man of leisure," he said sadly. "I have made the economies in my time and I have now the means to enjoy a life of idleness."

"I envy you."

"No, no, you would be unwise to do so. I can assure you, it is not so gay as it sounds." He sighed. "How true is the saying that man was forced to invent work in order to escape the strain of having to think."

M. Blondin threw up his hands.

"But there is so much! There is travel!"

"Yes, there is travel. Already I have done not so badly. This winter I shall visit Egypt, I think. The climate, they say, is superb! One will escape from the fogs, the greyness, the monotony of the constantly falling rain."

"Ah! Egypt," breathed M. Blondin.

"One can even voyage there now, I believe, by train, escaping all sea travel except the Channel."

"Ah, the sea, it does not agree with you?"

Hercule Poirot shook his head and shuddered slightly.

"I, too," said M. Blondin with sympathy. "Curious the effect it has upon the stomach."

"But only upon certain stomachs! There are people on whom the motion makes no impression whatever. They actually *enjoy* it!"

"An unfairness of the good God," said M. Blondin.

He shook his head sadly, and, brooding on the impious thought, withdrew.

Smooth-footed, deft-handed waiters ministered to the table. Toast Melba, butter, an ice pail, all the adjuncts to a meal of quality.

The Negro orchestra broke into an ecstasy of strange discordant noises. London danced.

Hercule Poirot looked on, registering impressions in his neat orderly mind.

How bored and weary most of the faces were! Some of those stout men, however, were enjoying themselves . . . whereas a patient endurance seemed to be the sentiment exhibited on their partners' faces. The fat woman in purple was looking radiant. . . . Undoubtedly the fat had certain compensations in life . . . a zest—a gusto—denied to those of more fashionable contours.

A good sprinkling of young people—some vacant looking—some bored—some definitely unhappy. How absurd to call youth the time of happiness—youth, the time of greatest vulnerability!

His glance softened as it rested on one particular couple. A well-matched pair—tall broad-shouldered man, slender delicate girl. Two bodies that moved in a perfect rhythm of happiness. Happiness in the place, the hour, and in each other.

The dance stopped abruptly. Hands clapped and it started again. After a second *encore* the couple returned to their table close by Poirot. The girl was flushed, laughing. As she sat, he could study her face, lifted laughing to her companion.

There was something else beside laughter in her eyes. Hercule Poirot shook his head doubtfully.

"She cares too much, that little one," he said to himself. "It is not safe. No, it is not safe."

And then a word caught his ear, "Egypt."

Their voices came to him clearly—the girl's young, fresh, arrogant, with just a trace of soft-sounding foreign R's, and the man's pleasant, low-toned, well-bred English.

"I'm *not* counting my chickens before they're hatched, Simon. I tell you Linnet won't let us down!"

"*I* might let *her* down."

"Nonsense—it's just the right job for you."

"As a matter of fact I think it is. . . . I haven't really any doubts as to my capability. And I mean to make good—for *your* sake!"

The girl laughed softly, a laugh of pure happiness.

"We'll wait three months—to make sure you don't get the sack—and then—"

"And then I'll endow thee with my worldly goods—that's the hang of it, isn't it?"

"And, as I say, we'll go to Egypt for our honeymoon. Damn the expense! I've always wanted to go to Egypt all my life. The Nile and the pyramids and the sand . . ."

He said, his voice slightly indistinct: "We'll see it together, Jackie . . . together. Won't it be marvellous?"

"I wonder. Will it be as marvellous to you as it is to me? Do you really care—as much as I do?"

Her voice was suddenly sharp—her eyes dilated—almost with fear.

The man's answer came quickly crisp, "Don't be absurd, Jackie."

But the girl repeated, "I wonder. . . ."

Then she shrugged her shoulders.

"Let's dance."

Hercule Poirot murmured to himself:

"*Un qui aime et un qui se laisse aimer*. Yes, I wonder too."

VII

Joanna Southwood said, "And suppose he's a terrible tough?"

Linnet shook her head. "Oh, he won't be. I can trust Jacqueline's taste."

Joanna murmured, "Ah, but people don't run true to form in love affairs."

Linnet shook her head impatiently. Then she changed the subject. "I must go and see Mr. Pierce about those plans."

"Plans?"

"Yes, some dreadful insanitary old cottages. I'm having them pulled down and the people moved."

"How sanitary and public-spirited of you, darling!"

"They'd have had to go anyway. Those cottages would have overlooked my new swimming pool."

"Do the people who lived in them like going?"

"Most of them are delighted. One or two are being rather stupid about it—really tiresome in fact. They don't seem to realize how vastly improved their living conditions will be!"

"But you're being quite high-handed about it, I presume."

"My dear Joanna, it's to their advantage really."

"Yes, dear, I'm sure it is. Compulsory benefit."

Linnet frowned. Joanna laughed.

"Come now, you *are* a tyrant, admit it. A beneficent tyrant if you like!"

"I'm not the least bit a tyrant."

"But you like your own way!"

"Not especially."

"Linnet Ridgeway, can you look me in the face and tell me of *any one occasion* on which you've failed to do exactly as you wanted?"

"Heaps of times."

"Oh, yes, 'heaps of times'—just like that—but no concrete example. And you simply can't think up one, darling, however hard you try! The triumphal progress of Linnet Ridgeway in her golden car."

Linnet said sharply, "You think I'm selfish?"

"No—just irresistible. The combined effect of money and charm. Everything goes down before you. What you can't buy with cash you buy with a smile. Result: Linnet Ridgeway, the Girl Who Has Everything."

"Don't be ridiculous, Joanna!"

"Well, haven't you got everything?"

"I suppose I have. . . . It sounds rather disgusting, somehow!"

"Of course it's disgusting, darling! You'll probably get terribly bored and blasé by and by. In the meantime, enjoy the triumphal progress in the golden car. Only I wonder, I really do wonder, what will happen when you want to go down a street which has a board up saying 'No Thoroughfare.'"

"Don't be idiotic, Joanna." As Lord Windlesham joined them, Linnet said, turning to him, "Joanna is saying the nastiest things to me."

"All spite, darling, all spite," said Joanna vaguely as she got up from her seat.

She made no apology for leaving them. She had caught the glint in Windlesham's eye.

He was silent for a minute or two. Then he went straight to the point.

"Have you come to a decision, Linnet?"

Linnet said slowly: "Am I being a brute? I suppose, if I'm not sure, I ought to say 'No'—"

He interrupted her.

"Don't say it. You shall have time—as much time as you want. But I think, you know, we should be happy together."

"You see," Linnet's tone was apologetic, almost childish, "I'm enjoying myself so much—especially with all this." She waved a hand. "I wanted to make Wode Hall into my real ideal of a country house, and I do think I've got it nice, don't you?"

"It's beautiful. Beautifully planned. Everything perfect. You're very clever, Linnet."

He paused a minute and went on: "And you like Charltonbury, don't you? Of course it wants modernizing and all that—but you're so clever at that sort of thing. You'd enjoy it."

"Why, of course, Charltonbury's divine."

She spoke with ready enthusiasm, but inwardly she was conscious of a sudden chill. An alien note had sounded, disturbing her complete satisfaction with life. She did not analyse the feeling at the moment, but later, when Windlesham had gone into the house, she tried to probe into the recesses of her mind.

Charltonbury—yes, that was it—she had resented the mention of Charltonbury. But why? Charltonbury was modestly famous. Windlesham's ancestors had held it since the time of Elizabeth. To be mistress of Charltonbury was a position unsurpassed in society. Windlesham was one of the most desirable *partis* in England.

Naturally he couldn't take Wode seriously. . . . It was not in any way to be compared with Charltonbury.

Ah, but Wode was *hers!* She had seen it, acquired it, rebuilt and re-dressed it, lavished money on it. It was her own possession—her kingdom.

But in a sense it wouldn't count if she married Windlesham. What would they want with two country places? And of the two, naturally Wode Hall would be the one to be given up.

She, Linnet Ridgeway, wouldn't exist any longer. She would be Countess of Windlesham, bringing a fine dowry to Charltonbury and its master. She would be queen consort, not queen any longer.

"I'm being ridiculous," said Linnet to herself.

But it was curious how she did hate the idea of abandoning Wode. . . .

And wasn't there something else nagging at her?

Jackie's voice with that queer blurred note in it saying: "I shall *die* if I can't marry him! I shall die. I shall die . . ."

So positive, so earnest. Did she, Linnet, feel like that about Windlesham? Assuredly she didn't. Perhaps she could never feel like that about anyone. It must be—rather wonderful—to feel like that. . . .

The sound of a car came through the open window.

Linnet shook herself impatiently. That must be Jackie and her young man. She'd go out and meet them.

She was standing in the open doorway as Jacqueline and Simon Doyle got out of the car.

"Linnet!" Jackie ran to her. "This is Simon. Simon, here's Linnet. She's just the most wonderful person in the world."

Linnet saw a tall, broad-shouldered young man, with very dark blue eyes, crisply curling brown hair, a square chin and a boyish, appealingly simple smile. . . .

She stretched out a hand. The hand that clasped hers was firm and warm. . . . She liked the way he looked at her, the *naïve* genuine admiration.

Jackie had told him she was wonderful, and he clearly thought that she was wonderful. . . .

A warm sweet feeling of intoxication ran through her veins.

"Isn't this all lovely?" she said. "Come in, Simon, and let me welcome my new land agent properly."

And as she turned to lead the way she thought: "I'm frightfully —frightfully happy. I like Jackie's young man . . . I like him enormously. . . ."

And then with a sudden pang, "Lucky Jackie. . . ."

VIII

Tim Allerton leant back in his wicker chair and yawned as he looked out over the sea. He shot a quick sidelong glance at his mother.

Mrs. Allerton was a good-looking, white-haired woman of fifty. By imparting an expression of pinched severity to her mouth every time she looked at her son, she sought to disguise the fact of her intense affection for him. Even total strangers were seldom deceived by this device and Tim himself saw through it perfectly.

He said, "Do you really like Majorca, Mother?"

"Well," Mrs. Allerton considered, "it's cheap."

"And cold," said Tim with a slight shiver.

He was a tall, thin young man, with dark hair and a rather narrow chest. His mouth had a very sweet expression; his eyes were sad and his chin was indecisive. He had long delicate hands.

Threatened by consumption some years ago, he had never displayed a really robust physique. He was popularly supposed "to write," but it was understood among his friends that inquiries as to literary output were not encouraged.

"What are you thinking of, Tim?"

Mrs. Allerton was alert. Her bright, dark-brown eyes looked suspicious.

Tim Allerton grinned at her.

"I was thinking of Egypt."

"Egypt?"

Mrs. Allerton sounded doubtful.

"Real warmth, darling. Lazy golden sands. The Nile. I'd like to go up the Nile, wouldn't you?"

"Oh, I'd *like* it." Her tone was dry. "But Egypt's expensive, my dear. Not for those who have to count the pennies."

Tim laughed. He rose, stretched himself. Suddenly he looked alive and eager. There was an excited note in his voice.

"The expense will be my affair. Yes, darling. A little flutter on the Stock Exchange. With thoroughly satisfactory results. I heard this morning."

"This morning?" said Mrs. Allerton sharply. "You only had one letter and that—"

She stopped and bit her lip.

Tim looked momentarily undecided whether to be amused or annoyed. Amusement gained the day.

"And that was from Joanna," he finished coolly. "Quite right, Mother. What a Queen of detectives you'd make! The famous Hercule Poirot would have to look to his laurels if you were about."

Mrs. Allerton looked rather cross.

"I just happened to see the handwriting—"

"And knew it wasn't that of a stockbroker? Quite right. As a matter of fact it was yesterday I heard from them. Poor Joanna's handwriting *is* rather noticeable—sprawls about all over the envelope like an inebriated spider."

"What does Joanna say? Any news?"

Mrs. Allerton strove to make her voice sound casual and ordinary. The friendship between her son and his second cousin, Joanna Southwood, always irritated her. Not, as she put it to herself, that there was "anything in it." She was quite sure there wasn't. Tim had never manifested a sentimental interest in Joanna, nor she in him. Their mutual attraction seemed to be founded on gossip and the possession of a large number of friends and acquaintances in common. They both liked people and discussing people. Joanna had an amusing if caustic tongue.

It was not because Mrs. Allerton feared that Tim might fall in love with Joanna that she found herself always becoming a little stiff in manner if Joanna were present or when letters from her arrived.

It was some other feeling hard to define—perhaps an unacknowledged jealousy in the unfeigned pleasure Tim always seemed to take in Joanna's society. He and his mother were such perfect companions that the sight of him absorbed and interested in another woman always startled Mrs. Allerton slightly. She fancied, too, that her own presence on these occasions set some barrier between the two members of the younger generation. Often she had come upon them eagerly absorbed in some conversation and, at sight of her, their talk had wavered, had seemed to include her rather too purposefully and as in duty bound. Quite definitely, Mrs. Allerton did not like Joanna Southwood. She thought her insincere, affected and essentially superficial. She found it very hard to prevent herself saying so in unmeasured tones.

In answer to her question, Tim pulled the letter out of his pocket and glanced through it. It was quite a long letter, his mother noted.

"Nothing much," he said. "The Devenishes are getting a divorce.

Old Monty's been had up for being drunk in charge of a car. Windlesham's gone to Canada. Seems he was pretty badly hit when Linnet Ridgeway turned him down. She's definitely going to marry this land agent person."

"How extraordinary! Is he very dreadful?"

"No, no, not at all. He's one of the Devonshire Doyles. No money, of course—and he was actually engaged to one of Linnet's best friends. Pretty thick, that."

"I don't think it's at all nice," said Mrs. Allerton, flushing.

Tim flashed her a quick affectionate glance.

"I know, darling. You don't approve of snaffling other people's husbands and all that sort of thing."

"In my day we had our standards," said Mrs. Allerton. "And a very good thing too! Nowadays young people seem to think they can just go about doing anything they choose."

Tim smiled.

"They don't only think it. They do it. *Vide* Linnet Ridgeway!"

"Well, I think it's horrid!"

Tim twinkled at her.

"Cheer up, you old die-hard! Perhaps I agree with you. Anyway, *I* haven't helped myself to anyone's wife or fiancée yet."

"I'm sure you'd never do such a thing," said Mrs. Allerton. She added with spirit, "I've brought you up properly."

"So the credit is yours, not mine."

He smiled teasingly at her as he folded the letter and put it away again. Mrs. Allerton let the thought just flash across her mind: "Most letters he shows to me. He only reads me snippets from Joanna's."

But she put the unworthy thought away from her, and decided, as ever, to behave like a gentlewoman.

"Is Joanna enjoying life?" she asked.

"So so. Says she thinks of opening a delicatessen shop in Mayfair."

"She always talks about being hard up," said Mrs. Allerton with a tinge of spite, "but she goes about everywhere and her clothes must cost her a lot. She's always beautifully dressed."

"Ah, well," said Tim, "she probably doesn't pay for them. No, Mother, I don't mean what your Edwardian mind suggests to you. I just mean quite literally that she leaves her bills unpaid."

Mrs. Allerton sighed.

"I never know how people manage to do that."

"It's a kind of special gift," said Tim. "If only you have sufficiently extravagant tastes, and absolutely no sense of money values, people will give you any amount of credit."

"Yes, but you come to the Bankruptcy Court in the end like poor Sir George Wode."

"You have a soft spot for that old horse coper—probably because he called you a rosebud in eighteen seventy-nine at a dance."

"I wasn't born in eighteen seventy-nine," Mrs. Allerton retorted with spirit. "Sir George has charming manners, and I won't have you calling him a horse coper."

"I've heard funny stories about him from people that know."

"You and Joanna don't mind what you say about people; anything will do so long as it's sufficiently ill-natured."

Tim raised his eyebrows.

"My dear, you're quite heated. I didn't know old Wode was such a favourite of yours."

"You don't realize how hard it is for him, having to sell Wode Hall. He cared terribly about that place."

Tim suppressed the easy retort. After all, who was he to judge? Instead he said thoughtfully:

"You know, I think you're not far wrong there. Linnet asked him to come down and see what she'd done to the place, and he refused quite rudely."

"Of course. She ought to have known better than to ask him."

"And I believe he's quite venomous about her—mutters things under his breath whenever he sees her. Can't forgive her for having given him an absolutely top price for the worm-eaten family estate."

"And you can't understand that?" Mrs. Allerton spoke sharply.

"Frankly," said Tim calmly, "I can't. Why live in the past? Why cling on to things that have been?"

"What are you going to put in their place?"

He shrugged his shoulders. "Excitement, perhaps. Novelty. The joy of never knowing what may turn up from day to day. Instead of inheriting a useless tract of land, the pleasure of making money for yourself—by your own brains and skill."

"A successful deal on the Stock Exchange in fact!"

He laughed. "Why not?"

"And what about an equal *loss* on the Stock Exchange?"

"That, dear, is rather tactless. And quite inappropriate today. . . . What about this Egypt plan?"

"Well—"

He cut in, smiling at her: "That's settled. We've both always wanted to see Egypt."

"When do you suggest?"

"Oh, next month. January's about the best time there. We'll enjoy the delightful society in this hotel a few weeks longer."

"Tim," said Mrs. Allerton reproachfully. Then she added guiltily: "I'm afraid I promised Mrs. Leech that you'd go with her to the police station. She doesn't understand any Spanish."

Tim made a grimace.

"About her ring? The blood-red ruby of the horse leech's daughter? Does she still persist in thinking it's been stolen? I'll go if you like, but it's a waste of time. She'll only get some wretched chambermaid into trouble. I distinctly saw it on her finger when she went into the sea that day. It came off in the water and she never noticed."

"She says she is quite sure she took it off and left it on her dressing-table."

"Well, she didn't. I saw it with my own eyes. The woman's a fool. Any woman's a fool who goes prancing into the sea in December, pretending the water's quite warm just because the sun happens to be shining rather brightly at the moment. Stout women oughtn't to be allowed to bathe anyway; they look so revolting in bathing dresses."

Mrs. Allerton murmured, "I really feel I ought to give up bathing."

Tim gave a shout of laughter.

"You? You can give most of the young things points and to spare."

Mrs. Allerton sighed and said, "I wish there were a few more young people for you here."

Tim Allerton shook his head decidedly.

"I don't. You and I get along rather comfortably without outside distractions."

"You'd like it if Joanna were here."

"I wouldn't." His tone was unexpectedly resolute. "You're all wrong there. Joanna amuses me, but I don't really like her, and to have her around much gets on my nerves. I'm thankful she isn't here. I should be quite resigned if I were never to see Joanna again."

He added, almost below his breath, "There's only one woman in the world I've got a real respect and admiration for, and I think, Mrs. Allerton, you know very well who that woman is."

His mother blushed and looked quite confused.

Tim said gravely: "There aren't very many really nice women in the world. You happen to be one of them."

IX

In an apartment overlooking Central Park in New York, Mrs. Robson exclaimed: "If that isn't just too lovely! You really are the luckiest girl, Cornelia."

Cornelia Robson flushed responsively. She was a big clumsy-looking girl with brown doglike eyes.

"Oh, it will be wonderful!" she gasped.

Old Miss Van Schuyler inclined her head in a satisfied fashion at this correct attitude on the part of poor relations.

"I've always dreamed of a trip to Europe," sighed Cornelia, "but I just didn't feel I'd ever get there."

"Miss Bowers will come with me as usual, of course," said Miss Van Schuyler, "but as a social companion I find her limited—very limited. There are many little things that Cornelia can do for me."

"I'd just love to, Cousin Marie," said Cornelia eagerly.

"Well, well, then that's settled," said Miss Van Schuyler. "Just run and find Miss Bowers, my dear. It's time for my eggnog."

Cornelia departed. Her mother said: "My dear Marie, I'm really *most* grateful to you! You know I think Cornelia suffers a lot from not being a social success. It makes her feel kind of mortified. If I could afford to take her to places—but you know how it's been since Ned died."

"I'm very glad to take her," said Miss Van Schuyler. "Cornelia has always been a nice handy girl, willing to run errands, and not so selfish as some of these young people nowadays."

Mrs. Robson rose and kissed her rich relative's wrinkled and slightly yellow face.

"I'm just ever so grateful," she declared.

On the stairs she met a tall capable looking woman who was carrying a glass containing a yellow foamy liquid.

"Well, Miss Bowers, so you're off to Europe?"

"Why, yes, Mrs. Robson."

"What a lovely trip!"

"Why, yes, I should think it would be very enjoyable."

"But you've been abroad before?"

"Oh, yes, Mrs. Robson. I went over to Paris with Miss Van Schuyler last Fall. But I've never been to Egypt before."

Mrs. Robson hesitated.

"I do hope—there won't be any—trouble."

She had lowered her voice. Miss Bowers, however, replied in her usual tone:

"Oh, *no*, Mrs. Robson; I shall take good care of *that*. I keep a very sharp look-out always."

But there was still a faint shadow on Mrs. Robson's face as she slowly continued down the stairs.

X

In his office down town Mr. Andrew Pennington was opening his personal mail. Suddenly his fist clenched itself and came down on his desk with a bang; his face crimsoned and two big veins stood out on his forehead. He pressed a buzzer on his desk and a smart looking stenographer appeared with commendable promptitude.

"Tell Mr. Rockford to step in here."

"Yes, Mr. Pennington."

A few minutes later, Sterndale Rockford, Pennington's partner, entered the office. The two men were not unlike—both tall, spare, with greying hair and clean-shaven, clever faces.

"What's up, Pennington?"

Pennington looked up from the letter he was re-reading. He said, "Linnet's married. . . ."

"*What?*"

"You heard what I said! Linnet Ridgeway's *married!*"

"How? When? Why didn't we hear about it?"

Pennington glanced at the calendar on his desk.

"She wasn't married when she wrote this letter, but she's married now. Morning of the fourth. That's today."

Rockford dropped into a chair.

"Whew! No warning? Nothing? Who's the man?"

Pennington referred again to the letter.

"Doyle. Simon Doyle."

"What sort of a fellow is he? Ever heard of him?"

"No. She doesn't say much. . . ." He scanned the lines of clear, upright handwriting. "Got an idea there's something hole-and-corner about the business. . . . That doesn't matter. The whole point is, she's married."

The eyes of the two men met. Rockford nodded.

"This needs a bit of thinking out," he said quietly.

"What are we going to do about it?"

"I'm asking you."

The two men sat silent. Then Rockford asked, "Got any plan?"

Pennington said slowly: "The *Normandie* sails today. One of us could just make it."

"You're crazy! What's the big idea?"

Pennington began, "Those British lawyers—" and stopped.

"What about 'em? Surely you're not going over to tackle 'em? You're mad!"

"I'm not suggesting that you—or I—should go to England."

"What's the big idea, then?"

Pennington smoothed out the letter on the table.

"Linnet's going to Egypt for her honeymoon. Expects to be there a month or more. . . ."

"Egypt—eh?"

Rockford considered. Then he looked up and met the other's glance.

"Egypt," he said; "*that's* your idea!"

"Yes—a chance meeting. Over on a trip. Linnet and her husband —honeymoon atmosphere. It might be done."

Rockford said doubtfully, "She's sharp, Linnet is . . . but—"

Pennington went on softly, "I think there might be ways of—managing it."

Again their eyes met. Rockford nodded.

"All right, big boy."

Pennington looked at the clock.

"We'll have to hustle—whichever of us is going."

"You go," said Rockford promptly. "You always made a hit with Linnet. 'Uncle Andrew.' That's the ticket!"

Pennington's face had hardened. He said, "I hope I can pull it off."

"You've got to pull it off," his partner said. "The situation's critical. . . ."

XI

William Carmichael said to the thin, weedy youth who opened the door inquiringly, "Send Mr. Jim to me, please."

Jim Fanthorp entered the room and looked inquiringly at his uncle. The older man looked up with a nod and a grunt.

"Humph, there you are."

"You asked for me?"

"Just cast an eye over this."

The young man sat down and drew the sheaf of papers toward him. The elder man watched him.

"Well?"

The answer came promptly, "Looks fishy to me, sir."

Again the senior partner of Carmichael, Grant & Carmichael uttered his characteristic grunt.

Jim Fanthorp re-read the letter which had just arrived by air mail from Egypt:

. . . It seems wicked to be writing business letters on such a day. We have spent a week at Mena House and made an expedition to the Fayum. The day after tomorrow we are going up the Nile to Luxor and Assuan by steamer, and perhaps on to Khartûm. When we went into Cook's this morning to see about our tickets who do you think was the first person I saw?—my American trustee, Andrew Pennington. I think you met him two years ago when he was over. I had no idea he was in Egypt and he had no idea that I was! Nor that I was married! My letter, telling him of my marriage, must just have missed him. He is actually going up the Nile on the same trip that we are. Isn't it a coincidence? Thank you so much for all you have done in this busy time. I—

As the young man was about to turn the page, Mr. Carmichael took the letter from him.

"That's all," he said. "The rest doesn't matter. Well, what do you think?"

His nephew considered for a moment—then he said:

"Well—I think—not a coincidence. . . ."

The other nodded approval.

"Like a trip to Egypt?" he barked out.

"You think that's advisable?"

"I think there's no time to lose."

"But why me?"

"Use your brains, boy; use your brains. Linnet Ridgeway has never met you; no more has Pennington. If you go by air you may get there in time."

"I—I don't like it, sir. What am I to do?"

"Use your eyes. Use your ears. Use your brains—if you've got any. And, if necessary—act."

"I—I don't like it."

"Perhaps not—but you've got to do it."

"It's—necessary?"

"In my opinion," said Mr. Carmichael, "it's absolutely vital."

XII

Mrs. Otterbourne, readjusting the turban of native material that she wore draped round her head, said fretfully:

"I really don't see why we shouldn't go on to Egypt. I'm sick and tired of Jerusalem."

As her daughter made no reply, she said, "You might at least answer when you're spoken to."

Rosalie Otterbourne was looking at a newspaper reproduction of a face. Below it was printed:

Mrs. Simon Doyle, who before her marriage was the well-known society beauty, Miss Linnet Ridgeway. Mr. and Mrs. Doyle are spending their holiday in Egypt.

Rosalie said, "You'd like to move on to Egypt, Mother?"

"Yes, I would," Mrs. Otterbourne snapped. "I consider they've treated us in a most cavalier fashion here. My being here is an advertisement—I ought to get a special reduction in terms. When I hinted as much, I consider they were most impertinent—*most* impertinent. I told them exactly what I thought of them."

The girl sighed. She said: "One place is very like another. I wish we could get right away."

"And this morning," went on Mrs. Otterbourne, "the manager actually had the impertinence to tell me that all the rooms had been booked in advance and that he would require ours in two days' time."

"So we've got to go somewhere."

"Not at all. I'm quite prepared to fight for my rights."

Rosalie murmured: "I suppose we might as well go on to Egypt. It doesn't make any difference."

"It's certainly not a matter of life or death," agreed Mrs. Otterbourne.

But there she was quite wrong—for a matter of life and death was exactly what it was.

PART II

EGYPT

CHAPTER I

"THAT'S HERCULE POIROT, the detective," said Mrs. Allerton.

She and her son were sitting in brightly painted scarlet basket chairs outside the Cataract Hotel at Assuan. They were watching the retreating figures of two people—a short man dressed in a white silk suit and a tall slim girl.

Tim Allerton sat up in an unusually alert fashion.

"That funny little man?" he asked incredulously.

"That funny little man!"

"What on earth's he doing out here?" Tim asked.

His mother laughed. "Darling, you sound quite excited. Why do men enjoy crime so much? I hate detective stories and never read them. But I don't think Monsieur Poirot is here with any ulterior motive. He's made a good deal of money and he's seeing life, I fancy."

"Seems to have an eye for the best looking girl in the place."

Mrs. Allerton tilted her head a little on one side as she considered the retreating backs of M. Poirot and his companion.

The girl by his side overtopped him by some three inches. She walked well, neither stiffly nor slouchingly.

"I suppose she *is* quite good-looking," said Mrs. Allerton.

She shot a little glance sideways at Tim. Somewhat to her amusement the fish rose at once.

"She's more than quite. Pity she looks so bad-tempered and sulky."

"Perhaps that's just expression, dear."

"Unpleasant young devil, I think. But she's pretty enough."

The subject of these remarks was walking slowly by Poirot's side. Rosalie Otterbourne was twirling an unopened parasol, and her expression certainly bore out what Tim had just said. She looked both sulky and bad-tempered. Her eyebrows were drawn together in a frown, and the scarlet line of her mouth was drawn downward.

They turned to the left out of the hotel gate and entered the cool shade of the public gardens.

Hercule Poirot was prattling gently, his expression that of beatific good humour. He wore a white silk suit, carefully pressed, and a panama hat and carried a highly ornamental fly whisk with a sham amber handle.

"—it enchants me," he was saying. "The black rocks of Elephantine, and the sun, and the little boats on the river. Yes, it is good to be alive."

He paused and then added, "You do not find it so, Mademoiselle?"

Rosalie Otterbourne said shortly: "It's all right, I suppose. I think Assuan's a gloomy sort of place. The hotel's half empty, and everyone's about a hundred—"

She stopped—biting her lip.

Hercule Poirot's eyes twinkled.

"It is true, yes, I have one leg in the grave."

"I—I wasn't thinking of you," said the girl. "I'm sorry. That sounded rude."

"Not at all. It is natural you should wish for companions of your own age. Ah, well, there is *one* young man, at least."

"The one who sits with his mother all the time? I like *her*—but I think he looks dreadful—so conceited!"

Poirot smiled.

"And I—am I conceited?"

"Oh, I don't think so."

She was obviously uninterested—but the fact did not seem to annoy Poirot. He merely remarked with placid satisfaction, "My best friend says that I am very conceited."

"Oh, well," said Rosalie vaguely, "I suppose you have something to be conceited about. Unfortunately crime doesn't interest me in the least."

Poirot said solemnly, "I am delighted to learn that you have no guilty secret to hide."

Just for a moment the sulky mask of her face was transformed as she shot him a swift questioning glance. Poirot did not seem to notice it as he went on:

"Madame, your mother, was not at lunch today. She is not indisposed, I trust?"

"This place doesn't suit her," said Rosalie briefly. "I shall be glad when we leave."

"We are fellow passengers, are we not? We both make the excursion up to Wâdi Halfa and the Second Cataract?"

"Yes."

They came out from the shade of the gardens onto a dusty stretch of road bordered by the river. Five watchful bead sellers, two vendors of postcards, three sellers of plaster scarabs, a couple of donkey boys and some detached but hopeful infantile riff-raff closed in upon them.

"You want beads, sir? Very good, sir. Very cheap. . . ."

"Lady, you want scarab? Look—great queen—very lucky. . . ."

"You look, sir—real lapis. Very good, very cheap. . . ."

"You want ride donkey, sir? This very good donkey. This donkey Whisky and Soda, sir. . . ."

"You want to go granite quarries, sir? This very good donkey. Other donkey very bad, sir, that donkey fall down. . . ."

"You want postcard—very cheap—very nice. . . ."

"Look, lady. . . . Only ten piastres—very cheap—lapis—this ivory. . . ."

"This very good fly whisk—this all amber. . . ."

"You go out in boat, sir? I got very good boat, sir. . . ."

"You ride back to hotel, lady? This first class donkey. . . ."

Hercule Poirot made vague gestures to rid himself of this human cluster of flies. Rosalie stalked through them like a sleep walker.

"It's best to pretend to be deaf and blind," she remarked.

The infantile riff-raff ran alongside murmuring plaintively: "Bakshish? Bakshish? Hip hip hurrah—very good, very nice. . . ."

Their gaily coloured rags trailed picturesquely, and the flies lay in clusters on their eyelids. They were the most persistent. The others fell back and launched a fresh attack on the next comer.

Now Poirot and Rosalie only ran the gauntlet of the shops—suave, persuasive accents here. . . .

"You visit my shop today, sir?" "You want that ivory crocodile, sir?" "You not been in my shop yet, sir? I show you very beautiful things."

They turned into the fifth shop and Rosalie handed over several rolls of films—the object of the walk.

Then they came out again and walked toward the river's edge.

One of the Nile steamers was just mooring. Poirot and Rosalie looked interestedly at the passengers.

"Quite a lot, aren't there?" commented Rosalie.

She turned her head as Tim Allerton came up and joined them. He was a little out of breath as though he had been walking fast.

They stood there for a moment or two and then Tim spoke.

"An awful crowd as usual, I suppose," he remarked disparagingly, indicating the disembarking passengers.

"They're usually quite terrible," agreed Rosalie.

All three wore the air of superiority assumed by people who are already in a place when studying new arrivals.

"Hullo!" exclaimed Tim, his voice suddenly excited. "I'm damned if that isn't Linnet Ridgeway."

If the information left Poirot unmoved, it stirred Rosalie's interest. She leaned forward and her sulkiness quite dropped from her as she asked: "Where? That one in white?"

"Yes, there with the tall man. They're coming ashore now. He's the new husband, I suppose. Can't remember her name now."

"Doyle," said Rosalie. "Simon Doyle. It was in all the newspapers. She's simply rolling, isn't she?"

"Only about the richest girl in England," replied Tim cheerfully.

The three lookers-on were silent watching the passengers come ashore. Poirot gazed with interest at the subject of the remarks of his companions. He murmured, "She is beautiful."

"Some people have got everything," said Rosalie bitterly.

There was a queer grudging expression on her face as she watched the other girl come up the gangplank.

Linnet Doyle was looking as perfectly turned out as if she were stepping onto the centre of the stage of a Revue. She had something too of the assurance of a famous actress. She was used to being looked at, to being admired, to being the centre of the stage wherever she went.

She was aware of the keen glances bent upon her—and at the same time almost unaware of them; such tributes were part of her life.

She came ashore playing a rôle, even though she played it unconsciously. The rich beautiful society bride on her honeymoon. She turned, with a little smile and a light remark, to the tall man by her side. He answered, and the sound of his voice seemed to interest Hercule Poirot. His eyes lit up and he drew his brows together.

The couple passed close to him. He heard Simon Doyle say:

"We'll try and make time for it, darling. We can easily stay a week or two if you like it here."

His face was turned toward her, eager, adoring, a little humble.

Poirot's eyes ran over him thoughtfully—the square shoulders, the bronzed face, the dark blue eyes, the rather childlike simplicity of the smile.

"Lucky devil," said Tim after they had passed. "Fancy finding an heiress who hasn't got adenoids and flat feet!"

"They look frightfully happy," said Rosalie with a note of envy in her voice. She added suddenly, but so low that Tim did not catch the words, "It isn't fair."

Poirot heard, however. He had been frowning somewhat perplexedly but now he flashed a quick glance toward her.

Tim said, "I must collect some stuff for my mother now."

He raised his hat and moved off. Poirot and Rosalie retraced their steps slowly in the direction of the hotel, waving aside fresh proffers of donkeys.

"So it is not fair, Mademoiselle?" asked Poirot gently.

The girl flushed angrily.

"I don't know what you mean."

"I am repeating what you said just now under your breath. Oh, yes, you did."

Rosalie Otterbourne shrugged her shoulders.

"It really seems a little too much for one person. Money, good looks, marvellous figure and—"

She paused and Poirot said:

"And love? Eh? And love? But you do not know—she may have been married for her money!"

"Didn't you see the way he looked at her?"

"Oh, yes, Mademoiselle. I saw all there was to see—indeed I saw something that you did not."

"What was that?"

Poirot said slowly: "I saw, Mademoiselle, dark lines below a woman's eyes. I saw a hand that clutched a sunshade so tight that the knuckles were white. . . ."

Rosalie was staring at him.

"What do you mean?"

"I mean that all is not the gold that glitters. I mean that, though this lady is rich and beautiful and beloved, there is all the same *something* that is not right. And I know something else."

"Yes?"

"I know," said Poirot, frowning, "that somewhere, at some time, I have heard that voice before—the voice of Monsieur Doyle—and I wish I could remember where."

But Rosalie was not listening. She had stopped dead. With the point of her sunshade she was tracing patterns in the loose sand. Suddenly she broke out fiercely:

"I'm odious. I'm quite odious. I'm just a beast through and through. I'd like to tear the clothes off her back and stamp on her lovely, arrogant, self-confident face. I'm just a jealous cat—but that's what I feel like. She's so horribly successful and poised and assured."

Hercule Poirot looked a little astonished by the outburst. He took her by the arm and gave her a friendly little shake.

"*Tenez*—you will feel better for having said that!"

"I just hate her! I've never hated anyone so much at first sight."

"Magnificent!"

Rosalie looked at him doubtfully. Then her mouth twitched and she laughed.

"*Bien,*" said Poirot, and laughed too.

They proceeded amicably back to the hotel.

"I must find Mother," said Rosalie, as they came into the cool, dim hall.

Poirot passed out on the other side onto the terrace overlooking the Nile. Here were little tables set for tea, but it was early still. He stood for a few moments looking at the river, then strolled down through the gardens.

Some people were playing tennis in the hot sun. He paused to watch them for a while, then went on down the steep path. It was there, sitting on a bench overlooking the Nile, that he came upon the girl of Chez Ma Tante. He recognized her at once. Her face, as he had seen it that night, was securely etched upon his memory. The expression on it now was very different. She was paler, thinner, and there were lines that told of a great weariness and misery of spirit.

He drew back a little. She had not seen him, and he watched her for a while without her suspecting his presence. Her small foot tapped impatiently on the ground. Her eyes, dark with a kind of smouldering fire, had a queer kind of suffering dark triumph in them. She was looking out across the Nile where the white-sailed boats glided up and down the river.

A face—and a voice. He remembered them both. This girl's face and the voice he had heard just now, the voice of a newly made bridegroom. . . .

And even as he stood there considering the unconscious girl, the next scene in the drama was played.

Voices sounded above. The girl on the seat started to her feet. Linnet Doyle and her husband came down the path. Linnet's voice was happy and confident. The look of strain and tenseness of muscle had quite disappeared. Linnet was happy.

The girl who was standing there took a step or two forward. The other two stopped dead.

"Hullo, Linnet," said Jacqueline de Bellefort. "So here you are! We

19426 lee

Date Requested: 2015/02/18 16:37:28
Date Delivered: 2015/02/18 16:45:25

# of items in request: 1
# of items not found: 0

Items in Request:

FICTION MYSTERY CHRIS
Perilous journeys of Hercule Poirot; including T
he mystery of the blue train, Death on the Nile,
 and Murder in Mesopotamia
Christie, Agatha, 1890-1976.

never seem to stop running into each other. Hullo, Simon, how are you?"

Linnet Doyle had shrunk back against the rock with a little cry. Simon Doyle's good-looking face was suddenly convulsed with rage. He moved forward as though he would have liked to strike the slim girlish figure.

With a quick birdlike turn of her head she signalled her realization of a stranger's presence. Simon turned his head and noticed Poirot. He said awkwardly, "Hullo, Jacqueline; we didn't expect to see you here."

The words were unconvincing in the extreme.

The girl flashed white teeth at them.

"Quite a surprise?" she asked. Then, with a little nod, she walked up the path.

Poirot moved delicately in the opposite direction. As he went he heard Linnet Doyle say:

"Simon—for God's sake! Simon—what can we do?"

CHAPTER II

DINNER WAS OVER. The terrace outside the Cataract Hotel was softly lit. Most of the guests staying at the hotel were there sitting at little tables.

Simon and Linnet Doyle came out, a tall, distinguished looking grey-haired man, with a keen, clean-shaven American face, beside them.

As the little group hesitated for a moment in the doorway, Tim Allerton rose from his chair near by and came forward.

"You don't remember me, I'm sure," he said pleasantly to Linnet, "but I'm Joanna Southwood's cousin."

"Of course—how stupid of me! You're Tim Allerton. This is my husband"—a faint tremor in the voice, pride, shyness?—"and this is my American trustee, Mr. Pennington."

Tim said, "You must meet my mother."

A few minutes later they were sitting together in a party—Linnet in the corner, Tim and Pennington each side of her, both talking to her, vying for her attention. Mrs. Allerton talked to Simon Doyle.

The swing doors revolved. A sudden tension came into the beautiful upright figure sitting in the corner between the two men. Then it relaxed as a small man came out and walked across the terrace.

Mrs. Allerton said: "You're not the only celebrity here, my dear. That funny little man is Hercule Poirot."

She had spoken lightly, just out of instinctive social tact to bridge an awkward pause, but Linnet seemed struck by the information.

"Hercule Poirot? Of course—I've heard of him. . . ."

She seemed to sink into a fit of abstraction. The two men on either side of her were momentarily at a loss.

Poirot had strolled across to the edge of the terrace, but his attention was immediately solicited.

"Sit down, Monsieur Poirot. What a lovely night."

He obeyed.

"*Mais oui, Madame,* it is indeed beautiful."

He smiled politely at Mrs. Otterbourne. What draperies of black ninon and that ridiculous turban effect! Mrs. Otterbourne went on in her high complaining voice:

"Quite a lot of notabilities here now, aren't there? I expect we shall see a paragraph about it in the papers soon. Society beauties, famous novelists—"

She paused with a slight mock-modest laugh.

Poirot felt, rather than saw, the sulky frowning girl opposite him flinch and set her mouth in a sulkier line than before.

"You have a novel on the way at present, Madame?" he inquired.

Mrs. Otterbourne gave her little self-conscious laugh again.

"I'm being dreadfully lazy. I really must set to. My public is getting terribly impatient—and my publisher, poor man! Appeals by every post! Even cables!"

Again he felt the girl shift in the darkness.

"I don't mind telling you, Monsieur Poirot, I am partly here for local colour. *Snow on the Desert's Face*—that is the title of my new book. Powerful—suggestive. Snow—on the desert—melted in the first flaming breath of passion."

Rosalie got up, muttering something, and moved away down into the dark garden.

"One must be strong," went on Mrs. Otterbourne, wagging the turban emphatically. "Strong meat—that is what my books are—all important. Libraries banned—no matter! I speak the truth. Sex—ah! Monsieur Poirot—why is everyone so afraid of sex? The pivot of the universe! You have read my books?"

"Alas, Madame! You comprehend, I do not read many novels. My work—"

Mrs. Otterbourne said firmly: "I must give you a copy of *Under the Fig Tree*. I think you will find it significant. It is outspoken—but it is *real!*"

"That is most kind of you, Madame. I will read it with pleasure."

Mrs. Otterbourne was silent a minute or two. She fidgeted with a long chain of beads that was wound twice round her neck. She looked swiftly from side to side.

"Perhaps—I'll just slip up and get it for you now."

"Oh, Madame, pray do not trouble yourself. Later—"

"No, no. It's no trouble." She rose. "I'd like to show you—"

"What is it, Mother?"

Rosalie was suddenly at her side.

"Nothing, dear. I was just going up to get a book for Monsieur Poirot."

"The *Fig Tree?* I'll get it."

"You don't know where it is, dear. I'll go."

"Yes, I do."

The girl went swiftly across the terrace and into the hotel.

"Let me congratulate you, Madame, on a very lovely daughter," said Poirot, with a bow.

"Rosalie? Yes, yes—she is good-looking. But she's very *hard,* Monsieur Poirot. And no sympathy with illness. She always thinks she knows best. She imagines she knows more about my health than I do myself—"

Poirot signalled to a passing waiter.

"A liqueur, Madame? A chartreuse? A crème de menthe?"

Mrs. Otterbourne shook her head vigorously.

"No, no. I am practically a teetotaller. You may have noticed I never drink anything but water—or perhaps lemonade. I cannot bear the taste of spirits."

"Then may I order you a lemon squash, Madame?"

He gave the order—one lemon squash and one Benedictine.

The swing door revolved. Rosalie passed through and came toward them, a book in her hand.

"Here you are," she said. Her voice was quite expressionless—almost remarkably so.

"Monsieur Poirot has just ordered me a lemon squash," said her mother.

"And you, Mademoiselle, what will you take?"

"Nothing." She added, suddenly conscious of the curtness, "Nothing, thank you."

Poirot took the volume which Mrs. Otterbourne held out to him. It still bore its original jacket, a gaily coloured affair representing a lady, with smartly shingled hair and scarlet fingernails, sitting on a tiger skin, in the traditional costume of Eve. Above her was a tree with the leaves of an oak, bearing large and improbably coloured apples.

It was entitled *Under the Fig Tree,* by Salome Otterbourne. On the inside was a publisher's blurb. It spoke enthusiastically of the superb courage and realism of this study of a modern woman's love life. "Fearless, unconventional, realistic," were the adjectives used.

Poirot bowed and murmured, "I am honoured, Madame."

As he raised his head, his eyes met those of the authoress's daughter. Almost involuntarily he made a little movement. He was astonished and grieved at the eloquent pain they revealed.

It was at that moment that the drinks arrived and created a welcome diversion.

Poirot lifted his glass gallantly.

"*A votre santé, Madame—Mademoiselle.*"

Mrs. Otterbourne, sipping her lemonade, murmured, "So refreshing—delicious!"

Silence fell on the three of them. They looked down to the shining black rocks in the Nile. There was something fantastic about them in the moonlight. They were like vast prehistoric monsters lying half out of the water. A little breeze came up suddenly and as suddenly died away. There was a feeling in the air of hush—of expectancy.

Hercule Poirot brought his gaze back to the terrace and its occupants. Was he wrong, or was there the same hush of expectancy there? It was like a moment on the stage when one is waiting for the entrance of the leading lady.

And just at that moment the swing doors began to revolve once more. This time it seemed as though they did so with a special air of importance. Everyone had stopped talking and was looking toward them.

A dark slender girl in a wine coloured evening frock came through. She paused for a minute, then walked deliberately across the terrace and sat down at an empty table. There was nothing flaunting, nothing out of the way about her demeanour, and yet it had somehow the studied effect of a stage entrance.

"Well," said Mrs. Otterbourne. She tossed her turbaned head. "She seems to think she is somebody, that girl!"

Poirot did not answer. He was watching. The girl had sat down in a place where she could look deliberately across at Linnet Doyle. Presently, Poirot noticed, Linnet Doyle leant forward and said something and a moment later got up and changed her seat. She was now sitting facing in the opposite direction.

Poirot nodded thoughtfully to himself.

It was about five minutes later that the other girl changed her seat to the opposite side of the terrace. She sat smoking and smiling quietly, the picture of contented ease. But always, as though unconsciously, her meditative gaze was on Simon Doyle's wife.

After a quarter of an hour Linnet Doyle got up abruptly and went into the hotel. Her husband followed her almost immediately.

Jacqueline de Bellefort smiled and twisted her chair round. She lit a cigarette and stared out over the Nile. She went on smiling to herself.

CHAPTER III

"MONSIEUR POIROT."

Poirot got hastily to his feet. He had remained sitting out on the terrace alone after everyone else had left. Lost in meditation he had been staring at the smooth shiny black rocks when the sound of his name recalled him to himself.

It was a well-bred, assured voice, a charming voice, although perhaps a trifle arrogant.

Hercule Poirot, rising quickly, looked into the commanding eyes of Linnet Doyle. She wore a wrap of rich purple velvet over her white satin gown and she looked more lovely and more regal than Poirot had imagined possible.

"You are Monsieur Hercule Poirot?" said Linnet.

It was hardly a question.

"At your service, Madame."

"You know who I am, perhaps?"

"Yes, Madame. I have heard your name. I know exactly who you are."

Linnet nodded. That was only what she had expected. She went on, in her charming autocratic manner: "Will you come with me into the card room, Monsieur Poirot? I am very anxious to speak to you."

"Certainly, Madame."

She led the way into the hotel. He followed. She led him into the deserted card room and motioned him to close the door. Then she sank down on a chair at one of the tables and he sat down opposite her.

She plunged straightaway into what she wanted to say. There were no hesitations. Her speech came flowingly.

"I have heard a great deal about you, Monsieur Poirot, and I know that you are a very clever man. It happens that I am urgently in need of someone to help me—and I think very possibly that you are the man who could do it."

Poirot inclined his head.

"You are very amiable, Madame, but you see, I am on holiday, and when I am on holiday I do not take cases."

"That could be arranged."

It was not offensively said—only with the quiet confidence of a young woman who had always been able to arrange matters to her satisfaction.

Linnet Doyle went on: "I am the subject, Monsieur Poirot, of an intolerable persecution. That persecution has got to stop! My own idea was to go to the police about it, but my—my husband seems to think that the police would be powerless to do anything."

"Perhaps—if you would explain a little further?" murmured Poirot politely.

"Oh, yes, I will do so. The matter is perfectly simple."

There was still no hesitation—no faltering. Linnet Doyle had a clear-cut businesslike mind. She only paused a minute so as to present the facts as concisely as possible.

"Before I met my husband, he was engaged to a Miss de Bellefort. She was also a friend of mine. My husband broke off his engagement to her—they were not suited in any way. She, I am sorry to say, took it rather hard. . . . I—am very sorry about that—but these things cannot be helped. She made certain—well, threats—to which I paid very little attention, and which, I may say, she has not attempted to carry out. But instead she has adopted the extraordinary course of—of following us about wherever we go."

Poirot raised his eyebrows.

"Ah—rather an unusual—er—revenge."

"Very unusual—and very ridiculous! But also—annoying."

She bit her lip.

Poirot nodded.

"Yes, I can imagine that. You are, I understand, on your honeymoon?"

"Yes. It happened—the first time—at Venice. She was there—at Danielli's. I thought it was just coincidence. Rather embarrassing, but that was all. Then we found her on board the boat at Brindisi. We—we understood that she was going on to Palestine. We left her, as we thought, on the boat. But—but when we got to Mena House she was there—waiting for us."

Poirot nodded.

"And now?"

"We came up the Nile by boat. I—I was half expecting to find her on board. When she wasn't there I thought she had stopped being so—so childish. But when we got here—she—she was here—waiting."

Poirot eyed her keenly for a moment. She was still perfectly composed, but the knuckles of the hand that was gripping the table were white with the force of her grip.

He said, "And you are afraid this state of things may continue?"

"Yes." She paused. "Of course the whole thing is idiotic! Jacqueline is making herself utterly ridiculous. I am surprised she hasn't got more pride—more dignity."

Poirot made a slight gesture.

"There are times, Madame, when pride and dignity—they go by the board! There are other—stronger emotions."

"Yes, possibly." Linnet spoke impatiently. "But what on earth can she hope to *gain* by all this?"

"It is not always a question of gain, Madame."

Something in his tone struck Linnet disagreeably. She flushed and said quickly: "You are right. A discussion of motives is beside the point. The crux of the matter is that this has got to be stopped."

"And how do you propose that that should be accomplished, Madame?" Poirot asked.

"Well—naturally—my husband and I cannot continue being subjected to this annoyance. There must be some kind of legal redress against such a thing."

She spoke impatiently. Poirot looked at her thoughtfully as he asked: "Has she threatened you in actual words in public? Used insulting language? Attempted any bodily harm?"

"No."

"Then, frankly, Madame, I do not see what you can do. If it is a young lady's pleasure to travel in certain places, and those places are the same where you and your husband find themselves—*eh bien*—what of it? The air is free to all! There is no question of her forcing herself upon your privacy? It is always in public that these encounters take place?"

"You mean there is nothing that I can do about it?"

Linnet sounded incredulous.

Poirot said placidly: "Nothing at all as far as I can see. Mademoiselle de Bellefort is within her rights."

"But—but it is maddening! It is *intolerable* that I should have to put up with this!"

Poirot said drily, "I sympathize with you, Madame—especially as I imagine that you have not often had to put up with things."

Linnet was frowning.

"There *must* be some way of stopping it," she murmured.

Poirot shrugged his shoulders.

"You can always leave—move on somewhere else," he suggested.

"Then she will follow!"

"Very possibly—yes."

"It's absurd!"

"Precisely."

"Anyway, why should I—we—run away? As though—as though—"

She stopped.

"Exactly, Madame. As though—! It is all there, is it not?"

Linnet lifted her head and stared at him.

"What do you mean?"

Poirot altered his tone. He leant forward; his voice was confidential, appealing. He said very gently, "Why do you mind so much, Madame?"

"Why? But it's maddening! Irritating to the last degree! I've told you why!"

Poirot shook his head.

"Not altogether."

"What do you mean?" Linnet asked again.

Poirot leant back, folded his arms and spoke in a detached impersonal manner.

"*Ecoutez,* Madame. I will recount to you a little history. It is that one day, a month or two ago, I am dining in a restaurant in London. At the table next to me are two people, a man and a girl. They are very happy, so it seems, very much in love. They talk with confidence of the future. It is not that I listen to what is not meant for me; they are quite oblivious of who hears them and who does not. The man's back is to me, but I can watch the girl's face. It is very intense. She is in love—heart, soul and body—and she is not of those who love lightly and often. With her it is clearly the life and the death. They are engaged to be married, these two; that is what I gather; and they talk of where they shall pass the days of their honeymoon. They plan to go to Egypt."

He paused. Linnet said sharply, "Well?"

Poirot went on: "That is a month or two ago, but the girl's face—I do not forget it. I know that I shall remember if I see it again. And I remember too the man's voice. And I think you can guess, Madame, when it is I see the one and hear the other again. It is here in Egypt. The man is on his honeymoon, yes—but he is on his honeymoon with another woman."

Linnet said sharply: "What of it? I had already mentioned the facts."

"The facts—yes."

"Well then?"

Poirot said slowly: "The girl in the restaurant mentioned a friend —a friend who, she was very positive, would not let her down. That friend, I think, was you, Madame."

Linnet flushed.

"Yes. I told you we had been friends."

"And she trusted you?"

"Yes."

She hesitated for a moment, biting her lip impatiently; then, as Poirot did not seem disposed to speak, she broke out:

"Of course the whole thing was very unfortunate. But these things happen, Monsieur Poirot."

"Ah! yes, they happen, Madame." He paused. "You are of the Church of England I presume?"

"Yes." Linnet looked slightly bewildered.

"Then you have heard portions of the Bible read aloud in church. You have heard of King David and of the rich man who had many flocks and herds and the poor man who had one ewe lamb—and of how the rich man took the poor man's one ewe lamb. That was something that happened, Madame."

Linnet sat up. Her eyes flashed angrily.

"I see perfectly what you are driving at, Monsieur Poirot! You think, to put it vulgarly, that I stole my friend's young man. Looking at the matter sentimentally—which is, I suppose, the way people of your generation cannot help looking at things—that is possibly true. But the real hard truth is different. I don't deny that Jackie was passionately in love with Simon, but I don't think you take into account that he may not have been equally devoted to her. He was very fond of her, but I think that even before he met me he was beginning to feel that he had made a mistake. Look at it clearly, Monsieur Poirot. Simon discovers that it is I he loves, not Jackie. What is he to do? Be heroically noble and marry a woman he does not care for—and thereby probably ruin three lives—for it is doubtful whether he could make Jackie happy under those circumstances? If he were actually married to her when he met me I agree that it *might* be his duty to stick to her—though I'm not really sure of that. If one person is unhappy the other suffers too. But an engagement is not really binding. If a mistake has been made, then surely it is better to face the fact before it is too late. I admit that it was very hard on Jackie, and I'm terribly sorry about it—but there it is. It was inevitable."

"I wonder."

She stared at him.

"What do you mean?"

"It is very sensible, very logical—all that you say! But it does not explain one thing."

"What is that?"

"Your own attitude, Madame. See you, this pursuit of you, you might take it in two ways. It might cause you annoyance—yes, or it might stir your pity—that your friend should have been so deeply hurt as to throw all regards for the conventions aside. But that is not the way you react. No, to you this persecution is *intolerable*—and why? It can be for one reason only—that you feel a sense of guilt."

Linnet sprang to her feet.

"How dare you? Really, Monsieur Poirot, this is going too far."

"But I do dare, Madame! I am going to speak to you quite frankly. I suggest to you that, although you may have endeavoured to gloss over the fact to yourself, you did deliberately set about taking your husband from your friend. I suggest that you felt strongly attracted to him at once. But I suggest that there was a moment when you hesitated, when you realized that there was a *choice*—that you could refrain or go on. I suggest that the initiative rested with *you*—not with Monsieur Doyle. You are beautiful, Madame; you are rich; you are clever, intelligent—and you have charm. You could have exercised that charm or you could have restrained it. You had everything, Madame, that life can offer. Your friend's life was bound up in one person. You knew that, but, though you hesitated, you did not hold your hand. You stretched it out and, like the rich man in the Bible, you took the poor man's one ewe lamb."

There was a silence. Linnet controlled herself with an effort and said in a cold voice, "All this is quite beside the point!"

"No, it is not beside the point. I am explaining to you just why the unexpected appearances of Mademoiselle de Bellefort have upset you so much. It is because, though she may be unwomanly and undignified in what she is doing, you have the inner conviction that she has right on her side."

"That's not true!"

Poirot shrugged his shoulders.

"You refuse to be honest with yourself."

"Not at all."

Poirot said gently, "I should say, Madame, that you have had a happy life, that you have been generous and kindly in your attitude toward others."

"I have tried to be," said Linnet. The impatient anger died out of her face. She spoke simply—almost forlornly.

"And that is why the feeling that you have deliberately caused injury to someone upsets you so much, and why you are so reluctant to admit the fact. Pardon me if I have been impertinent, but the psychology, it is the most important fact in a case."

Linnet said slowly: "Even supposing what you say were true—and I don't admit it, mind—what can be done about it now? One can't alter the past; one must deal with things as they are."

Poirot nodded.

"You have the clear brain. Yes, one cannot go back over the past. One must accept things as they are. And sometimes, Madame, that is all one can do—accept the consequences of one's past deeds."

"You mean," asked Linnet incredulously, "that I can do nothing—*nothing?*"

"You must have courage, Madame; that is what it seems like to me."

Linnet said slowly:

"Couldn't you—talk to Jackie—to Miss de Bellefort? Reason with her?"

"Yes, I could do that. I will do that if you would like me to do so. But do not expect much result. I fancy that Mademoiselle de Bellefort is so much in the grip of a fixed idea that nothing will turn her from it."

"But surely we can do *something* to extricate ourselves?"

"You could, of course, return to England and establish yourself in your own house."

"Even then, I suppose, Jacqueline is capable of planting herself in the village, so that I should see her every time I went out of the grounds."

"True."

"Besides," said Linnet slowly, "I don't think that Simon would agree to run away."

"What is his attitude in this?"

"He's furious—simply furious."

Poirot nodded thoughtfully.

Linnet said appealingly, "You will—talk to her?"

"Yes, I will do that. But it is my opinion that I shall not be able to accomplish anything."

Linnet said violently: "Jackie is extraordinary! One can't tell what she will do!"

"You spoke just now of certain threats she had made. Would you tell me what those threats were?"

Linnet shrugged her shoulders.

"She threatened to—well—kill us both. Jackie can be rather—Latin sometimes."

"I see." Poirot's tone was grave.

Linnet turned to him appealingly.

"You will act for me?"

"No, Madame." His tone was firm. "I will not accept a commission from you. I will do what I can in the interests of humanity. That, yes. There is here a situation that is full of difficulty and danger. I will do what I can to clear it up—but I am not very sanguine as to my chance of success."

Linnet Doyle said slowly, "But you will not act for *me?*"

"No, Madame," said Hercule Poirot.

CHAPTER IV

HERCULE POIROT FOUND Jacqueline de Bellefort sitting on the rocks directly overlooking the Nile. He had felt fairly certain that she had not retired for the night and that he would find her somewhere about the grounds of the hotel.

She was sitting with her chin cupped in the palms of her hands, and she did not turn her head or look round at the sound of his approach.

"Mademoiselle de Bellefort?" asked Poirot. "You permit that I speak to you for a little moment?"

Jacqueline turned her head slightly. A faint smile played round her lips.

"Certainly," she said. "You are Monsieur Hercule Poirot, I think? Shall I make a guess? You are acting for Mrs. Doyle, who has promised you a large fee if you succeed in your mission."

Poirot sat down on the bench near her.

"Your assumption is partially correct," he said, smiling. "I have just come from Madame Doyle, but I am not accepting any fee from her and, strictly speaking, I am not acting for her."

"Oh!"

Jacqueline studied him attentively.

"Then why have you come?" she asked abruptly.

Hercule Poirot's reply was in the form of another question.

"Have you ever seen me before, Mademoiselle?"

She shook her head.

"No, I do not think so."

"Yet I have seen you. I sat next to you once at Chez Ma Tante. You were there with Monsieur Simon Doyle."

A strange masklike expression came over the girl's face. She said, "I remember that evening. . . ."

"Since then," said Poirot, "many things have occurred."

"As you say, many things have occurred."

Her voice was hard with an undertone of desperate bitterness.

"Mademoiselle, I speak as a friend. Bury your dead!"

She looked startled.

"What do you mean?"

"Give up the past! Turn to the future! What is done is done. Bitterness will not undo it."

"I'm sure that that would suit dear Linnet admirably."

Poirot made a gesture.

"I am not thinking of her at this moment! I am thinking of *you*. You have suffered—yes—but what you are doing now will only prolong that suffering."

She shook her head.

"You're wrong. There are times when I almost enjoy myself."

"And that, Mademoiselle, is the worst of all."

She looked up swiftly.

"You're not stupid," she said. She added slowly, "I believe you mean to be kind."

"Go home, Mademoiselle. You are young; you have brains; the world is before you."

Jacqueline shook her head slowly.

"You don't understand—or you won't. Simon is my world."

"Love is not everything, Mademoiselle," Poirot said gently. "It is only when we are young that we think it is."

But the girl still shook her head.

"You don't understand." She shot him a quick look. "You know all about it, of course? You've talked to Linnet? And you were in the restaurant that night. . . . Simon and I loved each other."

"I know that you loved him."

She was quick to perceive the inflection of his words. She repeated with emphasis:

"*We loved each other*. And I loved Linnet. . . . I trusted her. She was my best friend. All her life Linnet has been able to buy everything she wanted. She's never denied herself anything. When she saw Simon she wanted him—and she just took him."

"And he allowed himself to be—bought?"

Jacqueline shook her dark head slowly.

"No, it's not quite like that. If it were, I shouldn't be here now. . . . You're suggesting that Simon isn't worth caring for. . . . If he'd married Linnet for her money, that would be true. But he didn't marry her for her money. It's more complicated than that. There's such a thing as *glamour*, Monsieur Poirot. And money helps that. Linnet had an 'atmosphere,' you see. She was the queen of a kingdom—the young princess—luxurious to her fingertips. It was like a stage setting. She had the world at her feet, one of the richest and most sought after peers in England wanting to marry her. And she stoops instead to the obscure Simon Doyle. . . . Do you wonder it went to his head?" She made a sudden gesture. "Look at the moon up there. You see her very plainly, don't you? She's very real. But if the sun were to shine you wouldn't be able to see her at all. It was rather like that. I was the moon. . . . When the sun came out, Simon couldn't see me any more. . . . He was dazzled. He couldn't see anything but the sun—Linnet."

She paused and then went on: "So you see it was—glamour. She went to his head. And then there's her complete assurance—her habit of command. She's so sure of herself that she makes other people sure. Simon was weak, perhaps; but then he's a very simple person. He would have loved me and me only if Linnet hadn't come along and snatched him up in her golden chariot. And I know—I know perfectly—that he wouldn't ever have fallen in love with her if she hadn't made him."

"That is what you think—yes."

"I *know* it. He loved me—he will always love me."

Poirot said, "Even now?"

A quick answer seemed to rise to her lips, then be stifled. She looked at Poirot and a deep burning colour spread over her face. She looked away; her head dropped down. She said in a low stifled voice: "Yes, I know. He hates me now. Yes, hates me. . . . He'd better be careful!"

With a quick gesture she fumbled in a little silk bag that lay on the seat. Then she held out her hand. On the palm of it was a small pearl-handled pistol—a dainty toy it looked.

"Nice little thing, isn't it?" she said. "Looks too foolish to be real, but it is real! One of those bullets would kill a man or a woman. And I'm a good shot." She smiled a faraway, reminiscent smile. "When I went home as a child with my mother, to South Carolina, my grandfather taught me to shoot. He was the old-fashioned kind that believes in shooting—especially where honour is concerned. My father, too, he fought several duels as a young man. He was a good swordsman. He killed a man once. That was over a woman. So you see, Monsieur Poirot"—she met his eyes squarely—"I've hot blood in me! I bought this when it first happened. I meant to kill one or other of them—the trouble was I couldn't decide which. Both of them would have been unsatisfactory. If I'd thought Linnet would have looked afraid—but she's got plenty of physical courage. She can stand up to physical action. And then I thought I'd—wait! That appealed to me more and more. After all, I could do it any time; it would be more fun to wait and—think about it! And then this idea came to my mind—to follow them! Whenever they arrived at some faraway spot and were together and happy, they should see *Me!* And it worked! It got Linnet badly—in a way nothing else could have done! It got right under her skin. . . . That was when I began to enjoy myself. . . . And there's nothing she can do about it! I'm always perfectly pleasant and polite! There's not a word they can take hold of! It's poisoning everything—everything—for them."

Her laugh rang out, clear and silvery.

Poirot grasped her arm.

"Be quiet. Quiet, I tell you."

Jacqueline looked at him.

"Well?" she asked. Her smile was definitely challenging.

"Mademoiselle, I beseech you, do not do what you are doing."

"Leave dear Linnet alone, you mean?"

"It is deeper than that. Do not open your heart to evil."

Her lips fell apart; a look of bewilderment came into her eyes.

Poirot went on gravely: "Because—if you do—evil will come. . . . Yes, very surely evil will come. . . . It will enter in and make its home within you, and after a little while it will no longer be possible to drive it out."

Jacqueline stared at him. Her glance seemed to waver, to flicker uncertainly.

She said, "I—don't know—" Then she cried out defiantly, "You can't stop me."

"No," said Hercule Poirot. "I cannot stop you." His voice was sad.

"Even if I were to—kill her, you couldn't stop me."

"No—not if you were willing to pay the price."

Jacqueline de Bellefort laughed.

"Oh, I'm not afraid of death! What have I got to live for, after all? I suppose you believe it's very wrong to kill a person who has injured you—even if they've taken away everything you had in the world?"

Poirot said steadily: "Yes, Mademoiselle. I believe it is the unforgivable offense—to kill."

Jacqueline laughed again.

"Then you ought to approve of my present scheme of revenge; because, you see, as long as it works, I shan't use that pistol. . . . But I'm afraid—yes, afraid sometimes—it all goes red—I want to hurt her—to stick a knife into her, to put my dear little pistol close against her head and then—just press with my finger— *Oh!*"

The exclamation startled him.

"What is it, Mademoiselle?"

She had turned her head and was staring into the shadows.

"Someone—standing over there. He's gone now."

Hercule Poirot looked round sharply.

The place seemed quite deserted.

"There seems no one here but ourselves, Mademoiselle." He got up. "In any case I have said all I came to say. I wish you good-night."

Jacqueline got up too. She said almost pleadingly, "You do understand—that I can't do what you ask me to do?"

Poirot shook his head.

"No—for you could do it! There is always a moment! Your friend Linnet—there was a moment, too, in which she could have held her hand. . . . She let it pass by. And if one does that, then one is committed to the enterprise and there comes no second chance."

"No second chance. . . ." said Jacqueline de Bellefort.

She stood brooding for a moment; then she lifted her head defiantly.

"Good-night, Monsieur Poirot."

He shook his head sadly and followed her up the path to the hotel.

CHAPTER V

On the following morning Simon Doyle joined Hercule Poirot as the latter was leaving the hotel to walk down to the town.

"Good-morning, Monsieur Poirot."

"Good-morning, Monsieur Doyle."

"You going to the town? Mind if I stroll along with you?"

"But certainly. I shall be delighted."

The two men walked side by side, passed out through the gateway and turned into the cool shade of the gardens. Then Simon removed his pipe from his mouth and said, "I understand, Monsieur Poirot, that my wife had a talk with you last night?"

"That is so."

Simon Doyle was frowning a little. He belonged to that type of men of action who find it difficult to put thoughts into words and who have trouble in expressing themselves clearly.

"I'm glad of one thing," he said. "You've made her realize that we're more or less powerless in the matter."

"There is clearly no legal redress," agreed Poirot.

"Exactly. Linnet didn't seem to understand that." He gave a faint smile. "Linnet's been brought up to believe that every annoyance can automatically be referred to the police."

"It would be pleasant if such were the case," said Poirot.

There was a pause. Then Simon said suddenly, his face going very red as he spoke:

"It's—it's infamous that she should be victimized like this! She's done nothing! If anyone likes to say I behaved like a cad, they're welcome to say so! I suppose I did. But I won't have the whole thing visited on Linnet. She had nothing whatever to do with it."

Poirot bowed his head gravely but said nothing.

"Did you—er—have you—talked to Jackie—Miss de Bellefort?"

"Yes, I have spoken with her."

"Did you get her to see sense?"

"I'm afraid not."

Simon broke out irritably: "Can't she see what an ass she's making of herself? Doesn't she realize that no decent woman would behave as she is doing? Hasn't she got any pride or self-respect?"

Poirot shrugged his shoulders.

"She has only a sense of—injury, shall we say?" he replied.

"Yes, but damn it all, man, decent girls don't behave like this! I admit I was entirely to blame. I treated her damned badly and all that. I should quite understand her being thoroughly fed up with me and never wishing to see me again. But this following me round—it's—it's *indecent!* Making a show of herself! What the devil does she hope to get out of it?"

"Perhaps—revenge!"

"Idiotic! I'd really understand better if she'd tried to do something melodramatic—like taking a pot shot at me."

"You think that would be more like her—yes?"

"Frankly I do. She's hot-blooded—and she's got an ungovernable temper. I shouldn't be surprised at her doing anything while she was in a white-hot rage. But this spying business—" He shook his head.

"It is more subtle—yes! It is intelligent!"

Doyle stared at him.

"You don't understand. It's playing hell with Linnet's nerves."

"And yours?"

Simon looked at him with momentary surprise.

"Me? I'd like to wring the little devil's neck."

"There is nothing, then, of the old feeling left?"

"My dear Monsieur Poirot—how can I put it? It's like the moon when the sun comes out. You don't know it's there any more. When once I'd met Linnet—Jackie didn't exist."

"*Tiens, c'est drôle ça!*" muttered Poirot.

"I beg your pardon."

"Your simile interested me, that is all."

Again flushing, Simon said: "I suppose Jackie told you that I'd only married Linnet for her money? Well, that's a damned lie! I wouldn't marry any woman for money! What Jackie doesn't understand is that it's difficult for a fellow when—when—a woman cares for him as she cared for me."

"Ah?"

Poirot looked up sharply.

Simon blundered on, "It—it—sounds a caddish thing to say, but Jackie was *too* fond of me!"

"*Un qui aime et un qui se laisse aimer,*" murmured Poirot.

"Eh? What's that you say? You see a man doesn't want to feel that a woman cares more for him than he does for her." His voice grew warm as he went on. "He doesn't want to feel *owned,* body and soul. It's that damned *possessive* attitude! This man is *mine*—he *be-*

longs to me! That's the sort of thing I can't stick—no man could stick! He wants to get away—to get free. He wants to own his woman; he doesn't want *her* to own *him.*"

He broke off, and with fingers that trembled slightly he lit a cigarette.

Poirot said, "And it is like that that you felt with Mademoiselle Jacqueline?"

"Eh?" Simon stared and then admitted: "Er—yes—well, yes, as a matter of fact I did. She doesn't realize that, of course. And it's not the sort of thing I could ever tell her. But I *was* feeling restless—and then I met Linnet, and she just swept me off my feet! I'd never seen anything so lovely. It was all so amazing. Everyone kowtowing to her—and then her singling out a poor chump like me."

His tone held boyish awe and astonishment.

"I see," said Poirot. He nodded thoughtfully. "Yes—I see."

"Why can't Jackie take it like a man?" demanded Simon resentfully.

A very faint smile twitched Poirot's upper lip.

"Well, you see, Monsieur Doyle, to begin with she is *not* a man."

"No, no—but I meant take it like a good sport! After all, you've got to take your medicine when it comes to you. The fault's all mine, I admit. But there it is! If you no longer care for a girl, it's simply madness to marry her. And, now that I see what Jackie's really like and the lengths she is likely to go to, I feel I've had rather a lucky escape."

"The lengths she is likely to go to," Poirot repeated thoughtfully. "Have you an idea, Monsieur Doyle, what those lengths are?"

Simon looked at him, rather startled.

"No—at least, what do you mean?"

"You know she carries a pistol about with her."

Simon frowned, then shook his head.

"I don't believe she'll use that—now. She might have done so earlier. But I believe it's got past that. She's just spiteful now—trying to take it out of us both."

Poirot shrugged his shoulders.

"It may be so," he said doubtfully.

"It's Linnet I'm worrying about," declared Simon, somewhat unnecessarily.

"I quite realize that," said Poirot.

"I'm not really afraid of Jackie doing any melodramatic shooting stuff, but this spying and following business has absolutely got Linnet on the raw. I'll tell you the plan I've made, and perhaps you can suggest improvements on it. To begin with, I've announced fairly openly that we're going to stay here ten days. But tomorrow the steamer *Karnak* starts from Shellâl to Wâdi Halfa. I propose to book passages on that under an assumed name. Tomorrow we'll go on an excursion to Philae. Linnet's maid can take the luggage. We'll join the *Karnak* at Shellâl. When Jackie finds we don't come back, it will be too late—we shall be well on our way. She'll assume we have given her the slip and gone back to Cairo. In fact I might even bribe the porter to say so. Inquiry at the tourist offices won't help her, because our names won't appear. How does that strike you?"

"It is well imagined, yes. And suppose she waits here till you return?"

"We may not return. We could go on to Khartûm and then perhaps by air to Kenya. She can't follow us all over the globe."

"No; there must come a time when financial reasons forbid. She has very little money, I understand."

Simon looked at him with admiration.

"That's clever of you. Do you know, I hadn't thought of that. Jackie's as poor as they make them."

"And yet she has managed to follow you so far?"

Simon said doubtfully:

"She's got a small income, of course. Something under two hundred a year, I imagine. I suppose—yes, I suppose she must have sold out the capital to do what she's doing."

"So that the time will come when she has exhausted her resources and is quite penniless?"

"Yes. . . ."

Simon wriggled uneasily. The thought seemed to make him uncomfortable. Poirot watched him attentively.

"No," he remarked. "No, it is not a pretty thought. . . ."

Simon said rather angrily, "Well, *I* can't help it!" Then he added, "What do you think of my plan?"

"I think it may work, yes. But it is, of course, a *retreat.*"

Simon flushed.

"You mean, we're running away? Yes, that's true. . . . But Linnet—"

Poirot watched him, then gave a short nod.

"As you say, it may be the best way. But remember, Mademoiselle de Bellefort has brains."

Simon said sombrely: "Someday, I feel, we've got to make a stand and fight it out. Her attitude isn't reasonable."

"Reasonable, *mon Dieu!*" cried Poirot.

"There's no reason why women shouldn't behave like rational beings," Simon asserted stolidly.

Poirot said drily: "Quite frequently they do. That is even more upsetting!" He added: "I, too, shall be on the *Karnak*. It is part of my itinerary."

"Oh!" Simon hesitated, then said, choosing his words with some embarrassment: "That isn't—isn't—er—on our account in any way? I mean I wouldn't like to think—"

Poirot disabused him quickly.

"Not at all. It was all arranged before I left London. I always make my plans well in advance."

"You don't just move on from place to place as the fancy takes you? Isn't the latter really pleasanter?"

"Perhaps. But to succeed in life every detail should be arranged well beforehand."

Simon laughed and said, "That is how the more skilful murderer behaves, I suppose."

"Yes—though I must admit that the most brilliant crime I remember and one of the most difficult to solve was committed on the spur of the moment."

Simon said boyishly, "You must tell us something about your cases on board the *Karnak*."

"No, no; that would be to talk—what do you call it—the shop."

"Yes, but your kind of shop is rather thrilling. Mrs. Allerton thinks so. She's longing to get a chance to cross-question you."

"Mrs. Allerton? That is the charming grey-haired woman who has such a devoted son?"

"Yes. She'll be on the *Karnak* too."

"Does she know that you—?"

"Certainly not," said Simon with emphasis. "Nobody knows. I've gone on the principle that it's better not to trust anybody."

"An admirable sentiment—and one which I always adopt. By the way, the third member of your party, the tall grey-haired man—"

"Pennington?"

"Yes. He is travelling with you?"

Simon said grimly: "Not very usual on a honeymoon, you were thinking? Pennington is Linnet's American trustee. We ran across him by chance in Cairo."

"*Ah vraiment!* You permit a question? She is of age, Madame your wife?"

Simon looked amused.

"She isn't actually twenty-one yet—but she hadn't got to ask anyone's consent before marrying me. It was the greatest surprise to Pennington. He left New York on the *Carmanic* two days before Linnet's letter got there telling him of our marriage, so he knew nothing about it."

"The *Carmanic*—" murmured Poirot.

"It was the greatest surprise to him when we ran into him at Shepheard's in Cairo."

"That was indeed the coincidence!"

"Yes, and we found that he was coming on this Nile trip—so naturally we foregathered; couldn't have done anything else decently. Besides that, it's been—well, a relief in some ways." He looked embarrassed again. "You see Linnet's been all strung up—expecting Jackie to turn up anywhere and everywhere. While we were alone together, the subject kept coming up. Andrew Pennington's a help that way; we have to talk of outside matters."

"Your wife has not confided in Mr. Pennington?"

"No." Simon's jaw looked aggressive. "It's nothing to do with anyone else. Besides, when we started on this Nile trip we thought we'd seen the end of the business."

Poirot shook his head.

"You have not seen the end of it yet. No—the end is not yet at hand. I am very sure of that."

"I say, Monsieur Poirot, you're not very encouraging."

Poirot looked at him with a slight feeling of irritation. He thought to himself: "The Anglo Saxon, he takes nothing seriously but playing games! He does not grow up."

Linnet Doyle—Jacqueline de Bellefort—both of them took the business seriously enough. But in Simon's attitude he could find nothing but male impatience and annoyance. He said: "You will permit me an impertinent question? Was it your idea to come to Egypt for your honeymoon?"

Simon flushed.

"No, of course not. As a matter of fact I'd rather have gone anywhere else, but Linnet was absolutely set upon it. And so—and so—"

He stopped rather lamely.

"Naturally," said Poirot gravely.

He appreciated the fact that, if Linnet Doyle was set upon anything, that thing had to happen.

He thought to himself: "I have now heard three separate accounts of the affair—Linnet Doyle's, Jacqueline de Bellefort's, Simon Doyle's. Which of them is nearest to the truth?"

CHAPTER VI

SIMON AND LINNET DOYLE set off on their expedition to Philae about eleven o'clock the following morning. Jacqueline de Bellefort, sitting on the hotel balcony, watched them set off in the picturesque sailing boat. What she did not see was the departure of a car—laden with luggage, and in which sat a demure-looking maid—from the front door of the hotel. It turned to the right in the direction of Shellâl.

Hercule Poirot decided to pass the remaining two hours before lunch on the island of Elephantine, immediately opposite the hotel.

He went down to the landing stage. There were two men just stepping into one of the hotel boats, and Poirot joined them. The men were obviously strangers to each other. The younger of them had arrived by train the day before. He was a tall, dark-haired young man, with a thin face and a pugnacious chin. He was wearing an extremely dirty pair of grey flannel trousers and a high-necked polo jumper singularly unsuited to the climate. The other was a slightly podgy middle-aged man who lost no time in entering into conversation with Poirot in idiomatic but slightly broken English. Far from taking part in the conversation, the younger man merely scowled at them both and then deliberately turned his back on them and proceeded to admire the agility with which the Nubian boatman steered the boat with his toes as he manipulated the sail with his hands.

It was very peaceful on the water, the great smooth slippery black rocks gliding by and the soft breeze fanning their faces. Elephantine was reached very quickly and on going ashore Poirot and his loquacious acquaintance made straight for the Museum. By this time the latter had produced a card which he handed to Poirot with a little bow. It bore the inscription:

Signor Guido Richetti, Archeologo.

Not to be outdone, Poirot returned the bow and extracted his own card. These formalities completed, the two men stepped into the Museum together, the Italian pouring forth a stream of erudite information. They were by now conversing in French.

The young man in the flannel trousers strolled listlessly round the Museum, yawning from time to time, and then escaped to the outer air.

Poirot and Signor Richetti at last followed him. The Italian was energetic in examining the ruins, but presently Poirot, espying a green-lined sunshade which he recognized on the rocks down by the river, escaped in that direction.

Mrs. Allerton was sitting on a large rock, a sketch-book by her side and a book on her lap.

Poirot removed his hat politely and Mrs. Allerton at once entered into conversation.

"Good-morning," she said. "I suppose it would be quite impossible to get rid of some of these awful children."

A group of small black figures surrounded her, all grinning and posturing and holding out imploring hands as they lisped "Bakshish" at intervals, hopefully.

"I thought they'd get tired of me," said Mrs. Allerton sadly. "They've been watching me for over two hours now—and they close in on me little by little; and then I yell 'Imshi' and brandish my sunshade at them and they scatter for a minute or two. And then they come back and stare and stare, and their eyes are simply disgusting, and so are their noses, and I don't believe I really like children—not unless they're more or less washed and have the rudiments of manners."

She laughed ruefully.

Poirot gallantly attempted to disperse the mob for her, but without avail. They scattered and then reappeared, closing in once more.

"If there were only any peace in Egypt, I should like it better," said Mrs. Allerton. "But you can never be alone anywhere. Someone is always pestering you for money, or offering you donkeys, or beads, or expeditions to native villages, or duck shooting."

"It is the great disadvantage, that is true," agreed Poirot.

He spread his handkerchief cautiously on the rock and sat somewhat gingerly upon it.

"Your son is not with you this morning?" he went on.

"No, Tim had some letters to get off before we leave. We're doing the trip to the Second Cataract, you know."

"I, too."

"I'm so glad. I want to tell you that I'm quite thrilled to meet you. When we were in Majorca, there was a Mrs. Leech there, and she was telling us the most wonderful things about you. She'd lost a ruby ring bathing, and she was just lamenting that you weren't there to find it for her."

"Ah, *parbleu*, but I am not the diving seal!"

They both laughed.

Mrs. Allerton went on:

"I saw you from my window walking down the drive with Simon Doyle this morning. Do tell me what you make of him? We're all so excited about him."

"Ah? Truly?"

"Yes. You know his marriage to Linnet Ridgeway was the greatest surprise. She was supposed to be going to marry Lord Windlesham and then suddenly she gets engaged to this man no one had ever heard of!"

"You know her well, Madame?"

"No, but a cousin of mine, Joanna Southwood, is one of her best friends."

"Ah, yes, I have read that name in the papers." He was silent a moment and then went on, "She is a young lady very much in the news, Mademoiselle Joanna Southwood."

"Oh, she knows how to advertise herself all right," snapped Mrs. Allerton.

"You do not like her, Madame?"

"That was a nasty remark of mine." Mrs. Allerton looked penitent. "You see I'm old-fashioned. I don't like her much. Tim and she are the greatest friends, though."

"I see," said Poirot.

His companion shot a quick look at him. She changed the subject.

"How very few young people there are out here! That pretty girl with the chestnut hair and the appalling mother in the turban is almost the only young creature in the place. You have talked to her a good deal, I notice. She interests me, that child."

"Why is that, Madame?"

"I feel sorry for her. You can suffer so much when you are young and sensitive. I think she is suffering."

"Yes, she is not happy, poor little one."

"Tim and I call her the 'sulky girl.' I've tried to talk to her once or twice, but she's snubbed me on each occasion. However I believe she's going on this Nile trip too, and I expect we'll have to be more or less all matey together, shan't we?"

"It is a possible contingency, Madame."

"I'm very matey really—people interest me enormously. All the different types." She paused, then said: "Tim tells me that that dark girl—her name is de Bellefort—is the girl who was engaged to Simon Doyle. It's rather awkward for them—meeting like this."

"It is awkward—yes," agreed Poirot.

Mrs. Allerton shot a quick glance at him.

"You know, it may sound foolish, but she almost frightened me. She looked so—intense."

Poirot nodded his head slowly.

"You were not far wrong, Madame. A great force of emotion is always frightening."

"Do people interest you too, Monsieur Poirot? Or do you reserve your interest for potential criminals?"

"Madame—that category would not leave many people outside it."

Mrs. Allerton looked a trifle startled.

"Do you really mean that?"

"Given the particular incentive, that is to say," Poirot added.

"Which would differ?"

"Naturally."

Mrs. Allerton hesitated—a little smile on her lips.

"Even I perhaps?"

"Mothers, Madame, are particularly ruthless when their children are in danger."

She said gravely, "I think that's true—yes, you're quite right."

She was silent a minute or two, then she said, smiling: "I'm trying to imagine motives for crime suitable for everyone in the hotel. It's quite entertaining. Simon Doyle for instance?"

Poirot said, smiling: "A very simple crime—a direct short-cut to his objective. No subtlety about it."

"And therefore very easily detected?"

"Yes; he would not be ingenious."

"And Linnet?"

"That would be like the Queen in your *Alice in Wonderland*, 'Off with her head.'"

"Of course. The divine right of monarchy! Just a little bit of the Naboth's vineyard touch. And the dangerous girl—Jacqueline de Bellefort—could *she* do a murder?"

Poirot hesitated for a minute or two, then he said doubtfully, "Yes, I think she could."

"But you're not sure?"

"No. She puzzles me, that little one."

"I don't think Mr. Pennington could do one, do you? He looks so desiccated and dyspeptic—with no red blood in him."

"But possibly a strong sense of self-preservation."

"Yes, I suppose so. And poor Mrs. Otterbourne in her turban?"

"There is always vanity."

"As a motive for murder?" Mrs. Allerton asked doubtfully.

"Motives for murder are sometimes very trivial, Madame."

"What are the most usual motives, Monsieur Poirot?"

"Most frequent—money. That is to say, gain in its various ramifications. Then there is revenge—and love, and fear, and pure hate, and beneficence—"

"Monsieur Poirot!"

"Oh, yes, Madame. I have known of—shall we say A?—being removed by B solely in order to benefit C. Political murders often come under that heading. Someone is considered to be harmful to civilization and is removed on that account. Such people forget that life and death are the affair of the good God."

He spoke gravely.

Mrs. Allerton said quietly: "I am glad to hear you say that. All the same, God chooses his instruments."

"There is danger in thinking like that, Madame."

She adopted a lighter tone.

"After this conversation, Monsieur Poirot, I shall wonder that there is anyone left alive!"

She got up.

"We must be getting back. We have to start immediately after lunch."

When they reached the landing stage they found the young man in the polo jumper just taking his place in the boat. The Italian was already waiting. As the Nubian boatman cast the sail loose and they started, Poirot addressed a polite remark to the stranger.

"There are very wonderful things to be seen in Egypt, are there not?"

The young man was now smoking a somewhat noisome pipe. He removed it from his mouth and remarked briefly and very emphatically, in astonishingly well-bred accents, "They make me sick."

Mrs. Allerton put on her pince-nez and surveyed him with pleasurable interest.

"Indeed? And why is that?" Poirot asked.

"Take the Pyramids. Great blocks of useless masonry, put up to minister to the egoism of a despotic bloated king. Think of the sweated masses who toiled to build them and died doing it. It makes me sick to think of the suffering and torture they represent."

Mrs. Allerton said cheerfully, "You'd rather have no Pyramids, no Parthenon, no beautiful tombs or temples—just the solid satisfaction of knowing that people got three meals a day and died in their beds."

The young man directed his scowl in her direction.

"I think human beings matter more than stones."

"But they do not endure as well," remarked Hercule Poirot.

"I'd rather see a well fed worker than any so-called work of art. What matters is the future—not the past."

This was too much for Signor Richetti, who burst into a torrent of impassioned speech not too easy to follow.

The young man retorted by telling everybody exactly what he thought of the capitalist system. He spoke with the utmost venom.

When the tirade was over they had arrived at the hotel landing stage.

Mrs. Allerton murmured cheerfully, "Well, well," and stepped ashore. The young man directed a baleful glance after her.

In the hall of the hotel Poirot encountered Jacqueline de Bellefort. She was dressed in riding clothes. She gave him an ironical little bow.

"I'm going donkey riding. Do you recommend the native villages, Monsieur Poirot?"

"Is that your excursion today, Mademoiselle? *Eh bien,* they are picturesque—but do not spend large sums on native curios."

"Which are shipped here from Europe? No, I am not so easy to deceive as that."

With a little nod she passed out into the brilliant sunshine.

Poirot completed his packing—a very simple affair, since his possessions were always in the most meticulous order. Then he repaired to the dining-room and ate an early lunch.

After lunch the hotel bus took the passengers for the Second Cataract to the station where they were to catch the daily express from Cairo on to Shellâl—a ten-minute run.

The Allertons, Poirot, the young man in the dirty flannel trousers and the Italian were the passengers. Mrs. Otterbourne and her daughter had made the expedition to the Dam and to Philae and would join the steamer at Shellâl.

The train from Cairo and Luxor was about twenty minutes late. However, it arrived at last, and the usual scenes of wild activity occurred. Native porters taking suitcases out of the train collided with other porters putting them in.

Finally, somewhat breathless, Poirot found himself, with an assortment of his own, the Allertons' and some totally unknown luggage, in one compartment, while Tim and his mother were elsewhere with the remains of the assorted baggage.

The compartment in which Poirot found himself was occupied by an elderly lady with a very wrinkled face, a stiff white stock, a good many diamonds and an expression of reptilian contempt for the majority of mankind.

She treated Poirot to an aristocratic glare and retired behind the pages of an American magazine. A big rather clumsy young woman of under thirty was sitting opposite her. She had eager brown eyes, rather like a dog's, untidy hair, and a terrific air of willingness to please. At intervals the old lady looked over the top of her magazine and snapped an order at her.

"Cornelia, collect the rugs." "When we arrive look after my dressing-case. On no account let anyone else handle it." "Don't forget my paper-cutter."

The train run was brief. In ten minutes' time they came to rest on the jetty where the S. S. *Karnak* was awaiting them. The Otterbournes were already on board.

The *Karnak* was a smaller steamer than the *Papyrus* and the *Lotus*, the First Cataract steamers, which are too large to pass through the locks of the Assuan dam. The passengers went on board and were shown their accommodation. Since the boat was not full, most of the passengers had accommodation on the promenade deck. The entire forward part of this deck was occupied by an observation saloon, all glass-enclosed, where the passengers could sit and watch the river unfold before them. On the deck below were a smoking-room and a small drawing-room and on the deck below that, the dining-saloon.

Having seen his possessions disposed in his cabin, Poirot came out on the deck again to watch the process of departure. He joined Rosalie Otterbourne, who was leaning over the side.

"So now we journey into Nubia. You are pleased, Mademoiselle?"

The girl drew a deep breath.

"Yes. I feel that one's really getting away from things at last."

She made a gesture with her hand. There was a savage aspect

about the sheet of water in front of them, the masses of rock without vegetation that came down to the water's edge—here and there a trace of houses abandoned and ruined as a result of the damming up of the waters. The whole scene had a melancholy, almost sinister charm.

"Away from *people,*" said Rosalie Otterbourne.

"Except those of our own number, Mademoiselle?"

She shrugged her shoulders. Then she said: "There's something about this country that makes me feel—wicked. It brings to the surface all the things that are boiling inside one. Everything's so unfair—so unjust."

"I wonder. You cannot judge by material evidence."

Rosalie muttered: "Look at—at some people's mothers—and look at mine. There is no God but Sex, and Salome Otterbourne is its Prophet." She stopped. "I shouldn't have said that, I suppose."

Poirot made a gesture with his hands.

"Why not say it—to me? I am one of those who hear many things. If, as you say, you boil inside—like the jam—*eh bien*, let the scum come to the surface, and then one can take it off with a spoon, so."

He made the gesture of dropping something into the Nile.

"There, it has gone."

"What an extraordinary man you are!" Rosalie said. Her sulky mouth twisted into a smile. Then she suddenly stiffened as she exclaimed: "Why, here are Mrs. Doyle and her husband! I'd no idea *they* were coming on this trip!"

Linnet had just emerged from a cabin half way down the deck. Simon was behind her. Poirot was almost startled by the look of her—so radiant, so assured. She looked positively arrogant with happiness. Simon Doyle, too, was a transformed being. He was grinning from ear to ear and looking like a happy schoolboy.

"This is grand," he said as he too leaned on the rail. "I'm really looking forward to this trip, aren't you, Linnet? It feels somehow, so much less touristy—as though we were really going into the heart of Egypt."

His wife responded quickly: "I know. It's so much—wilder, somehow."

Her hand slipped through his arm. He pressed it close to his side.

"We're off, Lin," he murmured.

The steamer was drawing away from the jetty. They had started on their seven-day journey to the Second Cataract and back.

Behind them a light silvery laugh rang out. Linnet whipped round.

Jacqueline de Bellefort was standing there. She seemed amused.

"Hullo, Linnet! I didn't expect to find *you* here. I thought you said you were staying at Assuan another ten days. This is a surprise!"

"You—you didn't—" Linnet's tongue stammered. She forced a ghastly conventional smile. "I—I didn't expect to see you either."

"No?"

Jacqueline moved away to the other side of the boat. Linnet's grasp on her husband's arm tightened.

"Simon—Simon—"

All Doyle's good-natured pleasure had gone. He looked furious. His hands clenched themselves in spite of his effort at self-control.

The two of them moved a little away. Without turning his head Poirot caught scraps of disjointed words:

". . . turn back . . . impossible . . . we could . . ." and then, slightly louder, Doyle's voice, despairing but grim: "We can't run away for ever, Lin. We've got to go through with it now. . . ."

It was some hours later. Daylight was just fading. Poirot stood in the glass-enclosed saloon looking straight ahead. The *Karnak* was going through a narrow gorge. The rocks came down with a kind of sheer ferocity to the river flowing deep and swift between them. They were in Nubia now.

He heard a movement and Linnet Doyle stood by his side. Her fingers twisted and untwisted themselves; she looked as he had never yet seen her look. There was about her the air of a bewildered child. She said:

"Monsieur Poirot, I'm afraid—I'm afraid of everything. I've never felt like this before. All these wild rocks and the awful grimness and starkness. Where are we going? What's going to happen? I'm afraid, I tell you. Everyone hates me. I've never felt like that before. I've always been nice to people—I've done things for them—and they hate me—lots of people hate me. Except for Simon, I'm surrounded by enemies. . . . It's terrible to feel—that there are people who hate you. . . ."

"But what is all this, Madame?"

She shook her head.

"I suppose—it's nerves. . . . I just feel that—everything's unsafe all round me."

She cast a quick nervous glance over her shoulder. Then she said abruptly: "How will all this end? We're caught here. Trapped! There's no way out. We've got to go on. I—I don't know where I am."

She slipped down onto a seat. Poirot looked down on her gravely; his glance was not untinged with compassion.

"How did she know we were coming on this boat?" she said. "How could she have known?"

Poirot shook his head as he answered, "She has brains, you know."

"I feel as though I shall never escape from her."

Poirot said: "There is one plan you might have adopted. In fact I am surprised that it did not occur to you. After all, with you, Madame, money is no object. Why did you not engage your own private dahabiyeh?"

Linnet shook her head rather helplessly.

"If we'd known about all this—but you see we didn't—then. And it was difficult. . . ." She flashed out with sudden impatience: "Oh! you don't understand half my difficulties. I've got to be careful with Simon. . . . He's—he's absurdly sensitive—about money. About my having so much! He wanted me to go to some little place in Spain with him—he—he wanted to pay all our honeymoon expenses himself. As if it *mattered!* Men are stupid! He's got to get used to—to—living comfortably. The mere idea of a dahabiyeh upset him—the—the needless expense. I've got to educate him—gradually."

She looked up, bit her lip vexedly, as though feeling that she had been led into discussing her difficulties rather too unguardedly.

She got up.

"I must change. I'm sorry, Monsieur Poirot. I'm afraid I've been talking a lot of foolish nonsense."

CHAPTER VII

Mrs. Allerton, looking quiet and distinguished in her simple black lace evening gown, descended two decks to the dining-room. At the door of it her son caught her up.

"Sorry, darling. I thought I was going to be late."

"I wonder where we sit." The saloon was dotted with little tables. Mrs. Allerton paused till the steward, who was busy seating a party of people, could attend to them.

"By the way," she added, "I asked little Hercule Poirot to sit at our table."

"Mother, you didn't!" Tim sounded really taken aback and annoyed.

His mother stared at him in surprise. Tim was usually so easy-going.

"My dear, do you mind?"

"Yes, I do. He's an unmitigated little bounder!"

"Oh, no, Tim! I don't agree with you."

"Anyway, what do we want to get mixed up with an outsider for? Cooped up like this on a small boat, that sort of thing is always a bore. He'll be with us morning, noon and night."

"I'm sorry, dear." Mrs. Allerton looked distressed. "I thought really it would amuse you. After all, he must have had a varied experience. And you love detective stories."

Tim grunted.

"I wish you wouldn't have these bright ideas, Mother. We can't get out of it now, I suppose?"

"Really, Tim, I don't see how we can."

"Oh, well, we shall have to put up with it, I suppose."

The steward came to them at this minute and led them to a table. Mrs. Allerton's face wore rather a puzzled expression as she followed him. Tim was usually so easy-going and good-tempered. This outburst was quite unlike him. It wasn't as though he had the ordinary Britisher's dislike—and mistrust—of foreigners. Tim was very cosmopolitan. Oh, well—she sighed. Men were incomprehensible! Even one's nearest and dearest had unsuspected reactions and feelings.

As they took their places, Hercule Poirot came quickly and silently into the dining-saloon. He paused with his hand on the back of the third chair.

"You really permit, Madame, that I avail myself of your kind suggestion?"

"Of course. Sit down, Monsieur Poirot."

"You are most amiable."

She was uneasily conscious that, as he seated himself, he shot a swift glance at Tim, and that Tim had not quite succeeded in masking a somewhat sullen expression.

Mrs. Allerton set herself to produce a pleasant atmosphere. As they drank their soup, she picked up the passenger list which had been placed beside her plate.

"Let's try and identify everybody," she suggested cheerfully. "I always think that's rather fun."

She began reading: "Mrs. Allerton, Mr. T. Allerton. That's easy enough! Miss de Bellefort. They've put her at the same table as the Otterbournes, I see. I wonder what she and Rosalie will make of each other. Who comes next? Dr. Bessner. Dr. Bessner? Who can identify Dr. Bessner?"

She bent her glance on a table at which four men sat together. "I think he must be the fat one with the closely shaved head and the moustache. A German, I should imagine. He seems to be enjoying his soup very much." Certain succulent noises floated across to them.

Mrs. Allerton continued: "Miss Bowers? Can we make a guess at Miss Bowers? There are three or four women— No, we'll leave her for the present. Mr. and Mrs. Doyle. Yes, indeed, the lions of this trip. She really is very beautiful, and what a perfectly lovely frock she is wearing."

Tim turned round in his chair. Linnet and her husband and Andrew Pennington had been given a table in the corner. Linnet was wearing a white dress and pearls.

"It looks frightfully simple to me," said Tim. "Just a length of stuff with a kind of cord round the middle."

"Yes, darling," said his mother. "A very nice manly description of an eighty-guinea model."

"I can't think why women pay so much for their clothes," Tim said. "It seems absurd to me."

Mrs. Allerton proceeded with her study of her fellow passengers. "Mr. Fanthorp must be one of the four at that table. The intensely quiet young man who never speaks. Rather a nice face, cautious but intelligent."

Poirot agreed.

"He is intelligent—yes. He does not talk, but he listens very attentively, and he also watches. Yes, he makes good use of his eyes. Not quite the type you would expect to find travelling for pleasure in this part of the world. I wonder what he is doing here."

"Mr. Ferguson," read Mrs. Allerton. "I feel that Ferguson must be our anti-capitalist friend. Mrs. Otterbourne, Miss Otterbourne. We know all about them. Mr. Pennington? Alias Uncle Andrew. He's a good-looking man, I think—"

"Now, Mother," said Tim.

"I think he's very good-looking in a dry sort of way," said Mrs. Allerton. "Rather a ruthless jaw. Probably the kind of man one reads about in the paper, who operates on Wall Street—or is it *in* Wall Street? I'm sure he must be extremely rich. Next—Monsieur Hercule Poirot—whose talents are really being wasted. Can't you get up a crime for Monsieur Poirot, Tim?"

But her well-meant banter only seemed to annoy her son anew. He scowled and Mrs. Allerton hurried on: "Mr. Richetti. Our Italian archaeological friend. Then Miss Robson and last of all Miss Van Schuyler. The last's easy. The very ugly old American lady who obviously feels herself the queen of the boat and who is clearly going to be very exclusive and speak to nobody who doesn't come up to the most exacting standards! She's rather marvellous, isn't she, really? A kind of period piece. The two women with her must be Miss Bowers and Miss Robson—perhaps a secretary, the thin one with pince-nez, and a poor relation, the rather pathetic young woman who is obviously enjoying herself in spite of being treated like a black slave. I think Robson's the secretary woman and Bowers is the poor relation."

"Wrong, Mother," said Tim, grinning. He had suddenly recovered his good humour.

"How do you know?"

"Because I was in the lounge before dinner and the old bean said to the companion woman: 'Where's Miss Bowers? Fetch her at once Cornelia.' And away trotted Cornelia like an obedient dog."

"I shall have to talk to Miss Van Schuyler," mused Mrs. Allerton.

Tim grinned again.

"She'll snub you, Mother."

"Not at all. I shall pave the way by sitting near her and conversing in low (but penetrating), well-bred tones, about any titled relation and friends I can remember. I think a casual mention of your second cousin, once removed, the Duke of Glasgow, would probably do the trick."

"How unscrupulous you are, Mother!"

Events after dinner were not without their amusing side to a student of human nature.

The socialistic young man (who turned out to be Mr. Ferguson as deduced) retired to the smoking-room, scorning the assemblage of passengers in the observation saloon on the top deck.

Miss Van Schuyler duly secured the best and most undraughty position there by advancing firmly on a table at which Mrs. Otterbourne was sitting and saying, "You'll excuse me, I am sure, but I *think* my knitting was left here!"

Fixed by a hypnotic eye, the turban rose and gave ground. Miss Van Schuyler established herself and her suite. Mrs. Otterbourne sat down near by and hazarded various remarks, which were met with such chilling politeness that she soon gave up. Miss Van Schuyler then sat in glorious isolation. The Doyles sat with the Allertons. Dr. Bessner retained the quiet Mr. Fanthorp as a companion. Jacqueline de Bellefort sat by herself with a book. Rosalie Otterbourne was restless. Mrs. Allerton spoke to her once or twice and tried to draw her into their group, but the girl responded ungraciously.

M. Hercule Poirot spent his evening listening to an account of Mrs. Otterbourne's mission as a writer.

On his way to his cabin that night he encountered Jacqueline de Bellefort. She was leaning over the rail and, as she turned her head, he was struck by the look of acute misery on her face. There was now no insouciance, no malicious defiance, no dark flaming triumph.

"Good-night, Mademoiselle."

"Good-night, Monsieur Poirot." She hesitated, then said, "You were surprised to find me here?"

"I was not so much surprised as sorry—very sorry. . . ."

He spoke gravely.

"You mean sorry—for *me*?"

"That is what I meant. You have chosen, Mademoiselle, the dangerous course. . . . As we here in this boat have embarked on a journey, so you too have embarked on your own private journey—a journey on a swift-moving river, between dangerous rocks, and heading for who knows what currents of disaster. . . ."

"Why do you say all this?"

"Because it is true. . . . You have cut the bonds that moored you to safety. I doubt now if you could turn back if you would."

She said very slowly, "That is true. . . ."

Then she flung her head back.

"Ah, well—one must follow one's star, wherever it leads."

"Beware, Mademoiselle, that it is not a false star. . . ."

She laughed and mimicked the parrot cry of the donkey boys: "That very bad star, sir! That star fall down. . . ."

He was just dropping off to sleep when the murmur of voices awoke him. It was Simon Doyle's voice he heard, repeating the same words he had used when the steamer left Shellâl.

"We've got to go through with it now. . . ."

"Yes," thought Hercule Poirot to himself, "we have got to go through with it now. . . ."

He was not happy.

CHAPTER VIII

THE STEAMER ARRIVED early next morning at Ez-Sebûa.

Cornelia Robson, her face beaming, a large flapping hat on her head, was one of the first to hurry on shore. Cornelia was not good at snubbing people. She was of an amiable disposition and disposed to like all her fellow creatures.

The sight of Hercule Poirot, in a white suit, pink shirt, large black bow tie and a white topee, did not make her wince as the aristocratic Miss Van Schuyler would assuredly have winced. As they walked together up an avenue of sphinxes, she responded readily to his conventional opening.

"Your companions are not coming ashore to view the temple?"

"Well, you see, Cousin Marie—that's Miss Van Schuyler—never gets up very early. She has to be very, very careful of her health. And of course she wanted Miss Bowers, that's her hospital nurse, to do things for her. And she said, too, that this isn't one of the best temples—but she was frightfully kind and said it would be quite all right for me to come."

"That was very gracious of her," said Poirot drily.

The ingenuous Cornelia agreed unsuspectingly.

"Oh, she's very kind. It's simply wonderful of her to bring me on this trip. I do feel I'm a lucky girl. I just could hardly believe it when she suggested to Mother that I should come too."

"And you have enjoyed it—yes?"

"Oh, it's been wonderful! I've seen Italy—Venice and Padua and Pisa—and then Cairo—only Cousin Marie wasn't very well in Cairo, so I couldn't get around much, and now this wonderful trip up to Wâdi Halfa and back."

Poirot said, smiling, "You have the happy nature, Mademoiselle."

He looked thoughtfully from her to the silent, frowning Rosalie, who was walking ahead by herself.

"She's very nice-looking, isn't she?" said Cornelia, following his glance. "Only kind of scornful looking. She's very English, of course. She's not as lovely as Mrs. Doyle. I think Mrs. Doyle's the loveliest, the most elegant woman I've ever seen! And her husband just worships the ground she walks on, doesn't he? I think that grey-haired lady is kind of distinguished looking, don't you? She's cousin to a

Duke, I believe. She was talking about him right near us last night. But she isn't actually titled herself, is she?"

She prattled on until the dragoman in charge called a halt and began to intone: "This temple was dedicated to Egyptian God Amun and the Sun God Rē-Harakhte—whose symbol was hawk's head . . ."

It droned on. Dr. Bessner, Baedeker in hand, mumbled to himself in German. He preferred the written word.

Tim Allerton had not joined the party. His mother was breaking the ice with the reserved Mr. Fanthorp. Andrew Pennington, his arm through Linnet Doyle's, was listening attentively, seemingly most interested in the measurements as recited by the guide.

"Sixty-five feet high, is that so? Looks a little less to me. Great fellow, this Rameses. An Egyptian live wire."

"A big business man, Uncle Andrew."

Andrew Pennington looked at her appreciatively.

"You look fine this morning, Linnet. I've been a mite worried about you lately. You've looked kind of peaky."

Chatting together, the party returned to the boat. Once more the *Karnak* glided up the river. The scenery was less stern now. There were palms, cultivation.

It was as though the change in the scenery had relieved some secret oppression that had brooded over the passengers. Tim Allerton had got over his fit of moodiness. Rosalie looked less sulky. Linnet seemed almost lighthearted.

Pennington said to her, "It's tactless to talk business to a bride on her honeymoon, but there are just one or two things—"

"Why, of course, Uncle Andrew." Linnet at once became businesslike. "My marriage has made a difference, of course."

"That's just it. Some time or other I want your signature to several documents."

"Why not now?"

Andrew Pennington glanced round. Their corner of the observation saloon was quite untenanted. Most of the people were outside on the deck space between the observation saloon and the cabins. The only occupants of the saloon were Mr. Ferguson—who was drinking beer at a small table in the middle, his legs, encased in their dirty flannel trousers, stuck out in front of him, whilst he whistled to himself in the intervals of drinking—M. Hercule Poirot, who was sitting close up to the front glass, intent on the panorama unfolding before him, and Miss Van Schuyler, who was sitting in a corner reading a book on Egypt.

"That's fine," said Andrew Pennington. He left the saloon.

Linnet and Simon smiled at each other—a slow smile that took a few minutes to come to full fruition.

"All right, sweet?" he asked.

"Yes, still all right. . . . Funny how I'm not rattled any more."

Simon said with deep conviction in his tone, "You're marvellous."

Pennington came back. He brought with him a sheaf of closely written documents.

"Mercy!" cried Linnet. "Have I got to sign all these?"

Andrew Pennington was apologetic.

"It's tough on you, I know, but I'd just like to get your affairs put in proper shape. First of all there's the lease of the Fifth Avenue property . . . then there are the Western Lands Concessions . . ."

He talked on, rustling and sorting the papers. Simon yawned.

The door to the deck swung open and Mr. Fanthorp came in. He gazed aimlessly round, then strolled forward and stood by Poirot looking out at the pale blue water and the yellow enveloping sands. . . .

"—you sign just there," concluded Pennington, spreading a paper before Linnet and indicating a space.

Linnet picked up the document and glanced through it. She turned back once to the first page, then, taking up the fountain pen Pennington had laid beside her, she signed her name *Linnet Doyle*. . . .

Pennington took away the paper and spread out another.

Fanthorp wandered over in their direction. He peered out through the side window at something that seemed to interest him on the bank they were passing.

"That's just the transfer," said Pennington. "You needn't read it."

But Linnet took a brief glance through it. Pennington laid down a third paper. Again Linnet perused it carefully.

"They're all quite straightforward," said Andrew. "Nothing of interest. Only legal phraseology."

Simon yawned again.

"My dear girl, you're not going to read the whole lot through, are you? You'll be at it till lunch time and longer."

"I always read everything through," said Linnet. "Father taught me to do that. He said there might be some clerical error."

Pennington laughed rather harshly.

"You're a grand woman of business, Linnet."

"She's much more conscientious than I'd be," said Simon, laughing. "I've never read a legal document in my life. I sign where they tell me to sign on the dotted line—and that's that."

"That's frightfully slipshod," said Linnet disapprovingly.

"I've no business head," declared Simon cheerfully. "Never had. A fellow tells me to sign—I sign. It's much the simplest way."

Andrew Pennington was looking at him thoughtfully. He said drily, stroking his upper lip, "A little risky sometimes, Doyle?"

"Nonsense," replied Simon. "I'm not one of those people who believe the whole world is out to do one down. I'm a trusting kind of fellow—and it pays, you know. I've hardly ever been let down."

Suddenly, to everyone's surprise, the silent Mr. Fanthorp swung round and addressed Linnet.

"I hope I'm not butting in, but you must let me say how much I admire your businesslike capacity. In my profession—er—I am a lawyer—I find ladies sadly unbusinesslike. Never to sign a document before you read it through is admirable—altogether admirable."

He gave a little bow. Then, rather red in the face, he turned once more to contemplate the banks of the Nile.

Linnet said rather uncertainly, "Er—thank you. . . ." She bit her lip to repress a giggle. The young man had looked so preternaturally solemn.

Andrew Pennington looked seriously annoyed.

Simon Doyle looked uncertain whether to be annoyed or amused.

The backs of Mr. Fanthorp's ears were bright crimson.

"Next, please," said Linnet, smiling up at Pennington.

But Pennington was looking decidedly ruffled.

"I think perhaps some other time would be better," he said stiffly. "As—er—Doyle says, if you have to read through all these we shall be here till lunch time. We mustn't miss enjoying the scenery. Anyway those first two papers were the only urgent ones. We'll settle down to business later."

"It's frightfully hot in here," Linnet said. "Let's go outside."

The three of them passed through the swing door. Hercule Poirot turned his head. His gaze rested thoughtfully on Mr. Fanthorp's back; then it shifted to the lounging figure of Mr. Ferguson who had his head thrown back and was still whistling softly to himself.

Finally Poirot looked over at the upright figure of Miss Van

Schuyler in her corner. Miss Van Schuyler was glaring at Mr. Ferguson.

The swing door on the port side opened and Cornelia Robson hurried in.

"You've been a long time," snapped the old lady. "Where've you been?"

"I'm so sorry, Cousin Marie. The wool wasn't where you said it was. It was in another case altogether—"

"My dear child, you are perfectly hopeless at finding anything! You are willing, I know, my dear, but you must try to be a little cleverer and quicker. It only needs *concentration.*"

"I'm so sorry, Cousin Marie. I'm afraid I am very stupid."

"Nobody need be stupid if they *try,* my dear. I have brought you on this trip, and I expect a little attention in return."

Cornelia flushed.

"I'm very sorry, Cousin Marie."

"And where is Miss Bowers? It was time for my drops ten minutes ago. Please go and find her at once. The doctor said it was most important—"

But at this stage Miss Bowers entered, carrying a small medicine glass.

"Your drops, Miss Van Schuyler."

"I should have had them at eleven," snapped the old lady. "If there's one thing I detest it's unpunctuality."

"Quite," said Miss Bowers. She glanced at her wrist-watch. "It's exactly half a minute to eleven."

"By my watch it's ten past."

"I think you'll find my watch is right. It's a perfect timekeeper. It never loses or gains." Miss Bowers was quite unperturbable.

Miss Van Schuyler swallowed the contents of the medicine glass.

"I feel definitely worse," she snapped.

"I'm sorry to hear that, Miss Van Schuyler."

Miss Bowers did not sound sorry. She sounded completely uninterested. She was obviously making the correct reply mechanically.

"It's too hot in here," snapped Miss Van Schuyler. "Find me a chair on the deck, Miss Bowers. Cornelia, bring my knitting. Don't be clumsy or drop it. And then I shall want you to wind some wool."

The procession passed out.

Mr. Ferguson sighed, stirred his legs and remarked to the world at large, "Gosh, I'd like to scrag that dame."

Poirot asked interestedly, "She is a type you dislike, eh?"

"Dislike? I should say so. What good has that woman ever been to anyone or anything? She's never worked or lifted a finger. She's just battened on other people. She's a parasite—and a damned unpleasant parasite. There are a lot of people on this boat I'd say the world could do without."

"Really?"

"Yes. That girl in here just now, signing share transfers and throwing her weight about. Hundreds and thousands of wretched workers slaving for a mere pittance to keep her in silk stockings and useless luxuries. One of the richest women in England, so someone told me—and never done a hand's turn in her life."

"Who told you she was one of the richest women in England?"

Mr. Ferguson cast a belligerent eye at him.

"A man you wouldn't be seen speaking to! A man who works with his hands and isn't ashamed of it! Not one of your dressed-up, foppish good-for-nothings."

His eye rested unfavourably on the bow tie and pink shirt.

"Me, I work with my brains and am not ashamed of it," said Poirot, answering the glance.

Mr. Ferguson merely snorted.

"Ought to be shot up—the lot of them!" he asserted.

"My dear young man," said Poirot, "what a passion you have for violence!"

"Can you tell me of any good that can be done without it? You've got to break down and destroy before you can build up."

"It is certainly much easier and much noisier and much more spectacular."

"What do *you* do for a living? Nothing at all, I bet. Probably call yourself a middle man."

"I am not a middle man. I am a top man," declared Hercule Poirot with slight arrogance.

"What *are* you?"

"I am a detective," said Hercule Poirot with the modest air of one who says "I am a King."

"Good God!" The young man seemed seriously taken aback. "Do you mean that girl actually totes about a dumb dick? Is she as careful of her precious skin as *that*?"

"I have no connection whatever with Monsieur and Madame Doyle," said Poirot stiffly. "I am on a holiday."

"Enjoying a vacation—eh?"

"And you? Is it not that you are on a holiday also?"

"Holiday!" Mr. Ferguson snorted. Then he added cryptically, "I'm studying conditions."

"Very interesting," murmured Poirot and moved gently out onto the deck.

Miss Van Schuyler was established in the best corner. Cornelia knelt in front of her, her arms outstretched with a skein of grey wool upon them. Miss Bowers was sitting very upright reading the *Saturday Evening Post.*

Poirot wandered gently onward down the starboard deck. As he passed round the stern of the boat he almost ran into a woman who turned a startled face toward him—a dark, piquant, Latin face. She was neatly dressed in black and had been standing talking to a big burly man in uniform—one of the engineers, by the look of him. There was a queer expression on both their faces—guilt and alarm. Poirot wondered what they had been talking about.

He rounded the stern and continued his walk along the port side. A cabin door opened and Mrs. Otterbourne emerged and nearly fell into his arms. She was wearing a scarlet satin dressing-gown.

"So sorry," she apologized. "Dear Mr. Poirot—so very sorry. The motion—just the motion, you know. Never did have any sea legs. If the boat would only keep still . . ." She clutched at his arm. "It's the pitching I can't stand. . . . Never really happy at sea. . . . And left all alone here hour after hour. That girl of mine—no sympathy—no understanding of her poor old mother who's done everything for her. . . ." Mrs. Otterbourne began to weep. "Slaved for her I have—worn myself to the bone—to the bone. A *grande amoureuse*—that's what I might have been—a *grande amoureuse*—sacrificed everything—everything. . . . And nobody cares! But I'll tell everyone—I'll tell them now—how she neglects me—how hard she is—making me come on this journey—bored to death. . . . I'll go and tell them now—"

She surged forward. Poirot gently repressed the action.

"I will send her to you, Madame. Re-enter your cabin. It is best that way—"

"No. I want to tell everyone—everyone on the boat—"

"It is too dangerous, Madame. The sea is too rough. You might be swept overboard."

Mrs. Otterbourne looked at him doubtfully.

"You think so. You really think so?"

"I do."

He was successful. Mrs. Otterbourne wavered, faltered and re-entered her cabin.

Poirot's nostrils twitched once or twice. Then he nodded and walked on to where Rosalie Otterbourne was sitting between Mrs. Allerton and Tim.

"Your mother wants you, Mademoiselle."

She had been laughing quite happily. Now her face clouded over. She shot a quick suspicious look at him and hurried along the deck.

"I can't make that child out," said Mrs. Allerton. "She varies so. One day she's friendly; the next day she's positively rude."

"Thoroughly spoilt and bad-tempered," said Tim.

Mrs. Allerton shook her head.

"No. I don't think it's that. I think she's unhappy."

Tim shrugged his shoulders.

"Oh, well, I suppose we've all got our private troubles." His voice sounded hard and curt.

A booming noise was heard.

"Lunch," cried Mrs. Allerton delightedly. "I'm starving."

That evening, Poirot noticed that Mrs. Allerton was sitting talking to Miss Van Schuyler. As he passed, Mrs. Allerton closed one eye and opened it again. She was saying, "Of course at Calfries Castle—the dear Duke—"

Cornelia, released from attendance, was out on the deck. She was listening to Dr. Bessner, who was instructing her somewhat ponderously in Egyptology as culled from the pages of Baedeker. Cornelia listened with rapt attention.

Leaning over the rail Tim Allerton was saying, "Anyhow, it's a rotten world. . . ."

Rosalie Otterbourne answered, "It's unfair; some people have everything."

Poirot sighed. He was glad that he was no longer young.

CHAPTER IX

On the Monday morning various expressions of delight and appreciation were heard on the deck of the *Karnak.* The steamer was moored to the bank and a few hundred yards away, the morning sun just striking it, was a great temple carved out of the face of the rock. Four colossal figures, hewn out of the cliff, look out eternally over the Nile and face the rising sun.

Cornelia Robson said incoherently: "Oh, Monsieur Poirot, isn't it wonderful? I mean they're so big and so peaceful—and looking at them makes one feel that one's so small and—and rather like an insect—and that nothing matters very much really, does it?"

Mr. Fanthorp, who was standing near by, murmured, "Very—er—impressive."

"Grand, isn't it?" said Simon Doyle, strolling up. He went on confidentially to Poirot: "You know, I'm not much of a fellow for temples and sight-seeing and all that, but a place like this sort of gets you, if you know what I mean. Those old Pharaohs must have been wonderful fellows."

The others had drifted away. Simon lowered his voice.

"I'm no end glad we came on this trip. It's—well, it's cleared things up. Amazing why it should—but there it is. Linnet's got her nerve back. She says it's because she's actually *faced* the business at last."

"I think that is very probable," said Poirot.

"She says that when she actually saw Jackie on the boat she felt terrible—and then, suddenly, it didn't matter any more. We're both agreed that we won't try and dodge her any more. We'll just meet her on her own ground and show her that this ridiculous stunt of hers doesn't worry us a bit. It's just damned bad form—that's all. She thought she'd got us badly rattled, but now, well, we just aren't rattled any more. That ought to show her."

"Yes," said Poirot thoughtfully.

"So that's splendid, isn't it?"

"Oh, yes, yes."

Linnet came along the deck. She was dressed in a soft shade of apricot linen. She was smiling. She greeted Poirot with no particular enthusiasm, just gave him a cool nod and then drew her husband away.

Poirot realized with a momentary flicker of amusement that he had not made himself popular by his critical attitude. Linnet was used to unqualified admiration of all she was or did. Hercule Poirot had sinned noticeably against this creed.

Mrs. Allerton, joining him, murmured:

"What a difference in that girl! She looked worried and not very happy at Assuan. Today she looks so happy that one might almost be afraid she was fey."

Before Poirot could respond as he meant, the party was called to order. The official dragoman took charge and the party was led ashore to visit Abu Simbel.

Poirot himself fell into step with Andrew Pennington.

"It is your first visit to Egypt—yes?" he asked.

"Why, no, I was here in nineteen twenty-three. That is to say, I was in Cairo. I've never been this trip up the Nile before."

"You came over on the *Carmanic,* I believe—at least so Madame Doyle was telling me."

Pennington shot a shrewd glance in his direction.

"Why, yes, that is so," he admitted.

"I wondered if you had happened to come across some friends of mine who were aboard—the Rushington Smiths."

"I can't recall anyone of that name. The boat was full and we had bad weather. A lot of passengers hardly appeared, and in any case the voyage is so short one doesn't get to know who is on board and who isn't."

"Yes, that is very true. What a pleasant surprise your running into Madame Doyle and her husband. You had no idea they were married?"

"No. Mrs. Doyle had written me, but the letter was forwarded on and I only received it some days after our unexpected meeting in Cairo."

"You have known her for very many years, I understand?"

"Why, I should say I have, Monsieur Poirot. I've known Linnet Ridgeway since she was just a cute little thing so high—" He made an illustrating gesture. "Her father and I were lifelong friends. A very remarkable man, Melhuish Ridgeway—and a very successful one."

"His daughter comes into a considerable fortune, I understand. . . . Ah, *pardon*—perhaps it is not delicate what I say there."

Andrew Pennington seemed slightly amused.

"Oh, that's pretty common knowledge. Yes, Linnet's a wealthy woman."

"I suppose, though, that the recent slump is bound to affect any stocks, however sound they may be?"

Pennington took a moment or two to answer. He said at last: "That, of course, is true to a certain extent. The position is very difficult in these days."

Poirot murmured, "I should imagine, however, that Madame Doyle has a keen business head."

"That is so. Yes, that is so. Linnet is a clever practical girl."

They came to a halt. The guide proceeded to instruct them on the subject of the temple built by the great Rameses. The four colossi of Rameses himself, one pair on each side of the entrance, hewn out of the living rock, looked down on the little straggling party of tourists.

Signor Richetti, disdaining the remarks of the dragoman, was busy examining the reliefs of Negro and Syrian captives on the bases of the colossi on either side of the entrance.

When the party entered the temple, a sense of dimness and peace came over them. The still vividly coloured reliefs on some of the inner walls were pointed out, but the party tended to break up into groups.

Dr. Bessner read sonorously in German from a Baedeker, pausing every now and then to translate for the benefit of Cornelia, who walked in a docile manner beside him. This was not to continue, however. Miss Van Schuyler, entering on the arm of the phlegmatic Miss Bowers, uttered a commanding "Cornelia, come here," and the instruction had perforce to cease. Dr. Bessner beamed after her vaguely through his thick lenses.

"A very nice maiden, that," he announced to Poirot. "She does not look so starved as some of these young women. No, she has the nice curves. She listens too, very intelligently; it is a pleasure to instruct her."

It fleeted across Poirot's mind that it seemed to be Cornelia's fate either to be bullied or instructed. In any case she was always the listener, never the talker.

Miss Bowers, momentarily released by the peremptory summons of Cornelia, was standing in the middle of the temple, looking about her with her cool, incurious gaze. Her reaction to the wonders of the past was succinct.

"The guide says the name of one of these gods or goddesses was Mut. Can you beat it?"

There was an inner sanctuary where sat four figures eternally presiding, strangely dignified in their dim aloofness.

Before them stood Linnet and her husband. Her arm was in his, her face lifted—a typical face of the new civilization, intelligent, curious, untouched by the past.

Simon said suddenly: "Let's get out of here. I don't like these four fellows—especially the one in the high hat."

"That's Amon, I suppose. And that one is Rameses. Why don't you like them? I think they're very impressive."

"They're a damned sight too impressive; there's something uncanny about them. Come out into the sunlight."

Linnet laughed but yielded.

They came out of the temple into the sunshine with the sand yellow and warm about their feet. Linnet began to laugh. At their feet in a row, presenting a momentarily gruesome appearance as though sawn from their bodies, were the heads of half a dozen Nubian boys. The eyes rolled, the heads moved rhythmically from side to side, the lips chanted a new invocation:

"Hip, hip *hurray!* Hip, hip *hurray!* Very good, very nice. Thank you very much."

"How absurd! How do they do it? Are they really buried very deep?"

Simon produced some small change.

"Very good, very nice, very expensive," he mimicked.

Two small boys in charge of the "show" picked up the coins neatly.

Linnet and Simon passed on. They had no wish to return to the boat, and they were weary of sight-seeing. They settled themselves with their backs to the cliff and let the warm sun bake them through.

"How lovely the sun is," thought Linnet. "How warm—how safe. . . . How lovely it is to be happy. . . . How lovely to be me—me . . . me . . . Linnet . . ."

Her eyes closed. She was half asleep, half awake, drifting in the midst of thought that was like the sand drifting and blowing.

Simon's eyes were open. They too held contentment. What a fool he'd been to be rattled that first night. . . . There was nothing to be rattled about. . . . Everything was all right. . . . After all, one could trust Jackie—

There was a shout—people running toward him waving their arms—shouting. . . .

Simon stared stupidly for a moment. Then he sprang to his feet and dragged Linnet with him.

Not a minute too soon. A big boulder hurtling down the cliff crashed past them. If Linnet had remained where she was she would have been crushed to atoms.

White-faced they clung together. Hercule Poirot and Tim Allerton ran up to them.

"*Ma foi,* Madame, that was a near thing."

All four instinctively looked up at the cliff. There was nothing to be seen. But there was a path along the top. Poirot remembered seeing some natives walking along there when they had first come ashore.

He looked at the husband and wife. Linnet looked dazed still—bewildered. Simon, however, was inarticulate with rage.

"God damn her!" he ejaculated.

He checked himself with a quick glance at Tim Allerton.

The latter said: "Phew, that was near! Did some fool bowl that thing over, or did it get detached on its own?"

Linnet was very pale. She said with difficulty, "I think—some fool must have done it."

"Might have crushed you like an eggshell. Sure you haven't got an enemy, Linnet?"

Linnet swallowed twice and found a difficulty in answering the light-hearted raillery.

"Come back to the boat, Madame," Poirot said quickly. "You must have a restorative."

They walked there quietly, Simon still full of pent-up rage, Tim trying to talk cheerfully and distract Linnet's mind from the danger she had run, Poirot with a grave face.

And then, just as they reached the gangplank, Simon stopped dead. A look of amazement spread over his face.

Jacqueline de Bellefort was just coming ashore. Dressed in blue gingham, she looked childish this morning.

"Good God!" said Simon under his breath. "So it *was* an accident, after all."

The anger went out of his face. An overwhelming relief showed so plainly that Jacqueline noticed something amiss.

"Good-morning," she said. "I'm afraid I'm a little on the late side."

She gave them all a nod and stepped ashore and proceeded in the direction of the temple.

Simon clutched Poirot's arm. The other two had gone on.

"My God, that's a relief. I thought—I thought—"

Poirot nodded. "Yes, yes, I know what you thought." But he himself still looked grave and preoccupied. He turned his head and noted carefully what had become of the rest of the party from the ship.

Miss Van Schuyler was slowly returning on the arm of Miss Bowers. A little further away Mrs. Allerton was standing laughing at the little Nubian row of heads. Mrs. Otterbourne was with her.

The others were nowhere in sight.

Poirot shook his head as he followed Simon slowly onto the boat.

CHAPTER X

"WILL YOU EXPLAIN TO ME, Madame, the meaning of the word 'fey'?"

Mrs. Allerton looked slightly surprised. She and Poirot were toiling slowly up to the rock overlooking the Second Cataract. Most of the others had gone up on camels, but Poirot had felt that the motion of the camel was slightly reminiscent of that of a ship. Mrs. Allerton had put it on the grounds of personal dignity.

They had arrived at Wâdi Halfa the night before. This morning two launches had conveyed all the party to the Second Cataract, with the exception of Signor Richetti, who had insisted on making an excursion of his own to a remote spot called Semna, which, he explained, was of paramount interest as being the gateway of Nubia in the time of Amenemhet III, and where there was a stele recording the fact that on entering Egypt Negroes must pay custom duties. Everything had been done to discourage this example of individuality, but with no avail. Signor Richetti was determined and had waved aside each objection: (1) that the expedition was not worth making, (2) that the expedition could not be made, owing to the impossibility of getting a car there, (3) that no car could be obtained to do the trip, (4) that a car would be a prohibitive price. Having scoffed at 1, expressed incredulity at 2, offered to find a car himself to 3, and bargained fluently in Arabic for 4, Signor Richetti had at last departed—his departure being arranged in a secret and furtive manner, in case some of the other tourists should take it into their heads to stray from the appointed paths of sight-seeing.

" 'Fey'?" Mrs. Allerton put her head on one side as she considered her reply. "Well, it's a Scotch word, really. It means the kind of exalted happiness that comes before disaster. You know—it's too good to be true."

She enlarged on the theme. Poirot listened attentively.

"I thank you, Madame. I understand now. It is odd that you should have said that yesterday—when Madame Doyle was to escape death so shortly afterward."

Mrs. Allerton gave a little shiver.

"It must have been a very near escape. Do you think some of those little black wretches rolled it over for fun? It's the sort of thing boys might do all over the world—not perhaps really meaning any harm."

Poirot shrugged his shoulders.

"It may be, Madame."

He changed the subject, talking of Majorca and asking various practical questions from the point of view of a possible visit.

Mrs. Allerton had grown to like the little man very much—partly perhaps out of a contradictory spirit. Tim, she felt, was always trying to make her less friendly to Hercule Poirot, whom he summarized firmly as "the worst kind of bounder." But she herself did not call him a bounder; she supposed it was his somewhat foreign exotic clothing which roused her son's prejudices. She herself found him an intelligent and stimulating companion. He was also extremely sympathetic. She found herself suddenly confiding in him her dislike of Joanna Southwood. It eased her to talk of the matter. And after all, why not? He did not know Joanna—would probably never meet her. Why should she not ease herself of that constantly borne burden of jealous thought?

At that same moment Tim and Rosalie Otterbourne were talking of her. Tim had just been half jestingly abusing his luck. His rotten health, never bad enough to be really interesting, yet not good enough for him to have led the life he would have chosen. Very little money, no congenial occupation.

"A thoroughly lukewarm, tame existence," he finished discontentedly.

Rosalie said abruptly, "You've got something heaps of people would envy you."

"What's that?"

"Your mother."

Tim was surprised and pleased.

"Mother? Yes, of course she is quite unique. It's nice of you to see it."

"I think she's marvellous. She looks so lovely—so composed and calm—as though nothing could ever touch her, and yet—and yet somehow she's always ready to be funny about things too. . . ."

Rosalie was stammering slightly in her earnestness.

Tim felt a rising warmth toward the girl. He wished he could return the compliment, but, lamentably, Mrs. Otterbourne was his idea of the world's greatest menace. The inability to respond in kind made him embarrassed.

Miss Van Schuyler had stayed in the launch. She could not risk the ascent either on a camel or on her legs. She had said snappily:

"I'm sorry to have to ask you to stay with me, Miss Bowers. I intended you to go and Cornelia to stay, but girls are so selfish. She rushed off without a word to me. And I actually saw her talking to that very unpleasant and ill-bred young man, Ferguson. Cornelia has disappointed me sadly. She has absolutely no social sense."

Miss Bowers replied in her usual matter-of-fact fashion.

"That's quite all right, Miss Van Schuyler. It would have been a hot walk up there, and I don't fancy the look of those saddles on the camels. Fleas, as likely as not."

She adjusted her glasses, screwed up her eyes to look at the party descending the hill and remarked: "Miss Robson isn't with that young man any more. She's with Dr. Bessner."

Miss Van Schuyler grunted.

Since she had discovered that Dr. Bessner had a large clinic in Czecho-Slovakia and a European reputation as a fashionable physician, she was disposed to be gracious to him. Besides, she might need his professional services before the journey was over.

When the party returned to the *Karnak* Linnet gave a cry of surprise.

"A telegram for me."

She snatched it off the board and tore it open.

"Why—I don't understand—potatoes, beetroots—what does it mean, Simon?"

Simon was just coming to look over her shoulder when a furious voice said, "Excuse me, that telegram is for me," and Signor Richetti snatched it rudely from her hand, fixing her with a furious glare as he did so.

Linnet stared in surprise for a moment, then turned over the envelope.

"Oh, Simon, what a fool I am! It's Richetti—not Ridgeway—and anyway of course my name isn't Ridgeway now. I must apologize."

She followed the little archaeologist up to the stern of the boat.

"I am so sorry, Signor Richetti. You see my name was Ridgeway before I married, and I haven't been married very long, and so—"

She paused, her face dimpled with smiles, inviting him to smile upon a young bride's faux pas.

But Richetti was obviously "not amused." Queen Victoria at her most disapproving could not have looked more grim.

"Names should be read carefully. It is inexcusable to be careless in these matters."

Linnet bit her lip and her colour rose. She was not accustomed to have her apologies received in this fashion. She turned away and, rejoining Simon, said angrily, "These Italians are really insupportable."

"Never mind, darling; let's go and look at that big ivory crocodile you liked."

They went ashore together.

Poirot, watching them walk up the landing stage, heard a sharp indrawn breath. He turned to see Jacqueline de Bellefort at his side. Her hands were clenched on the rail. The expression on her face, as she turned it toward him, quite startled him. It was no longer gay or malicious. She looked devoured by some inner consuming fire.

"They don't care any more." The words came low and fast. "They've got beyond me. I can't reach them. . . . They don't mind if I'm here or not. . . . I can't—I can't hurt them any more. . . ."

Her hands on the rail trembled.

"Mademoiselle—"

She broke in: "Oh, it's too late now—too late for warning. . . . You were right. I ought not to have come. Not on this journey. What did you call it? A journey of the soul? I can't go back; I've got to go on. And I'm going on. They shan't be happy together; they shan't. I'd kill him sooner. . . ."

She turned abruptly away. Poirot, staring after her, felt a hand on his shoulder.

"Your girl friend seems a trifle upset, Monsieur Poirot."

Poirot turned. He stared in surprise, seeing an old acquaintance.

"Colonel Race."

The tall bronzed man smiled.

"Bit of a surprise, eh?"

Hercule Poirot had come across Colonel Race a year previously in London. They had been fellow guests at a very strange dinner party—a dinner party that had ended in death for that strange man, their host.

Poirot knew that Race was a man of unadvertised goings and comings. He was usually to be found in one of the outposts of Empire where trouble was brewing.

"So you are here at Wâdi Halfa," he remarked thoughtfully.

"I am here on this boat."

"You mean?"

"That I am making the return journey with you to Shellâl."

Hercule Poirot's eyebrows rose.

"That is very interesting. Shall we, perhaps, have a little drink?"

They went into the observation saloon, now quite empty. Poirot ordered a whisky for the Colonel and a double orangeade full of sugar for himself.

"So you make the return journey with us," said Poirot as he sipped. "You would go faster, would you not, on the Government steamer, which travels by night as well as day?"

Colonel Race's face creased appreciatively.

"You're right on the spot as usual, Monsieur Poirot," he said pleasantly.

"It is, then, the passengers?"

"One of the passengers."

"Now which one, I wonder?" Hercule Poirot asked of the ornate ceiling.

"Unfortunately I don't know myself," said Race ruefully.

Poirot looked interested.

Race said: "There's no need to be mysterious to you. We've had a good deal of trouble out here—one way and another. It isn't the people who ostensibly lead the rioters that we're after. It's the men who very cleverly put the match to the gunpowder. There were three of them. One's dead. One's in prison. I want the third man—a man with five or six cold-blooded murders to his credit. He's one of the cleverest paid agitators that ever existed. . . . He's on this boat. I know that from a passage in a letter that passed through our hands. Decoded it said: 'X will be on the *Karnak* trip February seventh to thirteenth.' It didn't say under what name X would be passing."

"Have you any description of him?"

"No. American, Irish and French descent. Bit of a mongrel. That doesn't help us much. Have you got any ideas?"

"An idea—it is all very well," said Poirot meditatively.

Such was the understanding between them that Race pressed him no further. He knew that Hercule Poirot did not ever speak unless he was sure.

Poirot rubbed his nose and said unhappily, "There passes itself something on this boat that causes me much inquietude."

Race looked at him inquiringly.

"Figure to yourself," said Poirot, "a person A who has grievously wronged a person B. The person B desires the revenge. The person B makes the threats."

"A and B being both on this boat?"

Poirot nodded. "Precisely."

"And B, I gather, being a woman?"

"Exactly."

Race lit a cigarette.

"I shouldn't worry. People who go about talking of what they are going to do don't usually do it."

"And particularly is that the case with *les femmes,* you would say! Yes, that is true."

But he still did not look happy.

"Anything else?" asked Race.

"Yes, there is something. Yesterday the person A had a very near escape from death, the kind of death that might very conveniently be called an accident."

"Engineered by B?"

"No, that is just the point. B could have had nothing to do with it."

"Then it *was* an accident."

"I suppose so—but I do not like such accidents."

"You're quite sure B could have had no hand in it?"

"Absolutely."

"Oh, well, coincidences do happen. Who is A, by the way? A particularly disagreeable person?"

"On the contrary. A is a charming, rich and beautiful young lady."

Race grinned.

"Sounds quite like a novelette."

"*Peut-être.* But I tell you, I am not happy, my friend. If I am right, and after all I am constantly in the habit of being right"—Race smiled into his moustache at this typical utterance—"then there is matter for grave inquietude. And now, *you* come to add yet another complication. You tell me that there is a man on the *Karnak* who kills."

"He doesn't usually kill charming young ladies."

Poirot shook his head in a dissatisfied manner.

"I am afraid, my friend," he said. "I am afraid. . . . Today, I advised this lady, Madame Doyle, to go with her husband to Khartûm, not to return on this boat. But they would not agree. I pray to Heaven that we may arrive at Shellâl without catastrophe."

"Aren't you taking rather a gloomy view?"

Poirot shook his head.

"I am afraid," he said simply. "Yes, I, Hercule Poirot, am afraid. . . ."

CHAPTER XI

CORNELIA ROBSON STOOD inside the temple of Abu Simbel. It was the evening of the following day—a hot still evening. The *Karnak* was anchored once more at Abu Simbel to permit a second visit to be made to the temple, this time by artificial light. The difference this made was considerable, and Cornelia commented wonderingly on the fact to Mr. Ferguson, who was standing by her side.

"Why, you see it ever so much better now!" she exclaimed. "All those enemies having their heads cut off by the King—they just stand right out. That's a cute kind of castle there that I never noticed before. I wish Dr. Bessner was here, he'd tell me what it was."

"How you can stand that old fool beats me," said Ferguson gloomily.

"Why, he's just one of the kindest men I've ever met!"

"Pompous old bore."

"I don't think you ought to speak that way."

The young man gripped her suddenly by the arm. They were just emerging from the temple into the moonlight.

"Why do you stick being bored by fat old men—and bullied and snubbed by a vicious old harridan?"

"Why, Mr. Ferguson!"

"Haven't you got any spirit? Don't you know you're just as good as she is?"

"But I'm not!" Cornelia spoke with honest conviction.

"You're not as rich; that's all you mean."

"No, it isn't. Cousin Marie's very, very cultured, and—"

"Cultured!" The young man let go of her arm as suddenly as he had taken it. "That word makes me sick."

Cornelia looked at him in alarm.

"She doesn't like you talking to me, does she?" asked the young man.

Cornelia blushed and looked embarrassed.

"Why? Because she thinks I'm not her social equal! Pah! Doesn't that make you see red?"

Cornelia faltered out, "I wish you wouldn't get so mad about things."

"Don't you realize—and you an American—that everyone is born free and equal?"

"They're not," said Cornelia with calm certainty.

"My good girl, it's part of your constitution!"

"Cousin Marie says politicians aren't gentlemen," said Cornelia. "And of course people aren't equal. It doesn't make sense. I know I'm kind of homely looking, and I used to feel mortified about it sometimes, but I've got over that. I'd like to have been born elegant and beautiful like Mrs. Doyle, but I wasn't, so I guess it's no use worrying."

"Mrs. Doyle!" exclaimed Ferguson with deep contempt. "She's the sort of woman who ought to be shot as an example."

Cornelia looked at him anxiously.

"I believe it's your digestion," she said kindly. "I've got a special kind of pepsin that Cousin Marie tried once. Would you like to try it?"

Mr. Ferguson said, "You're impossible!"

He turned and strode away. Cornelia went on toward the boat. Just as she was crossing onto the gangway, he caught her up once more.

"You're the nicest person on the boat," he said. "And mind you remember it."

Blushing with pleasure Cornelia repaired to the observation saloon. Miss Van Schuyler was conversing with Dr. Bessner—an agreeable conversation dealing with certain royal patients of his.

Cornelia said guiltily, "I do hope I haven't been a long time, Cousin Marie."

Glancing at her watch the old lady snapped: "You haven't exactly hurried, my dear. And what have you done with my velvet stole?"

Cornelia looked round.

"Shall I see if it's in the cabin, Cousin Marie?"

"Of course it isn't! I had it just after dinner in here, and I haven't moved out of the place. It was on that chair."

Cornelia made a desultory search.

"I can't see it anywhere, Cousin Marie."

"Nonsense!" said Miss Van Schuyler. "Look about." It was an order such as one might give to a dog, and in her doglike fashion Cornelia obeyed. The quiet Mr. Fanthorp, who was sitting at a table near by, rose and assisted her. But the stole could not be found.

The day had been such an unusually hot and sultry one that most people had retired early after going ashore to view the temple. The Doyles were playing Bridge with Pennington and Race at a table in a corner. The only other occupant of the saloon was Hercule Poirot, who was yawning his head off at a small table near the door.

Miss Van Schuyler, making a Royal Progress bedward, with Cornelia and Miss Bowers in attendance, paused by his chair. He sprang politely to his feet, stifling a yawn of gargantuan dimensions.

Miss Van Schuyler said: "I have only just realized Who you are, Monsieur Poirot. I may tell you that I have heard of you from my old friend Rufus Van Aldin. You must tell me about your cases sometime."

Poirot, his eyes twinkling a little through their sleepiness, bowed in an exaggerated manner. With a kindly but condescending nod, Miss Van Schuyler passed on.

Poirot yawned once more. He felt heavy and stupid with sleep and could hardly keep his eyes open. He glanced over at the Bridge players, absorbed in their game, then at young Fanthorp, who was deep in a book. Apart from them the saloon was empty.

He passed through the swinging door out onto the deck. Jacqueline de Bellefort, coming precipitately along the deck, almost collided with him.

"Pardon, Mademoiselle."

She said, "You look sleepy, Monsieur Poirot."

He admitted it frankly.

"*Mais oui*—I am consumed with sleep. I can hardly keep my eyes open. It has been a day very close and oppressive."

"Yes." She seemed to brood over it. "It's been the sort of day when things—snap! Break! When one can't go on. . . ."

Her voice was low and charged with passion. She looked not at him, but toward the sandy shore. Her hands were clenched, rigid. . . .

Suddenly the tension relaxed. She said, "Good-night, Monsieur Poirot."

"Good-night, Mademoiselle."

Her eyes met his, just for a swift moment. Thinking it over the next day, he came to the conclusion that there had been appeal in that glance. He was to remember it afterward. . . .

Then he passed on to his cabin and she went toward the saloon.

Cornelia, having dealt with Miss Van Schuyler's many needs and fantasies, took some needlework with her back to the saloon. She herself did not feel in the least sleepy. On the contrary she felt wide awake and slightly excited.

The Bridge four were still at it. In another chair the quiet Fanthorp read a book. Cornelia sat down to her needlework.

Suddenly the door opened and Jacqueline de Bellefort came in. She stood in the doorway, her head thrown back. Then she pressed a bell and sauntered across to Cornelia and sat down.

"Been ashore?" she asked.

"Yes. I thought it was just fascinating in the moonlight."

Jacqueline nodded.

"Yes, lovely night. . . . A real honeymoon night."

Her eyes went to the Bridge table—rested a moment on Linnet Doyle.

The boy came in answer to the bell. Jacqueline ordered a double gin. As she gave the order Simon Doyle shot a quick glance at her. A faint line of anxiety showed between his eyebrows.

His wife said, "Simon, we're waiting for you to call."

Jacqueline hummed a little tune to herself. When the drink came, she picked it up, said, "Well, here's to crime," drank it off and ordered another.

Again Simon looked across from the Bridge table. His calls became slightly absent-minded. His partner, Pennington, took him to task.

Jacqueline began to hum again, at first under her breath, then louder:

"*He was her man and he did her wrong* . . ."

"Sorry," said Simon to Pennington. "Stupid of me not to return your lead. That gives 'em rubber."

Linnet rose to her feet.

"I'm sleepy. I think I'll go to bed."

"About time to turn in," said Colonel Race.

"I'm with you," agreed Pennington.

"Coming, Simon?"

Doyle said slowly: "Not just yet. I think I'll have a drink first."

Linnet nodded and went out. Race followed her. Pennington finished his drink and then followed suit.

Cornelia began to gather up her embroidery.

"Don't go to bed, Miss Robson," said Jacqueline. "Please don't. I feel like making a night of it. Don't desert me."

Cornelia sat down again.

"We girls must stick together," said Jacqueline.

She threw back her head and laughed—a shrill laugh without merriment.

The second drink came.

"Have something," said Jacqueline.

"No, thank you very much," replied Cornelia.

Jacqueline tilted back her chair. She hummed now loudly: "*He was her man and he did her wrong . . .*"

Mr. Fanthorp turned a page of *Europe from Within.*

Simon Doyle picked up a magazine.

"Really, I think I'll go to bed," said Cornelia. "It's getting very late."

"You can't go to bed yet," Jacqueline declared. "I forbid you to. Tell me all about yourself."

"Well—I don't know. There isn't much to tell," Cornelia faltered. "I've just lived at home, and I haven't been around much. This is my first trip to Europe. I'm just loving every minute of it."

Jacqueline laughed.

"You're a happy sort of person, aren't you? God, I'd like to be you."

"Oh! would you? But I mean—I'm sure—"

Cornelia felt flustered. Undoubtedly Miss de Bellefort was drinking too much. That wasn't exactly a novelty to Cornelia. She had seen plenty of drunkenness during Prohibition years. But there was something else. . . . Jacqueline de Bellefort was talking to her—was looking at her—and yet, Cornelia felt, it was as though, somehow, she was talking to someone else. . . .

But there were only two other people in the room, Mr. Fanthorp and Mr. Doyle. Mr. Fanthorp seemed quite absorbed in his book. Mr. Doyle was looking rather odd—a queer sort of watchful look on his face. . . .

Jacqueline said again, "Tell me all about yourself."

Always obedient, Cornelia tried to comply. She talked, rather heavily, going into unnecessary small details about her daily life. She was so unused to being the talker. Her rôle was so constantly that of listener. And yet Miss de Bellefort seemed to want to know. When Cornelia faltered to a standstill, the other girl was quick to prompt her.

"Go on—tell me more."

And so Cornelia went on ("Of course, Mother's very delicate—some days she touches nothing but cereals—") unhappily conscious that all she said was supremely uninteresting, yet flattered by the other girl's seeming interest. But was she interested? Wasn't she, somehow, listening to something else—or, perhaps, *for* something else? She was looking at Cornelia, yes, but wasn't there really *someone else*, sitting in the room.

"And of course we get very good art classes, and last winter I had a course of—"

(How late was it? Surely very late. She had been talking and talking. If only something definite would happen—)

And immediately, as though in answer to the wish, something did happen. Only, at the moment, it seemed very natural.

Jacqueline turned her head and spoke to Simon Doyle.

"Ring the bell, Simon. I want another drink."

Simon Doyle looked up from his magazine and said quietly: "The stewards have gone to bed. It's after midnight."

"I tell you I want another drink."

Simon said, "You've had quite enough drinks, Jackie."

She swung round at him.

"What damned business is it of yours?"

He shrugged his shoulders. "None."

She watched him for a minute or two. Then she said: "What's the matter, Simon? Are you afraid?"

Simon did not answer. Rather elaborately he picked up his magazine again.

Cornelia murmured, "Oh, dear—as late as that—I must—"

She began to fumble, dropped a thimble. . . .

Jacqueline said: "Don't go to bed. I'd like another woman here—to support me." She began to laugh again. "Do you know what Simon over there is afraid of? He's afraid *I'm* going to tell you the story of *my* life."

"Oh—er—" Cornelia spluttered a little.

Jacqueline said clearly, "You see, he and I were once engaged."

"Oh, really?"

Cornelia was the prey of conflicting emotions. She was deeply embarrassed but at the same time pleasurably thrilled. How—how *black* Simon Doyle was looking.

"Yes, it's a very sad story," said Jacqueline; her soft voice was low and mocking. "He treated me rather badly, didn't you, Simon?"

Simon Doyle said brutally: "Go to bed, Jackie. You're drunk."

"If you're embarrassed, Simon dear, you'd better leave the room."

Simon Doyle looked at her. The hand that held the magazine shook a little, but he spoke bluntly.

"I'm staying," he said.

Cornelia murmured for the third time, "I really must—it's so late—"

"You're not to go," said Jacqueline. Her hand shot out and held the other girl in her chair. "You're to stay and hear what I've got to say."

"Jackie," said Simon sharply, "you're making a fool of yourself! For God's sake, go to bed."

Jacqueline sat up suddenly in her chair. Words poured from her rapidly in a soft hissing stream.

"You're afraid of a scene, aren't you? That's because you're so English—so reticent! You want me to behave 'decently,' don't you? But I don't care whether I behave decently or not! You'd better get out of here quickly—because I'm going to talk—a lot."

Jim Fanthorp carefully shut his book, yawned, glanced at his watch, got up and strolled out. It was a very British and utterly unconvincing performance.

Jacqueline swung round in her chair and glared at Simon.

"You damned fool," she said thickly, "do you think you can treat me as you have done and get away with it?"

Simon Doyle opened his lips, then shut them again. He sat quite still as though he were hoping that her outburst would exhaust itself if he said nothing to provoke her further.

Jacqueline's voice came thick and blurred. It fascinated Cornelia, totally unused to naked emotions of any kind.

"I told you," said Jacqueline, "that I'd kill you sooner than see you go to another woman. . . . You don't think I meant that? *You're wrong.* I've only been—waiting! You're *my* man! Do you hear? You belong to me. . . ."

Still Simon did not speak. Jacqueline's hand fumbled a moment or two on her lap. She leant forward.

"I told you I'd kill you, and I meant it. . . ." Her hand came up suddenly with something in it that flashed and gleamed. "I'll shoot you like a dog—like the dirty dog you are. . . ."

Now at last Simon acted. He sprang to his feet, but at the same moment she pulled the trigger. . . .

Simon half twisted—fell across a chair. . . . Cornelia screamed and rushed to the door. Jim Fanthorp was on the deck leaning over the rail. She called to him.

"Mr. Fanthorp . . . Mr. Fanthorp. . . ."

He ran to her; she clutched at him incoherently. . . .

"She's shot him— Oh! she's shot him. . . ."

Simon Doyle still lay as he had fallen half into and across a chair. . . . Jacqueline stood as though paralysed. She was trembling violently, and her eyes, dilated and frightened, were staring at the crimson stain slowly soaking through Simon's trouser leg just below the knee where he held a handkerchief close against the wound. . . .

She stammered out:

"I didn't mean . . . Oh, my God, I didn't really mean . . ."

The pistol dropped from her nervous fingers with a clatter on the floor. She kicked it away with her foot. It slid under one of the settees.

Simon, his voice faint, murmured: "Fanthorp, for Heaven's sake —there's someone coming. . . . Say it's all right—an accident—something. There mustn't be a scandal over this."

Fanthorp nodded in quick comprehension. He wheeled round to the door where a startled Nubian face showed. He said: "All right —all right! Just fun!"

The black face looked doubtful, puzzled, then reassured. The teeth showed in a wide grin. The boy nodded and went off.

Fanthorp turned back.

"That's all right. Don't think anybody else heard. Only sounded like a cork, you know. Now the next thing—"

He was startled. Jacqueline suddenly began to weep hysterically.

"Oh, God, I wish I were dead. . . . I'll kill myself. I'll be better dead. . . . Oh, what have I done—what have I done?"

Cornelia hurried to her.

"Hush, dear, hush."

Simon, his brow wet, his face twisted with pain, said urgently:

"Get her away. For God's sake, get her out of here! Get her to her cabin, Fanthorp. Look here, Miss Robson, get that hospital nurse of yours." He looked appealingly from one to the other of them. "Don't leave her. Make quite sure she's safe with the nurse looking after her. Then get hold of old Bessner and bring him here. For God's sake, don't let any news of this get to my wife."

Jim Fanthorp nodded comprehendingly. The quiet young man was cool and competent in an emergency.

Between them he and Cornelia got the weeping, struggling girl out of the saloon and along the deck to her cabin. There they had more trouble with her. She fought to free herself; her sobs redoubled

"I'll drown myself . . . I'll drown myself. . . . I'm not fit to live. . . . Oh, Simon—Simon!"

Fanthorp said to Cornelia: "Better get hold of Miss Bowers. I'll stay while you get her."

Cornelia nodded and hurried out.

As soon as she left, Jacqueline clutched Fanthorp.

"His leg—it's bleeding—broken. . . . He may bleed to death. I must go to him. . . . Oh, Simon—Simon—how could I?"

Her voice rose. Fanthorp said urgently: "Quietly—quietly. . . . He'll be all right."

She began to struggle again.

"Let me go! Let me throw myself overboard. . . . Let me kill myself!"

Fanthorp, holding her by the shoulders, forced her back onto the bed.

"You must stay here. Don't make a fuss. Pull yourself together. It's all right, I tell you."

To his relief, the distraught girl did manage to control herself a little, but he was thankful when the curtains were pushed aside and the efficient Miss Bowers, neatly dressed in a hideous kimono, entered, accompanied by Cornelia.

"Now then," said Miss Bowers briskly, "what's all this?"

She took charge without any sign of surprise and alarm.

Fanthorp thankfully left the overwrought girl in her capable hands and hurried along to the cabin occupied by Dr. Bessner. He knocked and entered on the top of the knock.

"Dr. Bessner?"

A terrific snore resolved itself, and a startled voice asked: "So? What is it?"

By this time Fanthorp had switched the light on. The doctor blinked up at him, looking rather like a large owl.

"It's Doyle. He's been shot. Miss de Bellefort shot him. He's in the saloon. Can you come?"

The stout doctor reacted promptly. He asked a few curt questions, pulled on his bedroom slippers and a dressing-gown, picked up a little case of necessaries and accompanied Fanthorp to the lounge.

Simon had managed to get the window beside him open. He was leaning his head against it, inhaling the air. His face was a ghastly colour.

Dr. Bessner came over to him.

"Ha? So? What have we here?"

A handkerchief sodden with blood lay on the carpet and on the carpet itself was a dark stain.

The doctor's examination was punctuated with Teutonic grunts and exclamations.

"Yes, it is bad this. . . . The bone is fractured. And a big loss of blood. Herr Fanthorp, you and I must get him to my cabin. So—like this. He cannot walk. We must carry him, thus."

As they lifted him Cornelia appeared in the doorway. Catching sight of her, the doctor uttered a grunt of satisfaction.

"Ach, it is you? Goot. Come with us. I have need of assistance. You will be better than my friend here. He looks a little pale already."

Fanthorp emitted a rather sickly smile.

"Shall I get Miss Bowers?" he asked.

Dr. Bessner threw a considering glance over Cornelia.

"You will do very well, young lady," he announced. "You will not faint or be foolish, *hein?*"

"I can do what you tell me," said Cornelia eagerly.

Bessner nodded in a satisfied fashion.

The procession passed along the deck.

The next ten minutes was purely surgical and Mr. Jim Fanthorp did not enjoy it at all. He felt secretly ashamed of the superior fortitude exhibited by Cornelia.

"So, that is the best I can do," announced Dr. Bessner at last. "You have been a hero, my friend." He patted Simon approvingly on the shoulder. Then he rolled up his sleeve and produced a hypodermic needle.

"And now I will give you something to make you sleep. Your wife, what about her?"

Simon said weakly: "She needn't know till the morning. . . ." He went on: "I—you mustn't blame Jackie. . . . It's been all my fault. I treated her disgracefully . . . poor kid—she didn't know what she was doing. . . ."

Dr. Bessner nodded comprehendingly.

"Yes, yes—I understand. . . ."

"My fault—" Simon urged. His eyes went to Cornelia. "Someone—ought to—stay with her. She might—hurt herself—"

Dr. Bessner injected the needle. Cornelia said, with quiet competence: "It's all right, Mr. Doyle. Miss Bowers is going to stay with her all night. . . ."

A grateful look flashed over Simon's face. His body relaxed. His eyes closed. Suddenly he jerked them open. "Fanthorp?"

"Yes, Doyle."

"The pistol . . . ought not to leave it . . . lying about. The boys will find it in the morning. . . ."

Fanthorp nodded. "Quite right. I'll go and get hold of it now."

He went out of the cabin and along the deck. Miss Bowers appeared at the door of Jacqueline's cabin.

"She'll be all right now," she announced. "I've given her a morphine injection."

"But you'll stay with her?"

"Oh, yes. Morphia excites some people. I shall stay all night."

Fanthorp went on to the lounge.

Some three minutes later there was a tap on Bessner's cabin door.

"Dr. Bessner?"

"Yes?" The stout man appeared.

Fanthorp beckoned him out on the deck.

"Look here—I can't find that pistol. . . ."

"What is that?"

"The pistol. It dropped out of the girl's hand. She kicked it away and it went under a settee. It isn't under that settee now."

They stared at each other.

"But who can have taken it?"

Fanthorp shrugged his shoulders.

Bessner said: "It is curious, that. But I do not see what we can do about it."

Puzzled and vaguely alarmed, the two men separated.

CHAPTER XII

Hercule Poirot was just wiping the lather from his freshly shaved face when there was a quick tap on the door, and hard on top of it Colonel Race entered unceremoniously. He closed the door behind him.

He said: "Your instinct was quite correct. It's happened."

Poirot straightened up and asked sharply: "What has happened?"

"Linnet Doyle's dead—shot through the head last night."

Poirot was silent for a minute, two memories vividly before him—a girl in a garden at Assuan saying in a hard breathless voice, "I'd like to put my dear little pistol against her head and just press the trigger," and another more recent memory, the same voice saying, "One feels one can't go on—the kind of day when something breaks" —and that strange momentary flash of appeal in her eyes. What had been the matter with him not to respond to that appeal? He had been blind, deaf, stupid with his need for sleep. . . .

Race went on: "I've got some slight official standing; they sent for me, put it in my hands. The boat's due to start in half an hour, but it will be delayed till I give the word. There's a possibility, of course, that the murderer came from the shore."

Poirot shook his head.

Race acquiesced in the gesture.

"I agree. One can pretty well rule that out. Well, man, it's up to you. This is your show."

Poirot had been attiring himself with a neat-fingered celerity. He said now, "I am at your disposal."

The two men stepped out on the deck.

Race said: "Bessner should be there by now. I sent the stewar for him."

There were four cabins de luxe, with bathrooms, on the boat. O the two on the port side one was occupied by Dr. Bessner, the othe by Andrew Pennington. On the starboard side the first was occupie by Miss Van Schuyler, and the one next to it by Linnet Doyl Her husband's dressing cabin was next door.

A white-faced steward was standing outside the door of Linne Doyle's cabin. He opened the door for them and they passed insid Dr. Bessner was bending over the bed. He looked up and grunte as the other two entered.

S. S. KARNAK

PROMENADE DECK

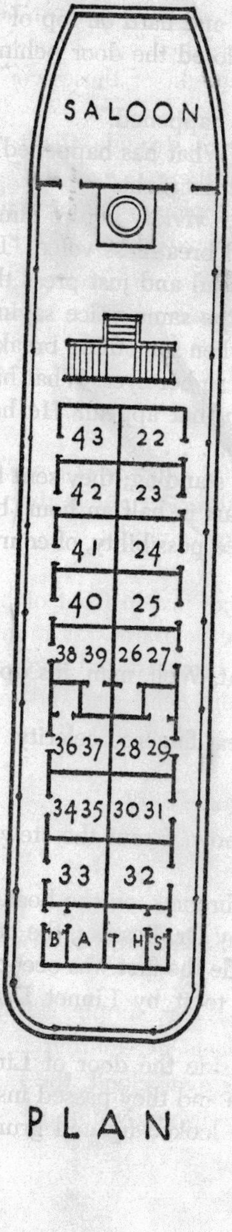

PLAN

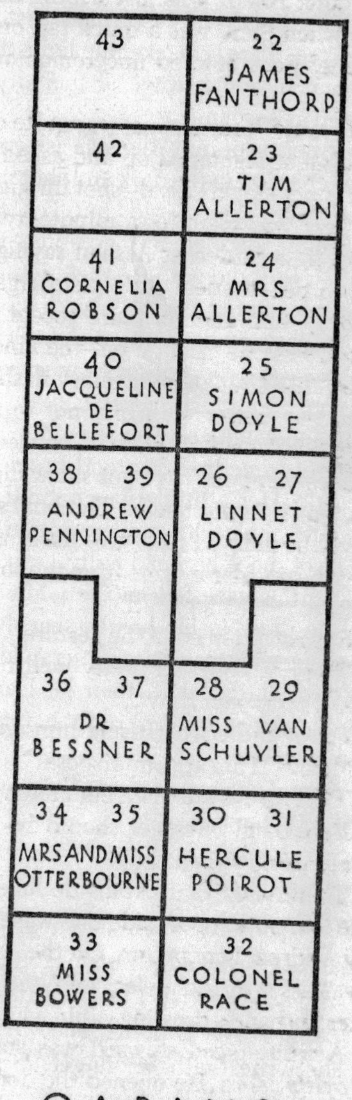

CABINS

"What can you tell us, Doctor, about this business?" asked Race.

Bessner rubbed his unshaven jaw meditatively.

"Ach! She was shot—shot at close quarters. See—here, just above the ear—that is where the bullet entered. A very little bullet—I should say a twenty-two. The pistol, it was held close against her head; see, there is blackening here, the skin is scorched."

Again in a sick wave of memory Poirot thought of those words uttered at Assuan.

Bessner went on: "She was asleep; there was no struggle; the murderer crept up in the dark and shot her as she lay there."

"*Ah! non!*" Poirot cried out. His sense of psychology was outraged. Jacqueline de Bellefort creeping into a darkened cabin, pistol in hand— No, it did not "fit," that picture.

Bessner stared at him through his thick lenses.

"But that is what happened, I tell you."

"Yes, yes. I did not mean what you thought. I was not contradicting you."

Bessner gave a satisfied grunt.

Poirot came up and stood beside him. Linnet Doyle was lying on her side. Her attitude was natural and peaceful. But above the ear was a tiny hole with an incrustation of dried blood round it.

Poirot shook his head sadly.

Then his gaze fell on the white painted wall just in front of him and he drew in his breath sharply. Its white neatness was marred by a big wavering letter J scrawled in some brownish-red medium.

Poirot stared at it, then he leaned over the dead girl and very gently picked up her right hand. One finger of it was stained a brownish-red.

"*Nom d'un nom d'un nom!*" ejaculated Hercule Poirot.

"Eh? What is that?"

Dr. Bessner looked up.

"Ach! *That.*"

Race said: "Well, I'm damned. What do you make of that, Poirot?"

Poirot swayed a little on his toes.

"You ask me what I make of it. *Eh bien,* it is very simple, is it not? Madame Doyle is dying; she wishes to indicate her murderer, and so she writes with her finger, dipped in her own blood, the initial letter of her murderer's name. Oh, yes, it is astonishingly simple."

"Ach! but—"

Dr. Bessner was about to break out, but a peremptory gesture from Race silenced him.

"So it strikes you like that?" he asked slowly.

Poirot turned round on him nodding his head.

"Yes, yes. It is, as I say, of an astonishing simplicity! It is so familiar, is it not? It has been done so often, in the pages of the romance of crime! It is now, indeed, a little *vieux jeu!* It leads one to suspect that our murderer is—old-fashioned!"

Race drew a long breath.

"I see," he said. "I thought at first—" He stopped.

Poirot said with a very faint smile: "That I believed in all the old clichés of melodrama? But pardon, Dr. Bessner, you were about to say—?"

Bessner broke out gutturally: "What do I say? Pah! I say it is absurd; it is the nonsense! The poor lady she died instantaneously. To dip her finger in the blood (and as you see, there is hardly any blood) and write the letter J upon the wall— Bah—it is the nonsense —the melodramatic nonsense!"

"*C'est l'enfantillage,*" agreed Poirot.

"But it was done with a purpose," suggested Race.

"That—naturally," agreed Poirot, and his face was grave.

"What does J stand for?" asked Race.

Poirot replied promptly: "J stands for Jacqueline de Bellefort, a young lady who declared to me less than a week ago that she would like nothing better than to—" he paused and then deliberately quoted, " 'to put my dear little pistol close against her head and then just press with my finger. . . .' "

"*Gott im Himmel!*" exclaimed Dr. Bessner.

There was a momentary silence. Then Race drew a deep breath and said: "Which is just what was done here?"

Bessner nodded.

"That is so, yes. It was a pistol of very small calibre—as I say probably a twenty-two. The bullet has got to be extracted, of course, before we can say definitely."

Race nodded in swift comprehension. Then he asked: "What about time of death?"

Bessner stroked his jaw again. His finger made a rasping sound. "I would not care to be too precise. It is now eight o'clock. I will say, with due regard to the temperature last night, that she has been dead certainly six hours and probably not longer than eight."

"That puts it between midnight and two A.M."

"That is so."

There was a pause. Race looked round.

"What about her husband? I suppose he sleeps in the cabin next door."

"At the moment," said Dr. Bessner, "he is asleep in my cabin."

Both men looked very surprised.

Bessner nodded his head several times.

"Ach, so. I see you have not been told about that. Mr. Doyle was shot last night in the saloon."

"Shot? By whom?"

"By the young lady, Jacqueline de Bellefort."

Race asked sharply, "Is he badly hurt?"

"Yes, the bone was splintered. I have done all that is possible at the moment, but it is necessary, you understand, that the fracture should be X-rayed as soon as possible and proper treatment given such as is impossible on this boat."

Poirot murmured, "Jacqueline de Bellefort."

His eyes went again to the J on the wall.

Race said abruptly: "If there is nothing more we can do here for the moment, let's go below. The management has put the smoking-room at our disposal. We must get the details of what happened last night."

They left the cabin. Race locked the door and took the key with him.

"We can come back later," he said. "The first thing to do is to get all the facts clear."

They went down to the deck below, where they found the Manager of the *Karnak* waiting uneasily in the doorway of the smoking-room.

The poor man was terribly upset and worried over the whole business, and was eager to leave everything in Colonel Race's hands.

"I feel I can't do better than leave it to you, sir, seeing your official position. I'd had orders to put myself at your disposal in the—er—other matter. If you will take charge, I'll see that everything is done as you wish."

"Good man! To begin with I'd like this room kept clear for me and for Monsieur Poirot during the inquiry."

"Certainly, sir."

"That's all at present. Go on with your own work. I know where to find you."

Looking slightly relieved the Manager left the room.

Race said, "Sit down, Bessner, and let's have the whole story of what happened last night."

They listened in silence to the doctor's rumbling voice.

"Clear enough," said Race, when he had finished. "The girl worked herself up, helped by a drink or two, and finally took a pot shot at the man with a twenty-two pistol. Then she went along to Linnet Doyle's cabin and shot her as well."

But Dr. Bessner was shaking his head.

"No, no. I do not think so. I do not think that was *possible.* For one thing she would not write her own initial on the wall; it would be ridiculous, *nicht wahr*?"

"She might," Race declared, "if she were as blindly mad and jealous as she sounds; she might want to—well—sign her name to the crime, so to speak."

Poirot shook his head.

"No, no, I do not think she would be as—as *crude* as that."

"Then there's only one reason for that J. It was put there by someone else deliberately to throw suspicion on her."

Bessner nodded.

"Yes, and the criminal was unlucky, because, you see, it is not only *unlikely* that the young Fräulein did the murder; it is also I think *impossible.*"

"How's that?"

Bessner explained Jacqueline's hysterics and the circumstances which had led Miss Bowers to take charge of her.

"And I think—I am sure—that Miss Bowers stayed with her all night."

Race said, "If that's so, it's going to simplify matters very much."

"Who discovered the crime?" Poirot asked.

"Mrs. Doyle's maid, Louise Bourget. She went to call her mistress as usual, found her dead, and came out and flopped into the steward's arms in a dead faint. He went to the Manager, who came to me. I got hold of Bessner and then came for you."

Poirot nodded.

Race said: "Doyle's got to know. You say he's asleep still?"

Bessner nodded. "Yes, he's still asleep in my cabin. I gave him a strong opiate last night."

Race turned to Poirot.

"Well," he said, "I don't think we need detain the doctor any longer, eh? Thank you, Doctor."

Bessner rose. "I will have my breakfast, yes. And then I will go back to my cabin and see if Mr. Doyle is ready to wake."

"Thanks."

Bessner went out. The two men looked at each other.

"Well, what about it, Poirot?" Race asked. "You're the man in charge. I'll take my orders from you. You say what's to be done."

Poirot bowed.

"*Eh bien,*" he said; "we must hold the court of inquiry. First of all, I think we must verify the story of the affair last night. That is to say, we must question Fanthorp and Miss Robson, who were the actual witnesses of what occurred. The disappearance of the pistol is very significant."

Race rang a bell and sent a message by the steward.

Poirot sighed and shook his head. "It is bad, this," he murmured. "It is bad."

"Have you any ideas?" asked Race curiously.

"My ideas conflict. They are not well arranged; they are not orderly. There is, you see, the big fact that this girl hated Linnet Doyle and wanted to kill her."

"You think she's capable of it?"

"I think so—yes." Poirot sounded doubtful.

"But not in this way? That's what's worrying you, isn't it? Not to creep into her cabin in the dark and shoot her while she was sleeping. It's the cold-bloodedness that strikes you as not ringing true?"

"In a sense, yes."

"You think that this girl, Jacqueline de Bellefort, is incapable of a premeditated cold-blooded murder?"

Poirot said slowly: "I am not sure, you see. She would have the brains—yes. But I doubt if, physically, she could bring herself to do the *act*. . . ."

Race nodded. "Yes, I see. . . . Well, according to Bessner's story, it would also have been physically impossible."

"If that is true it clears the ground considerably. Let us hope it is true." Poirot paused and then added simply: "I shall be glad if it is so, for I have for that little one much sympathy."

The door opened and Fanthorp and Cornelia came in. Bessner followed them.

Cornelia gasped out: "Isn't this just awful? Poor, poor Mrs. Doyle!

And she was so lovely too. It must have been a real *fiend* who could hurt her! And poor Mr. Doyle; he'll just go half crazy when he knows! Why, even last night he was so frightfully worried lest she should hear about his accident."

"That is just what we want you to tell us about, Miss Robson," said Race. "We want to know exactly what happened last night."

Cornelia began a little confusedly, but a question or two from Poirot helped matters.

"Ah, yes, I understand. After the Bridge, Madame Doyle went to her cabin. Did she really go to her cabin, I wonder?"

"She did," said Race. "I actually saw her. I said good-night to her at the door."

"And the time?"

"Mercy, I couldn't say," replied Cornelia.

"It was twenty past eleven," said Race.

"*Bien.* Then at twenty past eleven, Madame Doyle was alive and well. At that moment there was, in the saloon, who?"

Fanthorp answered: "Doyle was there. And Miss de Bellefort. Myself and Miss Robson."

"That's so," agreed Cornelia. "Mr. Pennington had a drink and then went off to bed."

"That was how much later?"

"Oh, about three or four minutes."

"Before half past eleven, then?"

"Oh, yes."

"So that there were left in the saloon you, Mademoiselle Robson, Mademoiselle de Bellefort, Monsieur Doyle and Monsieur Fanthorp. What were you all doing?"

"Mr. Fanthorp was reading a book. I'd got some embroidery. Miss de Bellefort was—she was—"

Fanthorp came to the rescue. "She was drinking pretty heavily."

"Yes," agreed Cornelia. "She was talking to me mostly and asking me about things at home. And she kept saying things—to me mostly, but I think they were kind of meant for Mr. Doyle. He was getting kind of mad at her, but he didn't say anything. I think he thought if he kept quiet she might simmer down."

"But she didn't?"

Cornelia shook her head.

"I tried to go once or twice, but she made me stay, and I was getting very, very uncomfortable. And then Mr. Fanthorp got up and went out—"

"It was a little embarrassing," said Fanthorp. "I thought I'd make an unobtrusive exit. Miss de Bellefort was clearly working up for a scene."

"And then she pulled out the pistol," went on Cornelia, "and Mr. Doyle jumped up to try and get it away from her, and it went off and shot him through the leg; and then she began to sob and cry—and I was scared to death and ran out after Mr. Fanthorp, and he came back with me, and Mr. Doyle said not to make a fuss, and one of the Nubian boys heard the noise of the shot and came along, but Mr. Fanthorp told him it was all right; and then we got Jacqueline away to her cabin, and Mr. Fanthorp stayed with her while I got Miss Bowers."

Cornelia paused breathless.

"What time was this?" asked Race.

Cornelia said again, "Mercy, I don't know," but Fanthorp answered promptly:

"It must have been about twenty minutes past twelve. I know that it was actually half past twelve when I finally got to my cabin."

"Now let me be quite sure on one or two points," said Poirot. "After Madame Doyle left the saloon, did any of you four leave it?"

"No."

"You are quite certain Mademoiselle de Bellefort did not leave the saloon at all?"

Fanthorp answered promptly: "Positive. Neither Doyle, Miss de Bellefort, Miss Robson, nor myself left the saloon."

"Good. That establishes the fact that Mademoiselle de Bellefort could not possibly have shot Madame Doyle before—let us say—twenty past twelve. Now, Mademoiselle Robson, you went to fetch Mademoiselle Bowers. Was Mademoiselle de Bellefort alone in her cabin during that period?"

"No, Mr. Fanthorp stayed with her."

"Good! So far, Mademoiselle de Bellefort has a perfect alibi. Mademoiselle Bowers is the next person to interview, but, before I send for her, I should like to have your opinion on one or two points. Monsieur Doyle, you say, was very anxious that Mademoiselle de Bellefort should not be left alone. Was he afraid, do you think, that she was contemplating some further rash act?"

"That is my opinion," said Fanthorp.

"He was definitely afraid she might attack Madame Doyle?"

"No." Fanthorp shook his head. "I don't think that was his idea at all. I think he was afraid she might—er—do something rash to herself."

"Suicide?"

"Yes. You see, she seemed completely sobered and heartbroken at what she had done. She was full of self-reproach. She kept saying she would be better dead."

Cornelia said timidly: "I think he was rather upset about her. He spoke—quite nicely. He said it was all his fault—that he'd treated her badly. He—he was really very nice."

Hercule Poirot nodded thoughtfully.

"Now about the pistol," he went on. "What happened to that?"

"She dropped it," said Cornelia.

"And afterward?"

Fanthorp explained how he had gone back to search for it, but had not been able to find it.

"Aha!" said Poirot. "Now we begin to arrive. Let us, I pray you, be very precise. Describe to me exactly what happened."

"Miss de Bellefort let it fall. Then she kicked it away from her with her foot."

"She sort of hated it," explained Cornelia. "I know just what she felt."

"And it went under a settee, you say. Now be very careful. Mademoiselle de Bellefort did not recover that pistol before she left the saloon?"

Both Fanthorp and Cornelia were positive on that point.

"*Précisément.* I seek only to be very exact, you comprehend. Then we arrive at this point. When Mademoiselle de Bellefort leaves the saloon the pistol is under the settee, and, since Mademoiselle de Bellefort is not left alone—Monsieur Fanthorp, Mademoiselle Robson or Mademoiselle Bowers being with her—she has no opportunity to get back the pistol after she left the saloon. What time was it, Monsieur Fanthorp, when you went back to look for it?"

"It must have been just before half past twelve."

"And how long would have elapsed between the time you and Dr. Bessner carried Monsieur Doyle out of the saloon until you returned to look for the pistol?"

"Perhaps five minutes—perhaps a little more."

"Then in that five minutes someone removes that pistol from where it lay out of sight under the settee. That someone was *not* Mademoiselle de Bellefort. Who was it? It seems highly probable that the person who removed it was the murderer of Madame Doyle. We may assume, too, that that person had overheard or seen something of the events immediately preceding."

"I don't see how you make that out," objected Fanthorp.

"Because," said Hercule Poirot, "you have just told us that the pistol was out of sight under the settee. Therefore it is hardly credible that it was discovered by *accident*. It was taken by someone who knew it was there. Therefore that someone must have assisted at the scene."

Fanthorp shook his head. "I saw no one when I went out on the deck just before the shot was fired."

"Ah, but you went out by the door on the starboard side."

"Yes. The same side as my cabin."

"Then if there had been anybody at the port door looking through the glass you would not have seen him?"

"No," admitted Fanthorp.

"Did anyone hear the shot except the Nubian boy?"

"Not as far as I know."

Fanthorp went on: "You see, the windows in here were all closed. Miss Van Schuyler felt a draught earlier in the evening. The swing doors were shut. I doubt if the shot would be at all clearly heard. It would only sound like the pop of a cork."

Race said, "As far as I know, no one seems to have heard the other shot—the shot that killed Mrs. Doyle."

"That we will inquire into presently," said Poirot. "For the moment we still concern ourselves with Mademoiselle de Bellefort. We must speak to Mademoiselle Bowers. But first, before you go"—he arrested Fanthorp and Cornelia with a gesture—"you will give me a little information about yourselves. Then it will not be necessary to call you again later. You first, Monsieur—your full name."

"James Lechdale Fanthorp."

"Address?"

"Glasmore House, Market Donnington, Northamptonshire."

"Your profession?"

"I am a lawyer."

"And your reasons for visiting this country?"

There was a pause. For the first time the impassive Mr. Fanthorp seemed taken aback. He said at last—almost mumbling the words, "Er—pleasure."

"Aha!" said Poirot. "You take the holiday; that is it, yes?"

"Er—yes."

"Very well, Monsieur Fanthorp. Will you give me a brief account of your own movements last night after the events we have just been narrating?"

"I went straight to bed."

"That was at—?"

"Just after half past twelve."

"Your cabin is number twenty-two on the starboard side—the one nearest the saloon?"

"Yes."

"I will ask you one more question. Did you hear anything—anything at all—after you went to your cabin?"

Fanthorp considered.

"I turned in very quickly. I *think* I heard a kind of splash just as I was dropping off to sleep. Nothing else."

"You heard a kind of splash? Near at hand?"

Fanthorp shook his head.

"Really, I couldn't say. I was half asleep."

"And what time would that be?"

"It might have been about one o'clock. I can't really say."

"Thank you, Monsieur Fanthorp. That is all."

Poirot turned his attention to Cornelia.

"And now, Mademoiselle Robson? Your full name?"

"Cornelia Ruth. And my address is The Red House, Bellfield, Connecticut."

"What brought you to Egypt?"

"Cousin Marie, Miss Van Schuyler, brought me along on a trip."

"Had you ever met Madame Doyle previous to this journey?"

"No, never."

"And what did you do last night?"

"I went right to bed after helping Dr. Bessner with Mr. Doyle's leg."

"Your cabin is—?"

"Forty-three on the port side—right next door to Miss de Bellefort."

"And did you hear anything?"

Cornelia shook her head.

"I didn't hear a thing."

"No splash?"

"No, but then I wouldn't, because the boat's against the bank my side."

Poirot nodded.

"Thank you, Mademoiselle Robson. Now perhaps you will be so kind as to ask Mademoiselle Bowers to come here."

Fanthorp and Cornelia went out.

"That seems clear enough," said Race. "Unless three independent witnesses are lying, Jacqueline de Bellefort couldn't have got hold of the pistol. But somebody did. And somebody overheard the scene. And somebody was B. F. enough to write a big J on the wall."

There was a tap on the door and Miss Bowers entered. The hospital nurse sat down in her usual composed, efficient manner. In answer to Poirot she gave her name, address, and qualifications, adding, "I've been looking after Miss Van Schuyler for over two years now."

"Is Mademoiselle Van Schuyler's health very bad?"

"Why, no, I wouldn't say that," replied Miss Bowers. "She's not very young, and she's nervous about herself, and she likes to have a nurse around handy. There's nothing serious the matter with her. She just likes plenty of attention, and she's willing to pay for it."

Poirot nodded comprehendingly. Then he said, "I understand that Mademoiselle Robson fetched you last night?"

"Why, yes, that's so."

"Will you tell me exactly what happened?"

"Well, Miss Robson just gave me a brief outline of what had occurred, and I came along with her. I found Miss de Bellefort in a very excited, hysterical condition."

"Did she utter any threats against Madame Doyle?"

"No, nothing of that kind. She was in a condition of morbid self-reproach. She'd taken a good deal of alcohol, I should say, and she was suffering from reaction. I didn't think she ought to be left. I gave her a shot of morphia and sat up with her."

"Now, Mademoiselle Bowers, I want you to answer this. Did Mademoiselle de Bellefort leave her cabin at all?"

"No, she did not."

"And you yourself?"

"I stayed with her until early this morning."

"You are quite sure of that."

"Absolutely sure."

"Thank you, Mademoiselle Bowers."

The nurse went out. The two men looked at each other.

Jacqueline de Bellefort was definitely cleared of the crime. Who then had shot Linnet Doyle?

CHAPTER XIII

RACE SAID: "Someone pinched the pistol. It wasn't Jacqueline de Bellefort. Someone knew enough to feel that his crime would be attributed to her. But that someone did not know that a hospital nurse was going to give her morphia and sit up with her all night. Add one thing more. Someone had already attempted to kill Linnet Doyle by rolling a boulder over the cliff; that someone was *not* Jacqueline de Bellefort. Who was it?"

Poirot said: "It will be simpler to say who it could not have been. Neither Monsieur Doyle, Madame Allerton, Monsieur Tim Allerton, Mademoiselle Van Schuyler nor Mademoiselle Bowers could have had anything to do with it. They were all within my sight."

"H'm," said Race; "that leaves rather a large field. What about motive?"

"That is where I hope Monsieur Doyle may be able to help us. There have been several incidents—"

The door opened and Jacqueline de Bellefort entered. She was very pale and she stumbled a little as she walked.

"I didn't do it," she said. Her voice was that of a frightened child. "I didn't do it. Oh, please believe me. Everyone will think I did it—but I didn't—I didn't. It's—it's awful. I wish it hadn't happened. I might have killed Simon last night; I was mad, I think. But I didn't do the other. . . ."

She sat down and burst into tears.

Poirot patted her on the shoulder.

"There, there. We know that you did not kill Madame Doyle. It is proved—yes, proved, *mon enfant*. It was not you."

Jackie sat up suddenly, her wet handkerchief clasped in her hand.

"But who did?"

"That," said Poirot, "is just the question we are asking ourselves. You cannot help us there, my child?"

Jacqueline shook her head.

"I don't know . . . I can't imagine. . . . No, I haven't the faintest idea." She frowned deeply. "No," she said at last. "I can't think of anyone who wanted her dead," her voice faltered a little, "except me."

Race said, "Excuse me a minute—just thought of something." He hurried out of the room.

Jacqueline de Bellefort sat with her head downcast, nervously twisting her fingers. She broke out suddenly: "Death's horrible—horrible! I—I hate the thought of it."

Poirot said: "Yes. It is not pleasant to think, is it, that now, at this very moment, someone is rejoicing at the successful carrying out of his or her plan."

"Don't—don't!" cried Jackie. "It sounds horrible, the way you put it."

Poirot shrugged his shoulders. "It is true."

Jackie said in a low voice: "I—I wanted her dead—and she *is* dead. . . . And, what is worse . . . she died—just like I said."

"Yes, Mademoiselle. She was shot through the head."

She cried out: "Then I was right, that night at the Cataract Hotel. There *was* someone listening!"

"Ah!" Poirot nodded his head. "I wondered if you would remember that. Yes, it is altogether too much of a coincidence—that Madame Doyle should be killed in just the way you described."

Jackie shuddered.

"That man that night—who can he have been?"

Poirot was silent for a minute or two, then he said in quite a different tone of voice, "You are sure it was a man, Mademoiselle?"

Jackie looked at him in surprise.

"Yes, of course. At least—"

"Well, Mademoiselle?"

She frowned, half closing her eyes in an effort to remember. She said slowly, "I *thought* it was a man. . . ."

"But now you are not so sure?"

Jackie said slowly: "No, I can't be certain. I just assumed it was a man—but it was really just a—a figure—a shadow. . . ."

She paused and then, as Poirot did not speak, she asked: "You think it must have been a woman? But surely none of the women on this boat can have wanted to kill Linnet?"

Poirot merely moved his head from side to side.

The door opened and Bessner appeared.

"Will you come and speak with Mr. Doyle, please, Monsieur Poirot. He would like to see you."

Jackie sprang up. She caught Bessner by the arm.

"How is he? Is he—all right?"

"Naturally he is not all right," replied Dr. Bessner reproachfully. "The bone is fractured, you understand."

"But he's not going to die?" cried Jackie.

"Ach, who said anything about dying? We will get him to civilization and there we will have an X-ray and proper treatment."

"Oh!" The girl's hands came together in a convulsive pressure. She sank down again on a chair.

Poirot stepped out onto the deck with the doctor and at that moment Race joined them. They went up to the promenade deck and along to Bessner's cabin.

Simon Doyle was lying propped with cushions and pillows, an improvised cage over his leg. His face was ghastly in colour, the ravages of pain with shock on top of it. But the predominant expression on his face was bewilderment—the sick bewilderment of a child.

He muttered: "Please come in. The doctor's told me—told me—about Linnet. . . . I can't believe it. I simply can't believe it's true."

"I know. It's a bad knock," said Race.

Simon stammered: "You know—Jackie didn't do it. I'm certain Jackie didn't do it! It looks black against her, I daresay, but she *didn't* do it. She—she was a bit tight last night, and all worked up, and that's why she went for me. But she wouldn't—she wouldn't do *murder* . . . not cold-blooded murder. . . ."

Poirot said gently: "Do not distress yourself, Monsieur Doyle. Whoever shot your wife, it was not Mademoiselle de Bellefort."

Simon looked at him doubtfully.

"Is that on the square?"

"But since it was not Mademoiselle de Bellefort," continued Poirot, "can you give us any idea of who it might have been?"

Simon shook his head. The look of bewilderment increased.

"It's crazy—impossible. Apart from Jackie nobody could have wanted to do her in."

"Reflect, Monsieur Doyle. Has she no enemies? Is there no one who has a grudge against her?"

Again Simon shook his head with the same hopeless gesture.

"It sounds absolutely fantastic. There's Windlesham, of course. She more or less chucked him to marry me—but I can't see a polite stick like Windlesham committing murder, and anyway he's miles away. Same thing with old Sir George Wode. He'd got a down on Linnet over the house—disliked the way she was pulling it about; but he's miles away in London, and anyway to think of murder in such a connection would be fantastic."

"Listen, Monsieur Doyle." Poirot spoke very earnestly. "On the first day we came on board the *Karnak* I was impressed by a little conversation which I had with Madame your wife. She was very upset—very distraught. She said—mark this well—that *everybody* hated her. She said she felt afraid—unsafe—as though *everyone* round her were an enemy."

"She was pretty upset at finding Jackie aboard. So was I," said Simon.

"That is true, but it does not quite explain those words. When she said she was surrounded by enemies, she was almost certainly exaggerating, but all the same she did mean more than one person."

"You may be right there," admitted Simon. "I think I can explain that. It was a name in the passenger list that upset her."

"A name in the passenger list? What name?"

"Well, you see, she didn't actually tell me. As a matter of fact I wasn't even listening very carefully. I was going over the Jacqueline business in my mind. As far as I remember, Linnet said something about doing people down in business, and that it made her uncomfortable to meet anyone who had a grudge against her family. You see, although I don't really know the family history very well, I gather that Linnet's mother was a millionaire's daughter. Her father was only just ordinary plain wealthy, but after his marriage he naturally began playing the markets or whatever you call it. And as a result of that, of course, several people got it in the neck. You know, affluence one day, the gutter the next. Well, I gather there was someone on board whose father had got up against Linnet's father and taken a pretty hard knock. I remember Linnet saying, 'It's pretty awful when people hate you without even knowing you.'"

"Yes," said Poirot thoughtfully. "That would explain what she said to me. For the first time she was feeling the burden of her inheritance and not its advantages. You are quite sure, Monsieur Doyle, that she did not mention this man's name?"

Simon shook his head ruefully.

"I didn't really pay much attention. Just said: 'Oh, nobody minds what happened to their fathers nowadays. Life goes too fast for that.' Something of that kind."

Bessner said drily: "Ach, but I can have a guess. There is certainly a young man with a grievance on board."

"You mean Ferguson?" asked Poirot.

"Yes. He spoke against Mrs. Doyle once or twice. I myself have heard him."

"What can we do to find out?" asked Simon.

Poirot replied: "Colonel Race and I must interview all the passengers. Until we have got their stories it would be unwise to form theories. Then there is the maid. We ought to interview her first of all. It would, perhaps, be as well if we did that here. Monsieur Doyle's presence might be helpful."

"Yes, that's a good idea," said Simon.

"Had she been with Mrs. Doyle long?"

"Just a couple of months, that's all."

"Only a couple of months!" exclaimed Poirot.

"Why, you don't think—"

"Had Madame any valuable jewellery?"

"There were her pearls," said Simon. "She once told me they were worth forty or fifty thousand." He shivered. "My God, do you think those damned pearls—"

"Robbery is a possible motive," said Poirot. "All the same it seems hardly credible. . . . Well, we shall see. Let us have the maid here."

Louise Bourget was that same vivacious Latin brunette whom Poirot had seen one day and noticed.

She was anything but vivacious now. She had been crying and looked frightened. Yet there was a kind of sharp cunning apparent in her face which did not prepossess the two men favourably toward her.

"You are Louise Bourget?"

"Yes, Monsieur."

"When did you last see Madame Doyle alive?"

"Last night, Monsieur. I wait in her cabin to undress her."

"What time was that?"

"It was some time after eleven, Monsieur. I cannot say exactly when. I undress Madame and put her to bed, and then I leave."

"How long did all that take?"

"Ten minutes, Monsieur. Madame was tired. She told me to put the lights out when I went."

"And when you had left her, what did you do?"

"I went to my own cabin, Monsieur, on the deck below."

"And you heard or saw nothing more that can help us?"

"How could I, Monsieur?"

"That, Mademoiselle, is for you to say, not for us," Hercule Poirot retorted.

She stole a sideways glance at him.

"But, Monsieur, I was nowhere near. . . . What could I have seen or heard? I was on the deck below. My cabin it was on the other side of the boat, even. It is impossible that I should have heard anything. Naturally, if I had been unable to sleep, if I had mounted the stairs, *then* perhaps I might have seen this assassin, this monster, enter or leave Madame's cabin, but as it is—"

She threw out her hands appealingly to Simon.

"Monsieur, I implore you—you see how it is? What can I say?"

"My good girl," said Simon harshly, "don't be a fool. Nobody thinks you saw or heard anything. You'll be quite all right. I'll look after you. Nobody's accusing you of anything."

Louise murmured, "Monsieur is very good," and dropped her eyelids modestly.

"We take it, then, that you saw and heard nothing?" asked Race impatiently.

"That is what I said, Monsieur."

"And you know of no one who had a grudge against your mistress?"

To the surprise of her listeners Louise nodded her head vigorously.

"Oh, yes. That I do know. To that question I can answer Yes most emphatically."

Poirot said, "You mean Mademoiselle de Bellefort?"

"She, certainly. But it is not of her I speak. There was someone else on this boat who disliked Madame, who was very angry because of the way Madame had injured him."

"Good Lord!" Simon exclaimed. "What's all this?"

Louise went on, still emphatically nodding her head with the utmost vigor.

"Yes, yes, yes, it is as I say! It concerns the former maid of Madame—my predecessor. There was a man, one of the engineers on this boat, who wanted her to marry him. And my predecessor, Marie her name was, she would have done so. But Madame Doyle, she made inquiries and she discovered that this Fleetwood already he had a wife—a wife of colour you understand, a wife of this country. She had gone back to her own people, but he was still married to her, you understand. And so Madame she told all this to Marie, and Marie she was very unhappy and she would not see Fleetwood any more. And this Fleetwood, he was infuriated, and when he found out that this Madame Doyle had formerly been Mademoiselle Linnet Ridgeway he tells me that he would like to kill her! Her interference ruined his life, he said."

Louise paused triumphantly.

"This is interesting," said Race.

Poirot turned to Simon.

"Had you any idea of this?"

"None whatever," Simon replied with patent sincerity. "I doubt if Linnet even knew the man was on the boat. She had probably forgotten all about the incident."

He turned sharply to the maid.

"Did you say anything to Mrs. Doyle about this?"

"No, Monsieur, of course not."

Poirot asked, "Do you know anything about your mistress's pearls?"

"Her pearls?" Louise's eyes opened very wide. "She was wearing them last night."

"You saw them when she came to bed?"

"Yes, Monsieur."

"Where did she put them?"

"On the table by the side as always."

"That is where you last saw them?"

"Yes, sir."

"Did you see them there this morning?"

A startled look came into the girl's face.

"Mon Dieu! I did not even look. I come up to the bed, I see—I see Madame; and then I cry out and rush out of the door, and I faint."

Hercule Poirot nodded his head.

"You did not look. But I, I have the eyes which notice, and there were no pearls on the table beside the bed this morning."

CHAPTER XIV

Hercule Poirot's observation had not been at fault. There were no pearls on the table by Linnet Doyle's bed.

Louise Bourget was bidden to make a search among Linnet's belongings. According to her, all was in order. Only the pearls had disappeared.

As they emerged from the cabin a steward was waiting to tell them that breakfast had been served in the smoking-room.

As they passed along the deck, Race paused to look over the rail.

"Aha! I see you have had an idea, my friend."

"Yes. It suddenly came to me, when Fanthorp mentioned thinking he had heard a splash, that I too had been awakened sometime last night by a splash. It's perfectly possible that, after the murder, the murderer threw the pistol overboard."

Poirot said slowly, "You really think that is possible, my friend?"

Race shrugged his shoulders.

"It's a suggestion. After all, the pistol wasn't anywhere in the cabin. First thing I looked for."

"All the same," said Poirot, "it is incredible that it should have been thrown overboard."

Race asked, "Where is it then?"

Poirot replied thoughtfully, "If it is not in Madame Doyle's cabin, there is, logically, only one other place where it could be."

"Where's that?"

"In Mademoiselle de Bellefort's cabin."

Race said thoughtfully: "Yes. I see—"

He stopped suddenly.

"She's out of her cabin. Shall we go and have a look now?"

Poirot shook his head.

"No, my friend, that would be precipitate. It may not yet have been put there."

"What about an immediate search of the whole boat?"

"That way we should show our hand. We must work with great care. It is very delicate, our position, at the moment. Let us discuss the situation as we eat."

Race agreed. They went into the smoking-room.

"Well," said Race as he poured himself out a cup of coffee, "we've got two definite leads. There's the disappearance of the pearls. And there's the man Fleetwood. As regards the pearls, robbery seems indicated, but—I don't know whether you'll agree with me—"

Poirot said quickly, "But it was an odd moment to choose?"

"Exactly. To steal the pearls at such a moment invites a close search of everybody on board. How then could the thief hope to get away with his booty?"

"He might have gone ashore and dumped it."

"The company always has a watchman on the bank."

"Then that is not feasible. Was the murder committed to divert attention from the robbery? No, that does not make sense; it is profoundly unsatisfactory. But supposing that Madame Doyle woke up and caught the thief in the act?"

"And therefore the thief shot her? But she was shot whilst she slept."

"So that too does not make sense. . . . You know, I have a little idea about those pearls—and yet—no—it is impossible. Because if my idea was right the pearls would not have disappeared. Tell me, what did you think of the maid?"

"I wondered," said Race slowly, "if she knew more than she said."

"Ah, you too had that impression."

"Definitely not a nice girl," said Race.

Hercule Poirot nodded. "Yes, I would not trust her, that one."

"You think she had something to do with the murder?"

"No, I would not say that."

"With the theft of the pearls, then?"

"That is more probable. She had only been with Madame Doyle a very short time. She may be a member of a gang that specializes in jewel robberies. In such a case there is often a maid with excellent references. Unfortunately we are not in a position to seek information on these points. And yet that explanation does not quite satisfy me. . . . Those pearls—ah, *sacré*, my little idea *ought* to be right. And yet nobody would be so imbecile—" He broke off.

"What about the man Fleetwood?"

"We must question him. It may be that we have there the solution. If Louise Bourget's story is true, he had a definite motive for revenge. He could have overheard the scene between Jacqueline and Monsieur Doyle, and when they have left the saloon he could have darted in and secured the gun. Yes, it is all quite possible. And that letter J scrawled in blood. That, too, would accord with a simple, rather crude nature."

"In fact, he's just the person we are looking for?"

"Yes—only—" Poirot rubbed his nose. He said with a slight grimace: "See you, I recognize my own weaknesses. It has been said of me that I like to make a case difficult. This solution that you put to me—it is too simple, too easy. I cannot feel that it really happened. And yet, that may be sheer prejudice on my part."

"Well, we'd better have the fellow here."

Race rang the bell and gave the order. Then he asked, "Any other —possibilities?"

"Plenty, my friend. There is, for example, the American trustee."

"Pennington?"

"Yes, Pennington. There was a curious little scene in here the other day." He narrated the happenings to Race. "You see—it is significant. Madame, she wanted to read all the papers before signing. So he makes the excuse of another day. And then, the husband, he makes a very significant remark."

"What was that?"

"He says—'I never read anything. I sign where I am told to sign.' You perceive the significance of that. Pennington did. I saw it in his eye. He looked at Doyle as though an entirely new idea had come into his head. Just imagine, my friend, that you have been left trustee to the daughter of an intensely wealthy man. You use, perhaps, that money to speculate with. I know it is so in all detective novels—but you read of it too in the newspapers. It happens, my friend, *it happens*."

"I don't dispute it," said Race.

"There is, perhaps, still time to make good by speculating wildly. Your ward is not yet of age. And then—she marries! The control passes from your hands into hers at a moment's notice! A disaster! But there is still a chance. She is on a honeymoon. She will perhaps be careless about business. A casual paper, slipped in among others, signed without reading . . . But Linnet Doyle was not like that. Honeymoon or no honeymoon, she was a business woman. And then her husband makes a remark, and a new idea comes to that desperate man who is seeking a way out from ruin. If Linnet Doyle were to die, her fortune would pass to her husband—and he would be easy to deal with; he would be a child in the hands of an astute man like Andrew Pennington. *Mon cher* Colonel, I tell you I *saw* the thought pass through Andrew Pennington's head. 'If only it were *Doyle* I had got to deal with . . .' That is what he was thinking."

"Quite possible, I daresay," said Race drily, "but you've no evidence."

"Alas, no."

"Then there's young Ferguson," said Race. "He talks bitterly enough. Not that I go by talk. Still, he *might* be the fellow whose father was ruined by old Ridgeway. It's a little far-fetched but it's *possible*. People do brood over bygone wrongs sometimes."

He paused a minute and then said, "And there's my fellow."

"Yes, there is 'your fellow' as you call him."

"He's a killer," said Race. "We know that. On the other hand, I can't see any way in which he could have come up against Linnet Doyle. Their orbits don't touch."

Poirot said slowly, "Unless, accidentally, she had become possessed of evidence showing his identity."

"That's possible, but it seems highly unlikely." There was a knock at the door. "Ah, here's our would-be bigamist."

Fleetwood was a big, truculent looking man. He looked suspiciously from one to the other of them as he entered the room. Poirot recognized him as the man he had seen talking to Louise Bourget.

Fleetwood asked suspiciously, "You wanted to see me?"

"We did," said Race. "You probably know that a murder was committed on this boat last night?"

Fleetwood nodded.

"And I believe it is true that you had reason to feel anger against the woman who was killed."

A look of alarm sprang up in Fleetwood's eyes.

"Who told you that?"

"You considered that Mrs. Doyle had interfered between you and a young woman."

"I know who told you that—that lying French hussy. She's a liar through and through, that girl."

"But this particular story happens to be true."

"It's a dirty lie!"

"You say that, although you don't know what it is yet."

The shot told. The man flushed and gulped.

"It is true, is it not, that you were going to marry the girl Marie, and that she broke it off when she discovered that you were a married man already?"

"What business was it of hers?"

"You mean, what business was it of Mrs. Doyle's? Well, you know, bigamy is bigamy."

"It wasn't like that. I married one of the locals out here. It didn't answer. She went back to her people. I've not seen her for half a dozen years."

"Still you were married to her."

The man was silent. Race went on:

"Mrs. Doyle, or Miss Ridgeway as she then was, found out all this?"

"Yes, she did, curse her! Nosing about where no one ever asked her to. I'd have treated Marie right. I'd have done anything for her. And she'd never have known about the other, if it hadn't been for that meddlesome young lady of hers. Yes, I'll say it, I *did* have a grudge against the lady, and I felt bitter about it when I saw her on this boat, all dressed up in pearls and diamonds and lording it all over the place, with never a thought that she'd broken up a man's life for him! I felt bitter all right, but if you think I'm a dirty murderer—if you think I went and shot her with a gun, well, that's a damned lie! I never touched her. And that's God's truth."

He stopped. The sweat was rolling down his face.

"Where were you last night between the hours of twelve and two?"

"In my bunk asleep—and my mate will tell you so."

"We shall see," said Race. He dismissed him with a curt nod. "That'll do."

"*Eh bien?*" inquired Poirot as the door closed behind Fleetwood.

Race shrugged his shoulders. "He tells quite a straight story. He's nervous, of course, but not unduly so. We'll have to investigate his alibi—though I don't suppose it will be decisive. His mate was probably asleep, and this fellow could have slipped in and out if he wanted to. It depends whether anyone else saw him."

"Yes, one must inquire as to that."

"The next thing, I think," said Race, "is whether anyone heard anything which might give us a clue to the time of the crime. Bessner places it as having occurred between twelve and two. It seems reasonable to hope that someone among the passengers may have heard the shot—even if they did not recognize it for what it was. I didn't hear anything of the kind myself. What about you?"

Poirot shook his head.

"Me, I slept absolutely like the log. I heard nothing—but nothing at all. I might have been drugged, I slept so soundly."

"A pity," said Race. "Well, let's hope we have a bit of luck with the people who have cabins on the starboard side. Fanthorp we've done. The Allertons come next. I'll send the steward to fetch them."

Mrs. Allerton came in briskly. She was wearing a soft grey striped silk dress. Her face looked distressed.

"It's too horrible," she said as she accepted the chair that Poirot placed for her. "I can hardly believe it. That lovely creature, with everything to live for—dead. I almost feel I can't believe it."

"I know how you feel, Madame," said Poirot sympathetically.

"I'm glad *you* are on board," said Mrs. Allerton simply. "You'll be able to find out who did it. I'm so glad it isn't that poor tragic girl."

"You mean Mademoiselle de Bellefort. Who told you she did not do it?"

"Cornelia Robson," replied Mrs. Allerton, with a faint smile. "You know, she's simply thrilled by it all. It's probably the only exciting thing that has ever happened to her, and probably the only exciting thing that ever will happen to her. But she's so nice that she's terribly ashamed of enjoying it. She thinks it's awful of her."

Mrs. Allerton gave a look at Poirot and then added: "But I mustn't chatter. You want to ask me questions."

"If you please. You went to bed at what time, Madame?"

"Just after half past ten."

"And you went to sleep at once?"

"Yes. I was sleepy."

"And did you hear anything—anything at all—during the night?"

Mrs. Allerton wrinkled her brows.

"Yes, I think I heard a splash and someone running—or was it the other way about? I'm rather hazy. I just had a vague idea that someone had fallen overboard at sea—a dream, you know—and then I woke up and listened, but it was all quite quiet."

"Do you know what time that was?"

"No, I'm afraid I don't. But I don't think it was very long after I went to sleep. I mean it was within the first hour or so."

"Alas, Madame, that is not very definite."

"No, I know it isn't. But it's no good my trying to guess, is it, when I haven't really the vaguest idea?"

"And that is all you can tell us, Madame?"

"I'm afraid so."

"Had you ever actually met Madame Doyle before?"

"No, Tim had met her. And I'd heard a good deal about her—

through a cousin of ours, Joanna Southwood, but I'd never spoken to her till we met at Assuan."

"I have one other question, Madame, if you will pardon me for asking."

Mrs. Allerton murmured with a faint smile, "I should love to be asked an indiscreet question."

"It is this. Did you, or your family, ever suffer any financial loss through the operations of Madame Doyle's father, Melhuish Ridgeway?"

Mrs. Allerton looked thoroughly astonished.

"Oh, no! The family finances have never suffered except by dwindling . . . you know, everything paying less interest than it used to. There's never been anything melodramatic about our poverty. My husband left very little money, but what he left I still have, though it doesn't yield as much as it used to yield."

"I thank you, Madame. Perhaps you will ask your son to come to us."

Tim said lightly, when his mother came to him: "Ordeal over? My turn now! What sort of things did they ask you?"

"Only whether I heard anything last night," said Mrs. Allerton. "And unluckily I didn't hear anything at all. I can't think why not. After all, Linnet's cabin is only one away from mine. I should think I'd have been bound to hear the shot. Go along, Tim; they're waiting for you."

To Tim Allerton Poirot repeated his previous question.

Tim answered: "I went to bed early, half past ten or so. I read for a bit. Put out my light just after eleven."

"Did you hear anything after that?"

"Heard a man's voice saying good-night, I think, not far away."

"That was I saying good-night to Mrs. Doyle," said Race.

"Yes. After that I went to sleep. Then, later, I heard a kind of hullabaloo going on, somebody calling Fanthorp, I remember."

"Mademoiselle Robson when she ran out from the observation saloon."

"Yes, I suppose that was it. And then a lot of different voices. And then somebody running along the deck. And then a splash. And then I heard old Bessner booming out something about 'Careful now' and 'Not too quick.'"

"You heard a splash?"

"Well, something of that kind."

"You are sure it was not a *shot* you heard?"

"Yes, I suppose it might have been . . . I did hear a cork pop. Perhaps that was the shot. I may have imagined the splash from connecting the idea of the cork with liquid pouring into a glass. . . . I know my foggy idea was that there was some kind of party on, and I wished they'd all go to bed and shut up."

"Anything more after that?"

Tim thought.

"Only Fanthorp barging round in his cabin next door. I thought he'd never get to bed."

"And after that?"

Tim shrugged his shoulders.

"After that—oblivion."

"You heard nothing more?"

"Nothing whatever."

"Thank you, Monsieur Allerton."

Tim got up and left the cabin.

CHAPTER XV

Race pored thoughtfully over a plan of the promenade deck of the *Karnak*.

"Fanthorp, young Allerton, Mrs. Allerton. Then an empty cabin —Simon Doyle's. Now who's on the other side of Mrs. Doyle's? The old American dame. If anyone heard anything, she should have done. If she's up we'd better have her along."

Miss Van Schuyler entered the room. She looked even older and yellower than usual this morning. Her small dark eyes had an air of venomous displeasure in them.

Race rose and bowed.

"We're very sorry to trouble you, Miss Van Schuyler. It's very good of you. Please sit down."

Miss Van Schuyler said sharply: "I dislike being mixed up in this. I resent it very much. I do not wish to be associated in any way with this—er—very unpleasant affair."

"Quite—quite. I was just saying to Monsieur Poirot that the sooner we took your statement the better, as then you need have no further trouble."

Miss Van Schuyler looked at Poirot with something approaching favour.

"I'm glad you both realize my feelings. I am not accustomed to anything of this kind."

Poirot said soothingly: "Precisely, Mademoiselle. That is why we wish to free you from unpleasantness as quickly as possible. Now you went to bed last night—at what time?"

"Ten o'clock is my usual time. Last night I was rather later, as Cornelia Robson, very inconsiderately, kept me waiting."

"*Très bien,* Mademoiselle. Now what did you hear after you had retired?"

Miss Van Schuyler said: "I sleep very lightly."

"*À merveille!* That is very fortunate for us."

"I was awakened by that rather flashy young woman, Mrs. Doyle's maid, who said, '*Bonne nuit, Madame*' in what I cannot but think an unnecessarily loud voice."

"And after that?"

"I went to sleep again. I woke up thinking someone was in my cabin, but I realized that it was someone in the cabin next door."

"In Madame Doyle's cabin?"

"Yes. Then I heard someone outside on the deck and then a splash."

"You have no idea what time this was?"

"I can tell you the time exactly. It was ten minutes past one."

"You are sure of that?"

"Yes. I looked at my little clock that stands by my bed."

"You did not hear a shot?"

"No, nothing of the kind."

"But it might possibly have been a shot that awakened you?"

Miss Van Schuyler considered the question, her toadlike head on one side.

"It might," she admitted rather grudgingly.

"And you have no idea what caused the splash you heard?"

"Not at all—I know perfectly."

Colonel Race sat up alertly.

"You know?"

"Certainly. I did not like this sound of prowling around. I got up and went to the door of my cabin. Miss Otterbourne was leaning over the side. She had just dropped something into the water."

"Miss Otterbourne?" Race sounded really surprised.

"Yes."

"You are quite sure it was Miss Otterbourne?"

"I saw her face distinctly."

"She did not see you?"

"I do not think so."

Poirot leant forward.

"And what did her face look like, Mademoiselle?"

"She was in a condition of considerable emotion."

Race and Poirot exchanged a quick glance.

"And then?" Race prompted.

"Miss Otterbourne went away round the stern of the boat and I returned to bed."

There was a knock at the door and the Manager entered. He carried in his hand a dripping bundle.

"We've got it, Colonel."

Race took the package. He unwrapped fold after fold of sodden velvet. Out of it fell a coarse handkerchief, faintly stained with pink, wrapped round a small pearl-handled pistol.

Race gave Poirot a glance of slightly malicious triumph.

"You see," he said, "my idea was right. It *was* thrown overboard."

He held the pistol out on the palm of his hand.

"What do you say, Monsieur Poirot? Is this the pistol you saw at the Cataract Hotel that night?"

Poirot examined it carefully; then he said quietly: "Yes—that is it. There is the ornamental work on it—and the initials J. B. It is an *article de luxe,* a very feminine production, but it is none the less a lethal weapon."

"Twenty-two," murmured Race. He took out the clip. "Two bullets fired. Yes, there doesn't seem much doubt about it."

Miss Van Schuyler coughed significantly.

"And what about my stole?" she demanded.

"Your stole, Mademoiselle?"

"Yes, that is my velvet stole you have here."

Race picked up the dripping folds of material.

"This is yours, Miss Van Schuyler?"

"Certainly it's mine!" the old lady snapped. "I missed it last night. I was asking everyone if they'd seen it."

Poirot questioned Race with a glance, and the latter gave a slight nod of assent.

"Where did you see it last, Miss Van Schuyler?"

"I had it in the saloon yesterday evening. When I came to go to bed I could not find it anywhere."

Race said quietly, "You realize what it's been used for?" He spread it out, indicating with a finger the scorching and several small holes. "The murderer wrapped it round the pistol to deaden the noise of the shot."

"Impertinence!" snapped Miss Van Schuyler. The colour rose in her wizened cheeks.

Race said, "I shall be glad, Miss Van Schuyler, if you will tell me the extent of your previous acquaintance with Mrs. Doyle."

"There was no previous acquaintance."

"But you knew of her?"

"I knew who she was, of course."

"But your families were not acquainted?"

"As a family we have always prided ourselves on being exclusive Colonel Race. My dear mother would never have dreamed of calling upon any of the Hartz family, who, outside their wealth, were nobodies."

"That is all you have to say, Miss Van Schuyler?"

"I have nothing to add to what I have told you. Linnet Ridgeway was brought up in England and I never saw her till I came aboard this boat."

She rose. Poirot opened the door for her and she marched out. The eyes of the two men met.

"That's her story," said Race, "and she's going to stick to it! It may be true. I don't know. But—Rosalie Otterbourne? I hadn't expected that."

Poirot shook his head in a perplexed manner. Then he brought down his hand on the table with a sudden bang.

"But it does not make sense," he cried. "*Nom d'un nom d'un nom!* It does not make sense."

Race looked at him.

"What do you mean exactly?"

"I mean that up to a point it is all the clear sailing. Someone wished to kill Linnet Doyle. Someone overheard the scene in the saloon last night. Someone sneaked in there and retrieved the pistol—Jacqueline de Bellefort's pistol, remember. Somebody shot Linnet Doyle with that pistol and wrote the letter J on the wall. . . . All so clear, is it not? All pointing to Jacqueline de Bellefort as the murderess. And then what does the murderer do. Leave the pistol—the damning pistol—Jacqueline de Bellefort's pistol, for everyone to find? No, he—or she—throws the pistol, that particularly damning bit of evidence, overboard. Why, my friend, why?"

Race shook his head. "It's odd."

"It is more than odd—it is *impossible!*"

"Not impossible, since it happened!"

"I do not mean that. I mean that the sequence of events is impossible. Something is wrong."

CHAPTER XVI

COLONEL RACE GLANCED curiously at his colleague. He respected—he had reason to respect—the brain of Hercule Poirot. Yet for the moment he did not follow the other's process of thought. He asked no question, however. He seldom did ask questions. He proceeded straightforwardly with the matter in hand.

"What's the next thing to be done? Question the Otterbourne girl?"

"Yes, that may advance us a little."

Rosalie Otterbourne entered ungraciously. She did not look nervous or frightened in any way—merely unwilling and sulky.

"Well," she asked, "what is it?"

Race was the spokesman.

"We're investigating Mrs. Doyle's death," he explained.

Rosalie nodded.

"Will you tell me what you did last night?"

Rosalie reflected a minute.

"Mother and I went to bed early—before eleven. We didn't hear anything in particular, except a bit of fuss outside Dr. Bessner's cabin. I heard the old man's German voice booming away. Of course I didn't know what it was all about till this morning."

"You didn't hear a shot?"

"No."

"Did you leave your cabin at all last night?"

"No."

"You are quite sure of that?"

Rosalie stared at him.

"What do you mean? Of course I'm sure of it."

"You did not, for instance, go round to the starboard side of the boat and throw something overboard?"

The colour rose in her face.

"Is there any rule against throwing things overboard?"

"No, of course not. Then you did?"

"No, I didn't. I never left my cabin, I tell you."

"Then if anyone says that they saw you—"

She interrupted him. "Who says they saw me?"

"Miss Van Schuyler."

"Miss Van Schuyler?" She sounded genuinely astonished.

"Yes. Miss Van Schuyler says she looked out of her cabin and saw you throw something over the side."

Rosalie said clearly, "That's a damned lie." Then, as though struck by a sudden thought, she asked, "What time was this?"

It was Poirot who answered.

"It was ten minutes past one, Mademoiselle."

She nodded her head thoughtfully. "Did she see anything else?"

Poirot looked at her curiously. He stroked his chin.

"See—no," he replied, "but she heard something."

"What did she hear?"

"Someone moving about in Madame Doyle's cabin."

"I see," muttered Rosalie.

She was pale now—deadly pale.

"And you persist in saying that you threw nothing overboard, Mademoiselle?"

"What on earth should I run about throwing things overboard for in the middle of the night?"

"There might be a reason—an innocent reason."

"Innocent?" repeated the girl sharply.

"That's what I said. You see, Mademoiselle, something *was* thrown overboard last night—something that was not innocent."

Race silently held out the bundle of stained velvet, opening it to display its contents.

Rosalie Otterbourne shrank back. "Was that—what—she was killed with?"

"Yes, Mademoiselle."

"And you think that I—I did it? What utter nonsense! Why on earth should I want to kill Linnet Doyle? I don't even know her!"

She laughed and stood up scornfully. "The whole thing is too ridiculous."

"Remember, Miss Otterbourne," said Race, "that Miss Van Schuyler is prepared to swear she saw your face quite clearly in the moonlight."

Rosalie laughed again. "That old cat? She's probably half blind anyway. It wasn't me she saw." She paused. "Can I go now?"

Race nodded and Rosalie Otterbourne left the room.

The eyes of the two men met. Race lighted a cigarette.

"Well, that's that. Flat contradiction. Which of 'em do we believe?"

Poirot shook his head. "I have a little idea that neither of them was being quite frank."

"That's the worst of our job," said Race despondently. "So many people keep back the truth for positively futile reasons. What's our next move? Get on with the questioning of the passengers?"

"I think so. It is always well to proceed with order and method."

Race nodded.

Mrs. Otterbourne, dressed in floating batik material, succeeded her daughter. She corroborated Rosalie's statement that they had both gone to bed before eleven o'clock. She herself had heard nothing of interest during the night. She could not say whether Rosalie had left their cabin or not. On the subject of the crime she was inclined to hold forth.

"The *crime passionnel!*" she exclaimed. "The primitive instinct—to kill! So closely allied to the sex instinct. That girl, Jacqueline, half Latin, hot-blooded, obeying the deepest instincts of her being, stealing forth, revolver in hand—"

"But Jacqueline de Bellefort did not shoot Madame Doyle. That we know for certain. It is proved," explained Poirot.

"Her husband, then," said Mrs. Otterbourne, rallying from the blow. "The blood lust and the sex instinct—a sexual crime. There are many well-known instances."

"Mr. Doyle was shot through the leg and he was quite unable to move—the bone was fractured," explained Colonel Race. "He spent the night with Dr. Bessner."

Mrs. Otterbourne was even more disappointed. She searched her mind hopefully.

"Of course!" she said. "How foolish of me! Miss Bowers!"

"Miss Bowers?"

"Yes. Naturally. It's so *clear* psychologically. Repression! The repressed virgin! Maddened by the sight of these two—a young husband and wife passionately in love with each other. Of course it was her! She's just the type—sexually unattractive, innately respectable. In my book, *The Barren Vine*—"

Colonel Race interposed tactfully: "Your suggestions have been most helpful, Mrs. Otterbourne. We must get on with our job now. Thank you so much."

He escorted her gallantly to the door and came back wiping his brow.

"What a poisonous woman! Whew! Why didn't somebody murder *her?*"

"It may yet happen," Poirot consoled him.

"There might be some sense in that. Whom have we got left? Pennington—we'll keep him for the end, I think. Richetti—Ferguson."

Signor Richetti was very voluble, very agitated.

"But what a horror, what an infamy—a woman so young and so beautiful—indeed an inhuman crime!"

Signor Richetti's hands flew expressively up in the air.

His answers were prompt. He had gone to bed early—very early. In fact immediately after dinner. He had read for a while—a very interesting pamphlet lately published—*Prähistorische Forschung in Kleinasien*—throwing an entirely new light on the painted pottery of the Anatolian foothills.

He had put out his light some time before eleven. No, he had not heard any shot. Not any sound like the pop of a cork. The only thing he had heard—but that was later, in the middle of the night—was a splash, a big splash, just near his porthole.

"Your cabin is on the lower deck, on the starboard side, is it not?"

"Yes, yes, that is so. And I hear the big splash." His arms flew up once more to describe the bigness of the splash.

"Can you tell me at all what time that was?"

Signor Richetti reflected.

"It was one, two, three hours after I go to sleep. Perhaps two hours."

"About ten minutes past one, for instance?"

"It might very well be, yes. Ah! but what a terrible crime—how inhuman. . . . So charming a woman. . . ."

Exit Signor Richetti, still gesticulating freely.

Race looked at Poirot. Poirot raised his eyebrows expressively, then shrugged his shoulders. They passed on to Mr. Ferguson.

Ferguson was difficult. He sprawled insolently in a chair.

"Grand to-do about this business!" he sneered. "What's it really matter? Lot of superfluous women in the world!"

Race said coldly, "Can we have an account of your movements last night, Mr. Ferguson?"

"Don't see why you should, but I don't mind. I mooched around a good bit. Went ashore with Miss Robson. When she went back to the boat I mooched around by myself for a while. Came back and turned in round about midnight."

"Your cabin is on the lower deck, starboard side?"

"Yes. I'm not up among the nobs."

"Did you hear a shot? It might only have sounded like the popping of a cork."

Ferguson considered. "Yes, I think I did hear something like a cork. . . . Can't remember when—before I went to sleep. But there were still a lot of people about then—commotion, running about on the deck above."

"That was probably the shot fired by Miss de Bellefort. You didn't hear another?"

Ferguson shook his head.

"Nor a splash?"

"A splash? Yes, I believe I did hear a splash. But there was so much row going on I can't be sure about it."

"Did you leave your cabin during the night?"

Ferguson grinned. "No, I didn't. And I didn't participate in the good work, worse luck."

"Come, come, Mr. Ferguson, don't behave childishly."

The young man reacted angrily.

"Why shouldn't I say what I think? I believe in violence."

"But you don't practise what you preach?" murmured Poirot. "I wonder."

He leaned forward.

"It was the man, Fleetwood, was it not, who told you that Linnet Doyle was one of the richest women in England?"

"What's Fleetwood got to do with this?"

"Fleetwood, my friend, had an excellent motive for killing Linnet Doyle. He had a special grudge against her."

Mr. Ferguson came up out of his seat like a Jack in the Box.

"So that's your dirty game, is it?" he demanded wrathfully. "Put it on to a poor devil like Fleetwood, who can't defend himself, who's got no money to hire lawyers. But I tell you this—if you try and saddle Fleetwood with this business you'll have me to deal with."

"And who exactly are you?" asked Poirot sweetly.

Mr. Ferguson got rather red.

"I can stick by my friends anyway," he said gruffly.

"Well, Mr. Ferguson, I think that's all we need for the present," said Race.

As the door closed behind Ferguson he remarked unexpectedly, "Rather a likable young cub, really."

"You don't think he is the man *you* are after?" asked Poirot.

"I hardly think so. I suppose he *is* on board. The information was very precise. Oh, well, one job at a time. Let's have a go at Pennington."

CHAPTER XVII

Andrew Pennington displayed all the conventional reactions of grief and shock. He was, as usual, carefully dressed. He had changed into a black tie. His long clean-shaven face bore a bewildered expression.

"Gentlemen," he said sadly, "this business has got me right down! Little Linnet—why, I remember her as the cutest little thing you can imagine. How proud of her Melhuish Ridgeway used to be, too! Well, there's no point in going into that. Just tell me what I can do; that's all I ask."

Race said, "To begin with, Mr. Pennington, did you hear anything last night?"

"No, sir, I can't say I did. I have the cabin right next to Dr. Bessner's, number forty—forty-one, and I heard a certain commotion going on in there round about midnight or so. Of course I didn't know what it was at the time."

"You heard nothing else? No shots?"

Andrew Pennington shook his head.

"Nothing whatever of that kind."

"And you went to bed at what time?"

"Must have been some time after eleven."

He leant forward.

"I don't suppose it's news to you to know that there's plenty of rumours going about the boat. That half French girl—Jacqueline de Bellefort—there was something fishy there, you know. Linnet didn't tell me anything, but naturally I wasn't born blind and deaf. There'd been some affair between her and Simon, some time, hadn't there? *Cherchez la femme*—that's a pretty good sound rule, and I should say you wouldn't have to *cherchez* far."

"You mean that in your belief Jacqueline de Bellefort shot Madame Doyle?" Poirot asked.

"That's what it looks like to me. Of course I don't *know* anything. . . ."

"Unfortunately we *do* know something!"

"Eh?" Mr. Pennington looked startled.

"We know that it is quite impossible for Mademoiselle de Bellefort to have shot Madame Doyle."

He explained carefully the circumstances. Pennington seemed reluctant to accept them.

"I agree it looks all right on the face of it—but this hospital nurse woman, I'll bet she didn't stay awake all night. She dozed off and the girl slipped out and in again."

"Hardly likely, Monsieur Pennington. She had administered a strong opiate, remember. And anyway a nurse is in the habit of sleeping lightly and waking when her patient wakes."

"It all sounds rather fishy to me," declared Pennington.

Race said, in a gently authoritative manner: "I think you must take it from me, Mr. Pennington, that we have examined all the possibilities very carefully. The result is quite definite—Jacqueline de Bellefort did not shoot Mrs. Doyle. So we are forced to look elsewhere. That is where we hope you may be able to help us."

"I?" Pennington gave a nervous start.

"Yes. You were an intimate friend of the dead woman's. You know the circumstances of her life, in all probability, much better than her husband does, since he only made her acquaintance a few months ago. You would know, for instance, of anyone who had a grudge against her. You would know, perhaps, whether there was anyone who had a motive for desiring her death."

Andrew Pennington passed his tongue over rather dry looking lips.

"I assure you, I have no idea. . . . You see Linnet was brought up in England. I know very little of her surroundings and associations."

"And yet," mused Poirot, "there was someone on board who was interested in Madame Doyle's removal. She had a near escape before, you remember, at this very place, when that boulder crashed down—Ah! but you were not there, perhaps?"

"No. I was inside the temple at the time. I heard about it afterward, of course. A very near escape. But possibly an accident, don't you think?"

Poirot shrugged his shoulders.

"One thought so at the time. Now—one wonders."

"Yes—yes, of course." Pennington wiped his face with a fine silk handkerchief.

Colonel Race went on: "Mrs. Doyle happened to mention someone being on board who bore a grudge—not against her personally, but against her family. Do you know who that could be?"

Pennington looked genuinely astonished.

"No, I've no idea."

"She didn't mention the matter to you?"

"No."

"You were an intimate friend of her father's—you cannot remember any business operations of his that might have resulted in ruin for some business opponent?"

Pennington shook his head helplessly. "No outstanding case. Such operations were frequent, of course, but I can't recall anyone who uttered threats—nothing of that kind."

"In short, Mr. Pennington, you cannot help us?"

"It seems so. I deplore my inadequacy, gentlemen."

Race interchanged a glance with Poirot, then he said: "I'm sorry too. We'd had hopes."

He got up as a sign the interview was at an end.

Andrew Pennington said: "As Doyle's laid up, I expect he'd like me to see to things. Pardon me, Colonel, but what exactly are the arrangements?"

"When we leave here we shall make a non-stop run to Shellâl, arriving there tomorrow morning."

"And the body?"

"Will be removed to one of the cold storage chambers."

Andrew Pennington bowed his head. Then he left the room.

Poirot and Race again interchanged a glance.

"Mr. Pennington," said Race, lighting a cigarette, "was not at all comfortable."

Poirot nodded. "And," he said, "Mr. Pennington was sufficiently perturbed to tell a rather stupid lie. He was *not* in the temple of Abu Simbel when that boulder fell. I—*moi qui vous parle*—can swear to that. I had just come from there."

"A very stupid lie," said Race, "and a very revealing one."

Again Poirot nodded.

"But for the moment," he said, and smiled, "we handle him with the gloves of kid, is it not so?"

"That was the idea," agreed Race.

"My friend, you and I understand each other to a marvel."

There was a faint grinding noise, a stir beneath their feet. The *Karnak* had started on her homeward journey to Shellâl.

"The pearls," said Race. "That is the next thing to be cleared up."

"You have a plan?"

"Yes." He glanced at his watch. "It will be lunch time in half an hour. At the end of the meal I propose to make an announcement—just state the fact that the pearls have been stolen, and that I must request everyone to stay in the dining-saloon while a search is conducted."

Poirot nodded approvingly.

"It is well imagined. Whoever took the pearls still has them. By giving no warning beforehand, there will be no chance of their being thrown overboard in a panic."

Race drew some sheets of paper toward him. He murmured apologetically: "I like to make a brief précis of the facts as I go along. It keeps one's mind free of confusion."

"You do well. Method and order, they are everything," replied Poirot.

Race wrote for some minutes in his small neat script. Finally he pushed the result of his labours toward Poirot.

"Anything you don't agree with there?"

Poirot took up the sheets. They were headed:

MURDER OF MRS. LINNET DOYLE

Mrs. Doyle was last seen alive by her maid, Louise Bourget. Time: 11.30 (approx).

From 11.30-12.20 following have alibis: Cornelia Robson, James Fanthorp, Simon Doyle, Jacqueline de Bellefort—*nobody else*—but crime almost certainly committed *after* that time, since it is practically certain that pistol used was Jacqueline de Bellefort's, which was then in her handbag. That her pistol was used is not *absolutely* certain until after post mortem and expert evidence re bullet—but it may be taken as overwhelmingly probable.

Probable course of events: X (murderer) was witness of scene between Jacqueline and Simon Doyle in observation saloon and noted where pistol went under settee. After the saloon was vacant, X procured pistol—his or her idea being that Jacqueline de Bellefort would be thought guilty of crime. On this theory certain people are automatically cleared of suspicion:

Cornelia Robson, since she had no opportunity to take pistol before James Fanthorp returned to search for it.

Miss Bowers—same.

Dr. Bessner—same.

N.B. Fanthorp is not definitely excluded from suspicion, since he could actually have pocketed pistol while declaring himself unable to find it.

Any other person could have taken the pistol during that ten minutes' interval.

Possible motives for the murder:

Andrew Pennington. This is on the assumption that he has been guilty of fraudulent practices. There is a certain amount of evidence in favour of that assumption, but not enough to justify making out a case against him. If it was he who rolled down the boulder, he is a man who can seize a chance when it presents itself. The crime, clearly, was not premeditated except in a *general* way. Last night's shooting scene was an ideal opportunity.

Objections to the theory of Pennington's guilt: *Why did he throw the pistol overboard, since it constituted a valuable clue against J. B.?*

Fleetwood. Motive, revenge. Fleetwood considered himself injured by Linnet Doyle. Might have overheard scene and noted position of pistol. He may have taken pistol because it was a handy weapon, rather than with the idea of throwing guilt on Jacqueline. This would fit in with throwing it overboard. *But if that were the case, why did he write J in blood on the wall?*

N.B. Cheap handkerchief found with pistol more likely to have belonged to a man like Fleetwood than to one of the well-to-do passengers.

Rosalie Otterbourne. Are we to accept Miss Van Schuyler's evidence or Rosalie's denial? Something *was* thrown overboard at that time and that something was presumably the pistol wrapped up in the velvet stole.

Points to be noted. Had Rosalie any motive? She may have disliked Linnet Doyle and even been envious of her—but as a motive for murder that seems grossly inadequate. The evidence against her can be convincing only if we discover an adequate motive. As far as we know, there is no previous knowledge or link between Rosalie Otterbourne and Linnet Doyle.

Miss Van Schuyler. The velvet stole in which pistol was wrapped belongs to Miss Van Schuyler. According to her own statement she last saw it in the observation saloon. She drew attention to its loss during the evening, and a search was made for it without success.

How did the stole come into the possession of X? Did X purloin it some time early in the evening? But if so, why? Nobody could tell, in advance, that there was going to be a scene between Jacqueline and Simon. Did X find the stole in the saloon when he went to get the pistol from under the settee? But if so, why was it not found when the search for it was made? Did it never leave Miss Van Schuyler's possession? That is to say: Did Miss Van Schuyler murder Linnet Doyle? Is her accusation of Rosalie Otterbourne a deliberate lie? If she did murder her, what was her motive?

Other possibilities:

Robbery as a motive. Possible, since the pearls have disappeared, and Linnet Doyle was certainly wearing them last night.

Someone with a grudge against the Ridgeway family. Possibly—again no evidence.

We know that there is a dangerous man on board—a killer. Here we have a killer and a death. May not the two be connected? But we should have to show that Linnet Doyle possessed dangerous knowledge concerning this man.

Conclusions: We can group the persons on board into two classes—those who had a possible motive or against whom there is definite evidence, and those who, as far as we know, are free of suspicion.

Group I	*Group II*
Andrew Pennington	Mrs. Allerton
Fleetwood	Tim Allerton
Rosalie Otterbourne	Cornelia Robson
Miss Van Schuyler	Miss Bowers
Louise Bourget (Robbery?)	Dr. Bessner
Ferguson (Political?)	Signor Richetti
	Mrs. Otterbourne
	James Fanthorp

Poirot pushed the paper back.

"It is very just, very exact, what you have written there."

"You agree with it?"

"Yes."

"And now what is your contribution?"

Poirot drew himself up in an important manner.

"Me, I pose to myself one question: '*Why* was the pistol thrown overboard?' "

"That's all?"

"At the moment, yes. Until I can arrive at a satisfactory answer to that question, there is no sense anywhere. That is—that *must* be the starting point. You will notice, my friend, that, in your summary of where we stand, you have not attempted to answer that point."

Race shrugged his shoulders.

"Panic."

Poirot shook his head perplexedly. He picked up the sodden velvet wrap and smoothed it out, wet and limp, on the table. His finger traced the scorched marks and the burnt holes.

"Tell me, my friend," he said suddenly. "You are more conversant with firearms than I am. Would such a thing as this, wrapped round a pistol, make much difference in muffling the sound?"

"No, it wouldn't. Not like a silencer, for instance."

Poirot nodded. He went on: "A man—certainly a man who had had much handling of firearms—would know that. But a woman—a woman would *not* know."

Race looked at him curiously. "Probably not."

"No. She would have read the detective stories where they are not always very exact as to details."

Race flicked the little pearl-handled pistol with his finger.

"This little fellow wouldn't make much noise anyway," he said. "Just a pop, that's all. With any other noise around, ten to one you wouldn't notice it."

"Yes, I have reflected as to that."

Poirot picked up the handkerchief and examined it.

"A man's handkerchief—but not a gentleman's handkerchief. *Ce cher* Woolworth, I imagine. Threepence at most."

"The sort of handkerchief a man like Fleetwood would own."

"Yes. Andrew Pennington, I notice, carries a very fine silk handkerchief."

"Ferguson?" suggested Race.

"Possibly. As a gesture. But then it ought to be a bandana."

"Used it instead of a glove, I suppose, to hold the pistol and obviate fingerprints." Race added, with slight facetiousness, " 'The Clue of the Blushing Handkerchief.' "

"Ah, yes. Quite a *jeune fille* colour, is it not?" He laid it down and returned to the stole, once more examining the powder marks.

"All the same," he murmured, "it is odd . . ."

"What's that?" Poirot said gently: "*Cette pauvre Madame Doyle.* Lying there so peacefully . . . with the little hole in her head. You remember how she looked?"

Race looked at him curiously. "You know," he said, "I've got an idea you're trying to tell me something—but I haven't the faintest idea what it is."

CHAPTER XVIII

THERE WAS A TAP on the door.

"Come in," Race called.

A steward entered.

"Excuse me, sir," he said to Poirot, "but Mr. Doyle is asking for you."

"I will come."

Poirot rose. He went out of the room and up the companionway to the promenade deck and along it to Dr. Bessner's cabin.

Simon, his face flushed and feverish, was propped up with pillows. He looked embarrassed.

"Awfully good of you to come along, Monsieur Poirot. Look here, there's something I want to ask you."

"Yes?"

Simon got still redder in the face.

"It's—it's about Jackie. I want to see her. Do you think—would you mind—would she mind, d'you think, if you asked her to come along here? You know I've been lying here thinking. . . . That wretched kid—she is only a kid after all—and I treated her damn badly—and—" He stammered to silence.

Poirot looked at him with interest.

"You desire to see Mademoiselle Jacqueline? I will fetch her."

"Thanks. Awfully good of you."

Poirot went on his quest. He found Jacqueline de Bellefort sitting huddled up in a corner of the observation saloon. There was an open book on her lap but she was not reading.

Poirot said gently: "Will you come with me, Mademoiselle? Monsieur Doyle wants to see you."

She started up. Her face flushed—then paled. She looked bewildered.

"Simon? He wants to see me—to see *me*?"

He found her incredulity moving.

"Will you come, Mademoiselle?"

"I—yes, of course I will."

She went with him in a docile fashion, like a child, but like a puzzled child.

Poirot passed into the cabin.

"Here is Mademoiselle."

She stepped in after him, wavered, stood still . . . standing there mute and dumb, her eyes fixed on Simon's face.

"Hullo, Jackie." He, too, was embarrassed. He went on: "Awfully good of you to come. I wanted to say—I mean—what I mean is—"

She interrupted him then. Her words came out in a rush—breathless, desperate.

"Simon—I didn't kill Linnet. You know I didn't do that. . . . I—I—was mad last night. Oh, can you ever forgive me?"

Words came more easily to him now.

"Of course. That's all right! Absolutely all right! That's what I wanted to say. Thought you might be worrying a bit, you know. . . ."

"*Worrying? A bit?* Oh! Simon!"

"That's what I wanted to see you about. It's quite all right, see, old girl? You just got a bit rattled last night—a shade tight. All perfectly natural."

"Oh, Simon! I might have killed you!"

"Not you. Not with a rotten little peashooter like that. . . ."

"And your leg! Perhaps you'll never walk again. . . ."

"Now, look here, Jackie, don't be maudlin. As soon as we get to Assuan they're going to put the X-rays to work, and dig out that tin pot bullet, and everything will be as right as rain."

Jacqueline gulped twice; then she rushed forward and knelt down by Simon's bed, burying her face and sobbing. Simon patted her awkwardly on the head. His eyes met Poirot's and, with a reluctant sigh, the latter left the cabin.

He heard broken murmurs as he went:

"How could I be such a devil? Oh, Simon! . . . I'm so dreadfully sorry. . . ."

Outside Cornelia Robson was leaning over the rail. She turned her head.

"Oh, it's you, Monsieur Poirot. It seems so awful somehow that it should be such a lovely day."

Poirot looked up at the sky.

"When the sun shines you cannot see the moon," he said. "But when the sun is gone—ah, when the sun is gone."

Cornelia's mouth fell open.

"I beg your pardon?"

"I was saying, Mademoiselle, that when the sun has gone down, we shall see the moon. That is so, is it not?"

"Why—why, yes—certainly."

She looked at him doubtfully.

Poirot laughed gently.

"I utter the imbecilities," he said. "Take no notice."

He strolled gently toward the stern of the boat. As he passed the next cabin he paused for a minute. He caught fragments of speech from within:

"Utterly ungrateful—after all I've done for you—no consideration for your wretched mother—no idea of what I suffer. . . ."

Poirot's lips stiffened as he pressed them together. He raised a hand and knocked.

There was a startled silence and Mrs. Otterbourne's voice called out, "Who's that?"

"Is Mademoiselle Rosalie there?"

Rosalie appeared in the doorway. Poirot was shocked at her appearance. There were dark circles under her eyes and drawn lines round her mouth.

"What's the matter?" she said ungraciously. "What do you want?"

"The pleasure of a few minutes' conversation with you, Mademoiselle. Will you come?"

Her mouth went sulky at once. She shot him a suspicious look. "Why should I?"

"I entreat you, Mademoiselle."

"Oh, I suppose—"

She stepped out on the deck, closing the door behind her.

"Well?"

Poirot took her gently by the arm and drew her along the deck, still in the direction of the stern. They passed the bathrooms and round the corner. They had the stern part of the deck to themselves. The Nile flowed away behind them.

Poirot rested his elbows on the rail. Rosalie stood up straight and stiff.

"Well?" she asked again, and her voice held the same ungracious tone.

Poirot spoke slowly, choosing his words. "I could ask you certain questions, Mademoiselle, but I do not think for one moment that you would consent to answer them."

"Seems rather a waste to bring me along here then."

Poirot drew a finger slowly along the wooden rail.

"You are accustomed, Mademoiselle, to carrying your own burdens. . . . But you can do that too long. The strain becomes too great. For you, Mademoiselle, the strain is becoming too great."

"I don't know what you are talking about," said Rosalie.

"I am talking about facts, Mademoiselle—plain ugly facts. Let us call the spade the spade and say it in one little short sentence. Your mother drinks, Mademoiselle."

Rosalie did not answer. Her mouth opened; then she closed it again. For once she seemed at a loss.

"There is no need for you to talk, Mademoiselle. I will do all the talking. I was interested at Assuan in the relations existing between you. I saw at once that, in spite of your carefully studied unfilial remarks, you were in reality passionately protecting her from something. I very soon knew what that something was. I knew it long before I encountered your mother one morning in an unmistakable state of intoxication. Moreover, her case, I could see, was one of secret bouts of drinking—by far the most difficult kind of case with which to deal. You were coping with it manfully. Nevertheless, she had all the secret drunkard's cunning. She managed to get hold of a secret supply of spirits and to keep it successfully hidden from you. I should not be surprised if you discovered its hiding place only yesterday. Accordingly, last night, as soon as your mother was really soundly asleep, you stole out with the contents of the *cache,* went round to the other side of the boat (since your own side was up against the bank) and cast it overboard into the Nile."

He paused.

"I am right, am I not?"

"Yes—you're quite right." Rosalie spoke with sudden passion. "I was a fool not to say so, I suppose! But I didn't want everyone to know. It would go all over the boat. And it seemed so—so silly—I mean—that I—"

Poirot finished the sentence for her.

"So silly that you should be suspected of committing a murder?"

Rosalie nodded.

Then she burst out again: "I've tried so hard to—keep everyone from knowing. . . . It isn't really her fault. She got discouraged. Her books didn't sell any more. People are tired of all that cheap sex stuff. . . . It hurt her—it hurt her dreadfully. And so she began to—to drink. For a long time I didn't know why she was so queer. Then, when I found out, I tried to—to stop it. She'd be all right for a bit, and then, suddenly, she'd start, and there would be dreadful quarrels and rows with people. It was awful." She shuddered. "I had always to be on the watch—to get her away . . .

"And then—she began to dislike me for it. She—she's turned right against me. I think she almost hates me sometimes. . . ."

"*Pauvre petite,*" said Poirot.

She turned on him vehemently.

"Don't be sorry for me. Don't be kind. It's easier if you're not." She sighed—a long heartrending sigh. "I'm so tired . . . I'm so deadly, deadly tired."

"I know," said Poirot.

"People think I'm awful. Stuck-up and cross and bad-tempered. I can't help it. I've forgotten how to be—to be nice."

"That is what I said to you; you have carried your burden by yourself too long."

Rosalie said slowly: "It is a relief—to talk about it. You—you've always been kind to me, Monsieur Poirot. I'm afraid I've been rude to you often."

"*La politesse,* it is not necessary between friends."

The suspicion came back to her face suddenly.

"Are you—are you going to tell everyone? I suppose you must, because of those damned bottles I threw overboard."

"No, no, it is not necessary. Just tell me what I want to know. At what time was this? Ten minutes past one?"

"About that, I should think. I don't remember exactly."

"Now tell me, Mademoiselle. Mademoiselle Van Schuyler saw *you,* did you see *her?*"

Rosalie shook her head.

"No, I didn't."

"She says that she looked out of the door of her cabin."

"I don't think I should have seen her. I just looked along the deck and then out to the river."

Poirot nodded.

"And did you see anyone—anyone at all, when you looked down the deck?"

There was a pause—quite a long pause. Rosalie was frowning. She seemed to be thinking earnestly.

At last she shook her head quite decisively.

"No," she said. "I saw nobody."

Hercule Poirot slowly nodded his head. But his eyes were grave.

CHAPTER XIX

People crept into the dining-saloon by ones and twos in a very subdued manner. There seemed a general feeling that to sit down eagerly to food displayed an unfortunate heartlessness. It was with an almost apologetic air that one passenger after another came and sat down at their tables.

Tim Allerton arrived some few minutes after his mother had taken her seat. He was looking in a thoroughly bad temper.

"I wish we'd never come on this blasted trip," he growled.

Mrs. Allerton shook her head sadly.

"Oh, my dear, so do I. That beautiful girl! It all seems such a *waste.* To think that anyone could shoot her in cold blood. It seems awful to me that anyone could do such a thing. And that other poor child."

"Jacqueline?"

"Yes; my heart aches for her. She looks so dreadfully unhappy."

"Teach her not to go round loosing off toy firearms," said Tim unfeelingly as he helped himself to butter.

"I expect she was badly brought up."

"Oh, for God's sake, Mother, don't go all maternal about it."

"You're in a shocking bad temper, Tim."

"Yes, I am. Who wouldn't be?"

"I don't see what there is to be cross about. It's just frightfully sad."

Tim said crossly: "You're taking the romantic point of view! What you don't seem to realize is that it's no joke being mixed up in a murder case."

Mrs. Allerton looked a little startled.

"But surely—"

"That's just it. There's no 'But surely' about it. Everyone on this damned boat is under suspicion—you and I as well as the rest of them."

Mrs. Allerton demurred. "Technically we are, I suppose—but actually it's ridiculous!"

"There's nothing ridiculous where murder's concerned! You may sit there, darling, just exuding virtue and conscious rectitude, but a lot of unpleasant policemen at Shellâl or Assuan won't take you at your face value."

"Perhaps the truth will be known before then."

"Why should it be?"

"Monsieur Poirot may find out."

"That old mountebank? He won't find out anything. He's all talk and moustaches."

"Well, Tim," said Mrs. Allerton, "I daresay everything you say is true, but, even if it is, we've got to go through with it, so we might as well make up our minds to it and go through with it as cheerfully as we can."

But her son showed no abatement of gloom.

"There's this blasted business of the pearls being missing, too."

"Linnet's pearls?"

"Yes. It seems somebody must have pinched 'em."

"I suppose that was the motive for the crime," said Mrs. Allerton.

"Why should it be? You're mixing up two perfectly different things."

"Who told you that they were missing?"

"Ferguson. He got it from his tough friend in the engine room, who got it from the maid."

"They were lovely pearls," declared Mrs. Allerton.

Poirot sat down at the table, bowing to Mrs. Allerton.

"I am a little late," he said.

"I expect you have been busy," Mrs. Allerton replied.

"Yes, I have been much occupied."

He ordered a fresh bottle of wine from the waiter.

"We're very catholic in our tastes," said Mrs. Allerton. "You drink wine always; Tim drinks whisky and soda, and I try all the different brands of mineral water in turn."

"*Tiens!*" said Poirot. He stared at her for a moment. He murmured to himself, "It is an idea, that. . . ."

Then, with an impatient shrug of his shoulders, he dismissed the sudden preoccupation that had distracted him and began to chat lightly of other matters.

"Is Mr. Doyle badly hurt?" asked Mrs. Allerton.

"Yes, it is a fairly serious injury. Dr. Bessner is anxious to reach Assuan so that his leg can be X-rayed and the bullet removed. But he hopes that there will be no permanent lameness."

"Poor Simon," said Mrs. Allerton. "Only yesterday he looked such a happy boy, with everything in the world he wanted. And now his beautiful wife killed and he himself laid up and helpless. I do hope, though—"

"What do you hope, Madame?" asked Poirot as Mrs. Allerton paused.

"I hope he's not too angry with that poor child."

"With Mademoiselle Jacqueline? Quite the contrary. He was full of anxiety on her behalf."

He turned to Tim.

"You know, it is a pretty little problem of psychology, that. All the time that Mademoiselle Jacqueline was following them from place to place, he was absolutely furious; but now, when she has actually shot him, and wounded him dangerously—perhaps made him lame for life—all his anger seems to have evaporated. Can you understand that?"

"Yes," said Tim thoughtfully, "I think I can. The first thing made him feel a fool—"

Poirot nodded. "You are right. It offended his male dignity."

"But now—if you look at it a certain way, it's *she* who's made a fool of herself. Everyone's down on her, and so—"

"He can be generously forgiving," finished Mrs. Allerton. "What children men are!"

"A profoundly untrue statement that women always make," murmured Tim.

Poirot smiled. Then he said to Tim, "Tell me, Madame Doyle's cousin, Miss Joanna Southwood, did she resemble Madame Doyle?"

"You've got it a little wrong, Monsieur Poirot. She was our cousin and Linnet's friend."

"Ah, pardon—I was confused. She is a young lady much in the news, that. I have been interested in her for some time."

"Why?" asked Tim sharply.

Poirot half rose to bow to Jacqueline de Bellefort, who had just come in and passed their table on the way to her own. Her cheeks were flushed and her eyes bright, and her breath came a little unevenly. As he resumed his seat Poirot seemed to have forgotten Tim's question. He murmured vaguely, "I wonder if all young ladies with valuable jewels were as careless as Madame Doyle was?"

"It is true, then, that they were stolen?" asked Mrs. Allerton.

"Who told you so, Madame?"

"Ferguson said so," Tim volunteered.

Poirot nodded gravely.

"It is quite true."

"I suppose," said Mrs. Allerton nervously, "that this will mean a lot of unpleasantness for all of us. Tim says it will."

Her son scowled, but Poirot had turned to him.

"Ah! you have had previous experience, perhaps? You have been in a house where there was a robbery?"

"Never," said Tim.

"Oh, yes, darling, you were at the Portarlingtons' that time—when that awful woman's diamonds were stolen."

"You always get things hopelessly wrong, Mother. I was there when it was discovered that the diamonds she was wearing round her fat neck were only paste! The actual substitution was probably done months earlier. As a matter of fact, a lot of people said she'd had it done herself!"

"Joanna said so, I expect."

"Joanna wasn't there."

"But she knew them quite well. And it's very like her to make that kind of suggestion."

"You're always down on Joanna, Mother."

Poirot hastily changed the subject. He had it in mind to make a really big purchase at one of the Assuan shops. Some very attractive purple and gold material at one of the Indian merchants. There would, of course, be the duty to pay, but—

"They tell me that they can—how do you say?—expedite it for me. And that the charges will not be too high. How think you, will it arrive all right?"

Mrs. Allerton said that many people, so she had heard, had had things sent straight to England from the shops in question and that everything had arrived safely.

"*Bien.* Then I will do that. But the trouble one has, when one is abroad, if a parcel comes out from England! Have you had experience of that? Have you had any parcels arrive since you have been on your travels?"

"I don't think we have, have we, Tim? You get books sometimes, but of course there is never any trouble about them."

"Ah, no, books are different."

Dessert had been served. Now, without any previous warning, Colonel Race stood up and made his speech.

He touched on the circumstances of the crime and announced the theft of the pearls. A search of the boat was about to be instituted, and he would be obliged if all the passengers would remain in the saloon until this was completed. Then, after that, if the passengers agreed, as he was sure they would, they themselves would be kind enough to submit to a search.

Poirot slipped nimbly along to his side. There was a little buzz and hum all round them. Voices doubtful, indignant, excited. . . .

Poirot reached Race's side and murmured something in his ear just as the latter was about to leave the dining-saloon.

Race listened, nodded assent, and beckoned a steward. He said a few brief words to him; then, together with Poirot, he passed out onto the deck, closing the door behind him.

They stood for a minute or two by the rail. Race lit a cigarette. "Not a bad idea of yours," he said. "We'll soon see if there's anything in it. I'll give 'em three minutes."

The door of the dining-saloon opened and the same steward to whom they had spoken came out. He saluted Race and said: "Quite right, sir. There's a lady who says it's urgent she should speak to you at once without any delay."

"Ah!" Race's face showed his satisfaction. "Who is it?"

"Miss Bowers, sir, the hospital nurse lady."

A slight shade of surprise showed on Race's face. He said: "Bring her to the smoking-room. Don't let anyone else leave."

"No, sir—the other steward will attend to that."

He went back into the dining-room. Poirot and Race went to the smoking-room.

"Bowers, eh?" murmured Race.

They had hardly got inside the smoking-room before the steward reappeared with Miss Bowers. He ushered her in and left, shutting the door behind him.

"Well, Miss Bowers?" Colonel Race looked at her inquiringly. "What's all this?"

Miss Bowers looked her usual composed, unhurried self. She displayed no particular emotion.

"You'll excuse me, Colonel Race," she said, "but under the circumstances I thought the best thing to do would be to speak to you at once"—she opened her neat black handbag—"and to return you these."

She took out a string of pearls and laid them on the table.

CHAPTER XX

If Miss Bowers had been the kind of woman who enjoyed creating a sensation, she would have been richly repaid by the result of her action.

A look of utter astonishment passed over Colonel Race's face as he picked up the pearls from the table.

"This is most extraordinary," he said. "Will you kindly explain, Miss Bowers?"

"Of course. That's what I've come to do." Miss Bowers settled herself comfortably in a chair. "Naturally it was a little difficult for me to decide what it was best for me to do. The family would naturally be averse to scandal of any kind, and they trust my discretion, but the circumstances are so very unusual that it really leaves me no choice. Of course, when you didn't find anything in the cabins, your next move would be a search of the passengers, and if the pearls were then found in my possession it would be rather an awkward situation and the truth would come out just the same."

"And just what is the truth? Did you take these pearls from Mrs. Doyle's cabin?"

"Oh, no, Colonel Race, of course not. Miss Van Schuyler did."

"Miss Van Schuyler?"

"Yes. She can't help it, you know, but she does—er—take things. Especially jewellery. That's really why I'm always with her. It's not her health at all; it's this little idiosyncrasy. I keep on the alert, and fortunately there's never been any trouble since I've been with her. It just means being watchful, you know. And she always hides the things she takes in the same place—rolled up in a pair of stockings—so that makes it very simple. I look each morning. Of course I'm a light sleeper, and I always sleep next door to her, and with the communicating door open if it's in a hotel, so that I usually hear. Then I go after her and persuade her to go back to bed. Of course it's been rather more difficult on a boat. But she doesn't usually do it at night. It's more just picking up things that she sees left about. Of course, pearls have a great attraction for her always."

Miss Bowers ceased speaking.

Race asked, "How did you discover they had been taken?"

"They were in her stockings this morning. I knew whose they were, of course. I've often noticed them. I went along to put them back, hoping that Mrs. Doyle wasn't up yet and hadn't discovered her loss. But there was a steward standing there, and he told me about the murder and that no one could go in. So then, you see, I was in a regular quandary. But I still hoped to slip them back in the cabin later, before their absence had been noticed. I can assure you I've passed a very unpleasant morning wondering what was the best thing to do. You see the Van Schuyler family is so *very* particular and exclusive. It would never do if this got into the newspapers. But that won't be necessary, will it?"

Miss Bowers really looked worried.

"That depends on circumstances," said Colonel Race cautiously. "But we shall do our best for you, of course. What does Miss Van Schuyler say to this?"

"Oh, she'll deny it, of course. She always does. Says some wicked person has put it there. She never admits taking anything. That's why if you catch her in time she goes back to bed like a lamb. Says she just went out to look at the moon. Something like that."

"Does Miss Robson know about this—er—failing?"

"No, she doesn't. Her mother knows, but she's a very simple kind of girl and her mother thought it best she should know nothing about it. I was quite equal to dealing with Miss Van Schuyler," added the competent Miss Bowers.

"We have to thank you, Mademoiselle, for coming to us so promptly," said Poirot.

Miss Bowers stood up.

"I'm sure I hope I've acted for the best."

"Be assured that you have."

"You see, what with there being a murder as well—"

Colonel Race interrupted her. His voice was grave.

"Miss Bowers, I am going to ask you a question, and I want to impress upon you that it has got to be answered truthfully. Miss Van Schuyler is unhinged mentally to the extent of being a kleptomaniac. Has she also a tendency to homicidal mania?"

Miss Bowers' answer came immediately: "Oh, dear me, no! Nothing of that kind. You can take my word for it absolutely. The old lady wouldn't hurt a fly."

The reply came with such positive assurance that there seemed nothing more to be said. Nevertheless Poirot did interpolate one mild inquiry.

"Does Miss Van Schuyler suffer at all from deafness?"

"As a matter of fact she does, Monsieur Poirot. Not so that you'd notice it any way, not if you were speaking to her, I mean. But quite often she doesn't hear you when you come into a room. Things like that."

"Do you think she would have heard anyone moving about in Mrs. Doyle's cabin, which is next door to her own?"

"Oh, I shouldn't think so—not for a minute. You see, the bunk is the other side of the cabin, not even against the partition wall. No, I don't think she would have heard anything."

"Thank you, Miss Bowers."

Race said, "Perhaps you will now go back to the dining-saloon and wait with the others?"

He opened the door for her and watched her go down the staircase and enter the saloon. Then he shut the door and came back to the table. Poirot had picked up the pearls.

"Well," said Race grimly, "that reaction came pretty quickly. That's a very cool-headed and astute young woman—perfectly capable of holding out on us still further if she thinks it suits her book. What about Miss Marie Van Schuyler now? I don't think we can eliminate her from the possible suspects. You know, she *might* have committed murder to get hold of those jewels. We can't take the nurse's word for it. She's all out to do the best for the family."

Poirot nodded in agreement. He was very busy with the pearls, running them through his fingers, holding them up to his eyes.

He said: "We may take it, I think, that part of the old lady's story to us was true. She *did* look out of her cabin and she *did* see Rosalie Otterbourne. But I don't think she *heard* anything or anyone in Linnet Doyle's cabin. I think she was just peering out from *her* cabin preparatory to slipping along and purloining the pearls."

"The Otterbourne girl was there, then?"

"Yes. Throwing her mother's secret *cache* of drink overboard."

Colonel Race shook his head sympathetically.

"So that's it! Tough on a young un."

"Yes, her life has not been very gay, *cette pauvre petite Rosalie.*"

"Well, I'm glad that's been cleared up. *She* didn't see or hear anything?"

"I asked her that. She responded—after a lapse of quite twenty seconds—that she saw nobody."

"Oh?" Race looked alert.

"Yes, it is suggestive, that."

Race said slowly: "If Linnet Doyle was shot round about ten minutes past one, or indeed any time after the boat had quieted down, it has seemed amazing to me that no one heard the shot. I grant you that a little pistol like that wouldn't make much noise, but all the same the boat would be deadly quiet, and any noise, even a gentle pop, should have been heard. But I begin to understand better now. The cabin on the forward side of hers was unoccupied—since her husband was in Dr. Bessner's cabin. The one aft was occupied by the Van Schuyler woman, who was deaf. That leaves only—"

He paused and looked expectantly at Poirot, who nodded.

"The cabin next to hers on the other side of the boat. In other words —Pennington. We always seem to come back to Pennington."

"We will come back to him presently with the kid gloves removed! Ah, yes, I am promising myself that pleasure."

"In the meantime we'd better get on with our search of the boat. The pearls still make a convenient excuse, even though they have been returned—but Miss Bowers is not likely to advertise that fact."

"Ah, these pearls!" Poirot held them up against the light once more. He stuck out his tongue and licked them; he even gingerly tried one of them between his teeth. Then, with a sigh, he threw them down on the table.

"Here are more complications, my friend," he said. "I am not an expert on precious stones, but I have had a good deal to do with them in my time and I am fairly certain of what I say. These pearls are only a clever imitation."

CHAPTER XXI

Colonel Race swore lustily.

"This damned case gets more and more involved." He picked up the pearls. "I suppose you've not made a mistake? They look all right to me."

"They are a very good imitation—yes."

"Now where does that lead us? I suppose Linnet Doyle didn't deliberately have an imitation made and bring it abroad with her for safety. Many women do."

"I think, if that were so, her husband would know about it."

"She may not have told him."

Poirot shook his head in a dissatisfied manner.

"No, I do not think that is so. I was admiring Madame Doyle's pearls the first evening on the boat—their wonderful sheen and lustre. I am sure that she was wearing the genuine ones then."

"That brings us up against two possibilities. First, that Miss Van Schuyler only stole the imitation string after the real ones had been stolen by someone else. Second, that the whole kleptomaniac story is a fabrication. Either Miss Bowers is a thief, and quickly invented the story and allayed suspicion by handing over the false pearls, or else that whole party is in it together. That is to say, they are a gang of clever jewel thieves masquerading as an exclusive American family."

"Yes," Poirot murmured. "It is difficult to say. But I will point out to you one thing—to make a perfect and exact copy of the pearls, clasp and all, good enough to stand a chance of deceiving Madame Doyle, is a highly skilled technical performance. It could not be done in a hurry. Whoever copied those pearls must have had a good opportunity of studying the original."

Race rose to his feet.

"Useless to speculate about it any further now. Let's get on with the job. We've got to find the real pearls. And at the same time we'll keep our eyes open."

They disposed first of the cabins occupied on the lower deck.

That of Signor Richetti contained various archaeological works in different languages, a varied assortment of clothing, hair lotions of a highly scented kind and two personal letters—one from an archaeological expedition in Syria, and one from, apparently, a sister in Rome. His handkerchiefs were all of coloured silk.

They passed on to Ferguson's cabin.

There was a sprinkling of communistic literature, a good many snapshots, Samuel Butler's *Erewhon* and a cheap edition of Pepys' Diary. His personal possessions were not many. Most of what outer clothing there was was torn and dirty; the underclothing, on the other hand, was of really good quality. The handkerchiefs were expensive linen ones.

"Some interesting discrepancies," murmured Poirot.

Race nodded. "Rather odd that there are absolutely no personal papers, letters, etc."

"Yes; that gives one to think. An odd young man, Monsieur Ferguson."

He looked thoughtfully at a signet ring he held in his hand, before replacing it in the drawer where he had found it.

They went along to the cabin occupied by Louise Bourget. The maid had her meals after the other passengers, but Race had sent word that she was to be taken to join the others. A cabin steward met them.

"I'm sorry, sir," he apologized, "but I've not been able to find the young woman anywhere. I can't think where she can have got to."

Race glanced inside the cabin. It was empty.

They went up to the promenade deck and started on the starboard side. The first cabin was that occupied by James Fanthorp. Here all was in meticulous order. Mr. Fanthorp travelled light, but all that he had was of good quality.

"No letters," said Poirot thoughtfully. "He is careful, our Mr. Fanthorp, to destroy his correspondence."

They passed on to Tim Allerton's cabin, next door.

There were evidences here of an Anglo Catholic turn of mind—an exquisite little triptych, and a big rosary of intricately carved wood. Besides personal clothing, there was a half completed manuscript, a good deal annotated and scribbled over, and a good collection of books, most of them recently published. There were also a quantity of letters thrown carelessly into a drawer. Poirot, never in the least scrupulous about reading other people's correspondence, glanced through them. He noted that amongst them there were no letters from Joanna Southwood. He picked up a tube of seccotine, fingered it absently for a minute or two, then said, "Let us pass on."

"No Woolworth handkerchiefs," reported Race, rapidly replacing the contents of a drawer.

Mrs. Allerton's cabin was the next. It was exquisitely neat, and a faint old-fashioned smell of lavender hung about it.

The two men's search was soon over. Race remarked as they left it, "Nice woman, that."

The next cabin was that which had been used as a dressing-room by Simon Doyle. His immediate necessities—pyjamas, toilet things, etc., had been moved to Bessner's cabin, but the remainder of his possessions were still there—two good-sized leather suitcases and a kit bag. There were also some clothes in the wardrobe.

"We will look carefully here, my friend," said Poirot, "for it is very possible that the thief hid the pearls here."

"You think it is likely?"

"But yes, indeed. Consider! The thief, whoever he or she may be, must know that sooner or later a search will be made, and therefore a hiding place in his or her own cabin would be injudicious in the extreme. The public rooms present other difficulties. But here is a cabin belonging to a man who cannot possibly visit it himself, so that, if the pearls are found here, it tells us nothing at all."

But the most meticulous search failed to reveal any trace of the missing necklace.

Poirot murmured "*Zut!*" to himself and they emerged once more on the deck.

Linnet Doyle's cabin had been locked after the body was removed, but Race had the key with him. He unlocked the door and the two men stepped inside.

Except for the removal of the girl's body, the cabin was exactly as it had been that morning.

"Poirot," said Race, "if there's anything to be found here, for God's sake go ahead and find it. You can if anyone can—I know that."

"This time you do not mean the pearls, *mon ami?*"

"No. The murder's the main thing. There may be something I overlooked this morning."

Quietly, deftly, Poirot went about his search. He went down on his knees and scrutinized the floor inch by inch. He examined the bed. He went rapidly through the wardrobe and chest of drawers. He went through the wardrobe trunk and the two costly suitcases. He looked through the expensive gold-fitted dressingcase. Finally he turned his attention to the washstand. There were various creams, powders, face lotions. But the only thing that seemed to interest Poirot were two little bottles labelled Nailex. He picked them up at last and brought them to the dressing-table. One, which bore the inscription Nailex Rose, was empty but for a drop or two of dark red fluid at the bottom. The other, the same size, but labelled Nailex Cardinal, was nearly full. Poirot uncorked first the empty, then the full one, and sniffed them both delicately.

An odour of pear drops billowed into the room. With a slight grimace he recorked them.

"Get anything?" asked Race.

Poirot replied by a French proverb, *"On ne prend pas les mouches avec le vinaigre."* Then he said with a sigh: "My friend, we have not been fortunate. The murderer has not been obliging. He has not dropped for us the cuff link, the cigarette end, the cigar ash—or, in the case of a woman, the handkerchief, the lipstick or the hair slide."

"Only the bottle of nail polish?"

Poirot shrugged his shoulders.

"I must ask the maid. There is something—yes—a little curious there."

"I wonder where the devil the girl's got to?" said Race.

They left the cabin, locking the door behind them, and passed on to that of Miss Van Schuyler.

Here again were all the appurtenances of wealth, expensive toilet fittings, good luggage, a certain number of private letters and papers all perfectly in order.

The next cabin was the double one occupied by Poirot, and beyond it that of Race.

"Hardly likely to hide 'em in either of these," said the Colonel.

Poirot demurred. "It might be. Once, on the Orient Express, I investigated a murder. There was a little matter of a scarlet kimono. It had disappeared, and yet it must be on the train. I found it—where do you think? In my own locked suitcase! Ah! it was an impertinence, that!"

"Well, let's see if anybody has been impertinent with you or me this time."

But the thief of the pearls had not been impertinent with Hercule Poirot or with Colonel Race.

Rounding the stern they made a very careful search of Miss Bowers' cabin but could find nothing of a suspicious nature. Her handkerchiefs were of plain linen with an initial.

The Otterbournes' cabin came next. Here, again, Poirot made a very meticulous search, but with no result.

The next cabin was Bessner's. Simon Doyle lay with an untasted tray of food beside him.

"Off my feed," he said apologetically.

He was looking feverish and very much worse than earlier in the day. Poirot appreciated Bessner's anxiety to get him as swiftly as possible to hospital and skilled appliances.

The little Belgian explained what the two of them were doing, and Simon nodded approval. On learning that the pearls had been restored by Miss Bowers, but proved to be merely imitation, he expressed the most complete astonishment.

"You are quite sure, Monsieur Doyle, that your wife did not have an imitation string which she brought abroad with her instead of the real ones?"

Simon shook his head decisively.

"Oh, no. I'm quite sure of that. Linnet loved those pearls and she wore 'em everywhere. They were insured against every possible risk, so I think that made her a bit careless."

"Then we must continue our search."

He started opening drawers. Race attacked a suitcase.

Simon stared. "Look here, you surely don't suspect old Bessner pinched them?" Poirot shrugged his shoulders.

"It might be so. After all, what do we know of Dr. Bessner? Only what he himself gives out."

"But he couldn't have hidden them in here without my seeing him."

"He could not have hidden anything *today* without your having seen him. But we do not know when the substitution took place. He may have effected the exchange some days ago."

"I never thought of that."

But the search was unavailing.

The next cabin was Pennington's. The two men spent some time in their search. In particular, Poirot and Race examined carefully a case full of legal and business documents, most of them requiring Linnet's signature.

Poirot shook his head gloomily. "These seem all square and above board. You agree?"

"Absolutely. Still, the man isn't a born fool. If there *had* been a compromising document there—a power of attorney or something of that kind—he'd be pretty sure to have destroyed it first thing."

"That is so, yes."

Poirot lifted a heavy Colt revolver out of the top drawer of the chest of drawers, looked at it and put it back.

"So it seems there are still some people who travel with revolvers," he murmured.

"Yes, a little suggestive, perhaps. Still, Linnet Doyle wasn't shot with a thing that size." Race paused and then said: "You know, I've thought of a possible answer to your point about the pistol being thrown overboard. Supposing that the actual murderer *did* leave it in Linnet Doyle's cabin, and that someone else—some second person—took it away and threw it into the river?"

"Yes, that is possible. I have thought of it. But it opens up a whole string of questions. Who was that second person? What interest had they in endeavouring to shield Jacqueline de Bellefort by taking away the pistol? What was that second person doing there? The only other person we know of who went into the cabin was Mademoiselle Van Schuyler. Was it conceivably Mademoiselle Van Schuyler who removed it? Why should *she* wish to shield Jacqueline de Bellefort? And yet—what other reason can there be for the removal of the pistol?"

Race suggested, "She may have recognized the stole as hers, got the wind up, and thrown the whole bag of tricks over on that account."

"The stole, perhaps, but would she have got rid of the pistol, too? Still, I agree that it is a possible solution. But it is clumsy—*bon Dieu*, it is clumsy. And you still have not appreciated one point about the stole—"

As they emerged from Pennington's cabin Poirot suggested that Race should search the remaining cabins, those occupied by Jacqueline, Cornelia and two empty ones at the end, while he himself had a few words with Simon Doyle.

Accordingly he retraced his steps along the deck and re-entered Bessner's cabin.

Simon said: "Look here, I've been thinking. I'm perfectly sure that those pearls were all right yesterday."

"Why is that, Monsieur Doyle?"

"Because, Linnet"—he winced as he uttered his wife's name—"was passing them through her hands just before dinner and talking about them. She knew something about pearls. I feel certain she'd have known if they were a fake."

"They were a very good imitation, though. Tell me, was Madame

Doyle in the habit of letting those pearls out of her hands? Did she ever lend them to a friend, for instance?"

Simon flushed with slight embarrassment.

"You see, Monsieur Poirot, it's difficult for me to say. . . . I—I—well, you see, I hadn't known Linnet very long."

"Ah, no, it was a quick romance—yours."

Simon went on.

"And so—really—I shouldn't know a thing like that. But Linnet was awfully generous with her things. I should think she might have done."

"She never for instance"—Poirot's voice was very smooth—"she never, for instance, lent them to Mademoiselle de Bellefort?"

"What d'you mean?" Simon flushed brick red, tried to sit up and, wincing, fell back. "What are you getting at? That Jackie stole the pearls? She didn't. I'll swear she didn't. Jackie's as straight as a die. The mere idea of her being a thief is ridiculous—absolutely ridiculous."

Poirot looked at him with gently twinkling eyes.

"Oh, la! la! la!" he said unexpectedly. "That suggestion of mine, it has indeed stirred up the nest of hornets."

Simon repeated doggedly, unmoved by Poirot's lighter note, "Jackie's straight!"

Poirot remembered a girl's voice by the Nile in Assuan saying, "I love Simon—and he loves me. . . ."

He had wondered which of the three statements he had heard that night was the true one. It seemed to him that it had turned out to be Jacqueline who had come closest to the truth.

The door opened and Race came in.

"Nothing," he said brusquely. "Well, we didn't expect it. I see the stewards coming along with their report as to the searching of the passengers."

A steward and stewardess appeared in the doorway. The former spoke first.

"Nothing, sir."

"Any of the gentlemen make any fuss?"

"Only the Italian gentleman, sir. He carried on a good deal. Said it was a dishonour—something of that kind. He'd got a gun on him too."

"What kind of a gun?"

"Mauser automatic twenty-five, sir."

"Italians are pretty hot-tempered," said Simon. "Richetti got in no end of a stew at Wâdi Halfa just because of a mistake over a telegram. He was darned rude to Linnet over it."

Race turned to the stewardess. She was a big handsome looking woman.

"Nothing on any of the ladies, sir. They made a good deal of fuss —except for Mrs. Allerton, who was as nice as nice could be. Not a sign of the pearls. By the way, the young lady, Miss Rosalie Otterbourne, had a little pistol in her handbag."

"What kind?"

"It was a very small one, sir, with a pearl handle. A kind of toy."

Race stared.

"Devil take this case," he muttered. "I thought we'd got *her* cleared of suspicion, and now— Does every girl on this blinking boat carry around pearl-handled toy pistols?"

He shot a question at the stewardess. "Did she show any feeling over your finding it?"

The woman shook her head. "I don't think she noticed. I had my back turned whilst I was going through the handbag."

"Still, she must have known you'd come across it. Oh, well, it beats me. What about the maid?"

"We've looked all over the boat, sir. We can't find her anywhere."

"What's this?" asked Simon.

"Mrs. Doyle's maid—Louise Bourget. She's disappeared."

"*Disappeared?*"

Race said thoughtfully: "She might have stolen the pearls. She is the one person who had ample opportunity to get a replica made."

"And then, when she found a search was being instituted, she threw herself overboard?" suggested Simon.

"Nonsense," replied Race, irritably. "A woman can't throw herself overboard in broad daylight, from a boat like this, without somebody realizing the fact. She's bound to be somewhere on board." He addressed the stewardess once more. "When was she last seen?"

"About half an hour before the bell went for lunch, sir."

"We'll have a look at her cabin anyway," said Race. "That may tell us something."

He led the way to the deck below. Poirot followed him. They unlocked the door of the cabin and passed inside.

Louise Bourget, whose trade it was to keep other people's belongings in order, had taken a holiday where her own were concerned.

Odds and ends littered the top of the chest of drawers; a suitcase gaped open, with clothes hanging out of the side of it and preventing it shutting; underclothing hung limply over the sides of the chairs.

As Poirot, with swift neat fingers, opened the drawers of the dressing-chest, Race examined the suitcase.

Louise's shoes were lined along by the bed. One of them, a black patent leather, seemed to be resting at an extraordinary angle, almost unsupported. The appearance of it was so odd that it attracted Race's attention.

He closed the suitcase and bent over the line of shoes. Then he uttered a sharp exclamation.

Poirot whirled round.

"*Qu'est ce qu'il y a?*"

Race said grimly: "She hasn't disappeared. She's here—under the bed. . . ."

CHAPTER XXII

THE BODY OF A DEAD WOMAN, who in life had been Louise Bourget, lay on the floor of her cabin. The two men bent over it.

Race straightened himself first.

"Been dead close on an hour, I should say. We'll get Bessner on to it. Stabbed to the heart. Death pretty well instantaneous, I should imagine. She doesn't look pretty, does she?"

"No."

Poirot shook his head with a slight shudder.

The dark feline face was convulsed, as though with surprise and fury, the lips drawn back from the teeth.

Poirot bent again gently and picked up the right hand. Something just showed within the fingers. He detached it and held it out to Race, a little sliver of flimsy paper coloured a pale mauvish pink.

"You see what it is?"

"Money," said Race.

"The corner of a thousand franc note, I fancy."

"Well, it's clear what happened," said Race. "She knew something—and she was blackmailing the murderer with her knowledge. We thought she wasn't being quite straight this morning."

Poirot cried out: "We have been idiots—fools! We should have known—then. What did she say? 'What could I have seen or heard? I was on the deck below. Naturally, if I had been unable to sleep, if I had mounted the stairs, *then* perhaps I might have seen this assassin, this monster, enter or leave Madame's cabin, but as it is—' Of course, that is what did happen! She did come up. She did see someone gliding into Linnet Doyle's cabin—or coming out of it. And, because of her greed, her insensate greed, she lies here—"

"And we are no nearer to knowing who killed her," finished Race disgustedly.

Poirot shook his head. "No, no. We know much more now. We know—we know almost everything. Only what we know seems incredible. . . . Yet it must be so. Only I do not see. Pah! what a fool I was this morning! We felt—both of us felt—that she was keeping something back, and yet we never realized the logical reason, blackmail."

"She must have demanded hush money straight away," said Race.

"Demanded it with threats. The murderer was forced to accede t that request and paid her in French notes. Anything there?"

Poirot shook his head thoughtfully. "I hardly think so. Many peopl take a reserve of money with them when travelling—sometimes fiv pound notes, sometimes dollars, but very often French notes as wel Possibly the murderer paid her all he had in a mixture of currencie Let us continue our reconstruction."

"The murderer comes to her cabin, gives her the money, and then—

"And then," said Poirot, "she counts it. Oh, yes, I know that clas She would count the money, and while she counted it she was com pletely off her guard. The murderer struck. Having done so succes fully, he gathered up the money and fled—not noticing that th corner of one of the notes was torn."

"We may get him that way," suggested Race doubtfully.

"I doubt it," said Poirot. "He will examine those notes, and wi probably notice the tear. Of course if he were of a parsimonious di position he would not be able to bring himself to destroy a *mille* not —but I fear—I very much fear that his temperament is just the op posite."

"How do you make that out?"

"Both this crime and the murder of Madame Doyle demande certain qualities—courage, audacity, bold execution, lightning actio those qualities do not accord with a saving, prudent disposition."

Race shook his head sadly. "I'd better get Bessner down," he sai

The stout doctor's examination did not take long. Accompanied b a good many Ach's and So's, he went to work.

"She has been dead not more than an hour," he announced. "Dea it was very quick—at once."

"And what weapon do you think was used?"

"Ach, it is interesting, that. It was something very sharp, very thi very delicate. I could show you the kind of thing."

Back again in his cabin he opened a case and extracted a lon delicate, surgical knife.

"It was something like that, my friend; it was not a common tab knife."

"I suppose," suggested Race smoothly, "that none of your ow knives are—er—missing, Doctor?"

Bessner stared at him; then his face grew red with indignatio

"What is that you say? Do you think I—I, Carl Bessner—who well-known is all over Austria—I with my clinics, my highly bo patients—I have killed a miserable little *femme de chambre*?! Ah, but it is ridiculous—absurd, what you say! None of my knives are missing—not one, I tell you. They are all here, correct, in their places. You can see for yourself. And this insult to my profession I will not forget."

Dr. Bessner closed his case with a snap, flung it down and stamped out onto the deck.

"Whew!" said Simon. "You've put the old boy's back up."

Poirot shrugged his shoulders. "It is regrettable."

"You're on the wrong tack. Old Bessner's one of the best, even though he is a kind of Boche."

Dr. Bessner reappeared suddenly.

"Will you be so kind as to leave me now my cabin? I have to do the dressing of my patient's leg."

Miss Bowers had entered with him and stood, brisk and professional, waiting for the others to go.

Race and Poirot crept out meekly. Race muttered something and went off. Poirot turned to his left. He heard scraps of girlish conversation, a little laugh. Jacqueline and Rosalie were together in the latter's cabin.

The door was open and the two girls were standing near it. As his shadow fell on them they looked up. He saw Rosalie Otterbourne smile at him for the first time—a shy welcoming smile—a little uncertain in its lines, as of one who does a new and unfamiliar thing.

"You talk the scandal, Mesdemoiselles?" he accused them.

"No, indeed," said Rosalie. "As a matter of fact we were just comparing lipsticks."

Poirot smiled. "*Les chiffons d'aujourd'hui,*" he murmured.

But there was something a little mechanical about his smile, and Jacqueline de Bellefort, quicker and more observant than Rosalie, saw it. She dropped the lipstick she was holding and came out upon the deck.

"Has something—what has happened now?"

"It is as you guess, Mademoiselle; something has happened."

"What?" Rosalie came out too.

"Another death," said Poirot.

Rosalie caught her breath sharply. Poirot was watching her narrowly. He saw alarm and something more—consternation—show for a minute or two in her eyes.

"Madame Doyle's maid has been killed," he told them bluntly.

"Killed?" cried Jacqueline. "*Killed,* do you say?"

"Yes, that is what I said." Though his answer was nominally to her, it was Rosalie whom he watched. It was Rosalie to whom he spoke as he went on: "You see, this maid she saw something she was not intended to see. And so—she was silenced, in case she should not hold her tongue."

"What was it she saw?"

Again it was Jacqueline who asked, and again Poirot's answer was to Rosalie. It was an odd little three-cornered scene.

"There is, I think, very little doubt what it was she saw," said Poirot. "She saw someone enter and leave Linnet Doyle's cabin on that fatal night."

His ears were quick. He heard the sharp intake of breath and saw the eyelids flicker. Rosalie Otterbourne had reacted just as he had intended she should.

"Did she say who it was she saw?" Rosalie asked.

Gently—regretfully—Poirot shook his head.

Footsteps pattered up the deck. It was Cornelia Robson, her eyes wide and startled.

"Oh, Jacqueline," she cried, "something awful has happened! Another dreadful thing!"

Jacqueline turned to her. The two moved a few steps forward. Almost unconsciously Poirot and Rosalie Otterbourne moved in the other direction.

Rosalie said sharply: "Why do you look at me? What have you got in your mind?"

"That is two questions you ask me. I will ask you only one in return. Why do you not tell me all the truth, Mademoiselle?"

"I don't know what you mean. I told you—everything—this morning."

"No, there were things you did not tell me. You did not tell me that you carry about in your handbag a small-calibre pistol with a pearl handle. You did not tell me all that you saw last night."

She flushed. Then she said sharply: "It's quite untrue. I haven' got a revolver."

"I did not say a revolver. I said a small pistol that you carry abou in your handbag."

She wheeled round, darted into her cabin and out again and thrus her grey leather handbag into his hands.

"You're talking nonsense. Look for yourself if you like."

Poirot opened the bag. There was no pistol inside.

He handed the bag back to her, meeting her scornful, triumphant glance.

"No," he said pleasantly. "It is not there."

"You see. You're not always right, Monsieur Poirot. And you're wrong about that other ridiculous thing you said."

"No, I do not think so."

"You're infuriating!" She stamped an angry foot. "You get an idea into your head, and you go on and on and on about it."

"Because I want you to tell me the truth."

"What is the truth? You seem to know it better than I do."

Poirot said: "You want me to tell what it was you saw? If I am right, will you admit that I am right? I will tell you my little idea. I think that when you came round the stern of the boat you stopped involuntarily because you saw a man come out of a cabin about half way down the deck—Linnet Doyle's cabin, as you realized next day. You saw him come out, close the door behind him, and walk away from you down the deck and—perhaps—enter one of the two end cabins. Now then, am I right, Mademoiselle?"

She did not answer.

Poirot said: "Perhaps you think it wiser not to speak. Perhaps you are afraid that, if you do, you too will be killed."

For a moment he thought she had risen to the easy bait, that the accusation against her courage would succeed where more subtle arguments would have failed.

Her lips opened—trembled—then, "I saw no one," said Rosalie Otterbourne.

CHAPTER XXIII

Miss Bowers came out of Dr. Bessner's cabin, smoothing her cuffs over her wrists.

Jacqueline left Cornelia abruptly and accosted the hospital nurse.

"How is he?" she demanded.

Poirot came up in time to hear the answer. Miss Bowers was looking rather worried.

"Things aren't going too badly," she said.

Jacqueline cried, "You mean, he's worse?"

"Well, I must say I shall be relieved when we get in and can get a proper X-ray done and the whole thing cleaned up under an anaesthetic. When do you think we shall get to Shellâl, Monsieur Poirot?"

"Tomorrow morning."

Miss Bowers pursed her lips and shook her head.

"It's very unfortunate. We are doing all we can, but there's always such a danger of septicaemia."

Jacqueline caught Miss Bowers' arm and shook it.

"Is he going to die? Is he going to die?"

"Dear me, no, Miss de Bellefort. That is, I hope not, I'm sure. The wound in itself isn't dangerous, but there's no doubt it ought to be X-rayed as soon as possible. And then, of course, poor Mr. Doyle ought to have been kept absolutely quiet today. He's had far too much worry and excitement. No wonder his temperature is rising. What with the shock of his wife's death, and one thing and another—"

Jacqueline relinquished her grasp of the nurse's arm and turned away. She stood leaning over the side, her back to the other two.

"What I say is, we've got to hope for the best always," said Miss Bowers. "Of course Mr. Doyle has a very strong constitution—one can see that—probably never had a day's illness in his life. So that's in his favour. But there's no denying that this rise in temperature is a nasty sign and—"

She shook her head, adjusted her cuffs once more, and moved briskly away.

Jacqueline turned and walked gropingly, blinded by tears, toward her cabin. A hand below her elbow steadied and guided her. She looked up through the tears to find Poirot by her side. She leaned on him a little and he guided her through the cabin door.

She sank down on the bed and the tears came more freely, punctuated by great shuddering sobs.

"He'll die! He'll die! I know he'll die. . . . And I shall have killed him. Yes, I shall have killed him. . . ."

Poirot shrugged his shoulders. He shook his head a little, sadly.

"Mademoiselle, what is done, is done. One cannot take back the accomplished action. It is too late to regret."

She cried out more vehemently: "I shall have killed him! And I love him so . . . I love him so."

Poirot sighed. "Too much. . . ."

It had been his thought long ago in the restaurant of M. Blondin. It was his thought again now.

He said, hesitating a little: "Do not, at all events, go by what Miss Bowers says. Hospital nurses, me, I find them always gloomy! The night nurse, always, she is astonished to find her patient alive in the evening; the day nurse, always, she is surprised to find him alive in the morning! They know too much, you see, of the possibilities that may arise. When one is motoring one might easily say to oneself, 'If a car came out from that crossroad—or if that lorry backed suddenly—or if the wheel came off the car that is approaching me—or if a dog jumped off the hedge onto my driving arm—*eh bien,* I should probably be killed!' But one assumes, and usually rightly, that none of these things *will* happen, and that one will get to one's journey's end. But if, of course, one has been in an accident, or seen one or more accidents, then one is inclined to take the opposite point of view."

Jacqueline asked, half smiling through her tears, "Are you trying to console me, Monsieur Poirot?"

"The *Bon Dieu* knows what I am trying to do! You should not have come on this journey."

"No—I wish I hadn't. It's been—so awful. But—it will be soon over now."

"*Mais oui—mais oui.*"

"And Simon will go to the hospital, and they'll give the proper treatment and everything will be all right."

"You speak like the child! 'And they lived happily ever afterward.' That is it, is it not?"

She flushed suddenly scarlet.

"Monsieur Poirot, I never meant—never—"

"It is too soon to think of such a thing! That is the proper hypocritical thing to say, is it not? But you are partly a Latin, Mademoiselle Jacqueline. You should be able to admit facts even if they do not sound very decorous. *Le roi est mort—vive le roi!* The sun has gone and the moon rises. That is so, is it not?"

"You don't understand. He's just sorry for me—awfully sorry for me, because he knows how terrible it is for me to know I've hurt him so badly."

"Ah, well," said Poirot. "The pure pity, it is a very lofty sentiment."

He looked at her half mockingly, half with some other emotion.

He murmured softly under his breath words in French:

"La vie est vaine.
Un peu d'amour,
Un peu de haine,
Et puis bonjour.

La vie est brève.
Un peu d'espoir,
Un peu de rêve,
Et puis bonsoir."

He went out again onto the deck. Colonel Race was striding along the deck and hailed him at once.

"Poirot. Good man! I want you. I've got an idea."

Thrusting his arm through Poirot's he walked him up the deck.

"Just a chance remark of Doyle's. I hardly noticed it at the time. Something about a telegram."

"Tiens—c'est vrai."

"Nothing in it, perhaps, but one can't leave any avenue unexplored. Damn it all, man, two murders, and we're still in the dark."

Poirot shook his head. "No, not in the dark. In the light."

Race looked at him curiously. "You have an idea?"

"It is more than an idea now. *I am sure.*"

"Since—when?"

"Since the death of the maid, Louise Bourget."

"Damned if I see it!"

"My friend, it is so clear—so clear. Only there are difficulties—embarrassments—impediments! See you, around a person like Linnet Doyle there is so much—so many conflicting hates and jealousies and envies and meannesses. It is like a cloud of flies, buzzing, buzzing. . . ."

"But you think you know?" The other looked at him curiously. "You wouldn't say so unless you were sure. Can't say I've any real light, myself. I've suspicions, of course. . . ."

Poirot stopped. He laid an impressive hand on Race's arm.

"You are a great man, mon Colonel. . . . You do not say 'Tell me. What is it that you think?' You know that if I could speak now I would. But there is much to be cleared away first. But think, think for a moment along the lines that I shall indicate. There are certain points. . . . There is the statement of Mademoiselle de Bellefort that someone overheard our conversation that night in the garden at Assuan. There is the statement of Monsieur Tim Allerton as to what he heard and did on the night of the crime. There are Louise Bourget's significant answers to our questions this morning. There is the fact that Madame Allerton drinks water, that her son drinks whisky and soda and that I drink wine. Add to that the fact of two bottles of nail polish and the proverb I quoted. And finally we come to the crux of the whole business, the fact that the pistol was wrapped up in a cheap handkerchief and a velvet stole and thrown overboard. . . ."

Race was silent a minute or two then he shook his head.

"No," he said, "I don't see it. Mind, I've got a faint idea what you're driving at, but as far as I can see, it doesn't work."

"But yes—but yes. You are seeing only half the truth. And remember this—we must start again from the beginning, since our first conception was entirely wrong."

Race made a slight grimace.

"I'm used to that. It often seems to me that's all detective work is, wiping out your false starts and beginning again."

"Yes, it is very true, that. And it is just what some people will not do. They conceive a certain theory, and everything has to fit into that theory. If one little fact will not fit it, they throw it aside. But it is always the facts that will not fit in that are significant. All along I have realized the significance of that pistol being removed from the scene of the crime. I knew that it meant something, but what that something was I only realized one little half hour ago."

"And I still don't see it!"

"But you will! Only reflect along the lines I indicated. And now let us clear up this matter of a telegram. That is, if the Herr Doktor will admit us."

Dr. Bessner was still in a very bad humour. In answer to their knock he disclosed a scowling face.

"What is it? Once more you wish to see my patient? But I tell you it is not wise. He has fever. He has had more than enough excitement today."

"Just one question," said Race. "Nothing more, I assure you."

With an unwilling grunt the doctor moved aside and the two men entered the cabin. Dr. Bessner, growling to himself, pushed past them.

"I return in three minutes," he said. "And then—positively—you go!"

They heard him stumping down the deck.

Simon Doyle looked from one to the other of them inquiringly. "Yes," he said, "what is it?"

"A very little thing," Race replied. "Just now, when the stewards were reporting to me, they mentioned that Signor Richetti had been particularly troublesome. You said that that didn't surprise you, as you knew he had a bad temper, and that he had been rude to your wife over some matter of a telegram. Now can you tell me about that incident?"

"Easily. It was at Wâdi Halfa. We'd just come back from the Second Cataract. Linnet thought she saw a telegram for her sticking up on the board. She'd forgotten, you see, that she wasn't called Ridgeway any longer, and Richetti and Ridgeway do look rather alike when written in an atrocious handwriting. So she tore it open, couldn't make head or tail of it, and was puzzling over it when this fellow Richetti came along, fairly tore it out of her hand and gibbered with rage. She went after him to apologize and he was frightfully rude to her about it."

Race drew a deep breath. "And do you know at all, Mr. Doyle, what was in that telegram?"

"Yes, Linnet read part of it out aloud. It said—"

He paused. There was a commotion outside. A high-pitched voice was rapidly approaching.

"Where are Monsieur Poirot and Colonel Race? I must see them *immediately!* It is most important. I have vital information. I— Are they with Mr. Doyle?"

Bessner had not closed the door. Only the curtain hung across the open doorway. Mrs. Otterbourne swept it to one side and entered like a tornado. Her face was suffused with colour, her gait slightly unsteady, her command of words not quite under her control.

"Mr. Doyle," she said dramatically, "I know who killed your wife!"

"What?"

Simon stared at her. So did the other two.

Mrs. Otterbourne swept all three of them with a triumphant glance. She was happy—superbly happy.

"Yes," she said. "My theories are completely vindicated. The deep, primeval, primordial urges—it may appear impossible—fantastic—but it is the truth!"

Race said sharply, "Do I understand that you have evidence in your possession to show who killed Mrs. Doyle?"

Mrs. Otterbourne sat down in a chair and leaned forward, nodding her head vigorously.

"Certainly I have. You will agree, will you not, that whoever killed Louise Bourget also killed Linnet Doyle—that the two crimes were committed by one and the same hand?"

"Yes, yes," said Simon impatiently. "Of course. That stands to reason. Go on."

"Then my assertion holds. I know who killed Louise Bourget; therefore I know who killed Linnet Doyle."

"You mean, you have a theory as to who killed Louise Bourget," suggested Race sceptically.

Mrs. Otterbourne turned on him like a tiger.

"No, I have exact knowledge. I *saw* the person with my own eyes."

Simon, fevered, shouted out: "For God's sake, start at the beginning. You know the person who killed Louise Bourget, you say."

Mrs. Otterbourne nodded.

"I will tell you exactly what occurred."

Yes, she was very happy—no doubt of it! This was her moment, her triumph! What of it if her books were failing to sell, if the stupid public that once had bought them and devoured them voraciously now turned to newer favourites? Salome Otterbourne would once again be notorious. Her name would be in all the papers. She would be principal witness for the prosecution at the trial.

She took a deep breath and opened her mouth.

"It was when I went down to lunch. I hardly felt like eating—all the horror of the recent tragedy— Well, I needn't go into that. Half way down I remember that I had—er—left something in my cabin. I told Rosalie to go on without me. She did."

Mrs. Otterbourne paused a minute.

The curtain across the door moved slightly as though lifted by the wind, but none of the three men noticed it.

"I—er—" Mrs. Otterbourne paused. Thin ice to skate over here, but it must be done somehow. "I—er—had an arrangement with one of the—er—*personnel* of the ship. He was to—er—get me something I needed, but I did not wish my daughter to know of it. She is inclined to be tiresome in certain ways—"

Not too good, this, but she could think of something that sounded better before it came to telling the story in court.

Race's eyebrows lifted as his eyes asked a question of Poirot.

Poirot gave an infinitesimal nod. His lips formed the word, "Drink."

The curtain across the door moved again. Between it and the door itself something showed with a faint steel blue gleam.

Mrs. Otterbourne continued: "The arrangement was that I should go round to the stern on the deck below this, and there I should find the man waiting for me. As I went along the deck a cabin door opened and somebody looked out. It was this girl—Louise Bourget, or whatever her name is. She seemed to be expecting someone. When she saw it was me, she looked disappointed and went abruptly inside again. I didn't think anything of it, of course. I went along just as I had said I would and got the—the stuff from the man. I paid him and—er—just had a word with him. Then I started back. Just as I came around the corner I saw someone knock on the maid's door and go into the cabin."

Race said, "And that person was—"

Bang!

The noise of the explosion filled the cabin. There was an acrid sour smell of smoke. Mrs. Otterbourne turned slowly sideways, as though in supreme inquiry, then her body slumped forward and she fell to the ground with a crash. From just behind her ear the blood flowed from a round neat hole.

There was a moment's stupefied silence. Then both the able-bodied men jumped to their feet. The woman's body hindered their movements a little. Race bent over her while Poirot made a catlike jump for the door and the deck.

The deck was empty. On the ground just in front of the sill lay a big Colt revolver.

Poirot glanced in both directions. The deck was empty. He then sprinted toward the stern. As he rounded the corner he ran into Tim Allerton, who was coming full tilt from the opposite direction

"What the devil was that?" cried Tim breathlessly.

Poirot said sharply, "Did you meet anyone on your way here?"

"Meet anyone? No."

"Then come with me." He took the young man by the arm and retraced his steps. A little crowd had assembled by now. Rosalie, Jacqueline and Cornelia had rushed out of their cabins. More people were coming along the deck from the saloon—Ferguson, Jim Fanthorp and Mrs. Allerton.

Race stood by the revolver. Poirot turned his head and said sharply to Tim Allerton, "Got any gloves in your pocket?"

Tim fumbled.

"Yes, I have."

Poirot seized them from him, put them on, and bent to examine the revolver. Race did the same. The others watched breathlessly.

Race said: "He didn't go the other way. Fanthorp and Ferguson were sitting on this deck lounge; they'd have seen him."

Poirot responded, "And Mr. Allerton would have met him if he'd gone aft."

Race said, pointing to the revolver: "Rather fancy we've seen this not so very long ago. Must make sure, though."

He knocked on the door of Pennington's cabin. There was no answer. The cabin was empty. Race strode to the right hand drawer of the chest and jerked it open. The revolver was gone.

"Settles that," said Race. "Now then, where's Pennington himself?"

They went out again on deck. Mrs. Allerton had joined the group. Poirot moved swiftly over to her.

"Madame, take Miss Otterbourne with you and look after her. Her mother has been"—he consulted Race with an eye and Race nodded —"killed."

Dr. Bessner came bustling along.

"*Gott im Himmel!* What is there now?"

They made way for him. Race indicated the cabin. Bessner went inside.

"Find Pennington," said Race. "Any fingerprints on that revolver?"

"None," said Poirot.

They found Pennington on the deck below. He was sitting in the little drawing-room writing letters. He lifted a handsome, clean-shaven face.

"Anything new?" he asked.

"Didn't you hear a shot?"

"Why—now you mention it—I believe I did hear a kind of a bang. But I never dreamed— Who's been shot?"

"Mrs. Otterbourne."

"*Mrs. Otterbourne?*" Pennington sounded quite astounded. "Well, you do surprise me. Mrs. Otterbourne." He shook his head. "I can't see that at all." He lowered his voice. "Strikes me, gentlemen, we've got a homicidal maniac aboard. We ought to organize a defence system."

"Mr. Pennington," said Race, "how long have you been in this room?"

"Why, let me see." Mr. Pennington gently rubbed his chin. "I should say a matter of twenty minutes or so."

"And you haven't left it?"

"Why no—certainly not."

He looked inquiringly at the two men.

"You see, Mr. Pennington," said Race, "Mrs. Otterbourne was shot with your revolver."

CHAPTER XXIV

Mr. Pennington was shocked. Mr. Pennington could hardly believe it.

"Why, gentlemen," he said, "this is a very serious matter. Very serious indeed."

"Extremely serious for you, Mr. Pennington."

"For me?" Pennington's eyebrows rose in startled surprise. "But, my dear sir, I was sitting quietly writing in here when that shot was fired."

"You have, perhaps, a witness to prove that?"

Pennington shook his head.

"Why, no—I wouldn't say that. But it's clearly impossible that I should have gone to the deck above, shot this poor woman (and why should I shoot her anyway?) and come down again with no one seeing me. There are always plenty of people on the deck lounge this time of day."

"How do you account for your pistol being used?"

"Well—I'm afraid I may be to blame there. Quite soon after getting aboard there was a conversation in the saloon one evening, I remember, about firearms, and I mentioned then that I always carried a revolver with me when I travel."

"Who was there?"

"Well, I can't remember exactly. Most people, I think. Quite a crowd, anyway."

He shook his head gently.

"Why, yes," he said. "I am certainly to blame there."

He went on: "First Linnet, then Linnet's maid, and now Mrs. Otterbourne. There seems no reason in it all!"

"There *was* reason," said Race.

"There was?"

"Yes. Mrs. Otterbourne was on the point of telling us that she had seen a certain person go into Louise's cabin. Before she could name that person she was shot dead."

Andrew Pennington passed a fine silk handkerchief over his brow.

"All this is terrible," he murmured.

Poirot said: "Monsieur Pennington, I would like to discuss certain aspects of the case with you. Will you come to my cabin in half an hour's time?"

"I should be delighted."

Pennington did not sound delighted. He did not look delighted either. Race and Poirot exchanged glances and then abruptly left the room.

"Cunning old devil," said Race, "but he's afraid. Eh?"

Poirot nodded. "Yes, he is not happy, our Monsieur Pennington."

As they reached the promenade deck again, Mrs. Allerton came out of her cabin and, seeing Poirot, beckoned him imperiously.

"Madame?"

"That poor child! Tell me, Monsieur Poirot, is there a double cabin somewhere that I could share with her? She oughtn't to go back to the one she shared with her mother, and mine is only a single one."

"That can be arranged, Madame. It is very good of you."

"It's mere decency. Besides, I'm very fond of the girl. I've always liked her."

"Is she very upset?"

"Terribly. She seems to have been absolutely devoted to that odious woman. That is what is so pathetic about it all. Tim says he believes she drank. Is that true?"

Poirot nodded.

"Oh, well, poor woman, one mustn't judge her, I suppose; but that girl must have had a terrible life."

"She did, Madame. She is very proud and she was very loyal."

"Yes, I like that—loyalty, I mean. It's out of fashion nowadays. She's an odd character, that girl—proud, reserved, stubborn, and terribly warm-hearted underneath, I fancy."

"I see that I have given her into good hands, Madame."

"Yes, don't worry. I'll look after her. She's inclined to cling to me in the most pathetic fashion."

Mrs. Allerton went back into the cabin. Poirot returned to the scene of the tragedy.

Cornelia was still standing on the deck, her eyes wide. She said: "I don't understand, Monsieur Poirot. How did the person who shot her get away without our seeing him?"

"Yes, how?" echoed Jacqueline.

"Ah," said Poirot, "it was not quite such a disappearing trick as you think, Mademoiselle. There were three distinct ways the murderer might have gone."

Jacqueline looked puzzled. She said, "Three?"

"He might have gone to the right, or he might have gone to the left, but I don't see any other way," puzzled Cornelia.

Jacqueline too frowned. Then her brow cleared.

She said: "Of course. He could move in two directions on one plane, but he could go at right angles to that plane too. That is, he couldn't go *up* very well, but he could go *down*."

Poirot smiled. "You have brains, Mademoiselle."

Cornelia said, "I know I'm just a plain mutt, but I still don't see."

Jacqueline said, "Monsieur Poirot means, darling, that he could swing himself over the rail and down onto the deck below."

"My!" gasped Cornelia. "I never thought of that. He'd have to be mighty quick about it, though. I suppose he could just do it?"

"He could do it easily enough," said Tim Allerton. "Remember, there's always a minute of shock after a thing like this. One hears a shot and one's too paralysed to move for a second or two."

"That was your experience, Monsieur Allerton?"

"Yes, it was. I just stood like a dummy for quite five seconds. Then I fairly sprinted round the deck."

Race came out of Bessner's cabin and said authoritatively: "Would you mind all clearing off? We want to bring out the body."

Everyone moved away obediently. Poirot went with them. Cornelia said to him with sad earnestness: "I'll never forget this trip as long as I live. Three deaths. . . . It's just like living in a nightmare."

Ferguson overheard her. He said aggressively: "That's because you're overcivilized. You should look on death as the Oriental does. It's a mere incident—hardly noticeable."

"That's all very well," Cornelia said. "They're not educated, poor creatures."

"No, and a good thing too. Education has devitalized the white races. Look at America—goes in for an orgy of culture. Simply disgusting."

"I think you're talking nonsense," said Cornelia flushing. "I attend lectures every winter on Greek Art and the Renaissance, and I went to some on Famous Women of History."

Mr. Ferguson groaned in agony. "Greek Art! Renaissance! Famous Women of History! It makes me quite sick to hear you. It's the *future* that matters, woman, not the past. Three women are dead on this boat. Well, what of it? They're no loss! Linnet Doyle and her money! The French maid—a domestic parasite. Mrs. Otterbourne—a useless fool of a woman. Do you think anyone really cares whether they're dead or not? *I* don't. I think it's a damned good thing!"

"Then you're wrong!" Cornelia blazed out at him. "And it makes me sick to hear you talk and talk, as though nobody mattered but *you*. I didn't like Mrs. Otterbourne much, but her daughter was ever so fond of her, and she's all broken up over her mother's death. I don't know much about the French maid, but I expect somebody was fond of her somewhere; and as for Linnet Doyle—well, apart from everything else, she was just lovely! She was so beautiful when she came into a room that it made a lump come in your throat. I'm homely myself, and that makes me appreciate beauty a lot more. She was as beautiful—just as a woman—as anything in Greek Art. And when anything beautiful's dead, it's a loss to the world. So there!"

Mr. Ferguson stepped back a space. He caught hold of his hair with both hands and tugged at it vehemently.

"I give it up," he said. "You're unbelievable. Just haven't got a bit of natural female spite in you anywhere." He turned to Poirot. "Do you know, sir, that Cornelia's father was practically ruined by Linnet Ridgeway's old man? But does the girl gnash her teeth when she sees the heiress sailing about in pearls and Paris models? No, she just bleats out, 'Isn't she beautiful?' like a blessed Baa Lamb. I don't believe she even felt sore at her."

Cornelia flushed. "I did—just for a minute. Poppa kind of died of discouragement, you know, because he hadn't made good."

"Felt sore for a minute! I ask you."

Cornelia flashed round on him.

"Well, didn't you say just now it was the future that mattered, not the past? All that was in the past, wasn't it? It's over."

"Got me there," said Ferguson. "Cornelia Robson, you're the only nice woman I've ever come across. Will you marry me?"

"Don't be absurd."

"It's a genuine proposal—even if it is made in the presence of Old Man Sleuth. Anyway, you're a witness, Monsieur Poirot. I've deliberately offered marriage to this female—against all my principles, because I don't believe in legal contracts between the sexes; but I don't think she'd stand for anything else, so marriage it shall be. Come on, Cornelia, say yes."

"I think you're utterly ridiculous," said Cornelia flushing.

"Why won't you marry me?"

"You're not serious," said Cornelia.

"Do you mean not serious in proposing or do you mean not serious in character?"

"Both, but I really meant character. You laugh at all sorts of serious things. Education and Culture—and—and Death. You wouldn't be *reliable*."

She broke off, flushed again, and hurried along into her cabin.

Ferguson stared after her. "Damn the girl! I believe she really means it. She wants a man to be reliable. *Reliable*—ye gods!" He paused and then said curiously: "What's the matter with you, Monsieur Poirot? You seem very deep in thought."

Poirot roused himself with a start.

"I reflect, that is all. I reflect."

"Meditation on Death. Death, the Recurring Decimal, by Hercule Poirot. One of his well-known monographs."

"Monsieur Ferguson," said Poirot, "you are a very impertinent young man."

"You must excuse me. I like attacking established institutions."

"And I am an established institution?"

"Precisely. What do you think of that girl?"

"Of Miss Robson?"

"Yes."

"I think that she has a great deal of character."

"You're right. She's got spirit. She looks meek, but she isn't. She's got guts. She's—oh, damn it, I want that girl. It mightn't be a bad move if I tackled the old lady. If I could once get her thoroughly against me, it might cut some ice with Cornelia."

He wheeled and went into the observation saloon. Miss Van Schuyler was seated in her usual corner. She looked even more arrogant than usual. She was knitting. Ferguson strode up to her. Hercule Poirot, entering unobtrusively, took a seat a discreet distance away and appeared to be absorbed in a magazine.

"Good-afternoon, Miss Van Schuyler."

Miss Van Schuyler raised her eyes for a bare second, dropped them again and murmured frigidly, "Er—good-afternoon."

"Look here, Miss Van Schuyler, I want to talk to you about something pretty important. It's just this. I want to marry your cousin."

Miss Van Schuyler's ball of wool dropped onto the ground and ran wildly across the saloon.

She said, in a venomous tone, "You must be out of your senses, young man."

"Not at all. I'm determined to marry her. I've asked her to marry me!"

Miss Van Schuyler surveyed him coldly, with the kind of speculative interest she might have accorded to an odd sort of beetle.

"Indeed? And I presume she sent you about your business."

"She refused me."

"Naturally."

"Not 'naturally' at all. I'm going to go on asking her till she agrees."

"I can assure you, sir, that I shall take steps to see that my young cousin is not subjected to any such persecution," said Miss Van Schuyler in a biting tone.

"What have you got against me?"

Miss Van Schuyler merely raised her eyebrows and gave a vehement tug to her wool, preparatory to regaining it and closing the interview.

"Come now," persisted Mr. Ferguson, "what have you got against me?"

"I should think that was quite obvious, Mr.—er—I don't know your name."

"Ferguson."

"Mr. Ferguson." Miss Van Schuyler uttered the name with definite distaste. "Any such idea is quite out of the question."

"You mean," said Ferguson, "that I'm not good enough for her?"

"I should think that would have been obvious to you."

"In what way am I not good enough?"

Miss Van Schuyler again did not answer.

"I've got two legs, two arms, good health and quite reasonable brains. What's wrong with that?"

"There is such a thing as social position, Mr. Ferguson."

"Social position is bunk!"

The door swung open and Cornelia came in. She stopped dead on seeing her redoubtable Cousin Marie in conversation with her would-be suitor.

The outrageous Mr. Ferguson turned his head, grinned broadly and called out: "Come along, Cornelia. I'm asking for your hand in marriage in the best conventional manner."

"Cornelia," said Miss Van Schuyler, and her voice was truly awful in quality, "*have you encouraged this young man?*"

"I—no, of course not—at least—not exactly—I mean—"

"What do you mean?"

"She hasn't encouraged me," said Mr. Ferguson helpfully. "I've done it all. She hasn't actually pushed me in the face, because she's got too kind a heart. Cornelia, your cousin says I'm not good enough for you. That, of course, is true, but not in the way she means it. My moral nature certainly doesn't equal yours, but her point is that I'm hopelessly below you socially."

"That, I think, is equally obvious to Cornelia," said Miss Van Schuyler.

"Is it?" Mr. Ferguson looked at her searchingly. "Is that why you won't marry me?"

"No, it isn't." Cornelia flushed. "If—if I liked you, I'd marry you no matter who you were."

"But you don't like me?"

"I—I think you're just outrageous. The way you say things . . . The *things* you say . . . I—I've never met anyone the least like you. I—"

Tears threatened to overcome her. She rushed from the room.

"On the whole," said Mr. Ferguson, "that's not too bad for a start." He leaned back in his chair, gazed at the ceiling, whistled, crossed his disreputable knees and remarked, "I'll be calling you Cousin yet."

Miss Van Schuyler trembled with rage. "Leave this room at once, sir, or I'll ring for the steward."

"I've paid for my ticket," said Mr. Ferguson. "They can't possibly turn me out of the public lounge. But I'll humour you." He sang softly, "Yo ho ho, and a bottle of rum." Rising, he sauntered nonchalantly to the door and passed out.

Choking with anger Miss Van Schuyler struggled to her feet. Poirot, discreetly emerging from retirement behind his magazine, sprang up and retrieved the ball of wool.

"Thank you, Monsieur Poirot. If you would send Miss Bowers to me—I feel quite upset—that insolent young man."

"Rather eccentric, I'm afraid," said Poirot. "Most of that family are. Spoilt, of course. Always inclined to tilt at windmills." He added carelessly, "You recognized him, I suppose?"

"Recognized him?"

"Calls himself Ferguson and won't use his title because of his advanced ideas."

"His *title?*" Miss Van Schuyler's tone was sharp.

"Yes, that's young Lord Dawlish. Rolling in money, of course, but he became a communist when he was at Oxford."

Miss Van Schuyler, her face a battleground of contradictory emotions, said, "How long have you known this, Monsieur Poirot?"

Poirot shrugged his shoulders.

"There was a picture in one of these papers—I noticed the resemblance. Then I found a signet ring with a coat of arms on it. Oh, there's no doubt about it, I assure you."

He quite enjoyed reading the conflicting expressions that succeeded each other on Miss Van Schuyler's face. Finally, with a gracious inclination of the head, she said, "I am very much obliged to you, Monsieur Poirot."

Poirot looked after her and smiled as she went out of the saloon. Then he sat down and his face grew grave once more. He was following out a train of thought in his mind. From time to time he nodded his head.

"*Mais oui,*" he said at last. "It all fits in."

CHAPTER XXV

RACE FOUND HIM still sitting there.

"Well, Poirot, what about it? Pennington's due in ten minutes. I'm leaving this in your hands."

Poirot rose quickly to his feet. "First, get hold of young Fanthorp."

"Fanthorp?" Race looked surprised.

"Yes. Bring him to my cabin."

Race nodded and went off. Poirot went along to his cabin. Race arrived with young Fanthorp a minute or two afterward.

Poirot indicated chairs and offered cigarettes.

"Now, Monsieur Fanthorp," he said, "to our business! I perceive that you wear the same tie that my friend Hastings wears."

Jim Fanthorp looked down at his neckwear with some bewilderment."

"It's an O.E. tie," he said.

"Exactly. You must understand that, though I am a foreigner, I know something of the English point of view. I know, for instance, that there are 'things which are done' and 'things which are not done.'"

Jim Fanthorp grinned.

"We don't say that sort of thing much nowadays, sir."

"Perhaps not, but the custom, it still remains. The Old School Tie is the Old School Tie, and there are certain things (I know this from experience) that the Old School Tie does not do! One of those things, Monsieur Fanthorp, is to butt into a private conversation unasked when one does not know the people who are conducting it."

Fanthorp stared.

Poirot went on: "But the other day, Monsieur Fanthorp, that is exactly what you did do. Certain persons were quietly transacting some private business in the observation saloon. You strolled near them, obviously in order to overhear what it was that was in progress, and presently you actually turned round and congratulated a lady—Madame Simon Doyle—on the soundness of her business methods."

Jim Fanthorp's face got very red. Poirot swept on, not waiting for a comment.

"Now that, Monsieur Fanthorp, was not at all the behaviour of one who wears a tie similar to that worn by my friend Hastings!

Hastings is all delicacy, would die of shame before he did such a thing! Therefore, taking that action of yours in conjunction with the fact that you are a very young man to be able to afford an expensive holiday, that you are a member of a country solicitor's firm, and therefore probably not extravagantly well off, and that you show no signs of recent illness such as might necessitate a prolonged visit abroad, I ask myself—and am now asking you—what is the reason for your presence on this boat?"

Jim Fanthorp jerked his head back.

"I decline to give you any information whatever, Monsieur Poirot. I really think you must be mad."

"I am not mad. I am very, very sane. Where is your firm? In Northampton; that is not very far from Wode Hall. What conversation did you try to overhear? One concerning legal documents. What was the object of your remark—a remark which you uttered with obvious embarrassment and malaise? Your object was to prevent Madame Doyle from signing any document unread."

He paused.

"On this boat we have had a murder, and following that murder two other murders in rapid succession. If I further give you the information that the weapon which killed Madame Otterbourne was a revolver owned by Monsieur Andrew Pennington, then perhaps you will realize that it is actually your duty to tell us all you can."

Jim Fanthorp was silent for some minutes. At last he said: "You have rather an odd way of going about things, Monsieur Poirot, but I appreciate the points you have made. The trouble is that I have no exact information to lay before you."

"You mean that it is a case, merely, of suspicion."

"Yes."

"And therefore you think it injudicious to speak? That may be true legally speaking. But this is not a court of law. Colonel Race and myself are endeavouring to track down a murderer. Anything that can help us to do so may be valuable."

Again Jim Fanthorp reflected. Then he said: "Very well. What is it you want to know?"

"Why did you come on this trip?"

"My uncle, Mr. Carmichael, Mrs. Doyle's English solicitor, sent me. He handled a good many of her affairs. In this way, he was often in correspondence with Mr. Andrew Pennington, who was Mrs. Doyle's American trustee. Several small incidents (I cannot enume ate them all) made my uncle suspicious that all was not quite as it should be."

"In plain language," said Race, "your uncle suspected that Pennington was a crook?"

Jim Fanthorp nodded, a faint smile on his face.

"You put it rather more bluntly than I should, but the main idea is correct. Various excuses made by Pennington, certain plausible explanations of the disposal of funds, aroused my uncle's distrust.

"While these suspicions of his were still nebulous, Miss Ridgeway married unexpectedly and went off on her honeymoon to Egypt. Her marriage relieved my uncle's mind, as he knew that on her return to England the estate would have to be formally settled and handed over.

"However, in a letter she wrote him from Cairo, she mentioned casually that she had unexpectedly run across Andrew Pennington. My uncle's suspicions became acute. He felt sure that Pennington, perhaps by now in a desperate position, was going to try and obtain signatures from her which would cover his own defalcations. Since my uncle had no definite evidence to lay before her, he was in a most difficult position. The only thing he could think of was to send me out here, travelling by air, with instructions to discover what was in the wind. I was to keep my eyes open and act summarily if necessary—a most unpleasant mission, I can assure you. As a matter of fact, on the occasion you mention I had to behave more or less as a cad! It was awkward, but on the whole I was satisfied with the result."

"You mean you put Madame Doyle on her guard?" asked Race.

"Not so much that, but I think I put the wind up Pennington. I felt convinced he wouldn't try any more funny business for some time, and by then I hoped to have got intimate enough with Mr. and Mrs. Doyle to convey some kind of a warning. As a matter of fact I hoped to do so through Doyle. Mrs. Doyle was so attached to Mr. Pennington that it would have been a bit awkward to suggest things to her about him. It would have been easier for me to approach the husband."

Race nodded.

Poirot asked: "Will you give me a candid opinion on one point, Monsieur Fanthorp? If you were engaged in putting a swindle over, would you choose Madame Doyle or Monsieur Doyle as a victim?"

Fanthorp smiled faintly.

"Mr. Doyle, every time. Linnet Doyle was very shrewd in business matters. Her husband, I should fancy, is one of those trustful fellows who know nothing of business and are always ready to 'sign on the dotted line' as he himself put it."

"I agree," said Poirot. He looked at Race. "And there's your motive."

Jim Fanthorp said: "But this is all pure conjecture. It isn't *evidence*."

Poirot replied, easily, "Ah, bah! we will get evidence!"

"How?"

"Possibly from Mr. Pennington himself."

Fanthorp looked doubtful.

"I wonder. I very much wonder."

Race glanced at his watch. "He's about due now."

Jim Fanthorp was quick to take the hint. He left them.

Two minutes later Andrew Pennington made his appearance. His manner was all smiling urbanity. Only the taut line of his jaw and the wariness of his eyes betrayed the fact that a thoroughly experienced fighter was on his guard.

"Well, gentlemen," he said, "here I am."

He sat down and looked at them inquiringly.

"We asked you to come here, Monsieur Pennington," began Poirot, "because it is fairly obvious that you have a very special and immediate interest in the case."

Pennington raised his eyebrows slightly.

"Is that so?"

Poirot said gently: "Surely. You have known Linnet Ridgeway, I understand, since she was quite a child."

"Oh! that—" His face altered, became less alert. "I beg pardon, I didn't quite get you. Yes, as I told you this morning, I've known Linnet since she was a cute little thing in pinafores."

"You were on terms of close intimacy with her father?"

"That's so. Melhuish Ridgeway and I were close—very close."

"You were so intimately associated that on his death he appointed you business guardian to his daughter and trustee to the vast fortune she inherited."

"Why, roughly, that is so." The wariness was back again. The note was more cautious. "I was not the only trustee, naturally; others were associated with me."

"Who have since died?"

"Two of them are dead. The other, Mr. Sterndale Rockford, is alive."

"Your partner?"

"Yes."

"Mademoiselle Ridgeway, I understand, was not yet of age when she married?"

"She would have been twenty-one next July."

"And in the normal course of events she would have come into control of her fortune then?"

"Yes."

"But her marriage precipitated matters?"

Pennington's jaw hardened. He shot out his chin at them aggressively.

"You'll pardon me, gentlemen, but what exact business is all this of yours?"

"If you dislike answering the question—"

"There's no dislike about it. I don't mind what you ask me. But I don't see the relevance of all this."

"Oh, but surely, Monsieur Pennington"—Poirot leaned forward, his eyes green and catlike—"there is the question of motive. In considering that, financial considerations must always be taken into account."

Pennington said sullenly, "By Ridgeway's will, Linnet got control of her dough when she was twenty-one or when she married."

"No conditions of any kind?"

"No conditions."

"And it is a matter, I am credibly assured, of millions."

"Millions it is."

Poirot said softly, "Your responsibility, Mr. Pennington, and that of your partner, has been a very grave one."

Pennington replied curtly: "We're used to responsibility. Doesn't worry us any."

"I wonder."

Something in his tone flicked the other man on the raw. He asked angrily, "What the devil do you mean?"

Poirot replied with an air of engaging frankness: "I was wondering, Mr. Pennington, whether Linnet Ridgeway's sudden marriage caused any—consternation, in your office?"

"Consternation?"

"That was the word I used."

"What the hell are you driving at?"

"Something quite simple. Are Linnet Doyle's affairs in the perfect order they should be?"

Pennington rose to his feet.

"That's enough. I'm through." He made for the door.

"But you will answer my question first?"

Pennington snapped, "They're in perfect order."

"You were not so alarmed when the news of Linnet Ridgeway's marriage reached you that you rushed over to Europe by the first boat and staged an apparently fortuitous meeting in Egypt."

Pennington came back toward them. He had himself under control once more.

"What you are saying is absolute balderdash! I didn't even know that Linnet was married till I met her in Cairo. I was utterly astonished. Her letter must have missed me by a day in New York. It was forwarded and I got it about a week later."

"You came over by the *Carmanic,* I think you said."

"That's right."

"And the letter reached New York after the *Carmanic* sailed?"

"How many times have I got to repeat it?"

"It is strange," said Poirot.

"What's strange?"

"That on your luggage there are no labels of the *Carmanic*. The only recent labels of transatlantic sailing are the *Normandie*. The *Normandie,* I remember, sailed two days after the *Carmanic*."

For a moment the other was at a loss. His eyes wavered.

Colonel Race weighed in with telling effect.

"Come now, Mr. Pennington," he said. "We've several reasons for believing that you came over on the *Normandie* and not by the *Carmanic,* as you said. In that case, you received Mrs. Doyle's letter before you left New York. It's no good denying it, for it's the easiest thing in the world to check up the steamship companies."

Andrew Pennington felt absent-mindedly for a chair and sat down. His face was impassive—a poker face. Behind that mask his agile brain looked ahead to the next move.

"I'll have to hand it you, gentlemen. You've been too smart for me. But I had my reasons for acting as I did."

"No doubt." Race's tone was curt.

"If I give them to you, it must be understood I do so in confidence."

"I think you can trust us to behave fittingly. Naturally I cannot give assurances blindly."

"Well—" Pennington sighed. "I'll come clean. There was some monkey business going on in England. It worried me. I couldn't do much about it by letter. The only thing was to come over and see for myself."

"What do you mean by monkey business?"

"I'd good reason to believe that Linnet was being swindled."

"By whom?"

"Her British lawyer. Now that's not the kind of accusation you can fling around anyhow. I made up my mind to come over right away and see into matters myself."

"That does great credit to your vigilance, I am sure. But why the little deception about not having received the letter?"

"Well, I ask you—" Pennington spread out his hands. "You can't butt in on a honeymoon couple without more or less coming down to brass tacks and giving your reasons. I thought it best to make the meeting accidental. Besides, I didn't know anything about the husband. He might have been mixed up in the racket for all I knew."

"In fact all your actions were actuated by pure disinterestedness," said Colonel Race drily.

"You've said it, Colonel."

There was a pause. Race glanced at Poirot. The little man leant forward.

"Monsieur Pennington, we do not believe a word of your story."

"The hell you don't! And what the hell do you believe?"

"We believe that Linnet Ridgeway's unexpected marriage put you in a financial quandary. That you came over post haste to try and find some way out of the mess you were in—that is to say, some way of gaining time. That, with that end in view, you endeavoured to obtain Madame Doyle's signature to certain documents—and failed. That on the journey up the Nile, when walking along the cliff top at Abu Simbel, you dislodged a boulder which fell and only very narrowly missed its object—"

"You're crazy."

"We believe that the same kind of circumstances occurred on the return journey. That is to say, an opportunity presented itself of putting Madame Doyle out of the way at a moment when her death would be almost certainly ascribed to the action of another person. We not only believe, but *know*, that it was your revolver which killed a woman who was about to reveal to us the name of the person who she had reason to believe killed both Linnet Doyle and the maid Louise—"

"Hell!" The forcible ejaculation broke forth and interrupted Poirot's stream of eloquence. "What are you getting at? Are you crazy? What motive had I to kill Linnet? I wouldn't get her money; that goes to her husband. Why don't you pick on him? *He's* the one to benefit—not me."

Race said coldly: "Doyle never left the lounge on the night of the tragedy till he was shot at and wounded in the leg. The impossibility of his walking a step after that is attested to by a doctor and a nurse—both independent and reliable witnesses. Simon Doyle could not have killed his wife. He could not have killed Louise Bourget. He most definitely did not kill Mrs. Otterbourne! You know that as well as we do."

"I know he didn't kill her." Pennington sounded a little calmer. "All I say is, why pick on me when I don't benefit by her death?"

"But, my dear sir," Poirot's voice came soft as a purring cat, "that is rather a matter of opinion. Madame Doyle was a keen woman of business, fully conversant of her own affairs and very quick to spot any irregularity. As soon as she took up the control of her property, which she would have done on her return to England, her suspicions were bound to be aroused. But now that she is dead and that her husband, as you have just pointed out, inherits, the whole thing is different. Simon Doyle knows nothing whatever of his wife's affairs except that she was a rich woman. He is of a simple, trusting disposition. You will find it easy to place complicated statements before him, to involve the real issue in a net of figures, and to delay settlement with pleas of legal formalities and the recent depression. I think that it makes a very considerable difference to you whether you deal with the husband or the wife."

Pennington shrugged his shoulders.

"Your ideas are—fantastic."

"Time will show."

"What did you say?"

"I said, 'Time will show!' This is a matter of three deaths—three murders. The law will demand the most searching investigation into the condition of Madame Doyle's estate."

He saw the sudden sag in the other's shoulders and knew that he had won. Jim Fanthorp's suspicions were well founded.

Poirot went on: "You've played—and lost. Useless to go on bluffing.

"You don't understand," Pennington muttered. "It's all square enough really. It's been this damned slump— Wall Street's been crazy. But I'd staged a comeback. With luck everything will be O.K. by the middle of June."

With shaking hands he took a cigarette, tried to light it, failed.

"I suppose," mused Poirot, "that the boulder was a sudden temptation. You thought nobody saw you."

"That was an accident. I swear it was an accident!" The man leant forward, his face working, his eyes terrified. "I stumbled and fell against it. I swear it was an accident. . . ."

The two men said nothing.

Pennington suddenly pulled himself together. He was still a wreck of a man, but his fighting spirit had returned in a certain measure. He moved toward the door.

"You can't pin that on me, gentlemen. It was an accident. And it wasn't I who shot her. D'you hear? You can't pin that on me either— and you never will."

He went out.

CHAPTER XXVI

As the door closed behind him, Race gave a deep sigh.

"We got more than I thought we should. Admission of fraud. Admission of attempted murder. Further than that it's impossible to go A man will confess, more or less, to attempted murder, but you won' get him to confess to the real thing."

"Sometimes it can be done," said Poirot. His eyes were dreamy-catlike.

Race looked at him curiously.

"Got a plan?"

Poirot nodded. Then he said ticking off the items on his fingers "The garden at Assuan. Mr. Allerton's statement. The two bottles o nail polish. My bottle of wine. The velvet stole. The stained hand kerchief. The pistol that was left on the scene of the crime. The deat of Louise. The death of Madame Otterbourne . . . Yes, it's all there Pennington didn't do it, Race!"

"What?" Race was startled.

"Pennington didn't do it. He had the motive, yes. He had the *wi* to do it, yes. He got as far as *attempting* to do it. *Mais c'est tou* For this crime, something was wanted that Pennington hasn't got This is a crime that needed audacity, swift and faultless executior courage, indifference to danger, and a resourceful, calculating brai Pennington hasn't got those attributes. He couldn't do a crime unles he knew it to be safe. This crime wasn't safe! It hung on a razor edg It needed boldness. Pennington isn't bold. He's only astute."

Race looked at him with the respect one able man gives to anothe

"You've got it all well taped," he said.

"I think so, yes. There are one or two things—that telegram, fc instance, that Linnet Doyle read. I should like to get that cleared up

"By Jove, we forgot to ask Doyle. He was telling us when poor ol Ma Otterbourne came along. We'll ask him again."

"Presently. First, I have someone else to whom I wish to speak

"Who's that?"

"Tim Allerton."

Race raised his eyebrows.

"Allerton? Well, we'll get him here."

He pressed a bell and sent the steward with a message.

Tim Allerton entered with a questioning look.

"Steward said you wanted to see me?"

"That is right, Monsieur Allerton. Sit down."

Tim sat. His face was attentive but very slightly bored.

"Anything I can do?" His tone was polite but not enthusiastic.

Poirot said: "In a sense, perhaps. What I really require is for you to listen."

Tim's eyebrows rose in polite surprise.

"Certainly. I'm the world's best listener. Can be relied on to say 'Oo-er!' at the right moments."

"That is very satisfactory. 'Oo-er!' will be very expressive. *Eh bien*, let us commence. When I met you and your mother at Assuan, Monsieur Allerton, I was attracted to your company very strongly. To begin with, I thought your mother was one of the most charming people I had ever met—"

The weary face flickered for a moment; a shade of expression came into it.

"She is—unique," he said.

"But the second thing that interested me was your mention of a certain lady."

"Really?"

"Yes, a Mademoiselle Joanna Southwood. You see, I had recently been hearing that name."

He paused and went on: "For the last three years there have been certain jewel robberies that have been worrying Scotland Yard a good deal. They are what may be described as Society robberies. The method is usually the same—the substitution of an imitation piece of jewellery for an original. My friend, Chief Inspector Japp, came to the conclusion that the robberies were not the work of one person, but of two people working in with each other very cleverly. He was convinced, from the considerable inside knowledge displayed, that the robberies were the work of people in a good social position. And finally his attention became riveted on Mademoiselle Joanna Southwood.

"Every one of the victims had been either a friend or acquaintance of hers, and in each case she had either handled or been lent the piece of jewellery in question. Also, her style of living was far in excess of her income. On the other hand it was quite clear that the actual robbery—that is to say the substitution—had *not* been accomplished by her. In some cases she had even been out of England during the period when the jewellery must have been replaced.

"So gradually a little picture grew up in Chief Inspector Japp's mind. Mademoiselle Southwood was at one time associated with a Guild of Modern Jewellery. He suspected that she handled the jewels in question, made accurate drawings of them, got them copied by some humble but dishonest working jeweller and that the third part of the operation was the successful substitution by another person—somebody who could have been proved never to have handled the jewels and never to have had anything to do with copies or imitations of precious stones. Of the identity of this other person Japp was ignorant.

"Certain things that fell from you in conversation interested me. A ring that had disappeared when you were in Majorca, the fact that you had been in a house-party where one of these fake substitutions had occurred, your close association with Mademoiselle Southwood. There was also the fact that you obviously resented my presence and tried to get your mother to be less friendly toward me. That might, of course, have been just personal dislike, but I thought not. You were too anxious to try and hide your distaste under a genial manner.

"*Eh bien*, after the murder of Linnet Doyle, it is discovered that her pearls are missing. You comprehend, at once I think of you! But I am not quite satisfied. For if you are working, as I suspect, with Mademoiselle Southwood (who was an intimate friend of Madame Doyle's) then substitution would be the method employed—not barefaced theft. But then, the pearls quite unexpectedly are returned, and what do I discover? That they are not genuine, but imitation.

"I know then who the real thief is. It was the imitation string which was stolen and returned—an imitation which you had previously substituted for the real necklace."

He looked at the young man in front of him. Tim was white under his tan. He was not so good a fighter as Pennington; his stamina was bad. He said, with an effort to sustain his mocking manner: "Indeed? And if so, what did I do with them?"

"That I know also."

The young man's face changed—broke up.

Poirot went on slowly: "There is only one place where they can be. I have reflected, and my reason tells me that that is so. Those pearls, Monsieur Allerton, are concealed in a rosary that hangs in your cabin. The beads of it are very elaborately carved. I think you had it made specially. Those beads unscrew, though you would never think sc to look at them. Inside each is a pearl, stuck with seccotine. Most police searchers respect religious symbols, unless there is something obviously queer about them. You counted on that. I endeavoured to find out how Mademoiselle Southwood sent the imitation necklace out to you. She must have done so, since you came here from Majorca on hearing that Madame Doyle would be here for her honeymoon. My theory is that it was sent in a book—a square hole being cut out of the pages in the middle. A book goes with the ends open and is practically never opened in the post."

There was a pause—a long pause. Then Tim said quietly: "You win! It's been a good game, but it's over at last. There's nothing for it now, I suppose, but to take my medicine."

Poirot nodded gently.

"Do you realize that you were seen that night?"

"Seen?" Tim started.

"Yes, on the night that Linnet Doyle died, someone saw you leave her cabin just after one in the morning."

Tim said: "Look here—you aren't thinking . . . It wasn't I who killed her! I'll swear that! I've been in the most awful stew. To have chosen that night of all others . . . God, it's been awful!"

Poirot said: "Yes, you must have had uneasy moments. But, now that the truth has come out, you may be able to help us. Was Madame Doyle alive or dead when you stole the pearls?"

"I don't know," Tim said hoarsely. "Honest to God, Monsieur Poirot, I don't know! I'd found out where she put them at night—on the little table by the bed. I crept in, felt very softly on the table and grabbed 'em, put down the others and crept out again. I assumed, of course, that she was asleep."

"Did you hear her breathing? Surely you would have listened for that?"

Tim thought earnestly.

"It was very still—very still indeed. No, I can't remember actually hearing her breathe."

"Was there any smell of smoke lingering in the air, as there would have been if a firearm had been discharged recently?"

"I don't think so. I don't remember it."

Poirot sighed.

"Then we are no further."

Tim asked curiously, "Who was it saw me?"

"Rosalie Otterbourne. She came round from the other side of the boat and saw you leave Linnet Doyle's cabin and go to your own."

"So it was she who told you."

Poirot said gently, "Excuse me; she did not tell me."

"But then, how do you know?"

"Because I am Hercule Poirot! I do not need to be told. When I taxed her with it, do you know what she said? She said, 'I saw nobody.' And she lied."

"But why?"

Poirot said in a detached voice: "Perhaps because she thought the man she saw was the murderer. It looked like that, you know."

"That seems to me all the more reason for telling you."

Poirot shrugged his shoulders. "She did not think so, it seems."

Tim said, a queer note in his voice: "She's an extraordinary sort of a girl. She must have been through a pretty rough time with that mother of hers."

"Yes, life has not been easy for her."

"Poor kid," Tim muttered. Then he looked toward Race.

"Well, sir, where do we go from here? I admit taking the pearls from Linnet's cabin and you'll find them just where you say they are. I'm guilty all right. But as far as Miss Southwood is concerned, I'm not admitting anything. You've no evidence whatever against her. How I got hold of the fake necklace is my own business."

Poirot murmured, "A very correct attitude."

Tim said with a flash of humour, "Always the gentleman!" He added: "Perhaps you can imagine how annoying it was to me to find my mother cottoning on to you! I'm not a sufficiently hardened criminal to enjoy sitting cheek by jowl with a successful detective just before bringing off a rather risky coup! Some people might get a kick out of it. I didn't. Frankly, it gave me cold feet."

"But it did not deter you from making your attempt?"

Tim shrugged his shoulders.

"I couldn't funk it to that extent. The exchange had to be made sometime and I'd got a unique opportunity on this boat—a cabin only two doors off, and Linnet herself so preoccupied with her own troubles that she wasn't likely to detect the change."

"I wonder if that was so—"

Tim looked up sharply. "What do you mean?"

Poirot pressed the bell. "I am going to ask Miss Otterbourne if she will come here for a minute."

Tim frowned but said nothing. A steward came, received the order and went away with the message.

Rosalie came after a few minutes. Her eyes, reddened with recent weeping, widened a little at seeing Tim, but her old attitude of suspicion and defiance seemed entirely absent. She sat down and with a new docility looked from Race to Poirot.

"We're very sorry to bother you, Miss Otterbourne," said Race gently. He was slightly annoyed with Poirot.

"It doesn't matter," the girl said in a low voice.

Poirot said: "It is necessary to clear up one or two points. When I asked you whether you saw anyone on the starboard deck at one-ten this morning, your answer was that you saw nobody. Fortunately I have been able to arrive at the truth without your help. Monsieur Allerton has admitted that he was in Linnet Doyle's cabin last night."

She flashed a swift glance at Tim. Tim, his face grim and set, gave a curt nod.

"The time is correct, Monsieur Allerton?"

Allerton replied, "Quite correct."

Rosalie was staring at him. Her lips trembled—fell apart. . . .

"But you didn't—you didn't—"

He said quickly: "No, I didn't kill her. I'm a thief, not a murderer. It's all going to come out, so you might as well know. I was after her pearls."

Poirot said, "Mr. Allerton's story is that he went to her cabin last night and exchanged a string of fake pearls for the real ones."

"Did you?" asked Rosalie. Her eyes, grave, sad, childlike, questioned his.

"Yes," said Tim.

There was a pause. Colonel Race shifted restlessly.

Poirot said in a curious voice: "That, as I say, is Monsieur Allerton's story, partially confirmed by your evidence. That is to say, there is evidence that he did visit Linnet Doyle's cabin last night, but there is no evidence to show why he did so."

Tim stared at him. "But you know!"

"What do I know?"

"Well—you know I've got the pearls."

"*Mais oui—mais oui!* I know you have the pearls, but I do not know when you got them. It may have been *before* last night. . . . You said just now that Linnet Doyle would not have noticed the substitution. I am not so sure of that. Supposing she *did* notice it. . . . Supposing, even, she knew who did it. . . . Supposing that last night she threatened to expose the whole business, and that you knew she meant to do so . . . and supposing that you overheard the scene in the saloon between Jacqueline de Bellefort and Simon Doyle and, as soon as the saloon was empty, you slipped in and secured the pistol, and then, an hour later, when the boat had quieted down, you crept along to Linnet Doyle's cabin and made quite sure that no exposure would come. . . ."

"My God!" said Tim. Out of his ashen face, two tortured, agonized eyes gazed dumbly at Hercule Poirot.

The latter went on: "But somebody else saw you—the girl Louise. The next day she came to you and blackmailed you. You must pay her handsomely or she would tell what she knew. You realized that to submit to blackmail would be the beginning of the end. You pretended to agree, made an appointment to come to her cabin just before lunch with the money. Then, when she was counting the notes, you stabbed her.

"But again luck was against you. Somebody saw you go to her cabin"—he half turned to Rosalie—"your mother. Once again you had to act—dangerously, foolhardily—but it was the only chance. You had heard Pennington talk about his revolver. You rushed into his cabin, got hold of it, listened outside Dr. Bessner's cabin door and shot Madame Otterbourne before she could reveal your name."

"No-o!" cried Rosalie. "He didn't! He didn't!"

"After that, you did the only thing you could do—rushed round the stern. And when I rushed after you, you had turned and pretended to be coming in the *opposite* direction. You had handled the revolver in gloves; those gloves were in your pocket when I asked for them. . . ."

Tim said, "Before God, I swear it isn't true—not a word of it." But his voice, ill assured and trembling, failed to convince.

It was then that Rosalie Otterbourne surprised them.

"Of course it isn't true! And Monsieur Poirot knows it isn't! He's saying it for some reason of his own."

Poirot looked at her. A faint smile came to his lips. He spread out his hands in token of surrender.

"Mademoiselle is too clever. . . . But you agree—it was a good case?"

"What the devil—" Tim began with rising anger, but Poirot held up a hand.

"There is a very good case against you, Monsieur Allerton. I wanted you to realize that. Now I will tell you something more pleasant. I have not yet examined that rosary in your cabin. It may be that, when I do, I shall find nothing there. And then, since Mademoiselle Otterbourne sticks to it that she saw no one on the deck last night, *eh bien*, there is no case against you at all. The pearls were taken by a kleptomaniac who has since returned them. They are in a little box on the table by the door, if you would care to examine them with Mademoiselle."

Tim got up. He stood for a moment unable to speak. When he did, his words seemed inadequate, but it is possible that they satisfied his listeners.

"Thanks!" he said. "You won't have to give me another chance."

He held the door open for the girl; she passed out and, picking up the little cardboard box, he followed her.

Side by side they went. Tim opened the box, took out the sham string of pearls and hurled it far from him into the Nile.

"There!" he said. "That's gone. When I return the box to Poirot the real string will be in it. What a damned fool I've been!"

Rosalie said in a low voice, "Why did you come to do it in the first place?"

"How did I come to start, do you mean? Oh, I don't know. Boredom—laziness—the fun of the thing. Such a much more attractive way of earning a living than just pegging away at a job. Sounds pretty sordid to you, I expect, but you know there was an attraction about it—mainly the risk, I suppose."

"I think I understand."

"Yes, but you wouldn't ever do it."

Rosalie considered for a moment or two, her grave young head bent.

"No," she said simply. "I wouldn't."

He said: "Oh, my dear—you're so lovely . . . so utterly lovely. Why wouldn't you say you'd seen me last night?"

"I thought—they might suspect you," Rosalie said.

"Did you suspect me?"

"No. I couldn't believe that you'd kill anyone."

"No. I'm not the strong stuff murderers are made of. I'm only a miserable sneakthief."

She put out a timid hand and touched his arm.

"Don't say that. . . ."

He caught her hand in his.

"Rosalie, would you—you know what I mean? Or would you always despise me and throw it in my teeth?"

She smiled faintly. "There are things you could throw in my teeth, too. . . ."

"Rosalie—darling . . ."

But she held back a minute longer.

"This—Joanna?"

Tim gave a sudden shout.

"Joanna? You're as bad as Mother. I don't care a damn about Joanna. She's got a face like a horse and a predatory eye. A most unattractive female."

Presently Rosalie said, "Your mother need never know about you."

"I'm not sure," Tim said thoughtfully. "I think I shall tell her. Mother's got plenty of stuffing, you know. She can stand up to things. Yes, I think I shall shatter her maternal illusions about me. She'll be so relieved to know that my relations with Joanna were purely of a business nature that she'll forgive me everything else."

They had come to Mrs. Allerton's cabin and Tim knocked firmly on the door. It opened and Mrs. Allerton stood on the threshold.

"Rosalie and I—" began Tim. He paused.

"Oh, my dears," said Mrs. Allerton. She folded Rosalie in her arms. "My dear, dear child . . . I always hoped—but Tim was so tiresome —and pretended he didn't like you. But of course I saw through *that!*"

Rosalie said in a broken voice: "You've been so sweet to me—always. I used to wish—to wish—"

She broke off and sobbed happily on Mrs. Allerton's shoulder.

CHAPTER XXVII

As the door closed behind Tim and Rosalie, Poirot looked somewhat apologetically at Colonel Race. The Colonel was looking rather grim.

"You will consent to my little arrangement, yes?" Poirot pleaded. "It is irregular—I know it is irregular, yes—but I have a high regard for human happiness."

"You've none for mine," said Race.

"That *jeune fille*, I have a tenderness toward her, and she loves that young man. It will be an excellent match; she has the stiffening he needs; the mother likes her; everything is thoroughly suitable."

"In fact the marriage has been arranged by heaven and Hercule Poirot. All I have to do is to compound a felony."

"But, *mon ami*, I told you, it was all conjecture on my part."

Race grinned suddenly.

"It's all right by me," he said. "I'm not a damned policeman, thank God! I daresay the young fool will go straight enough now. The girl's straight all right. No, what I'm complaining of is your treatment of *me!* I'm a patient man, but there are limits to my patience! *Do* you know who committed the three murders on this boat or *don't* you?"

"I do."

"Then why all this beating about the bush?"

"You think that I am just amusing myself with side issues? And it annoys you? But it is not that. Once I went professionally to an archaeological expedition—and I learnt something there. In the course of an excavation, when something comes up out of the ground, everything is cleared away very carefully all around it. You take away the loose earth, and you scrape here and there with a knife until finally your object is there, all alone, ready to be drawn and photographed with no extraneous matter confusing it. That is what I have been seeking to do—clear away the extraneous matter so that we can see the truth—the naked shining truth."

"Good," said Race. "Let's have this naked shining truth. It wasn't Pennington. It wasn't young Allerton. I presume it wasn't Fleetwood. Let's hear who it was for a change."

"My friend, I am just about to tell you."

There was a knock on the door. Race uttered a muffled curse.

It was Dr. Bessner and Cornelia. The latter was looking upset.

"Oh, Colonel Race," she exclaimed, "Miss Bowers has just told me about Cousin Marie. It's been the most dreadful shock. She said she couldn't bear the responsibility all by herself any longer, and that I'd better know, as I was one of the family. I just couldn't believe it at first, but Dr. Bessner here has been just wonderful."

"No, no," protested the doctor modestly.

"He's been so kind, explaining it all, and how people really can't help it. He's had kleptomaniacs in his clinic. And he's explained to me how it's very often due to a deep-seated neurosis."

Cornelia repeated the words with awe.

"It's planted very deeply in the subconscious; sometimes it's just some little thing that happened when you were a child. And he's cured people by getting them to think back and remember what that little thing was."

Cornelia paused, drew a deep breath, and started off again.

"But it's worrying me dreadfully in case it all gets out. It would be too, too terrible in New York. Why, all the tabloids would have it. Cousin Marie and Mother and everybody—they'd never hold up their heads again."

Race sighed. "That's all right," he said. "This is Hush Hush House."

"I beg your pardon, Colonel Race?"

"What I was endeavouring to say was that anything short of murder is being hushed up."

"Oh!" Cornelia clasped her hands. "I'm *so* relieved. I've just been worrying and worrying."

"You have the heart too tender," said Dr. Bessner, and patted her benevolently on the shoulder. He said to the others, "She has a very sensitive and beautiful nature."

"Oh, I haven't really. You're too kind."

Poirot murmured, "Have you seen any more of Mr. Ferguson?"

Cornelia blushed.

"No—but Cousin Marie's been talking about him."

"It seems the young man is highly born," said Dr. Bessner. "I must confess he does not look it. His clothes are terrible. Not for a moment does he appear a well-bred man."

"And what do you think, Mademoiselle?"

"I think he must be just plain crazy," said Cornelia.

Poirot turned to the doctor. "How is your patient?"

"Ach, he is going on splendidly. I have just reassured the little

Fräulein de Bellefort. Would you believe it, I found her in despair. Just because the fellow had a bit of a temperature this afternoon! But what could be more natural? It is amazing that he is not in a high fever now. But no, he is like some of our peasants; he has a magnificent constitution, the constitution of an ox. I have seen them with deep wounds that they hardly notice. It is the same with Mr. Doyle. His pulse is steady, his temperature only slightly above normal. I was able to pooh pooh the little lady's fears. All the same, it is ridiculous, *nicht wahr?* One minute you shoot a man; the next you are in hysterics in case he may not be doing well."

Cornelia said, "She loves him terribly, you see."

"Ach! but it is not sensible, that. If *you* loved a man, would you try and shoot him? No, you are sensible."

"I don't like things that go off with bangs anyway," said Cornelia.

"Naturally you do not. You are very feminine."

Race interrupted this scene of heavy approval. "Since Doyle is all right, there's no reason I shouldn't come along and resume our talk of this afternoon. He was just telling me about a telegram."

Dr. Bessner's bulk moved up and down appreciatively.

"Ho, ho, ho, it was very funny that! Doyle, he tells me about it. It was a telegram all about vegetables—potatoes, artichokes, leeks—Ach! pardon?"

With a stifled exclamation, Race had sat up in his chair.

"My God," he said. "So that's it! Richetti!"

He looked round on three uncomprehending faces.

"A new code—it was used in the South African rebellion. Potatoes mean machine guns, artichokes are high explosives—and so on. Richetti is no more an archaeologist than I am! He's a very dangerous agitator, a man who's killed more than once, and I'll swear that he's killed once again. Mrs. Doyle opened that telegram by mistake, you see. If she were ever to repeat what was in it before me, he knew his goose would be cooked!"

He turned to Poirot. "Am I right?" he asked. "Is Richetti the man?"

"He is *your* man," said Poirot. "I always thought there was something wrong about him! He was almost too word perfect in his rôle; he was all archaeologist, not enough human being."

He paused and then said: "But it was not Richetti who killed Linnet Doyle. For some time now I have known what I may express as the 'first half' of the murderer. Now I know the 'second half' also. The picture is complete. But you understand that, although I know what must have happened, I have no proof that it happened. Intellectually the case is satisfying. Actually it is profoundly unsatisfactory. There is only one hope—a confession from the murderer."

Dr. Bessner raised his shoulders sceptically. "Ach! but that—it would be a miracle."

"I think not. Not under the circumstances."

Cornelia cried out: "But who is it? Aren't you going to tell us?"

Poirot's eyes ranged quietly over the three of them. Race, smiling sardonically, Bessner, still looking sceptical, Cornelia, her mouth hanging a little open gazing at him with eager eyes.

"*Mais oui,*" he said. "I like an audience, I must confess. I am vain, you see. I am puffed up with conceit. I like to say, 'See how clever is Hercule Poirot!' "

Race shifted a little in his chair.

"Well," he asked gently, "just how clever *is* Hercule Poirot?"

Shaking his head sadly from side to side Poirot said: "To begin with I was stupid—incredibly stupid. To me the stumbling block was the pistol—Jacqueline de Bellefort's pistol. Why had that pistol not been left on the scene of the crime? The idea of the murderer was quite plainly to incriminate her. Why then did the murderer take it away? I was so stupid that I thought of all sorts of fantastic reasons. The real one was very simple. The murderer took it away because he *had* to take it away—because he had no choice in the matter."

CHAPTER XXVIII

"You and I, my friend," Poirot leaned toward Race, "started our investigation with a preconceived idea. That idea was that the crime was committed on the spur of the moment, without any preliminary planning. Somebody wished to remove Linnet Doyle and had seized their opportunity to do so at a moment when the crime would almost certainly be attributed to Jacqueline de Bellefort. It therefore followed that the person in question had overheard the scene between Jacqueline and Simon Doyle and had obtained possession of the pistol after the others had left the saloon.

"But, my friends, if that preconceived idea was wrong, the whole aspect of the case altered. And it *was* wrong! This was no spontaneous crime committed on the spur of the moment. It was, on the contrary, very carefully planned and accurately timed, with all the details meticulously worked out beforehand, even to the drugging of Hercule Poirot's bottle of wine on the night in question!

"But, yes, that is so! I was put to sleep so that there should be no possibility of my participating in the events of the night. It did just occur to me as a possibility. I drink wine; my two companions at table drink whisky and mineral water respectively. Nothing easier than to slip a dose of harmless narcotic into my bottle of wine—the bottles stand on the tables all day. But I dismissed the thought. It had been a hot day; I had been unusually tired; it was not really extraordinary that I should for once have slept heavily instead of lightly as I usually do.

"You see, I was still in the grip of the preconceived idea. If I had been drugged, that would have implied premeditation, it would mean that before seven-thirty, when dinner is served, the crime had already been decided upon; and that (always from the point of view of the preconceived idea) was absurd.

"The first blow to the preconceived idea was when the pistol was recovered from the Nile. To begin with, if we were right in our assumptions, the pistol ought never to have been thrown overboard at all. . . . And there was more to follow."

Poirot turned to Dr. Bessner.

"You, Dr. Bessner, examined Linnet Doyle's body. You will remember that the wound showed signs of scorching—that is to say, that the pistol had been placed close against the head before being fired."

Bessner nodded. "So. That is exact."

"But when the pistol was found it was wrapped in a velvet stole, and that velvet showed definite signs that a pistol had been fired through its folds, presumably under the impression that that would deaden the sound of the shot. But if the pistol had been fired through the velvet, there would have been no signs of burning on the victim's skin. Therefore, the shot fired through the stole could not have been the shot that killed Linnet Doyle. Could it have been the other shot—the one fired by Jacqueline de Bellefort at Simon Doyle? Again no, for there had been two witnesses of that shooting, and we knew all about it. It appeared, therefore, as though a *third* shot had been fired—one we knew nothing about. But only two shots had been fired from the pistol, and there was no hint or suggestion of another shot.

"Here we were face to face with a very curious unexplained circumstance. The next interesting point was the fact that in Linnet Doyle's cabin I found two bottles of coloured nail polish. Now ladies very often vary the colour of their nails, but so far Linnet Doyle's nails had always been the shade called Cardinal—a deep dark red. The other bottle was labelled Rose, which is a shade of pale pink, but the few drops remaining in the bottle were not pale pink but a bright red. I was sufficiently curious to take out the stopper and sniff. Instead of the usual strong odour of pear drops, the bottle smelt of vinegar! That is to say, it suggested that the drop or two of fluid in it was red ink. Now there is no reason why Madame Doyle should not have had a bottle of red ink, but it would have been more natural if she had had red ink in a red ink bottle and not in a nail polish bottle. It suggested a link with the faintly stained handkerchief which had been wrapped round the pistol. Red ink washes out quickly but always leaves a pale pink stain.

"I should perhaps have arrived at the truth with these slender indications, but an event occurred which rendered all doubt superfluous. Louise Bourget was killed in circumstances which pointed unmistakably to the fact that she had been blackmailing the murderer. Not only was a fragment of a *mille* franc note still clasped in her hand, but I remembered some very significant words she had used this morning.

"Listen carefully, for here is the crux of the whole matter. When I asked her if she had seen anything the previous night she gave this very curious answer: 'Naturally, if I had been unable to sleep, if I had mounted the stairs, *then* perhaps I might have seen this assassin, this monster, enter or leave Madame's cabin. . . .' Now what exactly did that tell us?"

Bessner, his nose wrinkling with intellectual interest, replied promptly, "It told you that she *had* mounted the stair."

"No, no; you fail to see the point. Why should she have said that, to *us?*"

"To convey a hint."

"But why *hint* to us? If she knows who the murderer is, there are two courses open to her—to tell us the truth, or to hold her tongue and demand money for her silence from the person concerned! But she does neither. She neither says promptly: 'I saw nobody. I was asleep.' Nor does she say, 'Yes, I saw someone, and it was so and so.' Why use that significant indeterminate rigmarole of words? *Parbleu,* there can be only one reason! She is hinting to the murderer; therefore the murderer must have been present at the time. But, besides myself and Colonel Race, only two people were present—Simon Doyle and Dr. Bessner."

The doctor sprang up with a roar.

"Ach! what is that you say? You accuse me? Again? But it is ridiculous—beneath contempt."

Poirot said sharply: "Be quiet. I am telling you what I thought at the time. Let us remain impersonal."

"He doesn't mean he thinks it's you now," said Cornelia soothingly.

Poirot went on quickly: "So it lay there—between Simon Doyle and Dr. Bessner. But what reason has Bessner to kill Linnet Doyle? None, so far as I know. Simon Doyle, then? But that was impossible! There were plenty of witnesses who could swear that Doyle never left the saloon that evening until the quarrel broke out. After that he was wounded and it would then have been physically impossible for him to have done so. Had I good evidence on both those points? Yes, I had the evidence of Mademoiselle Robson, of Jim Fanthorp and of Jacqueline de Bellefort as to the first, and I had the skilled testimony of Dr. Bessner and of Mademoiselle Bowers as to the other. No doubt was possible.

"So Dr. Bessner *must* be the guilty one. In favour of this theory there was the fact that the maid had been stabbed with a surgical knife. On the other hand Bessner had deliberately called attention to this fact.

"And then, my friends, a second perfectly indisputable fact became apparent to me. Louise Bourget's hint could not have been intended for Dr. Bessner, because she could perfectly well have spoken to him in private at any time she liked. There was one person, *and one person only,* who corresponded to her necessity—Simon Doyle! Simon Doyle was wounded, was constantly attended by a doctor, was in that doctor's cabin. It was to him therefore that she risked saying those ambiguous words, in case she might not get another chance. And I remembered how she had gone on, turning to him: 'Monsieur, I implore you—you see how it is? What can I say?' And his answer, 'My good girl, don't be a fool. Nobody thinks you saw or heard anything. You'll be quite all right. I'll look after you. Nobody's accusing you of anything.' That was the assurance she wanted, and she got it!"

Bessner uttered a colossal snort.

"Ach! it is foolish, that! Do you think a man with a fractured bone and a splint on his leg could go walking about the boat and stabbing people? I tell you, it was *impossible* for Simon Doyle to leave his cabin."

Poirot said gently: "I know. That is quite true. The thing was impossible. It was impossible, but it was also true! There could be only one logical meaning behind Louise Bourget's words.

"So I returned to the beginning and reviewed the crime in the light of this new knowledge. Was it possible that in the period preceding the quarrel Simon Doyle had left the saloon and the others had forgotten or not noticed it? I could not see that that was possible. Could the skilled testimony of Dr. Bessner and Mademoiselle Bowers be disregarded? Again I felt sure it could not. But, I remembered, there was a gap between the two. Simon Doyle had been alone in the saloon for a period of five minutes, and the skilled testimony of Dr. Bessner only applied to the time after that period. For that period we had only the evidence of visual appearance, and, though apparently that was perfectly sound, it was no longer certain. What had actually been *seen*—leaving assumption out of the question?

"Mademoiselle Robson had seen Mademoiselle de Bellefort fire her pistol, had seen Simon Doyle collapse onto a chair, had seen him clasp a handkerchief to his leg and seen that handkerchief gradually soak through red. What had Monsieur Fanthorp heard and seen? He heard a shot, he found Doyle with a red-stained handkerchief clasped to his leg. What had happened then? Doyle had been very insistent that Mademoiselle de Bellefort should be got away, that she should not be left alone. After that, he suggested that Fanthorp should get hold of the doctor.

"Accordingly Mademoiselle Robson and Monsieur Fanthorp go out with Mademoiselle de Bellefort and for the next five minutes they are busy, on the port side of the deck. Mademoiselle Bowers', Dr. Bessner's and Mademoiselle de Bellefort's cabins are all on the port side. Two minutes are all that Simon Doyle needs. He picks up the pistol from under the sofa, slips out of his shoes, runs like a hare silently along the starboard deck, enters his wife's cabin, creeps up to her as she lies asleep, shoots her through the head, puts the bottle that has contained the red ink on her washstand (it mustn't be found on him) runs back, gets hold of Mademoiselle Van Schuyler's velvet stole, which he has quietly stuffed down the side of a chair in readiness, muffles it round the pistol and fires a bullet into his leg. His chair into which he falls (in genuine agony this time) is by a window. He lifts the window and throws the pistol (wrapped up with the telltale handkerchief in the velvet stole) into the Nile."

"Impossible!" said Race.

"No, my friend, not *impossible*. Remember the evidence of Tim Allerton. He heard a pop—*followed* by a splash. And he heard something else—the footsteps of a man running—a man running past his door. But nobody should have been running along the starboard side of the deck. What he heard was the stockinged feet of Simon Doyle running past his cabin."

Race said: "I still say it's impossible. No man could work out the whole caboodle like that in a flash—especially a chap like Doyle who is slow in his mental processes."

"But very quick and deft in his physical actions!"

"That, yes. But he wouldn't be capable of thinking the whole thing out."

"But he did not think it out himself, my friend. That is where we were all wrong. It looked like a crime committed on the spur of the moment, but it was *not* a crime committed on the spur of the moment. As I say it was a very cleverly planned and well thought out piece of work. It could not be *chance* that Simon Doyle had a bottle of red ink in his pocket. No, it must be *design*. It was not *chance* that he had a plain unmarked handkerchief with him. It was not *chance* that Jacqueline de Bellefort's foot kicked the pistol under the settee, where it would be out of sight and unremembered until later."

"Jacqueline?"

"Certainly. The two halves of the murderer. What gave Simon his alibi? The shot fired by Jacqueline. What gave Jacqueline *her* alibi? The insistence of Simon, which resulted in a hospital nurse remaining with her all night. There, between the two of them, you get all the qualities you require—the cool, resourceful, planning brain, Jacqueline de Bellefort's brain, and the man of action to carry it out with incredible swiftness and timing.

"Look at it the right way, and it answers every question. Simon Doyle and Jacqueline had been lovers. Realize that they are still lovers, and it is all clear. Simon does away with his rich wife, inherits her money, and in due course will marry his old love. It was all very ingenious. The persecution of Madame Doyle by Jacqueline, all part of the plan. Simon's pretended rage. . . . And yet—there were lapses. He held forth to me once about possessive women—held forth with real bitterness. It ought to have been clear to me that it was his wife he was thinking about—not Jacqueline. Then his manner to his wife in public. An ordinary, inarticulate Englishman, such as Simon Doyle, is very embarrassed at showing any affection. Simon was not a really good actor. He overdid the devoted manner. That conversation I had with Mademoiselle Jacqueline, too, when she pretended that somebody had overheard. *I* saw no one. And there *was* no one! But it was to be a useful red herring later. Then one night on this boat I thought I heard Simon and Linnet outside my cabin. He was saying, 'We've got to go through with it now.' It was Doyle all right, but it was to Jacqueline he was speaking.

"The final drama was perfectly planned and timed. There was a sleeping draught for me, in case I might put an inconvenient finger in the pie. There was the selection of Mademoiselle Robson as a witness—the working up of the scene, Mademoiselle de Bellefort's exaggerated remorse and hysterics. She made a good deal of noise, in case the shot should be heard. *En vérité*, it was an extraordinarily clever idea. Jacqueline says she has shot Doyle; Mademoiselle Robson says so; Fanthorp says so—and when Simon's leg is examined he *has* been shot. It looks unanswerable! For both of them there is a perfect alibi—at the cost, it is true, of a certain amount of pain and risk to Simon Doyle, but it is necessary that his wound should definitely disable him.

"And then the plan goes wrong. Louise Bourget has been wakeful. She has come up the stairway and she has seen Simon Doyle run along to his wife's cabin and come back. Easy enough to piece together what has happened the following day. And so she makes her greedy bid for hush money, and in so doing signs her death warrant."

"But Mr. Doyle couldn't have killed *her?*" Cornelia objected.

"No, the other partner did that murder. As soon as he can, Simon Doyle asks to see Jacqueline. He even asks me to leave them alone together. He tells her then of the new danger. They must act at once. He knows where Bessner's scalpels are kept. After the crime the scalpel is wiped and returned, and then, very late and rather out of breath, Jacqueline de Bellefort hurries in to lunch.

"And still all is not well, for Madame Otterbourne has seen Jacqueline go into Louise Bourget's cabin. And she comes hot foot to tell Simon about it. Jacqueline is the murderess. Do you remember how Simon shouted at the poor woman? Nerves, we thought. But the door was open and he was trying to convey the danger to his accomplice. She heard and she acted—acted like lightning. She remembered Pennington had talked about a revolver. She got hold of it, crept up outside the door, listened and, at the critical moment, fired. She boasted once that she was a good shot, and her boast was not an idle one.

"I remarked after that third crime that there were three ways the murderer could have gone. I meant that he could have gone aft (in which case Tim Allerton was the criminal) he could have gone over the side (very improbable) or he could have gone into a cabin. Jacqueline's cabin was just two away from Dr. Bessner's. She had only to throw down the revolver, bolt into the cabin, ruffle her hair and fling herself down on the bunk. It was risky, but it was the only possible chance."

There was a silence, then Race asked, "What happened to the first bullet fired at Doyle by the girl?"

"I think it went into the table. There is a recently made hole there. I think Doyle had time to dig it out with a penknife and fling it through the window. He had, of course, a spare cartridge, so that it would appear that only two shots had been fired.

Cornelia sighed. "They thought of everything," she said. "It's—horrible!"

Poirot was silent. But it was not a modest silence. His eyes seemed to be saying: "You are wrong. They didn't allow for Hercule Poirot."

Aloud he said, "And now, Doctor, we will go and have a word with your patient."

CHAPTER XXIX

It was very much later that evening that Hercule Poirot came and knocked on the door of a cabin.

A voice said "Come in" and he entered.

Jacqueline de Bellefort was sitting in a chair. In another chair, close against the wall, sat the big stewardess.

Jacqueline's eyes surveyed Poirot thoughtfully. She made a gesture toward the stewardess.

"Can she go?"

Poirot nodded to the woman and she went out. Poirot drew up her chair and sat down near Jacqueline. Neither of them spoke. Poirot's face was unhappy.

In the end it was the girl who spoke first.

"Well," she said, "it is all over! You were too clever for us, Monsieur Poirot."

Poirot sighed. He spread out his hands. He seemed strangely dumb.

"All the same," said Jacqueline reflectively, "I can't really see that you had much proof. You were quite right, of course, but if we'd bluffed you out—"

"In no other way, Mademoiselle, could the thing have happened."

"That's proof enough for a logical mind, but I don't believe it would have convinced a jury. Oh, well—it can't be helped. You sprang it all on Simon, and he went down like a ninepin. He just lost his head utterly, poor lamb, and admitted everything." She shook her head. "He's a bad loser."

"But you, Mademoiselle, are a good loser."

She laughed suddenly—a queer, gay, defiant little laugh.

"Oh, yes, I'm a good loser all right." She looked at him.

She said suddenly and impulsively: "Don't mind so much, Monsieur Poirot! About me, I mean. You do mind, don't you?"

"Yes, Mademoiselle."

"But it wouldn't have occurred to you to let me off?"

Hercule Poirot said quietly, "No."

She nodded her head in quiet agreement.

"No, it's no use being sentimental. I might do it again. . . . I'm not a safe person any longer. I can feel that myself. . . ." She went on broodingly: "It's so dreadfully easy—killing people. And you begin to feel that it doesn't matter . . . that it's only *you* that matters! It's dangerous—that."

She paused, then said with a little smile: "You did your best for me, you know. That night at Assuan—you told me not to open my heart to evil. . . . Did you realize then what was in my mind?"

He shook his head.

"I only knew that what I said was true."

"It was true. I could have stopped, then, you know. I nearly did. . . . I could have told Simon that I wouldn't go on with it. . . . But then perhaps—"

She broke off. She said: "Would you like to hear about it? From the beginning?"

"If you care to tell me, Mademoiselle."

"I think I want to tell you. It was all very simple really. You see, Simon and I loved each other. . . ."

It was a matter-of-fact statement, yet, underneath the lightness of her tone, there were echoes. . . .

Poirot said simply, "and for you love would have been enough, but not for him."

"You might put it that way, perhaps. But you don't quite understand Simon. You see, he's always wanted money so dreadfully. He likes all the things you get with money—horses and yachts and sport—nice things, all of them, things a man ought to be keen about. And he'd never been able to have any of them. He's awfully simple, Simon is. He wants things just as a child wants them—you know—terribly.

"All the same he never tried to marry anybody rich and horrid. He wasn't that sort. And then we met—and—and that sort of settled things. Only we didn't see when we'd be able to marry. He'd had rather a decent job, but he'd lost it. In a way it was his own fault. He tried to do something smart over money, and got found out at once. I don't believe he really meant to be dishonest. He just thought it was the sort of thing people did in the City."

A flicker passed over her listener's face, but he guarded his tongue.

"There we were, up against it; and then I thought of Linnet and her new country house, and I rushed off to her. You know, Monsieur Poirot, I loved Linnet, really I did. She was my best friend, and I never dreamed that anything would ever come between us. I just thought how lucky it was she was rich. It might make all the difference to me and Simon if she'd give him a job. And she was awfully sweet about it and told me to bring Simon down to see her. It was about then you saw us that night at Chez Ma Tante. We were making whoopee, although we couldn't really afford it."

She paused, sighed, then went on: "What I'm going to say now is quite true, Monsieur Poirot. Even though Linnet is dead, it doesn't alter the truth. That's why I'm not really sorry about her, even now. She went all out to get Simon away from me. That's the absolute truth! I don't think she even hesitated for more than about a minute. I was her friend, but she didn't care. She just went baldheaded for Simon. . . .

"And Simon didn't care a damn about her! I talked a lot to you about glamour, but of course that wasn't true. He didn't want Linnet. He thought her good-looking but terribly bossy, and he hated bossy women! The whole thing embarrassed him frightfully. But he did like the thought of her money.

"Of course I saw that . . . and at last I suggested to him that it might be a good thing if he—got rid of me and married Linnet. But he scouted the idea. He said, money or no money, it would be hell to be married to her. He said his idea of having money was to have it himself—not to have a rich wife holding the purse strings. 'I'd be a kind of damned Prince Consort,' he said to me. He said, too, that he didn't want anyone but me. . . .

"I think I know when the idea came into his head. He said one day, 'If I'd any luck, I'd marry her and she'd die in about a year and leave me all the boodle.' And then a queer startled look came into his eyes. That was when he first thought of it. . . .

"He talked about it a good deal, one way and another—about how convenient it would be if Linnet died. I said it was an awful idea, and then he shut up about it. Then, one day, I found him reading up all about arsenic. I taxed him with it then, and he laughed and said: 'Nothing venture, nothing have! It's about the only time in my life I shall be near to touching a fat lot of money.'

"After a bit I saw that he'd made up his mind. And I was terrified—simply terrified. Because, you see, I realized that he'd never pull it off. He's so childishly simple. He'd have no kind of subtlety about it—and he's got no imagination. He would probably have just bunged arsenic into her and assumed the doctor would say she'd died of gastritis. He always thought things would go right.

"So I had to come into it, too, to look after him. . . ."

She said it very simply but in complete good faith. Poirot had no doubt whatever that her motive had been exactly what she said it was. She herself had not coveted Linnet Ridgeway's money, but she had loved Simon Doyle, had loved him beyond reason and beyond rectitude and beyond pity.

"I thought and I thought—trying to work out a plan. It seemed to me that the basis of the idea ought to be a kind of two-handed alibi. You know—if Simon and I could somehow or other give evidence against each other, but actually that evidence would clear us of everything. It would be easy enough for me to pretend to hate Simon. It was quite a likely thing to happen under the circumstances. Then, if Linnet was killed, I should probably be suspected, so it would be better if I was suspected right away. We worked out details little by little. I wanted it to be so that, if anything went wrong, they'd get me and not Simon. But Simon was worried about me.

"The only thing I was glad about was that I hadn't got to do *it*. I simply couldn't have! Not go along in cold blood and kill her when she was asleep! You see, I hadn't forgiven her—I think I could have killed her face to face, but not the other way. . . .

"We worked everything out carefully. Even then, Simon went and wrote a J in blood, which was a silly melodramatic thing to do. It's just the sort of thing he *would* think of! But it went off all right."

Poirot nodded.

"Yes. It was not your fault that Louise Bourget could not sleep that night. . . . And afterward, Mademoiselle?"

She met his eyes squarely.

"Yes," she said, "it's rather horrible, isn't it? I can't believe that I —did that! I know now what you meant by opening your heart to evil. . . . You know pretty well how it happened. Louise made it clear to Simon that she knew. Simon got you to bring me to him. As soon as we were alone together he told me what had happened. He told me what I'd got to do. I wasn't even horrified. I was so afraid—so deadly afraid. . . . That's what murder does to you. Simon and I were safe—quite safe—except for this miserable blackmailing French girl. I took her all the money we could get hold of. I pretended to grovel. And then, when she was counting the money, I—did it! It was quite easy. That's what's so horribly, horribly frightening about it. . . . It's so terribly easy. . . .

"And even then we weren't safe. Mrs. Otterbourne had seen me. She came triumphantly along the deck looking for you and Colonel Race. I'd no time to think. I just acted like a flash. It was almost exciting. I knew it was touch or go that time. That seemed to make it better. . . ."

She stopped again.

"Do you remember when you came into my cabin afterward? You said you were not sure why you had come. I was so miserable—so terrified. I thought Simon was going to die. . . ."

"And I—was hoping it," said Poirot.

Jacqueline nodded.

"Yes, it would have been better for him that way."

"That was not my thought."

Jacqueline looked at the sternness of his face.

She said gently: "Don't mind so much for me, Monsieur Poirot. After all, I've lived hard always, you know. If we'd won out, I'd have been very happy and enjoyed things and probably should never have regretted anything. As it is—well, one goes through with it."

She added: "I suppose the stewardess is in attendance to see I don't hang myself or swallow a miraculous capsule of prussic acid as people always do in books. You needn't be afraid! I shan't do that. It will be easier for Simon if I'm standing by."

Poirot got up. Jacqueline rose also. She said with a sudden smile: "Do you remember when I said I must follow my star? You said it might be a false star. And I said, 'That very bad star, that star fall down.'"

He went out onto the deck with her laughter ringing in his ears.

CHAPTER XXX

IT WAS EARLY DAWN when they came into Shellâl. The rocks came down grimly to the water's edge.

Poirot murmured, "*Quel pays sauvage!*"

Race stood beside him. "Well," he said, "we've done our job. I've arranged for Richetti to be taken ashore first. Glad we've got him. He's been a slippery customer, I can tell you. Given us the slip dozens of times."

He went on: "We must get hold of a stretcher for Doyle. Remarkable how he went to pieces."

"Not really," said Poirot. "That boyish type of criminal is usually intensely vain. Once prick the bubble of their self-esteem and it is finished! They go to pieces like children."

"Deserves to be hanged," said Race. "He's a cold-blooded scoundrel. I'm sorry for the girl—but there's nothing to be done about it."

Poirot shook his head.

"People say love justifies everything, but that is not true. . . . Women who care for men as Jacqueline cares for Simon Doyle are very dangerous. It is what I said when I saw her first. 'She cares too much, that little one!' It is true."

Cornelia Robson came up beside him.

"Oh," she said, "we're nearly in."

She paused a minute or two then added, "I've been with her."

"With Mademoiselle de Bellefort?"

"Yes. I felt it was kind of awful for her boxed up with that stewardess. Cousin Marie's very angry though, I'm afraid."

Miss Van Schuyler was progressing slowly down the deck toward them. Her eyes were venomous.

"Cornelia," she snapped, "you've behaved outrageously. I shall send you straight home."

Cornelia took a deep breath. "I'm sorry, Cousin Marie, but I'm not going home. I'm going to get married."

"So you've seen sense at last," snapped the old lady.

Ferguson came striding round the corner of the deck. He said: "Cornelia, what's this I hear? It's not true!"

"It's quite true," said Cornelia. "I'm going to marry Dr. Bessner. He asked me last night."

"And why are you going to marry him?" asked Ferguson furiously. "Simply because he's rich."

"No, I'm not," said Cornelia indignantly. "I like him. He's kind, and he knows a lot. And I've always been interested in sick folks and clinics, and I shall have just a wonderful life with him."

"Do you mean to say," asked Mr. Ferguson incredulously, "that you'd rather marry that disgusting old man than Me?"

"Yes, I would. You're not reliable! You wouldn't be at all a comfortable sort of person to live with. And he's *not* old. He's not fifty yet."

"He's got a stomach," said Mr. Ferguson venomously.

"Well, I've got round shoulders," retorted Cornelia. "What one looks like doesn't matter. He says I really could help him in his work, and he's going to teach me all about neuroses."

She moved away. Ferguson said to Poirot, "Do you think she really means that?"

"Certainly."

"She prefers that pompous old bore to Me?"

"Undoubtedly."

"The girl's mad," declared Ferguson.

Poirot's eyes twinkled.

"She is a woman of an original mind," he said. "It is probably the first time you have met one."

The boat drew in to the landing stage. A cordon had been drawn round the passengers. They had been asked to wait before disembarking.

Richetti, dark faced and sullen, was marched ashore by two engineers.

Then, after a certain amount of delay, a stretcher was brought. Simon Doyle was carried along the deck to the gangway.

He looked a different man—cringing, frightened, all his boyish insouciance vanished.

Jacqueline de Bellefort followed. A stewardess walked beside her. She was pale but otherwise looked much as usual. She came up to the stretcher.

"Hullo, Simon," she said.

He looked up at her quickly. The old boyish look came back to his face for a moment.

"I messed it up," he said. "Lost my head and admitted everything. Sorry, Jackie. I've let you down."

She smiled at him then.

"It's all right, Simon," she said. "A fool's game, and we've lost. That's all."

She stood aside. The bearer picked up the handles of the stretcher. Jacqueline bent down and tied the lace of her shoe. Then her hand went to her stocking top and she straightened up with something in her hand.

There was a sharp explosive "pop."

Simon Doyle gave one convulsed shudder and then lay still.

Jacqueline de Bellefort nodded. She stood for a minute, pistol in hand. She gave a fleeting smile at Poirot.

Then, as Race jumped forward, she turned the little glittering toy against her heart and pressed the trigger.

She sank down in a soft huddled heap.

Race shouted, "Where the devil did she get that pistol?"

Poirot felt a hand on his arm. Mrs. Allerton said softly, "You—knew?"

He nodded. "She had a pair of these pistols. I realized that when I heard that one had been found in Rosalie Otterbourne's handbag the day of the search. Jacqueline sat at the same table as they did. When she realized that there was going to be a search, she slipped it into the other girl's handbag. Later she went to Rosalie's cabin and got it back, after having distracted her attention with a comparison of lipsticks. As both she and her cabin had been searched yesterday, it wasn't thought necessary to do it again."

Mrs. Allerton said, "You wanted her to take that way out?"

"Yes. But she would not take it alone. That is why Simon Doyle has died an easier death than he deserved."

Mrs. Allerton shivered. "Love can be a very frightening thing."

"That is why most great love stories are tragedies."

Mrs. Allerton's eyes rested upon Tim and Rosalie, standing side by side in the sunlight, and she said suddenly and passionately, "But thank God, there is happiness in the world."

"As you say, Madame, thank God for it."

Presently the passengers went ashore.

Later the bodies of Louise Bourget and Mrs. Otterbourne were carried off the *Karnak*.

Lastly the body of Linnet Doyle was brought ashore, and all over the world wires began to hum, telling the public that Linnet Doyle, who had been Linnet Ridgeway, the famous, the beautiful, the wealthy Linnet Doyle was dead. . . .

Sir George Wode read about it in his London club, and Sterndale Rockford in New York, and Joanna Southwood in Switzerland, and it was discussed in the bar of the Three Crowns in Malton-under-Wode.

And Mr. Burnaby's lean friend said, "Well, it didn't seem fair, her having everything."

And Mr. Burnaby said acutely, "Well, it doesn't seem to have done her much good, poor lass."

But after a while they stopped talking about her and discussed instead who was going to win the Grand National. For, as Mr. Ferguson was saying at that minute in Luxor, it is not the past that matters but the future.

Murder in Mesopotamia

The EVENTS [illegible]

ago. Circumstances have [illegible]

a straightforward account [illegible]

There have been [illegible]

that important evidence [illegible]

kind. Those misconstructions [illegible]

American press.

For obvious reasons [illegible]

come from the pen of [illegible]

ably be supposed to be [illegible]

I therefore suggested [illegible]

dertake the task. [illegible]

fessional character of [illegible]

previous connection [illegible]

Iraq and she was an [illegible]

It was not very easy [illegible]

this task—in fact, [illegible]

professional career—[illegible]

curious reluctance [illegible]

was partly due to [illegible]

daughter Sheila. I [illegible]

criticize their parents [illegible]

delighted when their [illegible]

other objection was [illegible]

hoped I would "put the [illegible]

contrary, refused to [illegible]

style in my opinion is [illegible]

she calls Hercule Poirot [illegible]

in the next, such a [illegible]

moment she is, so to speak, [illegible]

tal nurses are great [illegible]

terest in what she is [illegible]

cuffs forgotten!

FOREWORD

BY

Giles Reilly, M.D.

The events chronicled in this narrative took place some four years ago. Circumstances have rendered it necessary, in my opinion, that a straightforward account of them should be given to the public. There have been the wildest and most ridiculous rumours suggesting that important evidence was suppressed and other nonsense of that kind. Those misconstructions have appeared more especially in the American press.

For obvious reasons it was desirable that the account should not come from the pen of one of the expedition staff, who might reasonably be supposed to be prejudiced.

I therefore suggested to Miss Amy Leatheran that she should undertake the task. She is obviously the person to do it. She has a professional character of the highest, she is not biased by having any previous connection with the University of Pittstown Expedition to Iraq and she was an observant and intelligent eye-witness.

It was not very easy to persuade Miss Leatheran to undertake this task—in fact, persuading her was one of the hardest jobs of my professional career—and even after it was completed she displayed a curious reluctance to let me see the manuscript. I discovered that this was partly due to some critical remarks she had made concerning my daughter Sheila. I soon disposed of that, assuring her that as children criticize their parents freely in print nowadays, parents are only too delighted when their offspring come in for their share of abuse! Her other objection was extreme modesty about her literary style. She hoped I would "put the grammar right and all that." I have, on the contrary, refused to alter so much as a single word. Miss Leatheran's style in my opinion is vigorous, individual and entirely apposite. If she calls Hercule Poirot "Poirot" in one paragraph and "Mr. Poirot" in the next, such a variation is both interesting and suggestive. At one moment she is, so to speak, "remembering her manners" (and hospital nurses are great sticklers for etiquette) and at the next her interest in what she is telling is that of a pure human being—cap and cuffs forgotten!

The only thing I have done is to take the liberty of writing a first chapter—aided by a letter kindly supplied by one of Miss Leatheran's friends. It is intended to be in the nature of a frontispiece—that is, it gives a rough sketch of the narrator.

CHAPTER I

FOREWORD

IN THE HALL of the Tigris Palace Hotel in Baghdad a hospital nurse was finishing a letter. Her fountain-pen drove briskly over the paper.

" . . . Well, dear, I think that's really all my news. I must say it's been nice to see a bit of the world—though England for me every time, thank you! The *dirt* and the *mess* in Baghdad you wouldn't believe—and not romantic at all like you'd think from the Arabian Nights! Of course, it's pretty just on the river, but the town itself is just awful—and no proper shops at all. Major Kelsey took me through the bazaars, and of course there's no denying they're *quaint*—but just a lot of rubbish and hammering away at copper pans till they make your head ache—and not what I'd like to use myself unless I was sure about the cleaning. You've got to be so careful of verdigris with copper pans.

"I'll write and let you know if anything comes of the job that Dr. Reilly spoke about. He said this American gentleman was in Baghdad now and might come and see me this afternoon. It's for his wife—she has 'fancies,' so Dr. Reilly said. He didn't say any more than that, and of course, dear, one knows what that *usually means* (but I hope not actually D.T.'s!). Of course, Dr. Reilly didn't say anything—but he had a look—if you know what I mean. This Dr. Leidner is an archæologist and is digging up a mound out in the desert somewhere for some American museum.

"Well, dear, I will close now. I thought what you told me about little Stubbins was simply *killing!* Whatever did Matron say?

"No more now.

"Yours ever,

"Amy Leatheran."

Enclosing the letter in an envelope, she addressed it to Sister Curshaw, St. Christopher's Hospital, London.

As she put the cap on her fountain-pen, one of the native boys approached her.

"A gentleman come see you. Dr. Leidner."

Nurse Leatheran turned. She saw a man of middle height with slightly stooping shoulders, a brown beard and gentle tired eyes.

Dr. Leidner saw a woman of thirty-five of erect, confident bearing. He saw a good-humoured face with slightly prominent blue eyes and glossy brown hair. She looked, he thought, just what a hospital nurse for a nervous case ought to look. Cheerful, robust, shrewd and matter of fact.

Nurse Leatheran, he thought, would do.

CHAPTER II

INTRODUCING AMY LEATHERAN

I DON'T PRETEND to be an author or to know anything about writing. I'm doing this simply because Dr. Reilly asked me to, and somehow when Dr. Reilly asks you to do a thing you don't like to refuse.

"Oh, but, doctor," I said, "I'm not literary—not literary at all."

"Nonsense!" he said. "Treat it as case notes, if you like."

Well, of course, you *can* look at it that way.

Dr. Reilly went on. He said that an unvarnished plain account of the Tell Yarimjah business was badly needed.

"If one of the interested parties writes it, it won't carry conviction. They'll say it's biased one way or another."

And of course that was true, too. I was in it all and yet an outsider, so to speak.

"Why don't you write it yourself, doctor?" I asked.

"I wasn't on the spot—you were. Besides," he added with a sigh, "my daughter won't let me."

The way he knuckles under to that chit of a girl of his is downright disgraceful. I had half a mind to say so, when I saw that his eyes were twinkling. That was the worst of Dr. Reilly. You never knew whether he was joking or not. He always said things in the same slow melancholy way—but half the time there was a twinkle underneath it.

"Well," I said doubtfully. "I suppose I *could*."

"Of course you could."

"Only I don't quite know how to set about it."

"There's a good precedent for that. Begin at the beginning, go on to the end and then leave off."

"I don't even know quite where and what the beginning was," I said doubtfully.

"Believe me, nurse, the difficulty of beginning will be nothing to the difficulty of knowing how to stop. At least that's the way it is with me when I have to make a speech. Some one's got to catch hold of my coat-tails and pull me down by main force."

"Oh, you're joking, doctor."

"It's profoundly serious I am. Now what about it?"

Another thing was worrying me. After hesitating a moment or two I said:

"You know, doctor, I'm afraid I might tend to be—well, a little *personal* sometimes."

"God bless my soul, woman, the more personal you are the better! This is a story of human beings—not dummies! Be personal—be prejudiced—be catty—be anything you please! Write the thing your own way. We can always prune out the bits that are libellous afterwards! You go ahead. You're a sensible woman, and you'll give a sensible common-sense account of the business."

So that was that, and I promised to do my best.

And here I am beginning, but as I said to the doctor, it's difficult to know just where to start.

I suppose I ought to say a word or two about myself. I'm thirty-two and my name is Amy Leatheran. I took my training at St. Christopher's and after that did two years' maternity. I did a certain amount of private work and I was for four years at Miss Bendix's Nursing Home in Devonshire Place. I came out to Iraq with a Mrs. Kelsey. I'd attended her when her baby was born. She was coming out to Baghdad with her husband and had already got a children's nurse booked who had been for some years with friends of hers out there. Their children were coming home and going to school, and the nurse had agreed to go to Mrs. Kelsey when they left. Mrs. Kelsey was delicate and nervous about the journey out with so young a child, so Major Kelsey arranged that I should come out with her and look after her and the baby. They would pay my passage home unless we found some one needing a nurse for the return journey.

Well, there is no need to describe the Kelseys—the baby was a little love and Mrs. Kelsey quite nice, though rather the fretting kind. I enjoyed the voyage very much. I'd never been a long trip on the sea before.

Dr. Reilly was on board the boat. He was a black-haired, long-faced man who said all sorts of funny things in a low, sad voice. I think he enjoyed pulling my leg and used to make the most extraordinary statements to see if I would swallow them. He was the civil surgeon at a place called Hassanieh—a day and a half's journey from Baghdad.

I had been about a week in Baghdad when I ran across him and he asked when I was leaving the Kelseys. I said that it was funny his asking that because as a matter of fact the Wrights (the other people

I mentioned) were going home earlier than they had meant to and their nurse was free to come straightaway.

He said that he had heard about the Wrights and that that was why he had asked me.

"As a matter of fact, nurse, I've got a possible job for you."

"A case?"

He screwed his face up as though considering.

"You could hardly call it a case. It's just a lady who has—shall we say—fancies?"

"Oh!" I said.

(One usually knows what *that* means—drink or drugs!)

Dr. Reilly didn't explain further. He was very discreet.

"Yes," he said. "A Mrs. Leidner. Husband's an American—an American Swede to be exact. He's the head of a large American dig."

And he explained how this expedition was excavating the site of a big Assyrian city something like Nineveh. The expedition house was not actually very far from Hassanieh, but it was a lonely spot and Dr. Leidner had been worried for some time about his wife's health.

"He's not been very explicit about it, but it seems she has these fits of recurring nervous terrors."

"Is she left alone all day amongst natives?" I asked.

"Oh, no, there's quite a crowd—seven or eight. I don't fancy she's ever alone in the house. But there seems to be no doubt that she's worked herself up into a queer state. Leidner has any amount of work on his shoulders, but he's crazy about his wife and it worries him to know she's in this state. He felt he'd be happier if he knew that some responsible person with expert knowledge was keeping an eye on her."

"And what does Mrs. Leidner herself think about it?"

Dr. Reilly answered gravely.

"Mrs. Leidner is a very lovely lady. She's seldom of the same mind about anything two days on end. But on the whole she favours the idea." He added, "She's an odd woman. A mass of affectation and, I should fancy, a champion liar—but Leidner seems honestly to believe that she is scared out of her life by something or other."

"What did she herself say to you, doctor?"

"Oh, she hasn't consulted me! She doesn't like me anyway—for several reasons. It was Leidner who came to me and propounded this plan. Well, nurse, what do you think of the idea? You'd see something of the country before you go home—they'll be digging for another two months. And excavation is quite interesting work."

After a moment's hesitation while I turned the matter over in my mind:

"Well," I said. "I really think I might try it."

"Splendid," said Dr. Reilly, rising. "Leidner's in Baghdad now. I'll tell him to come round and see if he can fix things up with you."

Dr. Leidner came to the hotel that afternoon. He was a middle-aged man with a rather nervous, hesitating manner. There was something gentle and kindly and rather helpless about him.

He sounded very devoted to his wife, but he was very vague about what was the matter with her.

"You see," he said, tugging at his beard in a rather perplexed manner that I later came to know to be characteristic of him, "my wife is really in a very nervous state. I—I'm quite worried about her."

"She is in good physical health?" I asked.

"Yes—oh, yes, I think so. No, I should not think there was anything the matter with her physically. But she—well—imagines things, you know."

"What kind of things?" I asked.

But he shied off from the point, merely murmuring perplexedly:

"She works herself up over nothing at all. . . . I really can see no foundations for these fears."

"Fears of what, Dr. Leidner?"

He said vaguely, "Oh, just—nervous terrors, you know."

Ten to one, I thought to myself, it's drugs. And he doesn't realize it! Lots of men don't. Just wonder why their wives are so jumpy and have such extraordinary changes of mood.

I asked whether Mrs. Leidner herself approved of the idea of my coming.

His face lighted up.

"Yes. I was surprised. Most pleasurably surprised. She said it was a very good idea. She said she would feel very much safer."

The word struck me oddly. *Safer.* A very queer word to use. I began to surmise that Mrs. Leidner might be a mental case.

He went on with a kind of boyish eagerness.

"I'm sure you'll get on very well with her. She's really a very charming woman." He smiled disarmingly. "She feels you'll be the greatest comfort to her. I felt the same as soon as I saw you. You look, if you will allow me to say so, so splendidly healthy and full of common sense. I'm sure you're just the person for Louise."

"Well, we can but try, Dr. Leidner," I said cheerfully. "I'm sure I hope I can be of use to your wife. Perhaps she's nervous of natives and coloured people?"

"Oh, dear me, no." He shook his head, amused at the idea. "My wife likes Arabs very much—she appreciates their simplicity and their sense of humour. This is only her second season—we have been married less than two years—but she already speaks quite a fair amount of Arabic."

I was silent for a moment or two, then I had one more try.

"Can't you tell me at all what it is your wife is afraid of, Dr. Leidner?" I asked.

He hesitated. Then he said slowly, "I hope—I believe—that she will tell you that herself."

And that's all I could get out of him.

CHAPTER III

GOSSIP

It was arranged that I should go to Tell Yarimjah the following week.

Mrs. Kelsey was settling into her house at Alwiyah, and I was glad to be able to take a few things off her shoulders.

During that time I heard one or two allusions to the Leidner expedition. A friend of Mrs. Kelsey's, a young squadron-leader, pursed his lips in surprise as he exclaimed:

"Lovely Louise. So that's her latest!" He turned to me. "That's our nickname for her, nurse. She's always known as Lovely Louise."

"Is she so very handsome then?" I asked.

"It's taking her at her own valuation. *She* thinks she is!"

"Now don't be spiteful, John," said Mrs. Kelsey. "You know it's not only she who thinks so! Lots of people have been very smitten by her."

"Perhaps you're right. She's a bit long in the tooth, but she has a certain attraction."

"You were completely bowled over yourself," said Mrs. Kelsey, laughing.

The squadron-leader blushed and admitted rather shamefacedly:

"Well, she has a way with her. As for Leidner himself, he worships the ground she walks on—and all the rest of the expedition has to worship too! It's expected of them!"

"How many are there altogether?" I asked.

"All sorts and nationalities, nurse," said the squadron-leader cheerfully. "An English architect, a French Father from Carthage—he does the inscriptions—tablets and things, you know. And then there's Miss Johnson. She's English too—sort of general bottle-washer. And a little plump man who does the photography—he's an American. And the Mercados. Heaven knows what nationality they are—Dagos of some kind! She's quite young—a snaky-looking creature—and oh! doesn't she hate Lovely Louise! And there are a couple of youngsters, and that's the lot. A few odd fish, but nice on the whole—don't you agree, Pennyman?"

He was appealing to an elderly man who was sitting thoughtfully twirling a pair of pince-nez.

The latter started and looked up.

"Yes—yes—very nice indeed. Taken individually, that is. Of course, Mercado is rather a queer fish—"

"He has such a very *odd* beard," put in Mrs. Kelsey. "A queer limp kind."

Major Pennyman went on without noticing her interruption.

"The young 'uns are both nice. The American's rather silent, and the English boy talks a bit too much. Funny, it's usually the other way round. Leidner himself is a delightful fellow—so modest and unassuming. Yes, individually they are all pleasant people. But somehow or other, I may have been fanciful, but the last time I went to see them I got a queer impression of something being wrong. I don't know what it was exactly. . . . Nobody seemed quite natural. There was a queer atmosphere of tension. I can explain best what I mean by saying that they all passed the butter to each other too politely."

Blushing a little, because I don't like airing my own opinions too much, I said:

"If people are too much cooped up together it's got a way of getting on their nerves. I know that myself from experience in hospital."

"That's true," said Major Kelsey, "but it's early in the season, hardly time for that particular irritation to have set in."

"An expedition is probably like our life here in miniature," said Major Pennyman. "It has its cliques and rivalries and jealousies."

"It sounds as though they'd got a good many new-comers this year," said Major Kelsey.

"Let me see." The squadron-leader counted them off on his fingers. "Young Coleman is new, so is Reiter. Emmott was out last year and so were the Mercados. Father Lavigny is a new-comer. He's come in place of Dr. Byrd, who was ill this year and couldn't come out. Carey, of course, is an old hand. He's been out ever since the beginning, five years ago. Miss Johnson's been out nearly as many years as Carey."

"I always thought they got on so well together at Tell Yarimjah," remarked Major Kelsey. "They seemed like a happy family—which is really surprising when one considers what human nature is! I'm sure Nurse Leatheran agrees with me."

"Well," I said. "I don't know that you're not right! The rows I've known in hospital and starting often from nothing more than a dispute about a pot of tea."

"Yes, one tends to get petty in close communities," said Major Pennyman. "All the same I feel there must be something more to it in this case. Leidner is such a gentle, unassuming man, with really a remarkable amount of tact. He's always managed to keep his expedition happy and on good terms with each other. And yet I *did* notice that feeling of tension the other day."

Mrs. Kelsey laughed.

"And you don't see the explanation? Why, it leaps to the eye!"

"What do you mean?"

"*Mrs.* Leidner, of course."

"Oh, come, Mary," said her husband, "she's a charming woman—not at all the quarrelsome kind."

"I didn't say she was quarrelsome. She *causes* quarrels!"

"In what way? And why should she?"

"Why? Why? Because she's bored. She's not an archæologist, only the wife of one. She's bored shut away from any excitements and so she provides her own drama. She amuses herself by setting other people by the ears."

"Mary, you don't know in the least. You're merely imagining."

"Of course I'm imagining! But you'll find I'm right. Lovely Louise doesn't look like the Mona Lisa for nothing! She mayn't mean any harm, but she likes to see what will happen."

"She's devoted to Leidner."

"Oh! I dare say. I'm not suggesting vulgar intrigues. But she's an *allumeuse,* that woman."

"Women are so sweet to each other," said Major Kelsey.

"I know. Cat, cat, cat, that's what you men say. But we're usually right about our own sex."

"All the same," said Major Pennyman thoughtfully, "assuming all Mrs. Kelsey's uncharitable surmises to be true, I don't think it would quite account for that curious sense of tension—rather like the feeling there is before a thunderstorm. I had the impression very strongly that the storm might break any minute."

"Now don't frighten nurse," said Mrs. Kelsey. "She's going there in three days' time and you'll put her right off."

"Oh, you won't frighten me," I said, laughing.

All the same I thought a good deal about what had been said. Dr. Leidner's curious use of the word "safer" recurred to me. Was it his wife's secret fear, unacknowledged or expressed perhaps, that was reacting on the rest of the party? Or was it the actual tension (or perhaps the unknown cause of it) that was reacting on *her* nerves?

I looked up the word "allumeuse" that Mrs. Kelsey had used in a dictionary, but couldn't get any sense out of it.

"Well," I thought to myself, "I must wait and see."

CHAPTER IV

I ARRIVE IN HASSANIEH

THREE DAYS LATER I left Baghdad.

I was sorry to leave Mrs. Kelsey and the baby, who was a little love and was thriving splendidly, gaining her proper number of ounces every week. Major Kelsey took me to the station and saw me off. I should arrive at Kirkuk the following morning, and there some one was to meet me.

I slept badly. I never sleep very well in a train and I was troubled by dreams.

The next morning, however, when I looked out of the window it was a lovely day and I felt interested and curious about the people I was going to see.

As I stood on the platform hesitating and looking about me I saw a young man coming towards me. He had a round pink face, and really, in all my life, I have never seen any one who seemed so exactly like a young man out of one of Mr. P. G. Wodehouse's books.

"Hallo, 'allo, 'allo," he said. "Are you Nurse Leatheran? Well, I mean you must be—I can see that. Ha ha! My name's Coleman. Dr. Leidner sent me along. How are you feeling? Beastly journey and all that? Don't I know these trains! Well, here we are—had any breakfast? This your kit? I say, awfully modest, aren't you? Mrs. Leidner has four suitcases and a trunk—to say nothing of a hat-box and a patent pillow, and this, that and the other. Am I talking too much? Come along to the old bus."

There was what I heard called later a station wagon waiting outside. It was a little like a wagonette, a little like a lorry and a little like a car. Mr. Coleman helped me in, explaining that I had better sit next to the driver so as to get less jolting.

Jolting! I wonder the whole contraption didn't fall to pieces! And nothing like a road—just a sort of track all ruts and holes. Glorious East indeed! When I thought of our splendid arterial roads in England it made me quite homesick.

Mr. Coleman leaned forward from his seat behind me and yelled in my ear a good deal.

"Track's in pretty good condition," he shouted just after we had all been thrown up in our seats till we nearly touched the roof.

And apparently he was speaking quite seriously.

"Very good for you—jogs the liver," he said. "You ought to know that, nurse."

"A stimulated liver won't be much good to me if my head's split open," I observed tartly.

"You should come along here after it's rained! The skids are glorious. Most of the time one's going sideways."

To this I did not respond.

Presently we had to cross the river, which we did on the craziest ferry-boat you can imagine. To my mind it was a mercy we ever got across, but every one seemed to think it was quite usual.

It took us about four hours to get to Hassanieh, which, to my surprise, was quite a big place. Very pretty it looked, too, before we got there from the other side of the river—standing up quite white and fairy-like with minarets. It was a bit different, though, when one had crossed the bridge and come right into it. Such a smell, and everything ramshackle and tumble-down, and mud and mess everywhere.

Mr. Coleman took me to Dr. Reilly's house, where, he said, the doctor was expecting me to lunch.

Dr. Reilly was just as nice as ever, and his house was nice too, with a bathroom and everything spick and span. I had a nice bath, and by the time I got back into my uniform and came down I was feeling fine.

Lunch was just ready and we went in, the doctor apologizing for his daughter, whom he said was always late.

We'd just had a very good dish of eggs in sauce when she came in and Dr. Reilly said, "Nurse, this is my daughter Sheila."

She shook hands, hoped I'd had a good journey, tossed off her hat, gave a cool nod to Mr. Coleman and sat down.

"Well, Bill," she said. "How's everything?"

He began to talk to her about some party or other that was to come off at the club, and I took stock of her.

I can't say I took to her much. A thought too cool for my liking. An off-hand sort of girl, though good-looking. Black hair and blue eyes—a pale sort of face and the usual lip-sticked mouth. She'd a cool, sarcastic way of talking that rather annoyed me. I had a probationer like her under me once—a girl who worked well, I'll admit, but whose manner always riled me.

It looked to me rather as though Mr. Coleman was gone on her. He stammered a bit, and his conversation became slightly more idiotic than it was before, if that was possible! He reminded me of a large stupid dog wagging its tail and trying to please.

After lunch Dr. Reilly went off to the hospital, and Mr. Coleman had some things to get in the town, and Miss Reilly asked me whether I'd like to see round the town a bit or whether I'd rather stop in the house. Mr. Coleman, she said, would be back to fetch me in about an hour.

"Is there anything to see?" I asked.

"There are some picturesque corners," said Miss Reilly. "But I don't know that you'd care for them. They're extremely dirty."

The way she said it rather nettled me. I've never been able to see that picturesqueness excuses dirt.

In the end she took me to the club, which was pleasant enough, overlooking the river, and there were English papers and magazines there.

When we got back to the house Mr. Coleman wasn't there yet, so we sat down and talked a bit. It wasn't easy somehow.

She asked me if I'd met Mrs. Leidner yet.

"No," I said. "Only her husband."

"Oh," she said. "I wonder what you'll think of her?"

I didn't say anything to that. And she went on:

"I like Dr. Leidner very much. Everybody likes him."

That's as good as saying, I thought, that you don't like his wife. I still didn't say anything and presently she asked abruptly:

"What's the matter with her? Did Dr. Leidner tell you?"

I wasn't going to start gossiping about a patient before I got there even, so I said evasively:

"I understand she's a bit run down and wants looking after."

She laughed—a nasty sort of laugh—hard and abrupt.

"Good God," she said. "Aren't nine people looking after her already enough?"

"I suppose they've all got their work to do," I said.

"Work to do? Of course they've got work to do. But Louise comes first—she sees to that all right."

"No," I said to myself. "You *don't* like her."

"All the same," went on Miss Reilly, "I don't see what she wants with a professional hospital nurse. I should have thought amateur assistance was more in her line; not some one who'll jam a thermometer in her mouth, and count her pulse and bring everything down to hard facts."

Well, I must admit it, I was curious.

"You think there's nothing the matter with her?" I asked.

"Of course there's nothing the matter with her! The woman's as strong as an ox. 'Dear Louise hasn't slept.' 'She's got black circles under her eyes.' Yes—put there with a blue pencil! Anything to get attention, to have everybody hovering round her, making a fuss of her!"

There was something in that, of course. I had (what nurse hasn't?) come across many cases of hypochondriacs whose delight it is to keep a whole household dancing attendance. And if a doctor or a nurse were to say to them, "There's nothing on earth the matter with you!" well, to begin with they wouldn't believe it, and their indignation would be as genuine as indignation can be.

Of course it was quite possible that Mrs. Leidner might be a case of this kind. The husband, naturally, would be the first to be deceived. Husbands, I've found, are a credulous lot where illness is concerned. But all the same, it didn't quite square with what I'd heard. It didn't, for instance, fit in with that word "safer."

Funny how that word had got kind of stuck in my mind.

Reflecting on it, I asked:

"Is Mrs. Leidner a nervous woman? Is she nervous, for instance, of living out far from anywhere?"

"What is there to be nervous of? Good heavens, there are ten of them! And they've got guards too—because of the antiquities. Oh, no, she's not nervous—at least—"

She seemed struck by some thought and stopped—going on slowly after a minute or two.

"It's odd your saying that."

"Why?"

"Flight-Lieutenant Jervis and I rode over the other day. It was in the morning. Most of them were up on the dig. She was sitting writing a letter and I suppose she didn't hear us coming. The boy who brings you in wasn't about for once, and we came straight up on to the verandah. Apparently she saw Flight-Lieutenant Jervis's shadow thrown on the wall—and she fairly screamed! Apologized, of course. Said she thought it was a strange man. A bit odd, that. I mean, even if it was a strange man, why get the wind up?"

I nodded thoughtfully.

Miss Reilly was silent, then burst out suddenly.

"I don't know what's the matter with them there this year. They've all got the jumps. Johnson goes about so glum she can't open her mouth. David never speaks if he can help it. Bill, of course, never stops, and somehow his chatter seems to make the others worse. Carey goes about looking as though something would snap any minute. And they all watch each other as though—as though— Oh, I don't know, but it's *queer*."

It was odd, I thought, that two such dissimilar people as Miss Reilly and Major Pennyman should have been struck in the same manner.

Just then Mr. Coleman came bustling in. Bustling was just the word for it. If his tongue had hung out and he had suddenly produced a tail to wag you wouldn't have been surprised.

"Hallo-allo," he said. "Absolutely the world's best shopper—that's me. Have you shown nurse all the beauties of the town?"

"She wasn't impressed," said Miss Reilly dryly.

"I don't blame her," said Mr. Coleman heartily. "Of all the one-horse tumble-down places!"

"Not a lover of the picturesque or the antique, are you, Bill? I can't think why you are an archæologist."

"Don't blame me for that. Blame my guardian. He's a learned bird —fellow of his college—browses among books in bedroom slippers—that kind of man. Bit of a shock for him to have a ward like me."

"I think it's frightfully stupid of you to be forced into a profession you don't care for," said the girl sharply.

"Not forced, Sheila, old girl, not forced. The old man asked if I had any special profession in mind, and I said I hadn't, and so he wangled a season out here for me."

"But haven't you any idea really what you'd *like* to do? You *must* have!"

"Of course I have. My idea would be to give work a miss altogether. What I'd like to do is to have plenty of money and go in for motor-racing."

"You're absurd!" said Miss Reilly.

She sounded quite angry.

"Oh, I realize that it's quite out of the question," said Mr. Coleman cheerfully. "So, if I've got to do something, I don't much care what it is so long as it isn't mugging in an office all day long. I was quite agreeable to seeing a bit of the world. Here goes, I said, and along I came."

"And a fat lot of use you must be, I expect!"

"There you're wrong. I can stand up on the dig and shout *'Y'Allah'* with anybody! And as a matter of fact I'm not so dusty at drawing. Imitating handwriting used to be my speciality at school. I'd have made a first-class forger. Oh, well, I may come to that yet. If my Rolls-Royce splashes you with mud as you're waiting for a bus, you'll know that I've taken to crime."

Miss Reilly said coldly:

"Don't you think it's about time you started instead of talking so much?"

"Hospitable, aren't we, nurse?"

"I'm sure Nurse Leatheran is anxious to get settled in."

"You're always sure of everything," retorted Mr. Coleman with a grin.

That was true enough, I thought. Cock-sure little minx.

I said dryly:

"Perhaps we'd better start, Mr. Coleman."

"Right you are, nurse."

I shook hands with Miss Reilly and thanked her, and we set off.

"Damned attractive girl, Sheila," said Mr. Coleman. "But always ticking a fellow off."

We drove out of the town and presently took a kind of track between green crops. It was very bumpy and full of ruts.

After about half an hour Mr. Coleman pointed to a big mound by the river bank ahead of us and said:

"Tell Yarimjah."

I could see little black figures moving about it like ants.

As I was looking they suddenly began to run all together down the side of the mound.

"Fidos," said Mr. Coleman. "Knocking off time. We knock off an hour before sunset."

The expedition house lay a little way back from the river.

The driver rounded a corner, bumped through an extremely narrow arch and there we were.

The house was built round a courtyard. Originally it had occupied only the south side of the courtyard with a few unimportant outbuildings on the east. The expedition had continued the building on the other two sides. As the plan of the house was to prove of special interest later, I append a rough sketch of it above.

All the rooms opened on to the courtyard, and most of the windows—the exception being in the original south building where there

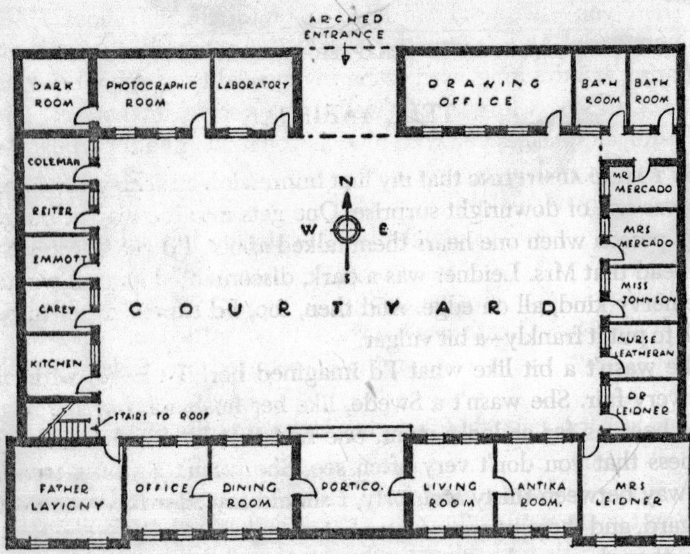

were windows giving on the outside country as well. These windows, however, were barred on the outside. In the south-west corner a staircase ran up to a long flat roof with a parapet running the length of the south side of the building which was higher than the other three sides.

Mr. Coleman led me along the east side of the courtyard and round to where a big open verandah occupied the centre of the south side. He pushed open a door at one side of it and we entered a room where several people were sitting round a tea table.

"Toodle-oodle-oo!" said Mr. Coleman. "Here's Sairey Gamp."

The lady who was sitting at the head of the table rose and came to greet me.

I had my first glimpse of Louise Leidner.

CHAPTER V

TELL YARIMJAH

I DON'T MIND ADMITTING that my first impression on seeing Mrs. Leidner was one of downright surprise. One gets into the way of imagining a person when one hears them talked about. I'd got it firmly into my head that Mrs. Leidner was a dark, discontented kind of woman. The nervy kind, all on edge. And then, too, I'd expected her to be—well, to put it frankly—a bit vulgar.

She wasn't a bit like what I'd imagined her! To begin with, she was very fair. She wasn't a Swede, like her husband, but she might have been as far as looks went. She had that blonde Scandinavian fairness that you don't very often see. She wasn't a young woman. Midway between thirty and forty, I should say. Her face was rather haggard, and there was some grey hair mingled with the fairness. Her eyes, though, were lovely. They were the only eyes I've ever come across that you might truly describe as violet. They were very large, and there were faint shadows underneath them. She was very thin and fragile-looking, and if I say that she had an air of intense weariness and was at the same time very much alive, it sounds like nonsense—but that's the feeling I got. I felt, too, that she was a lady through and through. And that means something—even nowadays.

She put out her hand and smiled. Her voice was low and soft with an American drawl in it.

"I'm so glad you've come, nurse. Will you have some tea? Or would you like to go to your room first?"

I said I'd have tea, and she introduced me to the people sitting round the table.

"This is Miss Johnson—and Mr. Reiter. Mrs. Mercado. Mr. Emmott. Father Lavigny. My husband will be in presently. Sit down here between Father Lavigny and Miss Johnson."

I did as I was bid and Miss Johnson began talking to me, asking about my journey and so on.

I liked her. She reminded me of a matron I'd had in my probationer days whom we had all admired and worked hard for.

She was getting on for fifty, I should judge, and rather mannish in appearance, with iron-grey hair cropped short. She had an abrupt, pleasant voice, rather deep in tone. She had an ugly rugged face with an almost laughably turned-up nose which she was in the habit of rubbing irritably when anything troubled or perplexed her. She wore a tweed coat and skirt made rather like a man's. She told me presently that she was a native of Yorkshire.

Father Lavigny I found just a bit alarming. He was a tall man with a great black beard and pince-nez. I had heard Mrs. Kelsey say that there was a French monk there, and I now saw that Father Lavigny was wearing a monk's robe of some white woollen material. It surprised me rather, because I always understood that monks went into monasteries and didn't come out again.

Mrs. Leidner talked to him mostly in French, but he spoke to me in quite fair English. I noticed that he had shrewd, observant eyes which darted about from face to face.

Opposite me were the other three. Mr. Reiter was a stout, fair young man with glasses. His hair was rather long and curly, and he had very round blue eyes. I should think he must have been a lovely baby, but he wasn't much to look at now! In fact he was just a little like a pig. The other young man had very short hair cropped close to his head. He had a long, rather humorous face and very good teeth, and he looked very attractive when he smiled. He said very little, though, just nodded if spoken to or answered in monosyllables. He, like Mr. Reiter, was an American. The last person was Mrs. Mercado, and I couldn't have a good look at her because whenever I glanced in her direction I always found her staring at me with a kind of hungry stare that was a bit disconcerting to say the least of it. You might have thought a hospital nurse was a strange animal the way she was looking at me. No manners at all!

She was quite young—not more than about twenty-five—and sort of dark and slinky-looking, if you know what I mean. Quite nice-looking in a kind of way, but rather as though she might have what my mother used to call "a touch of the tar-brush." She had on a very vivid pullover and her nails matched it in colour. She had a thin bird-like eager face with big eyes and rather a tight, suspicious mouth.

The tea was very good—a nice strong blend—not like the weak China stuff that Mrs. Kelsey always had and that had been a sore trial to me.

There was toast and jam and a plate of rock buns and a cutting cake. Mr. Emmott was very polite passing me things. Quiet as he was he always seemed to notice when my plate was empty.

Presently Mr. Coleman bustled in and took the place beyond Miss Johnson. There didn't seem to be anything the matter with *his* nerves. He talked away nineteen to the dozen.

Mrs. Leidner sighed once and cast a wearied look in his direction but it didn't have any effect. Nor did the fact that Mrs. Mercado, to whom he was addressing most of his conversation, was far too busy watching me to do more than make perfunctory replies.

Just as we were finishing, Dr. Leidner and Mr. Mercado came in from the dig.

Dr. Leidner greeted me in his nice kind manner. I saw his eyes go quickly and anxiously to his wife's face and he seemed to be relieved by what he saw there. Then he sat down at the other end of the table and Mr. Mercado sat down in the vacant place by Mrs. Leidner. He was a tall, thin, melancholy man, a good deal older than his wife, with a sallow complexion and a queer, soft, shapeless-looking beard. I was glad when he came in, for his wife stopped staring at me and transferred her attention to him, watching him with a kind of anxious impatience that I found rather odd. He himself stirred his tea dreamily and said nothing at all. A piece of cake lay untasted on his plate.

There was still one vacant place, and presently the door opened and a man came in.

The moment I saw Richard Carey I felt he was one of the handsomest men I'd seen for a long time—and yet I doubt if that were really so. To say a man is handsome and at the same time to say he looks like a death's head sounds a rank contradiction, and yet it was true. His head gave the effect of having the skin stretched unusually tightly over the bones—but they were beautiful bones. The lean line of jaw and temple and forehead was so sharply outlined that he reminded me of a bronze statue. Out of this lean brown face looked two of the brightest and most intensely blue eyes I have ever seen. He stood about six foot and was, I should imagine, a little under forty years of age.

Dr. Leidner said:

"This is Mr. Carey, our architect, nurse."

He murmured something in a pleasant, inaudible English voice and sat down by Mrs. Mercado.

Mrs. Leidner said:

"I'm afraid the tea is a little cold, Mr. Carey." He said:

"Oh, that's quite all right, Mrs. Leidner. My fault for being late. I wanted to finish plotting those walls."

Mrs. Mercado said, "Jam, Mr. Carey?"

Mr. Reiter pushed forward the toast.

And I remember Major Pennyman saying:

"I can explain best what I mean by saying that they all passed the butter to each other a shade too politely."

Yes, there was something a little odd about it. . . .

A shade formal. . . .

You'd have said it was a party of strangers—not people who had known each other—some of them—for quite a number of years.

CHAPTER VI

FIRST EVENING

AFTER TEA MRS. LEIDNER took me to show me my room.

Perhaps here I had better give a short description of the arrangement of the rooms. This was very simple and can easily be understood by a reference to the plan.

On either side of the big open porch were doors leading into the two principal rooms. That on the right led into the dining-room, where we had had tea. The one on the other side led into an exactly similar room (I have called it the living-room) which was used as a sitting-room and kind of informal workroom—that is, a certain amount of drawing (other than the strictly architectural) was done there, and the more delicate pieces of pottery were brought there to be pieced together. Through the living-room one passed into the antiquities-room where all the finds from the dig were brought in and stored on shelves and in pigeon-holes, and also laid out on big benches and tables. From the antika-room there was no exit save through the living-room.

Beyond the antika-room, but reached through a door which gave on the courtyard, was Mrs. Leidner's bedroom. This, like the other rooms on that side of the house, had a couple of barred windows looking out over the ploughed countryside. Round the corner next to Mrs. Leidner's room, but with no actual communicating door, was Dr. Leidner's room. This was the first of the rooms on the east side of the building. Next to it was the room that was to be mine. Next to me was Miss Johnson's, with Mr. and Mrs. Mercado's beyond. After that came two so-called bathrooms.

(When I once used that last term in the hearing of Dr. Reilly he laughed at me and said a bathroom was either a bathroom or not a bathroom! All the same, when you've got used to taps and proper plumbing, it seems strange to call a couple of mud-rooms with a tin hip-bath in each of them, and muddy water brought in kerosene tins, *bathrooms!*)

All this side of the building had been added by Dr. Leidner to the original Arab house. The bedrooms were all the same, each with a window and a door giving on to the courtyard.

Along the north side were the drawing-office, the laboratory and the photographic rooms.

To return to the verandah, the arrangement of rooms was much the same on the other side. There was the dining-room leading into the office where the files were kept and the cataloguing and typing were done. Corresponding to Mrs. Leidner's room was that of Father Lavigny, who was given the largest bedroom; he used it also for the decoding—or whatever you call it—of tablets.

In the south-west corner was the staircase running up to the roof. On the west side were first the kitchen quarters and then four small bedrooms used by the young men—Carey, Emmott, Reiter and Coleman.

At the north-west corner was the photographic-room with the dark-room leading out of it. Next to that the laboratory. Then came the only entrance—the big arched doorway through which we had entered. Outside were sleeping quarters for the native servants, the guard-house for the soldiers, and stables, etc., for the water horses. The drawing-office was to the right of the archway occupying the rest of the north side.

I have gone into the arrangements of the house rather fully here because I don't want to have to go over them again later.

As I say, Mrs. Leidner herself took me round the building and finally established me in my bedroom, hoping that I should be comfortable and have everything I wanted.

The room was nicely though plainly furnished—a bed, a chest of drawers, a wash-stand and a chair.

"The boys will bring you hot water before lunch and dinner—and in the morning, of course. If you want it any other time, go outside and clap your hands, and when the boy comes say, *jib mai' har*. Do you think you can remember that?"

I said I thought so and repeated it a little haltingly.

"That's right. And be sure and shout it. Arabs don't understand anything said in an ordinary 'English' voice."

"Languages are funny things," I said. "It seems odd there should be such a lot of different ones."

Mrs. Leidner smiled.

"There is a church in Palestine in which the Lord's Prayer is written up in—ninety, I think it is—different languages."

"Well!" I said, "I must write and tell my old aunt that. She *will* be interested."

Mrs. Leidner fingered the jug and basin absently and shifted the soap-dish an inch or two.

"I do hope you'll be happy here," she said. "And not get too bored."

"I'm not often bored," I assured her. "Life's not long enough for that."

She did not answer. She continued to toy with the wash-stand as though abstracted.

Suddenly she fixed her dark violet eyes on my face.

"What exactly did my husband tell you, nurse?"

Well, one usually says the same thing to a question of that kind.

"I gathered you were a bit run-down and all that, Mrs. Leidner," I said glibly. "And that you just wanted some one to look after you and take any worries off your hands."

She bent her head slowly and thoughtfully.

"Yes," she said. "Yes—that will do very well."

That was just a little bit enigmatic, but I wasn't going to question it. Instead I said:

"I hope you'll let me help you with anything there is to do in the house. You mustn't let me be idle."

She smiled a little.

"Thank you, nurse."

Then she sat down on the bed and, rather to my surprise, began to cross-question me rather closely. I say rather to my surprise because, from the moment I set eyes on her, I felt sure that Mrs. Leidner was a lady. And a lady, in my experience, very seldom displays curiosity about one's private affairs.

But Mrs. Leidner seemed anxious to know everything there was to know about me. Where I'd trained and how long ago. What had brought me out to the East. How it had come about that Dr. Reilly had recommended me. She even asked me if I had ever been in America or had any relations in America. One or two other questions she asked me that seemed quite purposeless at the time, but of which I saw the significance later.

Then, suddenly, her manner changed. She smiled—a warm sunny smile—and she said, very sweetly, that she was very glad I had come and that she was sure I was going to be a comfort to her.

She got up from the bed and said:

"Would you like to come up to the roof and see the sunset? It's usually very lovely about this time."

I agreed willingly.

As we went out of the room she asked:

"Were there many other people on the train from Baghdad? Any men?"

I said that I hadn't noticed anybody in particular. There had been two Frenchmen in the restaurant-car the night before. And a party of three men who I gathered from their conversation had to do with the Pipe line.

She nodded and a faint sound escaped her. It sounded like a small sigh of relief.

We went up to the roof together.

Mrs. Mercado was there, sitting on the parapet, and Dr. Leidner was bending over looking at a lot of stones and broken pottery that were laid out in rows. There were big things he called querns, and pestles and celts and stone axes, and more broken bits of pottery with queer patterns on them than I've ever seen all at once.

"Come over here," called out Mrs. Mercado. "Isn't it *too,* too beautiful?"

It certainly was a beautiful sunset. Hassanieh in the distance looked quite fairy-like with the setting sun behind it, and the River Tigris flowing between its wide banks looked like a dream river rather than a real one.

"Isn't it lovely, Eric?" said Mrs. Leidner.

The doctor looked up with abstracted eyes, murmured, "Lovely, lovely," perfunctorily and went on sorting potsherds.

Mrs. Leidner smiled and said:

"Archæologists only look at what lies beneath their feet. The sky and the heavens don't exist for them."

Mrs. Mercado giggled.

"Oh, they're very queer people—you'll soon find *that* out, nurse," she said.

She paused and then added:

"We are all *so* glad you've come. We've been so very worried about our dear Mrs. Leidner, haven't we, Louise?"

"Have you?"

Her voice was not encouraging.

"Oh, yes. She really has been *very* bad, nurse. All sorts of alarms and excursions. You know when anybody says to me of some one 'It's just nerves,' I always say: But what could be *worse?* Nerves are the core and centre of one's being, aren't they?"

"Puss, puss," I thought to myself.

Mrs. Leidner said dryly:

"Well, you needn't be worried about me any more, Marie. Nurse is going to look after me."

"Certainly I am," I said cheerfully.

"I'm sure that will make all the difference," said Mrs. Mercado. "We've all felt that she ought to see a doctor or do *something*. Her nerves have really been all to pieces, haven't they, Louise dear?"

"So much so that I seem to have got on *your* nerves with them," said Mrs. Leidner. "Shall we talk about something more interesting than my wretched ailments?"

I understood then that Mrs. Leidner was the sort of woman who could easily make enemies. There was a cool rudeness in her tone (not that I blamed her for it) which brought a flush to Mrs. Mercado's rather sallow cheeks. She stammered out something, but Mrs. Leidner had risen and had joined her husband at the other end of the roof. I doubt if he heard her coming till she laid her hand on his shoulder, then he looked up quickly. There was affection and a kind of eager questioning in his face.

Mrs. Leidner nodded her head gently. Presently, her arm through his, they wandered to the far parapet and finally down the steps together.

"He's devoted to her, isn't he?" said Mrs. Mercado.

"Yes," I said. "It's very nice to see."

She was looking at me with a queer, rather eager sidelong glance.

"What do you think is really the matter with her, nurse?" she asked, lowering her voice a little.

"Oh, I don't suppose it's much," I said cheerfully. "Just a bit run-down, I expect."

Her eyes still bored into me as they had done at tea. She said abruptly:

"Are you a mental nurse?"

"Oh, dear no!" I said. "What made you think that?"

She was silent for a moment, then she said:

"Do you know how queer she's been? Did Dr. Leidner tell you?"

I don't hold with gossiping about my cases. On the other hand, it's my experience that it's often very hard to get the truth out of the relatives, and until you know the truth you're often working in the dark and doing no good. Of course, when there's a doctor in charge, it's different. He tells you what it's necessary for you to know. But in this case there wasn't a doctor in charge. Dr. Reilly had never been called in professionally. And in my own mind I wasn't at all sure that Dr. Leidner had told me all he could have done. It's often the husband's instinct to be reticent—and more honour to him, I say. But all the same, the more I knew the better I could tell which line to take. Mrs. Mercado (whom I put down in my own mind as a thoroughly spiteful little cat) was clearly dying to talk. And frankly, on the human side as well as the professional, I wanted to hear what she had to say. You can put it that I was just every-day curious if you like.

I said, "I gather Mrs. Leidner's not been quite her normal self lately?"

Mrs. Mercado laughed disagreeably.

"Normal? I should say not. Frightening us to death. One night it was fingers tapping on her window. And then it was a hand without an arm attached. But when it came to a yellow face pressed against the window—and when she rushed to the window there was nothing there—well, I ask you, it *is* a bit creepy for all of us."

"Perhaps somebody was playing a trick on her," I suggested.

"Oh, no, she fancied it all. And only three days ago at dinner they were firing off shots in the village—nearly a mile away—and she jumped up and screamed out—it scared us all to death. As for Dr. Leidner, he rushed to her and behaved in the most ridiculous way. 'It's nothing, darling, it's nothing at all,' he kept saying. I think, you know, nurse, men sometimes *encourage* women in these hysterical fancies. It's a pity because it's a bad thing. Delusions shouldn't be encouraged."

"Not if they *are* delusions," I said dryly.

"What else could they be?"

I didn't answer because I didn't know what to say. It was a funny business. The shots and the screaming were natural enough—for any one in a nervous condition, that is. But this queer story of a spectral face and hand was different. It looked to me like one of two things—either Mrs. Leidner had made the story up (exactly as a child shows off by telling lies about something that never happened in order to make herself the centre of attraction) or else it was, as I had suggested, a deliberate practical joke. It was the sort of thing, I reflected, that an unimaginative hearty sort of young fellow like Mr. Coleman might think very funny. I decided to keep a close watch on him. Nervous patients can be scared nearly out of their minds by a silly joke.

Mrs. Mercado said with a sideways glance at me.

"She's very romantic-looking, nurse, don't you think so? The sort of woman things *happen* to."

"Have many things happened to her?" I asked.

"Well, her first husband was killed in the war when she was only twenty. I think that's very pathetic and romantic, don't you?"

"It's one way of calling a goose a swan," I said dryly.

"Oh! nurse. What an extraordinary remark!"

It was really a very true one. The amount of women you hear say, 'If Donald—or Arthur—or whatever his name was—had *only* lived." And I sometimes think but if he had, he'd have been a stout, unromantic, short-tempered, middle-aged husband as likely as not.

It was getting dark and I suggested that we should go down. Mrs. Mercado agreed and asked if I would like to see the laboratory. 'My husband will be there—working."

I said I would like to very much and we made our way there. The place was lighted by a lamp but it was empty. Mrs. Mercado showed me some of the apparatus and some copper ornaments that were being treated, and also some bones coated with wax.

"Where can Joseph be?" said Mrs. Mercado.

She looked into the drawing-office, where Carey was at work. He hardly looked up as we entered, and I was struck by the extraordinary look of strain on his face. It came to me suddenly: "This man is at the end of his tether. Very soon, something will snap." And I remembered somebody else had noticed that same tenseness about him.

As we went out again I turned my head for one last look at him. He was bent over his paper, his lips pressed very closely together, and that "death's head" suggestion of his bones very strongly marked. Perhaps it was fanciful, but I thought that he looked like a knight of old who was going into battle and knew he was going to be killed.

And again I felt what an extraordinary and quite unconscious power of attraction he had.

We found Mr. Mercado in the living-room. He was explaining the idea of some new process to Mrs. Leidner. She was sitting on a straight wooden chair, embroidering flowers in fine silks, and I was struck anew by her strange, fragile, unearthly appearance. She looked a fairy creature more than flesh and blood.

Mrs. Mercado said, her voice high and shrill:

"Oh, *there* you are, Joseph. We thought we'd find you in the lab."

He jumped up looking startled and confused, as though her entrance had broken a spell. He said stammeringly:

"I—I must go now. I'm in the middle of—the middle of—"

He didn't complete the sentence but turned towards the door.

Mrs. Leidner said in her soft, drawling voice:

"You must finish telling me some other time. It was very interesting."

She looked up at us, smiled rather sweetly but in a far-away manner, and bent over her embroidery again.

In a minute or two she said:

"There are some books over there, nurse. We've got quite a good selection. Choose one and sit down."

I went over to the bookshelf. Mrs. Mercado stayed for a minute or two, then, turning abruptly, she went out. As she passed me I saw her face and I didn't like the look of it. She looked wild with fury.

In spite of myself I remembered some of the things Mrs. Kelsey had said and hinted about Mrs. Leidner. I didn't like to think they were true because I liked Mrs. Leidner, but I wondered, nevertheless, if there mightn't perhaps be a grain of truth behind them.

I didn't think it was all her fault, but the fact remained that dear ugly Miss Johnson, and that common little spitfire Mrs. Mercado couldn't hold a candle to her in looks or in attraction. And after all men are men all over the world. You soon see a lot of that in my profession.

Mercado was a poor fish, and I don't suppose Mrs. Leidner really cared two hoots for his admiration—but his wife cared. If I wasn't mistaken, she minded badly and would be quite willing to do Mrs. Leidner a bad turn if she could.

I looked at Mrs. Leidner sitting there and sewing at her pretty flowers, so remote and far away and aloof. I felt somehow I ought to warn her. I felt that perhaps she didn't know how stupid and unreasoning and violent jealousy and hate can be—and how little it takes to set them smouldering.

And then I said to myself, "Amy Leatheran, you're a fool. Mrs. Leidner's no chicken. She's close on forty if she's a day, and she must know all about life there is to know."

But I felt that all the same perhaps she didn't.

She had such a queer untouched look.

I began to wonder what her life had been. I knew she'd only married Dr. Leidner two years ago. And according to Mrs. Mercado her first husband had died nearly twenty years ago.

I came and sat down near her with a book, and presently I went and washed my hands for supper. It was a good meal—some really excellent curry. They all went to bed early and I was glad for I was tired.

Dr. Leidner came with me to my room to see I had all I wanted. He gave me a warm handclasp and said eagerly:

"She likes you, nurse. She's taken to you at once. I'm so glad. I feel everything's going to be all right now."

His eagerness was almost boyish.

I felt, too, that Mrs. Leidner had taken a liking to me, and I was pleased it should be so.

But I didn't quite share his confidence. I felt, somehow, that there was more to it all than he himself might know.

There was *something*—something I couldn't get at. But I felt it in he air.

My bed was comfortable, but I didn't sleep well for all that. I lreamt too much.

The words of a poem by Keats, that I'd had to learn as a child, kept running through my head. I kept getting them wrong and it vorried me. It was a poem I'd always hated—I suppose because I'd nad to learn it whether I wanted to or not. But somehow when I voke up in the dark I saw a sort of beauty in it for the first time.

"*Oh, say what ails thee, knight at arms, alone—and* (what was t?)*—palely loitering* . . . ?" I saw the knight's face in my mind for he first time—and it was Mr. Carey's face—a grim, tense, bronzed ace like some of those poor young men I remembered as a girl luring the war . . . and I felt sorry for him—and then I fell off to leep again and I saw that the Belle Dame sans Merci was Mrs. Leidner and she was leaning sideways on a horse with an embroidery f flowers in her hands—and then the horse stumbled and everyvhere there were bones coated in wax, and I woke up all gooseesh and shivering, and told myself that curry never *had* agreed vith me at night.

CHAPTER VII

THE MAN AT THE WINDOW

I THINK I'D BETTER make it clear right away that there isn't going to be any local colour in this story. I don't know anything about archæology and I don't know that I very much want to. Messing about with people and places that are buried and done with doesn't make sense to me. Mr. Carey used to tell me that I hadn't got the archæological temperament and I've no doubt he was quite right.

The very first morning after my arrival Mr. Carey asked if I'd like to come and see the palace he was—*planning* I think he called it. Though how you can plan for a thing that's happened long ago I'm sure I don't know! Well, I said I'd like to, and to tell the truth, I was a bit excited about it. Nearly three thousand years old that palace was, it appeared. I wondered what sort of palaces they had in those days, and if it would be like the pictures I'd seen of Tutankhamen's tomb furniture. But would you believe it, there was nothing to see but *mud!* Dirty mud walls about two feet high—and that's all there was to it. Mr. Carey took me here and there telling me things—how this was the great court, and there were some chambers here and an upper storey and various other rooms that opened off the central court. And all I thought was, "But how does he *know?*" though, of course, I was too polite to say so. I can tell you it *was* a disappointment! The whole excavation looked like nothing but mud to me—no marble or gold or anything handsome—my aunt's house in Cricklewood would have made a much more imposing ruin! And those old Assyrians or whatever they were called themselves *kings.* When Mr Carey had shown me his old "palace," he handed me over to Father Lavigny, who showed me the rest of the mound. I was a little afraid of Father Lavigny, being a monk and a foreigner and having such a deep voice and all, but he was very kind—though rather vague Sometimes I felt it wasn't much more real to him than it was to me

Mrs. Leidner explained that later. She said that Father Lavigny was only interested in "written documents"—as she called them. They wrote everything on clay, these people, queer heathenish-looking marks too, but quite sensible. There were even school tablets—the teacher's lesson on one side and the pupil's effort on the back of it

I confess that that did interest me rather—it seemed so human, if you know what I mean.

Father Lavigny walked round the work with me and showed me what were temples or palaces and what were private houses, and also a place which he said was an early Akkadian cemetery. He spoke in a funny jerky way, just throwing in a scrap of information and then reverting to other subjects.

He said:

"It is strange that you have come here. Is Mrs. Leidner really ill, then?"

"Not exactly ill," I said cautiously.

He said:

"She is an odd woman. A dangerous woman, I think."

"Now what do you mean by that?" I said. "Dangerous? How dangerous?"

He shook his head thoughtfully.

"I think she is ruthless," he said. "Yes, I think she could be absolutely ruthless."

"If you'll excuse me," I said, "I think you're talking nonsense."

He shook his head.

"You do not know women as I do," he said.

And that was a funny thing, I thought, for a monk to say. But of course I suppose he might have heard a lot of things in confession. But that rather puzzled me, because I wasn't sure if monks heard confessions or if it was only priests. I supposed he *was* a monk with that long woollen robe—all sweeping up the dirt—and the rosary and all!

"Yes, she could be ruthless," he said musingly. "I am quite sure of that. And yet—though she is so hard—like stone, like marble—yet she is afraid. What is she afraid of?"

That, I thought, is what we should all like to know!

At least it was possible that her husband did know, but I didn't think any one else did.

He fixed me with a sudden bright, dark eye.

"It is odd here? You find it odd? Or quite natural?"

"Not quite natural," I said, considering. "It's comfortable enough as far as the arrangements go—but there isn't quite a comfortable feeling."

"It makes *me* uncomfortable. I have the idea"—he became suddenly a little more foreign—"that something prepares itself. Dr. Leidner, too, he is not quite himself. Something is worrying him also."

"His wife's health?"

"That perhaps. But there is more. There is—how shall I say it—an uneasiness."

And that was just it, there was an uneasiness.

We didn't say any more just then, for Dr. Leidner came towards us. He showed me a child's grave that had just been uncovered. Rather pathetic it was—the little bones—and a pot or two and some little specks that Dr. Leidner told me were a bead necklace.

It was the workmen that made me laugh. You never saw such a lot of scarecrows—all in long petticoats and rags, and their heads tied up as though they had toothache. And every now and then, as they went to and fro carrying away baskets of earth, they began to sing—at least I suppose it was meant to be singing—a queer sort of montonous chant that went on and on over and over again. I noticed that most of their eyes were terrible—all covered with discharge, and one or two looked half blind. I was just thinking what a miserable lot they were when Dr. Leidner said, "Rather a fine-looking lot of men, aren't they?" and I thought what a queer world it was and how two different people could see the same thing each of them the other way round. I haven't put that very well, but you can guess what I mean.

After a bit Dr. Leidner said he was going back to the house for a mid-morning cup of tea. So he and I walked back together and he told me things. When *he* explained, it was all quite different. I sort of *saw* it all—how it used to be—the streets and the houses, and he showed me ovens where they baked bread and said the Arabs used much the same kind of ovens nowadays.

We got back to the house and found Mrs. Leidner had got up. She was looking better to-day, not so thin and worn. Tea came in almost at once and Dr. Leidner told her what had turned up during the morning on the dig. Then he went back to work and Mrs. Leidner asked me if I would like to see some of the finds they had made up to date. Of course I said "Yes," so she took me through into the antika-room. There was a lot of stuff lying about—mostly broken pots it seemed to me—or else ones that were all mended and stuck together. The whole lot might have been thrown away, I thought.

"Dear, dear," I said, "it's a pity they're all so broken, isn't it? Are they really worth keeping?"

Mrs. Leidner smiled a little and she said:

"You mustn't let Eric hear you. Pots interest him more than anything else, and some of these are the oldest things we have—perhaps as much as seven thousand years old." And she explained how some of them came from a very deep cut on the mound down towards the bottom, and how, thousands of years ago, they had been broken and mended with bitumen, showing people prized their things just as much then as they do nowadays.

"And now," she said, "we'll show you something more exciting."

And she took down a box from the shelf and showed me a beautiful gold dagger with dark-blue stones in the handle.

I exclaimed with pleasure.

Mrs. Leidner laughed.

"Yes, everybody likes gold! Except my husband."

"Why doesn't Dr. Leidner like it?"

"Well, for one thing it comes expensive. You have to pay the workmen who find it the weight of the object in gold."

"Good gracious!" I exclaimed. "But why?"

"Oh, it's a custom. For one thing it prevents them from stealing. You see, if they *did* steal it wouldn't be for the archæological value but for the intrinsic value. They could melt it down. So we make it easy for them to be honest."

She took down another tray and showed me a really beautiful gold drinking-cup with a design of rams' heads on it.

Again I exclaimed.

"Yes, it is beautiful, isn't it? These came from a prince's grave. We found other royal graves but most of them had been plundered. This cup is our best find. It is one of the most lovely ever found anywhere. Early Akkadian. Unique."

Suddenly, with a frown, Mrs. Leidner brought the cup up close to her eyes and scratched at it delicately with her nail.

"How extraordinary! There's actually wax on it. Some one must have been in here with a candle."

She detached the little flake and replaced the cup in its place.

After that she showed me some queer little terra-cotta figurines —but most of them were just rude. Nasty minds those old people had, I say.

When we went back to the porch Mrs. Mercado was sitting polishing her nails. She was holding them out in front of her admiring the effect. I thought myself that anything more hideous than that orange red could hardly have been imagined.

Mrs. Leidner had brought with her from the antika-room a very delicate little saucer broken in several pieces, and this she now proceeded to join together. I watched her for a minute or two and then asked if I could help.

"Oh, yes, there are plenty more." She fetched quite a supply of broken pottery and we set to work. I soon got into the hang of it and she praised my ability. I suppose most nurses are handy with their fingers.

"How busy everybody is," said Mrs. Mercado. "It makes me feel dreadfully idle. Of course I *am* idle."

"Why shouldn't you be if you like?" said Mrs. Leidner.

Her voice was quite uninterested.

At twelve we had lunch. Afterwards Dr. Leidner and Mr. Mercado cleaned some pottery, pouring a solution of hydrochloric acid over it. One pot went a lovely plum colour and a pattern of bulls' horns came out on another one. It was really quite magical. All the dried mud that no washing would remove sort of foamed and boiled away.

Mr. Carey and Mr. Coleman went out on the dig and Mr. Reiter went off to the photographic room.

"What will you do, Louise?" Dr. Leidner asked his wife. "I suppose you'll rest for a bit?"

I gathered that Mrs. Leidner usually lay down every afternoon.

"I'll rest for about an hour. Then perhaps I'll go out for a short stroll."

"Good. Nurse will go with you, won't you?"

"Of course," I said.

"No, no," said Mrs. Leidner. "I like going alone. Nurse isn't to feel so much on duty that I'm not allowed out of her sight."

"Oh, but I'd like to come," I said.

"No, really, I'd rather you didn't." She was quite firm—almost peremptory. "I must be by myself every now and then. It's necessary to me."

I didn't insist, of course. But as I went off for a short sleep myself it struck me as odd that Mrs. Leidner, with her nervous terrors, should be quite content to walk by herself without any kind of protection.

When I came out of my room at half-past three the courtyard was deserted save for a little boy with a large copper bath who was washing pottery, and Mr. Emmott, who was sorting and arranging it. As I went towards them Mrs. Leidner came in through the archway.

She looked more alive than I had seen her yet. Her eyes shone and she looked uplifted and almost gay.

Dr. Leidner came out from the laboratory and joined her. He was showing her a big dish with bulls' horns on it.

"The prehistoric levels are being extraordinarily productive," he said. "It's been a good season so far. Finding that tomb right at the beginning was a real piece of luck. The only person who might complain is Father Lavigny. We've had hardly any tablets so far."

"He doesn't seem to have done very much with the few we have had," said Mrs. Leidner dryly. "He may be a very fine epigraphist but he's a remarkably lazy one. He spends all his afternoons sleeping."

"We miss Byrd," said Dr. Leidner. "This man strikes me as slightly unorthodox—though, of course, I'm not competent to judge. But one or two of his translations have been surprising to say the least of it. I can hardly believe, for instance, that he's right about that inscribed brick, and yet he must know."

After tea Mrs. Leidner asked me if I would like to stroll down to the river. I thought that perhaps she feared that her refusal to let me accompany her earlier in the afternoon might have hurt my feelings.

I wanted to her to know that I wasn't the touchy kind, so I accepted at once.

It was a lovely evening. A path led between barley fields and then through some flowering fruit trees. Finally we came to the edge of the Tigris. Immediately on our left was the Tell with the workmen singing in their queer monotonous chant. A little to our right was a big water-wheel which made a queer groaning noise. It used to set my teeth on edge at first. But in the end I got fond of it and it had a queer soothing effect on me. Beyond the water-wheel was the village from which most of the workmen came.

"It's rather beautiful, isn't it?" said Mrs. Leidner.

"It's very peaceful," I said. "It seems funny to me to be so far away from everywhere."

"Far from everywhere," repeated Mrs. Leidner. "Yes. Here at least one might expect to be safe."

I glanced at her sharply, but I think she was speaking more to herself than to me, and I don't think she realized that her words had been revealing.

We began to walk back to the house.

Suddenly Mrs. Leidner clutched my arm so violently that I nearly cried out.

"Who's that, nurse? What's he doing?"

Some little distance ahead of us, just where the path ran near the expedition house, a man was standing. He wore European clothes and he seemed to be standing on tiptoe and trying to look in at one of the windows.

As we watched he glanced round, caught sight of us, and immediately continued on the path towards us. I felt Mrs. Leidner's clutch tighten.

"Nurse," she whispered. "Nurse . . ."

"It's all right, my dear, it's all right," I said reassuringly.

The man came along and passed us. He was an Iraqi, and as soon as she saw him near to, Mrs. Leidner relaxed with a sigh.

"He's only an Iraqi after all," she said.

We went on our way. I glanced up at the windows as I passed. Not only were they barred, but they were too high from the ground to permit of any one seeing in, for the level of the ground was lower here than on the inside of the courtyard.

"It must have been just curiosity," I said.

Mrs. Leidner nodded.

"That's all. But just for a minute I thought—"

She broke off.

I thought to myself, "You thought *what?* That's what I'd like to know? *What* did you think?"

But I knew one thing now—that Mrs. Leidner was afraid of a definite flesh and blood person.

CHAPTER VIII

NIGHT ALARM

IT'S A LITTLE DIFFICULT to know exactly what to note in the week that followed my arrival at Tell Yarimjah.

Looking back as I do from my present standpoint of knowledge I can see a good many little signs and indications that I was quite blind to at the time.

To tell the story properly, however, I think I ought to try and recapture the point of view that I actually held—puzzled, uneasy, and increasingly conscious of *something* wrong.

For one thing *was* certain, that curious sense of strain and constraint was *not* imagined. It was genuine. Even Bill Coleman the insensitive commented upon it.

"This place gets under my skin," I heard him say. "Are they always such a glum lot?"

It was David Emmott to whom he spoke, the other assistant. I had taken rather a fancy to Mr. Emmott; his taciturnity was not, I felt sure, unfriendly. There was something about him that seemed very steadfast and reassuring in an atmosphere where one was uncertain what any one was feeling or thinking.

"No," he said in answer to Mr. Coleman. "It wasn't like this last year."

But he didn't enlarge on the theme, or say any more.

"What I can't make out is what it's all about," said Mr. Coleman in an aggrieved voice.

Emmott shrugged his shoulders but didn't answer.

I had a rather enlightening conversation with Miss Johnson. I liked her very much. She was capable, practical and intelligent. She had, it was quite obvious, a distinct hero worship for Dr. Leidner.

On this occasion she told me the story of his life since his young days. She knew every site he had dug, and the results of the dig. I would almost dare swear she could quote from every lecture he had ever delivered. She considered him, she told me, quite the finest field archæologist living.

"And he's so simple. So completely unworldly. He doesn't know the meaning of the word conceit. Only a really great man could be so simple."

"That's true enough," I said. "Big people don't need to throw their weight about."

"And he's so light-hearted too. I can't tell you what fun we used to have—he and Richard Carey and I—the first years we were out here. We were such a happy party. Richard Carey worked with him in Palestine, of course. Theirs is a friendship of ten years or so. Oh, well, I've known him for seven."

"What a handsome man Mr. Carey is," I said.

"Yes—I suppose he is."

She said it rather curtly.

"But he's just a little bit quiet, don't you think?"

"He usedn't to be like that," said Miss Johnson quickly. "It's only since—"

She stopped abruptly.

"Only since—?" I prompted.

"Oh, well." Miss Johnson gave a characteristic motion of her shoulders. "A good many things are changed nowadays."

I didn't answer. I hoped she would go on—and she did—prefacing her remarks with a little laugh as though to detract from their importance.

"I'm afraid I'm rather a conservative old fogy. I sometimes think that if an archæologist's wife isn't really interested, it would be wiser for her not to accompany the expedition. It often leads to friction."

"Mrs. Mercado—" I suggested.

"Oh, her!" Miss Johnson brushed the suggestion aside. "I was really thinking of Mrs. Leidner. She's a very charming woman—and one can quite understand why Dr. Leidner 'fell for her'—to use a slang term. But I can't help feeling she's out of place here. She—it unsettles things."

So Miss Johnson agreed with Mrs. Kelsey that it was Mrs. Leidner who was responsible for the strained atmosphere. But then where did Mrs. Leidner's own nervous fears come in?

"It unsettles *him*," said Miss Johnson earnestly. "Of course, I'm—well, I'm like a faithful but jealous old dog. I don't like to see him so worn out and worried. His whole mind ought to be on the work—not taken up with his wife and her silly fears! If she's nervous of coming to out-of-the-way places, she ought to have stayed in America. I've no patience with people who come to a place and then do nothing but grouse about it!"

And then, a little fearful of having said more than she meant to say, she went on:

"Of course I admire her very much. She's a lovely woman and she's got great charm of manner when she chooses."

And there the subject dropped.

I thought to myself that it was always the same way—wherever women are cooped up together, there's bound to be jealousy. Miss Johnson clearly didn't like her chief's wife (that was perhaps natural) and unless I was much mistaken Mrs. Mercado fairly hated her.

Another person who didn't like Mrs. Leidner was Sheila Reilly. She came out once or twice to the dig, once in a car and twice with some young man on a horse—on two horses I mean, of course. It was at the back of my mind that she had a weakness for the silent young American, Emmott. When he was on duty at the dig she used to stay talking to him, and I thought, too, that *he* admired *her*.

One day, rather injudiciously, I thought, Mrs. Leidner commented upon it at lunch.

"The Reilly girl is still hunting David down," she said with a little laugh. "Poor David, she chases you up on the dig even! How foolish girls are!"

Mr. Emmott didn't answer, but under his tan his face got rather red. He raised his eyes and looked right into hers with a very curious expression—a straight, steady glance with something of a challenge in it.

She smiled very faintly and looked away.

I heard Father Lavigny murmur something, but when I said "Pardon?" he merely shook his head and did not repeat his remark.

That afternoon Mr. Coleman said to me:

"Matter of fact I didn't like Mrs. L any too much at first. She used to jump down my throat every time I opened my mouth. But I've begun to understand her better now. She's one of the kindest women I've ever met. You find yourself telling her all the foolish scrapes you ever got into before you know where you are. She's got her knife into Sheila Reilly, I know, but then Sheila's been damned rude to her once or twice. That's the worst of Sheila—she's got no manners. And a temper like the devil!"

That I could well believe. Dr. Reilly spoilt her.

"Of course she's bound to get a bit full of herself, being the only young woman in the place. But that doesn't excuse her talking to Mrs. Leidner as though Mrs. Leidner were her great-aunt. Mrs. L's not exactly a chicken, but she's a damned good-looking woman. Rather like those fairy women who come out of marshes with lights and lure you away." He added bitterly, "You wouldn't find Sheila luring any one. All she does is to tick a fellow off."

I only remember two other incidents of any kind of significance. One was when I went to the laboratory to fetch some acetone to get the stickiness off my fingers from mending the pottery. Mr. Mercado was sitting in a corner, his head was laid down on his arms and I fancied he was asleep. I took the bottle I wanted and went off with it.

That evening, to my great surprise, Mrs. Mercado tackled me.

"Did you take a bottle of acetone from the lab?"

"Yes," I said. "I did."

"You know perfectly well that there's a small bottle always kept in the antika-room."

She spoke quite angrily.

"Is there? I didn't know."

"I think you did! You just wanted to come spying round. I know what hospital nurses are."

I stared at her.

"I don't know what you're talking about, Mrs. Mercado," I said with dignity. "I'm sure I don't want to spy on any one."

"Oh, no! Of course not. Do you think I don't know what you're here for?"

Really, for a minute or two I thought she must have been drinking. I went away without saying any more. But I thought it was very odd.

The other thing was nothing very much. I was trying to entice a pi dog pup with a piece of bread. It was very timid, however, like all Arab dogs—and was convinced I meant no good. It slunk away and I followed it—out through the archway and round the corner of the house. I came round so sharply that before I knew I had cannoned into Father Lavingy and another man who were standing together—and in a minute I realized that the second man was the same one Mrs. Leidner and I had noticed that day trying to peer through the window.

I apologized and Father Lavigny smiled, and with a word of farewell greeting to the other man he returned to the house with me.

"You know," he said, "I am very ashamed. I am a student of Oriental languages and none of the men on the work can understand me! It is humiliating, do you not think? I was trying my Arabic on that man, who is a townsman, to see if I got on better—but it still wasn't very successful. Leidner says my Arabic is too pure."

That was all. But it just passed through my head that it was odd the same man should still be hanging round the house.

That night we had a scare.

It must have been about two in the morning. I'm a light sleeper, as most nurses have to be. I was awake and sitting up in bed by the time that my door opened.

"Nurse, nurse!"

It was Mrs. Leidner's voice, low and urgent.

I struck a match and lighted the candle.

She was standing by the door in a long blue dressing-gown. She was looking petrified with terror.

"There's some one—some one—in the room next to mine. . . . I heard him—scratching on the wall."

I jumped out of bed and came to her.

"It's all right," I said. "I'm here. Don't be afraid, my dear."

She whispered:

"Get Eric."

I nodded and ran out and knocked on his door. In a minute he was with us. Mrs. Leidner was sitting on my bed, her breath coming in great gasps.

"I heard him," she said. "I heard him—scratching on the wall."

"Some one in the antika-room?" cried Dr. Leidner.

He ran out quickly—and it just flashed across my mind how differently these two had reacted. Mrs. Leidner's fear was entirely personal, but Dr. Leidner's mind leaped at once to his precious treasures.

"The antika-room!" breathed Mrs. Leidner. "Of course! How stupid of me."

And rising and pulling her gown round her, she bade me come with her. All traces of her panic-stricken fear had vanished.

We arrived in the antika-room to find Dr. Leidner and Father Lavigny. The latter had also heard a noise, had risen to investigate, and had fancied he saw a light in the antika-room. He had delayed to put on slippers and snatch up a torch and had found no one by the time he got there. The door, moreover, was duly locked, as it was supposed to be at night.

Whilst he was assuring himself that nothing had been taken, Dr. Leidner had joined him.

Nothing more was to be learned. The outside archway door was locked. The guard swore nobody could have got in from outside, but as they had probably been fast asleep this was not conclusive. There were no marks or traces of an intruder and nothing had been taken.

It was possible that what had alarmed Mrs. Leidner was the noise made by Father Lavigny taking down boxes from the shelves to assure himself that all was in order.

On the other hand, Father Lavigny himself was positive that he had (*a*) heard footsteps passing his window and (*b*) seen the flicker of a light, possibly a torch, in the antika-room.

Nobody else had heard or seen anything.

The incident is of value in my narrative because it led to Mrs. Leidner's unburdening herself to me on the following day.

CHAPTER IX

MRS. LEIDNER'S STORY

We had just finished lunch. Mrs. Leidner went to her room to rest as usual. I settled her on her bed with plenty of pillows and her book, and was leaving the room when she called me back.

"Don't go, nurse, there's something I want to say to you."

I came back into the room.

"Shut the door."

I obeyed.

She got up from the bed and began to walk up and down the room. I could see that she was making up her mind to something and I didn't like to interrupt her. She was clearly in great indecision of mind.

At last she seemed to have nerved herself to the required point. She turned to me and said abruptly:

"Sit down."

I sat down by the table very quietly. She began nervously:

"You must have wondered what all this is about?"

I just nodded without saying anything.

"I've made up my mind to tell you—everything! I must tell some one or I shall go mad."

"Well," I said. "I think really it would be just as well. It's not easy to know the best thing to do when one's kept in the dark."

She stopped in her uneasy walk and faced me.

"Do you know what I'm frightened of?"

"Some man," I said.

"Yes—but I didn't say whom—I said what."

I waited.

She said:

"*I'm afraid of being killed!*"

Well, it was out now. I wasn't going to show any particular concern. She was near enough hysterics as it was.

"Dear me," I said. "So that's it, is it?"

Then she began to laugh. She laughed and she laughed—and the tears ran down her face.

"The way you said that!" she gasped. "The way you said it . . ."

"Now, now," I said. "This won't do." I spoke sharply. I pushed her into a chair, went over to the wash-stand and got a cold sponge and bathed her forehead and wrists.

"No more nonsense," I said. "Tell me calmly and sensibly all about it."

That stopped her. She sat up and spoke in her natural voice.

"You're a treasure, nurse," she said. "You make me feel as though I'm six. I'm going to tell you."

"That's right," I said. "Take your time and don't hurry."

She began to speak, slowly and deliberately.

"When I was a girl of twenty I married. A young man in one of our state departments. It was in 1918."

"I know," I said. "Mrs. Mercado told me. He was killed in the war."

But Mrs. Leidner shook her head.

"That's what she thinks. That's what everybody thinks. The truth is something quite different. I was a queer patriotic, enthusiastic girl, nurse, full of idealism. When I'd been married a few months I discovered—by a quite unforeseeable accident—that my husband was a spy in German pay. I learned that the information supplied by him had led directly to the sinking of an American transport and the loss of hundreds of lives. I don't know what most people would have done. . . . But I'll tell you what I did. I went straight to my father, who was in the War Department, and told him the truth. Frederick *was* killed in the war—but he was killed in America—shot as a spy."

"Oh, dear, dear!" I ejaculated. "How terrible!"

"Yes," she said. "It was terrible. He was so kind, too—so gentle. . . . And all the time . . . But I never hesitated. Perhaps I was wrong."

"It's difficult to say," I said. "I'm sure I don't know what one would do."

"What I'm telling you was never generally known outside the state departments. Ostensibly my husband had gone to the front and had been killed. I had a lot of sympathy and kindness shown me as a war widow."

Her voice was bitter and I nodded comprehendingly.

"Lots of people wanted to marry me, but I always refused. I'd had too bad a shock. I didn't feel I could ever *trust* any one again."

"Yes, I can imagine feeling like that."

"And then I became very fond of a certain young man. I wavered.

An amazing thing happened! I got an anonymous letter—from Frederick—saying that if I ever married another man, he'd kill me!"

"From Frederick? From your dead husband?"

"Yes. Of course, I thought at first I was mad or dreaming. . . . At last I went to my father. He told me the truth. My husband hadn't been shot after all. He'd escaped—but his escape did him no good. He was involved in a train wreck a few weeks later and his dead body was found amongst others. My father had kept the fact of his escape from me, and since the man had died anyway he had seen no reason to tell me anything until now.

"But the letter I received opened up entirely new possibilities. Was it perhaps a fact that my husband was still alive?

"My father went into the matter as carefully as possible. And he declared that as far as one could humanly be sure the body that was buried as Frederick's *was* Frederick's. There had been a certain amount of disfiguration, so that he could not speak with absolute cast-iron certainty, but he reiterated his solemn belief that Frederick was dead and that this letter was a cruel and malicious hoax.

"The same thing happened more than once. If I seemed to be on intimate terms with any man, I would receive a threatening letter."

"In your husband's handwriting?"

She said slowly:

"That is difficult to say. I had no letters of his. I had only my memory to go by."

"There was no allusion or special form of words used that could make you sure?"

"No. There *were* certain terms—nicknames, for instance—private between us—if one of those had been used or quoted, then I should have been quite sure."

"Yes," I said thoughtfully. "That is odd. It looks as though it *wasn't* your husband. But is there any one else it could be?"

"There is a possibility. Frederick had a younger brother—a boy of ten or twelve at the time of our marriage. He worshipped Frederick and Frederick was devoted to him. What happened to this boy, William his name was, I don't know. It seems to me possible that, adoring his brother as fanatically as he did, he may have grown up regarding me as directly responsible for his death. He had always been jealous of me and may have invented this scheme by way of punishment."

"It's possible," I said. "It's amazing the way children do remember if they've had a shock."

"I know. This boy may have dedicated his life to revenge."

"Please go on."

"There isn't very much more to tell. I met Eric three years ago. I meant never to marry. Eric made me change my mind. Right up to our wedding day I waited for another threatening letter. None came. I decided that whoever the writer might be, he was either dead, or tired of his cruel sport. *Two days after our marriage I got this.*"

Drawing a small attaché-case which was on the table towards her, she unlocked it, took out a letter and handed it to me.

The ink was slightly faded. It was written in a rather womanish hand with a forward slant.

You have disobeyed. Now you cannot escape. You must be Frederick Bosner's wife only! You have got to die.

"I was frightened—but not so much as I might have been to begin with. Being with Eric made me feel safe. Then, a month later, I got a second letter."

I have not forgotten. I am making my plans. You have got to die. Why did you disobey?

"Does your husband know about this?"

Mrs. Leidner answered slowly.

"He knows that I am threatened. I showed him both letters when the second one came. He was inclined to think the whole thing a hoax. He thought also that it might be some one who wanted to blackmail me by pretending my first husband was alive."

She paused and then went on.

"A few days after I received the second letter we had a narrow escape from death by gas poisoning. Somebody entered our apartment after we were asleep and turned on the gas. Luckily I woke and smelled the gas in time. Then I lost my nerve. I told Eric how I had been persecuted for years, and I told him that I was sure this madman, whoever he might be, did really mean to kill me. I think that for the first time I really did think it *was* Frederick. There was always something a little ruthless behind his gentleness.

"Eric was still, I think, less alarmed than I was. He wanted to go to the police. Naturally I wouldn't hear of that. In the end we agreed that I should accompany him here, and that it might be wise if

I didn't return to America in the summer but stayed in London and Paris.

"We carried out our plan and all went well. I felt sure that now everything would be all right. After all, we had put half the globe between ourselves and my enemy.

"And then—a little over three weeks ago—I received a letter—with an Iraq stamp on it."

She handed me a third letter.

You thought you could escape. You were wrong. You shall not be false to me and live. I have always told you so. Death is coming very soon.

"And a week ago—*this!* Just lying on the table here. It had not even gone through the post."

I took the sheet of paper from her. There was just one phrase scrawled across it.

I have arrived.

She stared at me.

"You see? You understand? He's going to kill me. It may be Frederick—it may be little William—*but he's going to kill me.*"

Her voice rose shudderingly. I caught her wrist.

"Now—now," I said warningly. "Don't give way. We'll look after you. Have you got any sal volatile?"

She nodded towards the wash-stand and I gave her a good dose.

"That's better," I said, as the colour returned to her cheeks.

"Yes, I'm better now. But oh, nurse, do you see why I'm in this state. When I saw that man looking in through my window, I thought: *He's come*. . . . Even when *you* arrived I was suspicious. I thought you might be a man in disguise—"

"The idea!"

"Oh, I know it sounds absurd. But you might have been in league with him perhaps—not a hospital nurse at all."

"But that's nonsense!"

"Yes, perhaps. But I've got beyond sense."

Struck by a sudden idea, I said:

"You'd *recognize* your husband, I suppose?"

She answered slowly.

"I don't even know that. It's over fifteen years ago. I mightn't recognize his face."

Then she shivered.

"I saw it one night—but it was a *dead* face. There was a tap, tap,

tap on the window. And then I saw a face, a dead face, ghastly and grinning against the pane. I screamed and screamed. . . . And they said there wasn't anything there!"

I remembered Mrs. Mercado's story.

"You don't think," I said hesitatingly, "that you *dreamt* that?"

"I'm sure I didn't!"

I wasn't so sure. It was the kind of nightmare that was quite likely under the circumstances and that easily might be taken for a waking occurrence. However, I never contradict a patient. I soothed Mrs. Leidner as best I could and pointed out that if any stranger arrived in the neighbourhood it was pretty sure to be known.

I left her, I think, a little comforted, and I went in search of Dr. Leidner and told him of our conversation.

"I'm glad she's told you," he said simply. "It has worried me dreadfully. I feel sure that all those faces and tappings on the window-pane have been sheer imagination on her part. I haven't known what to do for the best. What do you think of the whole thing?"

I didn't quite understand the tone in his voice, but I answered promptly enough.

"It's possible," I said, "that these letters may be just a cruel and malicious hoax."

"Yes, that is quite likely. But what are we to *do*? They are driving her mad. I don't know what to think."

I didn't either. It had occurred to me that possibly a woman might be concerned. Those letters had a feminine note about them. Mrs. Mercado was at the back of my mind.

Supposing that by some chance she had learnt the facts of Mrs. Leidner's first marriage. She might be indulging her spite by terrorizing the other woman.

I didn't quite like to suggest such a thing to Dr. Leidner. It's so difficult to know how people are going to take things.

"Oh, well," I said cheerfully, "we must hope for the best. I think Mrs. Leidner seems happier already from just talking about it. That's always a help, you know. It's bottling things up that makes them get on your nerves."

"I'm very glad she has told you," he repeated. "It's a good sign. It shows she likes and trusts you. I've been at my wit's end to know what to do for the best."

It was on the tip of my tongue to ask him whether he'd thought of giving a discreet hint to the local police, but afterwards I was glad I hadn't done so.

What happened was this. On the following day Mr. Coleman was going in to Hassanieh to get the workmen's pay. He was also taking in all our letters to catch the air mail.

The letters, as written, were dropped into a wooden box on the dining-room window-sill. Last thing that night Mr. Coleman took them out and was sorting them out into bundles and putting rubber-bands round them.

Suddenly he gave a shout.

"What is it?" I asked.

He held out a letter with a grin.

"It's our Lovely Louise—she really *is* going balmly. She's addressed a letter to some one at 42nd Street, Paris, France. I don't think that can be right, do you? Do you mind taking it to her and asking what she *does* mean? She's just gone off to bed."

I took it from him and ran off to Mrs. Leidner with it and she amended the address.

It was the first time I had seen Mrs. Leidner's handwriting, and I wondered idly where I had seen it before, for it was certainly quite familiar to me.

It wasn't until the middle of the night that it suddenly came to me.

Except that it was bigger and rather more straggling, *it was extraordinarily like the writing on the anonymous letters.*

New ideas flashed through my head.

Had Mrs. Leidner conceivably written those letters *herself?*

And did Dr. Leidner half suspect the fact?

CHAPTER X

SATURDAY AFTERNOON

Mrs. Leidner told me her story on a Friday.

On Saturday morning there was a feeling of slight anticlimax in the air.

Mrs. Leidner, in particular, was inclined to be very off-hand with me and rather pointedly avoided any possibility of a *tête-à-tête*. Well, *that* didn't surprise me! I've had the same thing happen to me again and again. Ladies tell their nurses things in a sudden burst of confidence, and then, afterwards, they feel uncomfortable about it and wish they hadn't! It's only human nature.

I was very careful not to hint or remind her in any way of what she had told me. I purposely kept my conversation as matter-of-fact as possible.

Mr. Coleman had started in to Hassanieh in the morning, driving himself in the lorry with the letters in a knapsack. He also had one or two commissions to do for the members of the expedition. It was pay-day for the men, and he would have to go to the bank and bring out the money in coins of small denominations. All this was a long business and he did not expect to be back until the afternoon. I rather suspected he might be lunching with Sheila Reilly.

Work on the dig was usually not very busy on the afternoon of pay-day as at three-thirty the paying-out began.

The little boy, Abdullah, whose business it was to wash pots, was established as usual in the centre of the courtyard, and again as usual, kept up his queer nasal chant. Dr. Leidner and Mr. Emmott were going to put in some work on the pottery until Mr. Coleman returned, and Mr. Carey went up to the dig.

Mrs. Leidner went to her room to rest. I settled her as usual and then went to my own room, taking a book with me as I did not feel sleepy. It was then about a quarter to one, and a couple of hours passed quite pleasantly. I was reading *Death in a Nursing Home*—really a most exciting story—though I don't think the author knew much about the way nursing homes are run! At any rate I've never known a nursing home like that! I really felt inclined to write to the author and put him right about a few points.

When I put the book down at last (it was the red-haired parlourmaid and I'd never suspected her once!) and looked at my watch I was quite surprised to find it was twenty minutes to three!

I got up, straightened my uniform, and came out into the courtyard.

Abdullah was still scrubbing and still singing his depressing chant, and David Emmott was standing by him sorting the scrubbed pots, and putting the ones that were broken into boxes to await mending. I strolled over towards them just as Dr. Leidner came down the staircase from the roof.

"Not a bad afternoon," he said cheerfully. "I've made a bit of a clearance up there. Louise will be pleased. She's complained lately that there's not room to walk about. I'll go and tell her the good news."

He went over to his wife's door, tapped on it and went in.

It must, I suppose, have been about a minute and a half later that he came out again. I happened to be looking at the door when he did so. It was like a nightmare. He had gone in a brisk, cheerful man. He came out like a drunken one—reeling a little on his feet, and with a queer dazed expression on his face.

"Nurse—" he called in a queer, hoarse voice. "Nurse—"

I saw at once something was wrong, and I ran across to him. He looked awful—his face was all grey and twitching, and I saw he might collapse any minute.

"My wife . . ." he said. "My wife . . . Oh, my God . . ."

I pushed past him into the room. Then I caught my breath. Mrs. Leidner was lying in a dreadful huddled heap by the bed.

I bent over her. She was quite dead—must have been dead an hour at least. The cause of death was perfectly plain—a terrific blow on the front of the head just over the right temple. She must have got up from the bed and been struck down where she stood.

I didn't handle her more than I could help.

I glanced round the room to see if there was anything that might give a clue, but nothing seemed out of place or disturbed. The windows were closed and fastened, and there was no place where the murderer could have hidden. Obviously he had been and gone long ago.

I went out, closing the door behind me.

Dr. Leidner had collapsed completely now. David Emmott was with him and turned a white, inquiring face to me.

In a few low words I told him what had happened.

As I had always suspected, he was a first-class person to rely on in trouble. He was perfectly calm and self-possessed. Those blue eyes of his opened very wide, but otherwise he gave no sign at all.

He considered for a moment and then said:

"I suppose we must notify the police as soon as possible. Bill ought to be back any minute. What shall we do with Leidner?"

"Help me to get him into his room."

He nodded.

"Better lock this door first, I suppose," he said.

He turned the key in the lock of Mrs. Leidner's door, then drew it out and handed it to me.

"I guess you'd better keep this, nurse. Now then."

Together we lifted Dr. Leidner and carried him into his own room and laid him on his bed. Mr. Emmott went off in search of brandy. He returned, accompanied by Miss Johnson.

Her face was drawn and anxious, but she was calm and capable, and I felt satisfied to leave Dr. Leidner in her charge.

I hurried out into the courtyard. The station wagon was just coming in through the archway. I think it gave us all a shock to see Bill's pink, cheerful face as he jumped out with his familiar "Hallo, 'allo, 'allo! Here's the oof!" He went on gaily, "No highway robberies—"

He came to a halt suddenly. "I say, is anything up? What's the matter with you all? You look as though the cat had killed your canary."

Mr. Emmott said shortly:

"Mrs. Leidner's dead—killed."

"*What?*" Bill's jolly face changed ludicrously. He stared, his eyes goggling. "Mother Leidner dead! You're pulling my leg."

"Dead?" It was a sharp cry. I turned to see Mrs. Mercado behind me. "Did you say Mrs. Leidner had been *killed?*"

"Yes," I said. "Murdered."

"No!" she gasped. "Oh, no! I won't believe it. Perhaps she's committed suicide."

"Suicides don't hit themselves on the head," I said dryly. "It's murder all right, Mrs. Mercado."

She sat down suddenly on an upturned packing-case.

She said, "Oh, but this is horrible—*horrible* . . ."

Naturally it was horrible. We didn't need *her* to tell us so! I wondered if perhaps she was feeling a bit remorseful for the harsh feelings she had harboured against the dead woman, and all the spiteful things she had said.

After a minute or two she asked rather breathlessly:

"What are you going to do?"

Mr. Emmott took charge in his quiet way.

"Bill, you'd better get in again to Hassanieh as quick as you can. I don't know much about the proper procedure. Better get hold of Captain Maitland, he's in charge of the police here, I think. Get Dr. Reilly first. He'll know what to do."

Mr. Coleman nodded. All the facetiousness was knocked out of him. He just looked young and frightened. Without a word he jumped into the station wagon and drove off.

Mr. Emmott said rather uncertainly, "I suppose we ought to have a hunt round." He raised his voice and called:

"Ibrahim!"

"Na'am."

The house-boy came running. Mr. Emmott spoke to him in Arabic. A vigorous colloquy passed between them. The boy seemed to be emphatically denying something.

At last Mr. Emmott said in a perplexed voice:

"He says there's not been a soul here this afternoon. No stranger of any kind. I suppose the fellow must have slipped in without their seeing him."

"Of course he did," said Mrs. Mercado. "He slunk in when the boys weren't looking."

"Yes," said Mr. Emmott.

The slight uncertainty in his voice made me look at him inquiringly. He turned and spoke to the little pot-boy, Abdullah, asking him a question.

The boy replied vehemently at length.

The puzzled frown on Mr. Emmott's brow increased.

"I don't understand it," he murmured under his breath. "I don't understand it at all."

But he didn't tell me what he didn't understand.

CHAPTER XI

AN ODD BUSINESS

I'M ADHERING AS far as possible to telling only my personal part in the business. I pass over the events of the next two hours, the arrival of Captain Maitland and the police and Dr. Reilly. There was a good deal of general confusion, questioning, all the routine business, I suppose.

In my opinion we began to get down to brass tacks about five o'clock when Dr. Reilly asked me to come with him into the office.

He shut the door, sat down in Dr. Leidner's chair, motioned me to sit down opposite him, and said briskly:

"Now, then, nurse, let's get down to it. There's something damned odd here."

I settled my cuffs and looked at him inquiringly.

He drew out a notebook.

"This is for my own satisfaction. Now, what time was it exactly when Dr. Leidner found his wife's body?"

"I should say it was almost exactly a quarter to three," I said.

"And how do you know that?"

"Well, I looked at my watch when I got up. It was twenty to three then."

"Let's have a look at this watch of yours."

I slipped it off my wrist and held it out to him.

"Right to the minute. Excellent woman. Good, that's *that* fixed. Now did you form any opinion as to how long she'd been dead?"

"Oh, really, doctor," I said, "I shouldn't like to say."

"Don't be so professional. I want to see if your estimate agrees with mine."

"Well, I should say she'd been dead at least an hour."

"Quite so. I examined the body at half-past four and I'm inclined to put the time of death between 1.15 and 1.45. We'll say half-past one at a guess. That's near enough."

He stopped and drummed thoughtfully with his fingers on the table.

"Damned odd, this business," he said. "Can you tell me about it—you were resting, you say? Did you hear anything?"

"At half-past one? No, doctor. I didn't hear anything at half-past one or at any other time. I lay on my bed from a quarter to one until twenty to three and I didn't hear anything except that droning noise the Arab boy makes, and occasionally Mr. Emmott shouting up to Dr. Leidner on the roof."

"The Arab boy—yes."

He frowned.

At that moment the door opened and Dr. Leidner and Captain Maitland came in. Captain Maitland was a fussy little man with a pair of shrewd grey eyes.

Dr. Reilly rose and pushed Dr. Leidner into his chair.

"Sit down, man. I'm glad you've come. We shall want you. There's something very queer about this business."

Dr. Leidner bowed his head.

"I know." He looked at me. "My wife confided the truth to Nurse Leatheran. We mustn't keep anything back at this juncture, nurse, so please tell Captain Maitland and Dr. Reilly just what passed between you and my wife yesterday."

As nearly as possible I gave our conversation verbatim.

Captain Maitland uttered an occasional ejaculation. When I had finished he turned to Dr. Leidner.

"And this is all true, Leidner—eh?"

"Every word Nurse Leatheran has told you is correct."

"What an extraordinary story," said Dr. Reilly. "You can produce these letters?"

"I have no doubt they will be found amongst my wife's belongings."

"She took them out of the attaché-case on her table," I said.

"Then they are probably still there."

He turned to Captain Maitland and his usually gentle face grew hard and stern.

"There must be no question of hushing this story up, Captain Maitland. The one thing necessary is for this man to be caught and punished."

"You believe it actually is Mrs. Leidner's former husband?" I asked.

"Don't you think so, nurse?" asked Captain Maitland.

"Well, I think it is open to doubt," I said hesitatingly.

"In any case," said Dr. Leidner, "the man is a murderer—and I should say a dangerous lunatic also. He *must* be found, Captain Maitland. He must. It should not be difficult."

Dr. Reilly said slowly:

"It may be more difficult than you think . . . eh, Maitland?"

Captain Maitland tugged at his moustache without replying.

Suddenly I gave a start.

"Excuse me," I said, "but there's something perhaps I ought to mention."

I told my story of the Iraqi we had seen trying to peer through the window, and of how I had seen him hanging about the place two days ago trying to pump Father Lavigny.

"Good," said Captain Maitland, "we'll make a note of that. It will be something for the police to go on. The man may have some connection with the case."

"Probably paid to act as a spy," I suggested. "To find out when the coast was clear."

Dr. Reilly rubbed his nose with a harassed gesture.

"That's the devil of it," he said. "Supposing the coast wasn't clear—eh?"

I stared at him in a puzzled fashion.

Captain Maitland turned to Dr. Leidner.

"I want you to listen to me very carefully, Leidner. This is a review of the evidence we've got up to date. After lunch, which was served at twelve o'clock and was over by five and twenty to one, your wife went to her room accompanied by Nurse Leatheran, who settled her comfortably. You yourself went up to the roof, where you spent the next two hours, is that right?"

"Yes."

"Did you come down from the roof at all during that time?"

"No."

"Did any one come up to you?"

"Yes, Emmott did pretty frequently. He went to and fro between me and the boy, who was washing pottery down below."

"Did you yourself look over into the courtyard at all?"

"Once or twice—usually to call to Emmott about something."

"On each occasion the boy was sitting in the middle of the courtyard washing pots?"

"Yes."

"What was the longest period of time when Emmott was with you and absent from the courtyard?"

Dr. Leidner considered.

"It's difficult to say—perhaps ten minutes. Personally I should say two or three minutes, but I know by experience that my sense of time is not very good when I am absorbed and interested in what I am doing."

Captain Maitland looked at Dr. Reilly. The latter nodded. "We'd better get down to it," he said.

Captain Maitland took out a small notebook and opened it.

"Look here, Leidner, I'm going to read to you exactly what every member of your expedition was doing between one and two this afternoon."

"But surely—"

"Wait. You'll see what I'm driving at in a minute. First Mr. and Mrs. Mercado. Mr. Mercado says he was working in his laboratory. Mrs. Mercado says she was in her bedroom shampooing her hair. Miss Johnson says she was in the living-room taking impressions of cylinder seals. Mr. Reiter says he was in the dark-room developing plates. Father Lavigny says he was working in his bedroom. As to the two remaining members of the expedition, Carey and Coleman, the former was up on the dig and Coleman was in Hassanieh. So much for the members of the expedition. Now for the servants. The cook—your Indian chap—was sitting immediately outside the archway chatting to the guard and plucking a couple of fowls. Ibrahim and Mansur, the house-boys, joined him there at about 1.15. They both remained there laughing and talking until 2.30—*by which time your wife was already dead.*"

Dr. Leidner leaned forward.

"I don't understand—you puzzle me. What are you hinting at?"

"Is there any means of access to your wife's room except by the door into the courtyard?"

"No. There are two windows, but they are heavily barred—and besides, I think they were shut."

He looked at me questioningly.

"They were closed and latched on the inside," I said promptly.

"In any case," said Captain Maitland, "even if they had been open, no one could have entered or left the room that way. My fellows and I have assured ourselves of that. It is the same with all the other windows giving on the open country. They all have iron bars and all the bars are in good condition. To have got into your wife's room, a stranger *must* have come through the arched doorway into the courtyard. But we have the united assurances of the guard, the cook and the house-boy that *nobody did so.*"

Dr. Leidner sprang up.

"What do you mean? What do you mean?"

"Pull yourself together, man," said Dr. Reilly quietly. "I know it's a shock, but it's got to be faced. *The murderer didn't come from outside*—so he must have come from *inside.* It looks as though Mrs. Leidner must have been murdered *by a member of your own expedition.*"

CHAPTER XII

"I DIDN'T BELIEVE. . ."

"No. No!"

Dr. Leidner sprang up and walked up and down in an agitated manner.

"It's impossible what you say, Reilly. Absolutely impossible. One of *us?* Why, every single member of the expedition was devoted to Louise!"

A queer little expression pulled down the corners of Dr. Reilly's mouth. Under the circumstances it was difficult for him to say anything, but if ever a man's silence was eloquent his was at that minute.

"Quite impossible," reiterated Dr. Leidner. "They were all devoted to her. Louise had such wonderful charm. Every one felt it."

Dr. Reilly coughed.

"Excuse me, Leidner, but after all that's only your opinion. If any member of the expedition had disliked your wife they would naturally not advertise the fact to you."

Dr. Leidner looked distressed.

"True—quite true. But all the same, Reilly, I think you are wrong. I'm sure every one was fond of Louise."

He was silent for a moment or two and then burst out.

"This idea of yours is infamous. "It's—it's frankly incredible."

"You can't get away from—er—the facts," said Captain Maitland.

"Facts? Facts? Lies told by an Indian cook and a couple of Arab house-boys. You know these fellows as well as I do, Reilly; so do you, Maitland. Truth as truth means nothing to them. They say what you want them to say as a mere matter of politeness."

"In this case," said Dr. Reilly dryly, "they are saying what we *don't* want them to say. Besides, I know the habits of your household fairly well. Just outside the gate is a kind of social club. Whenever I've been over here in the afternoon I've always found most of your staff there. It's the natural place for them to be."

"All the same I think you are assuming too much. Why shouldn't this man—this devil—have got in earlier and concealed himself somewhere?"

"I agree that that is not actually impossible," said Dr. Reilly coolly.

"Let us assume that a stranger *did* somehow gain admission unseen. He would have to remain concealed until the right moment (and he certainly couldn't have done so in Mrs. Leidner's room, there is no cover there) and take the risk of being seen entering the room and leaving it—with Emmott and the boy in the courtyard most of the time."

"The boy. I'd forgotten the boy," said Dr. Leidner. "A sharp little chap. But surely, Maitland, the boy *must* have seen the murderer go into my wife's room?"

"We've elucidated that. The boy was washing pots the whole afternoon with one exception. Somewhere around half-past one—Emmott can't put it closer than that—he went up to the roof and was with you for ten minutes—that's right, isn't it?"

"Yes. I couldn't have told you the exact time but it must have been about that."

"Very good. Well, during that ten minutes, the boy, seizing his chance to be idle, strolled out and joined the others outside the gate for a chat. When Emmott came down he found the boy absent and called him angrily, asking him what he meant by leaving his work. As far as I can see, *your wife must have been murdered during that ten minutes.*"

With a groan, Dr. Leidner sat down and hid his face in his hands.

Dr. Reilly took up the tale, his voice quiet and matter-of-fact.

"The time fits in with my evidence," he said. "She'd been dead about three hours when I examined her. The only question is—who did it?"

There was a silence. Dr. Leidner sat up in his chair and passed a hand over his forehead.

"I admit the force of your reasoning, Reilly," he said quietly. "It certainly *seems* as though it were what people call 'an inside job.' But I feel convinced that somewhere or other there is a mistake. It's plausible but there must be a flaw in it. To begin with, you are assuming that an amazing coincidence has occurred."

"Odd that you should use that word," said Dr. Reilly.

Without paying any attention Dr. Leidner went on:

"My wife receives threatening letters. She has reason to fear a certain person. Then she is—killed. And you ask me to believe that she is killed—not by that person—but by some one entirely different! I say that that is ridiculous."

"It seems so—yes," said Dr. Reilly meditatively.

He looked at Captain Maitland. "Coincidence—eh? What do you say, Maitland? Are you in favour of the idea? Shall we put it up to Leidner?"

Captain Maitland gave a nod.

"Go ahead," he said shortly.

"Have you ever heard of a man called Hercule Poirot, Leidner?"

Dr. Leidner stared at him, puzzled.

"I think I have heard the name, yes," he said vaguely. "I once heard a Mr. Van Aldin speak of him in very high terms. He is a private detective, is he not?"

"That's the man."

"But surely he lives in London, so how will that help us?"

"He lives in London, true," said Dr. Reilly, "but this is where the coincidence comes in. He is now, not in London, but in Syria, and *he will actually pass through Hassanieh on his way to Baghdad tomorrow!*"

"Who told you this?"

"Jean Berat, the French consul. He dined with us last night and was talking about him. It seems he has been disentangling some military scandal in Syria. He's coming through here to visit Baghdad, and afterwards returning through Syria to London. How's that for a coincidence?"

Dr. Leidner hesitated a moment and looked apologetically at Captain Maitland.

"What do you think, Captain Maitland?"

"Should welcome co-operation," said Captain Maitland promptly. "My fellows are good scouts at scouring the countryside and investigating Arab blood feuds, but frankly, Leidner, this business of your wife's seems to me rather out of my class. The whole thing looks confoundedly fishy. I'm more than willing to have the fellow take a look at the case."

"You suggest that I should appeal to this man Poirot to help us?" said Dr. Leidner. "And suppose he refuses?"

"He won't refuse," said Dr. Reilly.

"How do you know?"

"Because I'm a professional man myself. If a really intricate case of say—cerebrospinal meningitis comes my way and I'm invited to take a hand, I shouldn't be able to refuse. This isn't an ordinary crime, Leidner."

"No," said Dr. Leidner. His lips twitched with sudden pain.

"Will you then, Reilly, approach this Hercule Poirot on my behalf?"

"I will."

Dr. Leidner made a gesture of thanks.

"Even now," he said slowly, "I can't realize it—that Louise is really dead."

I could bear it no longer.

"Oh! Dr. Leidner," I burst out. "I—I can't tell you how badly I feel about this. I've failed so badly in my duty. It was my job to watch over Mrs. Leidner—to keep her from harm."

Dr. Leidner shook his head gravely.

"No, no, nurse, you've nothing to reproach yourself with," he said slowly. "It's *I*, God forgive me, who am to blame. . . . *I didn't believe*—all along I didn't believe . . . I didn't dream for one moment that there was any *real* danger. . . ."

He got up. His face twitched.

"*I let her go to her death.* . . . Yes, I let her go to her death—*not believing*—"

He staggered out of the room.

Dr. Reilly looked at me.

"I feel pretty culpable too," he said. "I thought the good lady was playing on his nerves."

"I didn't take it really seriously either," I confessed.

"We were all three wrong," said Dr. Reilly gravely.

"So it seems," said Captain Maitland.

CHAPTER XIII

HERCULE POIROT ARRIVES

I DON'T THINK I shall ever forget my first sight of Hercule Poirot. Of course, I got used to him later on, but to begin with it was a shock, and I think every one else must have felt the same!

I don't know what I'd imagined—something rather like Sherlock Holmes—long and lean with a keen, clever face. Of course, I knew he was a foreigner, but I hadn't expected him to be *quite* as foreign as he was, if you know what I mean.

When you saw him you just wanted to laugh! He was like something on the stage or at the pictures. To begin with, he wasn't above five foot five, I should think—an odd plump little man, quite old, with an enormous moustache, and a head like an egg. He looked like a hairdresser in a comic play!

And this was the man who was going to find out who killed Mrs. Leidner!

I suppose something of my disgust must have shown in my face, for almost straightaway he said to me with a queer kind of twinkle:

"You disapprove of me, *ma sœur*? Remember, the pudding proves itself only when you eat it."

The proof of the pudding's in the eating, I *suppose* he meant. Well, that's a true enough saying, but I couldn't say I felt much confidence myself!

Dr. Reilly brought him out in his car soon after lunch on Sunday, and his first procedure was to ask us all to assemble together.

We did so in the dining-room, all sitting round the table. Mr. Poirot sat at the head of it with Dr. Leidner one side and Dr. Reilly the other.

When we were all assembled, Dr. Leidner cleared his throat and spoke in his gentle, hesitating voice.

"I dare say you have all heard of M. Hercule Poirot. He was passing through Hassanieh to-day, and has very kindly agreed to break his journey to help us. The Iraq police and Captain Maitland are, I am sure, doing their very best, but—but there are circumstances in the case"—he floundered and shot an appealing glance at Dr. Reilly—"there may, it seems, be difficulties. . . ."

"It is not all the square and overboard—no?" said the little man at the top of the table. Why, he couldn't even speak English properly!

"Oh, he *must* be caught!" cried Mrs. Mercado. "It would be unbearable if he got away!"

I noticed the little foreigner's eyes rest on her appraisingly.

"He? Who is *he*, madame?" he asked.

"Why, the murderer, of course."

"Ah! the murderer," said Hercule Poirot.

He spoke as though the murderer was of no consequence at all!

We all stared at him. He looked from one face to another.

"It is likely, I think," he said, "that you have none of you been brought in contact with a case of murder before?"

There was a general murmur of assent.

Hercule Poirot smiled.

"It is clear, therefore, that you do not understand the A.B.C. of the position. There are unpleasantnesses! Yes, there are a lot of unpleasantnesses. To begin with, there is *suspicion.*"

"Suspicion?"

It was Miss Johnson who spoke. Mr. Poirot looked at her thoughtfully. I had an idea that he regarded her with approval. He looked as though he were thinking, "Here is a sensible, intelligent person!"

"Yes, mademoiselle," he said. "Suspicion! Let us not make the bones about it. *You are all under suspicion here in this house.* The cook, the house-boy, the scullion, the pot-boy—yes, and all the members of the expedition too."

Mrs. Mercado started up, her face working.

"How *dare* you? How dare you say such a thing! This is odious—unbearable! Dr. Leidner—you can't sit here and let this man—and let this man—"

Dr. Leidner said wearily:

"Please try and be calm, Marie."

Mr. Mercado stood up too. His hands were shaking and his eyes were bloodshot.

"I agree. It is an outrage—an insult—"

"No, no," said Mr. Poirot. "I do not insult you. I merely ask you all to face facts. *In a house where murder has been committed, every inmate comes in for a certain share of suspicion.* I ask you what evidence is there that the murderer came from outside at all?"

Mrs. Mercado cried:

"But of course he did! It stands to reason! Why—" She stopped and said more slowly, "Anything else would be incredible!"

"You are doubtless correct, madame," said Poirot with a bow. "I explain to you only how the matter must be approached. First I assure myself of the fact that every one in this room is innocent. After that I seek the murderer elsewhere."

"Is it not possible that that may be a little late in the day?" asked Father Lavigny suavely.

"The tortoise, *mon père*, overtook the hare."

Father Lavigny shrugged his shoulders.

"We are in your hands," he said resignedly. "Convince yourself as soon as may be of our innocence in this terrible business."

"As rapidly as possible. It was my duty to make the position clear to you, so that you may not resent the impertinence of any questions I may have to ask. Perhaps, *mon père*, the Church will set an example?"

"Ask any questions you please of me," said Father Lavigny gravely.

"This is your first season out here?"

"Yes."

"And you arrived—when?"

"Three weeks ago almost to a day. That is, on the 27th of February."

"Coming from?"

"The Order of the *Pères Blancs* at Carthage."

"Thank you, *mon père*. Were you at any time acquainted with Mrs. Leidner before coming here?"

"No, I had never seen the lady until I met her here."

"Will you tell me what you were doing at the time of the tragedy?"

"I was working on some cuneiform tablets in my own room."

I noticed that Poirot had at his elbow a rough plan of the building.

"That is the room at the south-west corner corresponding to that of Mrs. Leidner on the opposite side?"

"Yes."

"At what time did you go to your room?"

"Immediately after lunch. I should say at about twenty minutes to one."

"And you remained there until—when?"

"Just before three o'clock. I had heard the station wagon come back—and then I heard it drive off again. I wondered why, and came out to see."

"During the time that you were there did you leave the room at all?"

"No, not once."

"And you heard or saw nothing that might have any bearing on the tragedy?"

"No."

"You have no window giving on the courtyard in your room?"

"No, both the windows give on the countryside."

"Could you hear at all what was happening in the courtyard?"

"Not very much. I heard Mr. Emmott passing my room and going up to the roof. He did so once or twice."

"Can you remember at what time?"

"No, I'm afraid I can't. I was engrossed in my work, you see."

There was a pause and then Poirot said:

"Can you say or suggest anything at all that might throw light on this business. Did you, for instance, notice anything in the days preceding the murder?"

Father Lavigny looked slightly uncomfortable.

He shot a half-questioning look at Dr. Leidner.

"That is rather a difficult question, monsieur," he said gravely. "If you ask me, I must reply frankly that in my opinion Mrs. Leidner was clearly in dread of some one or something. She was definitely nervous about strangers. I imagine she had a reason for this nervousness of hers—but I *know* nothing. She did not confide in me."

Poirot cleared his throat and consulted some notes that he held in his hand.

"Two nights ago I understand there was a scare of burglary."

Father Lavigny replied in the affirmative and retailed his story of the light seen in the antika-room and the subsequent futile search.

"You believe, do you not, that some unauthorized person was on the premises at that time?"

"I don't know what to think," said Father Lavigny frankly. "Nothing was taken or disturbed in any way. It might have been one of the house-boys—"

"Or a member of the expedition?"

"Or a member of the expedition. But in that case there would be no reason for the person not admitting the fact."

"But it *might* equally have been a stranger from outside?"

"I suppose so."

"Supposing a stranger *had* been on the premises, could he have concealed himself successfully during the following day and until the afternoon of the day following that?"

He asked the question half of Father Lavigny and half of Dr. Leidner. Both men considered the question carefully.

"I hardly think it would be possible," said Dr. Leidner at last with some reluctance. "I don't see where he could possibly conceal himself, do you, Father Lavigny?"

"No—no—I don't."

Both men seemed reluctant to put the suggestion aside.

Poirot turned to Miss Johnson.

"And you, mademoiselle? Do you consider such a hypothesis feasible?"

After a moment's thought Miss Johnson shook her head.

"No," she said. "I don't. Where could any one hide? The bedrooms are all in use and, in any case, are sparsely furnished. The dark-room, the drawing-office and the laboratory were all in use the next day—so were all these rooms. There are no cupboards or corners. Perhaps, if the servants were in collusion—"

"That is possible, but unlikely," said Poirot.

He turned once more to Father Lavigny.

"There is another point. The other day Nurse Leatheran here noticed you talking to a man outside. She had previously noticed that same man trying to peer in at one of the windows on the outside. It rather looks as though the man were hanging round the place deliberately."

"That is possible, of course," said Father Lavigny thoughtfully.

"Did you speak to this man first, or did he speak to you?"

Father Lavigny considered for a moment or two.

"I believe—yes, I am sure, that he spoke to me."

"What did he say?"

Father Lavigny made an effort of memory.

"He said, I think, something to the effect was this the American expedition house? And then something else about the Americans employing a lot of men on the work. I did not really understand him very well, but I endeavoured to keep up a conversation so as to improve my Arabic. I thought, perhaps, that being a townee he would understand me better than the men on the dig do."

"Did you converse about anything else?"

"As far as I remember, I said Hassanieh was a big town—and we then agreed that Baghdad was bigger—and I think he asked whether I was an Armenian or a Syrian Catholic—something of that kind."

Poirot nodded.

"Can you describe him?"

Again Father Lavigny frowned in thought.

"He was rather a short man," he said at last, "and squarely built. He had a very noticeable squint and was of fair complexion."

Mr. Poirot turned to me.

"Does that agree with the way you would describe him?" he asked.

"Not exactly," I said hesitatingly. "I should have said he was tall rather than short, and very dark complexioned. He seemed to me of a rather slender build. I didn't notice any squint."

Mr. Poirot gave a despairing shrug of the shoulders.

"It is always so! If you were of the police how well you would know it! The description of the same man by two different people—never does it agree. Every detail is contradicted."

"I'm fairly sure about the squint," said Father Lavigny. "Nurse Leatheran may be right about the other points. By the way, when I said *fair*, I only meant fair for an *Iraqi*. I expect nurse would call that dark."

"Very dark," I said obstinately. "A dirty dark-yellow colour."

I saw Dr. Reilly bite his lip and smile.

Poirot threw up his hands.

"*Passons!*" he said. "This stranger hanging about, he may be important—he may not. At any rate he must be found. Let us continue our inquiry."

He hesitated for a minute, studying the faces turned towards him round the table, then, with a quick nod, he singled out Mr. Reiter.

"Come, my friend," he said. "Let us have your account of yesterday afternoon."

Mr. Reiter's pink, plump face flushed scarlet.

"Me?" he said.

"Yes, you. To begin with, your name and your age?"

"Carl Reiter, twenty-eight."

"American—yes?"

"Yes, I come from Chicago."

"This is your first season?"

"Yes. I'm in charge of the photography."

"Ah, yes. And yesterday afternoon, how did you employ yourself?"

"Well—I was in the dark-room most of the time."

"*Most* of the time—eh?"

"Yes. I developed some plates first. Afterwards I was fixing up some objects to photograph."

"Outside?"

"Oh, no, in the photographic room."

"The dark-room opens out of the photographic room?"

"Yes."

"And so you never came outside the photographic room?"

"No."

"Did you notice anything that went on in the courtyard?"

The young man shook his head.

"I wasn't noticing anything," he explained. "I was busy. I heard the car come back, and as soon as I could leave what I was doing I came out to see if there was any mail. It was then that I—heard."

"And you began your work in the photographic room—when?"

"At ten minutes to one."

"Were you acquainted with Mrs. Leidner before you joined this expedition?"

The young man shook his head.

"No, sir. I never saw her till I actually got here."

"Can you think of *anything*—any incident—however small—that might help us?"

Carl Reiter shook his head.

He said helplessly:

"I guess I don't know anything at all, sir."

"Mr. Emmott?"

David Emmott spoke clearly and concisely in his pleasant soft American voice.

"I was working with the pottery from a quarter to one till a quarter to three—overseeing the boy Abdullah, sorting it, and occasionally going up to the roof to help Dr. Leidner."

"How often did you go up to the roof?"

"Four times, I think."

"For how long?"

"Usually a couple of minutes—not more. But on one occasion after I'd been working a little over half an hour I stayed as long as ten minutes—discussing what to keep and what to fling away."

"And I understand that when you came down you found the boy had left his place?"

"Yes. I called him angrily and he reappeared from outside the archway. He had gone out to gossip with the others."

"That was the only time he left his work?"

"Well, I sent him up once or twice to the roof with pottery."

Poirot said gravely:

"It is hardly necessary to ask you, Mr. Emmott, whether you saw any one enter or leave Mrs. Leidner's room during that time?"

Mr. Emmott replied promptly.

"I saw no one at all. Nobody even came out into the courtyard during the two hours I was working."

"And to the best of your belief it was half-past one when both you and the boy were absent and the courtyard was empty?"

"It couldn't have been far off that time. Of course, I can't say *exactly*."

Poirot turned to Dr. Reilly.

"That agrees with your estimate of the time of death, doctor?"

"It does," said Dr. Reilly.

Mr. Poirot stroked his great curled moustaches.

"I think we can take it," he said gravely, "that Mrs. Leidner met her death during that ten minutes."

CHAPTER XIV

ONE OF US?

There was a little pause—and in it a wave of horror seemed to float round the room.

I think it was at that moment that I first believed Dr. Reilly's theory to be right.

I *felt* that the murderer was in the room. Sitting with us—listening. *One of us . . .*

Perhaps Mrs. Mercado felt it too. For she suddenly gave a short sharp cry.

"I can't help it," she sobbed. "I—it's so *terrible!*"

"Courage, Marie," said her husband.

He looked at us apologetically.

"She is so sensitive. She feels things so much."

"I—I was so fond of Louise," sobbed Mrs. Mercado.

I don't know whether something of what I felt showed in my face, but I suddenly found that Mr. Poirot was looking at me, and that a slight smile hovered on his lips.

I gave him a cold glance, and at once he resumed his inquiry.

"Tell me, madame," he said, "of the way you spent yesterday afternoon?"

"I was washing my hair," sobbed Mrs. Mercado. "It seems awful not to have known anything about it. I was quite happy and busy."

"You were in your room?"

"Yes."

"And you did not leave it?"

"No. Not till I heard the car. Then I came out and I heard what had happened. Oh, it was *awful!*"

"Did it surprise you?"

Mrs. Mercado stopped crying. Her eyes opened resentfully.

"What do you mean, M. Poirot? Are you suggesting—"

"What should I mean, madame? You have just told us how fond you were of Mrs. Leidner. She might, perhaps, have confided in you."

"Oh, I see. . . . No—no, dear Louise never told me anything—anything *definite*, that is. Of course, I could see she was terribly worried and nervous. And there were those strange occurrences—hands tapping on the window and all that."

"Fancies, I remember you said," I put in, unable to keep silent.

I was glad to see that she looked momentarily disconcerted.

Once again I was conscious of Mr. Poirot's amused eye glancing in my direction.

He summed up in a business-like way.

"It comes to this, madame, you were washing your hair—you heard nothing and you saw nothing. Is there anything at all you can think of that would be a help to us in any way?"

Mrs. Mercado took no time to think.

"No, indeed there isn't. It's the deepest mystery! But I should say there is no doubt—no doubt *at all* that the murderer came from outside. Why, it stands to reason."

Poirot turned to her husband.

"And you, monsieur, what have you to say?"

Mr. Mercado started nervously. He pulled at his beard in an aimless fashion.

"Must have been. Must have been," he said. "Yet how could any one wish to harm her? She was so gentle—so kind—" He shook his head. "Whoever killed her must have been a fiend—yes, a fiend!"

"And you yourself, monsieur, how did you pass yesterday afternoon?"

"I?" he stared vaguely.

"You were in the laboratory, Joseph," his wife prompted him.

"Ah, yes, so I was—so I was. My usual tasks."

"At what time did you go there?"

Again he looked helplessly and inquiringly at Mrs. Mercado.

"At ten minutes to one, Joseph."

"Ah, yes, at ten minutes to one."

"Did you come out in the courtyard at all?"

"No—I don't think so." He considered. "No, I am sure I didn't."

"When did you hear of the tragedy?"

"My wife came and told me. It was terrible—shocking. I could hardly believe it. Even now, I can hardly believe it is true."

Suddenly he began to tremble.

"It is horrible—horrible . . ."

Mrs. Mercado came quickly to his side.

"Yes, yes, Joseph, we all feel that. But we mustn't give way. It makes it so much more difficult for poor Dr. Leidner."

I saw a spasm of pain pass across Dr. Leidner's face, and I guessed that this emotional atmosphere was not easy for him. He gave a half glance at Poirot as though in appeal. Poirot responded quickly.

"Miss Johnson?" he said.

"I'm afraid I can tell you very little," said Miss Johnson. Her cultured well-bred voice was soothing after Mrs. Mercado's shrill treble. She went on:

"I was working in the living-room—taking impressions of some cylinder seals on plasticine."

"And you saw or noticed nothing?"

"No."

Poirot gave her a quick glance. His ear had caught what mine had —a faint note of indecision.

"Are you quite sure, mademoiselle? Is there something that comes back to you vaguely?"

"No—not really—"

"Something you saw, shall we say, out of the corner of your eye hardly knowing you saw it."

"No, certainly not," she replied positively.

"Something you *heard* then. Ah, yes, something you are not quite sure whether you heard or not?"

Miss Johnson gave a short vexed laugh.

"You press me very closely, M. Poirot. I'm afraid you are encouraging me to tell you what I am, perhaps, only imagining."

"Then there *was* something you—shall we say—imagined?"

Miss Johnson said slowly, weighing her words in a detached way:

"I have imagined—since—that at some time during the afternoon I heard a very faint cry. . . . What I mean is that I dare say I *did* hear a cry. All the windows in the living-room were open and one hears all sorts of sounds from people working in the barley fields. But you see—since—I've got the idea into my head that it was—that it was Mrs. Leidner I heard. And that's made me rather unhappy. Because if I'd jumped up and run along to her room—well, who knows? I might have been in time . . ."

Dr. Reilly interposed authoritatively.

"Now, don't start getting that into your head," he said. I've no doubt but that Mrs. Leidner (forgive me, Leidner) was struck down almost as soon as the man entered the room, and it was that blow that killed her. No second blow was struck. Otherwise she would have had time to call for help and make a real outcry."

"Still, I might have caught the murderer," said Miss Johnson.

"What time was this, mademoiselle?" asked Poirot. "In the neighbourhood of half-past one?"

"It must have been about that time—yes." She reflected a minute.

"That would fit in," said Poirot thoughtfully. "You heard nothing else—the opening or shutting of a door, for instance?"

Miss Johnson shook her head.

"No, I do not remember anything of that kind."

"You were sitting at a table, I presume. Which way were you facing? The courtyard? The antika-room? The verandah? Or the open countryside?"

"I was facing the courtyard."

"Could you see the boy Abdullah washing pots from where you were?"

"Oh, yes, if I looked up, but of course, I was very intent on what I was doing. All my attention was on that."

"If any one had passed the courtyard window, though, you would have noticed it?"

"Oh, yes, I am almost sure of that."

"And nobody did so?"

"No."

"But if any one had walked, say, across the middle of the courtyard, would you have noticed that?"

"I think—probably not—unless, as I said before, I had happened to look up and out of the window."

"You did not notice the boy Abdullah leave his work and go out to join the other servants?"

"No."

"Ten minutes," mused Poirot. "That fatal ten minutes."

There was a momentary silence.

Miss Johnson lifted her head suddenly and said:

"You know, M. Poirot, I think I have unintentionally misled you. On thinking it over, I do not believe that I could possibly have heard any cry uttered in Mrs. Leidner's room from where I was. The antika-room lay between me and her—and I understand her windows were found closed."

"In any case, do not distress yourself, mademoiselle," said Poirot kindly. "It is not really of much importance."

"No, of course not. I understand that. But you see, it *is* of importance to me, because I feel I might have done something."

"Don't distress yourself, dear Anne," said Dr. Leidner with affection. "You must be sensible. What you heard was probably one Arab bawling to another some distance away in the fields."

Miss Johnson flushed a little at the kindliness of his tone. I even saw tears spring to her eyes. She turned her head away and spoke even more gruffly than usual.

"Probably was. Usual thing after a tragedy—start imagining things that aren't so at all."

Poirot was once more consulting his notebook.

"I do not suppose there is much more to be said. Mr. Carey?"

Richard Carey spoke slowly—in a wooden, mechanical manner.

"I'm afraid I can add nothing helpful. I was on duty at the dig. The news was brought to me there."

"And you know or can think of nothing helpful that occurred in the days immediately preceding the murder?"

"Nothing at all."

"Mr. Coleman?"

"I was right out of the whole thing," said Mr. Coleman with—was it just a shade of regret—in his tone. "I went into Hassanieh yesterday morning to get the money for the men's wages. When I came back Emmott told me what had happened and I went back in the bus to get the police and Dr. Reilly."

"And beforehand?"

"Well, sir, things were a bit jumpy—but you know that already. There was the antika-room scare and one or two before that—hands and faces at the window—you remember, sir," he appealed to Dr. Leidner, who bent his head in assent. "I think, you know, that you'll find some Johnny *did* get in from outside. Must have been an artful sort of beggar."

Poirot considered him for a minute or two in silence.

"You are an Englishman, Mr. Coleman?" he asked at last.

"That's right, sir. All British. See the trademark. Guaranteed genuine."

"This is your first season?"

"Quite right."

"And you are passionately keen on archæology?"

This description of himself seemed to cause Mr. Coleman some embarrassment. He got rather pink and shot the side look of a guilty schoolboy at Dr. Leidner.

"Of course—it's all very interesting," he stammered. "I mean—I'm not exactly a brainy chap . . ."

He broke off rather lamely. Poirot did not insist.

He tapped thoughtfully on the table with the end of his pencil and carefully straightened an inkpot that stood in front of him.

"It seems then," he said, "that that is as near as we can get for the moment. If any one of you thinks of something that has for the time being slipped his or her memory do not hesitate to come to me with it. It will be well now, I think, for me to have a few words alone with Dr. Leidner and Dr. Reilly."

It was the signal for a breaking up of the party. We all rose and filed out of the door. When I was half-way out, however, a voice recalled me.

"Perhaps," said Mr. Poirot, "Nurse Leatheran will be so kind as to remain. I think her assistance will be valuable to us."

I came back and resumed my seat at the table.

CHAPTER XV

POIROT MAKES A SUGGESTION

DR. REILLY HAD RISEN from his seat. When every one had gone out he carefully closed the door. Then, with an inquiring glance at Poirot, he proceeded to shut the window giving on the courtyard. The others were already shut. Then he, too, resumed his seat at the table.

"*Bien!*" said Poirot. "We are now private and undisturbed. We can speak freely. We have heard what the members of the expedition have to tell us and— But yes, *ma sœur,* what is it that you think?"

I got rather red. There was no denying that the queer little man had sharp eyes. He'd seen the thought passing through my mind—I suppose my face *had* shown a bit too clearly what I was thinking!

"Oh, it's nothing—" I said, hesitating.

"Come on, nurse," said Dr. Reilly. "Don't keep the specialist waiting."

"It's nothing really," I said hurriedly. "It only just passed through my mind, so to speak, that perhaps even if any one did know or suspect something it wouldn't be easy to bring it out in front of everybody else—or even, perhaps, in front of Dr. Leidner."

Rather to my astonishment, M. Poirot nodded his head in vigorous agreement.

"Precisely. Precisely. It is very just what you say there. But I will explain. That little reunion we have just had—it served a purpose. In England before the races you have a parade of the horses, do you not? They go in front of the grandstand so that every one may have an opportunity of seeing and judging them. That is the purpose of my little assembly. In the sporting phrase, I run my eye over the possible starters."

Dr. Leidner cried out violently, "I do not believe for one minute that *any* member of my expedition is implicated in this crime!"

Then, turning to me, he said authoritatively:

"Nurse, I should be much obliged if you would tell M. Poirot here and now exactly what passed between my wife and you two days ago."

Thus urged, I plunged straightaway into my story, trying as far as possible to recall the exact words and phrases Mrs. Leidner had used.

When I had finished, M. Poirot said:

"Very good. Very good. You have the mind neat and orderly. You will be of great service to me here."

He turned to Dr. Leidner.

"You have these letters?"

"I have them here. I thought that you would want to see them first thing."

Poirot took them from him, read them, and scrutinized them carefully as he did so. I was rather disappointed that he didn't dust powder over them or examine them with a microscope or anything like that—but I realized that he wasn't a very young man and that his methods were probably not very up to date. He just read them in the way that any one might read a letter.

Having read them he put them down and cleared his throat.

"Now," he said, "let us proceed to get our facts clear and in order. The first of these letters was received by your wife shortly after her marriage to you in America. There had been others but these she destroyed. The first letter was followed by a second. A very short time after the second arrived you both had a near escape from coal gas poisoning. You then came abroad and for nearly two years no further letters were received. They started again at the beginning of your season this year—that is to say, within the last three weeks. That is correct?"

"Absolutely."

"Your wife displayed every sign of panic and, after consulting Dr. Reilly, you engaged Nurse Leatheran here to keep your wife company and allay her fears?"

"Yes."

"Certain incidents occurred—hands tapping at the window—a spectral face—noises in the antika-room. You did not witness any of these phenomena yourself?"

"No."

"In fact nobody did except Mrs. Leidner?"

"Father Lavigny saw a light in the antika-room."

"Yes, I have not forgotten that."

He was silent for a minute or two, then he said:

"Had your wife made a will?"

"I do not think so."

"Why was that?"

"It did not seem worth it from her point of view."

"Is she not a wealthy woman?"

"Yes, during her lifetime. Her father left her a considerable sum of money in trust. She could not touch the principal. At her death it was to pass to any children she might have—and failing children to the Pittstown Museum."

Poirot drummed thoughtfully on the table.

"Then we can, I think," he said, "eliminate one motive from the case. It is, you comprehend, what I look for first. *Who benefits by the deceased's death?* In this case it is a museum. Had it been otherwise, had Mrs. Leidner died intestate but possessed of a considerable fortune, I should imagine that it would prove an interesting question as to who inherited the money—you—or a former husband. But there would have been this difficulty, the former husband would have had to resurrect himself in order to claim it, and I should imagine that he would then be in danger of arrest, though I hardly fancy that the death penalty would be exacted so long after the war. However, these speculations need not arise. As I say, I settle first the question of money. For the next step I proceed always to suspect the husband or wife of the deceased! In this case, in the first place, you are proved never to have gone near your wife's room yesterday afternoon, in the second place, you lose instead of gain by your wife's death, and in the third place—"

He paused.

"Yes?" said Dr. Leidner.

"In the third place," said Poirot slowly. "I can, I think, appreciate devotion when I see it. I believe, Dr. Leidner, that your love for your wife was the ruling passion of your life. It is so, is it not?"

Dr. Leidner answered quite simply:

"Yes."

Poirot nodded.

"Therefore," he said, "we can proceed."

"Hear, hear, let's get down to it," said Dr. Reilly with some impatience.

Poirot gave him a reproving glance.

"My friend, do not be impatient. In a case like this everything must be approached with order and method. In fact, that is my rule in every case. Having disposed of certain possibilities, we now approach a very important point. It is vital that, as you say—all the cards should be on the table—there must be nothing kept back."

"Quite so," said Dr. Reilly.

"That is why I demand the whole truth," went on Poirot.

Dr. Leidner looked at him in surprise.

"I assure you, M. Poirot, that I have kept nothing back. I have told you everything that I know. There have been no reserves."

"*Tout de même*, you have not told me *everything*."

"Yes, indeed. I cannot think of any detail that has escaped me."

He looked quite distressed.

Poirot shook his head gently.

"No," he said. "*You have not told me, for instance, why you installed Nurse Leatheran in the house.*"

Dr. Leidner looked completely bewildered.

"But I have explained that. It is obvious. My wife's nervousness—her fears . . ."

Poirot leaned forward. Slowly and emphatically he wagged a finger up and down.

"No, no, no. There is something there that is not clear. Your wife is in danger, yes—she is threatened with death, yes. You send—*not for the police*—not for a private detective even—but for a *nurse!* It does not make the sense, that!"

"I—I—" Dr. Leidner stopped. The colour rose in his cheeks. "I thought—" He came to a dead stop.

"Now we are coming to it," Poirot encouraged him. "You thought —what?"

Dr. Leidner remained silent. He looked harassed and unwilling.

"See you," Poirot's tone became winning and appealing, "it all rings true what you have told me, except for that. Why a *nurse?* There is an answer—yes. In fact, there can be only one answer. *You did not believe yourself in your wife's danger.*"

And then with a cry Dr. Leidner broke down.

"God help me," he groaned. "I didn't. I didn't."

Poirot watched him with the kind of attention a cat gives a mouse-hole—ready to pounce when the mouse shows itself.

"What *did* you think then?" he asked.

"I don't know. I don't know . . ."

"But you do know. You know perfectly. Perhaps I can help you—with a guess. *Did you, Dr. Leidner, suspect that these letters were all written by your wife herself?*"

There wasn't any need for him to answer. The truth of Poirot's guess was only too apparent. The horrified hand he held up, as though begging for mercy, told its own tale.

I drew a deep breath. So I *had* been right in my half-formed guess! I recalled the curious tone in which Dr. Leidner had asked me what I thought of it all. I nodded my head slowly and thoughtfully, and suddenly awoke to the fact that M. Poirot's eyes were on me.

"Did you think the same, nurse?"

"The idea did cross my mind," I said truthfully.

"For what reason?"

I explained the similarity of the handwriting on the letter that Mr. Coleman had shown me.

Poirot turned to Dr. Leidner.

"Had you, too, noticed that similarity?"

Dr. Leidner bowed his head.

"Yes, I did. The writing was small and cramped—not big and generous like Louise's, but several of the letters were formed the same way. I will show you."

From an inner breast pocket he took out some letters and finally selected a sheet from one which he handed to Poirot. It was part of a letter written to him by his wife. Poirot compared it carefully with the anonymous letters.

"Yes," he murmured. "Yes. There are several similarities—a curious way of forming the letter *s*, a distinctive *e*. I am not a handwriting expert—I cannot pronounce definitely (and for that matter, I have never found two handwriting experts who agree on any point whatsoever)—but one can at least say this—the similarity between the two handwritings is very marked. It seems highly probable that they were all written by the same person. But it is not *certain*. We must take all contingencies into mind."

He leaned back in his chair and said thoughtfully:

"There are three possibilities. First, the similarity of the handwriting is pure coincidence. Second, that these threatening letters were written by Mrs. Leidner herself for some obscure reason. Third, that they were written by some one *who deliberately copied her handwriting*. Why? There seems no sense in it. One of these three possibilities must be the correct one."

He reflected for a minute or two and then, turning to Dr. Leidner, he asked, with a resumal of his brisk manner.

"When the possibility that Mrs. Leidner herself was the author of these letters first struck you, what theory did you form?"

Dr. Leidner shook his head.

"I put the idea out of my head as quickly as possible. I felt it was monstrous."

"Did you search for no explanation?"

"Well," he hesitated, "I wondered if worrying and brooding over the past had perhaps affected my wife's brain slightly. I thought she might possibly have written those letters to herself without being conscious of having done so. That is possible, isn't it?" he added, turning to Dr. Reilly.

Dr. Reilly pursed up his lips.

"The human brain is capable of almost anything," he replied vaguely.

But he shot a lightning glance at Poirot, and as if in obedience to it, the latter abandoned the subject.

"The letters are an interesting point," he said. "But we must concentrate on the case as a whole. There are, as I see it, three possible solutions."

"Three?"

"Yes. Solution one: the simplest. Your wife's first husband is still alive. He first threatens her and then proceeds to carry out his threats. If we accept this solution, our problem is to discover how he got in or out without being seen.

"Solution two: Mrs. Leidner, for reasons of her own (reasons probably more easily understood by a medical man than a layman), writes herself threatening letters. The gas business is staged by her (remember, it was she who roused you by telling you she smelt gas). But, *if Mrs. Leidner wrote herself the letters, she cannot be in danger from the supposed writer.* We must, therefore, look elsewhere for the murderer. We must look, in fact, amongst the members of your staff. Yes," in answer to a murmur of protest from Dr. Leidner, "that is the only logical conclusion. To satisfy a private grudge one of them killed her. That person, I may say, was probably aware of the letters—or was at any rate aware that Mrs. Leidner feared or was pretending to fear some one. That fact, in the murderer's opinion, rendered the murder quite safe for him. He felt sure it would be put down to a mysterious outsider—the writer of the threatening letters.

"A variant of this solution is that the murderer actually wrote the letters himself, being aware of Mrs. Leidner's past history. But in that case it is not quite clear *why* the criminal should have copied Mrs. Leidner's own handwriting since, as far as we can see, it would be more to his or her advantage that they should appear to be written by an outsider.

"The third solution is the most interesting to my mind. I suggest that the letters are genuine. They are written by Mrs. Leidner's first husband (or his younger brother), *who is actually one of the expedition staff.*"

CHAPTER XVI

THE SUSPECTS

Dr. Leidner sprang to his feet.

"Impossible! Absolutely impossible! The idea is absurd!"

Mr. Poirot looked at him quite calmly but said nothing.

"You mean to suggest that my wife's former husband is one of the expedition *and that she didn't recognize him?*"

"Exactly. Reflect a little on the facts. Nearly twenty years ago your wife lived with this man for a few months. Would she know him if she came across him after that lapse of time? I think not. His face will have changed, his build will have changed—his voice may not have changed so much, but that is a detail he can attend to himself. And remember, *she is not looking for him amongst her own household.* She visualizes him as somewhere *outside*—a stranger. No, I do not think she would recognize him. And there is a second possibility. The young brother—the child of those days who was so passionately devoted to his elder brother. He is now a man. Will she recognize a child of ten or twelve years old in a man nearing thirty? Yes, there is young William Bosner to be reckoned with. Remember, his brother in his eyes may not loom as a traitor but as a patriot, a martyr for his own country—Germany. In his eyes *Mrs. Leidner* is the traitor—the monster who sent his beloved brother to death! A susceptible child is capable of great hero worship, and a young mind can easily be obsessed by an idea which persists into adult life."

"Quite true," said Dr. Reilly. "The popular view that a child forgets easily is not an accurate one. Many people go right through life in the grip of an idea which has been impressed on them in very tender years."

"*Bien.* You have these two possibilities. Frederick Bosner, a man by now of fifty odd, and William Bosner, whose age would be something short of thirty. Let us examine the members of your staff from these two points of view."

"This is fantastic," murmured Dr. Leidner. "*My* staff! The members of my own expedition."

"And consequently considered above suspicion," said Poirot dryly. "A very useful point of view. *Commençons!* Who could emphatically *not* be Frederick or William?"

"The women."

"Naturally. Miss Johnson and Mrs. Mercado are crossed off. Who else?"

"Carey. He and I have worked together for years before I even met Louise—"

"And also he is the wrong age. He is, I should judge, thirty-eight or nine, too young for Frederick, too old for William. Now for the rest. There is Father Lavigny and Mr. Mercado. Either of them might be Frederick Bosner."

"But, my dear sir," cried Dr. Leidner in a voice of mingled irritation and amusement, "Father Lavigny is known all over the world as an epigraphist and Mercado has worked for years in a well-known museum in New York. It is *impossible* that either of them should be the man you think!"

Poirot waved an airy hand.

"Impossible—impossible—I take no account of the word! The impossible, always I examine it very closely! But we will pass on for the moment. Who else have you? Carl Reiter, a young man with a German name, David Emmott—"

"He has been with me two seasons, remember."

"He is a young man with the gift of patience. *If* he committed a crime, it would not be in a hurry. All would be very well prepared."

Dr. Leidner made a gesture of despair.

"And lastly, William Coleman," continued Poirot.

"He is an Englishman."

"*Pourquoi pas?* Did not Mrs. Leidner say that the boy left America and could not be traced? He might easily have been brought up in England."

"You have an answer to everything," said Dr. Leidner.

I was thinking hard. Right from the beginning I had thought Mr. Coleman's manner rather more like a P. G. Wodehouse book than like a real live young man. Had he really been playing a part all the time?

Poirot was writing in a little book.

"Let us proceed with order and method," he said. "On the first count we have two names. Father Lavigny and Mr. Mercado. On the second we have Coleman, Emmott and Reiter.

"Now let us pass to the opposite aspect of the matter—means and opportunity. *Who amongst the expedition had the means and the opportunity of committing the crime?* Carey was on the dig, Coleman was in Hassanieh, you yourself were on the roof. That leaves us Father Lavigny, Mr. Mercado, Mrs. Mercado, David Emmott, Carl Reiter, Miss Johnson and Nurse Leatheran."

"Oh!" I exclaimed, and I bounded in my chair.

Mr. Poirot looked at me with twinkling eyes.

"Yes, I'm afraid, *ma sœur,* that you have got to be included. It would have been quite easy for you to have gone along and killed Mrs. Leidner while the courtyard was empty. You have plenty of muscle and strength, and she would have been quite unsuspicious until the moment the blow was struck."

I was so upset that I couldn't get a word out. Dr. Reilly, I noticed, was looking highly amused.

"Interesting case of a nurse who murdered her patients one by one," he murmured.

Such a look as I gave him!

Dr. Leidner's mind had been running on a different tack.

"Not Emmott, M. Poirot," he objected. "You can't include him. He was on the roof with me, remember, during that ten minutes."

"Nevertheless we cannot exclude him. He could have come down, gone straight to Mrs. Leidner's room, killed her, and *then* called the boy back. Or he might have killed her on one of the occasions when he had *sent the boy up to you.*"

Dr. Leidner shook his head, murmuring:

"What a nightmare! It's all so—fantastic."

To my surprise Poirot agreed.

"Yes, that is true. *This is a fantastic crime.* One does not often come across them. Usually murder is very sordid—very simple. But this is unusual murder . . . I suspect, Dr. Leidner, that your wife was an unusual woman."

He had hit the nail on the head with such accuracy that I jumped.

"Is that true, nurse?" he asked.

Dr. Leidner said quietly:

"Tell him what Louise was like, nurse. You are unprejudiced."

I spoke quite frankly.

"She was very lovely," I said. "You couldn't help admiring her and wanting to do things for her. I've never met any one like her before."

"Thank you," said Dr. Leidner and smiled at me.

"That is valuable testimony coming from an outsider," said Poirot politely. "Well, let us proceed. Under the heading of *means and opportunity* we have seven names. Nurse Leatheran, Miss Johnson, Mrs.

Mercado, Mr. Mercado, Mr. Reiter, Mr. Emmott and Father Lavigny."

Once more he cleared his throat. I've always noticed that foreigners can make the oddest noises.

"Let us for the moment assume that our third theory is correct. That is, that the murderer is Frederick or William Bosner, and that Frederick or William Bosner is a member of the expedition staff. By comparing both lists we can narrow down our suspects on this count to four. Father Lavigny, Mr. Mercado, Carl Reiter and David Emmott."

"Father Lavigny is out of the question," said Dr. Leidner with decision. "He is one of the *Pères Blancs* in Carthage."

"And his beard's quite real," I put in.

"*Ma sœur,*" said Poirot, "a murderer of the first class *never* wears a false beard!"

"How do you know the murderer is of the first class?" I asked rebelliously.

"Because if he were not, the whole truth would be plain to me at this instant—and it is not."

That's pure conceit, I thought to myself.

"Anyway," I said, reverting to the beard, "it must have taken quite a time to grow."

"That is a practical observation," said Poirot. Dr. Leidner said irritably:

"But it's ridiculous—quite ridiculous. Both he and Mercado are well-known men. They've been known for years."

Poirot turned to him.

"You have not the true vision. You do not appreciate an important point. *If Frederick Bosner is not dead—what has he been doing all these years?* He must have taken a different name. He must have built himself up a career."

"As a *Père Blanc?*" asked Dr. Reilly sceptically.

"It is a little fantastic that, yes," confessed Poirot. "But we cannot put it right out of court. Besides, there are other possibilities."

"The young 'uns?" said Reilly. "If you want my opinion, on the face of it there's only one of your suspects that's even plausible."

"And that is?"

"Young Carl Reiter. There's nothing actually against him, but come down to it and you've got to admit a few things—he's the right age, he's got a German name, he's new this year and he had the opportunity all right. He'd only got to pop out of his photographic place, cross the courtyard to do his dirty work and hare back again while the coast was clear. If any one were to have dropped into the photographic room while he was out of it, he can always say later that he was in the dark-room. I don't say he's your man but if you are going to suspect some one I say he's by far and away the most likely."

M. Poirot didn't seem very receptive. He nodded gravely but doubtfully.

"Yes," he said. "He is the most plausible, but it may not be so simple as all that."

Then he said:

"Let us say no more at present. I would like now if I may to examine the room where the crime took place."

"Certainly." Dr. Leidner fumbled in his pockets then looked at Dr. Reilly.

"Captain Maitland took it," he said.

"Maitland gave it to me," said Reilly. "He had to go off on that Kurdish business."

He produced the key.

Dr. Leidner said hesitatingly:

"Do you mind—if I don't— Perhaps, nurse—"

"Of course. Of course," said Poirot. "I quite understand. Never do I wish to cause you unnecessary pain. If you will be good enough to accompany me, *ma sœur*."

"Certainly," I said.

CHAPTER XVII

THE STAIN BY THE WASH-STAND

MRS. LEIDNER'S BODY had been taken to Hassanieh for the post-mortem, but otherwise her room had been left exactly as it was. There was so little in it that it had not taken the police long to go over it.

To the right of the door as you entered was the bed. Opposite the door were the two barred windows giving on the countryside. Between them was a plain oak table with two drawers that served Mrs. Leidner as a dressing-table. On the east wall there was a line of hooks with dresses hung up protected by cotton bags and a deal chest of drawers. Immediately to the left of the door was the wash-stand. In the middle of the room was a good-sized plain oak table with a blotter and inkstand and a small attaché-case. It was in the latter that Mrs. Leidner had kept the anonymous letters. The curtains were short strips of native material—white striped with orange. The floor was of stone with some goatskin rugs on it, three narrow ones of brown striped with white in front of the two windows and the wash-stand, and a larger better quality one of white with brown stripes lying between the bed and the writing-table.

There were no cupboards or alcoves or long curtains—nowhere, in fact, where any one could have hidden. The bed was a plain iron one with a printed cotton quilt. The only trace of luxury in the room were three pillows all made of the best soft and billowy down. Nobody but Mrs. Leidner had pillows like these.

In a few brief dry words Dr. Reilly explained where Mrs. Leidner's body had been found—in a heap on the rug beside the bed.

To illustrate his account, he beckoned me to come forward.

"If you don't mind, nurse?" he said.

I'm not squeamish. I got down on the floor and arranged myself as far as possible in the attitude in which Mrs. Leidner's body had been found.

"Leidner lifted her head when he found her," said the doctor. "But I questioned him closely and it's obvious that he didn't actually change her position."

"It seems quite straightforward," said Poirot. "She was lying on the bed, asleep or resting—some one opens the door, she looks up, rises to her feet—"

"And he struck her down," finished the doctor. "The blow would produce unconsciousness and death would follow very shortly. You see—"

He explained the injury in technical language.

"Not much blood, then?" said Poirot.

"No, the blood escaped internally into the brain."

"*Eh bien,*" said Poirot, "that seems straightforward enough—except for one thing. *If* the man who entered was a stranger, why did not Mrs. Leidner cry out at once for help? If she had screamed she would have been heard. Nurse Leatheran here would have heard her, and Emmott and the boy."

"That's easily answered," said Dr. Reilly dryly. "*Because it wasn't a stranger.*"

Poirot nodded.

"Yes," he said meditatively. "She may have been *surprised* to see the person—but she was not *afraid.* Then, as he struck, she *may* have uttered a half cry—too late."

"The cry Miss Johnson heard?"

"Yes, if she *did* hear it. But on the whole I doubt it. These mud walls are thick and the windows were closed."

He stepped up to the bed.

"You left her actually lying down?" he asked me. I explained exactly what I had done.

"Did she mean to sleep or was she going to read?"

"I gave her two books—a light one and a volume of memoirs. She usually read for a while and then sometimes dropped off for a short sleep."

"And she was—what shall I say—quite as usual?"

I considered.

"Yes. She seemed quite normal and in good spirits," I said. "Just a shade off-hand, perhaps, but I put that down to her having confided in me the day before. It makes people a little uncomfortable sometimes."

Poirot's eyes twinkled.

"Ah, yes, indeed, me, I know that well."

He looked round the room.

"And when you came in here after the murder, was everything as you had seen it before?"

I looked round also.

"Yes, I think so. I don't remember anything being different."

"There was no sign of the weapon with which she was struck?"

"No."

Poirot looked at Dr. Reilly.

"What was it in your opinion?"

The doctor replied promptly.

"Something pretty powerful of a fair size and without any sharp corners or edges. The rounded base of a statue, say—something like that. Mind you, I'm not suggesting that that *was* it. But that type of thing. The blow was delivered with great force."

"Struck by a strong arm? A man's arm?"

"Yes—unless—"

"Unless—what?"

Dr. Reilly said slowly:

"It is just possible that Mrs. Leidner might have been on her knees—in which case, the blow being delivered from above with a heavy implement, the force needed would not have been so great."

"*On her knees*," mused Poirot. "It is an idea—that."

"It's only an idea, mind," the doctor hastened to point out. "There's absolutely nothing to indicate it."

"But it's possible."

"Yes. And after all, in view of the circumstances, it's not fantastic. Her fear might have led her to kneel in supplication rather than to scream when her instinct would tell her it was too late—that nobody could get there in time."

"Yes," said Poirot thoughtfully. "It is an idea. . . ."

It was a very poor one, I thought. I couldn't for one moment imagine Mrs. Leidner on her knees to any one.

Poirot made his way slowly round the room. He opened the windows, tested the bars, passed his head through and satisfied himself that by no means could his shoulders be made to follow his head.

"The windows were shut when you found her," he said. "Were they also shut when you left her at a quarter to one?"

"Yes, they were always shut in the afternoon. There is no gauze over these windows as there is in the living-room and dining-room. They are kept shut to keep out the flies."

"And in any case no one could get in that way," mused Poirot. "And the walls are of the most solid—mud-brick—and there are no trap-doors and no sky-lights. No, there is only one way into this room—*through the door*. And there is only one way to the door—through the courtyard. And there is only one entrance to the courtyard—

through the archway. And outside the archway there were five people and they all tell the same story, and I do not think, me, that they are lying. . . . No, they are not lying. They are not bribed to silence. The murderer was *here*. . . ."

I didn't say anything. Hadn't I felt the same thing just now when we were all cooped up round that table?

Slowly Poirot prowled round the room. He took up a photograph from the chest of drawers. It was of an elderly man with a white goatee beard. He looked inquiringly at me.

"Mrs. Leidner's father," I said. "She told me so."

He put it down again and glanced over the articles on the dressing table—all of plain tortoiseshell—simple but good. He looked up at a row of books on a shelf, repeating the titles aloud.

"*Who Were the Greeks? Introduction to Relativity. Life of Lady Hester Stanhope. Crewe Train. Back to Methuselah. Linda Condon.* Yes, they tell us something, perhaps.

"She was not a fool, your Mrs. Leidner. She had a mind."

"Oh! she was a *very* clever woman," I said eagerly. "Very well read and up in everything. She wasn't a bit ordinary."

He smiled as he looked over at me.

"No," he said. "I've already realized that."

He passed on. He stood for some moments at the wash-stand where there was a big array of bottles and toilet creams.

Then, suddenly, he dropped on his knees and examined the rug.

Dr. Reilly and I came quickly to join him. He was examining a small dark brown stain, almost invisible on the brown of the rug. In fact it was only just noticeable where it impinged on one of the white stripes.

"What do you say, doctor?" he said. "Is that blood?"

Dr. Reilly knelt down.

"Might be," he said. "I'll make sure if you like?"

"If you would be so amiable."

Mr. Poirot examined the jug and basin. The jug was standing on the side of the wash-stand. The basin was empty, but beside the wash-stand there was an old kerosene tin containing slop water.

He turned to me.

"Do you remember, nurse? Was this jug *out* of the basin or *in* it when you left Mrs. Leidner at a quarter to one?"

"I can't be sure," I said after a minute or two. "I rather think it was standing in the basin."

"Ah?"

"But you see," I said hastily, "I only think so because it usually was. The boys leave it like that after lunch. I just feel that if it hadn't been in I should have noticed it."

He nodded quite appreciatively.

"Yes, I understand that. It is your hospital training. If everything had not been just so in the room, you would quite unconsciously have set it to rights hardly noticing what you were doing. And after the murder? Was it like it is now?"

I shook my head.

"I didn't notice then," I said. "All I looked for was whether there was any place any one could be hidden or if there were anything the murderer had left behind him."

"It's blood all right," said Dr. Reilly, rising from his knees. "Is it important?"

Poirot was frowning perplexedly. He flung out his hands with petulance.

"I cannot tell. How can I tell? It may mean nothing at all. I can say, if I like, that the murderer touched her—that there was blood on his hands—very little blood, but still blood—and so he came over here and washed them. Yes, it may have been like that. But I cannot jump to conclusions and say that it *was* so. That stain may be of no importance at all."

"There would have been very little blood," said Dr. Reilly dubiously. "None would have spurted out or anything like that. It would have just oozed a little from the wound. Of course, if he'd probed it at all . . ."

I gave a shiver. A nasty sort of picture came up in my mind. The vision of somebody—perhaps that nice pig-faced photographic boy, striking down that lovely woman and then bending over her probing the wound with his finger in an awful gloating fashion and his face, perhaps, quite different . . . all fierce and mad. . . .

Dr. Reilly noticed my shiver.

"What's the matter, nurse?" he said.

"Nothing—just goose-flesh," I said. "A goose walking over my grave."

Mr. Poirot turned round and looked at me.

"I know what you need," he said. "Presently when we have finished here and I go back with the doctor to Hassanieh we will take you with us. You will give Nurse Leatheran tea, will you not, doctor?"

"Delighted."

"Oh, no, doctor," I protested. "I couldn't think of such a thing."

M. Poirot gave me a little friendly tap on the shoulder. Quite an English tap, not a foreign one.

"You, *ma sœur,* will do as you are told," he said. "Besides, it will be of advantage to me. There is a good deal more that I want to discuss, and I cannot do it here where one must preserve the decencies. The good Dr. Leidner, he worshipped his wife and he is sure—oh, so sure—that everybody else felt the same about her! But that, in my opinion, would not be human nature! No, we want to discuss Mrs. Leidner with—how do you say—the gloves removed? That is settled then. When we have finished here, we take you with us to Hassanieh."

"I suppose," I said doubtfully, "that I ought to be leaving anyway. It's rather awkward."

"Do nothing for a day or two," said Dr. Reilly. "You can't very well go until after the funeral."

"That's all very well," I said. "And supposing I get murdered too, doctor?"

I said it half jokingly and Dr. Reilly took it in the same fashion and would, I think, have made some jocular response.

But M. Poirot, to my astonishment, stood stock still in the middle of the floor and clasped his hands to his head.

"Ah! if that were possible," he murmured. "It is a danger—yes—a great danger—and what can one do? How can one guard against it?"

"Why, M. Poirot," I said, "I was only joking! Who'd want to murder me, I should like to know?"

"You—or another," he said, and I didn't like the way he said it at all. Positively creepy.

"But why?" I persisted.

He looked at me very straight then.

"I joke, mademoiselle," he said, "and I laugh. *But there are some things that are no joke.* There are things that my profession has taught me. And one of these things, the most terrible thing, is this:

"*Murder is a habit . . .*"

CHAPTER XVIII

TEA AT DR. REILLY'S

BEFORE LEAVING, POIROT made a round of the expedition house and the outbuildings. He also asked a few questions of the servants at second hand—that is to say, Dr. Reilly translated the questions and answers from English into Arabic and vice versa.

These questions dealt mainly with the appearance of the stranger Mrs. Leidner and I had seen looking through the window and to whom Father Lavigny had been talking on the following day.

"Do you really think that fellow had anything to do with it?" asked Dr. Reilly when we were bumping along in his car on our way to Hassanieh.

"I like all the information there is," was Poirot's reply.

And really, that described his methods very well. I found later that there wasn't anything—no small scrap of insignificant gossip—in which he wasn't interested. Men aren't usually so gossipy.

I must confess I was glad of my cup of tea when we got to Dr. Reilly's house. M. Poirot, I noticed, put five lumps of sugar in his.

Stirring it carefully with his teaspoon he said:

"And now we can talk, can we not? We can make up our minds who is likely to have committed the crime."

"Lavigny, Mercado, Emmott or Reiter?" asked Dr. Reilly.

"No, no—that was theory number three. I wish to concentrate now on theory number two—leaving aside all question of a mysterious husband or brother-in-law turning up from the past. Let us discuss now quite simply which member of the expedition had the means and opportunity to kill Mrs. Leidner, and who is likely to have done so."

"I thought you didn't think much of that theory."

"Not at all. But I have some natural delicacy," said Poirot reproachfully. "Can I discuss in the presence of Dr. Leidner the motives likely to lead to the murder of his wife by a member of the expedition? That would not have been delicate at all. I had to sustain the fiction that his wife was adorable and that every one adored her!

"But naturally it was not like that at all. Now we can be brutal and impersonal and say what we think. We have no longer to consider people's feelings. And that is where Nurse Leatheran is going to help us. She is, I am sure, a very good observer."

"Oh, I don't know about that," I said.

Dr. Reilly handed me a plate of hot scones—"to fortify yourself," he said. They were very good scones.

"Come now," said M. Poirot in a friendly, chatty way. "You shall tell me, *ma sœur,* exactly what each member of the expedition felt towards Mrs. Leidner."

"I was only there a week, M. Poirot," I said.

"Quite long enough for one of your intelligence. A nurse sums up quickly. She makes her judgments and abides by them. Come, let us make a beginning. Father Lavigny, for instance?"

"Well, there now, I really couldn't say. He and Mrs. Leidner seemed to like talking together. But they usually spoke French and I'm not very good at French myself though I learnt it as a girl at school. I've an idea they talked mainly about books."

"They were, as you might say, companionable together—yes?"

"Well, yes, you might put it that way. But, all the same, I think Father Lavigny was puzzled by her and—well—almost annoyed by being puzzled, if you know what I mean."

And I told him of the conversation I had had with him out on the dig that first day when he had called Mrs. Leidner a "dangerous woman."

"Now that is very interesting," M. Poirot said. "And she—what do you think she thought of him?"

"That's rather difficult to say, too. It wasn't easy to know what Mrs. Leidner thought of people. Sometimes, I fancy, *he* puzzled *her.* I remember her saying to Dr. Leidner that he was unlike any priest she had ever known."

"A length of hemp to be ordered for Father Lavigny," said Dr. Reilly facetiously.

"My dear friend," said Poirot. "Have you not, perhaps, some patients to attend? I would not for the world detain you from your professional duties."

"I've got a whole hospital of them," said Dr. Reilly.

And he got up and said a wink was as good as a nod to a blind horse, and went out laughing.

"That is better," said Poirot. "We will have now an interesting conversation *tête-à-tête.* But you must not forget to eat your tea."

He passed me a plate of sandwiches and suggested my having a second cup of tea. He really had very pleasant, attentive manners.

"And now," he said, "let us continue with your impressions. Who was there who in your opinion did *not* like Mrs. Leidner?"

"Well," I said, "it's only my opinion and I don't want it repeated as coming from me."

"Naturally not."

"But in my opinion little Mrs. Mercado fairly hated her!"

"Ah! And Mr. Mercado?"

"He was a bit soft on her," I said. "I shouldn't think women apart from his wife had ever taken much notice of him. And Mrs. Leidner had a nice kind way of being interested in people and the things they told her. It rather went to the poor man's head, I fancy."

"And Mrs. Mercado—she was not pleased?"

"She was just plain jealous—that's the truth of it. You've got to be very careful when there's a husband and wife about, and that's a fact. I could tell you some surprising things. You've no idea the extraordinary things women get into their heads when it's a question of their husbands."

"I do not doubt the truth of what you say. So Mrs. Mercado was jealous? And she hated Mrs. Leidner?"

"I've seen her look at her as though she'd have liked to kill her—oh, gracious!" I pulled myself up. "Indeed, M. Poirot, I didn't mean to say—I mean that is, not for one moment—"

"No, no. I quite understand. The phrase slipped out. A very convenient one. And Mrs. Leidner, was she worried by this animosity of Mrs. Mercado's?"

"Well," I said, reflecting, "I don't really think she was worried at all. In fact, I don't even know whether she noticed it. I thought once of just giving her a hint—but I didn't like to. Least said soonest mended. That's what I say."

"You are doubtless wise. Can you give me any instances of how Mrs. Mercado showed her feelings?"

I told him about our conversation on the roof.

"So she mentioned Mrs. Leidner's first marriage," said Poirot thoughtfully. "Can you remember—in mentioning it—did she look at you as though she wondered whether you had heard a different version?"

"You think she may have known the truth about it?"

"It is a possiblity. She may have written those letters—and engineered a tapping hand and all the rest of it."

"I wondered something of the same kind myself. It seemed the kind of petty revengeful thing she might do."

"Yes. A cruel streak, I should say. But hardly the temperament for cold-blooded brutal murder unless, of course—"

He paused and then said:

"It is odd, that curious thing she said to you. *'I know why you are here.'* What did she mean by it?"

"I can't imagine," I said frankly.

"She thought you were there for some ulterior reason apart from the declared one. What reason? And why should she be so concerned in the matter. Odd, too, the way you tell me she stared at you all through tea the day you arrived."

"Well, she's not a lady, M. Poirot," I said primly.

"That, *ma sœur,* is an excuse but not an explanation."

I wasn't quite sure for the minute what he meant. But he went on quickly.

"And the other members of the staff?"

I considered.

"I don't think Miss Johnson liked Mrs. Leidner either very much. But she was quite open and above-board about it. She as good as admitted she was prejudiced. You see, she's very devoted to Dr. Leidner and had worked with him for years. And of course, marriage does change things—there's no denying it."

"Yes," said Poirot. "And from Miss Johnson's point of view it would be an unsuitable marriage. It would really have been much more suitable if Dr. Leidner had married *her.*"

"It would really," I agreed. "But there, that's a man all over. Not one in a hundred considers suitability. And one can't really blame Dr. Leidner. Miss Johnson, poor soul, isn't so much to look at. Now Mrs. Leidner was really beautiful—not young, of course—but oh! I wish you'd known her. There was something about her. . . . I remember Mr. Coleman saying she was like a thingummyjig that came to lure people into marshes. That wasn't a very good way of putting it but—oh, well—you'll laugh at me but there *was* something about her that was—well—unearthly."

"She could cast a spell—yes, I understand," said Poirot.

"Then I don't think she and Mr. Carey got on very well either," I went on. "I've an idea *he* was jealous just like Miss Johnson. He was always very stiff with her and so was she with him. You know—she passed him things and was very polite and called him Mr. Carey rather formally. He was an old friend of her husband's, of course, and some women can't stand their husband's old friends. They don't like to think that any one knew them before they did—at least that's rather a muddled way of putting it—"

"I quite understand. And the three young men? Coleman, you say, was inclined to be poetic about her."

I couldn't help laughing.

"It was funny, M. Poirot," I said. "He's such a matter-of-fact young man."

"And the other two?"

"I don't really know about Mr. Emmott. He's always so quiet and never says much. She was very nice to him always. You know—friendly—called him David and used to tease him about Miss Reilly and things like that."

"Ah, really? And did he enjoy that?"

"I don't quite know," I said doubtfully. "He'd just look at her. Rather funnily. You couldn't tell what he was thinking."

"And Mr. Reiter?"

"She wasn't always very kind to him," I said slowly. "I think he got on her nerves. She used to say quite sarcastic things to him."

"And did he mind?"

"He used to get very pink, poor boy. Of course, she didn't *mean* to be unkind."

And then suddenly, from feeling a little sorry for the boy, it came over me that he was very likely a cold-blooded murderer and had been playing a part all the time.

"Oh, M. Poirot," I exclaimed. "What do you think *really* happened?"

He shook his head slowly and thoughtfully.

"Tell me," he said. "You are not afraid to go back there to-night?"

"Oh, *no*," I said. "Of course, I remember what you said, but who would want to murder *me*?"

"I do not think that any one could," he said slowly. "That is partly why I have been so anxious to hear all you could tell me. No, I think —I am sure—you are quite safe."

"If any one had told me in Baghdad—" I began and stopped.

"Did you hear any gossip about the Leidners and the expedition before you came here?" he asked.

I told him about Mrs. Leidner's nickname and just a little of what Mrs. Kelsey had said about her.

In the middle of it the door opened and Miss Reilly came in. She had been playing tennis and had her racquet in her hand.

I gathered Poirot had already met her when he arrived in Hassanieh.

She said how do you do to me in her usual off-hand manner and picked up a sandwich.

"Well, M. Poirot," she said. "How are you getting on with our local mystery?"

"Not very fast, mademoiselle."

"I see you've rescued nurse from the wreck."

"Nurse Leatheran has been giving me valuable information about the various members of the expedition. Incidentally I have learnt a good deal—about the victim. And the victim, mademoiselle, is very often the clue to the mystery."

Miss Reilly said:

"That's rather clever of you, M. Poirot. It's certainly true that if ever a woman deserved to be murdered Mrs. Leidner was that woman!"

"Miss Reilly!" I cried, scandalized.

She laughed, a short, nasty laugh.

"Ah!" she said. "I thought you hadn't been hearing quite the truth. Nurse Leatheran, I'm afraid, was quite taken in, like many other people. Do you know, M. Poirot, I rather hope that this case isn't going to be one of your successes. I'd quite like the murderer of Louise Leidner to get away with it. In fact, I wouldn't much have objected to putting her out of the way myself."

I was simply disgusted with the girl. M. Poirot, I must say, didn't turn a hair. He just bowed and said quite pleasantly:

"I hope, then, that you have an alibi for yesterday afternoon?"

There was a moment's silence and Miss Reilly's racquet went clattering down on to the floor. She didn't bother to pick it up. Slack and untidy like all her sort! She said in a rather breathless voice:

"Oh, yes, I was playing tennis at the club. But, seriously, M. Poirot, I wonder if you know anything at all about Mrs. Leidner and the kind of woman she was?"

Again he made a funny little bow and said:

"You shall inform me, mademoiselle."

She hesitated a minute and then spoke with a callousness and lack of decency that really sickened me.

"There's a convention that one doesn't speak ill of the dead. That's stupid, I think. The truth's always the truth. On the whole it's better to keep your mouth shut about living people. You might conceivably injure them. The dead are past that. But the harm they've done lives after them sometimes. Not quite a quotation from Shakespeare but very nearly! Has nurse told you of the queer atmosphere there was at Tell Yarimjah? Has she told you how jumpy they all were? And how they all used to glare at each other like enemies? That was Louise Leidner's doing. When I was a kid out here three years ago they were the happiest, jolliest lot imaginable. Even last year they were pretty well all right. But this year there was a blight over them—and it was *her* doing. She was the kind of woman who won't let anybody else be happy! There *are* women like that and she was one of them! She wanted to break up things always. Just for fun—or for the sense of power—or perhaps just because she was made that way. And she was the kind of woman who had to get hold of every male creature within reach!"

"Miss Reilly," I cried, "I don't think that's true. In fact I *know* it isn't."

She went on without taking the least notice of me.

"It wasn't enough for her to have her husband adore her. She had to make a fool of that long-legged shambling idiot of a Mercado. Then she got hold of Bill. Bill's a sensible cove, but she was getting him all mazed and bewildered. Carl Reiter she just amused herself by tormenting. It was easy. He's a sensitive boy. And she had a jolly good go at David.

"David was better sport to her because he put up a fight. He felt her charm—but he wasn't having any. I think because he'd got sense enough to know that she didn't really care a damn. And that's why I hate her so. She's not sensual. She doesn't *want* affairs. It's just cold-blooded experiment on her part and the fun of stirring people up and setting them against each other. She dabbled in that too. She's the sort of woman who's never had a row with any one in her life—but rows always happen where she is! She *makes* them happen. She's a kind of female Iago. She *must* have drama. But she doesn't want to be involved *herself*. She's always outside pulling strings—looking on—enjoying it. Oh, do you see *at all* what I mean?"

"I see, perhaps, more than you know, mademoiselle," said Poirot.

I couldn't make his voice out. He didn't sound indignant. He sounded—oh, well, I can't explain it.

Sheila Reilly seemed to understand for she flushed all over her face.

"You can think what you choose," she said. "But I'm right about her. She was a clever woman and she was bored and she experimented—with people—like other people experiment with chemicals. She enjoyed working on poor old Johnson's feelings and seeing her bite on the bullet and control herself like the old sport she is. She liked goading little Mercado into a white-hot frenzy. She liked flicking *me* on the raw—and she could do it too, every time! She liked finding out things about people and holding it over them. Oh, I don't mean crude blackmail—I mean just letting them know that she *knew*—and leaving them uncertain what she meant to do about it. My God, though, that woman was an artist! There was nothing crude about *her* methods!"

"And her husband?" asked Poirot.

"She never wanted to hurt him," said Miss Reilly slowly. "I've never known her anything but sweet to him. I suppose she was fond of him. He's a dear—wrapped up in his own world—his digging and his theories. And he worshipped her and thought her perfection. That might have annoyed some women. It didn't annoy her. In a sense he lived in a fool's paradise—and yet it wasn't a fool's paradise because to him she was what he thought her. Though it's hard to reconcile that with—"

She stopped.

"Go on, mademoiselle," said Poirot.

She turned suddenly on me.

"What have you said about Richard Carey?"

"About Mr. Carey?" I asked, astonished.

"About her and Carey?"

"Well," I said, "I've mentioned that they didn't hit it off very well—"

To my surprise she broke into a fit of laughter.

"Didn't hit it off very well! You fool! He's head over ears in love with her. And it's tearing him to pieces—because he worships Leidner too. He's been his friend for years. That would be enough for her, of course. She's made it her business to come between them. But all the same I've fancied—"

"*Eh bien?*"

She was frowning, absorbed in thought.

"I've fancied that she'd gone too far for once—that she was not only biter but bit! Carey's attractive. He's as attractive as hell. . . . She was a cold devil—but I believe she could have lost her coldness with him. . . ."

"I think it's just scandalous what you're saying," I cried. "Why, they hardly spoke to each other!"

"Oh, didn't they?" She turned on me. "A hell of a lot you know about it. It was 'Mr. Carey' and 'Mrs. Leidner' in the house, but they used to meet outside. She'd walk down the path to the river. And he'd leave the dig for an hour at a time. They used to meet among the fruit trees.

"I saw him once just leaving her, striding back to the dig, and she was standing looking after him. I was a female cad, I suppose. I had some glasses with me and I took them out and had a good look at her face. If you ask me I believed she cared like hell for Richard Carey. . . ."

She broke off and looked at Poirot.

"Excuse my butting in on your case," she said with a sudden rather twisted grin, "but I thought you'd like to have the local colour correct."

And she marched out of the room.

"M. Poirot," I cried. "I don't believe one word of it all!"

He looked at me and he smiled, and he said (very queerly I thought):

"You can't deny, nurse, that Miss Reilly has shed a certain —illumination on the case."

CHAPTER XIX

A NEW SUSPICION

We couldn't say any more just then because Dr. Reilly came in, saying jokingly that he'd killed off the most tiresome of his patients.

He and M. Poirot settled down to a more or less medical discussion of the psychology and mental state of an anonymous letter-writer. The doctor cited cases that he had known professionally, and M. Poirot told various stories from his own experience.

"It is not so simple as it seems," he ended. "There is the desire for power and very often a strong inferiority complex."

Dr. Reilly nodded.

"That's why you often find that the author of anonymous letters is the last person in the place to be suspected. Some quiet inoffensive little soul who apparently can't say Boo to a goose—all sweetness and Christian meekness on the outside—and seething with all the fury of hell underneath!"

Poirot said thoughtfully:

"Should you say Mrs. Leidner had any tendency to an inferiority complex?"

Dr. Reilly scraped out his pipe with a chuckle.

"Last woman on earth I'd describe that way. No repressions about her. Life, life and more life—that's what she wanted—and got, too!"

"Do you consider it a possibility, psychologically speaking, that she wrote those letters?"

"Yes, I do. But if she did, the reason arose out of her instinct to dramatize herself. Mrs. Leidner was a bit of a film star in private life! She *had* to be the centre of things—in the limelight. By the law of opposites she married Leidner who's about the most retiring and modest man I know. He adored her—but adoration by the fireside wasn't enough for her. She had to be the persecuted heroine as well."

"In fact," said Poirot, smiling, "you don't subscribe to his theory that she wrote them and retained no memory of her act?"

"No, I don't. I didn't turn down the idea in front of him. You can't very well say to a man who's just lost a dearly loved wife that that same wife was a shameless exhibitionist, and that she drove him nearly crazy with anxiety to satisfy her sense of the dramatic. As a matter of fact it wouldn't be safe to tell any man the truth about his wife! Funnily enough, I'd trust most women with the truth about their husbands. Women can accept the fact that a man is a rotter, a swindler, a drug-taker, a confirmed liar, and a general swine without batting an eyelash and without its impairing their affection for the brute in the least! Women are wonderful realists."

"Frankly, Dr. Reilly, what *was* your exact opinion of Mrs. Leidner?"

Dr. Reilly lay back in his chair and puffed slowly at his pipe.

"Frankly—it's hard to say! I didn't know her well enough. She'd got charm—any amount of it. Brains, sympathy. . . . What else? She hadn't any of the ordinary unpleasant vices. She wasn't sensual or lazy or even particularly vain. She was, I've always thought (but I've no proofs of it), a most accomplished liar. What I don't know (and what I'd like to know) is whether she lied to herself or only to other people. I'm rather partial to liars myself. A woman who doesn't lie is a woman without imagination and without sympathy. I don't think she was really a man-hunter—she just liked the sport of bringing them down 'with my bow and arrow.' If you get my daughter on the subject—"

"We have had that pleasure," said Poirot with a slight smile.

"H'm," said Dr. Reilly. "She hasn't wasted much time! Shoved her knife into her pretty thoroughly, I should imagine! The younger generation has no sentiment towards the dead. It's a pity all young people are prigs! They condemn the 'old morality' and then proceed to set up a much more hard and fast code of their own. If Mrs. Leidner had had half a dozen affairs Sheila would probably have approved of her as 'living her life fully'—or 'obeying her blood instincts.' What she doesn't see is that Mrs. Leidner was acting true to type—*her* type. The cat *is* obeying its blood instinct when it plays with the mouse! It's made that way. Men aren't little boys to be shielded and protected. They've got to meet cat women—and faithful spaniel, yours-till-death adoring women, and henpecking nagging bird women—and all the rest of it! Life's a battlefield—not a picnic! I'd like to see Sheila honest enough to come off her high horse and admit that she hated Mrs. Leidner for good old thoroughgoing personal reasons. Sheila's about the only young girl in this place and she naturally assumes that she ought to have it all her own way with the young things in trousers. Naturally it annoys her when a woman, who in her view is middle-aged and who has already two husbands to her credit, comes along and licks her on her own ground. Sheila's a nice child, healthy and reasonably good-looking and attractive to the other sex as she should be. But Mrs. Leidner was something out of the ordinary in that line. She'd got just that sort of calamitous magic that plays the deuce with things—a kind of Belle Dame sans Merci."

I jumped in my chair. What a coincidence his saying that!

"Your daughter—I am not indiscreet—she has perhaps a *tendresse* for one of the young men out there?"

"Oh, I don't suppose so. She's had Emmott and Coleman dancing attendance on her as a matter of course. I don't know that she cares for one more than the other. There are a couple of young Air Force chaps too. I fancy all's fish that comes to her net at present. No, I think it's age daring to defeat youth that annoys her so much! She doesn't know as much of the world as I do. It's when you get to my age that you really appreciate a schoolgirl complexion and a clear eye and a firmly knit young body. But a woman over thirty can listen with rapt attention and throw in a word here and there to show the talker what a fine fellow he is—and few young men can resist that! Sheila's a pretty girl—but Louise Leidner was beautiful. Glorious eyes and that amazing golden fairness. Yes, she was a beautiful woman."

Yes, I thought to myself, he's right. Beauty's a wonderful thing. She *had* been beautiful. It wasn't the kind of looks you were jealous of—you just sat back and admired. I felt that first day I met her that I'd do *anything* for Mrs. Leidner!

All the same, that night as I was being driven back to the Tell Yarimjah (Dr. Reilly made me stay for an early dinner) one or two things came back to my mind and made me rather uncomfortable. At the time I hadn't believed a word of all Sheila Reilly's outpouring. I'd taken it for sheer spite and malice.

But now I suddenly remembered the way Mrs. Leidner had insisted on going for a stroll by herself that afternoon and wouldn't hear of me coming with her. I couldn't help wondering if perhaps, after all, she *had* been going to meet Mr. Carey. . . . And of course, it *was* a little odd, really, the way he and she spoke to each other so formally. Most of the others she called by their Christian names.

He never seemed to look at her, I remembered. That might be because he disliked her—or it might be just the opposite. . . .

I gave myself a little shake. Here I was fancying and imagining all sorts of things—all because of a girl's spiteful outbursts! It just showed how unkind and dangerous it was to go about saying that kind of thing.

Mrs. Leidner *hadn't* been like that at all. . . .

Of course, *she* hadn't liked Sheila Reilly. She'd really been—almost catty about her that day at lunch to Mr. Emmott.

Funny, the way he'd looked at her. The sort of way that you couldn't possibly tell what he was thinking. You never could tell what Mr. Emmott was thinking. He was so quiet. But very nice. A nice dependable person.

Now Mr. Coleman was a foolish young man if there ever was one!

I'd got to that point in my meditations when we arrived. It was just on nine o'clock and the big door was closed and barred.

Ibrahim came running with his great key to let me in.

We all went to bed early at Tell Yarimjah. There weren't any lights showing in the living-room. There was a light in the drawing-office and one in Dr. Leidner's office, but nearly all the other windows were dark. Every one must have gone to bed even earlier than usual.

As I passed the drawing-office to go to my room I looked in. Mr. Carey was in his shirt sleeves working over his big plan.

Terribly ill, he looked, I thought. So strained and worn. It gave me quite a pang. I don't know what there was about Mr. Carey—it wasn't what he *said* because he hardly said anything—and that of the most ordinary nature, and it wasn't what he *did*, for that didn't amount to much either—and yet you just couldn't help noticing him, and everything about him seemed to matter more than it would have about any one else. He just *counted*, if you know what I mean.

He turned his head and saw me. He removed his pipe from his mouth and said:

"Well, nurse, back from Hassanieh?"

"Yes, Mr. Carey. You're up working late. Everybody else seems to have gone to bed."

"I thought I might as well get on with things," he said. "I was a bit behind-hand. And I shall be out on the dig all to-morrow. We're starting digging again."

"Already?" I asked, shocked.

He looked at me rather queerly.

"It's the best thing, I think. I put it up to Leidner. He'll be in Hassanieh most of to-morrow seeing to things. But the rest of us will carry on here. You know it's not too easy all sitting round and looking at each other as things are."

He was right there, of course. Especially in the nervy, jumpy state every one was in.

"Well, of course you're right in a way," I said. "It takes one's mind off if one's got something to do."

The funeral, I knew, was to be the day after to-morrow.

He had bent over his plan again. I don't know why, but my heart just ached for him. I felt certain that he wasn't going to get any sleep.

"If you'd like a sleeping draught, Mr. Carey?" I said hesitatingly.

He shook his head with a smile.

"I'll carry on, nurse. Bad habit, sleeping draughts."

"Well, good-night, Mr. Carey," I said. "If there's anything I can do—"

"Don't think so, thank you, nurse. Good-night."

"I'm terribly sorry," I said, rather too impulsively I suppose.

"Sorry?" He looked surprised.

"For—for everybody. It's all so dreadful. But especially for you."

"For me? Why for me?"

"Well, you're such an old friend of them both."

"I'm an old friend of Leidner's. I wasn't a friend of hers particularly."

He spoke as though he had actually disliked her. Really, I wished Miss Reilly could have heard him!

"Well, good-night," I said and hurried along to my room.

I fussed around a bit in my room before undressing. Washed out some handkerchiefs and a pair of wash-leather gloves and wrote up my diary. I just looked out of my door again before I really started to get ready for bed. The lights were still on in the drawing-office and in the south building.

I supposed Dr. Leidner was still up and working in his office. I wondered whether I ought to go and say good-night to him. I hesitated about it—I didn't want to seem officious. He might be busy and not want to be disturbed. In the end, however, a sort of uneasiness drove me on. After all, it couldn't do any harm. I'd just say good-night, ask if there was anything I could do and come away.

But Dr. Leidner wasn't there. The office itself was lit up but there was no one in it except Miss Johnson. She had her head down on the table and was crying as though her heart would break.

It gave me quite a turn. She was such a quiet, self-controlled woman. It was pitiful to see her.

"Whatever is it, my dear?" I cried. I put my arm round her and patted her. "Now, now, this won't do at all. . . . You mustn't sit here crying all by yourself."

She didn't answer and I felt the dreadful shuddering sobs that were racking her.

"Don't, my dear, don't," I said. "Take a hold on yourself. I'll go and make you a cup of nice hot tea."

She raised her head and said:

"No, no, it's all right, nurse. I'm being a fool."

"What's upset you, my dear?" I asked.

She didn't answer at once, then she said:

"It's all too awful. . . ."

"Now don't start thinking of it," I told her. "What's happened has happened and can't be mended. It's no use fretting."

She sat up straight and began to pat her hair.

"I'm making rather a fool of myself," she said in her gruff voice. "I've been clearing up and tidying the office. Thought it was best to *do* something. And then—it all came over me suddenly—"

"Yes, yes," I said hastily. "I know. A nice strong cup of tea and a hot-water bottle in your bed is what you want," I said.

And she had them too. I didn't listen to any protests.

"Thank you, nurse," she said when I'd settled her in bed, and she was sipping her tea and the hot-water bottle was in. "You're a nice kind sensible woman. It's not often I make such a fool of myself."

"Oh, anybody's liable to do that at a time like this," I said, "what with one thing and another. The strain and the shock and the police here, there and everywhere. Why, I'm quite jumpy myself."

She said slowly in rather a queer voice:

"What you said in there is true. What's happened has happened and can't be mended. . . ."

She was silent for a minute or two and then said—rather oddly, I thought:

"She was never a nice woman!"

Well, I didn't argue the point. I'd always felt it was quite natural for Miss Johnson and Mrs. Leidner not to hit it off.

I wondered if, perhaps, Miss Johnson had secretly had a feeling that she was pleased Mrs. Leidner was dead, and had then been ashamed of herself for the thought.

I said:

"Now you go to sleep and don't worry about anything."

I just picked up a few things and set the room to rights. Stockings over the back of the chair and coat and skirt on a hanger. There was a little ball of crumpled paper on the floor where it must have fallen out of a pocket.

I was just smoothing it out to see whether I could safely throw it away when she quite startled me.

"Give that to me!"

I did so—rather taken aback. She'd called out so peremptorily. She snatched it from me—fairly snatched it—and then held it in the candle flame till it was burnt to ashes.

As I say, I was startled—and I just stared at her.

I hadn't had time to see what the paper was—she'd snatched it so quick. But funnily enough, as it burned it curled over towards me and I just saw that there were words written in ink on the paper.

It wasn't till I was getting into bed that I realized why they'd looked sort of familiar to me.

It was the same handwriting as that of the anonymous letters.

Was *that* why Miss Johnson had given way to a fit of remorse? Had it been her all along who had written those anonymous letters?

CHAPTER XX

MISS JOHNSON, MRS. MERCADO, MR. REITER

I DON'T MIND CONFESSING that the idea came as a complete shock to me. I'd never thought of associating *Miss Johnson* with the letters. Mrs. Mercado, perhaps. But Miss Johnson was a real lady, and so self-controlled and sensible.

But I reflected, remembering the conversation I had listened to that evening between M. Poirot and Dr. Reilly, that that might be just *why*.

If it were Miss Johnson who had written the letters it explained a lot. Mind you, I didn't think for a minute Miss Johnson had had anything to do with the murder. But I *did* see that her dislike of Mrs. Leidner might have made her succumb to the temptation of well—putting the wind up her—to put it vulgarly.

She might have hoped to frighten away Mrs. Leidner from the dig.

But then Mrs. Leidner had been murdered and Miss Johnson had felt terrible pangs of remorse—first for her cruel trick and also, perhaps, because she realized that those letters were acting as a very good shield to the actual murderer. No wonder she had broken down so utterly. She was, I was sure, a decent soul at heart. And it explained, too, why she had caught so eagerly at my consolation of "what's happened's happened and can't be amended."

And then her cryptic remark—her vindication of herself—"She was never a nice woman!"

The question was, what was *I* to do about it?

I tossed and turned for a good while and in the end decided I'd let M. Poirot know about it at the first opportunity.

He came out next day but I didn't get a chance of speaking to him what you might call privately.

We had just a minute alone together and before I could collect myself to know how to begin, he had come close to me and was whispering instructions in my ear.

"Me, I shall talk to Miss Johnson—and others, perhaps, in the living-room. You have the key of Mrs. Leidner's room still?"

"Yes," I said.

"*Très bien.* Go there, shut the door behind you and give a cry—not a scream—a cry. You understand what I mean—it is alarm—surprise that I want you to express—not mad terror. As for the excuse if you are heard—I leave that to you—the stepped toe or what you will."

At that moment Miss Johnson came out into the courtyard and there was no time for more.

I understood well enough what M. Poirot was after. As soon as he and Miss Johnson had gone into the living-room I went across to Mrs. Leidner's room and, unlocking the door, went in and pulled the door to behind me.

I can't say I didn't feel a bit of a fool standing up in an empty room and giving a yelp all for nothing at all. Besides, it wasn't so easy to know just how loud to do it. I gave a pretty loud "Oh" and then tried it a bit higher and a bit lower.

Then I came out again and prepared my excuse of a stepped (stubbed I *suppose* he meant!) toe.

But it soon appeared that no excuse would be needed. Poirot and Miss Johnson were talking together earnestly and there had clearly been no interruption.

"Well," I thought, "that settles that. Either Miss Johnson imagined that cry she heard or else it was something quite different."

I didn't like to go in and interrupt them. There was a deck-chair on the porch so I sat down there. Their voices floated out to me.

"The position is delicate, you understand," Poirot was saying. "Dr. Leidner—obviously he adored his wife—"

"He worshipped her," said Miss Johnson.

"He tells me, naturally, how fond all his staff was of her! As for them, what can they say? Naturally they say the same thing. It is politeness. It is decency. It *may* also be the truth! But also it may *not!* And I am convinced, mademoiselle, that the key to this enigma lies in a complete understanding of Mrs. Leidner's character. If I could get the opinion—the honest opinion—of every member of the staff, I might, from the whole, build up a picture. Frankly, that is why I am here to-day. I knew Dr. Leidner would be in Hassanieh. That makes it easy for me to have an interview with each of you here in turn, and beg your help."

"That's all very well," began Miss Johnson and stopped.

"Do not make me the British *clichés*," Poirot begged. "Do not say it is not the cricket or the football, that to speak anything but well of the dead is not done—that—*enfin*—there is loyalty! Loyalty, it is a pestilential thing in crime. Again and again it obscures the truth."

"I've no particular loyalty to Mrs. Leidner," said Miss Johnson dryly. There was indeed a sharp and acid tone in her voice. "Dr. Leidner's a different matter. And, after all, she was his wife."

"Precisely—precisely. I understand that you would not wish to speak against your chief's wife. But this is not a question of a testimonial. It is a question of sudden and mysterious death. If I am to believe that it is a martyred angel who has been killed it does not add to the easiness of my task."

"I certainly shouldn't call her an angel," said Miss Johnson and the acid tone was even more in evidence.

"Tell me your opinion, frankly, of Mrs. Leidner—as a woman."

"H'm! To begin with, M. Poirot, I'll give you this warning. I'm prejudiced. I am—we all were—devoted to Dr. Leidner. And, I suppose, when Mrs. Leidner came along, we were jealous. We resented the demands she made on his time and attention. The devotion he showed her irritated us. I'm being truthful, M. Poirot, and it isn't very pleasant for me. I resented her presence here—yes, I did, though, of course, I tried never to show it. It made a difference to us, you see."

"Us? You say us?"

"I mean Mr. Carey and myself. We're the two old-timers, you see. And we didn't much care for the new order of things. I suppose that's natural, though perhaps it was rather petty of us. But it *did* make a difference."

"What kind of a difference?"

"Oh! to everything. We used to have such a happy time. A good deal of fun, you know, and rather silly jokes, like people do who work together. Dr. Leidner was quite light-hearted—just like a boy."

"And when Mrs. Leidner came she changed all that?"

"Well, I suppose it wasn't her *fault*. It wasn't so bad last year. And please believe, M. Poirot, that it wasn't anything she *did*. She's always been charming to me—quite charming. That's why I've felt ashamed sometimes. It wasn't her fault that little things she said and did seemed to rub me up the wrong way. Really nobody could be nicer than she was."

"But nevertheless things were changed this season? There was a different atmosphere."

"Oh, entirely. Really, I don't know what it was. Everything seemed to go wrong—not with the work—I mean with us—our tempers and our nerves. All on edge. Almost the sort of feeling you get when there is a thunderstorm coming."

"And you put that down to Mrs. Leidner's influence?"

"Well, it was never like that before she came," said Miss Johnson dryly. "Oh! I'm a cross-grained, complaining old dog. Conservative—liking things always the same. You really mustn't take any notice of me, M. Poirot."

"How would you describe to me Mrs. Leidner's character and temperament?"

Miss Johnson hesitated for a moment. Then she said slowly:

"Well, of course, she was temperamental. A lot of ups and downs. Nice to people one day and perhaps wouldn't speak to them the next. She was very kind, I think. And very thoughtful for others. All the same you could see she had been thoroughly spoilt all her life. She took Dr. Leidner's waiting on her hand and foot as perfectly natural. And I don't think she ever really appreciated what a very remarkable—what a really great—man she had married. That used to annoy me sometimes. And of course she was terribly highly strung and nervous. The things she used to imagine and the states she used to get into! I was thankful when Dr. Leidner brought Nurse Leatheran here. It was too much for him having to cope both with his work and with his wife's fears."

"What is your own opinion of these anonymous letters she received?"

I had to do it. I leaned forward in my chair till I could just catch sight of Miss Johnson's profile turned to Poirot in answer to his question.

She was looking perfectly cool and collected.

"I think some one in America had a spite against her and was trying to frighten or annoy her."

"*Pas plus serieux que ça?*"

"That's my opinion. She was a very handsome woman, you know, and might easily have had enemies. I think those letters were written by some spiteful woman. Mrs. Leidner being of a nervous temperament took them seriously."

"She certainly did that," said Poirot. "But remember—the last of them arrived by hand."

"Well, I suppose that *could* have been managed if any one had given their minds to it. Women will take a lot of trouble to gratify their spite, M. Poirot."

They will indeed, I thought to myself!

"Perhaps you are right, mademoiselle. As you say, Mrs. Leidner was handsome. By the way, you know Miss Reilly, the doctor's daughter?"

"Sheila Reilly? Yes, of course."

Poirot adopted a very confidential, gossipy tone.

"I have heard a rumour (naturally I do not like to ask the doctor) that there was a *tendresse* between her and one of the members of Dr. Leidner's staff. Is that so, do you know?"

Miss Johnson appeared rather amused.

"Oh, young Coleman and David Emmott were both inclined to dance attendance. I believe there was some rivalry as to who was to be her partner in some event at the club. Both the boys went in on Saturday evenings to the club as a general rule. But I don't know that there was anything in it on her side. She's the only young creature in the place, you know, and so she's by way of being the belle of it. She's got the Air Force dancing attendance on her as well."

"So you think there is nothing in it?"

"Well—I don't know." Miss Johnson became thoughtful. "It is true that she comes out this way fairly often. Up to the dig and all that. In fact, Mrs. Leidner was chaffing David Emmott about it the other day—saying the girl was running after him. Which was rather a catty thing to say, I thought, and I don't think he liked it. . . . Yes, she was here a good deal. I saw her riding towards the dig on that awful afternoon." She nodded her head towards the open window. "But neither David Emmott nor Coleman were on duty that afternoon. Richard Carey was in charge. Yes, perhaps she *is* attracted to one of the boys—but she's such a modern unsentimental young woman that one doesn't know quite how seriously to take her. I'm sure I don't know which of them it is. Bill's a nice boy, and not nearly such a fool as he pretends to be. David Emmott is a dear—and there's a lot to him. He is the deep, quiet kind."

Then she looked quizzically at Poirot and said:

"But has this any bearing on the crime, M. Poirot?"

M. Poirot threw up his hands in a very French fashion.

"You make me blush, mademoiselle," he said. "You expose me as a mere gossip. But what will you, I am interested always in the love affairs of young people."

"Yes," said Miss Johnson with a little sigh. "It's nice when the course of true love runs smooth."

Poirot gave an answering sigh. I wondered if Miss Johnson was thinking of some love affair of her own when she was a girl. And I wondered if M. Poirot had a wife, and if he went on in the way you always hear foreigners do, with mistresses and things like that. He looks so comic I couldn't imagine it.

"Sheila Reilly has a lot of character," said Miss Johnson. "She's young and she's crude, but she's the right sort."

"I take your word for it, mademoiselle," said Poirot.

He got up and said, "Are there any other members of the staff in the house?"

"Marie Mercado is somewhere about. All the men are up on the dig to-day. I think they wanted to get out of the house. I don't blame them. If you'd like to go up to the dig—"

She came out on the verandah and said, smiling to me:

"Nurse Leatheran won't mind taking you, I dare say."

"Oh, certainly, Miss Johnson," I said.

"And you'll come back to lunch, won't you, M. Poirot?"

"Enchanted, mademoiselle."

Miss Johnson went back into the living-room where she was engaged in cataloguing.

"Mrs. Mercado's on the roof," I said. "Do you want to see her first?"

"It would be as well, I think. Let us go up."

As we went up the stairs I said:

"I did what you told me. Did you hear anything?"

"Not a sound."

"That will be a weight off Miss Johnson's mind at any rate," I said. "She's been worrying that she might have done something about it."

Mrs. Mercado was sitting on the parapet, her head bent down, and she was so deep in thought that she never heard us till Poirot halted opposite her and bade her good-morning.

Then she looked up with a start.

She looked ill this morning, I thought, her small face pinched and wizened and great dark circles under her eyes.

"*Encore moi,*" said Poirot. "I come to-day with a special object."

And he went on much in the same way as he had done to Miss Johnson, explaining how necessary it was that he should get a true picture of Mrs. Leidner.

Mrs. Mercado, however, wasn't as honest as Miss Johnson had been. She burst into fulsome praise which, I was pretty sure, was quite far removed from her real feelings.

"Dear, *dear* Louise! It's so hard to explain her to some one who didn't know her. She was such an *exotic* creature. Quite different from any one else. You felt that, I'm sure, nurse? A martyr to nerves, of course, and full of fancies, but one put up with things in her one wouldn't from any one else. And she was so *sweet* to us all, wasn't she, nurse? And so *humble* about herself—I mean she didn't know anything about archæology, and she was so eager to learn. Always asking my husband about the chemical processes for treating the metal objects and helping Miss Johnson to mend pottery. Oh, we were all *devoted* to her."

"Then it is not true, madame, what I have heard, that there was a certain tenseness—an uncomfortable atmosphere—here?"

Mrs. Mercado opened her opaque black eyes very wide.

"Oh! who *can* have been telling you that? Nurse? Dr. Leidner? I'm sure *he* would never notice anything, poor man."

And she shot a thoroughly unfriendly glance at me.

Poirot smiled easily.

"I have my spies, madame," he declared gaily. And just for a minute I saw her eyelids quiver and blink.

"Don't you think," asked Mrs. Mercado with an air of great sweetness, "that after an event of this kind, every one always pretends a lot of things that never were? You know—tension, atmosphere, a 'feeling that something was going to happen?' I think people just *make up* these things afterwards."

"There is a lot in what you say, madame," said Poirot.

"And it really *wasn't* true! We were a thoroughly happy family here."

"That woman is one of the most utter liars I've ever known," I said indignantly, when M. Poirot and I were clear of the house and walking along the path to the dig. "I'm sure she simply hated Mrs. Leidner really!"

"She is hardly the type to whom one would go for the truth," Poirot agreed.

"Waste of time talking to her," I snapped.

"Hardly that—hardly that. If a person tells you lies with her lips she is sometimes telling you truth with her eyes. What is she afraid of, little Madame Mercado? I saw fear in her eyes. Yes—decidedly she is afraid of something. It is very interesting."

"I've got something to tell you, M. Poirot," I said.

Then I told him all about my return the night before and my

strong belief that Miss Johnson was the writer of the anonymous letters.

"So *she's* a liar too!" I said. "The cool way she answered you this morning about these same letters!"

"Yes," said Poirot. "It was interesting, that. *For she let out the fact that she knew all about those letters.* So far they have not been spoken of in the presence of the staff. Of course, it is quite possible that Dr. Leidner told her about them yesterday. They are old friends, he and she. But if he did not—well—then it is curious and interesting, is it not?"

My respect for him went up. It was clever the way he had tricked her into mentioning the letters.

"Are you going to tackle her about them?" I asked.

Mr. Poirot seemed quite shocked by the idea.

"No, no, indeed. Always it is unwise to parade one's knowledge. Until the last minute I keep everything here." He tapped his forehead. "At the right moment—I make the spring—like the panther—and, *mon Dieu!* the consternation!"

I couldn't help laughing to myself at little M. Poirot in the rôle of a panther.

We had just reached the dig. The first person we saw was Mr. Reiter, who as busy photographing some walling.

It's my opinion that the men who were digging just hacked out walls wherever they wanted them. That's what it looked like anyway. Mr. Carey explained to me that you could feel the difference at once with a pick, and he tried to show me—but I never saw. When the man said "*Libn*"—mud-brick—it was just ordinary dirt and mud as far as I could see.

Mr. Reiter finished his photographs and handed over the camera and the plates to his boy and told him to take them back to the house.

Poirot asked him one or two questions about exposures and film packs and so on which he answered very readily. He seemed pleased to be asked about his work.

He was just tendering his excuses for leaving us when Poirot plunged once more into his set speech. As a matter of fact it wasn't quite a set speech because he varied it a little each time to suit the person he was talking to. But I'm not going to write it all down every time. With sensible people like Miss Johnson he went straight to the point, and with some of the others he had to beat about the bush a bit more. But it came to the same in the end.

"Yes, yes, I see what you mean," said Mr. Reiter. "But indeed, I do not see that I can be much help to you. I am new here this season and I did not speak much with Mrs. Leidner. I regret, but indeed I can tell you nothing."

There was something a little stiff and foreign in the way he spoke, though, of course, he hadn't got any accent—except an American one, I mean.

"You can at least tell me whether you liked or disliked her?" said Poirot with a smile.

Mr. Reiter got quite red and stammered:

"She was a charming person—most charming. And intellectual. She had a very fine brain—yes."

"*Bien!* You liked her. And she liked you?"

Mr. Reiter got redder still.

"Oh, I—I don't know that she noticed me much. And I was unfortunate once or twice. I was always unlucky when I tried to do anything for her. I'm afraid I annoyed her by my clumsiness. It was quite unintentional . . . I would have done *any*thing—"

Poirot took pity on his flounderings.

"Perfectly—perfectly. Let us pass to another matter. Was it a happy atmosphere in the house?"

"Please."

"Were you all happy together? Did you laugh and talk?"

"No—no, not exactly that. There was a little—stiffness."

He paused, struggling with himself, and then said:

"You see, I am not very good in company. I am clumsy. I am shy. Dr. Leidner always he has been most kind to me. But—it is stupid —I cannot overcome my shyness. I say always the wrong thing. I upset water jugs. I am unlucky."

He really looked like a large awkward child.

"We all do these things when we are young," said Poirot, smiling. "The poise, the *savoir faire,* it comes later."

Then with a word of farewell we walked on.

He said:

"That, *ma sœur,* is either an extremely simple young man or a very remarkable actor."

I didn't answer. I was caught up once more by the fantastic notion that one of these people was a dangerous and cold-blooded murderer. Somehow, on this beautiful still sunny morning, it seemed impossible.

CHAPTER XXI

MR. MERCADO, RICHARD CAREY

"They work in two separate places, I see," said Poirot, halting.

Mr. Reiter had been doing his photography on an outlying portion of the main excavation. A little distance away from us a second swarm of men were coming and going with baskets.

"That's what they call the deep cut," I explained. "They don't find much there, nothing but rubbishy broken pottery, but Dr. Leidner always says it's very interesting, so I suppose it must be."

"Let us go there."

We walked together slowly for the sun was hot.

Mr. Mercado was in command. We saw him below us talking to the foreman, an old man like a tortoise who wore a tweed coat over his long striped cotton gown.

It was a little difficult to get down to them as there was only a narrow path or stair and basket boys were going up and down it constantly, and they always seemed to be as blind as bats and never to think of getting out of the way.

As I followed Poirot down he said suddenly over his shoulder:

"Is Mr. Mercado right-handed or left-handed?"

Now that was an extraordinary question if you like!

I thought a minute, then:

"Right-handed," I said decisively.

Poirot didn't condescend to explain. He just went on and I followed him.

Mr. Mercado seemed rather pleased to see us.

His long melancholy face lit up.

M. Poirot pretended to an interest in archæology that I'm sure he couldn't have really felt, but Mr. Mercado responded at once.

He explained that they had already cut down through twelve levels of house occupation.

"We are now definitely in the fourth millennium," he said with enthusiasm.

I always thought a millennium was in the future—the time when everything comes right.

Mr. Mercado pointed out belts of ashes (how his hand did shake! I wondered if he might possibly have malaria) and he explained how the pottery changed in character, and about burials—and how they had had one level almost entirely composed of infant burials—poor little things—and about flexed position and orientation which seemed to mean the way the bones were lying.

And then suddenly, just as he was stooping down to pick up a kind of flint knife that was lying with some pots in a corner, he leapt into the air with a wild yell.

He spun round to find me and Poirot staring at him in astonishment.

He clapped his hand to his left arm.

"Something stung me—like a red-hot needle."

Immediately Poirot was galvanized into energy.

"Quick, *mon cher*, let us see. Nurse Leatheran!" I came forward.

He seized Mr. Mercado's arm and deftly rolled back the sleeve of his khaki shirt to the shoulder.

"There," said Mr. Mercado, pointing.

About three inches below the shoulder there was a minute prick from which the blood was oozing.

"Curious," said Poirot. He peered into the rolled-up sleeve. "I can see nothing. It was an ant, perhaps?"

"Better put on a little iodine," I said.

I always carry an iodine pencil with me, and I whipped it out and applied it. But I was a little absent-minded as I did so, for my attention had been caught by something quite different. Mr. Mercado's arm, all the way up the forearm to the elbow, was marked all over by tiny punctures. I knew well enough what *they* were—*the marks of a hypodermic needle.*

Mr. Mercado rolled down his sleeve again and recommenced his explanations. Mr. Poirot listened, but didn't try to bring the conversation round to the Leidners. In fact he didn't ask Mr. Mercado anything at all.

Presently we said good-bye to Mr. Mercado and climbed up the path again.

"It was neat that, did you not think so?" my companion asked.

"Neat?" I asked.

M. Poirot took something from behind the lapel of his coat and surveyed it affectionately. To my surprise I saw that it was a long sharp darning needle with a blob of sealing wax making it into a pin.

"M. Poirot," I cried, "did *you* do that?"

"I was the stinging insect—yes. And very neatly I did it, too, do you not think so? You did not see me."

That was true enough. *I* never saw him do it. And I'm sure Mr. Mercado hadn't suspected. He must have been quick as lightning.

"But, M. Poirot, why?" I asked.

He answered me by another question.

"Did you notice anything, sister?" he asked.

I nodded my head slowly.

"Hypodermic marks," I said.

"So now we know something about Mr. Mercado," said Poirot. "I suspected—but I did not *know*. It is always necessary to *know*."

"And you don't care how you set about it!" I thought, but didn't say.

Poirot suddenly clapped his hand to his pocket.

"Alas, I have dropped my handkerchief down there. I concealed the pin in it."

"I'll get it for you," I said and hurried back.

I'd got the feeling, you see, by this time, that M. Poirot and I were the doctor and nurse in charge of a case. At least, it was more like an operation and he was the surgeon. Perhaps I oughtn't to say so, but in a queer way I was beginning to enjoy myself.

I remember just after I'd finished my training, I went to a case in a private house and the need for an immediate operation arose, and the patient's husband was cranky about nursing homes. He just wouldn't hear of his wife being taken to one. Said it had to be done in the house.

Well, of course it was just splendid for me! Nobody else to have a look in! I was in charge of everything. Of course, I was terribly nervous—I thought of everything conceivable that doctor could want, but even then I was afraid I might have forgotten something. You never know with doctors. They ask for absolutely anything sometimes! But everything went splendidly! I had each thing ready as he asked for it, and he actually told me I'd done first rate after it was over—and that's a thing most doctors wouldn't bother to do! The G.P. was very nice too. And I ran the whole thing myself!

The patient recovered, too, so everybody was happy.

Well, I felt rather the same now. In a way M. Poirot reminded me of that surgeon. *He* was a little man, too. Ugly little man with a face like a monkey, but a wonderful surgeon. He knew instinctively just where to go. I've seen a lot of surgeons and I know what a lot of difference there is.

Gradually I'd been growing a kind of confidence in M. Poirot. I felt that he, too, knew exactly what he was doing. And I was getting to feel that it was my job to help him—as you might say—to have the forceps and the swabs and all handy just when he wanted them. That's why it seemed just as natural for me to run off and look for his handkerchief as it would have been to pick up a towel that a doctor had thrown on the floor.

When I'd found it and got back I couldn't see him at first. But at last I caught sight of him. He was sitting a little way from the mound talking to Mr. Carey. Mr. Carey's boy was standing near with that great big rod thing with metres marked on it, but just at that moment he said something to the boy and the boy took it away. It seemed he had finished with it for the time being.

I'd like to get this next bit quite clear. You see, I wasn't quite sure what M. Poirot did or didn't want me to do. He might, I mean, have sent me back for that handkerchief *on purpose*. To get me out of the way.

It was just like an operation over again. You've got to be careful to hand the doctor just what he wants and not what he *doesn't* want. I mean, suppose you gave him the artery forceps at the wrong moment, and were late with them at the right moment! Thank goodness I know my work in the theatre well enough. I'm not likely to make mistakes there. But in this business I was really the rawest of raw little probationers. And so I had to be particularly careful not to make any silly mistakes.

Of course, I didn't for one moment imagine that M. Poirot didn't want me to hear what he and Mr. Carey were saying. But he might have thought he'd get Mr. Carey to talk better if I wasn't there.

Now I don't want anybody to get it into their heads that I'm the kind of woman who goes about eavesdropping on private conversations. I wouldn't do such a thing. Not for a moment. Not however much I wanted to.

And what I mean is if it *had* been a private conversation I wouldn't for a moment have done what, as a matter of fact, I actually did do.

As I looked at it I was in a privileged position. After all, you hear many a thing when a patient's coming round after an anæsthetic. The patient wouldn't want you to hear it—and usually has no idea you *have* heard it—but the fact remains you *do* hear it. I just took it that Mr. Carey was the patient. He'd be none the worse for what he didn't know about. And if you think that I was just curious, well, I'll admit that I *was* curious. I didn't want to miss anything I could help.

All this is just leading up to the fact that I turned aside and went by a round-about way up behind the big dump until I was a foot from where they were, but concealed from them by the corner of the dump. And if any one says it was dishonourable I just beg to disagree. *Nothing* ought to be hidden from the nurse in charge of the case, though, of course, it's the doctor to say what shall be *done*.

I don't know, of course, what M. Poirot's line of approach had been but by the time I'd got there he was aiming straight for the bull's eye, so to speak.

"Nobody appreciates Dr. Leidner's devotion to his wife more than I do," he was saying. "But it is often the case that one learns more about a person from their enemies than from their friends."

"You suggest that their faults are more important than their virtues?" said Mr. Carey. His tone was dry and ironic.

"Undoubtedly—when it comes to murder. It seems odd that as far as I know nobody has yet been murdered for having too perfect a character! And yet perfection is undoubtedly an irritating thing."

"I'm afraid I'm hardly the right person to help you," said Mr. Carey. "To be perfectly honest, Mrs. Leidner and I didn't hit it off particularly well. I don't mean that we were in any sense of the word enemies, but we were not exactly friends. Mrs. Leidner was, perhaps, a shade jealous of my old friendship with her husband. I, for my part, although I admired her very much and thought she was an extremely attractive woman, was just a shade resentful of her influence over Leidner. As a result we were quite polite to each other, but not intimate."

"Admirably explained," said Poirot.

I could just see their heads, and I saw Mr. Carey's turn sharply as though something in M. Poirot's detached tone struck him disagreeably.

M. Poirot went on:

"Was not Dr. Leidner distressed that you and his wife did not get on together better?"

Carey hesitated a minute before saying:

"Really—I'm not sure. He never said anything. I always hoped he didn't notice it. He was very wrapped up in his work, you know."

"So the truth, according to you, is that you did not really like Mrs. Leidner?"

Carey shrugged his shoulders.

"I should probably have liked her very much if she hadn't been Leidner's wife."

He laughed as though amused by his own statement.

Poirot was arranging a little heap of broken potsherds. He said in a dreamy, far-away voice:

"I talked to Miss Johnson this morning. She admitted that she was prejudiced against Mrs. Leidner and did not like her very much, although she hastened to add that Mrs. Leidner had always been charming to her."

"All quite true, I should say," said Carey.

"So I believed. Then I had a conversation with Mrs. Mercado. She told me at great length how devoted she had been to Mrs. Leidner and how much she had admired her."

Carey made no answer to this, and after waiting a minute or two Poirot went on:

"That—I did not believe! Then I come to you and that which you tell me—well, again—I do not believe. . . ."

Carey stiffened. I could hear the anger—repressed anger—in his voice.

"I really cannot help your beliefs—or your disbeliefs, M. Poirot. You've heard the truth and you can take it or leave it as far as I am concerned."

Poirot did not grow angry. Instead he sounded particularly meek and depressed.

"Is it my fault what I do—or do not believe? I have a sensitive ear, you know. And then—there are always plenty of stories going about —rumours floating in the air. One listens—and perhaps—one learns something! Yes, there *are* stories. . . ."

Carey sprang to his feet. I could see clearly a little pulse that beat in his temple. He looked simply splendid! So lean and so brown— and that wonderful jaw, hard and square. I don't wonder women fell for that man.

"What stories?" he asked savagely.

Poirot looked sideways at him.

"Perhaps you can guess. The usual sort of story—about you and Mrs. Leidner."

"What foul minds people have!"

"*N'est-ce pas?* They are like dogs. However deep you bury an unpleasantness a dog will always root it up again."

"And you believe these stories?"

"I am willing to be convinced—of the truth," said Poirot gravely.

"I doubt if you'd know the truth if you heard it," Carey laughed rudely.

"Try me and see," said Poirot, watching him.

"I will then! You shall have the truth! I hated Louise Leidner—there's the truth for you! I hated her like hell!"

CHAPTER XXII

DAVID EMMOTT, FATHER LAVIGNY AND A DISCOVERY

TURNING ABRUPTLY AWAY, Carey strode off with long angry strides.

Poirot sat looking after him and presently he murmured:

"Yes—I see. . . ."

Without turning his head he said in a slightly louder voice:

"Do not come round the corner for a minute, nurse. In case he turns his head. Now it is all right. You have my handkerchief? Many thanks. You are most amiable."

He didn't say anything at all about my having been listening—and how he knew I *was* listening I can't think. He'd never once looked in that direction. I was rather relieved he didn't say anything. I mean, I felt all right with *myself* about it, but it might have been a little awkward explaining to him. So it was a good thing he didn't seem to want explanations.

"Do you think he did hate her, M. Poirot?" I asked.

Nodding his head slowly with a curious expression on his face, Poirot answered.

"Yes—I think he did."

Then he got up briskly and began to walk to where the men were working on the top of the mound. I followed him. We couldn't see any one but Arabs at first but we finally found Mr. Emmott lying face downwards blowing dust off a skeleton that had just been uncovered.

He gave his pleasant grave smile when he saw us.

"Have you come to see round?" he asked. "I'll be free in a minute."

He sat up, took his knife and began daintily cutting the earth away from round the bones, stopping every now and then to use either a bellows or his own breath. A very insanitary proceeding the latter, I thought.

"You'll get all sorts of nasty germs in your mouth, Mr. Emmott," I protested.

"Nasty germs are my daily diet, nurse," he said gravely. "Germs can't do anything to an archæologist—they just get naturally discouraged trying."

He scraped a little more away round the thigh bone. Then he

spoke to the foreman at his side directing him exactly what he wanted done.

"There," he said, rising to his feet. "That's ready for Reiter to photograph after lunch. Rather nice stuff she had in with her."

He showed us a little verdigrisy copper bowl and some pins. And a lot of gold and blue things that had been her necklace of beads.

The bones and all the objects were brushed and cleaned with a knife and kept in position ready to be photographed.

"Who is she?" asked Poirot.

"First millennium. A lady of some consequence perhaps. Skull looks rather odd—I must get Mercado to look at it. It suggests death by foul play."

"A Mrs. Leidner of two thousand odd years ago?" said Poirot.

"Perhaps," said Mr. Emmott.

Bill Coleman was doing something with a pick to a wall face.

David Emmott called something to him which I didn't catch and then started showing M. Poirot round.

When the short explanatory tour was over Emmott looked at his watch.

"We knock off in ten minutes," he said. "Shall we walk back to the house?"

"That will suit me excellently," said Poirot.

We walked slowly along the well-worn path.

"I expect you are all glad to get back to work again," said Poirot.

Emmott replied gravely:

"Yes, it's much the best thing. It's not been any too easy loafing about the house and making conversation."

"Knowing all the time *that one of you was a murderer.*"

Emmott did not answer. He made no gesture of dissent. I knew now that he had had a suspicion of the truth from the very first when he had questioned the house-boys.

After a few minutes he asked quietly:

"Are you gettting anywhere, M. Poirot?"

Poirot said gravely:

"Will you help me to get somewhere?"

"Why, naturally."

Watching him closely, Poirot said:

"The hub of the case is Mrs. Leidner. I want to know about Mrs. Leidner."

David Emmott said slowly:

"What do you mean by knowing about her?"

"I do not mean where she came from and what her maiden name was. I do not mean the shape of her face and the colour of her eyes. I mean her—herself."

"You think that counts in the case?"

"I am quite sure of it."

Emmott was silent for a moment or two, then he said:

"Maybe you're right."

"And that is where you can help me. You can tell me what sort of a woman she was."

"Can I? I've often wondered about it myself."

"Didn't you make up your mind on the subject?"

"I think I did in the end."

"*Eh bien?*"

But Mr. Emmott was silent for some minutes, then he said:

"What did nurse think of her? Women are said to sum up other women quickly enough, and a nurse has a wide experience of types."

Poirot didn't give me any chance of speaking even if I had wanted to. He said quickly:

"What I want to know is what a *man* thought of her?"

Emmott smiled a little.

"I expect they'd all be much the same." He paused and said, "She wasn't young, but I think she was about the most beautiful woman I've ever come across."

"That's hardly an answer, Mr. Emmott."

"It's not so far off one, M. Poirot."

He was silent a minute or two and then he went on:

"There used to be a fairy story I read when I was a kid. A Northern fairy story about the Snow Queen and Little Kay. I guess Mrs. Leidner was rather like that—always taking Little Kay for a ride."

"Ah, yes, a tale of Hans Andersen, is it not? And there was a girl in it. Little Gerda, was that her name?"

"Maybe. I don't remember much of it."

"Can't you go a little further, Mr. Emmott?"

David Emmott shook his head.

"I don't even know if I've summed her up correctly. She wasn't easy to read. She'd do a devilish thing one day, and a really fine one the next. But I think you're about right when you say that she's the hub of the case. That's what she always wanted to be—*at the centre of things.* And she liked to get *at* other people—I mean, she wasn't just satisfied with being passed the toast and the peanut butter, she wanted you to turn your mind and soul inside out for her to look at it."

"And if one did not give her that satisfaction?" asked Poirot.

"Then she could turn ugly!"

I saw his lips close resolutely and his jaws set.

"I suppose, Mr. Emmott, you would not care to express a plain unofficial opinion as to who murdered her?"

"I don't know," said Emmott. "I really haven't the slightest idea. I rather think that, if I'd been Carl—Carl Reiter, I mean—I would have had a shot at murdering her. She was a pretty fair devil to him. But, of course, he asks for it by being so darned sensitive. Just invites you to give him a kick in the pants."

"And did Mrs. Leidner give him—a kick in the pants?" inquired Poirot.

Emmott gave a sudden grin.

"No. Pretty little jabs with an embroidery needle—that was her method. He *was* irritating, of course. Just like some blubbering, poor-spirited kid. But a needle's a painful weapon."

I stole a glance at Poirot and thought I detected a slight quiver of his lips.

"But you don't really believe that Carl Reiter killed her?" he asked.

"No. I don't believe you'd kill a woman because she persistently made you look a fool at every meal."

Poirot shook his head thoughtfully.

Of course, Mr. Emmott made Mrs. Leidner sound quite inhuman. There was something to be said on the other side too.

There had been something terribly irritating about Mr. Reiter's attitude. He jumped when she spoke to him, and did idiotic things like passing her the marmalade again and again when he knew she never ate it. I'd have felt inclined to snap at him a bit myself.

Men don't understand how their mannerisms can get on women's nerves so that you feel you just have to snap.

I thought I'd just mention that to Mr. Poirot some time.

We had arrived back by now and Mr. Emmott offered Poirot a wash and took him into his room.

I hurried across the courtyard to mine.

I came out again about the same time they did and we were all making for the dining-room when Father Lavigny appeared in the doorway of his room and invited Poirot in.

Mr. Emmott came on round and he and I went into the dining-room together. Miss Johnson and Mrs. Mercado were there already, and after a few minutes Mr. Mercado, Mr. Reiter and Bill Coleman joined us.

We were just sitting down and Mercado had told the Arab boy to tell Father Lavigny lunch was ready when we were all startled by a faint, muffled cry.

I suppose our nerves weren't very good yet, for we all jumped, and Miss Johnson got quite pale and said:

"*What was that?* What's happened?"

Mrs. Mercado stared at her and said:

"My dear, what *is* the matter with you? It's some noise outside in the fields."

But at that minute Poirot and Father Lavigny came in.

"We thought some one was hurt," Miss Johnson said.

"A thousand pardons, mademoiselle," cried Poirot. "The fault is mine. Father Lavigny, he explains to me some tablets, and I take one to the window to see better—and, *ma foi,* not looking where I was going, I steb the toe, and the pain is sharp for the moment and I cry out."

"We thought it was another murder," said Mrs. Mercado, laughing.

"Marie!" said her husband.

His tone was reproachful and she flushed and bit her lip.

Miss Johnson hastily turned the conversation to the dig and what objects of interest had turned up that morning. Conversation all through lunch was sternly archæological.

I think we all felt it was the safest thing.

After we had had coffee we adjourned to the living-room. Then the men, with the exception of Father Lavigny, went off to the dig again.

Father Lavigny took Poirot through into the antika-room and I went with them. I was getting to know the things pretty well by now and I felt a thrill of pride—almost as though it were my own property—when Father Lavigny took down the gold cup and I heard Poirot's exclamation of admiration and pleasure.

"How beautiful! What a work of art!"

Father Lavigny agreed eagerly and began to point out its beauties with real enthusiasm and knowledge.

"No wax on it to-day," I said.

"Wax?" Poirot stared at me.

"Wax?" So did Father Lavigny.

I explained my remark.

"Ah, *je comprends,*" said Father Lavigny. "Yes, yes, candle grease."

That led direct to the subject of the midnight visitor. Forgetting my presence they both dropped into French and I left them together and went back into the living-room.

Mrs. Mercado was darning her husband's socks and Miss Johnson was reading a book. Rather an unusual thing for her. She usually seemed to have something to work at.

After a while Father Lavigny and Poirot came out, and the former excused himself on the score of work. Poirot sat down with us.

"A most interesting man," he said, and asked how much work there had been for Father Lavigny to do so far.

Miss Johnson explained that tablets had been scarce and that there had been very few inscribed bricks or cylinder seals. Father Lavigny, however, had done his share of work on the dig and was picking up colloquial Arabic very fast.

That led the talk to cylinder seals, and presently Miss Johnson fetched from a cupboard a sheet of impressions made by rolling them out on plasticine.

I realized as we bent over them, admiring the spirited designs, that these must be what she had been working at on that fatal afternoon.

As we talked I noticed that Poirot was rolling and kneading a little ball of plasticine between his fingers.

"You use a lot of plasticine, mademoiselle?" he asked.

"A fair amount. We seem to have got through a lot already this year—though I can't imagine how. But half our supply seems to have gone."

"Where is it kept, mademoiselle?"

"Here—in this cupboard."

As she replaced the sheet of impressions she showed him the shelf with rolls of plasticine, Durofix, photographic paste and other stationery supplies.

Poirot stooped down.

"And this—what is this, mademoiselle?"

He had slipped his hand right to the back and had brought out a curious crumpled object.

As he straightened it out we could see that it was a kind of mask, with eyes and mouth crudely painted on in Indian ink and the whole thing roughly smeared with plasticine.

"How perfectly extraordinary," cried Miss Johnson. "I've never seen it before. How did it get there? And what is it?"

"As to how it got there, well, one hiding-place is as good as another, and I presume that this cupboard would not have been turned out till the end of the season. As to what it *is*—that, too, I think, is not difficult to say. *We have here the face that Mrs. Leidner described.* The ghostly face seen in the semi-dusk outside her window—without body attached."

Mrs. Mercado gave a little shriek.

Miss Johnson was white to the lips. She murmured:

"Then it was *not* fancy. It was a trick—a wicked trick! But who played it?"

"Yes," cried Mrs. Mercado. "Who could have done such a wicked, wicked thing?"

Poirot did not attempt a reply. His face was very grim as he went into the next room, returned with an empty cardboard box in his hand and put the crumpled mask into it.

"The police must see this," he explained.

"It's horrible," said Miss Johnson in a low voice. "Horrible!"

"Do you think everything's hidden here somewhere?" cried Mrs. Mercado shrilly. "Do you think perhaps the weapon—the club she was killed with—all covered with blood still, perhaps . . . Oh! I'm frightened—I'm frightened . . ."

Miss Johnson gripped her by the shoulder.

"Be quiet," she said fiercely. "Here's Dr. Leidner. We mustn't upset him."

Indeed, at that very moment the car had driven into the courtyard. Dr. Leidner got out of it and came straight across and in at the living-room door. His face was set in lines of fatigue and he looked twice the age he had three days ago.

He said in a quiet voice:

"The funeral will be at eleven o'clock to-morrow. Major Deane will read the service."

Mrs. Mercado faltered something, then slipped out of the room.

Dr. Leidner said to Miss Johnson:

"You'll come, Anne?"

And she answered:

"Of course, my dear, we'll all come. Naturally."

She didn't say anything else, but her face must have expressed what her tongue was powerless to do, for his face lightened up with affection and a momentary ease.

"Dear Anne," he said. "You are such a wonderful comfort and help to me. My dear old friend."

He laid his hand on her arm and I saw the red colour creep up in her face as she muttered, gruff as ever:

"That's all right."

But I just caught a glimpse of her expression and knew that, for one short moment, Anne Johnson was a perfectly happy woman.

And another idea flashed across my mind. Perhaps soon, in the natural course of things, turning to his old friend for sympathy, a new and happy state of things might come about.

Not that I'm really a matchmaker, and of course it was indecent to think of such a thing before the funeral even. But after all, it *would* be a happy solution. He was very fond of her, and there was no doubt she was absolutely devoted to him and would be perfectly happy devoting the rest of her life to him. That is, if she could bear to hear Louise's perfections sung all the time. But women can put up with a lot when they've got what they want.

Dr. Leidner then greeted Poirot, asking him if he had made any progress.

Miss Johnson was standing behind Dr. Leidner and she looked hard at the box in Poirot's hand and shook her head, and I realized that she was pleading with Poirot not to tell him about the mask. She felt, I was sure, that he had enough to bear for one day.

Poirot fell in with her wish.

"These things march slowly, monsieur," he said.

Then, after a few desultory words, he took his leave.

I accompanied him out to his car.

There were half a dozen things I wanted to ask him, but somehow, when he turned and looked at me, I didn't ask anything after all. I'd as soon have asked a surgeon if he thought he'd made a good job of an operation. I just stood meekly waiting for instructions.

Rather to my surprise he said:

"Take care of yourself, my child."

And then he added:

"I wonder if it is well for you to remain here?"

"I must speak to Dr. Leidner about leaving," I said. "But I thought I'd wait until after the funeral."

He nodded in approval.

"In the meantime," he said, "do not try and find out too much. You understand, I do not want you to be clever!" And he added with a smile, "It is for you to hold the swabs and for me to do the operation."

Wasn't it funny, his actually saying that?

Then he said quite irrelevantly:

"An interesting man, that Father Lavigny."

"A monk being an archæologist seems odd to me," I said.

"Ah, yes, you are a Protestant. Me, I am a good Catholic. I know something of priests and monks."

He frowned, seemed to hesitate, then said:

"Remember, he is quite clever enough to turn you inside out if he likes."

If he was warning me against gossiping I felt that I didn't need any such warning!

It annoyed me and though I didn't like to ask him any of the things I really wanted to know, I didn't see why I shouldn't at any rate say one thing.

"You'll excuse me, M. Poirot," I said. "But it's 'stubbed your toe,' not *stepped* or *stebbed*."

"Ah? Thank you, *ma sœur*."

"Don't mention it. But it's just as well to get a phrase right."

"I will remember," he said—quite meekly for him.

And he got in the car and was driven away, and I went slowly back across the courtyard wondering about a lot of things.

About the hypodermic marks on Mr. Mercado's arm, and what drug it was he took. And about that horrid yellow smeared mask. And how odd it was that Poirot and Miss Johnson hadn't heard my cry in the living-room that morning, whereas we had all heard Poirot perfectly well in the dining-room at lunch time—and yet Father Lavigny's room and Mrs. Leidner's were just the same distance from the living-room and the dining-room respectively.

And then I felt rather pleased that I'd taught *Doctor* Poirot one English phrase correctly!

Even if he *was* a great detective he'd realize he *didn't* know *everything!*

CHAPTER XXIII

I GO PSYCHIC

THE FUNERAL WAS, I thought, a very affecting affair. As well as ourselves, all the English people in Hassanieh attended it. Even Sheila Reilly was there looking quiet and subdued in a dark coat and skirt. I hoped that she was feeling a little remorseful for all the unkind things she had said.

When we got back to the house I followed Dr. Leidner into the office and broached the subject of my departure. He was very nice about it, thanked me for what I had done (Done! I had been worse than useless) and insisted on my accepting an extra week's salary.

I protested because really I felt I'd done nothing to earn it.

"Indeed, Dr. Leidner, I'd rather not have any salary at all. If you'd just refund me my travelling expenses that's all I want."

But he wouldn't hear of that.

"You see," I said, "I don't feel I deserve it, Dr. Leidner. I mean, I've—well, I've failed. She—my coming didn't save her."

"Now don't get that idea into your head, nurse," he said earnestly. "After all, I didn't engage you as a female detective. I never dreamt my wife's life was in danger. I was convinced it was all nerves and that she'd worked herself up into a rather curious mental state. You did all any one could do. She liked and trusted you. And I think in her last days she felt happier and safer because of your being here. There's nothing for you to reproach yourself with."

His voice quivered a little and I knew what he was thinking. *He* was the one to blame for not having taken Mrs. Leidner's fears seriously.

"Dr. Leidner," I said curiously. "Have you ever come to any conclusion about those anonymous letters?"

He said with a sigh:

"I don't know what to believe. Has M. Poirot come to any definite conclusion?"

"He hadn't yesterday," I said, steering rather neatly, I thought, between truth and fiction. After all, he hadn't until I told him about Miss Johnson.

It was on my mind that I'd like to give Dr. Leidner a hint and see if he reacted. In the pleasure of seeing him and Miss Johnson together the day before, and his affection and reliance on her, I'd forgotten all about the letters. Even now I felt it was perhaps rather mean of me to bring it up. Even if she had written them, she had had a bad time after Mrs. Leidner's death. Yet I did want to see whether that particular possibility had ever entered Dr. Leidner's head.

"Anonymous letters are usually the work of a woman," I said. I wanted to see how he'd take it.

"I suppose they are," he said with a sigh. "But you seem to forget, nurse, that these may be genuine. They may actually be written by Frederick Bosner."

"No, I haven't forgotten," I said. "But I can't believe somehow that that's the real explanation."

"I do," he said. "It's all nonsense his being one of the expedition staff. That is just an ingenious theory of M. Poirot's. I believe that the truth is much simpler. The man is a madman, of course. He's been hanging round the place—perhaps in disguise of some kind. And somehow or other he got in on that fatal afternoon. The servants may be lying—they may have been bribed."

"I suppose it's possible," I said doubtfully.

Dr. Leidner went on with a trace of irritability.

"It is all very well for M. Poirot to suspect the members of my expedition. I am perfectly certain *none* of them have anything to do with it! I have worked with them. I *know* them!"

He stopped suddenly, then he said:

"Is that your experience, nurse? That anonymous letters are usually written by women?"

"It isn't always the case," I said. "But there's a certain type of feminine spitefulness that finds relief that way."

"I suppose you are thinking of Mrs. Mercado?" he said.

Then he shook his head.

"Even if she were malicious enough to wish to hurt Louise she would hardly have the necessary knowledge," he said.

I remembered the earlier letters in the attaché-case.

If Mrs. Leidner had left that unlocked and Mrs. Mercado had been alone in the house one day pottering about, she might easily have found them and read them. Men never seem to think of the simplest possibilities!

"And apart from her there is only Miss Johnson," I said, watching him.

"That would be quite ridiculous!"

The little smile with which he said it was quite conclusive. The idea of Miss Johnson being the author of the letters had never entered his head! I hesitated just for a minute—but I didn't say anything. One doesn't like giving away a fellow woman, and besides, I had been a witness of Miss Johnson's genuine and moving remorse. What was done was done. Why expose Dr. Leidner to a fresh disillusion on top of all his other troubles?

It was arranged that I should leave on the following day, and I had arranged through Dr. Reilly to stay for a day or two with the matron of the hospital whilst I made arrangements for returning to England either via Baghdad or direct via Nissibin by car and train.

Dr. Leidner was kind enough to say that he would like me to choose a memento from amongst his wife's things.

"Oh, no, really, Dr. Leidner," I said. "I couldn't. It's much too kind of you."

He insisted.

"But I should like you to have something. And Louise, I am sure, would have wished it."

Then he went on to suggest that I should have her tortoiseshell toilet set!

"Oh, no, Dr. Leidner! Why, that's a most *expensive* set. I couldn't, really."

"She had no sisters, you know—no one who wants these things. There is no one else to have them."

I could quite imagine that he wouldn't want them to fall into Mrs. Mercado's greedy little hands. And I didn't think he'd want to offer them to Miss Johnson.

He went on kindly:

"You just think it over. By the way, here is the key of Louise's jewel case. Perhaps you will find something there you would rather have. And I should be very grateful if you would pack up—all—all her clothes. I dare say Reilly can find a use for them amongst some of the poor Christian families in Hassanieh."

I was very glad to be able to do that for him, and I expressed my willingness.

I set about it at once.

Mrs. Leidner had only had a very simple wardrobe with her and it was soon sorted and packed up into a couple of suitcases. All her papers had been in the small attaché-case. The jewel case contained a few simple trinkets—a pearl ring, a diamond brooch, a small string of pearls, one or two plain gold bar brooches of the safety-pin type, and a string of large amber beads.

Naturally I wasn't going to take the pearls or the diamonds, but I hesitated a bit between the amber beads and the toilet set. In the end, however, I didn't see why I shouldn't take the latter. It was a kindly thought on Dr. Leidner's part, and I was sure there wasn't any patronage about it. I'd take it in the spirit it had been offered without any false pride. After all, I *had* been fond of her.

Well, that was all done and finished with. The suitcases packed, the jewel case locked up again and put separate to give to Dr. Leidner with the photograph of Mrs. Leidner's father and one or two other personal little odds and ends.

The room looked bare and forlorn emptied of all its accoutrements, when I'd finished. There was nothing more for me to do—and yet somehow or other I shrank from leaving the room. It seemed as though there were something still to do there—something I ought to *see*—or something I ought to have *known*.

I'm not superstitious but the idea *did* pop into my head that perhaps Mrs. Leidner's spirit was hanging about the room and trying to get in touch with me.

I remember once at the hospital some of us girls got a planchette and really it wrote some very remarkable things.

Perhaps, although I'd never thought of such a thing, I might be mediumistic.

As I say, one gets all worked up to imagine all sorts of foolishness sometimes.

I prowled round the room uneasily, touching this and that. But, of course, there wasn't anything in the room but bare furniture. There was nothing slipped behind drawers or tucked away. I couldn't hope for anything of that kind.

In the end (it sounds rather batty, but as I say, one gets worked up) I did rather a queer thing.

I went and lay down on the bed and closed my eyes.

I deliberately tried to forget who and what I was. I tried to think myself back to that fatal afternoon. I was Mrs. Leidner lying here resting, peaceful and unsuspicious.

It's extraordinary how you can work yourself up.

I'm a perfectly normal matter-of-fact individual—not the least little bit spooky, but I tell you that after I'd lain there about five minutes I began to *feel* spooky.

I didn't try to resist. I deliberately encouraged the feeling.

I said to myself:

"I'm Mrs. Leidner. I'm Mrs. Leidner. I'm lying here—half asleep. Presently—very soon now—the door's going to open."

I kept on saying that—as though I were hypnotizing myself.

"It's just about half-past one . . . it's just about the time. . . . The door is going to open . . . *the door is going to open.* . . . I shall see who comes in. . . ."

I kept my eyes glued on that door. Presently it was going to open. I should *see* it open. And I should see *the person who opened it.*

I must have been a little over-wrought that afternoon to imagine I could solve the mystery that way.

But I did believe it. A sort of chill passed down my back and settled in my legs. They felt numb—paralyzed.

"You're going into a trance," I said. "And in that trance you'll see . . ."

And once again I repeated monotonously again and again:

"The door is going to open—the door is going to open. . . ."

The cold numbed feeling grew more intense.

And then, slowly, *I saw the door just beginning to open.*

It was horrible.

I've never known anything so horrible before or since.

I was paralyzed—chilled through and through. I couldn't move. For the life of me I couldn't have moved.

And I was terrified. Sick and blind and dumb with terror.

That slowly opening door.

So noiseless.

In a minute I should see . . .

Slowly—slowly—wider and wider.

Bill Coleman came quietly in.

He must have had the shock of his life!

I bounded off the bed with a scream of terror and hurled myself across the room.

He stood stock still, his blunt pink face pinker and his mouth opened wide with surprise.

"Hallo-allo-allo," he said. "What's up, nurse?"

I came back to reality with a crash.

"Goodness, Mr. Coleman," I said. "How you startled me!"

"Sorry," he said with a momentary grin.

I saw then that he was holding a little bunch of scarlet ranunculus in his hand. They were pretty little flowers and they grew wild on the sides of the Tell. Mrs. Leidner had been very fond of them.

He blushed and got rather red as he said:

"One can't get any flowers or things in Hassanieh. Seemed rather rotten not to have any flowers for the grave. I thought I'd just nip in here and put a little posy in that little pot thing she always had flowers in on her table. Sort of show she wasn't forgotten—eh? A bit asinine, I know, but—well—I mean to say—"

I thought it was very nice of him. He was all pink with embarrassment like Englishmen are when they've done anything sentimental. I thought it was a very sweet thought.

"Why, I think that's a very nice idea, Mr. Coleman," I said.

And I picked up the little pot and went and got some water in it and we put the flowers in.

I really thought much more of Mr. Coleman for this idea of his. It showed he had a heart and nice feelings about things.

He didn't ask me again what made me let out such a squeal and I'm thankful he didn't. I should have felt a fool explaining.

"Stick to common sense in future, woman," I said to myself as I settled my cuffs and smoothed my apron. "You're not cut out for this psychic stuff."

I bustled about doing my own packing and kept myself busy for the rest of the day.

Father Lavigny was kind enough to express great distress at my leaving. He said my cheerfulness and common sense had been such a help to everybody. Common sense! I'm glad he didn't know about my idiotic behaviour in Mrs. Leidner's room.

"We have not seen M. Poirot to-day," he remarked.

I told him that Poirot had said he was going to be busy all day sending off telegrams.

Father Lavigny raised his eyebrows.

"Telegrams? To America?"

"I suppose so. He said 'All over the world!' but I think that was rather a foreign exaggeration."

And then I got rather red, remembering that Father Lavigny was a foreigner himself.

He didn't seem offended though, just laughed quite pleasantly and asked me if there were any news of the man with the squint.

I said I didn't know but I hadn't heard of any.

Father Lavigny asked me again about the time Mrs. Leidner and I had noticed the man and how he had seemed to be standing on tiptoe and peering through the window.

"It seems clear the man had some overwhelming interest in Mrs. Leidner," he said thoughtfully. "I have wondered since whether the man could possibly have been a European got up to look like an Iraqi?"

That was a new idea to me and I considered it carefully. I had taken it for granted that the man was a native, but of course, when I came to think of it, I was really going by the cut of his clothes and the yellowness of his skin.

Father Lavigny declared his intention of going round outside the house to the place where Mrs. Leidner and I had seen the man standing.

"You never know, he might have dropped something. In the detective stories the criminal always does."

"I expect in real life criminals are more careful," I said.

I fetched some socks I had just finished darning and put them on the table in the living-room for the men to sort out when they came in, and then, as there was nothing much more to do, I went up on the roof.

Miss Johnson was standing there but she didn't hear me. I got right up to her before she noticed me.

But long before that I'd seen that there was something very wrong.

She was standing in the middle of the roof staring straight in front of her, and there was the most awful look on her face. As though she'd seen something she couldn't possibly believe.

It gave me quite a shock.

Mind you, I'd seen her upset the other evening, but this was quite different.

"My dear," I said, hurrying to her, "whatever's the matter?"

She turned her head at that and stood looking at me—almost as if she didn't see me.

"What is it?" I persisted.

She made a queer sort of grimace—as though she were trying to swallow but her throat were too dry. She said hoarsely:

"I've just seen something."

"What have you seen? Tell me. Whatever can it be? You look all in."

She gave an effort to pull herself together, but she still looked pretty dreadful.

She said, still in that same dreadful choked voice.

"I've seen how some one could come in from outside—and no one would ever guess."

I followed the direction of her eyes but I couldn't see anything. Mr. Reiter was standing in the door of the photographic room and Father Lavigny was just crossing the courtyard—but there was nothing else.

I turned back puzzled and found her eyes fixed on mine with the strangest expression in them.

"Really," I said, "I don't see what you mean. Won't you explain?"

But she shook her head.

"Not now. Later. We *ought* to have seen. Oh, we ought to have seen!"

"If you'd only tell me—"

But she shook her head.

"I've got to think it out first."

And pushing past me, she went stumbling down the stairs.

I didn't follow her as she obviously didn't want me with her. Instead I sat down on the parapet and tried to puzzle things out. But I didn't get anywhere. There was only the one way into the courtyard—through the big arch. Just outside it I could see the water-boy and his horse and the Indian cook talking to him. Nobody could have passed them and come in without their seeing him.

I shook my head in perplexity and went downstairs again.

CHAPTER XXIV

MURDER IS A HABIT

We all went to bed early that night. Miss Johnson had appeared at dinner and had behaved more or less as usual. She had, however, a sort of dazed look, and once or twice quite failed to take in what other people said to her.

It wasn't somehow a very comfortable sort of meal. You'd say, I suppose, that that was natural enough in a house where there'd been a funeral that day. But I know what I mean.

Lately our meals had been hushed and subdued, but for all that there had been a feeling of comradeship. There had been sympathy with Dr. Leidner in his grief and a fellow feeling of being all in the same boat amongst the others.

But to-night I was reminded of my first meal there—when Mrs. Mercado had watched me and there had been that curious feeling as though something might snap any minute.

I'd felt the same thing—only very much intensified—when we'd sat round the dining-room table with Poirot at the head of it.

To-night it was particularly strong. Every one was on edge—jumpy—on tenterhooks. If any one had dropped something I'm sure somebody would have screamed.

As I say, we all separated early afterwards. I went to bed almost at once. The last thing I heard as I was dropping off to sleep was Mrs. Mercado's voice saying good-night to Miss Johnson just outside my door.

I dropped off to sleep at once—tired by my exertions and even more by my silly experience in Mrs. Leidner's room. I slept heavily and dreamlessly for several hours.

I awoke when I did awake with a start and a feeling of impending catastrophe. Some sound had woken me, and as I sat up in bed listening I heard it again.

An awful sort of agonized choking groan.

I had lit my candle and was out of bed in a twinkling. I snatched up a torch, too, in case the candle should blow out. I came out of my door and stood listening. I knew the sound wasn't far away. It came again—from the room immediately next to mine—Miss Johnson's room.

I hurried in. Miss Johnson was lying in bed, her whole body contorted in agony. As I set down the candle and bent over her, her lips moved and she tried to speak—but only an awful hoarse whisper came. I saw that the corners of her mouth and the skin of her chin were burnt a kind of greyish white.

Her eyes went from me to a glass that lay on the floor evidently where it had dropped from her hand. The light rug was stained a bright red where it had fallen. I picked it up and ran a finger over the inside, drawing back my hand with a sharp exclamation. Then I examined the inside of the poor woman's mouth.

There wasn't the least doubt what was the matter. Somehow or other, intentionally or otherwise, she'd swallowed a quantity of corrosive acid—oxalic or hydrochloric, I suspected.

I ran out and called to Dr. Leidner and he woke the others, and we worked over her for all we were worth, but all the time I had an awful feeling it was no good. We tried a strong solution of carbonate of soda—and followed it with olive oil. To ease the pain I gave her a hypodermic of morphine sulphate.

David Emmott had gone off to Hassanieh to fetch Dr. Reilly, but before he came it was over.

I won't dwell on the details. Poisoning by a strong solution of hydrochloric acid (which is what it proved to be) is one of the most painful deaths possible.

It was when I was bending over her to give her the morphia that she made one ghastly effort to speak. It was only a horrible strangled whisper when it came.

"The window . . ." she said. *"Nurse . . . the window . . ."*

But that was all—she couldn't go on. She collapsed completely.

I shall never forget that night. The arrival of Dr. Reilly. The arrival of Captain Maitland. And finally with the dawn, Hercule Poirot.

He it was who took me gently by the arm and steered me into the dining-room where he made me sit down and have a cup of good strong tea.

"There, *mon enfant,*" he said, "that is better. You are worn out."

Upon that, I burst into tears.

"It's too awful," I sobbed. "It's been like a nightmare. Such awful suffering. And her eyes . . . Oh, M. Poirot—her eyes . . ."

He patted me on the shoulder. A woman couldn't have been kinder.

"Yes, yes—do not think of it. You did all you could."

"It was one of the corrosive acids."

"It was a strong solution of hydrochloric acid."

"The stuff they use on the pots?"

"Yes. Miss Johnson probably drank it off before she was fully awake. That is—unless she took it on purpose."

"Oh, M. Poirot, what an awful idea!"

"It is a possibility, after all. What do you think?"

I considered for a moment and then shook my head decisively. "I don't believe it. No, I don't believe it for a moment." I hesitated and then said, "I think she found out something yesterday afternoon."

"What is that you say? She found out something?"

I repeated to him the curious conversation we had had together.

Poirot gave a low soft whistle.

"*La pauvre femme!*" he said. "She said she wanted to think it over—eh? That is what signed her death warrant. If she had only spoken out—then—at once."

He said:

"Tell me again her exact words?"

I repeated them.

"She saw how some one could have come in from outside without any of you knowing? Come, *ma sœur*, let us go up to the roof and you shall show me just where she was standing."

We went up to the roof together and I showed Poirot the exact spot where Miss Johnson had stood.

"Like this?" said Poirot. "Now what do I see? I see half the courtyard—and the archway—and the doors of the drawing-office and the photographic room and the laboratory. Was there any one in the courtyard?"

"Father Lavigny was just going towards the archway and Mr. Reiter was standing in the door of the photographic room."

"And still I do not see in the least how any one could come in from outside and none of you know about it. . . . But *she* saw . . ."

He gave it up at last, shaking his head.

"*Sacré nom d'un chien—va!* What *did* she see?"

The sun was just rising. The whole eastern sky was a riot of rose and orange and pale, pearly grey.

"What a beautiful sunrise," said Poirot gently.

The river wound away to our left and the Tell stood up outlined in gold colour. To the south were the blossoming trees and the peaceful cultivation. The water-wheel groaned in the distance—a faint unearthly sound. In the north were the slender minarets and the clustering fairy whiteness of Hassanieh.

It was all incredibly beautiful.

And then, close at my elbow, I heard Poirot give a long deep sigh.

"Fool that I have been," he murmured. "When the truth is so clear —so clear."

CHAPTER XXV

SUICIDE OR MURDER?

I HADN'T TIME to ask Poirot what he meant, for Captain Maitland was calling up to us and asking us to come down.

We hurried down the stairs.

"Look here, Poirot," he said. "Here's another complication. The monk fellow is missing."

"Father Lavigny?"

"Yes. Nobody noticed it till just now. Then it dawned on somebody that he was the only one of the party not around, and we went to his room. His bed's not been slept in and there's no sign of him."

The whole thing was like a bad dream. First Miss Johnson's death and then the disappearance of Father Lavigny.

The servants were called and questioned, but they couldn't throw any light on the mystery. He had last been seen at about eight o'clock the night before. Then he had said he was going out for a stroll before going to bed.

Nobody had seen him come back from that stroll.

The big doors had been closed and barred at nine o'clock as usual. Nobody, however, remembered unbarring them in the morning. The two house-boys each thought the other one must have done the unfastening.

Had Father Lavigny ever returned the night before? Had he, in the course of his earlier walk, discovered anything of a suspicious nature, gone out to investigate it later, and perhaps fallen a third victim?

Captain Maitland swung round as Dr. Reilly came up with Mr. Mercado behind him.

"Hallo, Reilly. Got anything?"

"Yes. The stuff came from the laboratory here. I've just been checking up the quantities with Mercado. It's H.C.L. from the lab."

"The laboratory—eh? Was it locked up?"

Mr. Mercado shook his head. His hands were shaking and his face was twitching. He looked a wreck of a man.

"It's never been the custom," he stammered. "You see—just now—we're using it all the time. I—nobody ever dreamt—"

"Is the place locked up at night?"

"Yes—all the rooms are locked. The keys are hung up just inside the living-room."

"So if any one had a key to that they could get the lot."

"Yes."

"And it's a perfectly ordinary key, I suppose?"

"Oh, yes."

"Nothing to show whether she took it herself from the laboratory?" asked Captain Maitland.

"She didn't," I said loudly and positively.

I felt a warning touch on my arm. Poirot was standing close behind me.

And then something rather ghastly happened.

Not ghastly in itself—in fact it was just the incongruousness that made it seem worse than anything else.

A car drove into the courtyard and a little man jumped out. He was wearing a sun helmet and a short thick trench coat.

He came straight to Dr. Leidner, who was standing by Dr. Reilly, and shook him warmly by the hand.

"*Vous voilà, mon cher,*" he cried. "Delighted to see you. I passed this way on Saturday afternoon—en route to the Italians at Fugima. I went to the dig but there wasn't a single European about and alas! I cannot speak Arabic. I had not time to come to the house. This morning I leave Fugima at five—two hours here with you—and then I catch the convoy on. *Eh bien,* and how is the season going?"

It was ghastly.

The cheery voice, the matter-of-fact manner, all the pleasant sanity of an everyday world now left far behind. He just bustled in, knowing nothing and noticing nothing—full of cheerful bonhomie.

No wonder Dr. Leidner gave an inarticulate gasp and looked in mute appeal at Dr. Reilly.

The doctor rose to the occasion.

He took the little man (he was a French archæologist called Verrier who dug in the Greek islands, I heard later) aside and explained to him what had occurred.

Verrier was horrified. He himself had been staying at an Italian dig right away from civilization for the last few days and had heard nothing.

He was profuse in condolences and apologies, finally striding over to Dr. Leidner and clasping him warmly by both hands.

"What a tragedy! My God, what a tragedy! I have no words. *Mon pauvre collègue.*"

And shaking his head in one last ineffectual effort to express his feelings, the little man climbed into his car and left us.

As I say, that momentary introduction of comic relief into tragedy seemed really more gruesome than anything else that had happened.

"The next thing," said Dr. Reilly firmly, "is breakfast. Yes, I insist. Come, Leidner, you must eat."

Poor Dr. Leidner was almost a complete wreck. He came with us to the dining-room and there a funereal meal was served. I think the hot coffee and fried eggs did us all good, though no one actually felt they wanted to eat. Dr. Leidner drank some coffee and sat twiddling his bread. His face was grey, drawn with pain and bewilderment.

After breakfast, Captain Maitland got down to things.

I explained how I had woken up, heard a queer sound and had gone into Miss Johnson's room.

"You say there was a glass on the floor?"

"Yes. She must have dropped it after drinking."

"Was it broken?"

"No, it had fallen on the rug. (I'm afraid the acid's ruined the rug, by the way.) I picked the glass up and put it back on the table."

"I'm glad you've told us that. There are only two sets of fingerprints on it, and one set is certainly Miss Johnson's own. The other must be yours."

He was silent for a moment, then he said:

"Please go on."

I described carefully what I'd done and the methods I had tried, looking rather anxiously at Dr. Reilly for approval. He gave it with a nod.

"You tried everything that could possibly have done any good," he said. And though I was pretty sure I had done so, it was a relief to have my belief confirmed.

"Did you know exactly what she had taken?" Captain Maitland asked.

"No—but I could see, of course, that it was a corrosive acid."

Captain Maitland asked gravely:

"Is it your opinion, nurse, that Miss Johnson deliberately administered this stuff to herself?"

"Oh, no," I exclaimed. "I never thought of such a thing!"

I don't know why I was so sure. Partly, I think, because of M. Poirot's hints. His "murder is a habit" had impressed itself on my mind. And then one doesn't readily believe that any one's going to commit suicide in such a terribly painful way.

I said as much and Captain Maitland nodded thoughtfully.

"I agree that it isn't what one would choose," he said. "But if any one were in great distress of mind and this stuff were easily available it might be taken for that reason."

"*Was* she in great distress of mind?" I asked doubtfully.

"Mrs. Mercado says so. She says that Miss Johnson was quite unlike herself at dinner last night—that she hardly replied to anything that was said to her. Mrs. Mercado is quite sure that Miss Johnson was in terrible distress over something and that the idea of making away with herself had already occurred to her."

"Well, I don't believe it for a moment," I said bluntly.

Mrs. Mercado indeed! Nasty slinking little cat!

"Then what *do* you think?"

"I think she was murdered," I said bluntly.

He rapped out his next question sharply. I felt rather that I was in the orderly room.

"Any reasons?"

"It seems to me by far and away the most possible solution."

"That's just your private opinion. There was no reason why the lady should be murdered?"

"Excuse me," I said, "there was. She found out something."

"Found out something? What did she find out?"

I repeated our conversation on the roof word for word.

"She refused to tell you what her discovery was?"

"Yes. She said she must have time to think it over."

"But she was very excited by it?"

"Yes."

"*A way of getting in from outside.*" Captain Maitland puzzled over it, his brows knit. "Had you no idea at all of what she was driving at?"

"Not in the least. I puzzled and puzzled over it but I couldn't even get a glimmering."

Captain Maitland said:

"What do you think, M. Poirot?"

Poirot said:

"I think you have there a possible motive."

"For murder?"

"For murder."

Captain Maitland frowned.

"She wasn't able to speak before she died?"

"Yes, she just managed to get out two words."

"What were they?"

"*The window . . .*"

"The window?" repeated Captain Maitland. "Did you understand to what she was referring?"

I shook my head.

"How many windows were there in her bedroom?"

"Just the one."

"Giving on the courtyard?"

"Yes."

"Was it open or shut? Open, I seem to remember. But perhaps one of you opened it?"

"No, it was open all the time. I wondered—"

I stopped.

"Go on, nurse."

"I examined the window, of course, but I couldn't see anything unusual about it. I wondered whether, perhaps, somebody changed the glasses that way."

"Changed the glasses?"

"Yes. You see, Miss Johnson always takes a glass of water to bed with her. I think that glass must have been tampered with and a glass of acid put there in its place."

"What do you say, Reilly?"

"If it's murder, that was probably the way it was done," said Dr. Reilly promptly. "No ordinary moderately observant human being would drink a glass of acid in mistake for one of water—if they were in full possession of their waking faculties. But if any one's accustomed to drinking off a glass of water in the middle of the night, that person might easily stretch out an arm, find the glass in the accustomed place, and still half asleep, toss off enough of the stuff to be fatal before realizing what had happened."

Captain Maitland reflected a minute.

"I'll have to go back and look at that window. How far is it from the head of the bed?"

I thought.

"With a very long stretch you could just reach the little table that stands by the head of the bed."

"The table on which the glass of water was?"

"Yes."

"Was the door locked?"

"No."

"So whoever it was could have come in that way and made the substitution?"

"Oh, yes."

"There would be more risk that way," said Dr. Reilly. "A person who is sleeping quite soundly will often wake up at the sound of a footfall. If the table could be reached from the window it would be the safer way."

"I'm not only thinking of the glass," said Captain Maitland absent-mindedly.

Rousing himself, he addressed me once again.

"It's your opinion that when the poor lady felt she was dying she was anxious to let you know that somebody had substituted acid for water through the open window? Surely the person's *name* would have been more to the point?"

"She mayn't have known the name," I pointed out.

"Or it would have been more to the point if she'd managed to hint what it was that she had discovered the day before?"

Dr. Reilly said:

"When you're dying, Maitland, you haven't always got a sense of proportion. One particular fact very likely obsesses your mind. That a murderous hand had come through the window may have been the principal fact obsessing her at the minute. It may have seemed to her important that she should let people know that. In my opinion she wasn't far wrong either. It *was* important! She probably jumped to the fact that you'd think it was suicide. If she could have used her tongue freely, she'd probably have said 'It wasn't suicide. I didn't take it myself. Somebody else must have put it near my bed *through the window.*'"

Captain Maitland drummed with his fingers for a minute or two without replying. Then he said:

"There are certainly two ways of looking at it. It's either suicide or murder. Which do you think, Dr. Leidner?"

Dr. Leidner was silent for a minute or two, then he said quietly and decisively:

"Murder. Anne Johnson wasn't the sort of woman to kill herself."

"No," allowed Captain Maitland. "Not in the normal run of things.

But there might be circumstances in which it would be quite a natural thing to do."

"Such as?"

Captain Maitland stooped to a bundle which I had previously noticed him place by the side of his chair. He swung it on to the table with something of an effort.

"There's something here that none of you know about," he said. "We found it under her bed."

He fumbled with the knot of the covering, then threw it back revealing a heavy great quern or grinder.

That was nothing in itself—there were a dozen or so already found in the course of the excavations.

What riveted our attention on this particular specimen was a dull, dark stain and a fragment of something that looked like hair.

"That'll be your job, Reilly," said Captain Maitland. "But I shouldn't say that there's much doubt about this being the instrument with which Mrs. Leidner was killed!"

CHAPTER XXVI

NEXT IT WILL BE ME!

It was rather horrible. Dr. Leidner looked as though he were going to faint and I felt a bit sick myself.

Dr. Reilly examined it with professional gusto.

"No fingerprints, I presume?" he threw out.

"No fingerprints."

Dr. Reilly took out a pair of forceps and investigated delicately.

"H'm—a fragment of human tissue—and hair—fair blonde hair. That's the unofficial verdict. Of course, I'll have to make a proper test, blood group, etc., but there's not much doubt. Found under Miss Johnson's bed? Well, well—so *that's* the big idea. She did the murder, and then, God rest her, remorse came to her and she finished herself off. It's a theory—a pretty theory."

Dr. Leidner could only shake his head helplessly.

"Not Anne—not Anne," he murmured.

"I don't know where she hid this to begin with," said Captain Maitland. "Every room was searched after the first crime."

Something jumped into my mind and I thought, "In the stationery cupboard," but I didn't say anything.

"Wherever it was, she became dissatisfied with its hiding-place and took it into her own room, which had been searched with all the rest. Or perhaps she did that after making up her mind to commit suicide."

"I don't believe it," I said aloud.

And I couldn't somehow believe that kind nice Miss Johnson had battered out Mrs. Leidner's brains. I just couldn't *see* it happening! And yet it *did* fit in with some things—her fit of weeping that night, for instance. After all, I'd said "remorse" myself—only I'd never thought it was remorse for anything but the smaller more insignificant crime.

"I don't know what to believe," said Captain Maitland. "There's the French Father's disappearance to be cleared up too. My men are out hunting around in case he's been knocked on the head and his body rolled into a convenient irrigation ditch."

"Oh! I remember now—" I began.

Every one looked towards me inquiringly.

"It was yesterday afternoon," I said. "He'd been cross-questioning me about the man with a squint who was looking in at the window that day. He asked me just where he'd stood on the path and then he said he was going out to have a look round. He said in detective stories the criminal always dropped a convenient clue."

"Damned if any of my criminals ever do," said Captain Maitland. "So that's what he was after, was it? By jove, I wonder if he *did* find anything. A bit of a coincidence if both he and Miss Johnson discovered a clue to the identity of the murderer at practically the same time."

He added irritably, "Man with a squint? Man with a squint? There's more in this tale of that fellow with a squint than meets the eye. I don't know why the devil my fellows can't lay hold of him?"

"Probably because he hasn't got a squint," said Poirot quietly.

"Do you mean he faked it? Didn't know you could fake an actual squint."

Poirot merely said:

"A squint can be a very useful thing."

"The devil it can! I'd give a lot to know where that fellow is now, squint or no squint!"

"At a guess," said Poirot, "he has already passed the Syrian frontier."

"We've warned Tell Kotchek and Abu Kemal—all the frontier posts, in fact."

"I should imagine that he took the route through the hills. The route lorries sometimes take when running contraband."

Captain Maitland grunted.

"Then we'd better telegraph Deir ez Zor?"

"I did so yesterday—warning them to look out for a car with two men in it whose passports will be in the most impeccable order."

Captain Maitland favoured him with a stare.

"*You* did, did you? Two men—eh?"

Poirot nodded.

"There are two men in this."

"It strikes me, M. Poirot, that you've been keeping quite a lot of things up your sleeve."

Poirot shook his head.

"No," he said. "Not really. The truth came to me only this morning when I was watching the sun rise. A very beautiful sunrise."

I don't think that any of us had noticed that Mrs. Mercado was in the room. She must have crept in when we were all taken aback by the production of that horrible great blood-stained stone.

But now, without the least warning, she set up a noise like a pig having its throat cut.

"Oh, my God!" she cried. "I see it all. I see it all now. *It was Father Lavigny.* He's mad—religious mania. He thinks women are sinful. *He's killing them all.* First Mrs Leidner—then Miss Johnson. And next it will be *me*. . . ."

With a scream of frenzy she flung herself across the room and clutched at Dr. Reilly's coat.

"I won't stay here, I tell you! I won't stay here a day longer. There's danger. There's danger all round. He's hiding somewhere—waiting his time. He'll spring out on me!"

Her mouth opened and she began screaming again.

I hurried over to Dr. Reilly, who had caught her by the wrists. I gave her a sharp slap on each cheek and with Dr. Reilly's help, I sat her down in a chair.

"Nobody's going to kill you," I said. "We'll see to that. Sit down and behave yourself."

She didn't scream any more. Her mouth closed and she sat looking at me with startled, stupid eyes.

Then there was another interruption. The door opened and Sheila Reilly came in.

Her face was pale and serious. She came straight to Poirot.

"I was at the post office early, M. Poirot," she said, "and there was a telegram there for you—so I brought it along."

"Thank you, mademoiselle."

He took it from her and tore it open while she watched his face.

It did not change, that face. He read the telegram, smoothed it out, folded it up neatly and put it in his pocket.

Mrs. Mercado was watching him. She said in a choked voice: "Is that—from America?"

He shook his head.

"No, madame," he said. "It is from Tunis."

She stared at him for a moment as though she did not understand, then with a long sigh, she leant back in her seat.

"Father Lavigny," she said. "I *was* right. I've always thought there was something queer about him. He said things to me once . . . I suppose he's mad. . . ." She paused and then said, "I'll be quiet. But I *must* leave this place. Joseph and I can go in and sleep at the Rest House."

"Patience, madame," said Poirot. "I will explain everything."

Captain Maitland was looking at him curiously.

"Do you consider you've definitely got the hang of this business?" he demanded.

Poirot bowed.

It was a most theatrical bow. I think it rather annoyed Captain Maitland.

"Well," he barked. "Out with it, man."

But that wasn't the way Hercule Poirot did things. I saw perfectly well that he meant to make a song and dance of it. I wondered if he really *did* know the truth, or if he was just showing off.

He turned to Dr. Reilly.

"Will you be so good, Dr. Reilly, as to summon the others?"

Dr. Reilly jumped up and went off obligingly. In a minute or two the other members of the expedition began to file into the room. First Reiter and Emmott. Then Bill Coleman. Then Richard Carey and finally Mr. Mercado.

Poor man, he really looked like death. I suppose he was mortally afraid that he'd get hauled over the coals for carelessness in leaving dangerous chemicals about.

Every one seated themselves round the table very much as we had done on the day M. Poirot arrived. Both Bill Coleman and David Emmott hesitated before they sat down, glancing towards Sheila Reilly. She had her back to them and was standing looking out of the window.

"Chair, Sheila?" said Bill.

David Emmott said in his low pleasant drawl, "Won't you sit down?"

She turned then and stood for a minute looking at them. Each was indicating a chair, pushing it forward. I wondered whose chair she would accept.

In the end she accepted neither.

"I'll sit here," she said brusquely. And she sat down on the edge of a table quite close to the window.

"That is," she added, "if Captain Maitland doesn't mind my staying?"

I'm not quite sure what Captain Maitland would have said. Poirot forestalled him.

"Stay by all means, mademoiselle," he said. "It is, indeed, necessary that you should."

She raised her eyebrows.

"Necessary?"

"That is the word I used, mademoiselle. There are some questions I shall have to ask you."

Again her eyebrows went up but she said nothing further. She turned her face to the window as though determined to ignore what went on in the room behind her.

"And now," said Captain Maitland, "perhaps we shall get at the truth!"

He spoke rather impatiently. He was essentially a man of action. At this very moment I feel sure that he was fretting to be out and doing things—directing the search for Father Lavigny's body, or alternatively sending out parties for his capture and arrest.

He looked at Poirot with something akin to dislike.

"If the beggar's got anything to say, why doesn't he say it?"

I could see the words on the tip of his tongue.

Poirot gave a slow appraising glance at us all, then rose to his feet.

I don't know what I expected him to say—something dramatic certainly. He was that kind of person.

But I certainly didn't expect him to start off with a phrase in Arabic.

Yet that is what happened. He said the words slowly and solemnly—and really quite religiously, if you know what I mean.

"*Bismillahi ar rahman ar rahim.*"

And then he gave the translation in English.

"In the name of Allah, the Merciful, the Compassionate."

CHAPTER XXVII

BEGINNING OF A JOURNEY

"Bismillahi ar rahman ar rahim. That is the Arab phrase used before starting out on a journey. *Eh bien,* we too, start on a journey. A journey into the past. A journey into the strange places of the human soul."

I don't think that up till that moment I'd ever felt any of the so-called "glamour of the East." Frankly, what had struck me was the *mess* everywhere. But suddenly, with M. Poirot's words, a queer sort of vision seemed to grow up before my eyes. I thought of words like Samarkand and Ispahan—and of merchants with long beards—and kneeling camels—and staggering porters carrying great bales on their backs held by a rope round the forehead—and women with henna-stained hair and tattooed faces kneeling by the Tigris and washing clothes, and I heard their queer, wailing chants and the far-off groaning of the water-wheel. . . .

They were mostly things I'd seen and heard and thought nothing much of. But now, somehow they seemed *different*—like a piece of fusty old stuff you take into the light and suddenly see the rich colours of an old embroidery. . . .

Then I looked round the room we were sitting in and I got a queer feeling that what M. Poirot said was true—we *were* all starting on a journey. We were here together now, but we were all going our different ways.

And I looked at every one as though, in a sort of way, I were seeing them for the first time—*and* for the last time—which sounds stupid, but it was what I felt all the same.

Mr. Mercado was twisting his fingers nervously—his queer light eyes with their dilated pupils were staring at Poirot. Mrs. Mercado was looking at her husband. She had a strange watchful look like a tigress waiting to spring. Dr. Leidner seemed to have shrunk in some curious fashion. This last blow had just crumpled him up. You might almost say he wasn't in the room at all. He was somewhere far away in a place of his own. Mr. Coleman was looking straight at Poirot. His mouth was slightly open and his eyes protruded. He looked almost idiotic. Mr. Emmott was looking down at his feet and I couldn't see his face properly. Mr. Reiter looked bewildered. His mouth was pushed out in a pout and that made him look more like a nice clean pig than ever. Miss Reilly was looking steadily out of the window. I don't know what she was thinking or feeling. Then I looked at Mr. Carey, and somehow his face hurt me and I looked away. There we were, all of us. And somehow I felt that when M. Poirot had finished we'd all be somewhere quite different. . . .

It was a queer feeling. . . .

Poirot's voice went quietly on. It was like a river running evenly between its banks . . . running to the sea. . . .

"From the very beginning, I have felt that to understand this case one must seek not for external signs or clues, but for the truer clues of the clash of personalities and the secrets of the heart.

"And I may say that though I have now arrived at what I believe to be the true solution of the case, *I have no material proof of it.* I *know* it is so, because it *must* be so, because *in no other way* can every single fact fit into its ordered and recognized place.

"And that, to my mind, is the most satisfying solution there can be."

He paused and then went on:

"I will start my journey at the moment when I myself was brought into the case—when I had it presented to me as an accomplished happening. Now, every case, in my opinion, has a definite *shape* and *form.* The pattern of this case, to my mind, all revolved round the personality of Mrs. Leidner. Until I knew *exactly what kind of a woman Mrs. Leidner was* I should not be able to know why she was murdered and who murdered her.

"That, then, was my starting point—the personality of Mrs. Leidner.

"There was also one other psychological point of interest—the curious state of tension described as existing amongst the members of the expedition. This was attested to by several different witnesses—some of them outsiders—and I made a note that although hardly a starting point, it should nevertheless be borne in mind during my investigations.

"The accepted idea seemed to be that it was directly the result of Mrs. Leidner's influence on the members of the expedition, but for reasons which I will outline to you later this did not seem to me entirely acceptable.

"To start with, as I say, I concentrated solely and entirely on the personality of Mrs. Leidner. I had various means of assessing that personality. There were the reactions she produced in a number of people, all varying widely in character and temperament, and there was what I could glean by my own observation. The scope of the latter was naturally limited. But I *did* learn certain facts.

"Mrs. Leidner's tastes were simple and even on the austere side. She was clearly not a luxurious woman. On the other hand, some embroidery she had been doing was of an extreme fineness and beauty. That indicated a woman of fastidious and artistic taste. From the observation of the books in her bedroom I formed a further estimate. She had brains, and I also fancied that she was, essentially, an egoist.

"It had been suggested to me that Mrs. Leidner was a woman whose main preoccupation was to attract the opposite sex—that she was, in fact, a sensual woman. This I did not believe to be the case.

"In her bedroom I noticed the following books on a shelf: *Who Were the Greeks? Introduction to Relativity, Life of Lady Hester Stanhope, Back to Methuselah, Linda Condon, Crewe Train.*

"She had, to begin with, an interest in culture and in modern science—that is, a distinct intellectual side. Of the novels *Linda Condon,* and in a lesser degree *Crewe Train,* seemed to show that Mrs. Leidner had a sympathy and interest in the independent woman—unencumbered or entrapped by man. She was also obviously interested by the personality of Lady Hester Stanhope. *Linda Condon* is an exquisite study of the worship of her own beauty by a woman. *Crewe Train* is a study of a passionate individualist. *Back to Methuselah* is in sympathy with the intellectual rather than the emotional attitude to life. I felt that I was beginning to understand the dead woman.

"I next studied the reactions of those who had formed Mrs. Leidner's immediate circle—and my picture of the dead woman grew more and more complete.

"It was quite clear to me from the accounts of Dr. Reilly and others that Mrs. Leidner was one of those women who are endowed by Nature not only with beauty but with the kind of calamitous magic which sometimes accompanies beauty and can, indeed, exist independently of it. Such women usually leave a trail of violent happenings behind them. They bring disaster—sometimes on others—sometimes on themselves.

"I was convinced that Mrs. Leidner was a woman who essentially worshipped *herself* and who enjoyed more than anything else the sense of *power*. Wherever she was, she *must* be the centre of the universe. And every one round her, man or woman, had got to acknowledge her sway. With some people that was easy. Nurse Leatheran, for instance, a generous-natured woman with a romantic imagination, was captured instantly and gave in ungrudging manner full appreciation. But there was a second way in which Mrs. Leidner exercised her sway—the way of fear. Where conquest was too easy she indulged a more cruel side to her nature—but I wish to reiterate emphatically that it was not what you might call *conscious* cruelty. It was as natural and unthinking as is the conduct of a cat with a mouse. Where consciousness came in, she was essentially kind and would often go out of her way to do kind and thoughtful actions for other people.

"Now of course the first and most important problem to solve was the problem of the anonymous letters. Who had written them and why? I asked myself: Had Mrs. Leidner written them *herself?*

"To answer this problem it was necessary to go back a long way—to go back, in fact, to the date of Mrs. Leidner's first marriage. It is here we start on our journey proper. The journey of Mrs. Leidner's life.

"First of all we must realize that the Louise Leidner of all those years ago is essentially the same Louise Leidner of the present time.

"She was young then, of remarkable beauty—that same haunting beauty that affects a man's spirit and senses as no mere material beauty can—and she was already essentially an egoist.

"Such women naturally revolt from the idea of marriage. They may be attracted by men, but they prefer to belong to themselves. They are truly *La Belle Dame sans Merci* of the legend. Nevertheless Mrs. Leidner *did* marry—and we can assume, I think, that her husband must have been a man of a certain force of character.

"Then the revelation of his traitorous activities occurs and Mrs. Leidner acts in the way she told Nurse Leatheran. She gave information to the Government.

"Now I submit that there was a psychological significance in her action. She told Nurse Leatheran that she was a very patriotic idealistic girl and that that feeling was the cause of her action. But it is a well-known fact that we all tend to deceive ourselves as to the motives for our own actions. Instinctively we select the best-sounding motive! Mrs. Leidner may have believed herself that it was patriotism that inspired her action, but I believe myself that it was really the outcome of an unacknowledged desire to get rid of her husband! She disliked domination—she disliked the feeling of belonging to some one else—in fact she disliked playing second fiddle. She took a patriotic way of regaining her freedom.

"But underneath her consciousness was a gnawing sense of guilt which was to play its part in her future destiny.

"We now come directly to the question of the letters. Mrs. Leidner was highly attractive to the male sex. On several occasions she was attracted by them—but in each case a threatening letter played its part and the affair came to nothing.

"Who wrote those letters? Frederick Bosner or his brother William or *Mrs. Leidner herself?*

"There is a perfectly good case for either theory. It seems clear to me that Mrs. Leidner was one of those women who do inspire devouring devotions in men, the type of devotion which can become an obsession. I find it quite possible to believe in a Frederick Bosner to whom Louise, his wife, mattered more than anything in the world! She had betrayed him once and he dared not approach her openly, but he was determined at least that she should be his or no one's. He preferred her death to her belonging to another man.

"On the other hand, if Mrs. Leidner had, deep down, a dislike of entering into the marriage bond, it is possible that she took this way of extricating herself from difficult positions. She was a huntress who, the prey once attained, had no further use for it! Craving drama in her life, she invented a highly satisfactory drama—a resurrected husband forbidding the banns! It satisfied her deepest instincts. It made her a romantic figure, a tragic heroine, and it enabled her not to marry again.

"This state of affairs continued over a number of years. Every time there was any likelihood of marriage—a threatening letter arrived.

"*But now we come to a really interesting point.* Dr. Leidner came upon the scene—and no forbidding letter arrived! Nothing stood in the way of her becoming Mrs. Leidner. Not until *after* her marriage did a letter arrive.

"At once we ask ourselves—why?

"Let us take each theory in turn.

"*If* Mrs. Leidner wrote the letters herself the problem is easily explained. Mrs. Leidner really *wanted* to marry Dr. Leidner. And so she *did* marry him. But in that case, *why did she write herself a letter afterwards?* Was her craving for drama too strong to be suppressed?

And why only those two letters? After that no other letter was received until a year and a half later.

"Now take the other theory, that the letters were written by her first husband, Frederick Bosner (or his brother). Why did the threatening letter arrive *after* the marriage? Presumably Frederick could not have *wanted* her to marry Leidner. Why, then, did he not stop the marriage? He had done so successfully on former occasions. And why, *having waited till the marriage had taken place*, did he then resume his threats?

"The answer, an unsatisfactory one, is that he was somehow or other unable to protest sooner. He may have been in prison or he may have been abroad.

"There is next the attempted gas poisoning to consider. It seems extremely unlikely that it was brought about by an outside agency. The likely persons to have staged it were Dr. and Mrs. Leidner themselves. There seems no conceivable reason why *Dr.* Leidner should do such a thing, so we are brought to the conclusion that *Mrs.* Leidner planned and carried it out herself.

"Why? More drama?

"After that Dr. and Mrs. Leidner go abroad and for eighteen months they lead a happy, peaceful life with no threats of death to disturb it. They put that down to having successfully covered their traces, but such an explanation is quite absurd. In these days going abroad is quite inadequate for that purpose. And especially was that so in the case of the Leidners. He was the director of a museum expedition. By inquiry at the museum, Frederick Bosner could at once have obtained his correct address. Even granting that he was in too reduced circumstances to pursue the couple himself, there would be no bar to his continuing his threatening letters. And it seems to me that a man with his obsession would certainly have done so.

"Instead nothing is heard of him until nearly two years later when the letters are resumed.

"*Why* were the letters resumed?

"A very difficult question—most easily answered by saying that Mrs. Leidner was bored and wanted more drama. But I was not quite satisfied with that. This particular form of drama seemed to me a shade too vulgar and too crude to accord well with her fastidious personality.

"The only thing to do was to keep an open mind on the question.

"There were three definite possibilities: (1) the letters were written by Mrs. Leidner herself; (2) they were written by Frederick Bosner (or young William Bosner); (3) they might have been written *originally* by either Mrs. Leidner or her first husband, but they were now *forgeries*—that is, they were being written by a *third* person who was aware of the earlier letters.

"I now come to direct consideration of Mrs. Leidner's entourage.

"I examined first the actual opportunities that each member of the staff had had for committing the murder.

"Roughly, on the face of it, *any one* might have committed it (as far as opportunity went), with the exception of three persons.

"Dr. Leidner, by overwhelming testimony, had never left the roof. Mr. Carey was on duty at the mound. Mr. Coleman was in Hassanieh.

"But those alibis, my friends, were not *quite* as good as they looked. I except Dr. Leidner's. There is absolutely no doubt that he was on the roof all the time and did not come down until quite an hour and a quarter after the murder had happened.

"But was it *quite* certain that Mr. Carey was on the mound all the time?

"And had Mr. Coleman *actually been in Hassanieh* at the time the murder took place?"

Bill Coleman reddened, opened his mouth, shut it and looked round uneasily.

Mr. Carey's expression did not change.

Poirot went on smoothly.

"I also considered one other person who, I satisfied myself, would be perfectly capable of committing murder *if she felt strongly enough*. Miss Reilly has courage and brains and a certain quality of ruthlessness. When Miss Reilly was speaking to me on the subject of the dead woman, I said to her, jokingly, that I hoped she had an alibi. I think Miss Reilly was conscious then that she had had in her heart the desire, at least, to kill. At any rate she immediately uttered a very silly and purposeless lie. She said she had been playing tennis on that afternoon. The next day I learned from a casual conversation with Miss Johnson that far from playing tennis, Miss Reilly *had actually been near this house at the time of the murder*. It occurred to me that Miss Reilly, if not guilty of the crime, might be able to tell me something useful."

He stopped and then said quietly:

"Will you tell us, Miss Reilly, what you *did* see that afternoon?"

The girl did not answer at once. She still looked out of the window without turning her head, and when she spoke it was in a detached and measured voice.

"I rode out to the dig after lunch. It must have been about a quarter to two when I got there."

"Did you find any of your friends on the dig?"

"No, there seemed to be no one there but the Arab foreman."

"You did not see Mr. Carey?"

"No."

"Curious," said Poirot. "No more did M. Verrier when he went there that same afternoon."

He looked invitingly at Carey, but the latter neither moved nor spoke.

"Have you any explanation, Mr. Carey?"

"I went for a walk. There was nothing of interest turning up."

"In which direction did you go for a walk?"

"Down by the river."

"Not back towards the house?"

"No."

"I suppose," said Miss Reilly, "that you were waiting for some one who didn't come."

He looked at her but didn't answer.

Poirot did not press the point. He spoke once more to the girl.

"Did you see anything else, mademoiselle?"

"Yes. I was not far from the expedition house when I noticed the expedition lorry drawn up in a wadi. I thought it was rather queer. Then I saw Mr. Coleman. He was walking along with his head down as though he were searching for something."

"Look here," burst out Mr. Coleman. "I—"

Poirot stopped him with an authoritative gesture.

"Wait. Did you speak to him, Miss Reilly?"

"No, I didn't."

"Why?"

The girl said slowly:

"Because, from time to time, he started and looked round with an extraordinary furtive look. It—gave me an unpleasant feeling. I turned my horse's head and rode away. I don't think he saw me. I was not very near and he was absorbed in what he was doing."

"Look here," Mr. Coleman was not to be hushed any longer. "I've got a perfectly good explanation for what—I admit—looks a bit fishy. As a matter of fact, the day before I had slipped a jolly fine cylinder seal into my coat pocket instead of putting it in the antika-room—forgot all about it. And then I discovered I'd been and lost it out of my pocket—dropped it somewhere. I didn't want to get into a row about it so I decided I'd have a jolly good search on the quiet. I was pretty sure I'd dropped it on the way to or from the dig. I rushed over my business in Hassanieh. Sent a walad to do some of the shopping and got back early. I stuck the bus where it wouldn't show and had a jolly good hunt for over an hour. And didn't find the damned thing at that! Then I got into the bus and drove on to the house. Naturally, every one thought I'd just got back."

"And you did not undeceive them?" asked Poirot sweetly.

"Well, that was pretty natural under the circumstances, don't you think?"

"I hardly agree," said Poirot.

"Oh, come now—don't go looking for trouble—that's *my* motto! But you can't fasten anything on me. I never went into the courtyard, and you can't find any one who'll say I did."

"That, of course, has been the difficulty," said Poirot. "The evidence of the servants that *no one entered the courtyard from outside*. But it occurred to me, upon reflection, that that was really *not* what they had said. They had sworn that *no stranger* had entered the premises. They had not been asked *if a member of the expedition* had done so."

"Well, you ask them," said Coleman. "I'll eat my hat if they saw me or Carey either."

"Ah! but that raises rather an interesting question. They would notice *a stranger* undoubtedly—but would they have even *noticed* a member of the expedition? The members of the staff are passing in and out all day. The servants would hardly notice their going and coming. It is possible, I think, that either Mr. Carey or Mr. Coleman *might* have entered and the servants' minds would have no remembrance of such an event."

"Bunkum!" said Mr. Coleman.

Poirot went on calmly:

"Of the two, I think Mr. Carey was the least likely to be noticed going or coming. Mr. Coleman had started to Hassanieh in the car that morning and he would be expected to return in it. His arrival on foot would therefore be noticeable."

"Of course it would!" said Coleman.

Richard Carey raised his head. His deep-blue eyes looked straight at Poirot.

"Are you accusing me of murder, M. Poirot?" he asked.

His manner was quite quiet but his voice had a dangerous undertone.

Poirot bowed to him.

"As yet I am only taking you all on a journey—my journey towards the truth. I had now established one fact—that all the members of the expedition staff, and also Nurse Leatheran, could in actual *fact* have committed the murder. That there was very little likelihood of some of them having committed it was a secondary matter.

"I had examined *means* and *opportunity.* I next passed to *motive.* I discovered that *one and all of you could be credited with a motive!*"

"Oh! M. Poirot," I cried. "Not *me!* Why, I was a stranger. I'd only just come."

"*Eh bien, ma sœur,* and was not that *just what Mrs. Leidner had been fearing?* A *stranger* from *outside?*"

"But—but— Why, Dr. Reilly knew all about me! He suggested my coming!"

"How much did he really know about you? *Mostly what you yourself had told him.* Impostors have passed themselves off as hospital nurses before now."

"You can write to St. Christopher's," I began.

"For the moment will you silence yourself. Impossible to proceed while you conduct this argument. I do not say I suspect you *now.* All I say is that, keeping the open mind, you might quite easily be some one other than you pretended to be. There are many successful female impersonators, you know. Young William Bosner might be something of that kind."

I was about to give him a further piece of my mind. Female impersonator indeed! But he raised his voice and hurried on with such an air of determination that I thought better of it.

"I am going now to be frank—brutally so. It is necessary. I am going to lay bare the underlying structure of this place.

"I examined and considered every single soul here. To begin with Dr. Leidner, I soon convinced myself that his love for his wife was the mainspring of his existence. He was a man torn and ravaged with grief. Nurse Leatheran I have already mentioned. If she were a female impersonator she was a most amazingly successful one, and

I inclined to the belief that she was exactly what she said she was—a thoroughly competent hospital nurse."

"Thank you for nothing," I interposed.

"My attention was immediately attracted towards Mr. and Mrs. Mercado, who were both of them clearly in a state of great agitation and unrest. I considered first Mrs. Mercado. Was she capable of murder and if so for what reasons?

"Mrs. Mercado's physique was frail. At first sight it did not seem possible that she could have had the physical strength to strike down a woman like Mrs. Leidner with a heavy stone implement. If, however, Mrs. Leidner had been on her knees at the time, the thing would at least be *physically possible.* There are ways in which one woman can induce another to go down on her knees. Oh! not emotional ways! For instance, a woman might be turning up the hem of a skirt and ask another woman to put in the pins for her. The second woman would kneel on the ground quite unsuspectingly.

"But the motive? Nurse Leatheran had told me of the angry glances she had seen Mrs. Mercado direct at Mrs. Leidner. Mr. Mercado had evidently succumbed easily to Mrs. Leidner's spell. But I did not think the solution was to be found in mere jealousy. I was sure Mrs. Leidner was not in the least interested really in Mr. Mercado—and doubtless Mrs. Mercado was aware of the fact. She might be furious with her for the moment, but for *murder* there would have to be greater provocation. But Mrs. Mercado was essentially a fiercely maternal type. From the way she looked at her husband I realized, not only that she loved him, but that she would fight for him tooth and nail—and more than that—*that she envisaged the possibility of having to do so.* She was constantly on her guard and uneasy. The uneasiness was for him—not for herself. And when I studied Mr. Mercado I could make a fairly easy guess at what the trouble was. I took means to assure myself of the truth of my guess. Mr. Mercado was a drug addict—in an advanced stage of the craving.

"Now I need probably not tell you all that the taking of drugs over a long period has the result of considerably blunting the moral sense.

"Under the influence of drugs a man commits actions that he would not have dreamed of committing a few years earlier before he began the practice. In some cases a man has committed murder—and it has been difficult to say whether he was wholly responsible for his actions or not. The law of different countries varies slightly on that point. The chief characteristic of the drug-fiend criminal is overweening confidence in his own cleverness.

"I thought it possible that there was some discreditable incident, perhaps a criminal incident, in Mr. Mercado's past which his wife had somehow or other succeeded in hushing up. Nevertheless his career hung on a thread. If anything of this past incident were bruited about, Mr. Mercado would be ruined. His wife was always on the watch. But there was Mrs. Leidner to be reckoned with. She had a sharp intelligence and a love of power. She might even induce the wretched man to confide in her. It would just have suited her peculiar temperament to feel she knew a secret which she could reveal at any minute with disastrous effects.

"Here, then, was a possible motive for murder on the part of the Mercados. To protect her mate, Mrs. Mercado, I felt sure, would stick at nothing! Both she and her husband had had the opportunity—during that ten minutes when the courtyard was empty."

Mrs. Mercado cried out, "It's not *true!*"

Poirot paid no attention.

"I next considered Miss Johnson. Was *she* capable of murder?

"I thought she was. She was a person of strong will and iron self-control. Such people are constantly repressing themselves—and one day the dam bursts! But if Miss Johnson had committed the crime it could only be for some reason connected with Dr. Leidner. If in any way she felt convinced that Mrs. Leidner was spoiling her husband's life, then the deep unacknowledged jealousy far down in her would leap at the chance of a plausible motive and give itself full rein.

"Yes, Miss Johnson was distinctly a possibility.

"Then there were the three young men.

"First Carl Reiter. If, by any chance, one of the expedition staff was William Bosner, then Reiter was by far the most likely person. But if he *was* William Bosner, then he was certainly a most accomplished actor! If he were merely *himself*, had he any reason for murder?

"Regarded from Mrs. Leidner's point of view, Carl Reiter was far too easy a victim for good sport. He was prepared to fall on his face and worship immediately. Mrs. Leidner despised undiscriminating adoration—and the door-mat attitude nearly always brings out the worst side of a woman. In her treatment of Carl Reiter Mrs. Leidner displayed really deliberate cruelty. She inserted a gibe here—a prick there. She made the poor young man's life a hell to him."

Poirot broke off suddenly and addressed the young man in a personal, highly confidential manner.

"*Mon ami,* let this be a lesson to you. You are a *man.* Behave, then, like a *man!* It is against Nature for a man to grovel. Women and Nature have almost exactly the same reactions! Remember it is better to take the largest plate within reach and fling it at a woman's head than it is to wriggle like a worm whenever she looks at you!"

He dropped his private manner and reverted to his lecture style.

"Could Carl Reiter have been goaded to such a pitch of torment that he turned on his tormentor and killed her? Suffering does queer things to a man. I could not be *sure* that it was *not* so!

"Next, William Coleman. His behavior, as reported by Miss Reilly, is certainly suspicious. If he was the criminal it could only be because his cheerful personality concealed the hidden one of William Bosner. I do not think William Coleman, as William Coleman, has the temperament of a murderer. His faults might lie in another direction. Ah! perhaps Nurse Leatheran can guess what they would be?"

"How *did* the man do it? I'm sure I didn't look as though I was thinking anything at all.

"It's nothing really," I said, hesitating. "Only if it's to be all truth, Mr. Coleman *did* say once himself that he would have made a good forger."

"A good point," said Poirot. "Therefore if he had come across some of the old threatening letters, he could have copied them without difficulty."

"Oy, oy, oy!" called out Mr. Coleman. "This is what they call a frame-up."

Poirot swept on.

"As to his being or not being William Bosner, such a matter is difficult of verification. But Mr. Coleman has spoken of a *guardian*—not of a father—and there is nothing definitely to veto the idea."

"Tommyrot," said Mr. Coleman. "Why all of you listen to this chap beats me."

"Of the three young men there remains Mr. Emmott," went on Poirot. "He again might be a possible shield for the identity of William Bosner. Whatever *personal* reasons he might have for the removal of Mrs. Leidner I soon realized that I should have no means of learning them from him. He could keep his own counsel remarkably well, and there was not the least chance of provoking him nor of tricking him into betraying himself on any point. Of all the expedition he seemed to be the best and most dispassionate judge of Mrs. Leidner's personality. I think that he always knew her for exactly what she was—but what impression her personality made on him I was unable to discover. I fancy that Mrs. Leidner herself must have been provoked and angered by his attitude.

"I may say that of all the expedition, *as far as character and capability were concerned,* Mr. Emmott seemed to me the most fitted to bring a clever and well-timed crime off satisfactorily."

For the first time Mr. Emmott raised his eyes from the toes of his boots.

"Thank you," he said.

There seemed to be just a trace of amusement in his voice.

"The last two people on my list were Richard Carey and Father Lavigny.

"According to the testimony of Nurse Leatheran and others, Mr. Carey and Mrs. Leidner disliked each other. They were both civil with an effort. Another person, Miss Reilly, propounded a totally different theory to account for their attitude of frigid politeness.

"I soon had very little doubt that Miss Reilly's explanation was the correct one. I acquired my certitude by the simple expedient of provoking Mr. Carey into reckless and unguarded speech. It was not difficult. As I soon saw, he was in a state of high nervous tension. In fact he was—and is—very near a complete nervous breakdown. A man who is suffering up to the limit of his capacity can seldom put up much of a fight.

"Mr. Carey's barriers came down almost immediately. He told me, with a sincerity that I did not for a moment doubt, that he hated Mrs. Leidner.

"And he was undoubtedly speaking the truth. He *did* hate Mrs. Leidner. But *why* did he hate her?

"I have spoken of women who have a calamitous magic. But men have that magic too. There are men who are able without the least effort to attract women. What they call in these days *le sex appeal!* Mr. Carey had this quality very strongly. He was to begin with being devoted to his friend and employer, and indifferent to his employer's wife. That did not suit Mrs. Leidner. She *must* dominate—and she set herself out to capture Richard Carey. But here, I believe, something entirely unforeseen took place. She herself, for perhaps the first time in her life, fell a victim to an overmastering passion. She fell in love—really in love—with Richard Carey.

"And he—was unable to resist her. Here is the truth of the terrible state of nervous tension that he has been enduring. He has been a man torn by two opposing passions. He loved Louise Leidner—yes, but he also hated her. He hated her for undermining his loyalty to his friend. There is no hatred so great as that of a man who has been made to love a woman against his will.

"I had here all the motive that I needed. I was convinced that *at certain moments* the most natural thing for Richard Carey to do would have been to strike with all the force of his arm at the beautiful face that had cast a spell over him.

"All along I had felt sure that the murder of Louise Leidner was a *crime passionnel.* In Mr. Carey I had found an ideal murderer for that type of crime.

"There remains one other candidate for the title of murderer—Father Lavigny. My attention was attracted to the good Father straightaway by a certain discrepancy between his description of the strange man who had been seen peering in at the window and the one given by Nurse Leatheran. In all accounts given by different witnesses there is usually *some* discrepancy, but this was absolutely glaring. Moreover, Father Lavigny insisted on a certain characteristic—a squint—which ought to make identification much easier.

"But very soon it became apparent that *while Nurse Leatheran's description was substantially accurate,* Father Lavigny's was *nothing of the kind.* It looked almost as though Father Lavigny was deliberately misleading us—as though he did *not want the man caught.*

"But in that case *he must know something about this curious person.* He had been seen talking to the man but we had only his word for what they had been talking about.

"What had the Iraqi been doing when Nurse Leatheran and Mrs. Leidner saw him? Trying to peer through the window—Mrs. Leidner's window, so they thought, but I realized when I went and stood where they had been, that it might equally have been *the antika-room window.*

"The night after that an alarm was given. Some one was in the antika-room. Nothing proved to have been taken, however. The interesting point to me is that when Dr. Leidner got there he found

Father Lavigny there before him. Father Lavigny tells his story of seeing a light. *But again we have only his word for it.*

"I begin to get curious about Father Lavigny. The other day when I make the suggestion that Father Lavigny may be Frederick Bosner Dr. Leidner pooh-poohs the suggestion. He says Father Lavigny is a well-known man. I advance the supposition that Frederick Bosner, who has had nearly twenty years to make a career for himself, under a new name, may very possibly *be* a well-known man by this time! All the same, I do not think that he has spent the intervening time in a religious community. A very much simpler solution presents itself.

"Did any one at the expedition know Father Lavigny by sight before he came? Apparently not. Why then should not it be *some one impersonating the good Father?* I found out that a telegram had been sent to Carthage on the sudden illness of Dr. Byrd, who was to have accompanied the expedition. To intercept a telegram, what could be easier? As to the work, there was no other epigraphist attached to the expedition. With a smattering of knowledge a clever man *might* bluff his way through. There had been very few tablets and inscriptions so far, and already I gathered that Father Lavigny's pronouncements had been felt to be somewhat unusual.

"It looked very much as though Father Lavigny were an *impostor.*

"But was he Frederick Bosner?

"Somehow affairs did not seem to be shaping themselves that way. The truth seemed likely to lie in quite a different direction.

"I had a lengthy conversation with Father Lavigny. I am a practising Catholic and I know many priests and members of religious communities. Father Lavigny struck me as not ringing quite true to his rôle. But he struck me, on the other hand, as familiar in quite a different capacity. I *had* met men of his type quite frequently—but they were not members of a religious community. Far from it!

"I began to send off telegrams.

"And then, unwittingly, Nurse Leatheran gave me a valuable clue. We were examining the gold ornaments in the antika-room and she mentioned a trace of wax having been found adhering to a gold cup. Me, I say, 'Wax?' and Father Lavigny, he said 'Wax?' and his tone was enough! I knew in a flash exactly what he was doing here."

Poirot paused and addressed himself directly to Dr. Leidner.

"I regret to tell you, monsieur, that the gold cup in the antika-room, the gold dagger, the hair ornaments and several other things *are not the genuine articles found by you.* They are very clever electrotypes. Father Lavigny, I have just learned by this last answer to my telegrams, is none other than Raoul Menier, one of the cleverest thieves known to the French police. He specializes in thefts from museums of *objets d'art* and such like. Associated with him is Ali Yusuf, a semi-Turk, who is a first-class working jeweller. Our first knowledge of Menier was when certain objects in the Louvre were found not to be genuine—in every case it was discovered that a distinguished archæologist *not known previously by sight to the director* had recently had the handling of the spurious articles when paying a visit to the Louvre. On inquiry all these distinguished gentlemen denied having paid a visit to the Louvre at the times stated!

"I have learned that Menier was in Tunis preparing the way for a theft from the Holy Fathers when your telegram arrived. Father Lavigny, who was in ill-health, was forced to refuse, but Menier managed to get hold of the telegram and substitute one of acceptance. He was quite safe in doing so. Even if the monks should read in some paper (in itself an unlikely thing) that Father Lavigny was in Iraq they would only think that the newspapers had got hold of a half truth as so often happens.

"Menier and his accomplice arrived. The latter is seen when he is reconnoitering the antika-room from outside. The plan is for Father Lavigny to take wax impressions. Ali then makes clever duplicates. There are always certain collectors who are willing to pay a good price for genuine antiques and will ask no embarrassing questions. Father Lavigny will effect the substitution of the fake for the genuine article—preferably at night.

"And that is doubtless what he was doing when Mrs. Leidner heard him and gave the alarm. What can he do? He hurriedly makes up a story of having seen a light in the antika-room.

"That 'went down,' as you say, very well. But Mrs. Leidner was no fool. She may have remembered the trace of wax she had noticed and then put two and two together. And if she did, what will she do then? Would it not be *dans son caractère* to do nothing at once, but to enjoy herself by letting hints slip to the discomfiture of Father Lavigny. She will let him see that she suspects—but not that she *knows.* It is, perhaps, a dangerous game, but she enjoys a dangerous game.

"And perhaps she plays that game too long. Father Lavigny sees the truth, and strikes before she realizes what he means to do.

"Father Lavigny is Raoul Menier—a thief. Is he also—a *murderer?*"

Poirot paced the room. He took out a handkerchief, wiped his forehead and went on:

"That was my position this morning. There were eight distinct possibilities and I did not know which of these possibilities was the right one. I still did not know *who was the murderer.*

"But murder is a habit. The man or woman who kills once will kill again.

"And by the second murder, the murderer was delivered into my hands.

"All along it was ever present in the back of my mind that some one of these people might have knowledge that they had kept back —knowledge incriminating the murderer.

"If so, that person would be in danger.

"My solicitude was mainly on account of Nurse Leatheran. She had an energetic personality and a brisk inquisitive mind. I was terrified of her finding out more than it was safe for her to know.

"As you all know, a second murder did take place. But the victim was not Nurse Leatheran—it was Miss Johnson.

"I like to think that I should have reached the correct solution anyway by pure reasoning, but it is certain that Miss Johnson's murder helped me to it much quicker.

"To begin with, one suspect was eliminated—Miss Johnson herself —for I did not for a moment entertain the theory of suicide.

"Let us examine now the facts of this second murder.

"Fact one: On Sunday evening Nurse Leatheran finds Miss Johnson in tears, and that same evening Miss Johnson burns a fragment of a letter which nurse believes to be in the same handwriting as that of the anonymous letters.

"Fact two: The evening before her death Miss Johnson is found by Nurse Leatheran standing on the roof in a state that nurse describes as one of incredulous horror. When nurse questions her she says, 'I've seen how some one could come in from outside—and no one would ever guess.' She won't say any more. Father Lavigny is crossing the courtyard and Mr. Reiter is at the door of the photographic room.

"Fact three: Miss Johnson is found dying. The only words she can manage to articulate are 'the window—the window—'

"Those are the facts, and these are the problems with which we are faced:

"What is the truth of the letters?

"What did Miss Johnson see from the roof?

"What did she mean by 'the window—the window'?

"*Eh bien,* let us take the second problem first as the easiest of solution. I went up with Nurse Leatheran and I stood where Miss Johnson had stood. From there she could see the courtyard and the archway and the north side of the building and two members of the staff. Had her words anything to do with either Mr. Reiter or Father Lavigny?

"Almost at once a possible explanation leaped to my brain. If a stranger came in from *outside* he could only do so in *disguise.* And there was only *one* person whose general appearance lent itself to such an impersonation. Father Lavigny! With a sun helmet, sun glasses, black beard and a monk's long woollen robe, a stranger could pass in without the servants *realizing* that a stranger had entered.

"Was *that* Miss Johnson's meaning? Or had she gone further? Did she realize that Father Lavigny's whole *personality* was a disguise. That he was some one other than he pretended to be?

"Knowing what I did know about Father Lavigny I was inclined to call the mystery solved. Raoul Menier was the murderer. He had killed Mrs. Leidner to silence her before she could give him away. Now *another person lets him see that she has penetrated his secret.* She, too, must be removed.

"And so everything is explained! The second murder. Father Lavigny's flight—minus robe and beard. (He and his friend are doubtless careering through Syria with excellent passports as two commercial travellers.) His action in placing the blood-stained quern under Miss Johnson's bed.

"As I say, I was almost satisfied—but not quite. For the perfect solution must explain *everything*—and this does not do so.

"It does not explain, for instance, why Miss Johnson should say 'the window—the window,' as she was dying. It does not explain her fit of weeping over the letter. It does not explain her mental attitude on the roof—her incredulous horror and her refusal to tell Nurse Leatheran what it was that *she now suspected or knew.*

"It was a solution that fitted the *outer* facts, but it did not satisfy the *psychological* requirements.

"And then, as I stood on the roof, going over in my mind those three points: the letters, the roof, the window, I *saw*—just as Miss Johnson had seen!

"*And this time what I saw explained everything!*"

CHAPTER XXVIII

JOURNEY'S END

POIROT LOOKED ROUND. Every eye was now fixed upon him. There had been a certain relaxation—a slackening of tension. Now the tension suddenly returned.

There was something coming . . . something . . .

Poirot's voice, quiet and unimpassioned, went on:

"The letters, the roof, 'the window' . . . Yes, everything was explained—everything fell into place.

"I said just now that three men had alibis for the time of the crime. Two of those alibis I have shown to be worthless. I saw now my great—my amazing mistake. The third alibi was worthless too. Not only *could* Dr. Leidner have committed the murder—but I was convinced that he *had* committed it."

There was a silence, a bewildered uncomprehending silence. Dr. Leidner said nothing. He seemed lost in his far-away world still. David Emmott, however, stirred uneasily and spoke.

"I don't know what you mean to imply, M. Poirot. I told you that Dr. Leidner never left the roof until at least a quarter to three. That is the absolute truth. I swear it solemnly. I am not lying. And it would have been quite impossible for him to have done so without my seeing him."

Poirot nodded.

"Oh, I believe you. *Dr. Leidner did not leave the roof*. That is an undisputed fact. But what I saw—and what Miss Johnson had seen—was *that Dr. Leidner could murder his wife from the roof without leaving it.*"

We all stared.

"The *window*," cried Poirot. "*Her* window! That is what I realized—just as Miss Johnson realized it. Her window was directly underneath, on the side away from the courtyard. And Dr. Leidner was alone up there with no one to witness his actions. And those heavy stone querns and grinders were up there all ready to his hand. So simple, so very simple, granted one thing—*that the murderer had the opportunity to move the body before any one else saw it.* . . . Oh, it is beautiful—of an unbelievable simplicity!

"Listen—it went like this:

"Dr. Leidner is on the roof working with the pottery. He calls you up, Mr. Emmott, and while he holds you in talk he notices that, as usually happens, the small boy takes advantage of your absence to leave his work and go outside the courtyard. He keeps you with him ten minutes, then he let you go and as soon as you are down below shouting to the boy he sets his plan in operation.

"He takes from his pocket the plasticine-smeared mask with which he has already scared his wife on a former occasion and dangles it over the edge of the parapet till it taps on his wife's window.

"That, remember, is the window giving on the countryside facing the opposite direction to the courtyard.

"Mrs. Leidner is lying on her bed half asleep. She is peaceful and happy. Suddenly the mask begins tapping on the window and attracts her attention. But it is not dusk now—it is broad daylight—there is nothing terrifying about it. She recognizes it for what it is—a crude form of trickery! She is not frightened but indignant. She does what any other woman would do in her place. Jumps off the bed, opens the window, passes her head through the bars and turns her face upwards to see who is playing the trick on her.

"Dr. Leidner is waiting. He has in his hands, poised and ready, a heavy quern. At the psychological moment *he drops it*. . . .

"With a faint cry (heard by Miss Johnson) Mrs. Leidner collapses on the rug underneath the window.

"Now there is a hole in this quern, and through that Dr. Leidner had previously passed a cord. He has now only to haul in the cord and bring up the quern. He replaces the latter neatly, blood-stained side down, amongst the other objects of that kind on the roof.

"Then he continues his work for an hour or more till he judges the moment has come for the second act. He descends the stairs, speaks to Mr. Emmott and Nurse Leatheran, crosses the courtyard and enters his wife's room. This is the explanation he himself gives of his movements there.

"*'I saw my wife's body in a heap by the bed. For a moment or two I felt paralyzed as though I couldn't move. Then at last I went and knelt down by her and lifted up her head. I saw she was dead. . . . At last I got up. I felt dazed and as though I were drunk. I managed to get to the door and call out.'*

"A perfectly possible account of the actions of a grief-dazed man. Now listen to what I believe to be the truth. Dr. Leidner enters the room, hurries to the window, and having pulled on a pair of gloves, closes and fastens it, then picks up his wife's body and transports it to a position between the bed and the door. Then he notices a slight stain on the window-side rug. He cannot change it with the other rug, they are a different size, but he does the next best thing. He puts the stained rug in front of the wash-stand and the rug from the wash-stand under the window. *If* the stain is noticed, it will be connected with the *wash-stand*—not with the *window*—a very important point. There must be no suggestion that the window played any part in the business. Then he comes to the door and acts the part of the overcome husband, and that, I imagine, is not difficult. For he *did* love his wife."

"My good man," cried Dr. Reilly impatiently, "if he loved her, why did he kill her? Where's the motive? Can't you speak, Leidner? Tell him he's mad."

Dr. Leidner neither spoke nor moved.

Poirot said:

"Did I not tell you all along that this was a *crime passionnel*? Why did her first husband, Frederick Bosner, threaten to kill her? Because he loved her. . . . And in the end, you see, he made his boast good. . . .

"*Mais oui—mais oui—once I realize that it is Dr. Leidner who did the killing* everything falls into place. . . .

"For the second time I recommence my journey from the beginning—Mrs. Leidner's first marriage—the threatening letters—her second marriage. The letters prevented her marrying any other man—but they did not prevent her marrying Dr. Leidner. How simple that is—*if Dr. Leidner is actually Frederick Bosner.*

"Once more let us start our journey—from the point of view this time of young Frederick Bosner.

"To begin with he loves his wife Louise with an overpowering passion such as only a woman of her kind can evoke. She betrays him. He is sentenced to death. He escapes. He is involved in a railway accident but he manages to emerge with a second personality—*that of a young Swedish archæologist, Eric Leidner,* whose body is badly disfigured and who will be conveniently buried as Frederick Bosner.

"What is the new Eric Leidner's attitude to the woman who was willing to send him to his death? First and most important, *he still loves her.* He sets to work to build up his new life. He is a man of great ability, his profession is congenial to him and he makes a success of it. *But he never forgets the ruling passion of his life.* He keeps himself informed of his wife's movements. Of one thing he is cold-bloodedly determined (remember Mrs. Leidner's own description of him to Nurse Leatheran—gentle and kind but ruthless), *she shall belong to no other man.* Whenever he judges it necessary he despatches a letter. He imitates some of the peculiarities of her handwriting in case she should think of taking his letters to the police. Women who write sensational anonymous letters to themselves are such a common phenomenon that the police will be sure to jump to that solution given the likeness of the handwriting. At the same time he leaves her in doubt as to whether he is really alive or not.

"At last, after many years, he judges that the time has arrived; he re-enters her life. All goes well. His wife never dreams of his real identity. He is a well-known man. The upstanding, good-looking young fellow is now a middle-aged man with a beard and stooping shoulders. And so we see history repeating itself. As before, Frederick is able to dominate Louise. For the second time she consents to marry him. *And no letter comes to forbid the banns.*

"But *afterwards* a letter *does* come. Why?

"I think that Dr. Leidner was taking no chances. The intimacy of marriage *might* awaken a memory. He wishes to impress on his wife, once and for all, *that Eric Leidner and Frederick Bosner are two* different people. So much so that a threatening letter comes from the former on account of the latter. The rather puerile gas poisoning business follows—arranged by Dr. Leidner, of course. Still with the same object in view.

"After that he is satisfied. No more letters need come. They can settle down to happy married life together.

"And then, after nearly two years, *the letters recommence.*

"*Why? Eh bien,* I think I know. *Because the threat underlying the letters was always a genuine threat.* (That is why Mrs. Leidner has always been frightened. She *knew* her Frederick's gentle but ruthless nature.) *If she belongs to any other man but him he would kill her. And she has given herself to Richard Carey.*

"And so, having discovered this, cold-bloodedly, calmly, Dr. Leidner prepares the scene for murder.

"You see now the important part played by Nurse Leatheran? Dr. Leidner's rather curious conduct (it puzzled me at the very first) in securing her services for his wife is explained. It was vital that a reliable professional witness should be able to state incontrovertibly that Mrs. Leidner had been dead *over an hour* when her body was found—that is, that she had been killed at a time when *everybody could swear her husband was on the roof*. A suspicion *might* have arisen that he had killed her when he entered the room and found the body—but that was out of the question when a trained hospital nurse would assert positively that she had already been dead an hour.

"Another thing that is explained is the curious state of tension and strain that had come over the expedition this year. I never from the first thought that that could be attributed solely to *Mrs.* Leidner's influence. For several years this particular expedition had had a reputation for happy good-fellowship. In my opinion the state of mind of a community is always directly due to the influence of the man at the top. Dr. Leidner, quiet though he was, was a man of great personality. It was due to his tact, to his judgment, to his sympathetic manipulation of human beings that the atmosphere had always been such a happy one.

"If there was a change, therefore, the change must be due to the man at the top—in other words, to Dr. Leidner. It was *Dr.* Leidner, not Mrs. Leidner, who was responsible for the tension and uneasiness. No wonder the staff felt the change without understanding it. The kindly genial Dr. Leidner, outwardly the same, was only playing the part of himself. The real man was an obsessed fanatic plotting to kill.

"And now we will pass on to the second murder—that of Miss Johnson. In tidying up Dr. Leidner's papers in the office (a job she took on herself unasked, craving for something to do) she must have come on some unfinished draft of one of the anonymous letters.

"It must have been both incomprehensible and extremely upsetting to her! Dr. Leidner has been deliberately terrorizing his wife! She cannot understand it—but it upsets her badly. It is in this mood that Nurse Leatheran discovers her crying.

"I do not think at the moment that she suspected Dr. Leidner of being the murderer, but my experiments with sounds in Mrs. Leidner's and Father Lavigny's rooms are not lost upon her. She realizes that if it *was* Mrs. Leidner's cry she heard, *the window in her room must have been open, not shut*. At the moment that conveys nothing vital to her, *but she remembers it*.

"Her mind goes on working—ferreting its way towards the truth. Perhaps she makes some reference to the letters which Dr. Leidner understands and his manner changes. She may see that he is, suddenly, afraid.

"But Dr. Leidner *cannot* have killed his wife! He was on the *roof* all the time.

"And then, one evening, as she herself is on the roof puzzling about it, the truth comes to her in a flash. Mrs. Leidner has been killed from up *here*, through the open window.

"It was at that minute that Nurse Leatheran found her.

"And immediately, her old affection reasserting itself, she puts up a quick camouflage. Nurse Leatheran must not guess the horrifying discovery she has just made.

"She looks deliberately in the opposite direction (towards the courtyard) and makes a remark suggested to her by Father Lavigny's appearance as he crosses the courtyard.

"She refuses to say more. She has got to 'think things out.'

"And Dr. Leidner, who has been watching her anxiously, *realizes that she knows the truth.* She is not the kind of woman to conceal her horror and distress from him.

"It is true that as yet she has not given him away—but how long can he depend upon her?

"Murder is a habit. That night he substitutes a glass of acid for her glass of water. There is just a chance she may be believed to have deliberately poisoned herself. There is even a chance she may be considered to have done the first murder and has now been overcome with remorse. To strengthen the latter idea he takes the quern from the roof and puts it under her bed.

"No wonder that poor Miss Johnson, in her death agony, could only try desperately to impart her hard-won information. Through 'the window,' *that* is how Mrs. Leidner was killed, *not* through the door—through the *window*. . . .

"And so thus, everything is explained, everything falls into place. . . . Psychologically perfect.

"But there is no proof. No proof at all. . . ."

None of us spoke. We were lost in a sea of horror. . . . Yes, and not only horror. Pity, too.

Dr. Leidner had neither moved nor spoken. He sat just as he had done all along. A tired, worn, elderly man.

At last he stirred slightly and looked at Poirot with gentle tired eyes.

"No," he said, "there is no proof. But that does not matter. You knew that I would not deny truth. . . . I have never denied truth . . . I think—really—I am rather glad . . . I'm so tired . . ."

Then he said simply:

"I'm sorry about Anne. That was bad—senseless—it wasn't *me!* And she suffered, too, poor soul. Yes, that wasn't me. It was fear. . . ."

A little smile just hovered on his pain-twisted lips.

"You would have made a good archæologist, M. Poirot. You have the gift of re-creating the past.

"It was all very much as you said.

"I loved Louise and I killed her . . . If you'd known Louise you'd have understood. . . . No, I think you understand anyway. . . .

CHAPTER XXIX

L'ENVOI

THERE ISN'T REALLY any more to say about things.

They got "Father" Lavigny and the other man just as they were going on board a steamer at Beyrouth.

Sheila Reilly married young Emmott. I think that will be good for her. He's no door-mat—he'll keep her in her place. She'd have ridden roughshod over poor Bill Coleman.

I nursed him, by the way, when he had appendicitis a year ago. I got quite fond of him. His people were sending him out to farm in South Africa.

I've never been out East again. It's funny—sometimes I wish I could. I think of the noise the water-wheel made and the women washing, and that queer haughty look that camels give you—and I get quite a homesick feeling. After all, perhaps dirt isn't really so unhealthy as one is brought up to believe!

Dr. Reilly usually looks me up when he's in England, and as I said, it's he who's got me into this. "Take it or leave it," I said to him. "I know the grammar's all wrong and it's not properly written or anything like that—but there it is."

And he took it. Made no bones about it. It will give me a queer feeling if it's ever printed.

M. Poirot went back to Syria and about a week later he went home on the Orient Express and got himself mixed up in another murder. He was clever, I don't deny it, but I shan't forgive him in a hurry for pulling my leg the way he did. Pretending to think I might be mixed up in the crime and not a real hospital nurse at all!

Doctors are like that sometimes. Will have their joke, some of them will, and never think of *your* feelings!

I've thought and thought about Mrs. Leidner and what she was really like. . . . Sometimes it seems to me she was just a terrible woman—and other times I remember how nice she was to me and how soft her voice was—and her lovely fair hair and everything—and I feel that perhaps, after all, she was more to be pitied than blamed. . . .

And I can't help but pity Dr. Leidner. I know he was a murderer twice over, but it doesn't seem to make any difference. He was so dreadfully fond of her. It's awful to be fond of any one like that.

Somehow, the more I get older, and the more I see of people and sadness and illness and everything, the sorrier I get for every one. Sometimes, I declare, I don't know what's become of the good strict principles my aunt brought me up with. A very religious woman she was, and most particular. There wasn't one of our neighbours whose faults she didn't know backwards and forwards. . . .

Oh, dear, it's quite true what Dr. Reilly said. How does one stop writing? If I could find a really good telling phrase.

I must ask Dr. Reilly for some Arab one.

Like the one M. Poirot used.

In the name of Allah, the Merciful, the Compassionate . . .

Something like that.

THE END